"The prolific bestselling author of historical saga . . . has put together a superb anthology of thirty Western short fictions written in the last one hundred years. Many of the stories are appearing here for the first time since they were published in the '30s, '40s, and '50s, but their appeal is as fresh as ever."

—Publishers Weekly

"The best-kept secret of American literature is the brilliance of the Western short story. That savvy master of fiction, John Jakes, has gathered some dazzling stories here, written by some of the finest fiction authors of the twentieth century. This is a collection you'll relish, read again and again, and keep among the classics on your bookshelves."

—Richard S. Wheeler

"A superb collection that tells you why the Western will never die."

—David Nevin

"A whopping collection of John Jakes's favorite tales . . . I had a lot of fun. . . . If you have any nostalgic feeling left for that uniquely American literary genre, you will, too."

—The Hilton Head Island Packet

"This superb collection . . . is entertaining not only for Western fans, but for other readers as well."

—The Tampa Tribune and Times

"This is an excellent retrospective, as well as a look into the future of the immortal Western, and for those unfamiliar with it, the best introduction to the genre today."

— Rocky Mountain News

A Century
of Great Western
Stories

———

Edited by
John Jakes

A Tom Doherty Associates Book
New York

A CENTURY OF GREAT WESTERN STORIES

Copyright © 2000 by John Jakes

Book design by Jane Adele Regina

A Forge Book
Published by Tom Doherty Associates, LLC
175 Fifth Avenue
New York, NY 10010

www.tor.com

Forge® is a registered trademark of Tom Doherty Associates, LLC.

Library of Congress Cataloging-in-Publication Data

A century of great Western stories / edited by John Jakes.
p. cm.
"A Tom Doherty Associates book."
Includes bibliographical references.
ISBN 0-312-86986-X (hc)
ISBN 0-312-86985-1 (pbk)
1. Western stories. 2. Frontier and pioneer life—West (U.S.)—Fiction. 3. West (U.S.)
—Social life and customs—Fiction.   I. Jakes, John, 1932–
PS648.W4 C46 2000
813'.087408—dc21
99-462096

Printed in the United States of America

D 20

Copyrights for
A Century of Great Western Stories

Copyrights

Contents

Introduction

What Happened to the Western?

by John Jakes

I

THIS COLLECTION CELEBRATES a literary form prized and read by millions around the world for more than a hundred years. With the invaluable help of Dr. Martin Greenberg and John Helfers of Tekno-Books, I have gathered together what are generally considered to be the best of the very best Western short stories of the past century. For everyone involved with developing and organizing the project, it has been a labor of love.

I got my start with Westerns via the movies, in Terre Haute, Indiana, in 1939. I remember the powerful impression made on a young kid by *Dodge City* and *Stagecoach*. I became a writer of Westerns in the 1950s, producing a couple of dozen short stories and novelettes for the pulps, mostly those for Popular Publications (screaming yellow covers—cover paintings illustrating some form of hideous sagebrush peril—nearly every story title ending with an exclam or two!!).

Today you can't find pulps, let alone a single national magazine that regularly prints Western fiction. A great venue for some of the best disappeared when *The Saturday Evening Post* and *Collier's* and the other so-called slicks fell out of favor and profitability after the 1940s. A recent attempt to create a short story magazine using Louis L'Amour's name on the masthead lasted but a couple of years.

The Western story, clearly, has been ailing for a long time. In a rapidly changing world it has gone the way of parental spanking, presidential candor, marital fidelity, and literate movie dialogue. Some fear it will end up, sooner rather than later, just like the bustle, the buggy whip, the dodo and the passenger pigeon. We'll explore that question shortly.

I am not a social scientist, but I can point to a day that the Western in all its forms took sick.

II

May 27, 1977, Friday, was the start of a Memorial Day weekend. We were living in Dayton, Ohio, where I buried myself each morning in a remodeled coal cellar, to battle implacable deadlines that unexpected success and skyrocketing sales had imposed on *The Kent Family Chronicles*.

That Friday night our son Mike went out to a suburban movie palace, with friends or on a date. He came home excited, having seen a largely unheralded science-fiction movie opening that day. He said we had to see it and extracted a promise that we would.

Next afternoon my wife, Rachel, and I set out. Around 4:30, after the curtains parted and the John Williams fanfare blared, there went sliding up the screen the kind of lettering I remembered from Saturday afternoon serials. Previous chapters were always summarized with this slanted lettering: it shrank as it ascended to the top of the frame where it disappeared, big lettering in the meantime continuing to roll up from the bottom. A man I'd never heard of, George Lucas, had remembered those serials, and put a new 70s version on the screen.

Once the slanted text concluded, a deep, almost intestinal rumbling began. And from the top of the frame, against a sea of stars, there appeared the prow of this *spaceship* descending into the picture, steadily revealed as ever *bigger*, ever *longer*—my God, I'd never seen anything so huge, or hugely spectacular, on any screen, not in all my years of traipsing to double features two and three times a week.

Star Wars was by turns flashy and corny, but most of all it was exciting, filled throughout with those visual tricks now shrugged off as "just more special effects." In 1977 they were truly special, although looking at "Star Wars" many times since, I see the shortcuts resulting from a tight budget. In the Death Star conference room, the ball-caster chairs are the kind found in any office furniture store at the time the picture was shot.

Though we didn't know it then, *Star Wars* would change many things. It heralded a flood tide of SF as well as nongenre pictures that depend on special effects of steadily escalating cost and dazzle to attract audiences. Clint Eastwood sardonically says, "Today the star of the picture is the explosion."

To my mind, *Star Wars* is a conventional Saturday afternoon cowboy vs. bad men picture decked out with stunning visuals. I didn't see that at first. For years, devoted moviegoers had thrilled to Technicolor vistas of Western scenery; suddenly we could thrill to Technicolor vistas of starry galaxies and fantastic rocketry. It seemed a completely new game.

But it wasn't. The Western just changed clothes. Horse opera became space opera. And as old-fashioned Westerns on the screen began to suffer, so too did Westerns on the page.

In fairness, maybe it was time for a sea change. The Western movie formula was just that—trite and too familiar. Same goes for most Western fiction.

The 60s and 70s saw a significant drop-off of interest in subjects traditionally taught in school, among them history. The new, younger audience cared less and less about our common past, including the saga of frontier expansion. Sometimes they hardly knew about it, thanks to bad texts, bad teachers, and de-emphasis on academics in favor of "social behavior," driver's ed., *et al.*

A recent analysis of American college students showed that less than one-third are enrolled in the liberal arts. The rest are taking job-specific, career-oriented courses. Any wonder that the audience for old-style Westerns with their dubious history, quaint lathered horses, endless chases, saloon gun-fights, bad men pitching off roof peaks in the final face-off, eroded rapidly when newer, glitzier visions of humanity came along?

Changes in distribution and marketing patterns for mass-market books played a part in downsizing the availability of Western fiction. Tom Doherty, president and publisher of the house bringing you this book, is a man of long experience in popular fiction. Tom observes, "The Western was always strongest in its mass-market format so, more than most publishing categories, it was hurt by radical restructuring of the wholesale and rack jobber distribution systems across North America. It was also hurt by the decline of the mall bookstore, but it seems unlikely that wholesale consolidation will go much further . . . and the latest credible forecast of consumer book spending predicts a compound yearly increase of five percent over the next five years [2000–2005]. . . . People who could cross the Rockies in covered wagons should be able to find a way to deal with the problems of book distribution."

In spite of adverse trends in publishing, there are still traditional Western novels to read and enjoy. I regularly see paperback Westerns from major trade houses in wire spinners at convenience stores, K-Marts, and similar outlets.

At the same time, smaller presses are publishing nonformula novels by talented new writers. Quite interesting changes have taken place in these novels. No longer are they written entirely by men, or women hiding behind male pseudonyms. Increasing numbers of women are writing about the West from the long-ignored feminist viewpoint. Whether this will reinvigorate the genre, as some claim, remains a question.

No longer do all Westerns reflect a macho, all-white-and-all-right view of Western history. No longer are Native Americans exclusively villains, fiendishly fighting to stem the red, white, and blue tide of Manifest Destiny (a.k.a. land-grabbing). No longer are minority characters either non-existent or burlesqued. No longer are novels dealing with the Western experience confined to the relatively few years from the close of the Civil War to the opening of the twentieth century. Writers range freely throughout our history, and even into prehistory. One major distributor of paperbacks created a new category, "Americana," to encompass some of these new, evolving approaches to the Western. All to the good.

But friend, if you're looking to read new Westerns in a shorter form—a three thousand- or five thousand-word story, for instance—you might as well forget it.

In its effort to list markets for short stories, the bulletin of Western Writers of America leaves me depressed. You can submit your story to low-pay/no-pay publications such as (I'm making these up, but they're representative) *Bit & Bridle Tales* or *Wyoming Feed & Seed Journal,* but that's about it. Any contemporary writer looking to make even lunch money from Western stories had better lope to a fast-food outlet for a part-time job.

It's sad, because, as this collection sets out to establish, there lies behind us a whole century of wonderful, compelling Western short stories. Yes, some of them are steeped in the outdated techniques and mores of their time, but what fiction isn't? These stories carry, if not in all cases a deep love of the Western land and heritage that inspired them, then certainly a profound interest.

Thinking about this introduction, however, it struck me that instead of dwelling exclusively on the past, I could more profitably look ahead, trying to glimpse the future of Western fiction in the next hundred years. Personally I suspected the outlook was bleak, but I didn't want to rely on my own opinion.

I asked half a dozen outstanding writers of Westerns for their views, with surprisingly affirmative results.

III

My first respondent was the former president of Western Writers of America, Dale Walker. Dale is a friend, and a writer of excellent nonfiction about the West. He writes occasional fiction, too. And he has keen eyes:

"The old Western story—that scion of Buntline and Beadle, the pulps and 50,000-word 'paperback original,' ten percent myth and ninety percent horse apple—is dead and has been, Louis L'Amour reprints notwithstanding, for at least a decade. But the passing of the old formulaic Western does not translate to the death of the story of the Old American West. Nobody is writing 'Westerns' now, nor will they in the twenty-first century, but there will always be literature inspired by our greatest national experience, the westward movement."

Miles Hood Swarthout, a screenwriter of note and the son of author Glendon Swarthout (*The Shootist* et al.) sounded a similar note:

"Old warhorses like the stories about Custer, Buffalo Bill, Wild Bill Hickok, Billy the Kid, Calamity Jane, Annie Oakley, the Earps and the James boys, the cattle drives, the Oregon Trail migration, and the Gold Rush have just been done to death. Time for a change!"

Loren Estleman is one of the best and most original writers of contemporary Westerns. Loren's the president elect of Western Writers of America, and outspoken:

"The 'traditional Western' is hackery, pure and simple; none of the authentic classics can be so categorized, and the Max Brands and Frank Grubers who typified it are responsible for the form's subliterary status . . ."[1]

Loren continues, "The death of the so-called 'traditional Western' is not mourned by serious artists, who realize that none of the great Westerns were traditional, and that to cast off the chains of the pulp past is to open the horizon."

The least sanguine of all my respondents is one of the most talented writers of this generation, Elmore Leonard. His clean, powerful prose and remarkable evocation of character, often grim, just as often funny, have made him, deservedly, a literary star as well as a popular success.[2] Dutch Leonard wrote me only a few days after receiving a glowing advance review for his collection of Western stories, *The Tonto Woman*. The review said it "might even revive the moribund Western literary genre," to which the author replied to me, "I really don't see it happening. Did *Lonesome Dove* revive the market? A Western now and then might take off, but I don't see one book or even a few reviving the genre."

The more confident response was Loren Estleman's:

"I don't agree that the Western is in any sort of danger and as president-elect of WWA I'm making it my first order of business to persuade Western writers to stop spreading prophecies of doom. . . . People take you at your own evaluation."

Writing of past sins, celluloid variety, Loren sounded a note similar to that in his comment about prose writers. After referring to the overwhelming success of *Dances with Wolves, Unforgiven,* and *Lonesome Dove,* he said, "A bunch of hack directors killed the spark by dumping on us the same old clichés in *Bad Girls, Lightning Jack,* and *The Quick and the Dead*. . . . What I find interesting is that *Wyatt Earp* was considered a big enough

---

[1] Of necessity, Max Brand is included in this collection, represented by what many consider his finest short story. His popularity and mind-blowing output can't be ignored.

[2] We would have liked to include "3:10 to Yuma," arguably Leonard's finest Western story, in this book, but the rights to his Western stories were unavailable at the time of publication.

disappointment to end the Western, while *Waterworld* and *The Postman*, bigger disasters both, did not stop Hollywood from filming science fiction."[3]

Judy Alter, a Texan, has written distinguished fiction and nonfiction about Western women. "I think there will always be a market for innovative approaches to Western material," she said, citing as examples Cormac McCarthy and Tony Hillerman.

Richard S. Wheeler has won awards for his Western fiction, and written and edited admirable works of American history. He admits the Western has its problems, but is not daunted by them:

"Urbanization, technology, and increasing distance from the frontier period may operate against the genre. But Westerns were really not about the frontier; they were about character. They taught several generations of Americans the virtues that set us apart here in the New World, and equipped each of us to cope. From Westerns we learned about courage, bravery, loyalty, and optimism. . . . Critics of the genre condemn it for just that reason: it supplies standards and ideals the critics don't like. . . . There is a profound thirst for stories that have admirable heroes we all want to emulate."[4]

Then what kind of books and stories will be written? What kind of pictures shot? Miles Hood Swarthout gave an interesting answer:

"As we approach the millennium, another important transition period in America's rather short history, I think you'll find that the most thoughtful writers . . . may also be exploring the *transitional periods* of our past two centuries."

Miles cites as examples of works that explore what he calls transitional eras Charles Frazier's *Cold Mountain* (end of the Civil War); the film *Sommersby* (ditto); *The Good Old Boys* (traditional cowboy facing the onslaught of change, in both Elmer Kelton's novel and the film directed by Tommy Lee Jones); and *The Shootist*, for which Miles cowrote the screenplay, from his father's novel about the end of an era, and of the life of one of the last gunfighters—ironically, the end of the life of a Western icon, too: it was John Wayne's last movie.

"The best writers," he concludes, "will be more effectively mining the nooks and crannies of the Western myth . . . the transitional periods in the conquering and settling of the American West—the cracks and historical crevices hiding lesser-known characters and events whose mostly true stories cry out to be told."

---

3 It's hard for me to fathom the reason *The Postman* tanked with such speed and completeness. I found it a watchable three hours, no worse than scores of other pictures and, in some respects, better. I submit that it, too, is a Western. Post-Atomic, but a Western.

4 As I write this in late autumn of 1998, and cast an eye at Washington, I can only murmur a thoroughly bipartisan, "Amen."

Richard Wheeler sees the more familiar West continuing to exert a strong hold on readers:

"The pessimistic historical revisionists have one thing wrong. Westering people brimmed with optimism and joy, and their high spirits and laughter dissolved their tribulations. The mythic Western catches that. 'Realistic' literature about the West usually doesn't.

"There is ongoing demand for historical Westerns, and I expect . . . big, serious novels that realistically portray our frontier life, and explore the human condition, will continue to sell. There is so much Western history that has never appeared in novels that the future of this sort of work seems boundless."

To which Loren Estleman adds, "The American Western has risen after its death more times than Wile E. Coyote. . . . The truth is that the Western cannot by its very nature be defeated. . . . General acceptance of the Western as our nation's only unique contribution to world literature is just around a very close corner."

Tom Doherty concludes, "No category trends steadily upward, but those of value do not disappear. The Western is fundamental to the understanding of the men and women who opened and won a continent. They farmed and fought and built a nation destined to become the richest and most powerful on earth. They were a diverse people and, as a people, made mistakes, but most of us share a real pride in what they accomplished. There is value in telling their story, and many who wish to hear."

IV

So there you are. Heartening words.

Maybe it's necessary to mourn the passing of the much-loved "traditional" Western story, novel, and film—driven to the grave not only by Mr. Lucas and his clever colleagues, but by triteness and bad writing. Maybe we must say adios to the past by celebrating it in a collection like this one, then move on to some of those new vistas described for us by some very talented writers. If we're at all convinced by their arguments, we should look forward eagerly to the new directions and new techniques of presentation.

And maybe if all those good predictions come true, another hundred years from now another team of editors may put together another celebratory anthology, and show us how the Western short story went on, thriving in ways we can't possibly imagine at this moment.

I've but one regret: that I won't be around to read it, and cheer.

Hilton Head Island,
South Carolina
1 December 1999

Preface

In the beginning . . .

by John Jakes

IN THE BEGINNING there was the 19th-century dime novel.

As I wrote in my essay *The Western and How We Got It*,[1] "The Western was, in its first life, an Eastern. . . . The earliest dime novels were created in the tradition of Cooper, (William Gilmore) Simms, and Sir Walter Scott. The very first one of them, *Malaeska: The Indian Wife of the White Hunter,* was published in June 1860 by the firm of Beadle and Company of William Street, New York. The work . . . had already appeared as a prize story in a magazine called *The Ladies' Companion.*" The "frontier" which the story explored for the wide-eyed reader was the Catskill mountains of New York.

Edmund Pearson described this new publishing format as ". . . a thin little book . . . about six inches high and four inches broad . . . the covers were of saffron paper—the book was a 'yellow-backed Beadle.'" Though clerics, parents, and other guardians of morality soon viewed Beadle novels as insidious threats, millions read and came to love these thrill-packed tales of honorable heroes, pure heroines, and rotten villains, encased in layers of purple prose in which dialogue frequently ended with one or more exclams (!!!).

Over the years the dime novel's format changed. Beadle's plain saffron covers were replaced by illustrations, usually engravings but later luridly colored line art. Whatever the package, the popularity of the contents lasted well into the first decade of the 20th century, by which time the Western story as we know it was emerging in general fiction magazines.

Was there literary value in dime novels? Apart from the pleasure they provided, hardly. The critic E. F. Bleiler in his introduction to a collection of eight representative dime novels observes, ". . . *Malaeska* . . . was an adult story, reasonably well told, a competent example of early Victorian

[1] *The Arbor House Treasury of Great Western Stories,* ed. Pronzini Greenberg, Arbor House, 1982.

commercial writing. It would be pleasant to say that the dime novel held to this level, but it would not be true. . . . What began as a marketing venture for adult books ended as an almost entirely juvenile form."

Dime novels typically featured series characters: a detective (Old King Brady, Nick Carter); a clever inventor (Frank Reade, Jack Wright); a college athlete (Frank Merriwell); or, once the reading public became aware of major events and figures in the Western expansion, frontiersmen (Deadwood Dick *et al.*) A bright star in this constellation, discovered and first written about in 1869 by Edward Zane Carroll Judson under the pseudonym Ned Buntline, was William F. Cody. Cody's chief chronicler, however, was an ex-Confederate soldier of fortune, Colonel Prentiss Ingraham. An excerpt from *Adventures of Buffalo Bill from Boyhood to Manhood* (subtitled "Deeds of Daring and Romantic Incidents in the Life of Wm. F. Cody, the Monarch of Bordermen"), will demonstrate the Ingraham style. The story was published in *Beadle's Boys Library* in 1881. In Chapter XXX, "The Yellow Hand Duel," Ingraham writes:

> "The scout and the chief came within a hundred yards of each other.
> "Then the Indian cried out in his own tongue:
> "'I know Pa-e-has-ka the Great White Hunter and want to fight him.'"
> "'Then come on, you red devil, and have it out,' shouted Buffalo Bill."

Soon the scout and the Cheyenne brave are locked in hand-to-hand combat. The fight, "hardly five seconds in duration," ends predictably:

> "Buffalo Bill had driven his knife into the broad red breast, and then tore from his head the scalp and feather war-bonnet, and waving it over his head, shouted in ringing tones:
> "*Bravo! The first scalp to avenge Custer!*" (Italics are Ingraham's.)

Because the settled East was insatiably curious about the Wild West, it was probably inevitable that famous bad men became dime-novel heroes or, to use a modern term, anti-heroes.

Foremost among these were the James brothers. After their initial appearance, they quickly became so popular, other publishers featured them too. At one time Street and Smith published both *Jesse James Stories* and *The James Boys Weekly*. E. F. Bleiler again:

"Many of these stories were completely fictional, and had no relationship whatever to the historical doings of Jesse and Frank. A typical example is *Jesse James's Diamond Deal, or Robbing the Red Hands* . . . [1902], in which Jesse destroys a criminal secret society and hijacks their loot. Of all the major publishers only Beadle refused to chronicle the nefarious doings of the Jameses."

In the 1890s publishers had already discovered cross merchandising. A famous dime-novel detective challenged the outlaws in his own publication, in a story entitled *The James Boys in Boston, or Old King Brady and the Car of Gold.*

While the various authors writing Frank and Jesse stories couldn't hide the history of the brothers, they could at least put a literary spin on their characters. Consider this short selection from *Frank James on the Trail* (1882), author unknown. The speaker is Frank himself:

> " 'Stow it!' " thundered the bushranger. 'Don't try any of your gibberish with me. I ain't been very particular in my life about knocking a fellow on the head if he stood in my way, but if I did a trifle more, I never put a pal's life in my pocket and drunk out his heart's blood in the nearest saloon. No; the James boys never sold a pal or sneaked a swag. Frank always went straight to his work, whether it was a man or a bank. No; he'd stand or fall like a man, not like a cur that would bite you in your sleep, and sell your wisen[2] to the rope as he would a bale of wool or a cask of tallow.' "

From these purple roots grew the form we celebrate in this collection.

---

2 Meaning unclear. Possibly it's a variant of "wisent," a word commonly used in the 1860s–80s as a synonym for bison. See *Random House Dictionary of the English Language.* Using this interpretation, however, the line still makes no sense.

A Century
of Great Western
Stories

Louis L'Amour was the most successful Western writer of all time, selling 15,000–20,000 books a day at the height of his popularity. He wrote the kind of action fiction beloved by so many generations of Americans, with strong heroes, evil villains, proud, energetic heroines, and all of the excitement and danger that the West represented. His novels include such masterpieces as *Hondo, Shalako, Down the Long Hills, The Cherokee Trail,* and *Last of the Breed.* His most famous series was the Sacketts saga, later made into several television movies. And yet, often overlooked in all his success, was the gentler and more philosophic side of L'Amour, as demonstrated in this wonderful story.

The Gift of Cochise

Louis L'Amour

Tense, and white to the lips, Angie Lowe stood in the door of her cabin with a double-barreled shotgun in her hands. Besides the door was a Winchester '73, and on the table inside the house were two Walker Colts.

Facing the cabin were twelve Apaches on ragged calico ponies, and one of the Indians had lifted his hand palm outward. The Apache sitting the white-splashed bay pony was Cochise.

Beside Angie were her seven-year-old son Jimmy and her five-year-old daughter Jane.

Cochise sat his pony in silence; his black, unreadable eyes studied the woman, the children, the cabin, and the small garden. He looked at the two ponies in the corral and the three cows. His eyes strayed to the small stack of hay cut from the meadow, and to the few steers farther up the canyon.

Three times the warriors of Cochise had attacked this solitary cabin and three times they had been turned back. In all, they had lost seven men, and three had been wounded. Four ponies had been killed. His braves reported that there was no man in the house, only a woman and two children, so Cochise had come to see for himself this woman who was so certain a shot with a rifle and who killed his fighting men.

These were some of the same fighting men who had outfought, outguessed, and outrun the finest American army on record, an army outnumbering the Apaches by a hundred to one. Yet a lone woman with two small children had fought them off, and the woman was scarcely more than a girl. And she was prepared to fight now. There was a glint of admiration in

the old eyes that appraised her. The Apache was a fighting man, and he respected fighting blood.

"Where is your man?"

"He has gone to El Paso." Angie's voice was steady, but she was frightened as she had never been before. She recognized Cochise from descrip-
tions, and she knew that if he decided to kill or capture her it would be
done. Until now, the sporadic attacks she had fought off had been those of
casual bands of warriors who raided her in passing.

"He has been gone a long time. How long?"

Angie hesitated, but it was not in her to lie. "He has been gone four
months."

Cochise considered that. No one but a fool would leave such a woman,
or such fine children. Only one thing could have prevented his return.
"Your man is dead," he said.

Angie waited, her heart pounding with heavy, measured beats. She had
guessed long ago that Ed had been killed but the way Cochise spoke did
not imply that Apaches had killed him, only that he must be dead or he
would have returned.

"You fight well," Cochise said. "You have killed my young men."

"Your young men attacked me." She hesitated then added, "They stole
my horses."

"Your man is gone. Why do you not leave?"

Angie looked at him with surprise. "Leave? Why, this is my home. This
land is mine. This spring is mine. I shall not leave."

"This was an Apache spring," Cochise reminded her reasonably.

"The Apache lives in the mountains," Angie replied. "He does not need
this spring. I have two children, and I do need it."

"But when the Apache comes this way, where shall he drink? His throat
is dry and you keep him from water."

The very fact that Cochise was willing to talk raised her hopes. There
had been a time when the Apache made no war on the white man.
"Cochise speaks with a forked tongue," she said. "There is water yonder."
She gestured toward the hills, where Ed had told her there were springs.
"But if the people of Cochise come in peace they may drink at this spring."

The Apache leader smiled faintly. Such a woman would rear a nation of
warriors. He nodded at Jimmy. "The small one—does he also shoot?"

"He does," Angie said proudly, "and well, too!" She pointed at an up-
thrust leaf of prickly pear. "Show them, Jimmy."

The prickly pear was an easy two hundred yards away, and the Winchester was long and heavy, but he lifted it eagerly and steadied it against the
doorjamb as his father had taught him, held his sight an instant, then fired.
The bud on top of the prickly pear disintegrated.

There were grunts of appreciation from the dark-faced warriors. Cochise chuckled.

"The little warrior shoots well. It is well you have no man. You might raise an army of little warriors to fight my people."

"I have no wish to fight your people," Angie said quietly. "Your people have your ways, and I have mine. I live in peace when I am left in peace. I did not think," she added with dignity, "that the great Cochise made war on women!"

The Apache looked at her, then turned his pony away. "My people will trouble you no longer," he said. "You are the mother of a strong son."

"What about my two ponies?" she called after him. "Your young men took them from me."

Cochise did not turn or look back, and the little cavalcade of riders followed him away. Angie stepped back into the cabin and closed the door. Then she sat down abruptly, her face white, the muscles in her legs trembling.

When morning came, she went cautiously to the spring for water. Her ponies were back in the corral. They had been returned during the night.

Slowly, the days drew on. Angie broke a small piece of the meadow and planted it. Alone, she cut hay in the meadow and built another stack. She saw Indians several times, but they did not bother her. One morning, when she opened the door, a quarter of an antelope lay on the step, but no Indian was in sight. Several times, during the weeks that followed, she saw moccasin tracks near the spring.

Once, going out at daybreak, she saw an Indian girl dipping water from the spring. Angie called to her, and the girl turned quickly, facing her. Angie walked toward her, offering a bright red silk ribbon. Pleased at the gift, the Apache girl left.

And the following morning there was another quarter of an antelope on her step—but she saw no Indian.

Ed Lowe had built the cabin in West Dog Canyon in the spring of 1871, but it was Angie who chose the spot, not Ed. In Sante Fe they would have told you that Ed Lowe was good-looking, shiftless, and agreeable. He was, also, unfortunately handy with a pistol.

Angie's father had come from County Mayo to New York and from New York to the Mississippi, where he became a tough, brawling river boatman. In New Orleans, he met a beautiful Cajun girl and married her. Together, they started west for Santa Fe, and Angie was born en route. Both parents died of cholera when Angie was fourteen. She lived with an Irish family for the following three years, then married Ed Lowe when she was seventeen.

Santa Fe was not good for Ed, and Angie kept after him until they started south. It was Apache country, but they kept on until they reached the old Spanish ruin in West Dog. Here there were grass, water, and shelter from the wind. There was fuel, and there were pinons and game. And Angie, with an Irish eye for the land, saw that it would grow crops.

The house itself was built on the ruins of the old Spanish building, using the thick walls and the floor. The location had been admirably chosen for defense. The house was built in a corner of the cliff, under the sheltering overhang, so that approach was possible from only two directions, both covered by an easy field of fire from the door and windows.

For seven months, Ed worked hard and steadily. He put in the first crop, he built the house, and proved himself a handy man with tools. He repaired the old plow they had bought, cleaned out the spring, and paved and walled it with slabs of stone. If he was lonely for the carefree companions of Santa Fe, he gave no indication of it. Provisions were low, and when he finally started off to the south, Angie watched him go with an ache in her heart.

She did not know whether she loved Ed. The first flush of enthusiasm had passed, and Ed Lowe had proved something less than she had believed. But he had tried, she admitted. And it had not been easy for him. He was an amiable soul, given to whittling and idle talk, all of which he missed in the loneliness of the Apache country. And when he rode away, she had no idea whether she would ever see him again. She never did.

Santa Fe was far and away to the north, but the growing village of El Paso was less than a hundred miles to the west, and it was there Ed Lowe rode for supplies and seed.

He had several drinks—his first in months—in one of the saloons. As the liquor warmed his stomach, Ed Lowe looked around agreeably. For a moment, his eyes clouded with worry as he thought of his wife and children back in Apache country, but it was not in Ed Lowe to worry for long. He had another drink and leaned on the bar, talking to the bartender. All Ed had ever asked of life was enough to eat, a horse to ride, an occasional drink, and companions to talk with. Not that he had anything important to say. He just liked to talk.

Suddenly a chair grated on the floor, and Ed turned. A lean, powerful man with a shock of uncut black hair and a torn, weather-faded shirt stood at bay. Facing him across the table were three hard-faced young men, obviously brothers.

Ches Lane did not notice Ed Lowe watching from the bar. He had eyes only for the men facing him. "You done that deliberate!" The statement was a challenge.

The broad-chested man on the left grinned through broken teeth. "That's right, Ches. I done it deliberate. You killed Dan Tolliver on the Brazos."

"He made the quarrel." Comprehension came to Ches. He was boxed, and by three of the fighting, blood-hungry Tollivers.

"Don't make no difference," the broad-chested Tolliver said. "'Who sheds a Tolliver's blood, by a Tolliver's hand must die!'"

Ed Lowe moved suddenly from the bar. "Three to one is long odds," he said, his voice low and friendly. "If the gent in the corner is willin', I'll side him."

Two Tollivers turned toward him. Ed Lowe was smiling easily, his hand hovering near his gun. "You stay out of this!" one of the brothers said harshly.

"I'm in," Ed replied. "Why don't you boys light a shuck?"

"No, by—!" The man's hand dropped for his gun, and the room thundered with sound.

Ed was smiling easily, unworried as always. His gun flashed up. He felt it leap in his hand, saw the nearest Tolliver smashed back, and he shot him again as he dropped. He had only time to see Ches Lane with two guns out and another Tolliver down when something struck him through the stomach and he stepped back against the bar, suddenly sick.

The sound stopped, and the room was quiet, and there was the acrid smell of powder smoke. Three Tollivers were down and dead, and Ed Lowe was dying. Ches Lane crossed to him.

"We got 'em," Ed said, "we sure did. But they got me."

Suddenly his face changed. "Oh Lord in heaven, what'll Angie do?" And then he crumpled over on the floor and lay still, the blood staining his shirt and mingling with the sawdust.

Stiff-faced, Ches looked up. "Who was Angie?" he asked.

"His wife," the bartender told him. "She's up northeast somewhere, in Apache country. He was tellin' me about her. Two kids, too."

Ches Lane stared down at the crumpled, used-up body of Ed Lowe. The man had saved his life.

One he could have beaten, two he might have beaten; three would have killed him. Ed Lowe, stepping in when he did, had saved the life of Ches Lane.

"He didn't say where?"

"No."

Ches Lane shoved his hat back on his head. "What's northeast of here?"

The bartender rested his hands on the bar. "Cochise," he said.

For more than three months, whenever he could rustle the grub, Ches Lane quartered the country over and back. The trouble was, he had no lead to the location of Ed Lowe's homestead. An examination of Ed's horse revealed nothing. Lowe had bought seed and ammunition, and the seed indicated a good water supply, and the ammunition implied trouble. But in the country there was always trouble.

A man had died to save his life, and Ches Lane had a deep sense of obligation. Somewhere that wife waited, if she was still alive, and it was up to him to find her and look out for her. He rode northeast, cutting for sign, but found none. Sandstorms had wiped out any hope of back-trailing Lowe. Actually, West Dog Canyon was more east than north, but this he had no way of knowing.

North he went, skirting the rugged San Andreas Mountains. Heat baked him hot, dry winds parched his skin. His hair grew dry and stiff and alkali-whitened. He rode north, and soon the Apaches knew of him. He fought them at a lonely water hole, and he fought them on the run. They killed his horse, and he switched his saddle to the spare and rode on. They cornered him in the rocks, and he killed two of them and escaped by night.

They trailed him through the White Sands, and he left two more for dead. He fought fiercely and bitterly, and would not be turned from his quest. He turned east through the lava beds and still more east to the Pecos. He saw only two white men, and neither knew of a white woman.

The bearded man laughed harshly. "A woman alone? She wouldn't last a month! By now the Apaches got her, or she's dead. Don't be a fool! Leave this country before you die here."

Lean, wind-whipped, and savage, Ches Lane pushed on. The Mescaleros cornered him in Rawhide Draw and he fought them to a standstill. Grimly, the Apaches clung to his trail.

The sheer determination of the man fascinated them. Bred and born in a rugged and lonely land, the Apaches knew the difficulties of survival; they knew how a man could live, how he must live. Even as they tried to kill this man, they loved him, for he was one of their own.

Lane's jeans grew ragged. Two bullet holes were added to the old black hat. The slicker was torn; the saddle, so carefully kept until now, was scratched by gravel and brush. At night he cleaned his guns and by day he scouted the trails. Three times he found lonely ranch houses burned to the ground, the buzzard- and coyote-stripped bones of their owners lying nearby.

Once he found a covered wagon, its canvas flopping in the wind, a man lying sprawled on the seat with a pistol near his hand. He was dead and his wife was dead, and their canteens rattled like empty skulls.

Leaner every day, Ches Lane pushed on. He camped one night in a canyon near some white oaks. He heard a hoof click on stone and he backed away from his tiny fire, gun in hand.

The riders were white men, and there were two of them. Joe Tompkins and Wiley Lynn were headed west, and Ches Lane could have guessed why. They were men he had known before, and he told them what he was doing.

Lynn chuckled. He was a thin-faced man with lank yellow hair and dirty fingers. "Seems a mighty strange way to get a woman. There's some as comes easier."

"This ain't for fun," Ches replied shortly. "I got to find her."

Tompkins stared at him. "Ches, you're crazy! That gent declared himself in of his own wish and desire. Far's that goes, the gal's dead. No woman could last this long in Apache country."

At daylight, the two men headed west, and Ches Lane turned south.

Antelope and deer are curious creatures, often led to their death by curiosity. The longhorn, soon going wild on the plains, acquires the same characteristic. He is essentially curious. Any new thing or strange action will bring his head up and his ears alert. Often a longhorn, like a deer, can be lured within a stone's throw by some queer antic, by a handkerchief waving, by a man under a hide, by a man on foot.

This character of the wild things holds true of the Indian. The lonely rider who fought so desperately and knew the desert so well soon became a subject of gossip among the Apaches. Over the fires of many a rancheria they discussed this strange rider who seemed to be going nowhere, but always riding, like a lean wolf dog on a trail. He rode across the mesas and down the canyons; he studied signs at every water hole; he looked long from every ridge. It was obvious to the Indians that he searched for something—but what?

Cochise had come again to the cabin in West Dog Canyon. "Little warrior too small," he said, "too small for hunt. You join my people. Take Apache for man."

"No." Angie shook her head. "Apache ways are good for the Apache, and the white man's ways are good for white men—and women."

They rode away and said no more, but that night, as she had on many other nights after the children were asleep, Angie cried. She wept silently, her head pillowed on her arms. She was as pretty as ever, but her face was thin, showing the worry and struggle of the months gone by, the weeks and months without hope.

The crops were small but good. Little Jimmy worked beside her. At night, Angie sat alone on the steps and watched the shadows gather down the long canyon, listening to the coyotes yapping from the rim of the Guadalupes, hearing the horses blowing in the corral. She watched, still hopeful, but now she knew that Cochise was right: Ed would not return.

But even if she had been ready to give this up, the first home she had known, there could be no escape. Here she was protected by Cochise. Other Apaches from other tribes would not so willingly grant her peace.

At daylight she was up. The morning air was bright and balmy, but soon it would be hot again. Jimmy went to the spring for water, and when breakfast was over, the children played while Angie sat in the shade of a huge old cottonwood and sewed. It was a Sunday, warm and lovely. From time to time, she lifted her eyes to look down the canyon, half smiling at her own foolishness.

The hard-packed earth of the yard was swept clean of dust; the pans hanging on the kitchen wall were neat and shining. The children's hair had been clipped, and there was a small bouquet on the kitchen table.

After awhile, Angie put aside her sewing and changed her dress. She did her hair carefully, and then, looking in her mirror, she reflected with sudden pain that she *was* pretty, and that she was only a girl.

Resolutely, she turned from the mirror and, taking up her Bible, went back to the seat under the cottonwood. The children left their playing and came to her, for this was a Sunday ritual, their only one. Opening the Bible, she read slowly.

". . . though I walk through the valley of the shadow of death. I will fear no evil; for thou art with me; thy rod and thy staff, they comfort me. Thou preparest a table before me in the presence of mine enemies: thou . . ."

"Mommy." Jimmy tugged at her sleeve. "Look!"

CHES LANE HAD reached a narrow canyon by midafternoon and decided to make camp. There was a small possibility he would find another such spot, and he was dead tired, his muscles sodden with fatigue. The canyon was one of those unexpected gashes in the cap rock that gave no indication of its presence until you came right on it. After some searching, Ches found a route to the bottom and made camp under a wind-hollowed overhang. There was water, and there was a small patch of grass.

After his horse had a drink and a roll on the ground, it began cropping eagerly at the rich, green grass, and Ches built a smokeless fire of some ancient driftwood in the canyon bottom. It was his first hot meal in days, and when he had finished he put out his fire, rolled a smoke, and leaned back contentedly.

Before darkness settled, he climbed to the rim and looked over the country. The sun had gone down, and the shadows were growing long. After a half hour of study, he decided there was no living thing within miles, except for the usual desert life. Returning to the bottom, he moved his horse to fresh grass, then rolled in his blanket. For the first time in a month, he slept without fear.

He woke up suddenly in the broad daylight. The horse was listening to something, his head up. Swiftly, Ches went to the horse and led it back under the overhang. Then he drew on his boots, rolled his blankets, and saddled the horse. Still he heard no sound.

Climbing the rim again, he studied the desert and found nothing. Returning to his horse, he mounted up and rode down the canyon toward the flatland beyond. Coming out of the canyon mouth, he rode right into the middle of a war party of more than twenty Apaches—invisible until suddenly they stood up behind rocks, their rifles leveled. And he didn't have a chance.

Swiftly, they bound his wrists to the saddle horn and tied his feet. Only then did he see the man who led the party. It was Cochise.

He was a lean, wiry Indian of past fifty, his black hair streaked with gray, his features strong and clean-cut. He stared at Lane, and there was nothing in his face to reveal what he might be thinking.

Several of the younger warriors pushed forward, talking excitedly and waving their arms. Ches Lane understood some of it, but he sat straight in the saddle, his head up, waiting. Then Cochise spoke and the party turned, and, leading his horse, they rode away.

The miles grew long and the sun was hot. He was offered no water and he asked for none. The Indians ignored him. Once a young brave rode near and struck him viciously. Lane made no sound, gave no indication of pain. When they finally stopped, it was beside a huge anthill swarming with big, red desert ants.

Roughly, they quickly untied him and jerked him from his horse. He dug in his heels and shouted at them in Spanish. "The Apaches are women! They tie me to the ants because they are afraid to fight me!"

An Indian struck him, and Ches glared at the man. If he must die, he would show them how it should be done. Yet he knew the unpredictable nature of the Indian, of his great respect for courage.

"Give me a knife, and I'll kill any of your warriors!"

They stared at him, and one powerfully built Apache angrily ordered them to get on with it. Cochise spoke, and the big warrior replied angrily.

Ches Lane nodded at the antihill. "Is this the death for a fighting man? I have fought your strong men and beaten them. I have left no trail for them to follow, and for months I have lived among you, and now only by accident have you captured me. Give me a knife," he added grimly, "and I will fight *him!*" He indicated the big, black-faced Apache.

The warrior's cruel mouth hardened, and he struck Ches across the face.

The white man tasted blood and fury. "Woman!" Ches said. "Coyote! You are afraid!" Ches turned on Cochise, as the Indians stood irresolute. "Free my hands and let me fight!" he demanded. "If I win, let me go free."

Cochise said something to the big Indian. Instantly, there was stillness. Then an Apache sprang forward and, with a slash of his knife, freed Lane's hands. Shaking loose the thongs, Ches Lane chafed his wrists to bring back the circulation. An Indian threw a knife at his feet. It was his own bowie knife.

Ches took off his riding boots. In sock feet, his knife gripped low in his hand, its cutting edge up, he looked at the big warrior.

"I promise you nothing," Cochise said in Spanish, "but an honorable death."

The big warrior came at him on cat feet. Warily, Ches circled. He had not only to defeat this Apache but to escape. He permitted himself a side glance toward his horse. It stood alone. No Indian held it.

The Apache closed swiftly, thrusting wickedly with the knife. Ches, who had learned knife-fighting in the bayou country of Louisiana, turned his hip sharply, and the blade slid past him. He struck swiftly, but the Apache's forward movement deflected the blade, and it failed to penetrate. However, as it swept up between the Indian's body and arm, it cut a deep gash in the warrior's left armpit.

The Indian sprang again, like a clawing cat, streaming blood. Ches moved aside, but a backhand sweep nicked him, and he felt the sharp bite of the blade. Turning, he paused on the balls of his feet.

He had had no water in hours. His lips were cracked. Yet he sweated now, and the salt of it stung his eyes. He stared into the malevolent black eyes of the Apache, then moved to meet him. The Indian lunged, and Ches sidestepped like a boxer and spun on the ball of his foot.

The sudden side step threw the Indian past him, but Ches failed to drive the knife into the Apache's kidney when his foot rolled on a stone. The point left a thin red line across the Indian's back. The Indian was quick. Before Ches could recover his balance, he grasped the white man's knife wrist. Desperately, Ches grabbed for the Indian's knife hand and got the wrist, and they stood there straining, chest to chest.

Seeing his chance, Ches suddenly let his knees buckle, then brought up his knee and fell back, throwing the Apache over his head to the sand. Instantly, he whirled and was on his feet, standing over the Apache. The warrior had lost his knife, and he lay there, staring up, his eyes black with hatred.

Coolly, Ches stepped back, picked up the Indian's knife, and tossed it to him contemptuously. There was a grunt from the watching Indians, and then his antagonist rushed. But loss of blood had weakened the warrior, and Ches stepped in swiftly, struck the blade aside, then thrust the point of his blade hard against the Indian's belly.

Black eyes glared into his without yielding. A thrust, and the man would be disemboweled, but Ches stepped back. "He is a strong man," Ches said in Spanish. "It is enough that I have won."

Deliberately, he walked to his horse and swung into the saddle. He looked around, and every rifle covered him.

So he had gained nothing. He had hoped that mercy might lead to mercy, that the Apaches' respect for a fighting man would win his freedom. He had failed. Again they bound him to his horse, but they did not take his knife from him.

When they camped at last, he was given food and drink. He was bound again, and a blanket was thrown over him. At daylight they were again in the saddle. In Spanish he asked where they were taking him, but they gave no indication of hearing. When they stopped again, it was beside a pole corral, near a stone cabin.

WHEN JIMMY SPOKE, Angie got quickly to her feet. She recognized Cochise with a start of relief, but she saw instantly that this was a war party. And then she saw the prisoner.

Their eyes met and she felt a distinct shock. He was a white man, a big, unshaven man who badly needed both a bath and a haircut, his clothes ragged and bloody. Cochise gestured at the prisoner.

"No take Apache man, you take white man. This man good for hunt, good for fight. He strong warrior. You take 'em."

Flushed and startled, Angie stared at the prisoner and caught a faint glint of humor in his dark eyes.

"Is this here the fate worse than death I hear tell of?" he inquired gently.

"Who are you?" she asked, and was immediately conscious that it was an extremely silly question.

The Apaches had drawn back and were watching curiously. She could do nothing for the present but accept the situation. Obviously they intended to do her a kindness, and it would not do to offend them. If they had not brought this man to her, he might have been killed.

"Name's Ches Lane, ma'am," he said. "Will you untie me? I'd feel a lot safer."

"Of course." Still flustered, she went to him and untied his hands. One Indian said something, and the others chuckled; then, with a whoop, they swung their horses and galloped off down the canyon.

Their departure left her suddenly helpless, the shadowy globe of her loneliness shattered by this utterly strange man standing before her, this big, bearded man brought to her out of the desert.

She smoothed her apron, suddenly pale as she realized what his delivery to her implied. What must he think of her? She turned away quickly. "There's hot water," she said hastily, to prevent his speaking. "Dinner is almost ready."

She walked quickly into the house and stopped before the stove, her mind a blank. She looked around her as if she had suddenly woken up in a strange place. She heard water being poured into the basin by the door, and heard him take Ed's razor. She had never moved the box. To have moved it would—

"Sight of work done here, ma'am."

She hesitated, then turned with determination and stepped into the doorway. "Yes, Ed—"

"You're Angie Lowe."

Surprised, she turned toward him, and recognized his own startled awareness of her. As he shaved, he told her about Ed, and what had happened that day in the saloon.

"He—Ed was like that. He never considered consequences until it was too late."

"Lucky for me he didn't."

He was younger looking with his beard gone. There was a certain quiet dignity in his face. She went back inside and began putting plates on the table. She was conscious that he had moved to the door and was watching her.

"You don't have to stay," she said. "You owe me nothing. Whatever Ed did, he did because he was that kind of person. You aren't responsible."

He did not answer, and when she turned again to the stove, she glanced swiftly at him. He was looking across the valley.

There was a studied deference about him when he moved to a place at the table. The children stared, wide-eyed and silent; it had been so long since a man sat at this table.

Angie could not remember when she had felt like this. She was awkwardly conscious of her hands, which never seemed to be in the right place or doing the right things. She scarcely tasted her food, nor did the children.

Ches Lane had no such inhibitions. For the first time, he realized how hungry he was. After the half-cooked meat of lonely, trailside fires, this was tender and flavored. Hot biscuits, desert honey . . . suddenly he looked up, embarrassed at his appetite.

"You were really hungry," she said.

"Man can't fix much, out on the trail."

Later, after he'd got his bedroll from his saddle and unrolled it on the hay in the barn, he walked back to the house and sat on the lowest step. The sun was gone, and they watched the cliffs stretch their red shadows across the valley. A quail called plaintively, a mellow sound of twilight.

"You needn't worry about Cochise," she said. "He'll soon be crossing into Mexico."

"I wasn't thinking about Cochise."

That left her with nothing to say, and she listened again to the quail and watched a lone bright star in the sky.

"A man could get to like it here," he said quietly.

John M. Cunningham's most famous story is "The Tin Star," which moviegoers around the globe know better as the legendary Western film *High Noon*. As with most of his stories and novels, "The Tin Star" takes a familiar situation and gives it new life. Cunningham has always been careful to give us real people and carefully drawn backdrops for his stories. He has a reporter's eye for the one right detail that brings a setting to vivid life. His novels include *Warhorse* and *Starfall*.

The Tin Star

John M. Cunningham

Sheriff Doane looked at his deputy and then down at the daisies he had picked for his weekly visit, lying wrapped in newspaper on his desk. "I'm sorry to hear you say that, Toby. I was kind of counting on you to take over after me."

"Don't get me wrong, Doane," Toby said, looking through the front window. "I'm not afraid. I'll see you through this shindig. I'm not afraid of Jordan or young Jordan or any of them. But I want to tell you now. I'll wait till Jordan's train gets in. I'll wait to see what he does. I'll see you through whatever happens. After that, I'm quitting."

Doane began kneading his knuckles, his face set against the pain as he gently rubbed the arthritic, twisted bones. He said nothing.

Toby looked around, his brown eyes troubled in his round, olive-skinned face. "What's the use of holding down a job like this? Look at you. What'd you ever get out of it? Enough to keep you eating. And what for?"

Doane stopped kneading his arthritic hands and looked down at the star on his shirtfront. He looked from it to the smaller one on Toby's. "That's right," he said. "They don't even hang the right ones. You risk your life catching somebody, and the damned juries let them go so they can come back and shoot at you. You're poor all your life, you got to do everything twice, and in the end they pay you off in lead. So you can wear a tin star. It's a job for a dog, son."

Toby's voice did not rise, but his eyes were a little wider in his round, gentle face. "Then why keep on with it? What for? I've been working for you for two years—trying to keep the law so sharp-nosed money-grabbers can get rich, while we piddle along on what the county pays us. I've seen men I used to bust playing marbles going up and down this street on four-hundred-dollar saddles, and what've I got? Nothing. Not a damned thing."

There was a little smile around Doane's wide mouth. "That's right, Toby. It's all for free. The headaches, the bullets and everything, all for free. I found that out long ago." The mock-grave look vanished. "But somebody's got to be around and take care of things." He looked out of the window at the people walking up and down the crazy boardwalks. "I like it free. You know what I mean? You don't get a thing for it. You've got to risk everything. And you're free inside. Like the larks. You know the larks? How they get up in the sky and sing when they want to? A pretty bird. A very pretty bird. That's the way I like to feel inside."

Toby looked at him without expression. "That's the way you look at it. I don't see it. I've only got one life. You talk about doing it all for nothing, and that gives you something. What? What've you got now, waiting for Jordan to come?"

"I don't know yet. We'll have to wait and see."

Toby turned back to the window. "All right, but I'm through. I don't see any sense in risking your neck for nothing."

"Maybe you will," Doane said, beginning to work on his hands again.

"Here comes Mettrick. I guess he don't give up so easy. He's still got that resignation in his hand."

"I guess he doesn't," Doane said. "But I'm through listening. Has young Jordan come out of the saloon yet?"

"No," Toby said, and stepped aside as the door opened. Mettrick came in.

"Now listen, Doane," he burst out, "for the last time—"

"Shut up, Percy," Doane said. "Sit down over there and shut up or get out."

The flare went out of the mayor's eyes. "Doane," he moaned, "you are the biggest—"

"Shut up," Doane said. "Toby, has he come out yet?"

Toby stood a little back from the window, where the slant of golden sunlight, swarming with dust, wouldn't strike his white shirt.

"Yes. He's got a chair. He's looking this way, Doane. He's still drinking. I can see a bottle on the porch beside him."

"I expected that. Not that it makes much difference." He looked down at the bunch of flowers.

Mettrick, in the straight chair against the wall, looked up at him, his black eyes scornful in his long, hopeless face.

"Don't make much difference? Who the hell do you think you are, Doane? God? It just means he'll start the trouble without waiting for his stinking brother, that's all it means." His hand was shaking, and the white paper hanging listlessly from his fingers fluttered slightly. He looked at it angrily and stuck it out at Doane. "I gave it to you. I did the best I could. Whatever happens, don't be blaming me, Doane. I gave you a chance to resign, and if—" He left off and sat looking at the paper in his hand as though it were a dead puppy of his that somebody had run a buggy over.

Doane, standing with the square, almost chisel-pointed tips of his fingers just touching the flowers, turned slowly, with the care of movement he would have used around a crazy horse. "I know you're my friend, Percy. Just take it easy, Percy. If I don't resign, it's not because I'm ungrateful."

"Here comes Staley with the news," Toby said from the window. "He looks like somebody just shot his grandma."

Percy Mettrick laid his paper on the desk and began smoothing it out ruefully. "It's not as though it were dishonorable, Doane. You should have quit two years ago, when your hands went bad. It's not dishonorable now. You've still got time."

He glanced up at the wall clock. "It's only three. You've got an hour before he gets in . . . you can take your horse . . ." As Mettrick talked to himself, Doane looking slantwise at him with his little smile, and he grew more cheerful. "Here." He jabbed a pen out of Doane. "Sign it and get out of town."

The smile left Doane's mouth. "This is an elective office. I don't have to take orders, even if you are mayor." His face softened. "It's simpler than you think Percy. When they didn't hang Jordan, I knew this day would come. Five years ago, I knew it was coming, when they gave him that silly sentence. I've been waiting for it."

"But not to commit suicide," Mettrick said in a low voice, his eyes going down to Doane's gouty hands. Doane's knobby, twisted fingers closed slowly into fists, as though hiding themselves; his face flushed slightly.

"I may be slow, but I can still shoot."

The mayor stood up and went slowly over to the door.

"Good-bye, Doane."

"I'm not saying good-bye, Percy. Not yet."

"Good-bye," Mettrick repeated, and went out of the door.

Toby turned from the window. His face was tight around the mouth. "You should have resigned like he said, Doane. You ain't a match for one of them alone, much less two of them together. And if Pierce and Frank Colby come, too, like they was all together before—"

"Shut up, shut up," Doane said. "For God's sake, shut up." He sat down suddenly at the desk and covered his face with his hands. "Maybe the pen changes a man." He was sitting stiff, hardly breathing.

"What are you going to do, Doane?"

"Nothing. I can't do anything until they start something. I can't do a thing. . . . Maybe the pen changes a man. Sometimes it does. I remember—"

"Listen, Doane." Toby said, his voice, for the first time, urgent. "It maybe changes some men, but not Jordan. It's already planned, what they're going to do. Why else would young Jordan be over there, watching? He's come three hundred miles for this."

"I've seen men go in the pen hard as rock and come out peaceful and settle down. Maybe Jordan—"

Toby's face relapsed into dullness. He turned back to the window listlessly. Doane's hands dropped.

"You don't think that's true, Toby?"

Toby sighed. "You know it isn't so, Doane. He swore he'd get you. That's the truth."

Doane's hands came up again in front of his face, but this time he was looking at them, his big gray eyes going quickly from one to the other, almost as though he were afraid of them. He curled his fingers slowly into fists, and uncurled them slowly, pulling with all his might, yet slowly. A thin sheen on his face reflected the sunlight from the floor. He got up.

"Is he still there?" he asked.

"Sure, he's still there."

"Maybe he'll get drunk. Dead drunk."

"You can't get a Jordan that drunk."

Doane stood with feet apart, looking at the floor, staring back and forth along one of the cracks. "Why didn't they hang him?" he asked the silence in the room.

"Why didn't they hang him?" he repeated, his voice louder.

Toby kept his post by the window, not moving a muscle in his face, staring out at the man across the street. "I don't know," he said. "For murder, they should. I guess they should've, but they didn't."

Doane's eyes came again to the flowers, and some of the strain went out of his face. Then suddenly his eyes closed and he gave a long sigh, and then, luxuriously stretched his arms. "Good God!" he said, his voice easy again. "It's funny how it comes over you like that." He shook his head violently. "I don't know why it should. It's not the first time. But it always does."

"I know," Toby said.

"It just builds up and then it busts."

"I know."

"The train may be late."

Toby said nothing.

"You never can tell," Doane said, buckling on his gun belt. "Things may have changed with Jordan. Maybe won't even come. You never can tell. I'm going up to the cemetery as soon as we hear from Staley."

"I wouldn't. You'd just tempt young Jordan to start something."

"I've been going up there every Sunday since she died."

"We'd best both just stay in here. Let them make the first move."

Feet sounded on the steps outside and Doane stopped breathing for a second. Staley came in, his face pinched, tight and dead, his eyes on the floor. Duane looked him over carefully.

"Is it on time?" he asked steadily.

Staley looked up, his faded blue eyes distant, pointed somewhere over Doane's head. "Mr. Doane, you ain't handled this thing right. You should've drove young Jordan out of town." His hand went to his chest and he took off his deputy's badge.

"What are you doing?" Doane asked sharply.

"If you'd of handled it right, we could have beat this," Staley said, his voice louder.

"You know nobody's done nothing yet," Toby said softly, his gentle brown eyes on Staley. "There's nothing we can do until they start something."

"I'm quitting, Mr. Doane," Staley said. He looked around for someplace to put the star. He started for the desk, hesitated, and then awkwardly, with a peculiar diffidence, laid the star gently on the windowsill.

Doane's jaw began to jut a little. "You still haven't answered my question. Is the train on time?"

"Yes. Four-ten. Just on time." Staley stood staring at Doane, then swallowed. "I saw Frank Colby. He was in the livery putting up his horse. He'd had a long ride on that horse. I asked him what he was doing in town—friendly like." He ducked his head and swallowed again. "He didn't know I was a deputy, I had my star off." He looked up again. "They're all meeting together, Mr. Doane. Young Jordan, and Colby and Pierce. They're going to meet Jordan when he comes in. The same four."

"So you're quitting," Doane said.

"Yes, sir. It ain't been handled right."

Toby stood looking at him, his gentle eyes dull. "Get out," he said, his voice low and tight.

Staley looked at him, nodded, and tried to smile, which was too weak to last. "Sure."

Toby took a step toward him. Staley's eyes were wild as he stood against the door. He tried to back out of Toby's way.

"Get out," Toby said again, and his small brown fist flashed out. Staley stepped backward and fell down the steps in a sprawling heap, scrambled to his feet and hobbled away. Toby closed the door slowly. He stood rubbing his knuckles, his face red and tight.

"That didn't do any good," Doane said softly.

Toby turned on him. "It couldn't do no harm," he said acidly, throwing the words into Doane's face.

"You want to quit, too?" Doane asked, smiling.

"Sure, I want to quit," Toby shot out. "Sure. Go on to your blasted cemetery, go on with your flowers, old man—" He sat down suddenly on the straight chair. "Put a flower up there for me, too."

Doane went to the door. "Put some water on the heater, Toby. Set out the liniment that the vet gave me. I'll try it again when I get back. It might do some good yet."

He let himself out and stood in the sunlight on the porch, the flowers drooping in his hand, looking against the sun across the street at the dim figure under the shaded porch.

Then he saw the two other shapes hunkered against the front of the saloon in the shade of the porch, one on each side of young Jordan, who sat tilted back in a chair. Colby and Pierce. The glare of the sun beat back from the blinding white dust and fought shimmering in the air.

Doane pulled the brim of his hat farther down in front and stepped slowly down to the board sidewalk, observing carefully from squinted eyes, and just as carefully avoiding any pause which might be interpreted as a challenge.

Young Jordan had the bottle to his lips as Doane came out. He held it there for a moment motionless, and then, as Doane reached the walk, he passed the bottle slowly sideward to Colby and leaned forward, away from the wall, so that the chair came down softly. He sat there, leaning forward slightly, watching while Doane untied his horse. As Doane mounted, Jordan got up. Colby's hand grabbed one of his arms. He shook it off and untied his own horse from the rail.

Doane's mouth tightened and his eyes looked a little sad. He turned his horse, and holding the flowers so the jog would not rattle off the petals, headed up the street, looking straight ahead.

The hoofs of his horse made soft, almost inaudible little plops in the deep dust. Behind him he heard a sudden stamping of hooves and then the harsh splitting and crashing of wood. He looked back. Young Jordan's horse was up on the sidewalk, wild-eyed and snorting, with young Jordan leaning forward half out of the saddle, pushing himself back from the horse's neck, back off the horn into the saddle, swaying insecurely. And as Jordan managed the horse off the sidewalk Doane looked quickly forward again, his eyes fixed distantly ahead and blank.

He passed men he knew, and out of the corner of his eye he saw their glances slowly follow him, calm, or gloomy, or shrewdly speculative. As he passed, he knew their glances were shifting to the man whose horse was softly coming behind him. It was like that all the way up the street. The flowers were drooping markedly now.

The town petered out with a few Mexican shacks, the road dwindled to broad ruts, and the sage was suddenly on all sides of him, stretching away toward the heat-obscured mountains like an infinite multitude of gray-green sheep. He turned off the road and began the slight ascent up the little hill whereon the cemetery lay. Grasshoppers shrilled invisibly in the sparse, dried grass along the track, silent as he came by, and shrilled again as he passed, only to become silent again as the other rider came.

He swung off at the rusty wire Missouri gate and slipped the loop from the post, and the shadow of the other slid tall across his path and stopped. Doane licked his lips quickly and looked up, his grasp tightening on the now sweat-wilted newspaper. Young Jordan was sitting his horse, open-mouthed, leaning forward with his hands on the pommel to support himself, his eyes vague and dull. His lips were wet and red, and hung in a slight smile.

A lark made the air sweet over to the left, and then Doane saw it, rising into the air. It hung in the sun, over the cemetery. Moving steadily and avoiding all suddenness, Doane hung his reins over the post.

"You don't like me, do you?" young Jordan said. A long thread of saliva descended from the corner of his slackly smiling mouth.

Doane's face set into a sort of blank preparedness. He turned and started slowly through the gate, his shoulders hunched up and pulled backward.

Jordan got down from the saddle, and Doane turned toward him slowly. Jordan came forward straight enough, with his feet apart, braced against staggering. He stopped three feet from Doane, bent forward, his mouth slightly open.

"You got any objections to me being in town?"

"No," Doane said, and stood still.

Jordan thought that over, his eyes drifting idly sideways for a moment. Then they came back, to a finer focus this time, and he said, "Why not?" hunching forward again, his hands open and held away from the holsters at his hips.

Doane looked at the point of his nose. "You haven't done anything, Jordan. Except get drunk. Nothing to break the law."

"I haven't done nothing," Jordan said, his eyes squinting away at one of the small, tilting tombstones. "By God, I'll do something. Whadda I got to do?" He drew his head back, as though he were farsighted, and squinted. "Whadda I got to do to make you fight, huh?"

"Don't do anything," Doane said quietly, keeping his voice even. "Just go back and have another drink. Have a good time."

"You think I ain't sober enough to fight?" Jordan slipped his right gun out of its holster, turning away from Doane. Doane stiffened. "Wait, mister," Jordan said.

He cocked the gun. "See that bird?" He raised the gun into the air, squinting along the barrel. The bright nickel of its finish gleamed in the sun. The lark wheeled and fluttered. Jordan's arm swung unsteadily in a small circle.

He pulled the trigger and the gun blasted. The lark jumped in the air, flew away about twenty feet, and began circling again, catching insects.

"Missed 'im," Jordan mumbled, lowering his arm and wiping sweat off his forehead. "Damn it, I can't see!" He raised his arm again. Again the heavy blast cracked Doane's ears. Down in the town near the Mexican huts, he could see tiny figures run out into the street.

The bird didn't jump this time, but darted away out of sight over the hill.

"Got 'im," Jordan said, scanning the sky. His eyes wandered over the graveyard for a moment, looking for the bird's body. "Now you see?" he said, turning to Doane, his eyes blurred and watering with the sun's glare. "I'm going down and shoot up the damned town. Come down and stop me, you old—"

He turned and lurched sideways a step, straightened himself out, and walked more steadily toward his horse, laughing to himself. Doane turned away, his face sick, and trudged slowly up the hill, his eyes on the ground.

He stopped at one of the newer graves. The headstone was straight on this one. He looked at it, his face changing expression. "Here lies Cecelia Doane, born 1837, died 1885, the loyal wife . . ."

He stooped and pulled a weed from the side of the grave, then pulled a bunch of withered stems from a small green funnel by the headstone, and awkwardly took the fresh flowers out of the newspaper. He put the flowers into the funnel, wedging them firmly down into the bottom, and set it down again. He stood up and moved back, wiping sweat from his eyes.

A sudden shout came from the gate, and the sharp crack of a quirt. Doane turned with a befuddled look.

Jordan was back on his horse, beating Doane's. He had looped the reins over its neck so that it would run free. It was tearing away down the slope headed back for town.

Doane stood with his hat in his hand, his face suddenly beet red. He took a step after Jordan, and then stood still, shaking a little. He stared fixedly after him, watching him turn into the main road and toward the main street again. Then, sighing deeply, he turned back to the grave. Folding the newspaper, he began dusting off the heavy slab, whispering to himself. "No, Cissie. I could have gone. But, you know—it's my town."

He straightened up, his face flushed, put on his hat, and slapping the folded paper against his knee, started down the path. He got to the Missouri gate, closed it, and started down the ruts again.

A SHOT CAME from the town, and he stopped. Then there were two more, sharp spurts of sound coming clear and definite across the sage. He made out a tiny figure in a blue shirt running along a sidewalk.

He stood stock-still, the grasshoppers singing in a contented chorus all around him in the bright yellow glare. A train whistle came faint from off the plain, and he looked far across it. He made out the tiny trailed plume of smoke.

His knees began to quiver very slightly and he began to walk, very slowly, down the road.

Then suddenly there was a splatter of shots from below. The train whistle came again, louder, a crying wail of despair in the burning, brilliant, dancing air.

He began to hurry, stumbling a little in the ruts. And then he stopped short, his face open in fear. "My God, my empty horse, those shots— Toby, no!" He began to run, shambling, awkward and stumbling, his face ashen.

From the end of the street, as he hobbled panting past the tight-shut Mexican shanties, he could see a blue patch in the dust in front of the saloon, and shambled to a halt. It wasn't Toby, whoever it was, lying there facedown: face buried in the deep, pillowing dust, feet still on the board sidewalk where the man had been standing.

The street was empty. None of the faces he knew looked at him now. He drew one of his guns and cocked it and walked fast up the walk, on the saloon side.

A shot smashed ahead of him and he stopped, shrinking against a storefront. Inside, through the glass door, he could see two pale faces in the murk. Blue powder smoke curled out from under the saloon porch ahead of him.

Another shot smashed, this time from his office. The spurt of smoke, almost invisible in the sunlight, was low down in the doorway. Two horses were loose in the street now, his own, standing alert up past the saloon, and young Jordan's, half up on the boardwalk under one of the porches.

He walked forward, past young Jordan's horse, to the corner of the saloon building. Another shot slammed out of his office door, the bullet smacking the window ahead of him. A small, slow smile grew on his mouth. He looked sideways at the body in the street. Young Jordan lay with the back of his head open to the sun, crimson and brilliant, his bright nickel gun still in his right hand, its hammer still cocked, unfired.

The train whistle moaned again, closer.

"Doane," Toby called from the office door, invisible. "Get out of town." There was a surge of effort in the voice, a strain that made it almost a squeal. "I'm shot in the leg. Get out before they get together."

A door slammed somewhere. Doane glanced down between the saloon and the store beside it. Then he saw, fifty yards down the street, a figure come out of another side alley and hurry away down the walk toward the station. From the saloon door another shot slammed across the street. Toby held his fire.

Doane peered after the running figure, his eyes squinting thoughtfully. The train's whistle shrieked again like the ultimatum of an approaching conqueror at the edge of town, and in a moment the ground under his feet began to vibrate slightly and the hoarse roar of braking wheels came up the street.

He turned back to young Jordan's horse, petted it around the head a moment, and then took it by the reins close to the bit. He guided it across the street, keeping its body between him and the front of the saloon, without drawing fire, and went on down the alley beside his office. At the rear door he hitched the horse and went inside.

Toby was on the floor, a gun in his hand, his hat beside him, peering out across the sill. Doane kept low, beneath the level of the window, and crawled up to him. Toby's left leg was twisted peculiarly and blood leaked steadily out from the boot top onto the floor. His face was sweating and very pale, and his lips were tight.

"I thought he got you," Toby said, keeping his eyes on the saloon across the street. "I heard those shots and then your horse came bucketing back down the street. I got Jordan. Colby got me in the leg before I got back inside."

"Never mind about that. Come on, get on your feet if you can and I'll help you on the horse in back. You can get out of town and I'll shift for myself."

"I think I'm going to pass out. I don't want to move. It won't hurt no worse getting killed than it does now. The hell with the horse! Take it yourself."

Doane looked across the street, his eyes moving over the door and the windows carefully, inch by inch.

"I'm sorry I shot him," Toby said. "It's my fault. And it's my fight now, Doane. Clear out."

Doane turned and scuttled out of the back. He mounted the horse and rode down behind four stores. He turned up another alley, dashed across the main street, down another alley, then back up behind the saloon.

He dismounted, his gun cocked in his hand. The back door of the place was open and he got through it quickly, the sound of his boot heels dimmed under the blast of a shot from the front of the saloon. From the dark rear of the room, he could see Pierce, crouched behind the bar, squinting through a bullet hole in the stained-glass bottom half of the front window.

There was a bottle of whisky standing on the bar beside Pierce; he reached out a hand and tilted the bottle up to his mouth, half turning toward Doane as he did so. Pierce kept the bottle to his lips, pretending to drink, and, with his right hand invisible behind the bar, brought his gun into line with Doane.

The tip of Pierce's gun came over the edge of the bar, the rest of him not moving a hair, and Doane, gritting his teeth, squeezed slowly and painfully on his gun trigger. The gun flamed and bucked in his hand, and he dropped it, his face twisting in agony. The bottle fell out of Pierce's hand and spun slowly on the bar. Pierce sat there for a moment before his head fell forward and he crashed against the edge of the bar and slipped down out of sight.

Doane picked up his gun with his left hand and walked forward to the bar, holding his right hand like a crippled paw in front of him. The bottle had stopped revolving. Whisky inside it, moving back and forth, rocked it gently. He righted it and took a short pull at the neck, and in a moment the pain lines relaxed in his face. He went to the batwing doors and pushed one of them partly open.

"Toby!" he called.

There was no answer from across the street, and then he saw the barrel of a revolver sticking out of his office door, lying flat, and behind it one hand, curled loosely and uselessly around the butt.

He looked down the street. The train stood across it. A brakeman moved along the cars slowly, his head down. There was nobody else in sight.

He started to step out, and saw then two men coming up the opposite walk, running fast. Suddenly one of them stopped, grabbing the other by the arm, and pointed at him. He stared back for a moment, seeing Jordan clearly now, the square, hard face unchanged except for its pallor, bleak and bony as before.

Doane let the door swing to and continued to watch them over the top of it. They talked for a moment. Then Colby ran back down the street—well out of effective range—sprinted across it and disappeared. Down the street the engine, hidden by some buildings, chuffed angrily, and the cars began to move again. Jordan stood still, leaning against the front of a building, fully exposed, a hard smile on his face.

Doane turned and hurried to the back door. It opened outward. He slammed and bolted it, then hurried back to the front and waited, his gun ready. He smiled as the back door rattled, turned, fired a shot at it, and listened. For a moment there was no sound. Then something solid hit it, bumped a couple of times, and silence came again.

From the side of the building, just beyond the corner where Pierce's body lay, a shot crashed. The gun in the office door jumped out of the hand and spun wildly. The hand lay still.

He heard Jordan's voice from down the street, calling, the words formed slowly, slightly spaced.

"Is he dead?"

"Passed out," Colby called back.

"I'm going around back to get him. Keep Doane inside." Jordan turned and disappeared down an alley.

Doane leaned across the bar, knocked bottles off the shelves of the back bar, and held his pistol on the corner of the wall, about a foot above the floor.

"Pierce," he said.

"Throw out your guns," Pierce answered.

Doane squinted at the corner, moved his gun slightly, and fired. He heard a cry of pain, then curses; saw the batwing doors swing slightly. Then he turned and ran for the back door. He threw back the bolt and pushed on the door. It wouldn't give. He threw himself against it. It gave a little at the bottom. Pierce had thrown a stake up against it to keep him locked in. He ran back to the front.

Across the street, he could see somebody moving in his office, dimly, beyond the window. Suddenly the hand on the floor disappeared.

"Come on out, you old—," Pierce said, panting. "You only skinned me." His voice was closer than before, somewhere between the door and the corner of the building, below the level of the stained glass.

Then Doane saw Toby's white shirt beyond the window opposite. Jordan was holding him up, and moving toward the door. Jordan came out on the porch, hugging Toby around the chest, protecting himself with the limp body. With a heave he sent Toby flying down the steps, and jumped back out of sight. Toby rolled across the sidewalk and fell into the street, where he lay motionless.

Doane looked stupidly at Toby, then at young Jordan, still lying with his feet cocked up on the sidewalk.

"He ain't dead, Doane," Jordan called. "Come and get him if you want him alive." He fired through the window. Dust jumped six inches from Toby's head. "Come on out, Doane, and shoot it out. You got a chance to save him." The gun roared again, and dust jumped a second time beside Toby's head, almost in the same spot.

"Leave the kid alone," Doane called. "This fight's between you and me."

"The next shot kills him, Doane."

Doane's face sagged white and he leaned against the side of the door. He could hear Pierce breathing heavily in the silence, just outside. He pushed himself away from the door and drew a breath through clenched teeth. He cocked his pistol and strode out, swinging around. Pierce fired from the sidewalk, and Doane aimed straight into the blast and pulled as he felt himself flung violently around by Pierce's bullet.

Pierce came up from the sidewalk and took two steps toward him, opening and shutting a mouth that was suddenly full of blood, his eyes wide and wild, and then pitched down at his feet.

Doane's right arm hung useless, his gun at his feet. With his left hand he drew his other gun and stepped out from the sidewalk, his mouth wide open, as though he were gasping for breath or were about to scream, and took two steps toward Toby as Jordan came out of the office door, firing. The slug caught Doane along the side of his neck, cutting the shoulder muscle, and his head fell over to one side. He staggered on, firing. He saw Toby trying to get up, saw Jordan fall back against the building, red running down the front of his shirt, and the smile gone.

Jordan stood braced against the building, holding his gun in both hands, firing as he slid slowly down. One bullet took Doane in the stomach, another in the knee. He went down, flopped forward, and dragged himself up to where Toby lay trying to prop himself up on one elbow. Doane knelt there like a dog, puking blood into the dust, blood running out of his nose, but his gray eyes almost indifferent, as though there were one man dying and another watching.

He saw Jordan lift his gun with both hands and aim it toward Toby, and as the hammer fell, he threw himself across Toby's head and took it in the back. He rolled off onto his back and lay staring into the sky.

Upside down, he saw Toby take his gun and get up on one elbow, level it at Jordan and fire, and then saw Toby's face, over his, looking down at him as the deputy knelt in the street.

They stayed that way for a long moment, while Doane's eyes grew more and more dull and the dark of his blood in the white dust grew broader. His breath was coming hard, in small, sharp gasps.

"There's nothing in it, kid," he whispered. "Only a tin star. They don't hang the right ones. You got to fight everything twice. It's a job for a dog."

"Thank you, Doane."

"It's all for free. You going to quit, Toby?"

Toby looked down at the gray face, the mouth and chin and neck crimson, the gray eyes dull. Toby shook his head. His face was hard as a rock.

Doane's face suddenly looked a little surprised, his eyes went past Toby to the sky. Toby looked up. A lark was high above them, circling and fluttering, directly overhead. "A pretty bird," Doane mumbled. "A very pretty bird."

His head turned slowly to one side, and Toby looked down at him and saw him as though fast asleep.

He took Doane's gun in his hand, and took off Doane's star, and sat there in the street while men slowly came out of stores and circled about them. He sat there unmoving, looking at Doane's half-averted face, holding the two things tightly, one in each hand, like a child with a broken toy, his face soft and blurred, his eyes unwet.

After awhile the lark went away. He looked up at the men, and saw Mettrick.

"I told him he should have resigned," Mettrick said, his voice high. "He could have taken his horse—"

"Shut up," Toby said. "Shut up or get out." His eyes were sharp and his face placid and set. He turned to another of the men. "Get the doc," he said. "I've got a busted leg. And I've got a lot to do."

The man looked at him, a little startled, and then ran.

Killers' Country!

Dan Cushman

1. First Blood for the Sagers

It was before dawn when the eight men rode from Colton's place, and still only midmorning when they topped the ridge beyond Squawblanket Springs and caught their first sight of the town of Maverly.

There Hooks Colton brought his horse around with a hard twist of the brutal, half-breed bit he always used, and sat with his heavy legs ram-rodding the stirrups. He rolled a cigarette while his narrow, pale gray eyes roved the limitless sage flats broken by the bright-shining roofs of Maverly and the long line of the Northern Pacific railroad.

His brother, Lester Colton, a dirty, red-whiskered man, rode up beside him and said, "Train smoke."

The smoke was far away, a smudge blending with gray clay hills.

Hooks said, "That's the local freight. Leaves Maverly about seven. Passenger train won't be 'long till two-fifteen."

"Think he'll really have the guts to come back?"

"He's got guts enough. All them Sagers got guts."

Hooks was about thirty, so raw-boned and powerful it set him apart from his five brothers, big and hard-muscled though they were. This morning they were especially rough-looking and taciturn, each with a Winchester in his saddle scabbard and a Colt at his hip. Besides Hooks and his five brothers, there was his stepbrother Babe, and a little sharp-faced puncher by the name of Wiley Gray.

Hooks said, "Yes, I expect he'll be on it. Unless he knows us Coltons are meeting him." His lips twisted down when he said that, and he turned to let his eyes rest on Babe. Babe was about seventeen, big as a Colton, but with a broader, more even-featured face. "How about it, Babe? You think Tom Sager will know we're riding to meet him?"

Babe had uncontrollable fear of Hooks Colton, and he raised his voice a trifle too much in an effort to hide it, "Why ask *me*?"

"You know why. Because you been hanging around Lily Sager." There was a raw, challenging quality in Hooks's voice. He was both handsome and predatory, and the voice fit him. Women had always fancied Hooks, and it had cut his pride when first Miss Grahame, the schoolteacher, and then fifteen-year-old Lily Sager had shown a preference for Babe. Hooks knew that Babe was scared of him, and he said, "Listen, kid, you lie to me and I'll slap it back down your throat. Paw ain't here for you to hide behind today. We all know you been sneaking over there in the coulee to see Lily Sager."

Babe wanted to stand up to him. He wasn't a coward. He could climb on a bronc that Hooks would be scared to get in the same corral with, yet when he faced Hooks he turned gutless. It had been like that ever since he'd watched Hooks kill that Flying W rep six years ago. The rep had gone for his gun first, but Hooks just reared back, with that big arm coming up, jerking the gun, firing. A single, inescapable second of time. Sometimes in the middle of the night Babe would still wake up and remember that rep, bullet-hit and falling with that awful, shocked expression in his eyes.

Hooks gave him a contemptuous look and turned his shoulder, and Lester said, "You been seeing her, Babe?"

"Maybe I have and maybe I haven't." His heart knocked at his ribs and sweat felt clammy along his hairline. It made his answer come back more violently than he'd intended.

Lester rubbed his tobacco-spattered whiskers and said, "Don't let that lip run away with you. I don't give a damn about the girl. I don't give a damn if you do beat Hooks's speed. But if you tipped her off that we're going down to meet her brother . . ."

"I never told her anything. If you don't trust me, then why'd you tell me anything? Why—"

"We trust you. You're here, and you're alive. That's proof we trust you."

Hooks had turned again, and his predatory eyes were this time fixed on Lester. "What d'you mean, beat my speed? If I really wanted a woman do you think I'd let that apple-cheeked—"

"All right, let it lie. So you never got turned down by the teacher, and you never called on Lily Sager. We got enough fighting cut out for us today. Let's drift in there to Maverly and have a look around. You can't tell about that damned Dad Sager. He get an idea we're greeting his boy home from the pen he'll likely have half the rustlers from the breaks backing him."

The Coltons had been trying to get hold of the Old Fort fields ever since the big blizzard of '87. They'd pushed the Sagers to the edge of the badlands by overgrazing the range until it looked like it had been sheeped off. They'd branded Sager calves and the Sagers had branded theirs. Finally, young Tom Sager had gone too far and had taken to slapping his iron on calves from the Flying R and the 88 and had ended up in Deer Lodge with a four-year sentence, which now had been commuted to two. It hadn't helped the Coltons that he was in jail. Old Rufe wanted to buy, and the meadows were in Tom's name, and when he wrote, Tom hadn't answered his letters. But today he was coming home, and old Rufe, his back bent like a Blackfoot bow from kidney stones, had sent his boys in to greet him.

As they were heading down toward Six-Mile Creek, young Delbert Colton dropped back and rode beside Babe. Delbert had a nasal obstruction that made his mouth hang open and had won him the name Fishface. He was Babe's age, give or take a couple of months, and they'd grown up together since the day old Rufe married Babe's widowed mother and took her away from her job as waitress in the depot beanery at Miles City. Fishface had always been a sneak, the only one in the Colton family.

Now Fishface grinned and said, "You better leave Hooks's girl alone. He might let you chase around with that Grahame woman, but if you try fooling around—"

"Keep quiet about Miss Grahame."

"Look here, now—"

"I said to keep quiet about Miss Grahame."

Andy Colton, who was next younger than Hooks, overheard them and said, "You better look out for him today, Fish. He sounds like he's drunk cougar milk."

The sun, rising higher, became hot and reflected off the whitish gumbo earth into their faces. Sage grew high. It slapped their stirrups and gave off a suffocating, dusty odor. It was close to noon when they rode through the outskirt shacks of Maverly.

The town was warped and unpainted. It boasted one tree—a box elder in the yard of the railroad sectionhouse. It had been long since the last rain, and Main Street was a strip of dust between platform sidewalks and false-fronted buildings.

Babe looked over at Andy, who was riding beside him and said, "What if Tom Sager won't sell?"

"He will."

"But what if he don't?"

"Why, I don't know. Maybe we'll give him what he *really* had coming when he started running our brands three years ago."

"He served his time."

"He served two years in a stone house letting tax money feed him. What a rustler needs is ten minutes on the end of a stiff rope. What's wrong, Babe? You sound like you might be backin' Sager's hand."

"It's just I don't think it'll do us any good to gun him down."

"Maybe. And it won't do *him* any good either."

"You can't just ride up and shoot him."

Lester turned and said, "We'll let him eat first." Lester was the oldest of the bunch, and he had a slouched, easy-seeming manner that made his underlying cruelty a little worse when he chose to show it. "Why can't we just ride up and shoot him? Who's here to stop us? Walt Baker? I'll lay dollars against buffalo chips he lights out for the deep coulees half an hour after we hit town. Walt didn't get elected sheriff for any reason except he needed the pay. He's hell on an Injun kid that steals a five-dollar saddle, but he won't stand between the Coltons and anybody."

A wagon freight outfit was loading up at the railway warehouse, and heavy-booted mule drivers mingled with the cowboys in town. A buckboard with a team of bay broncs was tied to the hitch rack in front of the J-B Mercantile. They wore Sager's Lazy S horse brand.

Sager was a widower with only the two children, but he was an early settler with friends in the country, and he stood well with the rustlers and wolfers down in the breaks. The prospect that he might have come with a few guns backing him made the Coltons a trifle wary.

THE COLTONS PASSED the Sager buckboard silent and set-jawed, pretending not to notice. Hooks said something and swung down at the hitch rack in front of the Lone Cabin saloon.

The others followed him, limped around on stiffened legs to get the feel of the ground after so many hours in the saddle. Babe stood at the rack with his gaze traveling automatically to the mercantile's front door. He could see the outline of a girl just beyond the screen, and he knew it was Lily Sager.

Fishface noticed him and nudged Hooks, saying, "Guess who he seen!"

Hooks glanced at the door, and back at Babe. His face was big-boned and hollow in the cheeks. Grayish under his tan. He'd always wanted Lily. He'd wanted her worse than anything else in his existence.

But Hooks kept control of himself. He turned and stepped to the sidewalk. He hitched his sagging gun belt. His Levi's were wrinkled, and they stuck to the insides of his stud-horse legs. He shot another glance at the girl and clumped across to the Lone Cabin's swinging doors.

Lily Sager had been watching him, and she must have thought he was out of sight, for now she stepped outside. She was a pretty kid, deeply tanned, slim and supple as a boy from riding. She usually wore boots and pants and kept her hair in a knot under her sombrero, but today she had on a dress, slippers, and a mail-order white bonnet. Her hair was combed in curls that fell to her shoulders.

She said, "Babe!"

Babe finished tying his bronc and cut across to the mercantile's high platform walk. He knew all the Coltons were watching him—that everybody along the street was watching him—but he managed to look casual enough and walk with a good jingle of his star-roweled spurs.

Lily was biting down on her underlip, and he could see the rapid beat of an artery in her throat. She was scared. He never remembered seeing her scared before.

She said, "Babe, what are you going to do?" Then she changed it, saying, "What are *they* going to do?"

"Meet the train."

"They came to get Tommy. They came to kill him."

"They're here to get those Old Fort fields. Won't he sell?"

"You know how Tommy is. He hates the Coltons. He even hates you. He wouldn't sell for all the money in Powder River County."

"I don't know what to say, Lily. You know I can't do anything about those fellows. Not when they're on the prod. Why don't you send a telegram to him in Iron City? Tell him to get off—"

"He wouldn't leave the train because of the Coltons. You know he wouldn't."

He had his Stetson off, turning it around in his hands. "I don't know what to say, Lily."

"Then they plan on gunning him down?"

"I don't know. It depends on . . . . things. Depends on what Tom does. You and your dad come in alone?"

She hesitated, and he had the uncomfortable feeling that there was something she didn't want to tell him because he was a Colton. Then she said, "Blackfoot Charley came on horseback. I don't know where he is."

Hooks had gone inside the saloon, but the rest of the Coltons were in a tight, hard-eyed knot at the door, watching him.

"I got to go," he said. "You see how it is."

"Yes, I see."

He left with the warm impression of her hand in his. Her last words stuck with him. She *saw*. He wondered if she'd seen how yellow-gutted he was when it came to Hooks Colton.

THE INTERIOR OF the Lone Cabin was dim and damp after the bright heat of outside. It smelled of stale beer. Hooks was at the bar, his heel notched on the rail, and one elbow propped. He kept his eyes on Babe all the way across the room. His thumb was hooked in his pants band, just above his .45. For a sick moment Babe thought maybe he'd force things to a show-down right then. It was unreasonable, but Babe knew he was more scared of Hooks than he was of dying. He had a .45 of his own, practically a twin of the one Hooks carried, and he knew how to draw it and shoot it, but still he was physically incapable of facing the man.

Lester—lean, unkempt, and four years the eldest of the Colton boys, came up beside Hooks and jolted him with his shoulder, saying, "Have a drink."

Hooks pushed away and kept his eyes on Babe. "What were you telling her?"

Babe's throat was tight, and his voice had a strange sound to his ears as he answered, "I told her I was in town."

Wiley Gray and a couple of the Colton boys laughed.

Hooks said, "You think you're a pretty smart button since you learned all that stuff from the books the schoolteacher lent you. You think you're one step above us Coltons. You think because old Rufe was damned fool enough to sign over a fourth of his property to that biscuit-shootin' mother of yours you can fall into—"

"Keep still about Ma!" She'd been dead for three years, but the Coltons never got over hating her. He was still scared of Hooks, and he thought Hooks was going to kill him, but he raised his voice and said, "You men-tion my mother again—"

Lester Colton said, "Shut up!" and rammed him so hard he staggered and had to grab the edge of the bar to keep from going down. Hooks moved a step clear of the bar with his right hand hanging down, its back forward, just like that day he shot the flying W rep.

Babe pulled himself up. He came with a lunge, and Lester hit him. His fist traveled no more than eighteen inches but it struck like a sledge. Babe was down with the slivery floor beneath his hands.

Lester said, "Live a while, kid. Live a while. Wait till we settle with Sager, then you go ahead and get shot if you want to."

BABE STOOD UP. All the Coltons except Hooks were grinning at him. There was a bottle and empty glass on the bar. He poured one and downed it. He remained dizzy for a while, but the liquor helped bring him around He saw Hooks and Lester walking out the door.

"Maybe you should've stayed home," Fishface said.

"You go to hell!"

"You see?" Andy said. "A bust on the jaw don't stop that one. He's been drinkin' cougar's milk."

Jeef Colton looked at his watch. "Train due at two-fifteen?" he asked the bartender.

"Two o'clock sharp. They changed it."

"We got an hour and a half. Let's put the nose bag on."

Babe went with Clint, Jeef, and Wiley Gray to a Chinese café. They never had fresh pork and eggs except when they came to town, so that's what they ordered. When they went outside forty-five minutes later, a saloon tramp named Dod Price got hold of Jeef's shirt and said, "Guess who pulled out? The sheriff. Walt Baker."

"Left town?"

"Sure. Said he had a hurry-up call in Johnnytown. Somebody shot. I'll lay dollars he ain't headed toward a shootin', but away from one."

Jeef laughed and gave him four bits for a drink. Jeef was twenty and proud of being one of the tough Coltons.

Andy saw them a few minutes later and came from a saloon. "Walt Baker just lit out," he said.

"I know," Clint said. "You better lay off tanglefoot till we're through with Sager, or Hooks will get mean again."

"To hell with Hooks." Andy looked at Babe. "Ain't that what you say? To hell with him." His lips twisted down in a nasty smile. "What do you want to take all that for? Show him you're not scared of him. You ain't, are you?"

"No, I'm not scared of him!"

"I'll tell him you said so." They were all grinning now. "Won't we, boys? We'll tell him he said so."

The buckboard was no longer in front of the mercantile. Jeef asked if the Sagers had pulled out, and Andy said no, they'd driven to the Climax stable.

Babe looked at his dollar watch when it was 1:22; and again when it was 1:35.

They went back to the Lone Cabin. A freight wagon with a six-mule team was tied to the hitch rack, and some drivers were inside, drinking and talking loud. They quieted when the Coltons came in. Babe had the feeling that the whole town was keyed like a set trap, waiting for the train to arrive.

He looked at his watch again, but less than three minutes had passed. Lester Colton walked in.

"Where's Hooks?" Andy asked.

"Up at the depot," Lester said, and poured himself a drink. "Saw Dad Sager. Talked to him."

"What'd he say?"

"Nothing. Just stood there, looking mean and stubborn. I told him we weren't wanting to get rough. Told him we wanted to buy. Would pay five thousand. He said he didn't own the Old Fort fields. Said Tommy did. I said, 'Will Tommy sell?' He said, 'Wait and talk to him,' and I said, 'We damned well intend to.'"

"Who'll talk to him—Hooks?"

"Me." Lester finished his drink, hitched his Colt and said, "All right, let's drift. It's about time."

TRAIN SMOKE MADE a dark smudge in the west. They turned a corner at the brick-fronted bank and caught sight of the depot. Lily was there, her dress looking very bright in the afternoon sun. Dad Sager was with her. He'd married when he was past forty, and now he looked more like he should be her grandfather. Dad wasn't very big, and he had a brace of .45s strapped on. It looked funny to see him weighted down like that. Babe knew he intended to give one of the guns to Tom as soon as he got off the train. The buckboard wasn't there. Dad didn't intend to leave immediately. He'd been a big rancher when the Coltons were still living in a dugout shanty, and it wouldn't be his style to let them run him out of town.

A moment later he saw Hooks. He was at the far end of the platform, slouched with an elbow on the rail.

Lester spat tobacco juice and said, "There won't be trouble, but spread out, just in case. Andy, you keep the boys down here. I'll get over by the freight shed door. That's where the passengers will get off."

The train appeared, distorted by a heat wave until it looked a hundred feet high. At a quarter-mile it shrank to perspective, and rolled in, came to a rumbling stop. Nervous from apprehension though he was, Babe still thought of when he was little, and his mother hashed in the depot beanery at Miles. Always met the trains.

Lily Sager ran along the still-moving coaches and was these to meet her brother when he climbed down with a cheap black suitcase in his hand. He was about twenty-two, taller than his dad. A hardness had replaced some of the hell-and-be-damned good looks that had made him the darling of half the women in the houses across the tracks at the time he was taken away.

He dropped his suitcase and lifted Lily off her feet. Then he put her down and beat his father on the back. They were still at it when Lester slouched up, dribbled some tobacco juice, and spoke to him.

Babe couldn't hear what they were saying, but they talked for a quarter minute and Lester turned away. "We made a long ride to settle this, Tom. You think about it," Lester said.

The Coltons drifted back toward town. Hooks caught up with Lester and said, "What the hell? I didn't ride twenty-five miles just to chippy around with that jailbird! What the hell goes?"

"Let him talk it over with the old man. The papers are in the bank vault and he'll have to get 'em before we can close the deal. I ain't lettin' him leave town."

There was still trouble brewing, and everyone knew it. Men stood around the fronts of buildings, watching. Some of the freight outfits were loaded and ready to hit the road toward Musselshell but none of the drivers budged.

The Sagers went inside the Territorial House, Maverly's big, ramshackle hotel. About forty minutes later Wiley Gray came around to where the Coltons were loafing with their backs against the iron rails that protected the big front windows of the mercantile and said, "They're havin' grub."

Lester said, "About through?"

"Down to apple pie."

"I'll go over and meet 'em." Hooks started to go along but Lester said, "I can handle that brand-runner alone."

Lester, the eldest, had always fancied himself as top man among the Coltons. He carried a couple of notches in his .45, and he also fancied himself as a gunman. He'd loosened his gun belt a few holes on his arrival, but the holster wasn't tied down, and it swung back and forth, cuffing his lean right flank as he crossed the street. He had an ambling walk, a way of seeming to stumble every three or four steps. He took the high step to the platform in front of the Territorial and craned his neck to see through the windows. Just then Tom Sager came out.

Tom had evidently been watching for him. He had one of his father's guns thrust through his belt of braided natural tan and black leather thongs. Prison-braid belt.

Their first words didn't reach across the street, but Babe heard Lester shout, "Well, make up your mind! I'll give you just exactly ten minutes."

Lester spun and jumped down from the platform. He was at midstreet, taking long strides, when Tom came to the edge and said, "I don't need that long. You can have your answer now. You can go to hell."

Lester turned with his right arm long and loose. He drew with a high, upward jerk of his shoulder, but Tom Sager was a trifle ahead of him. He crouched so the gun barrel in the band of his pants was horizontal. He drew with a straight back movement and fired.

THE BULLET HIT Lester when he had his gun half-lifted. It came at an angle downward from the platform walk. It hit him low in the chest and went all the way through, cuffing a puff of dust near the hitch rack of the Lone Cabin saloon.

It knocked Lester back. He caught himself, lunged, turned halfway around. He fired wildly, straight down the street. Then he folded and fell, with his sweat-stained hat under him and his face in the dirt.

One of the Coltons fired a long-range shot at Tom Sager. It cut slivers from a window casing and shattered glass. Tom fired one shot in return, then Dad grabbed him by the arm, and both of them started away on the run.

The Coltons were all trying to get forward, but the scattering crowd blocked their way. Tom and Dad headed across a side street toward Whal's blacksmith shop.

Hooks shouted, "Andy, you and Jeef get around behind. We'll smoke 'em out of there."

Babe found himself half-toppled over a hitch rack. A freight team tied to it was fighting back, terrified by the shooting, threatening to break loose. The thought occurred to him that the blacksmith shop would end by being a death trap if Andy and Jeef got them from behind. In that case, they were cooked.

He drew his jackknife and cut the tie rope. In another couple of seconds the team was stampeding down the street with the tandem freight wagons careening and banging behind them.

Andy and Jeff had to dive head foremost out of the way. The rear wagon overturned with a splintering smash. The six-mule team dragged it for thirty yards before its drawbar gave way. The Sagers were gone from the blacksmith shop by then. They headed on, among shacks and sheds, up the knoll topped by the Climax livery barn.

The Coltons cut loose on them from better than a hundred yards. It was long-range for their six-shooters. Not one of them had thought to get his Winchester from his scabbard. When they tried to get close, they were driven back by .30-30 bullets.

Lily was still at the hotel, but there were more than two guns up there. Babe remembered she'd said Blackfoot Charley was in town. He was a wolfer, and some said a horse-rustler, from out in the breaks.

The shooting was furious for several minutes. Jeef tried to circle the barn and come up close in the cover of some wrecked wagons and took a slug in the arm. Shock put him flat on his face and Babe thought he was mortally wounded. He holstered his six-shooter and crawled up the knoll after him.

"Get the hell away from me," Jeef said through his teeth. "I'm goin' up there and—"

Babe got him down and used his jackknife to remove the sleeve from his shirt. The bullet had cut upward, following muscle without shattering the bone. He was bleeding badly and it took a tight bandage to stop it.

When he was finished, Jeef wasn't so anxious to crawl onto the barn. He lay on his side and cursed through his teeth, calling Tom Sager every vile thing he could lay his tongue to.

"You see how he went for his gun? Lester's back turned and he was already reaching for his gun. Dirty yella-gut . . ."

The shooting settled down. Some of the Coltons came up with Winchesters. There was no way to get close, though. Not in the daylight.

After half an hour a posse of townsmen came up on the Coltons from behind. The jailer, Sy Blaney, aimed a sawed-off shotgun at Hooks and shouted, "Toss that rifle aside. All o' you!"

Hooks said, "If you think we're going to let that cow thief get out of town after him killin' Lester—"

"You can't fight the whole country," Blaney said. He was scared of the Coltons, but he had twenty men at his back. "There was a killin' here, I'll grant, but it's a wonder some woman or kid ain't shot already the way that stuff's whistlin' around." He jerked the shotgun at the stable, "It's the sheriff's job to bring them in."

"Baker's not here."

Lyle Stone, part-owner of the Musselshell Wagon-Freight Line said, "No, Baker's not here. *You* saw to that. You Coltons may be running things in the hills, but you're not running things in Maverly."

Hooks' lip curled. One side of his face was soot-grimed from black powdersmoke that had squirted from the worn mechanism of his gun. He was bleeding from a glancing slug of lead, and it left him a grim and savage sight. "What are you going to do, Lyle? Run us out of town?"

"You be to hell and gone out of Maverly by sundown!"

He hooked his thumb at the barn. "How about them?"

"They'll be out of town, too."

2. The Warriors Gather

It was after midnight when the Coltons, on their way home, stopped at Squawblanket Springs. By then Jeef's arm was bothering him, so he had a hard time staying in the saddle. They found an old kettle at an abandoned shanty, and put water on a sagebrush fire.

"Should o' waited in Maverly till the doc showed," Wiley Gray said.

Jeef's arm was swollen till he couldn't close his fingers, but he had enough left to manage a swagger and say, "I don't need no sawbones for that scratch. If I'd had my way we'd have followed them Sagers and gunned 'em down."

Hooks looked down at him with the sagebrush fire underlighting his face, accentuating lean lines of it. "Sure, kid. We'll get 'em. We'll pay 'em back for Lester. But we got time. We'll let the country quiet down a little."

Wiley Gray tore a strip off his Injun-weave saddle blanket, soaked it in boiling water, fished it, and held it to drain on the point of his knife. When it was cool enough to touch without scalding, he wrapped it around Jeef's bullet-ripped arm. The pain of it made Jeef bare his teeth and stiffen the tendons of his neck, but he took it without a sound.

Wiley said again, "We should have waited for the doc. Get jaundice in one o' these and it'll finish you."

Babe was hunkered, feeding twigs into the fire. He knew Hooks was watching him.

After a while, Hooks said in a voice that seemed casual, "Babe, where were you standin' when Lester got it?"

"Between Jeef and Clint."

Hooks said to his brothers, "Was he?"

"Yeah," Jeef said through teeth gritted from pain.

Hooks said to Babe, "From where you were, you ought to seen how that freight outfit got loose."

Babe shook his head. He couldn't trust his voice to answer. He was certain none of the Coltons had seen him cut the team loose. Hooks was guessing. If he *knew* he wouldn't fool around with questions.

Hooks said, "I went around and found the team at the freight shed. The tie rope wasn't broken—it had been cut."

Babe knew he was lying. He'd left them for twenty minutes or so late in the afternoon, but he'd gone to Garver's furniture store to pick out a coffin. Babe glanced around. All except Jeef were watching him, a circle of grim faces, turned coppery by firelight. They'd kill him if they knew. He had the awful feeling that they could read his thoughts through his eyeballs. He managed to laugh. He broke a twig and poked it under the kettle. His hand shook so violently the twig scattered sparks. Andy saw it and twisted a smile from one side of his mouth.

"What's wrong, kid?"

He cried, "Stop bullyraggin' me!" Sweat ran down his cheeks and mixed with the quarter inch of fuzz, which, at seventeen, was all the whiskers he was man enough to grow.

Andy said, "Yeah, quit it or he'll run and squeal to Rufe and you know how he gets. He'll have another *visitation*."

Andy was referring to his father, who'd come out of a fever with the conviction that he'd been visited by Babe's dead mother, with the result that he sat right down and signed over the fourth interest of his estate he'd promised in case she died before he did. Up until then it hadn't been too bad living with the Colton boys. Now they were on him, trying to make it so tough he'd quit the country.

Hooks said, "Notice you haven't got your gun on." Babe had taken it off and hooked it over the saddle horn on dismounting. Hooks laughed, spat in the fire, and turned away.

THE SUN WAS up, shining hot on the Colton home ranch when they sighted it from a pine-studded ridge. Rufe hobbled out on his diamond-willow cane to meet them. He was still a big man, though shrunken by his sickness of the last three years.

"Where's Lester?" he shouted when they were still two hundred yards away. "What happened? Did that rustler come in on the cars? Did he sign it over?"

Hooks rode ahead and swung down in front of his father before answering, "He came, he didn't sign anything over, and Lester's dead."

The news hit the old man hard, and he seemed to be ready to cave in right there. Then he commenced swinging his diamond willow cane and screaming, "Lester killed? You mean he got shot? You trying' to tell me that dirty rustler killed him?" He was getting his answer each time from Hooks's expression. "Is that what you mean? No rustler's going to gun a Colton down." The others were there by that time, and he looked around at their faces. "What did you do? You don't mean you let 'em shoot your brother down without—"

"Yes, that's what I mean!" Hooks shouted in the old man's face so violently he fell back a step. "Lester bulled into it alone, and he got himself outdrawn. We went for 'em, but they holed up in the livery barn."

"And you let 'em get out of town."

"Yes, they got out of town. Stone had his regulators out. We couldn't fight 'em all. But we'll get 'em, Pa. We'll get them Sagers. And we'll get the Old Fort fields, too."

Rufe Colton had been after those flats that ran east and west from Old Fort Ludloe since the blizzard of '87. In the spring of that year, when every breeze carried the stink of longhorn carcasses, Rufe had stood in the front door of the bunkhouse and announced to his boys that Montana would never be worth a hoot in hell as a cattle country unless a man was able to cut hay for the tough winters. With that in mind he'd ridden down from his hills and observed the level ground near the Old Fort. It had always been better than average grass, and the water of Elk Creek would make it grow deep as the belly of a horse. However, the land was military reserve, held on lease by the Sagers, and with it went the first water rights on Elk Creek.

Once Rufe got an idea he wasn't one to lay it aside, and for four years the chief thing he did was scheme to get those fields away from the Sagers. He was still at it, and that night, after the boys got some sleep, he held a meeting at the house.

Rufe opened the meeting by saying that Hooks was right in coming home instead of riding over to get the Sagers. After all, it had been an open gunfight. The thing to do was not go for the Sagers and risk getting the whole country down on them, but make the Sagers go for *them*. Furthermore, Rufe had schemed out a surefire way. The Sagers depended on Elk Creek for water, and he proposed to divert it along the old placer ditch and dump it down Shawnegan Coulee to the badlands.

Babe hadn't been at the meeting. He was sent out on the hooligan wagon with Jim Skinner, and spent the next three weeks at the Alkali Coulee line camp. Coming home, he crossed the deep gorge of Shawnegan Coulee and found eight inches of roily water rushing along its bottom. That night when he reached the home ranch there was another meeting in progress.

He walked up from the corrals and heard old Rufe through open door and windows shouting and beating his diamond willow cane on the floor. "I tell you, that's just a good way to get the whole range down on us! Listen here to me, every damn one of you—"

"Dad!" Clint Colton said, and the old man stopped. Clint had heard the jingle of Babe's spurs.

Babe walked through the door, into the lamplight, and said, "Hello." The Coltons were sitting around with their chairs tilted against the wall, boot heels notched in the rungs. Nobody spoke for a few seconds, then Rufe said, "Hello, Babe. How's things with them steers on the Arrow Range?"

"Eighteen head down with the bluebelly. Rest all right, except the Tip Top outfit has been pushing in across those benches at the northwest."

Usually a piece of news like that was enough to send Rufe into a screaming, cane-beating rage, but he didn't even flinch tonight.

He said, "We been talkin' about—"

Hooks barked, "It don't concern him, Pa. I say if you have a man's job, leave the kids out of it."

Rufe thought and said, "You et? Well then get the hell down to the cookhouse and quit snooping around."

Babe sat at the cookhouse table while the Chinaman, Ho Chu, fried steak for him. He ate as fast as he could, went out, circled some sheds to the house, and listened from the shadow of a box elder tree. Whole sentences reached him there, depending on who was talking, but the conversation was too far along and he couldn't tell just what they were planning to do.

After a while, Fishface came out and looked around. He stood for the better part of a minute, long and gangling, smoking a cigarette. Then he tossed it away and started on the roundabout path to the cookhouse. By hurrying, Babe cut back behind the sheds and was seated on the bench, rolling a cigarette, when Fishface came up.

"Oh." It was a blow to Fishface's crafty mind to see him there.

"Looking for me?"

"Yeah." He didn't know quite what to say. "You happen to run across that salt-and-pepper bronc of mine over on the Arrow?"

Babe shook his head. Fishface still hesitated. Something had made him suspicious, and finding Babe there hadn't completely satisfied him. He looked through the grease-clotted screen at Ho Chu who was inside, digging ashes from the stove hopper. He might have asked the Chinese and found out that Babe had been gone and come back. He didn't, though.

He left, and Babe could hear his spurs as they tinkled all the way to the house.

AFTER GRUB PILE next morning Babe said he was going to the Toston Flats in search of his gray long-horse, but instead, once the home ranch was out of sight, he took the wagon road down Elk Creek to the Old Fort flats, arriving shortly past noon.

He had an idea that Hooks Colton had someone spying on the Sager ranch, and it was a problem how he'd find Lily Sager without going there. He decided to wait awhile. There was a well at the old fort from which he managed to scoop half a bucket of water. The water was cold, and good despite the slight flavor of alkali. He drank, watered his horse, and dipped another bucket to rinse sweat and dirt off his face. He stood, letting the breeze dry him off, and saw a rider come into view over the rim of Elk Creek about three miles away. Ten minutes later the man was close enough so Babe recognized him. It was Blackfoot Charley, the wolfer who'd been backing the Sagers that day at Maverly.

Babe stepped out and called him by name, and Charley, who was about to pass the fort buildings on the south, drew up, bent over to get his Winchester from the scabbard, and, holding it across the pommel, jogged over. He was a quarter-breed, a dirty old man with ragged hair and whiskers. He used long stirrups, and rode with the long-legged spraddle of one who's accustomed to riding bareback. When he was close enough to recognize Babe he put the rifle back, spat tobacco juice, and called, "Babe, if Tom Sager saw you on his range he'd be minded to cut you down. They gettin' ready for a ruckus over this water."

"Put 'em in a bad way?"

"Sure did. Ain't been a dribble down the crick bottom in eight-nine days. Now the potholes are dryin' up. Dad drove four hundred head down to Emory Springs in the breaks, but they'll have the coulee bottoms et off in a week. You're damn right it puts 'em in a bad way, but don't say a word that I'm tellin' you."

"I wouldn't carry stories to the Coltons or the Sagers, either one."

"I know that or else I wouldn't have told you. Why in the hell don't you get out from between this ruckus? If I was a young puncher I'd make for the Milk River country."

Babe shrugged his shoulders and laughed. He was thinking that was just what the Coltons wanted.

Charley said, "Coltons tryin' to get Tom and his dad to start something, ain't they?"

Babe didn't answer that. He said, "I'm going to take a sleep here at the fort. If you happen to see Lily . . ."

"Yeah, I might happen to see her."

Babe kept out of sight among the roofless log walls through the long hours of the afternoon, sunset, twilight. It was almost dark and he'd given up hope of seeing her when his bronc stopped cropping grass and upped his head. Babe walked out and saw a rider silhouetted against the sky. It was Lily.

She saw him, rode up, and swung down in her precise, small-booted manner before saying a word. She was dressed in Levi's, a blue shirt open at the throat; a Stetson was on the back of her head with her hair knotted beneath it. She looked like a boy except when she turned and one could see the developing curve of her body.

She walked up and said, "Babe! I was scared you wouldn't wait around."

The quality of her voice was always a shock to him. Not once a month did he talk to a woman. She was quite close, with one hand lifted as though to lay it on his breast. He was aware of a faint perfume—the odor of the store-soap she used. He said her name, and she answered, "Yes?"

THERE WAS SOMETHING eager in her tone. A thought came that made him weak and sweaty. For a moment he forgot all about the fight brewing between Coltons and Sagers. Out on the lonesome prairie, or sleeping on the floor of the line shack, he'd dreamed of such a meeting with her and the things he'd say. But now he couldn't force himself, and when he felt that he had to say something it was, "Pretty tough on your dad, getting the creek shut off."

"We'll get water!" The fierceness of her response was a surprise to him.

"What's he going to do?"

"Don't worry about us. Tommy will see to it that the Coltons get back as good as they give."

"Lily, that's why I came to you. I'm not a spy, riding here behind the Coltons' backs, but I don't want a lot of killing, either. They *want* him to start this trouble."

Her head was high, and she said, "Tommy's no fool! He knows all about the Coltons waiting to bushwhack him when he tries to get at the dam. But don't think he won't do anything."

She was proud of Tom. He'd done as much to break their father as the big blizzard had, but he had a dash that appealed to women.

She said, "You don't believe me, do you? Well listen, and—"

"You better keep it to yourself. I'm a Colton. For all you know I might carry it back home."

She laid her hand on his arm and said, "Oh, Babe! I know you wouldn't do that."

He cried. "You don't know any such thing. They get an idea I know something they'd kick my ribs in to find out. Maybe I'd tell. I don't want to know what plan he's got up his sleeve. But I'll tell you this, if he starts anything the Coltons will be waiting for him. Once he makes a move, all hell will break loose."

Her voice and the tilt of her head were challenging. "Maybe we can raise a little of that ourselves. Don't think it'll be just Dad and Tommy. We'll have some men to back us, too."

"Sure, McGruder and the Henry boys and Blackfoot Charley from down in the breaks. If you Sagers start throwing in with that bunch of horse-rustlers the whole country will be down on you and Hooks can do what he likes."

She said bitterly, "I suppose you want us to give up."

"Old Rufe is sick of the business, too. You Sagers are one up on them now, with Lester in his grave, so why don't you go ahead and sell your lease on these fields? Get your price. Make it ten thousand. He might go for that, and the fields aren't worth any such amount to you."

"If you think we'd ever sell to the Coltons!" Anger brought her to the verge of tears. "You own a fourth of that spread, don't you? Is *that* why you're here?"

"Lily, you know it isn't."

She started away and he seized her by the arms. She had a wiry, rapid strength and almost slipped away.

She sobbed, "Let me go!"

"I came because of you. And on account of me, too, if you want to know it. I don't know what would happen if this broke out in a range war. I'd have to choose sides or leave the country."

She stopped struggling and looked up with her face so close he could feel her warm breath on his neck. "Which side would it be?"

"Yours, of course." The thought came to him of riding with the Sagers against Hooks. It was all right to brag about it when Hooks wasn't there, but down inside he wondered if he'd have the guts. Maybe Blackfoot Charley was right. Maybe he ought to drift to the Milk River country. Drift with his tail between his legs. He said to her. "Talk to Tom—to your dad. Try to keep him from tearing this thing wide open. It's a last chance!"

"All right." The fight had burned out of her now. "I'll do what I can."

He said good-bye to her a few minutes later and watched her ride away in the early darkness. He saddled and let his bronc take it at an easy wolf trot toward the brush of Elk Creek. Before dropping down to the wagon road he turned and sat for a while, watching for another sight of her, but the moon wasn't up, and all he could see were the elongated, dark shapes of the Old Fort buildings, and, miles away, the bird-track gullies where the badlands commenced encroaching on the prairie rim.

A LIGHT APPEARED near one of the buildings. It was dim, elusive, so even while watching it he wasn't quite sure it was there. Like the ghost fire sometimes given off by rotting wood in the beaver ponds back in the hills. It went out, and with a sick jolt it occurred to him that the light had come from a match in someone's cupped hands.

He thought of Hooks. He could have followed him from the ranch, lain all day by the creek, and approached under the cover of night. But that wouldn't be Hooks's style. Besides, Hooks wouldn't let him ride off. Fishface. Yes, it would be Fishface. He'd been suspicious the night before, and he'd been sitting on the corral fence that morning, watching as Babe had ridden away.

Babe wheeled his horse and rode slowly back toward the fort. He kept feeling his gun butt. He didn't know what he'd do if he caught up with him. He wondered how much he'd heard. He couldn't even remember just what had been said. He knew he hadn't given away any secrets except that the Coltons wanted them to attack, and he hadn't been very loud in saying that. It wasn't what Fishface heard, but what he'd *say* he heard.

He was a quarter way back to the fort when he glimpsed a rider heading south toward the hills at a good gallop. He turned and rode parallel with the man's course until he reached the hills. There he slanted over, hoping to intercept him at Dogtown Coulee, but the maneuver wasn't successful. After a half-hour wait he rode back to the home ranch.

He turned his horse in the corral, went in the barn, lit a lantern, and found Fish's saddle. The cinch was still damp—cold to the touch. It hadn't been there more than an hour. He walked on the bunkhouse, climbed in his bunk, and lay back with no thought of sleep. Next thing he realized someone yelled, "Go get it or starve!" and the cookhouse bell was banging.

He was scrubbing when Hooks walked up and said, "Find that long-horse?"

"No." He pretended his eyes were full of soap so he'd have time to think. There was no use of lying—Hooks knew. He rubbed dry and looked up to meet Hooks's quartz-hard eyes. "Didn't hunt for him."

"What did you hunt for?"

"I rode down toward the fort and saw Lily."

Hooks laughed with a hard twist of his mouth and said, "You got your guts."

No more was said about it. After breakfast Rufe sent him to the mailbox, eight miles away on the Middlefork stage road. When he got back all the Coltons except Rufe and Fishface had gone somewhere. The following night he was sitting in the bunkhouse, bending close to read a book in the light of a bacon-grease-dip, when Hooks came in, stiff-legged from hard riding.

"Hello, Babe," he said in a velvety voice. "Never thought of it till now, but I forgot to give you a birthday present."

He had something rolled up in his hand. Babe could feel the skin of his forehead draw tight from shock as he realized what it was. It was a belt—the prison-braid black and cream belt that Tommy Sager had been wearing in his black serge trousers that day he got off the train at Maverly.

Still smiling, Hooks tossed it to him. Then he clumped off in his stiff-tired manner to the dark, bunk-lined depths of the room.

3. The Back-shooter

The air now seemed suffocating. Babe blew out the grease-dip, and went outside. The night was cool, as it always was there in the hills no matter how hot the day, but sweat streaked down his cheeks. There was no doubt in his mind that Hooks had killed Tom Sager. He wondered if something Lily said that night had tipped him off.

He stood in the dark barn until thoughts became sorted in his mind. He knew he couldn't go on living with the Coltons. He had his choice of joining the Sagers or quitting the country.

He took his saddle down from the peg, then he put it back. There were some things he'd have to get at the bunkhouse. He'd wait until tomorrow.

He went back inside, lay down in his bunk. He could hear the heavy breathing sounds of men. In the blackness he had the feeling that Hooks Colton was lying, his eyes wide, listening.

The belt was gone from the table when he got up. Hooks sat in the house, eating. He didn't say anything when Babe came in. Babe put off packing his war bag, then, about midmorning, Andy and Clint came in, galloping hard, and had a talk with Hooks down by the corrals. Ho Chu saw them and put the skillet on, but they roped fresh horses and set off without eating, and Hooks went with them.

Babe had a hunch that things were getting ready to pop. He decided to wait awhile. He saddled and rode southwestward, through the hill notch where they'd disappeared. He saw no sign of the Coltons and made a wide swing to the north until he looked down on the soda-white flats where Wolf Creek sank away after leaving the hills. There for the first time he saw riders—five men in single file heading eastward through fields of sage belly-deep to their mounts. They were miles off, and he couldn't tell who they were. Men from the 88, maybe, riding to town.

He returned to the home ranch as the sun sank, brownish-red from a grass fire.

At midnight Clint Colton and a cowboy named Will Roberts rode in and hitched up in the spring wagon. Jeef had been shot through both shoulders and they were going to bring him in from the Lone Tree

Springs. The grass fire had been at Beaver Meadows and it had burned a strip half a mile wide and three long.

Clint said, "Always Jeef that gets it. Never satisfied but what he's double-brave. He'll be double-brave one o' these times with a ton of dirt on his chest."

They brought Jeef in and he lay on his stomach in the cookhouse while Wiley Gray cleaned out the wound and bandaged it. It was painful, but not necessarily serious. The bullet, fired from long range, had struck him across the right shoulder, shattered the bone and glanced downward across his back, missed his spine and came out near his left armpit without touching the big vein or artery.

"Dirty rustler outfit!" Jeef saying. "I'm going down there and blast the insides out of that dirty rustler outfit."

Wiley said, "Not for three or four weeks you won't."

Hooks said, "We'll get 'em, Jeef. We'll get 'em before any four weeks are up."

Babe had put the facts together and assumed someone had fired the meadows, the Colton winter range, and laid an ambush when the boys rode to fight it, but he heard them talking and learned the fire had been accidentally set by some Gros Ventres who were digging camas roots, while Jeef had been shot many miles to the north while he was riding the brush of Red Willow Creek.

NEXT EVENING, JUST before dark, Sheriff Walt Baker and Jim Conover, his deputy, rode up on the Elk Creek road.

Baker was a good-looking, tall man of forty, once foreman of the Warbonnet, which had been bankrupted by the hard winter of '87; Conover was a short, blunt man ten years his senior who had been deputy under one sheriff after another ever since the county was organized twelve years before.

Hooks strode down the slope from the big house to meet them. He called them by name and shouted, "Hey, Fish, tell Ho to put on the skillet." Then, as Baker swung to the ground, "You come to see about Jeef?"

"What about him?"

"Somebody tried to drygulch him down on the Red Willow. He's got a broke shoulder, and maybe he'll die if the poison sets in." Conover cursed and looked sympathetic. Hooks went on with a saw-edge quality in his voice, "First Lester and now Jeef. How long do you think us Coltons are going to take this, Sheriff?"

"I'm doing what I can. You know how it is with me. A county the size of Ioway, and three men to cover it." He looked in Hooks's face and said, "You hear about Tom Sager?"

"What about him?"

"Somebody killed him."

He stood back, looking surprised. Then he snorted breath from his nostrils. "I'll have to get back to my black suit."

Old Rufe hobbled down in time to overhear him. "Why you come here? You think we drygulched him? That what you think?"

"I'm going every place. Damn it, Tom gets killed, you Coltons ought to know the first thing folks'll say."

Andy grinned and said, "Where'd you find the dirty rustler?"

"By those alkali sinks where Wolf Crick comes out."

Babe had been looking down on the sinks that afternoon.

Andy asked, "Was he shot?"

"Yes."

Babe said, "Shot in the back!" A cold anger had settled in him. Anger, and a hatred of Hooks Colton that for a second overrode his fear, and made him say it. The words struck Hooks and made his shoulder muscles bulge to fill the sun-bleached fabric of his shirt. He started to swing around with his right arm long as though to reach for the gun at his hip, but he stopped himself tense and furious, without his eyes once resting on Babe, without saying a word.

"Why, yes," Baker said, "he was shot in the back. A .30-30, I'd say, but there was no way of being sure because the bullet went all the way through. Somebody took the belt off his pants. Like an Injun countin' coup."

Babe couldn't trust himself among the Coltons. He walked to the bunkhouse and sat on the split-pine bench out front. Against lamplight from the cookhouse he could see Hooks Colton. He was thinking Hooks didn't follow Tom out of Maverly that day because he was scared. He didn't have the guts to face Tom. He waited on his belly with a rifle and shot him in the back.

He went inside the bunkhouse, lighted the grease-dip, went to his bunk, filled his war sack, and made a blanket roll around it. He carried it on his shoulder to the barn and went back for his Winchester and his new Colt .45, silver-mounted, which he'd won in the keno lottery at Miles City the autumn before.

He stopped in the door of the barn with the Winchester in his hands, swung the lever down, and by moonlight saw the brassy glint of cartridge ready to go in the chamber. Hooks was inside the cookhouse, his head and shoulder visible through the window. It was about a hundred paces. Without levering the cartridge in, he lifted the gun and took aim. Hooks's faded blue shirt looked white by lamplight and made a perfect target against the knife-edge front sight. It would be easy—too easy.

HE DIDN'T CATCH his horse. He stood in the barn, and was still watching when Walt Baker and his deputy mounted and rode away down the wagon road. Baker wouldn't stay in the country. Now he'd made the motions of doing his duty it was a safe bet he'd get as far away as he decently could.

Hooks came out, called "Andy!" and walked toward the house.

This was the chance Babe had waited for. Now he could catch a horse and leave without being noticed. He put it off. He watched and saw their shadows passing in front of the windows as they seated themselves—the Coltons and the picked punchers of their rough-tough crew. He left his war bag and saddle in a box stall, with his Winchester leaning against them, and walked up the rise of ground, around the oat sheds to the box elder tree. They were talking inside, but quietly, and only a mutter of voices reached him.

He crept forward, found concealment beneath the pole-roofed awning that ran along that side of the house, remained crouched for a minute with one shoulder against the log wall.

Someone said, "I'm not waiting for that," and came through the door. The sound of boots and spurs seemed right atop him. Shadows loomed big. Clint Colton, Roberts, and a breed by the name of Joe Plain. They didn't look his way. They passed and were so close he caught the tepee smoke odor of Joe's gauntlet gloves.

". . . No pinto for that kind of a job," he heard Clint say while their boots crunched down the path. "I'll take that big black. . . ."

Joe Plain said, "Dapple's hardest to see in the dark. . . ."

Babe took a deep breath. He could hear his pulse. He waited for it to slow down, conquered an impulse to run, and moved forward until he was stopped by lamplight flooding from an open window.

There he could hear Hooks talking in clipped, restrained syllables. "Clint'll be at the claybanks by midnight. Well, maybe not. What time you got?"

A voice he recognized as Clayton Gotschall's said, "Ten past nine."

"Then say one-thirty. That'll put 'em at Blackfoot Charley's by three, and get McGruder on the way."

Wiley Gray said, "If they catch McGruder alone. Never tell about them damn horse-rustlers. Might find six men in that shack."

"We'll gamble on that."

Andy said, "That leaves Jinks Henry and the Sagers for us."

"We'll get Henry about when they get Blackfoot. Ought to put us at the Sagers by daybreak."

"What about the girl?"

After four or five seconds Hooks said, "That's up to her."

Wiley Gray said, "I seen her shoot one time over at the Fourth of July picnic, and she can cut the eyes out of a snake."

Hooks raised his raw, mean voice. "It's up to her!"

Andy laughed and said, "Maybe we ought to send Babe."

"That yellow pup?"

Babe scarcely noticed they were talking about him. All he could think of was Lily Sager. He knew how Hooks was. If he couldn't have her, he'd rather see her dead. Hooks would kill her himself if it worked out so the others weren't around to check him.

He moved back, one shoulder against the wall, step after step beneath the awning until he was at the lower edge of the house. There he felt safe to stand and start walking away, but someone was between him and the oat shed. Tall, gangling Fishface. He'd been placed there on watch.

Babe checked the impulse to leap out of sight. He stood perfectly rigid, knowing by the fellow's slack manner that he hadn't been seen. Fishface kept scraping at something with his boot toe. Then he turned and, seizing the opportunity, Babe crept to the box elder shadow, on up rising ground for fifty yards to some patchy buck brush that gave waist-high concealment.

He made a wide circle and came up to the corrals from the creek side in time to hear Clint and his men as they splashed across shallow water and up a rocky slope through a stiff tangle of serviceberry.

When they were gone he climbed over the corral rails, roped a big gelding, saddled him, and went inside for his war bag and Winchester. Suddenly, though the darkness was complete, he knew someone else was in the barn—was standing still, listening.

He made a guess and said, "Hello, Fish."

He heard the man's startled movement, and then his keyed-up voice, "Hello. What in hell you doing?"

Babe shifted his position and saw Fishface shadowed against the other door. Fish was retreating, bent a trifle, his right hand resting on the butt of his gun.

BABE WALKED TOWARD him. His boots were soundless in the cover of manure and rotted hay. They maintained the same distance apart, and when he was about to the door Fishface spoke.

"Why you saddlin' the horse?"

"Why you think?"

"You were listenin', weren't you? I thought I saw—" He stopped; he suddenly realized he'd made a mistake in letting Babe know. They were alone here. Fishface didn't have his brothers to back him.

Babe said, "You thought you saw me but you weren't sure, so you came down to check up. Now what, Fish?"

"Nothing. I ain't got nothin' agin' you. Honest, Babe—"

Fishface took two steps back while he was talking. That placed him just outside the door. He spun and took three long-legged leaps. He had his gun out. Moonlight struck it with a bluish gleam. He turned on his third step, and the gun exploded with a white flash that seemed to be right in Babe's face, but the bullet flew high and ripped a board over the barn door.

Babe had already drawn. He hesitated a quarter-second, unable to distinguish man from shadow, then shot. The bullet struck Fishface and knocked him on his back.

He lay with arms outflung and his mouth open, front teeth prominent like a dead prairie dog's, and Babe thought his bullet had hit him through the heart, but he was down from the shock of a wound through the fleshy part of his neck, and the shock left him suddenly. He twisted over, ran stumbling, dodging through the dark. The sound of gunfire brought men from the house. "Babe. He heard. He heard you. He's saddled and ready to tell 'em. By the barn . . ."

Babe kept hearing him. He found his Winchester in the barn, started away, and came back for two boxes of shells in his war bag. He had to open the gate, lead his horse through. Someone saw him. A gun cut the darkness and the bullet seemed to scorch him.

The gelding was bucking when he reached the saddle. He managed to find the other stirrup and stayed for a couple of jumps until he could get the animal to running.

He was around the corral with gunfire still raking the dark. He rode through the creek and up a trail-narrow cleft along the dirt bank where serviceberry bushes tore at his clothes.

Clayton Gotschall, with a Winchester in his hands, ran around the corrals and took a snap shot at him. Babe had his own rifle out and fired a second later just as his horse, slowed by steepness, looked for footing, and the bullet was close enough to put Gotschall on his belly amid the slather of mud and manure by the creek.

He swung over the crest and down a steel dip into more brush. He cursed his luck. He'd been beaten out of his chance to warn the Sagers. He still might get there ahead of them but it would only be a few minutes, and not enough to make much difference when you considered the number of men the Coltons could throw at the place.

This trail was a tough one, through one dip after another, and every one of them clogged with thorns. After a mile he cut back to the wagon road.

4. The Victors

He stopped for a moment, heard a man shout in the distance, the *clack* of a hoof on stone. He turned down the wagon road, pushing the gelding hard, but not too hard.

The miles that took him out of the hills gave him time to think of his best course. Straight across at the end of the Old Fort fields lay Jinks Henry's place. The Sager home ranch was sharply to his right, seven or eight miles farther along. Going to Jinks's house first would take him only a mile or so out of his way, and he usually had a puncher working for him. With a little help they might hole up in the rimrocks a couple miles this side of the Sager place, stop the Coltons, and raise enough of a shooting row to let Dad and Lily know there was trouble afoot.

Halfway across the meadows he stopped and scanned the country behind of him. A file of riders had emerged on a hillside, silhouetted by moonlight. He counted six. He wondered who the extra ones were. Alderdyce, probably, and the pale-eyed fellow who'd just hired out—the one calling himself the Alberta Kid.

He had a good start. Ten or twelve minutes. The gelding wasn't fast, but he could take the long going. It showed now as he drove hard across the remaining miles of flats, and down the coulee to Jinks Henry's house.

A shepherd dog commenced barking when he was still a quarter-mile off. He could see a cluster of corrals, a horse shed, and the dark shack beyond, perched on a shelf above the coulee bottom.

The dog stopped barking, and that told him that his master was somewhere around. He pulled in and called, "Jinks! Where are you?" He rode on, warily. "Jinks, this is Babe. Babe Colton." He saw movement by the house and the shine of a gun with its blue worn off. "Jinks, that you?"

"Yes, what'n hell do you want?" When he saw Babe coming straight across the coulee he slapped his rifle with his palm, making its lever rattle, and said, "Stop where y'are!"

Babe was close enough so he didn't have to yell. He stopped in some mud that seeped from a spring on the coulee side and told him what the Coltons were up to.

"What do you want *me* to do?" Jinks said.

"You here alone?"

"Yes."

Babe cursed through his teeth. "You want to help me head 'em off? They figured on coming here, but now they'll go straight for the Sagers. Think the two of us can stand them off at the sandstone pillars?"

Jinks shuffled forward. He was barefooted, dressed only in shirt and underwear. He was about fifty, a veteran of the Civil War—a Union veteran, which didn't add to his popularity in a country where two-thirds of the men had ridden up from Texas. He squinted at Babe's face.

"You out to fight your brothers?"

"They're not my brothers."

"No, they sure as hell ain't." With a sudden decision he leaned his rifle against an old gold rocker and started for the house. "I got to get my boots and pants. Toss a saddle on that bay bronc."

JINKS WAS DRESSED and down at the corrals before Babe had found the bridle. Jinks got it and fought the bronc all around the corral, wheezing and saying, "Easy boy—damn Injun bronc!" under his breath. "You jest take it easy!"

Babe would have headed back to the main trail, but Jinks said, "This way," and took him up the steep side to a ridge bearing on its crest the rain-deepened channels of the old travois tracks where Indians once traveled between Fort Ludloe and Piperock Crossing on the river. "This looks like a long way around, but it'll get us there sooner."

They followed forking ridges to the sand-rock cliffs and pillars that overlooked the coulee about three miles above Sager's home ranch. There, in a wild jumble of rock and juniper, they left their horses and clambered downward across sharp-edged boulders big as wagon boxes.

"There! Up-coulee!" Babe grabbed Jinks and pulled him down. Six men were in sight, coming down-coulee, easing their broncs warily.

He left Jinks and clambered along the broken slope towards them. He stopped, waited, levered a spent cartridge from his gun, felt the slight grab of lead as a fresh one went in. They were almost directly below at a range of one hundred and fifty yards when he aimed barely ahead of the lead horse and fired.

The bullet pounded dust that looked white as flour in the moonlight. Jinks cut loose a second later, and the six men scattered; three of them left their horses and dived to the first cover available; one broke toward the far wall at a gallop, and there, at far range, swung down and hunkered with his rifle behind a boulder; two others turned back the way they'd come and kept riding until they were a quarter-mile out of range and there stopped to appraise the situation. A bullet struck the rock by Babe's cheek and left him temporarily blind from powdered fragments. He moved to new positions one after another and fired his gun dry.

Those two up at the coulee would stand watching. They might come around to the ridge and attack from behind. He loaded up and shot dry again. The gun was hot and its action stiff from the gumming corrosion of black powder. He spat on it and kept working it back and forth while he watched the two start a steep climb up the far side. They wouldn't attack from behind. Their destination would be the Sager place.

He crawled back and found Jinks Henry. Jinks had his back to a boulder, looking at a wrist wound. "Got me with a sliver o' lead," he grumbled. He twisted and got his bandanna from his hip pocket. He wrapped it around and tried to pull it tight with his teeth.

Babe did it for him, and Jinks rolled back with his rifle over the edge of rock. He said, "Got one of 'em. Know who I think it was. Your old pal Hooks."

Every mile of his ride that night Babe had been certain that he'd end by facing Hooks. He was sure that Hooks was one of those who'd ridden to

Sager's. He tried to tell himself he wasn't glad. But he was. It was like walking down a corridor to die only to find freedom at the other end.

He said, "Then who rode toward Sager's?"

"That's what I was going to ask you."

"Can you handle things here?"

"I'll handle 'em. I'm harder to drag out than a badger out of a bar'l. What you got in mind?"

"I'm going on to the Sager place."

"All right, but don't do nothing foolish."

BABE CRAWLED UPHILL among the rocks. His gelding was tied to a sagebrush. He got him free, led him fifty yards around the hill without drawing a shot. Then a gun drove him to cover, and the horse tore away and galloped back around the hill, head to one side, dragging bridle.

Babe had no chance of catching him without exposing himself, so, with his rifle across his thighs, he slid downhill from rock to rock, digging his boots and spurs to check his descent. He stopped by a rock reef, tried to skirt it, but that rifle had shifted position and put him to cover again.

It had been a mistake coming down. He had no choice but to retrace his course upward among the rocks. As he climbed, the sound of distant gunfire came to him. That was from the Sager place.

He abandoned caution, sprang to his feet, and ran along the steep sidehill while that rifle, now better than a hundred yards off, dug dirt around his boots. He found a little gully, slid down it through rock and sagebrush, and following it he reached the coulee bottom a quarter-mile below the pillars.

His boot heels kept turning on rocks and tufts of grass as he ran. He stopped to get his breath and kick his spurs off. A ruddy light appeared over one of the round-topped hills. It died and rose again higher than before. It marked the position of the Sager place. They'd set fire to one of the buildings. He ran harder though his Colt, loaded belt, and extra Winchester cartridges in his hip pocket all weighted him down. Flame under-lit the billowing smoke, and to his nostrils came the odor of burning hay and wood.

The coulee was pinched down between walls of sand rock, then it widened and he had a view of the ranch.

It was the house burning. Upset against it was a half-burned buggy. The buggy had been loaded with hay, set afire, and rolled down the incline from the barn.

Someone was still inside the house. Gunfire ripped back and forth between there and the barn. The ground steepened. It slowed Babe to a faltering trot as he ran toward the barn. The fire, which had been enclosed in the rear room of the house, started to run along the ridge pole.

A voice he recognized as Clayton Gotschall's: "Hey, they're runnin' for the root cellar. Let's go get them hounds!"

Sixty yards away he located Gotschall, on his belly behind a heap of aspen corral poles. Gotschall heard him and twisted around. He did it with a catlike motion, rising enough to get one knee under him. He brought his rifle up but he shot too soon and the bullet whipped air a couple feet to Babe's left. Babe, still moving forward, fired from the waist.

The Winchester slug struck Gotschall in the midsection and doubled him like he'd been hit by a sledge. He took three dead man's steps and collapsed, with head and knees hitting the ground at the same instant.

"Gotschall!" a man shouted from the barn loft, and the shock of his voice was like a knife in Babe's middle. The voice belonged to Hooks Colton.

BABE KEPT GOING and half fell when he reached black shadow inside the barn. He got hold of something—it was a harness box—pulled himself to his feet. He fought air to his tortured lungs and got the dizziness of near-collapse from his brain.

Hooks! It was another man dead in the coulee. He should have gone gutless again. He was up against it now, the final showdown, the thing he always knew would come. It occurred to him that Hooks would probably kill him. It didn't seem important. The shock and crash of fighting had done something to him.

He groped, touched a ladder. The ladder to the loft. He started to climb. The second step brought him to a glassless window, and even at that distance he could feel heat from the burning house. Flames lay a bright circle around it. A man was down on the ground. Shot through the legs, trying to drag forward. Dad Sager.

A second later, Lily ran into sight. She was barefooted, her hair down. She'd had time to pull on a pair of Levi's and push the nightgown into the top of them. She had a rifle in one hand.

Lily reached her father, bent over him, got one arm under his shoulder, tried to lift him to his feet.

Hooks shouted her name. "Lily! Lily, come here!"

His voice seemed to be right over Babe's head, only a few feet away.

Lily let go and reached back for her rifle. Hooks fired—his bullet, aimed downward, dug dirt under Dad Sager's legs. Hooks laughed when he saw her lower the gun.

If Babe had any fear holding him, the sound of Hooks Colton killed it. His hatred of the man drove him forward, up the ladder. His Winchester clattered as he made the loft. Hooks heard him and cried, "Gotschall?"

Babe stood up, the rifle in his hands. He took one step. He could see nothing.

Hooks's voice, a new edge in it. "Gotschall?"

Babe said, "No, Hooks. Not Gotschall. He's dead."

Hooks fired, but Babe had expected it and moved. The gun flash was less than a dozen yards away. Babe returned it, and sidestepped as he did so. There were four more explosions, two from each gun.

Then a ringing silence, the air still carrying the rock of close-held concussion. Both men on the move. Babe touched the wall with one shoulder. There were holes here and there where hay could be forked down to the mangers. He'd have to look out. He drew cartridges from his pocket, fed them through the spring opening of the magazine.

A board creaked. He stood without breathing. The sound was repeated again, again, each time changing position, and so he was able to get a rough impression of Hooks's movement across the loft floor. It stopped for several seconds, and he was aware of a slight tremble. The floor had been released of weight. Hooks, a big man, had dropped below.

Babe heard the scuff of boots and knew he was running. He sprang to the ladder, laid down his Winchester, and dropped.

The Winchester still above, he laid his hand on his Colt, stepped into the central passage.

Hooks was running, back turned, silhouetted against the far door.

"Hooks!" Babe shouted.

HOOKS STOPPED AND spun around. He had his six-shooter in his hand. Babe drew with a half pivot and brought the gun up as he turned. He hesitated a fifth of a second, that brief instant a man needs to freeze on his target when it's more than twenty paces away. Their guns exploded almost in unison.

Babe felt the whip of burnt powder as the bullet went past his cheek. Hooks was hit. He was knocked backward. He dropped his gun. It struck his heavy-muscled thigh. Thudded to the floor. His right boot heel flipped over and dumped him. By ruddy, reflected light Babe was aware of his shocked eyes, his sagging moth.

"I'm . . . hit!" he said in a raw whisper. Like he was telling it to himself. "Got me." Then some focus came into his eyes. "What more you want?"

He was crouched, sitting on his heels, his hands far forward, fingers on the barn floor. He fell back, and with a dragging movement the fingers of his right hand found the gun, and he blazed wildly.

Babe fired twice, walking forward. One of the bullets knocked Hooks down, the other hit with a force that seemed to lift him an inch and drop him again.

Still, despite the awful shocking power of those .45 slugs, he managed to get to his knees, to his feet. He lurched into the firelight, a huge, stumbling, bent-over figure with both arms wrapped around his chest. There he fell, facedown, the toes of his boots together, heels out, his wicked, Mexican-roweled spurs making little pinpoint circles of reflection.

Babe kept walking and stood over him. Made sure he was dead. He had no feeling of sorrow, none of triumph. He just looked at him and knew he was dead.

Lily said his name. "Babe!" He turned and she was there, close enough to reach, to touch. She'd been there he didn't know how long. Stood there while their bullets roared by.

He rammed his gun back in the holster. It seemed natural that she should be in his arms. Her cheeks glistened from tears. She pressed her head against his breast and said his name over and over.

He said, "Your dad!"

They ran together and found him sitting up, trying to tear a bandage for his leg. It was bleeding badly. Lily found a dish towel that had been hanging over the line, and, soaking full, it slowly checked the flow of blood.

Dawn was coming. House now a smoldering oblong of logs. Jinks Henry rode up with Blackfoot Charley and one of the McGruder boys.

Jinks said, "That was Alderdyce I got, and he wasn't dead. So I guess Hooks got away after all."

"He's in the barn," Babe said.

He looked in Babe's eyes and said, "Oh." He understood and let it drop there. Then he said, "Blackfoot and Mick, here, got stirred up before Clint's bunch made a show. They came cross-country and scared off the ones we tackled. You think they'll bounce back on us today, Babe?"

"They won't," he said.

Babe hitched a team to the buckboard and asked Blackfoot to help him with Hooks. It wasn't easy looking at him, and he was glad when Blackfoot brought the tarp. All Babe's hatred was gone. Gone, with sour feeling left behind.

Lily ran up to him and said, "Babe, you're not going back there and—"

"Yes, I'm taking him home to Rufe. I stayed around to inherit my share of the place, so I guess I stayed around for this, too."

"Babe, they'll kill you up there."

"Don't worry. I'll be back. Don't you see? I have to face them today. They'll understand. I'll really be talking the Coltons' own language today. I ought to know. I guess I'm sort of a Colton myself."

The first great novel of the Old West, and a prototype for hundreds of others over the past eighty years, was Owen Wister's *The Virginian*, published in April of 1902. A bestseller for more than ten years, it led Wister (an easterner, curiously enough, educated at Harvard) to write other memorable Western adventures, among them the novel *Lin McLean* and numerous short stories collected under such titles as *Members of the Family* and *When the West Was West*. "Timberline," which first appeared in *The Saturday Evening Post* on March 7, 1908, is one of his (undeservedly) lesser known stories; it is a pleasure to reprint it here.

Timberline

Owen Wister

Just as the blaze of the sun seems to cast wild birds, when, by yielding themselves they invite it, into a sort of trance, so that they sit upon the ground tilted sidewise, their heads in the air, their beaks open, their wings hanging slack, their feathers ruffled and their eyes vacantly fixed, so must the spot of yellow at which I had sat staring steadily and idly have done something like this to me—given me a spell of torpor in which all thoughts and things receded far away from me. It was a yellow poster, still wet from rain.

A terrifying thunderstorm had left all space dumb and bruised, as it were, with the heavy blows of its noise. The damp seemed to make the yellow paper yellower, the black letters blacker. A dollar sign, figures and zeros, exclamation points, and the two blackest words of all: *reward* and *murder*, were what stood out of the yellow.

Two feet from it, on the same shed, was another poster, white, concerning some stallion, his place of residence, and his pedigree. This also I had read, with equal inattention and idleness, but my eyes had been drawn to the yellow spot and held by it.

Not by its news; the news was now old, since at every cabin and station dotted along our lonely road the same poster had appeared. They had discussed it, and whether he would be caught, and how much money he had got from his victim.

The body hadn't been found on Owl Creek for a good many weeks. Funny his friend hadn't turned up. If they'd killed him, why wasn't his body on Owl Creek, too? If he'd got away, why didn't he turn up? Such comments, with many more, were they making at Lost Soldier, Bull Spring, Crook's Gap, and Sweetwater Bridge.

I sat in the wagon waiting for Scipio Le Moyne to come out of the house; there in my nostrils was the smell of the wet sage brush and of the wet straw and manure, and there, against the gray sky, was an afterimage of the yellow poster, square, huge, and blue. It moved with my eyes as I turned them to get rid of the annoying vision, and it only slowly dissolved away over the head of the figure sitting on the corral with its back to me, the stocktender of this stage section. He sang, *"If that I was where I would be, Then should I be where I am not; Here am I where I must be, And where I would be I cannot."*

I could not see the figure's face, or that he moved. One boot was twisted between the bars of the corral to hold him steady, its trodden heel was worn to a slant; from one seat pocket a soiled rag protruded and through a hole below this a piece of his red shirt or drawers stuck out. A coat much too large for him hung from his neck rather than from his shoulders, and the damp, limp hat that he wore, with its spotted, unraveled hatband, somehow completed the suggestion that he was not alive at all, but had been tied together and stuffed and set out in joke. Certainly there were no birds, or crops to frighten birds from; the only thing man had sown the desert with at Rongis was empty bottles. These lay everywhere.

As he sat and repeated his song there came from his back and his hat and his voice an impression of loneliness, poignant and helpless. A windmill turned and turned and creaked near the corral, adding its note of forlornness to the song.

A man put his head out of the house. "Stop it," he said, and shut the door again.

The figure obediently climbed down and went over to the windmill, where he took hold of the rope hanging from its rudder and turned the contrivance slowly out of the wind, until the wheel ceased revolving.

The man put his head out of the house, this second time speaking louder: "I didn't say stop that. I said stop it; stop your damned singing." He withdrew his head immediately.

The boy—the mild, new yellow hair on his face was the unshaven growth of adolescence—stood a long while looking at the door in silence, with eyes and mouth expressing futile injury. Finally he thrust his hands into bunchy pockets, and said, "I ain't no two-bit man."

He watched the door, as if daring it to deny this, then, as nothing happened, he slowly drew his hands from the bunchy pockets, climbed the corral at the spot nearest him, twisted the boot between the bars, and sat as before only without singing.

Thus we sat waiting, I for Scipio to come out of the house with the information he had gone in for, while the boy waited for nothing. *Waiting for nothing* was stamped plain upon him from head to foot. This boy's eye-brows were insufficient, and his front was as ragged as his back. He just sat and waited.

Presently the same man put his head out of the door. "You after sheep?" I nodded.

"I could a-showed you sheep. Rams. Horns as big as your thigh—bigger 'n *your* thigh. That was before tenderfeet came in and spoiled this country. Counted seven thousand on that there butte one morning before break-fast. Seven thousand and twenty-three, if you want exact figgers. Quit your staring!" This was addressed to the boy on the corral. "Why, you're not a-going without another?" This convivial question was to Scipio, who now came out of the house and across to me with the news that he had failed on what he had went in for.

"I could a-showed you sheep—" resumed the man, but I was now at-tending to Scipio.

"He don't know anything," said Scipio, "nor any of 'em in there. But we haven't got this country rounded up yet. He's just come out of a week of snake fits, and, by the way it looks, he'll enter on another about tomor-row morning. But drink can't stop *him* lying."

"Bad weather," said the man, watching us make ready to continue our long drive. "Lot o' lightning loose in the air right now. Kind o' weather you're liable to see fire on the horns of the stock some night."

This sounded like such a good one that I encouraged him. "We have nothing like that in the East."

"Hm. Guess you've not. Guess you never seen sixteen thousand steers with a light at the end of every horn in the herd."

"Are they going to catch that man?" inquired Scipio, pointing to the yellow poster.

"Catch him? Them" No! But I could tell 'em where he's went. He's went to Idaho."

"Thought the '76 outfit had sold Auctioneer," Scipio continued con-versationally.

"That stallion? No! But I could tell 'em they'd ought to." This was his good-bye to us; he removed himself and his alcoholic omniscience into the house.

"Wait," I said to Scipio as he got in and took the reins from me. "I'm going to deal some magic to you. Look at that poster. No, not the stallion, the yellow one. Keep looking at it hard." While he obeyed me I made solemn passes with my hands over his head. "Now look anywhere you please."

Scipio looked across the corral at the gray sky. A slight stiffening of figure ensued, and he knit his brows. Then he rubbed a hand over his eyes and looked again.

"You after sheep?" It was the boy sitting on the corral. We paid him no attention.

"It's about gone," said Scipio, rubbing his eyes again. "Did you do that to me? Of course you didn't! What did?"

I adopted the manner of the professor who lectured on light to me when I was nineteen. "The eye being normal in structure and focus, the color of an afterimage of the negative variety is complementary to that of the object causing it. If, for instance, a yellow disk (or lozenge in this case) be attentively observed, the yellow-perceiving elements of the retina become fatigued. Hence, when the mixed rays which constitute white light fall upon that portion of the retina which has thus been fatigued, the rays which produce the sensation of yellow will cause less effect than the other rays for which the eye has been fatigued. Therefore, white light to an eye fatigued for yellow will appear blue—blue being yellow's complementary color. Now, shall I go on?" I asked.

"Don't y'u!" Scipio begged. "I'd sooner believe y'u done it to me."

"I can show you sheep." It was the boy again. We had not noticed him come from the corral to our wagon, by which he now stood. His eyes were eagerly fixed upon me; as they looked into mine they seemed almost burning with some sort of appeal.

"Hello, Timberline!" said Scipio, not at all unkindly. "Still holding your job here? Well, you better stick to it. You're inclined to drift some."

He touched the horses and we left the boy standing and looking after us, lonely and baffled.

"Why Timberline?" I asked after several miles.

"Well, he came into this country the long, lanky innocent kid you saw him, and he'd always get too tall in the legs for his latest pair of pants. They'd be half up to his knees. So we called him that. Guess he's most forgot his real name."

"What is his real name?"

"I've quite forgot."

This much talk did for us for two or three miles more.

"Do you suppose the man really did go to Idaho?" I asked then.

"They do go there—and they go everywhere else that's convenient—Canada, San Francisco, some Indian reservation. He'll never get found. I expect like as not he killed the confederate along with the victims—it's claimed there was a cook along, too. He's never showed up. It's a bad proposition to get tangled up with a murderer."

I sat thinking of this and that and the other.

"That was a superior lie about the lights on the steers' horns," I remarked next.

Scipio shoved one hand under his hat and scratched his head. "They say that's so," he said. "I've heard it. Never seen it. But—tell y'u—he ain't got brains enough to invent a thing like that. And he's too conceited to tell another man's lie."

"There's St. Elmo's fire," I pondered. "That's genuine."

Scipio desired to know about this, and I told him of the lights that are seen at the ends of the yards and spars of ships at sea in atmospheric conditions of a certain kind. He let me also tell him of the old Breton sailor belief that these lights are the souls of dead sailor men come back to pray for the living in peril; but stopped me soon when I attempted to speak of charged thunderclouds, and the positive, and the negative, and conductors and Leyden jars.

"That's a heap worse than the other stuff about yellow and blue," he objected. "Here's Broke Axle. We'll camp here."

SCIPIO'S SLEEP WAS superior to mine, coming sooner, burying him deeper from the world of wakefulness. Thus, he did not become aware of a figure sitting by our little fire of embers, whose presence penetrated my thinner sleep until my eyes opened and saw it. I lay still, drawing my gun stealthily into a good position and thinking what were best to do; but he must have heard me.

"Lemme show you sheep."

"What's that?" It was Scipio starting to life and action.

"Don't shoot Timberline," I said. "He's come to show us sheep."

Scipio sat staring stupefied at the figure by the embers, and then he slowly turned his head around to me, and I thought he was going to pour out one of those long corrosive streams of comment that usually burst from him when he was enough surprised. But he was too much surprised.

"His name is Henry Hall," he said to me very mildly. "I've just remembered it."

The patient figure by the embers rose. "There's sheep in the Washakie Needles. Lots and lots and lots. I seen 'em myself in the spring. I can take you right to 'em. Don't make me go back and be stocktender." He recited all this in a sort of rising rhythm until the last sentence, in which the entreaty shook his voice.

"Washakie Needles is the nearest likely place," muttered Scipio.

"If you don't get any you needn't to pay me any," urged the boy; and he stretched out an arm to mark his words and his prayer.

We sat in our beds and he stood waiting by the embers to hear his fate, while nothing made a sound but Broke Axle.

"Why not?" I said. "We were talking a ways back of taking on a third man."

"A man," said Scipio. "Yes."

"I can cook, I can pack. I can cook good bread, and I can show you sheep, and if I don't you won't have to pay me a cent," stated the boy.

"He sure means what he says," Scipio commented. "It's your trip."

Thus it was I came to hire Timberline.

Dawn showed him in the same miserable rags he wore on my first sight of him at the corral, and these provided his sole visible property of any kind; he didn't possess a change of anything, he hadn't brought away from Rongis so much as a handkerchief tied up with things inside it. Most wonderful of all, he owned not even a horse—and in that country in those days five dollars' worth of horse was within the means of almost anybody.

But he was unclean, as I had feared. He washed his one set of rags, and his skin-and-bones body, by the light of that first sunrise on Broke Axle, and this proved a habit with him, which made all the more strange his neglect to throw the rags away and wear the new clothes I bought as we passed through Lander, and gave him.

"Timberline," said Scipio the next day, "If Anthony Comstock came up in the country he'd jail you."

"Who's he?" Timberline screamed sharply.

"He lives in New York and he's agin the nood. That costume of yours is getting close on to what they claim Venus and other Greek statuary used to wear."

After this Timberline put on the Lander clothes, but we found that he kept the rags next to his skin. This clinging to such worthless things seemed probably the result of destitution, of having had nothing, day after day and month after month.

His help in camp was real, not merely well-meant; the curious haze or blur in which his mind had seemed to be at the corral cleared away, and he was worth his wages. What he had said he could do he did, and more. And yet, when I looked at him he was somehow forever pitiful.

"Do you think anything is the matter with him?" I asked Scipio.

"Only just one thing. He'd oughtn't never have been born."

We continued along the trail, engrossed in our several thoughts, and I could hear Timberline, behind us with the packhorses, singing: *"If that I was where I would be. Then should I be where I am not."*

OUR MODE OF travel had changed at Fort Washakie: we had left the wagon and put ourselves and our baggage upon horses because we should presently be in a country where wagons could not go.

Once the vigorous words of some bypasser on a horse caused Scipio and me to discuss dropping the Washakie Needles for the country at the head of Green River. None of us had ever been in the Green River country, while Timberline evidently knew the Washakie Needles well, and this decided us. But Timberline had been thrown into the strangest agitation by our uncertainty. He had said nothing, but he walked about, coming near, going away, sitting down, getting up, instead of placidly watching his fire and cooking; until at last I told him not to worry, that I should keep him and pay him in any case. Then he spoke.

"I didn't hire to go to Green River."

"What have you got against Green River?"

"I hired to go to the Washakie Needles."

His agitation left him immediately upon our turning our faces in that direction. What had so disturbed him we could not guess; but, later that day, Scipio rode up to me, bursting with a solution. He had visited a freighter's camp, and the freighter, upon learning our destination, had said he supposed we were "after the reward."

It did not get through my head at once, but when Scipio reminded me of the yellow poster and the murder, it got through fast enough; the body had been found on Owl Creek, and the middle fork of Owl Creek headed among the Washakie Needles. There might be another body—the other Eastern man who had never been seen since—and there was a possible third, the confederate, the cook; many held it was the murderer's best policy to destroy him as well.

So now we had Timberline accounted for satisfactorily to ourselves: he was "after the reward." We never said this to him, but we worked out his steps from the start. As stocktender at Rongis he had seen that yellow poster pasted up, and had read it, day after day, with its promise of what to him was a fortune. My sheep hunt had dropped like a providence into his hand.

We got across the hot country where rattlesnakes were thick, where neither man lived nor water ran, and came to the first lone habitation in this new part of the world—a new set of mountains, a new set of creeks. A man stood at the door, watching us come.

"Do you know him?" I asked Scipio.

"Well, I've heard of him," said Scipio. "He went and married a squaw."

We were now opposite the man's door. "You folks after the reward?" said he.

"After mountain sheep," I replied, somewhat angry.

We camped some ten miles beyond him, and the next day crossed a not high range, stopping near another cabin at noon. Two men were living here, cutting hay in a wild park. They gave us a quantity of berries they had picked and we gave them some potatoes.

"After the reward?" said one of them as we rode away, and I contradicted him with temper.

"Lie to 'em," said Scipio. "Say yes."

Something had begun to weigh upon our cheerfulness in this new country. The reward dogged us, and we met strange actions of people, twice. We came upon some hot sulphur springs and camped near them, with a wide creek between us and another camp. Those people—two men and two women—emerged from their tent, surveyed us, nodded to us, and settled down again.

Next morning they had vanished; we could see empty bottles where they had been. And once, coming out of a little valley, we sighted close to us through cottonwoods a horseman leading a packhorse coming out of the next little valley. He did not nod to us, but pursued his parallel course some three hundred yards off, until a rise in the ground hid him for a while; when this was passed he was no longer where he should have been, abreast of us, but far to the front, galloping away. That was our last sight of him.

We spoke of these actions a little. Did these people suspect us, or were they afraid we suspected them? All we ever knew was that suspicion now closed down upon all things like a change of climate.

I DROVE UP the narrowing canyon of Owl Creek, a constant prey to such ill-ease, such distaste for continuing my sheep hunt here, that shame alone prevented my giving it up and getting into another country out of sight and far away from these Washakie Needles, these twin spires of naked rock that rose in front of us now, high above the clustered mountaintops, closing the canyon in, shutting the setting sun away.

"He *can* talk when he wants to." This was Scipio, riding behind me.

"What has Timberline been telling you?"

"Nothing. But he's telling himself a heap of something." In the rear of our single-file party Timberline rode, and I could hear him. It was a relief to have a practical trouble threatening us; if the boy was going off his head we should have something real to deal with. But when I had chosen a camp and we were unsaddling and throwing the packs on the ground, Timberline was in his customary silence.

Next morning, the three of us left camp. It was a warm summer in the valley by the streaming channel of our creek, and the quiet days smelled of the pines. By three o'clock we stood upon a lofty, wet, slippery ledge that fell away on three sides, sheer or broken, to the summer and the warmth thousands of feet below. Here it began to be very cold, and to the west the sky now clotted into advancing lumps of thick thunderclouds, black, weaving and merging heavily and swiftly in a fierce rising wind.

We got away from this promontory to follow a sheep trail, and as we went along the backbone of the mountain, two or three valleys off to the right long black streamers let down from the cloud. They hung and wavered mistily close over the pines that did not grow within a thousand feet of our high level. I gazed hard at the streamers and discerned water, or something pouring down in them. Above our heads the day was still serene, and we had a chance to make camp without a wetting.

"No! No!" said Timberline hoarsely. "See there! We can get them. We're above them. They don't see us."

I saw no sheep where he pointed but he insisted they had merely moved behind a point, and so we went on to a junction of the knife-ridges upon which a second storm was hastening from the southwest over deep valleys that we turned our backs on to creep near the Great Washakie Needles.

Below us there was a new valley like the bottom of a cauldron; on the far side of the cauldron the air, like a stroke of magic became thick white and through it leaped the first lightning, a blinding violet. A sheet of the storm crossed over to us, the cauldron sank from sight in its white sea, and the hail cut my face, so I bowed it down. On the ground I saw what looked like a tangle of old footprints in the hard-crusted mud.

These the pellets of the swarming hail soon filled. This tempest of flying ice struck my body, my horse, raced over the ground like spray on the crest of breaking waves, and drove me to dismount and sit under the horse, huddled together even as he was huddled against the fury and the biting pain of the hail.

From under the horse's belly I looked out upon a chaos of shooting, hissing white, through which, in every direction, lightning flashed and leaped, while the fearful crashes behind the curtain of the hail sounded as if I should see a destroyed world when the curtain lifted. The place was so flooded with electricity that I gave up the shelter of my horse, and left my rifle on the ground, and moved away from the vicinity of these points of attraction.

At length the hailstones fell more gently, the near view opened, revealing white winter on all save the steep, gray needles; the thick white curtain of hail departed slowly, the hail where I was fell more scantily still.

Something somewhere near my head set up a delicate sound. It seemed in my hat. I rose and began to wander, bewildered by this. The hail was now falling very fine and gentle, when suddenly I was aware of its stinging me behind my ear more sharply than it had done before. I turned my face in its direction and found its blows harmless, while the stinging in my ear grew sharper. The hissing continued close to my head wherever I walked. It resembled the little watery escape of gas from a charged bottle whose cork is being slowly drawn.

I was now more really disturbed than I had been during the storm's worst, and meeting Scipio, who was also wandering, I asked if he felt anything. He nodded uneasily, when, suddenly—I know not why—I snatched my hat off. The hissing was in the brim, and it died out as I looked at the leather binding and the stitches.

I expected to see some insect there, or some visible person for the noise. I saw nothing, but the pricking behind my ear had also stopped. Then I knew my wet hat had been charged like a Leyden jar with electricity Scipio, who had watched me, jerked his hat off also.

"Lights on steer horns are nothing to this," I began, when he cut me short with an exclamation.

Timberline, on his knees, with a frightful countenance, was tearing off his clothes. He had felt the prickling, but it caused him thought different from mine.

"Leave me go!" he screamed. "I didn't push you over! He made me push you. I never knowed his game. I was only the cook. I wish't I'd followed you. There! There! Take it back! There's your money! I never spent a cent of it!"

And from those rags he had cherished he tore the bills that had been sewed in them. But this confession seemed not to stop the stinging. He rose, stared wildly, and screaming wildly, "You got it all," plunged into the cauldron from our sight. The fluttered money—some of the victim's, hush-money hapless Timberline had accepted from the murderer—was only five ten-dollar bills; but it had been enough load of guilt to draw him to the spot of the crime.

We found the two bodies, the old and the new, and buried them both. But the true murderer was not caught, and no one ever claimed the reward.

Jack London (1876–1916) was a master of the adventure story whose novel, *The Call of the Wild,* will live forever as the definitive example of the American spirit. An adventurer himself, he knew what he wrote, having spent parts of his early life living as a hobo, searching for gold in Alaska, and even serving time in prison for oyster pirating. Much of his work, such as his science-fiction novel, *The Scarlet Plague,* contains considerable political content, a strange combination of Marxism and rugged individualism. But he also wrote knowingly of the frontier and the search for wealth, as in this powerful story.

All Gold Canyon

Jack London

It was the green heart of the canyon, where the walls swerved back from the rigid plain and relieved their harshness of line by making a little sheltered nook and filling it to the brim with sweetness and roundness and softness. Here all things rested. Even the narrow stream ceased its turbulent down-rush long enough to form a quiet pool. Knee-deep in the water, with drooping head and half-shut eyes, drowsed a red-coated, many-antlered buck.

On one side, beginning at the very lip of the pool, was a tiny meadow, a cool, resilient surface of green that extended to the base of the frowning wall. Beyond the pool a gentle slope of earth ran up and up to meet the opposing wall. Fine grass covered the slope—grass that was spangled with flowers, with here-and-there patches of color, orange and purple and golden. Below, the canyon was shut in. There was no view. The walls leaned together abruptly, and the canyon ended in a chaos of rocks, moss-covered and hidden by a green screen of vines and creepers and boughs of trees. Up the canyon rose far hills and peaks, the big foothills, pine-covered and remote. And far beyond, like clouds upon the border of the sky, towered minarets of white, where the sierra's eternal snows flashed austerely the blazes of the sun.

There was no dust in the canyon. The leaves and flowers were clean and virginal. The grass was young velvet. Over the pool three cottonwoods sent their snowy fluffs fluttering down the quiet air. On the slope the blossoms of the wine-wooded manzanita filled the air with springtime odors, while the leaves, wise with experience, were already beginning their vertical twist against the coming aridity of summer. In the open spaces on the slope, beyond the farthest shadow-reach of the manzanita, poised the mariposa lilies, like so many flights of jeweled moths suddenly arrested and on the verge of trembling into flight again. Here and there that woods harlequin, the madrone, permitting itself to be caught in the act of changing its pea-green trunk to madder red, breathed its fragrance into the air from great clusters of waxen bells. Creamy white were these bells, shaped like lilies of the valley, with the sweetness of perfume that is of the springtime.

There was not a sigh of wind. The air was drowsy with its weight of perfume. It was a sweetness that would have been cloying had the air been heavy and humid. But the air was sharp and thin. It was as starlight transmuted into atmosphere, shot through and warmed by sunshine, and flower-drenched with sweetness.

An occasional butterfly drifted in and out through the patches of light and shade. And from all about rose the low and sleepy hum of mountain bees—feasting Sybarites that jostled one another good-naturedly at the board, nor found time for rough discourtesy. So quietly did the little stream drip and ripple its way through the canyon that it spoke only in faint and occasional gurgles. The voice of the stream was as a drowsy whisper, ever interrupted by dozings and silences, ever lifted again in the awakenings.

The motion of all things was a drifting in the heart of the canyon. Sunshine and butterflies drifted in and out among the trees. The hum of the bees and the whisper of the stream were a drifting of sound. And the drifting sound and drifting color seemed to weave together in the making of a delicate and intangible fabric which was the spirit of the place. It was a spirit of peace that was not of death, but of smooth-pulsing life, of quietude that was not silence, of movement that was not action, of repose that was quick with existence without being violent with struggle and travail. The spirit of the place was the spirit of the peace of the living, somnolent with the easement and content of prosperity, and undisturbed by rumors of far wars.

The red-coated many-antlered buck acknowledged the lordship of the spirit of the place and dozed knee-deep in the cool, shaded pool. There seemed no flies to vex him and he was languid with rest. Sometimes his ears moved when the stream awoke and whispered; but they moved lazily, with foreknowledge that it was merely the stream grown garrulous at discovery that it had slept.

But there came a time when the buck's ears lifted and tensed with swift eagerness for sound. His head was turned down the canyon. His sensitive, quivering nostrils scented the air. His eyes could not pierce the green screen through which the stream rippled away, but to his ears came the voice of a man. It was a steady, monotonous, singsong voice. Once the buck heard the harsh clash of metal upon rock. At the sound he snorted with a sudden start that jerked him through the air from water to meadow, and his feet sank into the young velvet while he pricked his ears and again scented the air. Then he stole across the tiny meadow, pausing once and again to listen, and faded away out of the canyon like a wraith, soft-footed and without sound.

The clash of steel-shod soles against the rocks began to be heard, and the man's voice grew louder. It was raised in a sort of chant and became distinct with nearness, so that the words could be heard.

> *"Tu'n around an' tu'n yo' face*
> *Untoe them sweet hills of grace*
>   *(D' pow'rs of sin yo' am scornin'!).*
> *Look about an' look aroun'*
> *Fling yo' sin-pack on d' groun'*
>   *(Yo' will meet wid d' Lord in d' mornin'!)."*

A sound of scrambling accompanied the song, and the spirit of the place fled away on the heels of the red-coated buck. The green screen was burst asunder, and a man peered out at the meadow and the pool and the sloping sidehill. He was a deliberate sort of man. He took in the scene with one embracing glance, then ran his eyes over the details to verify the general impression. Then, and not until then, did he open his mouth in vivid and solemn approval.

"Smoke of life an' snakes of purgatory! Will you just look at that! Wood an' water an' grass an' a sidehill! A pocket-hunter's delight an' a cayuse's paradise! Cool green for tired eyes! Pink pills for pale people ain't in it. A secret pasture for prospectors and a resting place for tired burros. It's just booful!"

He was a sandy-complexioned man in whose face geniality and humor seemed the salient characteristics. It was a mobile face, quick-changing to inward mood and thought. Thinking was in him a visible process. Ideas chased across his face like wind flaws across the surface of a lake. His hair, sparse and unkempt of growth, was an indeterminate and colorless as his complexion. It would seem that all the color of his frame had gone into his eyes, for they were startlingly blue. Also, they were laughing and merry eyes, within them much of the naiveté and wonder of the child; and yet, in an unassertive way, they contained much of calm self-reliance and strength of purpose founded upon self-experience and experience of the world.

From out the screen of vines and creepers, he flung ahead of him a miner's pick and shovel and gold-pan. Then he crawled out himself into the open. He was clad in faded overalls and black cotton shirt, with hob-nailed brogans on his feet, and on his head a hat whose shapelessness and stains advertised the rough usage of wind and rain and sun and camp smoke. He stood erect, seeing wide-eyed the secrecy of the scene and sensuously inhaling the warm, sweet breath of the canyon garden through nostrils that dilated and quivered with delight. His eyes narrowed to laughing slits of blue, his face wreathed itself in joy, and his mouth curled in a smile as he cried aloud, "Jumping dandelions and happy hollyhocks, but that smells good to me! Talk about your attar o' roses an' cologne factories! They ain't in it!"

He had the habit of soliloquy. His quick-changing facial expressions might tell every thought and mood, but the tongue, perforce, ran hard after, repeating, like a second Boswell.

The man lay down on the lip of the pool and drank long and deep of its water. "Tastes good to me," he murmured, lifting his head and gazing across the pool at the sidehill, while he wiped his mouth with the back of his hand. The sidehill attracted his attention. Still lying on his stomach, he studied the hill formation long and carefully. It was a practiced eye that traveled up the slope to the crumbling canyon wall and back and down again to the edge of the pool. He scrambled to his feet and favored the sidehill with a second survey.

"Look good to me," he concluded, picking up his pick and shovel and gold-pan.

He crossed the stream below the pool, stepping agilely from stone to stone. Where the sidehill touched the water he dug up a shovelful of dirt and put it into the gold-pan. He squatted down, holding the pan in his two hands, and partly immersing it in the stream. Then he imparted to the pan a deft circular motion that sent the water sluicing in and out through the dirt and gravel. The larger and the lighter particles worked to the surface, and these, by a skillful dipping movement of the pan, he spilled out and over the edge. Occasionally, to expedite matters, he rested the pan and with his fingers raked out the large pebbles and pieces of rock.

The contents of the pan diminished rapidly until only fine dirt and the smallest bits of gravel remained. At this stage he began to work very deliberately and carefully. It was fine washing, and he washed fine and finer, with a keen scrutiny and delicate and fastidious touch. At last the pan seemed empty of everything but water; but with a quick semicircular flirt that sent the water flying over the shallow rim into the stream, he disclosed a layer of black sand on the bottom of the pan. So thin was this layer that it was like a streak of paint. He examined it closely. In the midst of it was a tiny golden speck. He dribbled a little water in over the depressed edge of the pan. With a quick flirt he sent the water sluicing across the bottom, turning the grains of black sand over and over. A second tiny golden speck rewarded his effort.

The washing had now become very fine—fine beyond all need of ordinary placer mining. He worked the black sand, a small portion at a time, up the shallow rim of the pan. Each small portion he examined sharply, so that his eyes saw every grain of it before he allowed it to slide over the edge and away. Jealously, bit by bit, he let the black sand slip away. A golden speck, no larger than a pinpoint, appeared on the rim, and by his manipulation of the water it returned to the bottom of the pan. And in such fashion another speck was disclosed, and another. Great was his care of them. Like a shepherd he herded his flock of golden specks so that not one should be lost. At last, of the pan of dirt nothing remained but his golden herd. He counted it, and then, after all his labor, sent it flying out of the pan was one final swirl of water.

But his blue eyes were shining with desire as he rose to his feet. "Seven," he muttered aloud, asserting the sum of the specks for which he had toiled so hard and which he had so wantonly thrown away. "Seven," he repeated, with the emphasis of one trying to impress a number on his memory.

He stood still a long while, surveying the hillside. In his eyes was a curiosity, new-aroused and burning. There was an exultance about his bearing and a keenness like that of a hunting animal catching the fresh scent of game.

He moved down the stream a few steps and took a second panful of dirt.

Again came the careful washing, the jealous herding of the golden specks, and the wantonness with which he sent them flying into the stream. His golden herd diminished. "Four, five," he muttered, and repeated, "five."

He could not forbear another survey of the hill before filling the pan farther down the stream. His golden herds diminished. "Four, three, two, two, one," were his memory tabulations as he moved down the stream. When but one speck of gold rewarded his washing, he stopped and built a fire of dry twigs. Into this he thrust the gold-pan and burned it till it was blue black. He held up the pan and examined it critically. Then he nodded approbation. Against such a color-background he could defy the tiniest yellow speck to elude him.

Still moving down the stream, he panned again. A simple speck was his reward. A third pan contained no gold at all. Not satisfied with this, he panned three times again, taking his shovels of dirt within a foot of one another. Each pan proved empty of gold, and the fact, instead of discouraging him, seemed to give him satisfaction. His elation increased with each barren washing, until he arose, exclaiming jubilantly, "If it ain't the real thing, may God knock off my head with sour apples!"

Returning to where he had started operations, he began to pan up the stream. At first his golden herds increased—increased prodigiously. "Fourteen, eighteen, twenty-one, twenty-six," ran his memory tabulations. Just above the pool he struck his richest pan—thirty-five colors.

"Almost enough to save," he remarked regretfully as he allowed the water to sweep them away.

The sun climbed to the top of the sky. The man worked on. Pan by pan, he went up the stream, the tally of results steadily decreasing.

"It's just booful, the way it peters out," he exulted when a shovelful of dirt contained no more than a single speck of gold.

And when no specks at all were found in several pans, he straightened up and favored the hillside with a confident glance.

"Ah, ha! Mr. Pocket!" he cried out, as though to an auditor hidden somewhere above him beneath the surface of the slope.

"Ah, ha! Mr. Pocket! I'm a-comin', an' I'm shorely gwine to get yer! You heah me, Mr. Pocket? I'm gwine to get yer as shore as punkins ain't cauliflowers!"

He turned and flung a measuring glance at the sun poised above him in the azure of the cloudless sky. Then he went down the canyon, following the line of shovel holes he had made in filling the pans. He crossed the stream below the pool and disappeared through the green screen. There was little opportunity for the spirit of the place to return with its quietude and repose, for the man's voice, raised in ragtime song, still dominated the canyon with possession.

After a time, with a greater clashing of steel-shod feet on rock, he returned. The green screen was tremendously agitated. It surged back and forth in the throes of a struggle. There was a loud grating and clanging of metal. The man's voice leaped to a higher pitch and was sharp with imperativeness. A large body plunged and panted. There was a snapping and ripping and rending, and amid a shower of falling leaves a horse burst through the screen. On its back was a pack, and from this trailed broken vines and torn creepers. The animal gazed with astonished eyes at the scene into which it had been precipitated, then dropped its head to the grass and began contentedly to graze. A second horse scrambled into view, slipping once on the mossy rocks and regaining equilibrium when its hooves sank into the yielding surface of the meadow. It was riderless, though on its back was a high-horned Mexican saddle, scarred and discolored by long usage.

The man brought up the rear. He threw off pack and saddle, with an eye to camp location, and gave the animals their freedom to graze. He unpacked his food and got out frying pan and coffeepot. He gathered an armful of dry wood, and with a few stones made a place for his fire.

"My!" he said, "but I've got an appetite. I could scoff iron filings an' horseshoe nails an' thank you kindly, ma'am, for a second helpin'."

He straightened up, and while he reached for matches in the pocket of his overalls, his eyes traveled across the pool to the sidehill. His fingers had clutched the matchbox, but they relaxed their hold and the hand came out empty. The man wavered perceptibly. He looked at his preparations for cooking and he looked at the hill.

"Guess I'll take another whack at her," he concluded, starting to cross the stream.

"They ain't no sense in it, I know," he mumbled apologetically. "But keepin' grub back an hour ain't goin' to hurt none, I reckon."

A few feet back from his first of test pans he started a second line. The sun dropped down the western sky, the shadows lengthened, but the man worked on. He began a third line of test pans. He was crosscutting the hillside, line by line as he ascended. The center of each line produced the richest pans, while the end came where no colors showed in the pan. And as he ascended the hillside the lines grew perceptibly shorter. The regularity with which their length diminished served to indicate that somewhere up the slope the last line would be so short as to have scarcely length at all, and that beyond could come only a point. The design was growing into an inverted V. The converging sides of the V marked the boundaries of the gold-bearing dirt.

The apex of the V was evidently the man's goal. Often he ran his eye along the converging sides and on up the hill, trying to divine the apex, the point where the gold-bearing dirt must cease. Here resided Mr. Pocket—for so the man familiarly addressed the imaginary point above him on the slope, crying out, "Come down out o' that, Mr. Pocket! Be right smart an' agreeable, an' come down!

"All right," he would add later, in a voice resigned to determination. "All right, Mr. Pocket. It's plain to me I got to come right up an' snatch you out baldheaded. An' I'll do it! I'll do it!" he would threaten still later.

Each pan he carried down to the water to wash, and as he went higher up the hill the pans grew richer, until he began to save the gold in an empty baking-powder can which he carried carelessly in his hip pocket. So engrossed was he in his toil that he did not notice the long twilight of oncoming night. It was not until he tried vainly to see the gold colors in the bottom of the pan that he realized the passage of time. He straightened up abruptly. An expression of whimsical wonderment and awe overspread his face as he drawled, "Gosh darn my buttons! If I didn't plumb forget dinner!"

He stumbled across the stream in the darkness and lighted his long-delayed fire. Flapjacks and bacon and warmed-over beans constituted his supper. Then he smoked a pipe by the smoldering coals, listening to the night noises and watching the moonlight stream through the canyon. After that he unrolled his bed, took off his heavy shoes, and pulled the blankets up to his chin. His face showed white in the moonlight, like the face of a corpse. But it was a corpse that knew its resurrection, for the man rose suddenly on one elbow and gazed across at his hillside.

"Good night, Mr. Pocket," he called sleepily. "Good night."

He slept through the early gray of morning until the direct rays of the sun smote his closed eyelids, when he awoke with a start and looked about him until he had established the continuity of his existence and identified his present self with the days previously lived.

To dress, he had merely to buckle on his shoes. He glanced at his fireplace and at his hillside, wavered, but fought down the temptation and started the fire.

"Keep yer shirt on, Bill; keep yer shirt on," he admonished himself. "What's the good of rushin'? No use in getting' all het up an' sweaty. Mr. Pocket'll wait for you. He ain't a-runnin' away before you can get your breakfast. Now, what you want, Bill, is something fresh in yer bill o' fare. So it's up to you to go an' get it."

He cut a short pole at the water's edge and drew from one of his pockets a bit of line and a draggled fly that had once been a royal coachman.

"Mebbe they'll bite in the early morning," he muttered, as he made his first cast into the pool. And a moment later he was gleefully crying, "What'd I tell you, eh? What'd I tell you?"

He had no reel nor any inclination to waste time, and by main strength, and swiftly, he drew out of the water a flashing ten-inch trout. Three more, caught in rapid succession, furnished his breakfast. When he came to the stepping-stones on his way to his hillside, he was stuck by a sudden thought, and paused.

"I'd just better take a hike downstream a ways," he said. "There's no tellin' who may be snoopin' around."

But he crossed over on the stones, and with a "I really oughter take that hike," the need of the precaution passed out of his mind, and he fell to work.

At nightfall he straightened up. The small of his back was stiff from stooping toil, and as he put his hand behind him to soothe the protesting muscles, he said, "Now what d'ye think of that? I clean forgot my dinner again! If I don't watch out, I'll sure be degeneratin' into a two-meal-a-day crank.

"Pockets is the hangedest things I ever see for makin' a man absentminded," he communed that night, as he crawled into his blankets. Nor did he forget to call up the hillside, "Good night, Mr. Pocket! Good night!"

Rising with the sun, and snatching a hasty breakfast, he was early at work. A fever seemed to be growing in him, nor did the increasing richness of the test pans allay this fever. There was a flush in his cheek other than that made by the heat of the sun, and he was oblivious to fatigue and the passage of time. When he filled a pan with dirt, he ran down the hill to wash it; nor could he forbear running up the hill again, panting and stumbling profanely, to refill the pan.

He was now a hundred yards from the water, and the inverted V was assuming definite proportions. The width of the pay dirt steadily decreased, and the man extended in his mind's eye the sides of the V to their meeting place far up the hill. This was his goal, the apex of the V, and he panned many times to locate it.

"Just about two yards above that manzanita bush an' a yard to the right," he finally concluded.

Then the temptation seized him. "As plain as the nose on your face," he said, as he abandoned his laborious crosscutting and climbed to the indicated apex. He filled a pan and carried it down the hill to wash. It contained no trace of gold. He dug deep, and he dug shallow, filling and washing a dozen pans, and was unrewarded even by the tiniest golden speck. He was enraged at having yielded to the temptation, and berated himself blasphemously and pridelessly. Then he went down the hill and took up the crosscutting.

"Slow an' certain, Bill; slow an' certain," he crooned. "Shortcuts to fortune ain't in your line, an' it's about time you know it. Get wise, Bill; get wise. Slow an' certain's the only hand you can play; so get to it, an' keep to it, too."

As the crosscuts decreased, showing that the sides of the V were converging, the depth of the V increased. The gold trace was dipping into the hill. It was only at thirty inches beneath the surface that he could get colors in his pan. The dirt he found at twenty-five inches from the surface, and at thirty-five inches, yielded barren pans. At the base of the V, by the water's edge, he had found the gold colors at the grass roots. The higher he went up the hill, the deeper the gold dipped. To dig a hole three feet deep in order to get one test pan was a task of no mean magnitude; while between the man and the apex intervened an untold number of such holes to be dug. "An' there's no tellin' how much deeper it'll pitch," he sighed in a moment's pause while his fingers soothed his aching back.

Feverish with desire, with aching back and stiffening muscles, with pick and shovel gouging and mauling the soft brown earth, the man toiled up the hill. Before him was the smooth slope, spangled with flowers and made sweet with their breath. Behind him was devastation. It looked like some terrible eruption breaking out on the smooth skin of the hill. His slow progress was like that of a slug, befouling beauty with a monstrous trail.

Though the dipping gold trace increased the man's work, he found consolation in the increasing richness of the pans. Twenty cents, thirty cents, fifty cents, sixty cents, were the values of the gold found in the pans, and at nightfall he washed his banner pan, which gave him a dollar's worth of gold dust from a shovelful of dirt.

"I'll just bet it's my luck to have some inquisitive one come buttin' in here on my pasture," he mumbled sleepily that night as he pulled the blankets up to his chin.

Suddenly he sat upright. "Bill!" he called sharply. "Now, listen to me, Bill; d'ye hear! It's up to you, tomorrow mornin', to mosey round an' see what you can see. Understand? Tomorrow morning, an' don't you forget it!"

He yawned and glanced across at his sidehill. "Good night, Mr. Pocket," he called.

In the morning he stole a march on the sun, for he had finished breakfast when its first rays caught him, and he was climbing the wall of the canyon where it crumbled away and gave footing. From the outlook at the top he found himself in the midst of loneliness. As far as he could see, chain after chain of mountains heaved themselves into his vision. To the east his eyes, leaping the miles between range and range and between many ranges, brought up at last against the white-peaked sierras—the main crest, where the backbone of the Western world reared itself against the sky! To the north and south he could see more distinctly the cross systems that broke through the main trend of the sea of mountains. To the west the ranges fell away, one behind the other, diminishing and fading into the gentle foothills that, in turn, descended into the great valley which he could not see.

And in all that mighty sweep of earth he saw no sign of man nor of the handiwork of man—save only the torn bosom of the hillside at his feet. The man looked long and carefully. Once, far down his own canyon, he thought he saw in the air a faint hint of smoke. He looked again and decided that it was the purple haze of the hills made dark by a convolution of the canyon wall at its back.

"Hey, you, Mr. Pocket!" he called down into the canyon. "Stand out from under! I'm a-comin', Mr. Pocket! I'm a-comin'!"

The heavy brogans on the man's feet made him appear clumsyfooted, but he swung down from the giddy height as lightly and airily as a mountain goat. A rock, turning under his foot on the edge of the precipice, did not disconcert him. He seemed to know the precise time required for the turn to culminate in disaster, and in the meantime he utilized the false footing itself for the momentary earth contact necessary to carry him on into safety. Where the earth sloped so steeply that it was impossible to stand for a second upright, the man did not hesitate. His foot pressed the impossible surface for but a fraction of the fatal second and gave him the bound that carried him onward. Again, where even the fraction of a second's footing was out of the question, he would swing his body past by a moment's handgrip on a jutting knob of rock, a crevice, or a precariously rooted shrub. At last, with a wild leap and yell, he exchanged the face of the wall for an earthslide and finished the descent in the midst of several tons of sliding earth and gravel.

His first pan of the morning washed out over two dollars in coarse gold. It was from the center of the V. To either side the diminution in the values of the pans was swift. His lines of crosscutting holes were growing very short. The converging sides of the inverted V were only a few yards apart. Their meeting point was only a few yards above him. But the pay streak was dipping deeper and deeper into the earth. By early afternoon he was sinking the test holes five feet before the pans could show the gold trace.

For that matter, the gold trace had become something more than a trace; it was a placer mine in itself, and the man resolved to come back after he had found the pocket and work over the ground. But the increasing richness of the pans began to worry him. By late afternoon the worth of the pans had grown to three and four dollars. The man scratched his head perplexedly and looked a few feet up the hill at the manzanita bush that marked approximately the apex of the V. He nodded his head and said oracularly, "It's one o' two things, Bill; one o' two things. Either Mr. Pocket's spilled himself all out an' down the hill, or else Mr. Pocket's so rich you maybe won't be able to carry him all away with you. And that'd be an awful shame, wouldn't it, now?" He chuckled at contemplation of so pleasant a dilemma.

Nightfall found him by the edge of the stream, his eyes wrestling with the gathering darkness over the washing of a five-dollar pan.

"Wisht I had an electric light to go on working," he said.

He found sleep difficult that night. Many times he composed himself and closed his eyes for slumber to overtake him; but his blood pounded with too strong a desire, and many times his eyes opened and he murmured wearily, "Wisht it was sunup."

Sleep came to him in the end, but his eyes were open with the first paling of the stars, and the gray of dawn caught him with breakfast and climbing the hillside in the direction of the secret abiding-place of Mr. Pocket.

The first crosscut the man made, there was space for only three holes, so narrow had become the pay streak and so close was he to the fountainhead of the golden stream he had been following for four days.

"Be ca'm, Bill; be ca'm," he admonished himself, as he broke ground for the final hole where the sides of the V had at last come together in a point.

"I've got the almighty cinch on you, Mr. Pocket, an' you can't lose me," he said many times as he sank the hole deeper and deeper.

Four feet, five feet, six feet, he dug his way down into the earth. The digging grew harder. His pick grated on broken rock. He examined the rock. "Rotten quartz" was his conclusion as, with the shovel, he cleared the bottom of the hole of loose dirt. He attacked the crumbling quartz with the pick, bursting the disintegrating rock asunder with every stroke.

He thrust his shovel into the loose mass. His eye caught a gleam of yellow. He dropped the shovel and squatted suddenly on his heels. As a farmer rubs the clinging earth from fresh-dug potatoes, so the man, a piece of rotten quartz held in both hands, rubbed the dirt away.

"Sufferin' Sardanopolis!" he cried. "Lumps an' chunks of it! Lumps an' chunks of it!"

It was only half rock he held in his hand. The other half was virgin gold. He dropped it into his pan and examined another piece. Little yellow was to be seen, but with his strong fingers he crumbled the rotten quartz away till both hands were filled with glowing yellow. He rubbed the dirt away from fragment after fragment, tossing them into the gold-pan. It was a treasure hole. So much had the quartz rotted away that there was less of it than there was of gold. Now and again he found a piece to which no rock clung—a piece that was all gold. A chunk where the pick had laid open the heart of the gold glittered like a handful of yellow jewels, and he cocked his head at it and slowly turned it around and over to observe the rich play of the light upon it.

"Talk about yer too-much-gold diggin's!" the man snorted contemptuously. "Why, this diggin' 'd make it look like thirty cents. This diggin' is all gold. An' right here an' now I name this yere canyon All Gold Canyon, b'gosh!"

Still squatting on his heels, he continued examining the fragments and tossing them into the pan. Suddenly there came to him a premonition of danger. It seemed a shadow had fallen upon him. But there was no shadow. His heart had given a great jump up into his throat and was choking him. Then his blood slowly chilled, and he felt the sweat of his shirt cold against his flesh.

He did not spring up nor look around. He did not move. He was considering the nature of the premonition he had received, trying to locate the source of the mysterious force that had warned him, striving to sense the imperative presence of the unseen thing that threatened him. There is an aura of things hostile, made manifest by messengers too refined for the senses to know; and this aura he felt, but knew not how he felt it. His was the feeling as when a cloud passes over the sun. It seemed that between him and life had passed something dark and smothering and menacing; a gloom, as it were, that swallowed up life and made for death—his death.

Every force of his being impelled him to spring up and confront the unseen danger, but his soul dominated the panic, and he remained squatting on his heels, in his hands a chunk of gold. He did not dare to look around, but he knew by now that there was something behind him and above him. He made believe to be interested in the gold in his hand. He examined it critically, turned it over and over, and rubbed the dirt from it. And all the time he knew that something behind him was looking at the gold over his shoulder.

Still feigning interest in the chunk of gold in his hand, he listened intently and he heard the breathing of the thing behind him. His eyes searched the ground in front of him for a weapon, but he saw only the uprooted gold, worthless to him now in his extremity. There was his pick, a handy weapon on occasion; but this was not such an occasion. The man realized his predicament. He was in a narrow hole that was seven feet deep. His head did not come to the surface of the ground. He was in a trap.

He remained squatting on his heels. He was quite cool and collected; but his mind, considering every factor, showed him only his helplessness. He continued rubbing the dirt from the quartz fragments and throwing the gold into the pan. There was nothing else for him to do. Yet he knew that he would have to rise up, sooner or later, and face the danger that breathed at his back. The minutes passed, and with the passage of each minute he knew that by so much he was nearer the time when he must stand up, or else—and his wet shirt went cold against his flesh again at the thought—he might receive death as he stooped there over his treasure.

Still he squatted on his heels, rubbing dirt from gold and debating in just what manner he should rise up. He might rise up with a rush and claw his way out of the hole to meet whatever threatened on the even footing above ground. Or he might rise up slowly and carelessly, and feign casually to discover the thing that breathed at his back. His instinct and every fighting fiber of his body favored the mad, clawing rush to the surface. His intellect, and the craft thereof, favored the slow and cautious meeting with the thing that menaced and which he could not see. And while he debated, a loud, crashing noise burst in his ear. At the same instant he received a stunning blow on the left side of his back, and from the point of impact felt a rush of flame through his flesh. He sprang up in the air but, halfway to his feet, collapsed. His body crumpled in like a leaf withered in sudden heat, and he came down, his chest across his pan of gold, his face in the dirt and rock, his legs tangled and twisted because of the restricted space at the bottom of the hole. His legs twitched convulsively several times. His body was shaken with a mighty ague. There was a slow expansion of the lungs, accompanied by a deep sigh. Then the air was slowly, very slowly, exhaled, and his body as slowly flattened itself down into inertness.

Above, revolver in hand, a man was peering down over the edge of the hole. He peered for a long time at the prone and motionless body beneath him. After awhile the stranger sat down on the edge of the hole so that he could see into it, and rested the revolver on his knee. Reaching his hand into a pocket, he drew out a wisp of brown paper. Into this he dropped a few crumbs of tobacco. The combination became a cigarette, brown and squat, with the ends turned in. Not once did he take his eyes from the body at the bottom of the hole. He lighted the cigarette and drew its smoke into his lungs with a caressing intake of the breath. He smoked slowly. Once the cigarette went out and he relighted it. And all the while he studied the body beneath him.

In the end he tossed the cigarette stub away and rose to his feet. He moved to the edge of the hole. Spanning it, a hand resting on each edge, and with the revolver still in the right hand, he muscled his body down into the hole. While his feet were yet a yard from the bottom, he released his hands and dropped down.

At the instant his feet struck bottom he saw the pocket-miner's arm leap out, and his own legs knew a swift, jerking grip that overthrew him. In the nature of the jump his revolver hand was above his head. Swiftly as the grip had flashed about his legs, just as swiftly he brought the revolver down. He was still in the air, his fall in process of completion, when he pulled the trigger. The explosion was deafening in the confined space. The smoke filled the hole so that he could see nothing. He struck the bottom on his back, and like a cat the pocket-miner's body was on top of him. Even as the miner's body passed on top, the stranger crooked in his right arm to fire; and even in that instant the miner, with a quick thrust of elbow, struck his wrist. The muzzle was thrown up and the bullet thudded into the dirt of the side of the hole.

The next instant the stranger felt the miner's hand grip his wrist. The struggle was now for the revolver. Each man strove to turn it against the other's body. The smoke in the hole was clearing. The stranger, lying on his back, was beginning to see dimly. But suddenly he was blinded by a handful of dirt deliberately flung into his eyes by his antagonist. In that moment of shock his grip on the revolver was broken. In the next moment he felt a smashing darkness descend upon his brain, and in the midst of the darkness even the darkness ceased.

But the pocket-miner fired again and again, until the revolver was empty. Then he tossed it from him and, breathing heavily, sat down on the dead man's legs.

The miner was sobbing and struggling for breath. "Measly skunk!" he panted, "a-campin' on my trail an' lettin' me do the work, an' then shootin' me in the back!"

He was half crying from anger and exhaustion. He peered at the face of the dead man. It was sprinkled with loose dirt and gravel, and it was difficult to distinguish the features.

"Never laid eyes on him before," the minor concluded his scrutiny. "Just a common an' ordinary thief, hang him! An' he shot me in the back! He shot me in the back!"

He opened his shirt and felt himself, front and back, on his left side.

"Went clean through, and no harm done!" he cried jubilantly. "I'll bet he aimed all right; but he drew the gun over when he pulled the trigger—the cur! But I fixed 'm! Oh, I fixed 'm!"

His fingers were investigating the bullet hole in his side, and a shade of regret passed over his face. "It's goin' to be stiffer'n hell," he said. "An' it's up to me to get mended an' get out o' here."

He crawled out of the hole and went down the hill to his camp. Half an hour later he returned, leading his packhorse. His open shirt disclosed the rude bandages with which he had dressed his wound. He was slow and awkward with his left-hand movements, but that did not prevent his using the arm.

The bight of the pack rope under the dead man's shoulders enabled him to heave the body out of the hole. Then he set to work gathering up his gold. He worked steadily for several hours, pausing often to rest his stiffening shoulder and to exclaim, "He shot me in the back, the measly skunk! He shot me in the back!"

When his treasure was quite cleaned up and wrapped securely into a number of blanket-covered parcels he made an estimate of his value.

"Four hundred pounds, or I'm a Hottentot," he concluded. "Say two hundred in quartz an' dirt—that leaves two hundred pounds of gold. Bill! Wake up! Two hundred pounds of gold! Forty thousand dollars! An' it's yourn—all yourn!"

He scratched his head delightedly and his fingers blundered into an unfamiliar groove. They quested along it for several inches. It was a crease through his scalp where the second bullet had ploughed.

He walked angrily over to the dead man.

"You would, would you?" he bullied. "You would, eh? Well, I fixed you good an' plenty, an' I'll give you a decent burial, too. That's more 'n you'd have done for me."

He dragged the body to the edge of the hole and toppled it in. It struck the bottom with a dull crash, on its side, the face twisted up to the light. The miner peered down at it.

"An' you shot me in the back!" he said accusingly.

With pick and shovel he filled the hole. Then he loaded the gold on his horse. It was too great a load for the animal, and when he had gained his camp he transferred part of it to his saddle horse. Even so, he was compelled to abandon a portion of his outfit—pick and shovel and gold-pan, extra food and cooking utensils, and diverse odds and ends.

The sun was at the zenith when the man forced the horses at the screen of vines and creepers. To climb the huge boulders the animals were compelled to uprear and struggle blindly through the tangled mass of vegetation. Once the saddle horse fell heavily and the man removed the pack to get the animal on its feet. After it started on its way again the man thrust his head out from among the leaves and peered up at the hillside.

"The measly skunk!" he said, and disappeared.

There was a ripping and tearing of vines and boughs. The trees surged back and forth, marking the passage of the animals through the midst of them. There was a clashing of steel-shod hoofs on stone, and now and again a sharp cry of command. Then the voice of the man was raised in song.

> *"Tu'n around an' tu'n yo' face*
> *Untoe them sweet hills of grace*
> *(D' pow'rs of sin you' am scornin'!).*
> *Look about an' look aroun'*
> *Fling yo' sin-pack on d' groun'*
> *(Yo' will meet wid d' Lord in d' mornin'!)."*

The song grew faint and fainter, and through the silence crept back the spirit of the place. The stream once more drowsed and whispered; the hum of the mountain bees rose sleepily. Down through the perfume-weighted air fluttered the snowy fluffs of the cottonwoods. The butterflies drifted in and out among the trees, and over all blazed the quiet sunshine. Only remained the hoof marks in the meadow and the torn hillside to mark the boisterous trail of the life that had broken the peace of the place and passed on.

B. M. (Bertha Muzzy) Bower (1871–1940) was the first woman to write traditional cowboy stories. Beginning with *Chip of the Flying U*, she published more than seventy novels of the old and new West, most of them featuring the often humorous adventures of Chip and his comrades on the Flying U ranch. "The Lamb of the Flying U," which recounts the spectacular and surprising fashion in which a seeming tenderfoot named Pink is initiated into the flock, is one of several shorter works about the ranch and its "Happy Family." She was extremely popular during the first four decades of this century, but at her best she was more than simply an entertainer. Her depiction of the day-to-day conditions of cowboys provided a vivid and realistic portrayal of life on a large cattle ranch circa the 1880s. She knew whereof she wrote: she herself grew up on just such a ranch.

The Lamb of the Flying U

B. M. Bower

"'Scuse me," said a voice behind Chip Bennett, foreman of the Flying U. "Lookin' for men?"

For two days the Flying U herd had grazed within five miles of Dry Lake waiting for boxcars along the Montana Central line, which had never come. Then two of his men had gone to town on a spree and continued missing. They were not top hands, but every hand is vital in shipping time, so Chip had ridden into town to bring them back, or acquire facsimiles thereof.

He twisted his head to look down at a dandified little fellow who was staring up at him with bright blue eyes. He wore a silk shirt, neatly pressed gray trousers held up by a russet belt, and gleaming tan shoes. Golden hair, freshly barbered, just showed its edges under an immaculate Panama hat. The foreman was slightly taken aback.

"Sorry, son," he muttered. "I want men to *work*."

The fashion plate flashed a pair of dimples that any woman would have envied.

"My mammy done tol' me," he murmured, "never to judge a book by its cover."

"We were speakin' of *men*," Chip reminded him. "And work. I can't quite see you punchin' cows in them duds. Look me up when you've growed a bit, son."

A hand on his arm stopped him as he was turning away again. "Say, did you ever hear of Old Eagle Creek Smith of the Cross L?"

"Why, sure," said Chip. "I—"

"—Or of Rowdy Vaughan, or a fellow up on Milk River they call Pink?"

"I'll say!" Chip Bennett turned back. "I've heard tell of Eagle Creek Smith. And Pink—they say he's a bronc fighter and a little devil. Why?"

The blonde shoved his Panama back and grinned into Chip's face. "Nothin'," he said. "I'm glad to meet yuh. I'm Pink."

Chip digested that in silence, his suddenly alerted eyes measuring the slender figure from Panama to polished shoe tips. "You travelin' in disguise?" he asked.

"It's a long story," Pink said, and sighed. He found an empty case, upended it in the shade, and sat down to roll a cigarette. "I helped Rowdy Vaughan trail a herd of Cross L stock across the Canadian line, bein' a friend of his an' anxious to do him a favor. But I ain't long in our friendly neighbor country to the north when one of them boneheaded grangers gets unfriendly and I has to scatter his features around a bit to pound some sense into his thick skull.

"Then up rises a bunch of redcoats and I fogs it back across the line just about one jump ahead of the Mounties. I headed back to the Upper Milk River, but the old bunch was gone and it was plumb lonesome, so I sold my saddle an' gatherin' and reformed from punchin' cows."

He grinned his engaging, dimpled grin. "Well, I took the rattlers back to Minnesota and spent all winter with the home folks chewin' the fatted calf. It was mighty nice, too, except that the female critters outnumbered the males back there and each one carries a bear trap an' a pair of handcuffs. I dodged the traps as long as I could, but I seen I was getting' right gun-shy, so I sloped.

"Besides, even though I'd swore off cowpunchin', I was getting plumb mad at all the fences surroundin' everything, and lonesome to straddle a cayuse again. Seems like cow nursin' is in my blood after all. For Pete's sake, old-timer, stake me to a string! You won't be sorry."

Chip sat down on a neighboring case and regarded the dapper little figure. Such words, coming from those girlishly rosy lips, had an odd effect of unreality. But Pink plainly was in earnest. His eyes were pleading and wistful.

"You're it!" said Chip. "You can go right to work. Seems you're the man I've been looking for, only I didn't recognize yuh on sight. We've got a heap of work ahead, and only five decent men in the outfit. It's the Flying U. Those five have worked years for the outfit."

"I sure savvy that bunch," Pink declared sweetly. "I've heard of the Happy Family before. Ain't you one of them?"

Chip Bennett grinned. "I was," he admitted, a shade of regret in his voice. "But last spring I got married, and settled down. I'm one of the firm now, so I had to reform. The rest are a pretty salty bunch, but you'll get on all right, seein' you're not the pilgrim you look. Got an outfit?"

"Sure. Bought one, brand new, in the Falls. It's over at the hotel now, with a haughty, buckskin-colored suitcase." Pink pulled the silver belt-buckle of his russet belt straight and patted his pink and blue tie.

"Well, if you're ready, I'll get the horses and we'll drift. By the way, how shall I write you on the book?"

Pink stooped and with his handkerchief carefully wiped the Dry Lake dust from his shiny shoes.

"Yuh won't crawfish on me, if I tell yuh?" he inquired anxiously, standing up.

"Of course not." Chip looked his surprise.

"Well, it ain't *my* fault, but my lawful, legal name is Percival Cadwallader Perkins."

"Wha-at?"

"Percival Cad-*wall*-ader Perkins. Shall I get yuh something to take with it?"

Chip, with his pencil poised in air, stared again. "It's sure a heavy load to carry," he observed solemnly "How do you spell that second shift?"

Pink told him. "Ain't it fierce?" he wanted to know. "My mother must have sure been light-minded when I was born, but there are two grand-fathers who wanted a kid named after 'em. Them two names sure make a combination. You know what Cadwallader means, in the dictionary?"

"Lord, no!" said Chip, putting away his book.

"Battle-arranger," Pink told him sadly. "Now, wouldn't that jostle yuh? It's true, too. It has sure arranged a lot of battles for me. When I went to school, I had to lick about six kids a day. At last, seein' the name was mine and I couldn't chuck it, I throwed in with an expugilist and learned how to fight proper. Since then things come easier. I ain't afraid now to wear my name on my hatband."

"I wouldn't," said Chip dryly. "Hike over and get your haughty new war bag. We've got to be in camp by dinner time."

A MILE OUT Pink looked down at his festal garments and smiled. "I expect I'll be pickings for your Happy Family when they see me in these war togs," he remarked.

Chip Bennett studied him meditatively. "I was just wondering," he said slowly, "if the Happy Family wouldn't be pickings for *you*."

Pink dimpled and said nothing.

The Happy Family were at dinner when Chip and Pink dismounted by the bed tent and went over to where the men were sitting. The Happy Family received them with decorous silence. Chip got plate, knife, fork, and spoon and started for the stove.

"Help yourself to the tools, then come over and fill up," he invited Pink over his shoulder. "You'll soon get used to things here."

The Happy Family looked guardedly at one another. This wasn't a chance visitor, then. He was going to work!

Weary Davidson, sitting cross-legged in the shade of a wagon wheel, looked at Pink, fumbling shyly among the knives and forks, and whistled absently: "Oh, tell me, pretty maiden, are there any more at home like you?"

Pink glanced at him quickly and retreated inside the tent. Every man of them knew the stranger had caught Weary's meaning. They smiled discreetly at their plates.

After dinner—during which Cal Emmett tested the tenderness of the newcomer with tales of his life as a desperado—Pink asked Chip if he should change his clothes and get ready to go to work.

Chip told him it wouldn't be a bad idea, and Pink, carrying his haughty suitcase and another bulky bundle, disappeared into the bed tent.

"By golly!" spoke up Slim.

"Where did you pluck that modest flower, Chip?" Jack Bates wanted to know.

Chip sifted some tobacco into a paper. "I picked it in town," he told them. "I hired it to punch cows, and its name is—wait a minute." He put away the tobacco sack, got out his book, and turned the leaves. "Its name is Percival Cadwallader Perkins."

"Oh, mamma! Percival Cadwolloper Perkins!" Weary looked stunned. "Yuh want to double the guard tonight, Chip. That name'll sure stampede the bunch."

"He's sure a sweet young thing—mama's precious lamb broke out of the home corral!" said Jack Bates. "I'll bet yuh a tall, yellow-haired mamma with flowing widow's weeds'll be out here hunting him up inside a week. We got to be gentle with Cadwolloper."

The reappearance of Pink cut short the discussion. He still wore his Panama, and the dainty pink-and-white striped silk shirt, the gray trousers, and russet-leather belt with silver buckle. But around his neck, nestling under his rounded chin, was a gorgeous rose-pink silk handkerchief, of the hue that he always wore, and that had given him the nickname of "Pink."

His white hands were hidden in a pair of wonderful silk-embroidered buckskin gauntlets. His gray trousers were tucked into number-four tan riding boots, with silk-stitched tops. A shiny new pair of silver-mounted spurs jingled from his heels.

He smiled trustfully at Chip Bennett, got out papers and tobacco, and rolled a cigarette.

"If there's anything I hate," Cal remarked irrelevantly to the crowd, "it's to see a girl smoke!"

Pink looked up and opened his lips to speak, then thought better of it. The cavvy came jingling up, and Pink turned to watch. To him the thudding hoofs were sweet music for which he had hungered long.

"Weary, you and Cal better relieve the boys on herd," Chip Bennett called. "I'll get you a horse, P-Perkins"—he had almost said "Pink"—"and you can go along with Cal."

"Yes, sir," said Pink, with a docility that would have amazed any who knew him well. He followed Chip out to the corral, where Cal and Weary were already inside with their ropes, among the circling mass.

Chip led out a little cow-pony that could almost day-herd without a rider of any sort, and Pink bridled him before the covertly watching crew. He did not do it as quickly as he might have done, for he deliberately fumbled the buckle and pinned one ear of the pony down flat with the head-stall.

Happy Jack, who had been standing herd disconsolately with two aliens, stared open-mouthed at Pink's approach and rode hastily to camp, fair bursting with questions and comments.

The herd, twelve hundred range-fattened steers, grazed quietly on a hillside a half mile from camp. Pink ran a quick, appraising eye over the bunch, estimating correctly the number and noting their splendid condition.

"Never saw so many cattle in one bunch before, did yuh?" queried Cal, misinterpreting the glance.

Pink shook his head. "Does one man own all those cows?" he wanted to know.

"Yeah—and then some. This is just a few that we're shipping to get 'em out of the way of the real herds."

"How many are there?" asked Pink.

Cal turned his back upon his conscience and winked at Weary. "Oh, only nine thousand, seven hundred and twenty-one," he lied boldly. "Last bunch we gathered was fifty-one thousand, six hundred and twenty-nine and a half. Er—the half," he explained hastily in answer to Pink's look of unbelief, "was a calf that we let in by mistake. I caught it and took it back to its mother."

"I should think," Pink ventured hesitatingly, "it would be hard to find its mother. I don't see how you could tell."

"Well," said Cal gravely, sliding sidewise in the saddle, "it's this way. A calf is always like its mother, hair for hair. This calf had white hind feet, one white ear, and the deuce of diamonds on its left side. All I had to do was ride the range till I found the cow that matched."

"Oh!" Pink looked convinced.

Weary, smiling to himself, rode off to take his station at the other side of the herd. Even the Happy Family must place duty before pleasure, and Cal started down along the nearest edge of the bunch. Pink showed inclination to follow.

"You stay where you're at, sonny," Cal told him over his shoulder.

"What must I do?" Pink straightened his Panama.

Cal's voice came back to him faintly: "Just don't bother the cattle."

"Good advice, that," Pink commented amusedly. He prepared for a lazy afternoon and enjoyed every minute.

On the way back to camp at supper time, Pink looked as if he had something on his mind. Cal and Weary exchanged glances.

"I'd like to ask," Pink began timidly, "how you fed that calf—before you found his mother. Didn't he get pretty hungry?"

"Why, I carried a bottle of milk along," Cal lied fluently. "When the bottle went empty I'd catch a cow and milk her. All range cows'll gentle right down, if yuh know the right way to approach 'em. That's a secret that we don't tell just everybody."

That settled it, of course. Pink dismounted stiffly and walked painfully to the cook tent. Ten months out of saddle told even upon Pink, and made for extreme discomfort.

When he had eaten hungrily, responding to the ironical sociability of his fellow with a brevity which only his soft voice saved from brusqueness, he unrolled his new bed and lay down with not a thought for the part he was playing. He heard with indifference Weary's remark outside, that "Cadwolloper's about all in. Day-herding's too strenuous for him." The last that came to him, someone was chanting: "Mamma had a precious lamb, his cheeks were red and rosy; And when he rode the festive bronc, he tumbled on his nosey. . . ."

There was more, but Pink had gone to sleep and so missed it.

At sundown he awoke and saddled the night horse Chip Bennett had caught for him, then went to bed again. When shaken gently for middle guard, he dressed sleepily, donned a pair of white angora chaps, and stumbled out into the moonlight.

Guided and coached by Cal, he took his station and began that monotonous round which had been a part of life he loved best. Though stiff and sore from unaccustomed riding, Pink felt content to be where he was, watching the quiet land and the slumbering herd, with the moon swimming through the drifting gray clouds above. Twice in a complete round, he met Cal going in the opposite direction. At the second round Cal stopped him.

"How yuh coming?" he queried cheerfully.

"All right, thank you," said Pink.

"Yuh want to watch out for a lop-horned critter over on the other side," Cal went on, in confidential tones. "He keeps trying to sneak out of the bunch. Don't let him get away. If he goes, take after him and fog him back."

"He won't get away from me, if I can help it," Pink promised, and Cal rode on, with Pink smiling maliciously after him.

As Pink neared the opposite side, a dim shape angled slowly out before him, moving aimlessly away from the sleeping herd. Pink followed. Farther they moved, and faster. Into a little hollow went the critter and circled. Pink took down his rope, let loose a good ten feet of it, and spurred unexpectedly close.

Whack! The rope landed with precision on the bowed shoulders of Cal. "Yuh will try to fool me, will yuh?" *Whack!* "I guess I can point out a critter that won't stray out uh the bunch again for a spell!" *Whack!*

Cal straightened in the saddle, gasping astonishment, pulled up with a jerk, and got off in an unlovely mood.

"Here's where yuh get yourn, yuh little mama's lamb!" Cal cried angrily. "Climb down and get your ears cuffed proper, yuh pink little smart aleck! Thump *me* with a rope, will yuh?"

Pink got down. Immediately they mixed. Presently Cal stretched the long length of him in the grass, with Pink sitting comfortably upon his middle. Cal looked up at the dizzying swim of the moon, saw new and uncharted stars, and nearer, dimly revealed in the half-light, the self-satisfied, cherubic face of Pink.

Cal tried to rise and discovered a surprising state of affairs. He could scarcely move. The more he tried the more painful became Pink's hold on him. He blinked and puzzled over the mystery.

"Of all the bone-headed, feeble-minded sons-uh-guns," announced Pink melodiously, "you sure take the sour-dough biscuit. You're plumb tame. A lady could handle yuh. *You* cuff my ears proper? That's a laugh."

Cal, battered as to features and bewildered as to mind, blinked again and grinned feebly.

"Yuh try an old gag that I wore out in Wyoming," went on Pink, warming to the subject. "Loadin' me with stuff that wouldn't bring the heehaw from a sheepherder! Bah! You're extinct. Say" —Pink's fists kneaded Cal's diaphragm—"are yuh *all* ba-a-d?"

"Oh, Lord! No. I'm dead gentle. Lemme up."

"D'yuh think that critter will quit the bunch ag'in tonight?"

"He ain't liable to," Cal assured him. "Say, who are yuh, anyhow?"

"I'm Percival Cadwallader Perkins. Do you like that name?"

"Ouch! It—it's *bully!*"

"You're a liar," said Pink, getting up. "Furthermore, yuh old chucklehead, yuh ought to know better than try to run a blazer on me. Your best girl happens to be my cousin."

Cal scrambled slowly and painfully to his feet. "Then you're Milk River Pink!" He sighed. "I might of guessed it."

"I cannot tell a lie," Pink said. "Only, plain Pink'll do for me. Where do yuh suppose the bunch is by this time?"

They mounted and rode back together. Cal was deeply thoughtful.

"Say," he said suddenly, just as they parted to ride their rounds, "the boys'll be tickled plumb to death. We've been wishin' you'd blow in here ever since the Cross L quit the country."

Pink drew rein and looked back, resting one hand on the cantle. "Yuh needn't break your neck spreading the glad tidings," he warned. "Let 'em find out, the same as you done."

"Sure," agreed Cal, passing his fingers gingerly over his swollen face. "I ain't no hog. I'm willin' for 'em to have some sport with yuh, too."

THE NEXT MORNING when Cal Emmett appeared at breakfast with a slight limp and several inches of cuticle missing from his features, the Happy Family learned that his horse had fallen down with him as he was turning a stray back into the herd.

Chip Bennett hid a smile behind his coffee cup.

It was Weary Davidson that afternoon on dayherd who indulged his mendacity for the benefit of Pink. His remarks were but paving-stones for a scheme hatched overnight by the Happy Family.

Weary began by looking doleful and emptying his lungs in sorrowful sighs. Pink rose obediently to the bait and asked if he felt bad, but Weary only sighed the more. Then, growing confidential, he told how he had dreamed a dream the night before. With picturesque language, he detailed the horror of it. He was guilty of murder, he confessed, and the crime weighed heavily on his conscience.

"Not only that," he went on, "but I know that death is camping on my trail. That dream haunts me. I feel that my days are numbered in words of one syllable. That dream'll come true. You see if it don't!"

"I—I wouldn't worry over just a bad dream, Mr. Weary," comforted Pink.

"But that ain't all. I woke up in a cold sweat, and went outside. And there in the clouds, perfect as life, I seen a posse of men gallopin' up from the south. Down south," he explained sadly, "sleeps my victim—a white-headed, innocent old man. That posse is sure headed for me, Mr. Perkins."

Pink's eyes widened. He looked like a child listening to a story of goblins. "If I can help you, Mr. Weary, I will," he promised with wide-eyed generosity.

"Will yuh be my friend? Will yuh let me lean on yuh in my dark hours?" Weary's voice shook with emotion.

Pink said that he would, and he seemed very sympathetic and anxious for Weary's safety.

When Pink went out that night to stand his shift, he found Weary at his side instead of Cal. Weary explained that Cal was feeling shaky on account of that fall he had got, and, as Weary couldn't sleep anyway, he had offered to stand in Cal's place. Pink scented mischief.

This night the moon shone brightly at intervals, with patches of silvery clouds racing before the wind and chasing black splotches of shadows over the sleeping land. For all that, the cattle lay quiet, and the monotony of circling the herd was often broken by Weary and Pink with little talks, as they turned and rode together.

"Mr. Perkins, fate's a-crowding me close," said Weary gloomily, when an hour had gone by. "I feel as if I had—What in . . . what was that?"

Voices raised in excited talk came faintly on the wind. With a glance toward the cattle, Weary turned his horse and, beckoning Pink to follow, rode out to the right.

"It's the posse!" he growled. "They'll go to the herd to look for me. Mr. Perkins, the time has come to fly. If only I had a horse that could drift!"

Pink thought he caught the meaning. "Is . . . is mine any good, Mr. Weary?" he quavered. "If he is, you can have him. I . . . I'll stay and fool them as . . . long as I can."

"Perkins," said Weary solemnly, "you're sure all right! Let that posse think you're the man they want for half an hour, and I'm safe. I'll never forget yuh!"

He had not thought of changing horses, but the temptation mastered him. He was riding a little sorrel, Glory by name, that could beat even the Happy Family itself for unexpected deviltry. Yielding to Pink's persuasions, he changed mounts, clasped Pink's hand affectionately, and sped away just as the posse appeared over a rise, riding furiously.

Pink, playing his part, started toward them, then wheeled and sped away in the direction that would lead them off Weary's trail. That is, he sped for ten rods or so. After that he seemed to revolve on an axis. And there was an astonishing number of revolutions to the minute.

The stirrups were down in the dark somewhere below the farthest reach of Pink's toes—he never once located them. But Pink was not known all over Northern Montana as a bronc-peeler for nothing. He surprised Glory even more than that deceitful bit of horseflesh had surprised Pink. While his quirt swung methodically, he looked often over his shoulder for the posse and wondered why it did not appear.

The posse, however, at that moment had run into troubles of its own. Happy Jack, not having a night horse saddled, had borrowed one not remarkable for its surefootedness. No sooner had they sighted their quarry than Jack's horse stepped in a hole and went headlong—which was bad enough. When the horse got up, he planted a foot hastily on Jack's diaphragm and then bolted straight for the peacefully slumbering herd—which was worse.

With stirrup straps snapping like pistol shots, he tore down through the dreaming cattle, with nothing to stop him. The herd did not wait for explanations. As the posse afterward said, it quit the earth, while they gathered around the fallen Jack and tried to discover whether it was a doctor or coroner who was needed.

It was neither, cowboys being notoriously tough. Jack rebounded from the earth, spitting out sand and a choice collection of words which he had been saving for just such an occasion. The other cowboys would have admired to stay and listen, but stern duty called. The herd was gone, the horse was gone, and so was Pink.

Hoofbeats heralded Weary's return, already laughing at his joke and expecting to see a crestfallen Pink surrounded by his captors. Instead he saw Jack emitting language and the cowboys scrambling for their horses to go hunt for the herd.

"Mama mine!" said Weary feebly. He knew at once that it was useless to try and compete with Jack when that worthy was going at full steam. Instead he turned his horse and headed back to camp as fast as he could go.

Chip woke up as Weary crawled into the tent and grabbed the foreman by the shoulder.

"Saddle my horse," he mumbled. "I'm ready."

"Chip!" Weary gasped. "Cadwolloper's gone!"

"Huh Who? Oh." Chip's face showed disgust as he removed his shoulder gently and lay down again. "Hell, don't let that worry yuh."

Weary was puzzled but game. "Then it's all right," he said. And added as an afterthought, "The herd's gone, too."

"What!" Chip bounded out of bed like an uncoiled spring. Language began to pour out of him, and the blushing Weary afterwards testified that, when really wound up, he far outclassed Jack.

By sunrise, the hard-riding members of the once-Happy Family came upon the herd. It was quietly grazing in a little coulee and Pink was holding them, all by his lonesome.

"Yuh low-down, spavined, wind-broke, jug-headed bunch of locoed sheepherders!" Pink roared, his blue eyes flashing. "If yuh think the whole bunch of yuh are capable of holding these critters now that they've run theirselves out, you can take over an' let me go get some breakfast! When I took this job, Chip told me I'd be workin' with men! Don't make me laugh!

"On Milk River they'd tie a picket rope to every one of yuh to keep you from gettin' lost between the bunkhouse and the cook shack. And jokes!

Oh, Mother! Next time you try to play a joke on somebody, Mr. Weary, don't pick out a horse so feeble that he's like to fall down before anybody climbs aboard him. I thought this Glory would put on a show from all the braggin' about him. What a disappointment. I'm plumb wore out, but not from his buckin'. From tryin' to keep him awake! Come get him and give me somethin' that's half-alive!"

The erstwhile Happy Family gulped, blinked, and shuffled its feet under the tirade. The joke had backfired with a crash and they wanted nothing now but holes to crawl into.

Then, amazingly, the fire died out of Pink's voice and eyes. He slid to the ground and came forward. The dimples flashed as he held out his hand to Weary.

"Meet Milk River Pink," he said.

Then the uproar broke loose as the Happy Family crowded around to pound his back and shake his hand.

Thomas Thompson's career is the sort that most of his contemporaries looked upon with great admiration and at least a bit of envy. Born in 1913, he graduated from high school in 1930 and embarked on a variety of careers that included sailing, working as a nightclub entertainer, and selling furniture. But by 1940, he was working as a full-time writer, his fiction leading him to such great positions as associate producer and writer of the *Bonanza* TV series and the story consultant for the Temple Houston crime dramas. Thompson's writing displays genre virtues at their best—his stories and books are tight, precise, and laid out with maximum drama, all these being virtues he no doubt learned by writing for motion pictures and television.

Gun Job

Thomas Thompson

He was married in June, and he gave up his job as town marshal the following September, giving himself time to get settled on the little ranch he bought before the snows set in. That first winter was mild, and now, with summer in the air, he walked down the main street of the town and thought of his own calf crop and of his own problems, a fine feeling after fifteen years of thinking of the problems of others. He wasn't Marshal Jeff Anderson any more. He was Jeff Anderson, private citizen, beholden to no man, and that was the way he wanted it.

He gave the town his quick appraisal, a tall, well-built man who was nearing forty and beginning to think about it, and every building and every alley held a memory for him, some amusing, some tragic. The town had a Sunday morning peacefulness on it, a peacefulness Jeff Anderson had worked for. It hadn't always been this way. He inhaled deeply, a contented man, and he caught the scent of freshly sprinkled dust that came from the dampened square of street in front of the ice cream parlor. There was a promise of heat in the air and already the thick, warm scent of the tar weed was drifting down from the yellow slopes in back of the town. He kept to the middle of the street, enjoying his freedom, not yet free of old habits, and he headed for the marshal's office, where the door was closed, the shade drawn.

This was his Sunday morning pleasure, this brief tour of the town that had claimed him for so long. It was the same tour he had made every Sunday morning for fifteen years; but now he could enjoy the luxury of knowing he was making it because he wanted to, not because it was his job. A man who had built a bridge or a building could sit back and look at his finished work, remembering the fun and the heartache that had gone into it, but he didn't need to chip away personally at its rust or take a pot of paint to its scars.

In front of the marshal's office Anderson paused, remembering it all, not missing it, just remembering; then he turned and pushed open the door, the familiarity of the action momentarily strong on him. The floor was worn and his own boot heels had helped wear it; the desk was scarred and some of those spur marks were as much his own as his own initials would have been. He grinned at the new marshal and said, "Caught any criminals lately?"

The man behind the desk glanced up, his face drawn, expressionless, his eyes worried. He tried to joke. "How could I?" he said. "You ain't been in town since last Sunday." He took one foot off the desk and kicked a straight chair toward Jeff. "How's the cow business?"

"Good," Jeff said. "Mighty good." He sat down heavily and stretched his long legs, pushed his battered felt hat back on his thinning, weather-bleached hair, and made himself a cigarette. He saw the papers piled on the desk, and glancing at the clock, he knew it was nearly time to let the two or three prisoners exercise in the jail corridor. A feeling of well-being engulfed him. These things were another man's responsibility now, not Jeff Anderson's. "How's it with you, Billy?" he asked.

The answer came too quickly, the answer of a man who was nervous or angry, or possibly both. "You ought to know, Jeff. The mayor and the council came to see you, didn't they?"

Annoyance clouded Jeff Anderson's gray eyes. He hadn't liked the idea of the city fathers going behind the new marshal's back. If they didn't like the job Billy was doing, they should have gone to Billy, not to Jeff. But that was typical of the city council. Jeff had known three mayors and three different councils during his long term in office, and they usually ran to a pattern. A few complaints and they got panicky and started going off in seven directions at once. They seemed to think that because Jeff had recommended Billy for this job, the job was still Jeff's responsibility. "They made the trip for nothing, Billy," Jeff said. "If you're worried about me wanting your job, you can forget it. I told them that plain."

"They'll keep asking you, Jeff."

"They'll keep getting no for an answer," Jeff said.

Billy Lang sat at his desk and stared at the drawn shade of the front window, the thumb of his left hand toying nervously with the badge on his calfskin vest. He was a small man with eternally pink cheeks and pale blue eyes. He wore a full white mustache, and there was a cleft in his chin. He was married and had five children, and most of his life he had clerked in a store. When Jeff Anderson recommended him for this job Billy took it because it paid more and because the town was quiet. But now there was trouble, and Billy was sorry he had ever heard of the job. He said, "You can't blame them for wanting you back, Jeff. You did a good job."

There was no false modesty in Jeff Anderson. He had done a good job here and he knew it. He had handled his job exactly the way he felt it should be handled and he had backed down to no one. But it hadn't been all roses, either. He grinned. "Regardless of what a man does, there's some who won't like it."

"Like Hank Fetterman?"

Jeff shrugged. Hank Fetterman was a cattleman. Sometimes Hank got the idea that he ought to take this town over and run it the way he once had. Hank hadn't gotten away with it when Jeff was marshal. Thinking about it now, it didn't seem to matter much to Jeff one way or the other, and it was hard to remember that his fight with Hank Fetterman had once been important. It had been a long time ago and things had changed. "Hank's not a bad sort," Jeff said.

"He's in town," Billy Lang said. "Did you know that?"

Jeff felt that old, familiar tightening of his stomach muscles, the signal of trouble ahead. He inhaled deeply, let the smoke trickle from his nostrils, and the feeling went away. Hank Fetterman was Jeff Anderson's neighbor now, and Jeff was a rancher, not a marshal. "I'm in town too," he said. "So are fifty other people. There's no law against it."

"You know what I mean, Jeff," Billy Lang said. "You talked to Rudy Svitac's boy."

Jeff moved uneasily in his chair. Billy Lang was accusing him of meddling, and Jeff didn't like it. Jeff had never had anything to do with the marshal's job since his retirement, and he had promised himself he never would. It was Billy's job, and Billy was free to run it his own way. But when a twelve-year-old kid who thought you were something special asked you a straight question you gave him a straight answer. It had nothing to do with the fact that you had once been a marshal—

"Sure, Billy," Jeff said. "I talked to Rudy's boy. He came to see me about it just the way he's been coming to see me about things ever since he was big enough to walk. The kid needs somebody to talk to, I guess, so he comes to me. He's not old country like his folks. He was born here; he thinks American. I guess it's hard for the boy to understand them. I told him to have his dad see you, Billy."

"He took your advice," Billy Lang said. "Three days ago." He turned over a paper. "Rudy Svitac came in and swore out a warrant against Hank Fetterman for trespassing. He said his boy told him it was the thing to do."

Jeff had a strange feeling that he was suddenly two people. One was Jeff Anderson, ex-marshal, the man who had recommended Billy Lang for this job. As such, he should offer Billy some advice right here and now. The other person was Jeff Anderson, private citizen, a man with a small ranch and a fine wife and a right to live his own life. And that was the Jeff Anderson that was important. Jeff Anderson, the rancher, grinned. "Hank pawin' and bellerin' about it, is he?"

"I don't know, Jeff," Billy Lang said. "I haven't talked to Hank about it. I'm not sure I'm going to."

Jeff glanced quickly at the new marshal, surprised, only half believing what he had heard. He had recommended Billy for this job because he figured he and Billy thought along the same lines. Surely Billy knew that if you gave Hank Fetterman an inch, he would take a mile. . . .

He caught himself quickly, realizing suddenly that it was none of his business how Billy Lang thought. There were plenty of businessmen in town who had argued loudly and openly that Jeff Anderson's methods of law enforcement had been bad for their cash registers. They had liked the old days when Hank Fetterman was running things and the town was wide open. Maybe they wanted it that way again. Every man was entitled to his own opinion, and Billy Lang was entitled to handle his job in his own way. This freedom of thought and action that Jeff prized so highly had to work for everyone. He stood up and clapped a hand affectionately on Billy Lang's shoulder, anxious to change the conversation. "That's up to you, Billy," he said. "It's sure none of my affair." His grin widened. "Come on over to the saloon and I'll buy a drink."

Billy Lang stared at the drawn shade, and he thought of Hank Fetterman, a man who was big in this country, waiting over at the saloon. Hank Fetterman knew there was a warrant out for his arrest; the whole town knew it by now. You didn't need to tell a thing like that. It just got around. And before long, people would know who the law was in this town, Hank Fetterman or Billy Lang. Billy colored slightly, and there was perspiration on his forehead. "You go ahead and have your drink, Jeff," he said. "I've got some paperwork to do." He didn't look up.

Jeff went outside and the gathering heat of the day struck the west side of the street and brought a resinous smell from the old boards of the false-fronted buildings. He glanced at the little church, seeing Rudy Svitac's spring wagon there, remembering that the church hadn't always been here; then he crossed over toward the saloon, the first business building this town had erected. He had been in a dozen such towns, and it was always the same. The saloons and the deadfalls came first, the churches and the schools later. Maybe that proved something. He didn't know. He had just stepped onto the board sidewalk when he saw the druggist coming toward him. The druggist was also the mayor, a sanctimonious little man, dried up by his own smallness. "Jeff, I talked to Billy Lang," the mayor said. His voice was thin and reedy. "I wondered if you might reconsider . . ."

"No," Jeff Anderson said. He didn't break his stride. He walked by the mayor and went into the saloon. Two of Hank Fetterman's riders were standing by the piano, leaning on it, and one of them was fumbling out a one-finger tune, cursing when he missed a note. Hank Fetterman was at the far end of the bar, and Jeff went and joined him. A little cow talk was good of a Sunday morning, and Hank Fetterman knew cows. The two men at the piano started to sing.

Hank Fetterman's glance drifted lazily to Jeff Anderson and then away. His smile was fleeting. "How are you, Jeff?"

"Good enough," Jeff said. "Can I buy you a drink?"

"You twisted my arm," Hank Fetterman said.

Hank Fetterman was a well-built man with a weathered face. His brows were heavy and they pinched together toward the top, forming a perfect diamond of clean, hairless skin between his deep-set eyes. His voice was quiet, his manner calm. Jeff thought of the times he had crossed this man, enforcing the no-gun ordinance, keeping Hank's riders in jail overnight to cool them off. He had no regrets over the way he had handled Hank in the past. It had nothing to do with his feeling toward Hank now or in the future. He saw that Hank was wearing a gun and he smiled inwardly. That was like Hank. Tell him he couldn't do something and that was exactly what he wanted to do. "Didn't figure on seeing you in town," Jeff said. "Thought you and the boys were on roundup."

"I had a little personal business come up," Hank Fetterman said. "You know about it?"

Jeff shrugged. "Depends on what it is."

The pale smile left Hank Fetterman's eyes but not his lips. "Rudy Svitac is telling it around that I ran a bunch of my cows through his corn. He claims I'm trying to run him out of the country."

Jeff had no trouble concealing his feelings. It was a trick he had learned a long time ago. He leaned his elbows on the bar and turned his shot glass slowly in its own wet circle. Behind him Hank Fetterman's two cowboys broke into a boisterous ribald song. The bartender wiped his face with his apron and glanced out the front window across toward the marshal's office. Jeff Anderson downed his drink, tossed the shot glass in the air, and caught it with a down sweep of his hand. "You're used to that kind of talk, Hank." He set the shot glass on the bar.

"You're pretty friendly with the Svitacs, aren't you, Jeff?" Hank Fetterman asked. He was leaning with his back to the bar, his elbows behind him. His position made the holstered gun he wore obvious.

Again, just for a moment, Jeff Anderson was two people. He remembered the man he wanted to be. "I don't reckon anybody's very friendly with the Svitacs," he said. "They're hard to know. I think a lot of their boy. He's a nice kid."

Slowly the smile came back into Hank Fetterman's amber eyes. He turned around and took the bottle and poured a drink for himself and one for Jeff. "That forty acres of bottom land you were asking me about for a calf pasture," he said. "I've been thinking about it. I guess I could lease it to you all right."

"That's fine, Hank," Jeff Anderson said. "I can use it." He doffed his glass to Hank and downed his drink. It didn't taste right, but he downed it anyway. The two cowboys started to scuffle and one of them collided with a table. It overturned with a crash.

"Please, Hank," the bartender said. "They're gonna get me in trouble . . ." His voice trailed off and his eyes widened. A man had come through the door. He stood there, blinking the bright sun out of his eyes. Jeff Anderson felt his heart start to pump heavily, slowly, high in his chest. "Morning, Mr. Svitac," the bartender mumbled.

Rudy Svitac stood in the doorway, a thick dull man with black hair and brows that met across the bridge of his nose and a forehead that sloped. Jeff saw the rusty suit the man wore on Sundays, the suit that had faint soil stains on the knees because this man could not leave the soil alone, even on Sundays. He had to kneel down and feel the soil with his fingers, feeling the warmth and the life of it; for the soil was his book and his life and it was the only thing he understood completely and perhaps the only thing that understood him. He looked at Jeff, not at Hank Fetterman. "Is no good," Rudy Svitac said. "My son says I must talk to Billy Lang. I talk to Billy Lang, but he does nothing. Is no good."

A thick silence settled in the room and the two cowboys who had been scuffling quit it now and stood there looking at the farmer. Hank Fetterman said, "Say what's on your mind, Svitac."

"You broke my fence," Rudy Svitac said. "You drive your cows in my corn and spoil my crop. All winter I wait to plant my crop and now is grow fine and you drive your cows in."

"Maybe you're mistaken, Svitac," Hank Fetterman said.

"My boy says is for judge to decide," Rudy Svitac said. "My boy tell me to go to Billy Lang and he will make a paper and judge will decide. My boy says is fair. Is America." Rudy Svitac stared unblinkingly. He shook his head slowly. "Is not so. I want my money. You broke my fence."

"You're a liar, Svitac," Hank Fetterman said. He moved away from the bar, slowly. He looked steadily at Jeff Anderson, then he glanced across the street toward the marshal's office. The door was still closed, the shade still drawn. Hank Fetterman smiled. He walked forward and gripped Rudy Svitac by the shirtfront. For a moment he held the man that way, pulling him close, then he shoved, and Rudy Svitac stumbled backward, out through the door, and his heel caught on a loose board in the sidewalk. He fell hard and for a long time he lay there, his dull, steady eyes staring at Jeff

Anderson; then he turned and pushed himself up and he stood there looking at the dust on his old suit. He dropped his head and looked at the dust and he reached with his fingers and touched it. One of Hank Fetterman's cowboys started to laugh.

Across the street Jeff Anderson saw the blind on the window of the marshal's office move aside and then drop back into place, and immediately the door opened and Billy Lang was hurrying across the street. He came directly to Rudy Svitac and put his hand on Svitac's arm and jerked him around. "What's going on here?" Billy Lang demanded.

"Svitac came in looking for trouble," Hank Fetterman said. "I threw him out." Hank was standing in the doorway, directly alongside Jeff. For a brief moment Hank Fetterman's amber eyes met Jeff's gaze and Jeff saw the challenge. If you don't like it, do something about it, Hank Fetterman was saying. I want to know how you stand in this thing and I want to know now.

There was a dryness in Jeff Anderson's mouth. He had backed Hank Fetterman down before; he could do it again. But for what? One hundred and fifty dollars a month and a chance to get killed? Jeff had had fifteen years of that. A man had a right to live his own life. He looked up toward the church and the doors were just opening and people were coming out to stand on the porch, a small block of humanity suddenly aware of trouble. Jeff saw his wife Elaine, and he knew her hand was at her throat, twisting the fabric of her dress the way she did. He thought of the little ranch and of the things he and Elaine had planned for the future, and then he looked at Billy Lang and he knew Billy wasn't going to buck Hank Fetterman. So Jeff could make a stand, and it would be his own stand and he would be right back into it again just the way he had been for fifteen years. There was a thick line of perspiration on Jeff's upper lip. "That's the way it was, Billy," Jeff said.

He saw the quick smile cross Hank Fetterman's face, the dull acceptance and relief in Billy Lang's eyes. "Get out of town, Svitac," Billy Lang said. "I'm tired of your troublemaking. If Hank's cows got in your corn, it was an accident."

"Is no accident," Rudy Svitac said stubbornly. "Is for judge to decide. My son says—"

"It was an accident," Billy Lang said. "Make your fences stronger." He didn't look at Jeff. He glanced at Hank Fetterman and made his final capitulation. "Sorry it happened, Hank."

For a long moment Rudy Svitac stared at Billy Lang, at the star on Billy's vest, remembering that this star somehow had a connection with the stars in the flag. His son Anton had explained it, saying that Jeff Anderson said it was so, so it must be so. But it wasn't so. Hank Fetterman wasn't in jail. They weren't going to do anything about the ruined corn. The skin wrinkled between Rudy Svitac's eyes, and there was perspiration on his face and his lips moved thickly but no sound came out. He could not understand. Thirteen years he had lived in this America, but still he could not understand. His son had tried to tell him the things they taught in the schools and the things Jeff Anderson said were so; but Rudy had his soil to work and his crops to plant, and when a man's back was tired his head did not work so good. Rudy Svitac knew only that if the jimson weed grew in the potato patch, you cut it out. And the wild morning-glory must be pulled out by the roots. No one came to do these things for a man. A man did these chores himself. He turned and walked solidly up the street toward where he had left his spring wagon by the church.

His wife Mary was there, a thick, tired woman who never smiled nor ever complained, and watching them, Jeff saw Anton, their son, a boy of twelve with an old man's face, a boy who had always believed every word Jeff Anderson said. Jeff saw young Anton looking down the street toward him, and he remembered the boy's serious brown eyes and the thick, black hair that always stood out above his ears and lay rebelliously far down his neck. He remembered the hundred times he had talked to young Anton, patiently explaining things so Anton would understand, learning his own beliefs from the process of explaining them in simple words. And Anton would listen and then repeat to his parents in Bohemian, telling them this was so because Jeff Anderson said it was so. A bright boy with an unlimited belief in the future, in a household where there was no future. At times it seemed to Jeff almost as if God had looked upon Rudy and Mary Svitac and wanted to compensate in some way, so he had given them Anton.

Jeff saw Rudy reaching into the bed of the wagon. He saw Mary protest once; then Mary stood there, resigned, and now the boy had his father's arm and there was a brief struggle. The father shook the boy off, and now Rudy had a rifle and he was coming back down the street, walking slowly, down the middle of the street, the rifle in the crook of his arm.

Billy Lang moved. He met Rudy halfway, and he held out his hand. Jeff saw Rudy hesitate, take two more steps; and now Billy was saying something and Rudy dropped his head and let his chin lie on his chest. The boy came running up, and he took the rifle out of his father's hand and the crowd in front of the saloon expelled its breath. Jeff felt the triumph come into Hank Fetterman. He didn't need to look at the man. He could feel it.

The slow, wicked anger was inside Hank Fetterman, goaded by his ambition, his sense of power, and the catlike eagerness was in his eyes. "No Bohunk tells lies about me and gets away with it," he murmured. "No Bohunk comes after me with a gun and gets a second chance." His hand dropped and rested on the butt of his holstered six-shooter, and then the thumb of his left hand touched Jeff Anderson's arm. "Have a drink with me, Jeff?"

Jeff saw Elaine standing in front of the church, and he could feel her anxiety reaching through the hot, troubled air. And he saw the boy there in the street, the gun in his hands, his eyes, bewildered, searching Jeff Anderson's face. "I reckon I won't have time, Hank," Jeff said. He walked up the street, and now the feeling of being two people was strong in him, and there was a responsibility to Billy Lang that he couldn't deny. He had talked Billy into taking this job. It was a lonely job, and there was never a lonelier time than when a man was by himself in the middle of the street. He came close to Billy and he said, "Look, Billy, if you can take a gun away from one man, you can take a gun away from another."

Billy looked at him. Billy's hands were shaking, and there was sweat on his face. "A two-year-old kid could have taken that gun away from Rudy, and you know it," he said. He reached up swiftly and unpinned the badge from his vest. He handed it across. "You want it?"

Jeff looked at that familiar piece of metal, and he could feel the boy's eyes on him; and then he looked up and he saw Elaine there on the church porch, and he thought of his own dreams and of the plans he and Elaine had made for the future. "No, Billy," he said. "I don't want it."

"Then let it lay there," Billy Lang said. He dropped the badge into the dust of the street and hurried off, a man who had met defeat and accepted it, a man who could now go back to the clothing store and sell shirts and suits and overalls because that was the job he could do best. There was no indignity in Billy Lang's defeat. He had taken a role that he wasn't equipped to handle, and he was admitting it.

The boy said, "Mr. Jeff, I don't understand. You told me once—"

"We'll talk about it later, Anton," Jeff said. "Tell your dad to go home." He walked swiftly toward Elaine, swallowing against the sourness in his throat.

They drove out of town, Jeff and Elaine Anderson, toward their own home and their own life; and now the full heat of the day lay on the yellow slopes, and the dry air crackled with the smell of dust and the cured grass, and the leather seat of the buggy was hot to the touch. A mile out of town Jeff stopped in the shade of a sycamore, and put up the top. He moved with dull efficiency, pausing momentarily to glance up as Hank Fetterman and his two riders passed on their way back to the ranch. He got back into the buggy and unwrapped the lines from the whipstock, and Elaine said, "If there's anything you want to say, Jeff . . ."

How could he say it? He couldn't, for the thing that was most in his mind had nothing to do with the matter at hand, and yet it had everything to do with it and it couldn't be explained. For he was thinking not of Hank Fetterman nor of Rudy Svitac, but of a colored lithograph, a town promotion picture that had once hung on every wall in this town. It showed wide tree-lined streets, a tremendous townhouse with a flag half as large as the building flying from a mast, and lesser pennants, all mammoth, rippling from every building. Tiny men in cutaway coats and top hats leisurely strolled the avenues, and high-wheeled bicycles rolled elegantly past gleaming black victorias on the street of exclusive shops, while three sleek trains chuffed impatiently at the station. The railroad had put on a large land promotion around here when the road was first built. They had offered excursion trips free so that people could see the charms of New Canaan. They had handed out these lithos of the proposed town by the bushel. For a while New Canaan bustled with activity, and men bought town lots staked out in buffalo grass. And then the bubble burst, and New Canaan settled back to what it was before—a place called Alkali at the edge of open cattle range. And young Anton Svitac had come to see Marshal Jeff Anderson for the first time and he had come about that picture.

Jeff remembered how the boy had looked that day, no more than six years old, his eyes too large for his old-man's face, his voice a mirror of the seriousness of thought that was so much a part of him. He had come to Jeff Anderson because Jeff Anderson was authority, and already young Anton had learned that in America authority was for everyone. "My father and mother do not understand," he said. "They do not speak English." He unrolled the lithograph and put his finger on it, and then indicated the town of Alkali with a spread hand. "Is not the same," he said. "Is not so."

There were dreams in that boy's eyes, and they were about to be snuffed out; and Jeff Anderson didn't want it to happen. "Sure it's so, Anton," he heard himself saying. "It's not what it is today, it's what's going to be tomorrow, see?" He remembered the trouble he had with the words, and then it was all there and he was telling it to Anton, telling it so this boy could go home and tell it to a work-bent man and a tired woman. "It's like America, see? Some of the things aren't right where you can touch them. Maybe some of the things you see are ugly. But the picture is always there to look at, and you keep thinking about the picture, and you keep working and making things better all the time, see? America isn't something you cut off like a piece of cake and say 'there it is.' You keep on looking ahead to what it's going to be, and you keep working hard for it all the time, and you keep right on knowing it's going to be good because you've got the picture there to look at. You never stop working and say, 'Now the job is done,' because it never is. You see that, Anton?"

The boy hadn't smiled. This was a big thing and a boy didn't smile about big things. He rolled the lithograph carefully. "I see," he said. "Is good. I will tell my father. We will keep the picture."

Those were Jeff Anderson's thoughts, and how could he tell them, even to Elaine; for they had so little to do with the matter at hand and yet they had everything to do with it.

And Elaine, looking at her husband now, respected his silence. She remembered the three long years she was engaged to this man before they were married, years in which she had come to know him so well because she loved him so well. She knew him even better now. He was a man who was born to handle trouble, and a piece of tin on his vest or a wife at his side couldn't change the man he was born to be. She knew that and she didn't want to change him, but a woman couldn't help being what she was either and a woman could be afraid, especially at a time like this when there was so much ahead. She wanted to help him. "Maybe the Svitacs would be better off some place else," she said. "They never have made the place pay."

And that was exactly the same argument he had used on himself; but now, hearing it put into words, he didn't like the sound of it and he wanted to argue back. His voice was rough. "I reckon they look on it as home," he said. "The boy was born there. I reckon it sort of ties you to a place if your first one is born there."

She closed her eyes tightly, knowing that she was no longer one person but three, knowing the past was gone and the future would always be ahead, and it was her job to help secure that future as much as it was Jeff's job. She opened her eyes and looked at her husband, still afraid, for that was her way; but somehow prouder and older now. She folded her hands in her lap and the nervousness was gone. "I suppose we'll feel that way too, Jeff," she said. "It will always be our town after our baby is born here. I talked to the doctor yesterday—"

He felt the hard knot in the pit of his stomach. Then the coldness ran up his spine, and it was surprise and fear and a great swelling pride; and the feeling crawled up his neck, and every hair on his head was an individual hair, and the hard lump was in his throat. He moved on the seat, suddenly concerned for her comfort. "You feel all right, honey? Is there anything I can do?"

She didn't laugh at him any more than Anton had laughed at him that day in the office. She reached over and put her hand on his hand, and she smiled. As they drove down the lane the great pride was inside him, swelling against him until he felt that the seat of the buggy was no longer large enough to contain him. He helped her out of the buggy, his motions exaggerated in their kindness; and he took her arm and helped her up the front steps.

The coolness of the night still lingered in the little ranch house, for she had left the shades drawn; and now she went to the west windows and lifted the shades slightly, and she could see down the lane and across the small calf pasture where a thin drift of dust from their buggy wheels still lingered. There was a loneliness to Sunday after church, a stillness on the ranch. She glanced toward the barn, and Jeff was unharnessing the mare and turning her into the corral, his back broad, his movements deliberate;

and she saw him stand for a moment and look down the creek toward where Rudy Svitac's place cornered on Hank Fetterman's huge, unfenced range.

He came into the house later, into the cool living room, and he sat down in his big chair with a gusty sigh, and pulled off his boots and stretched his legs. "Good to be home," he said. "Good to have nothing to do." He raised his eyes to meet hers and they both knew he was lying. There was always something to do.

The moment he was sure, she knew it was easier for him, but he still had to be positive that she understood that now it was different. Once he made this move there would be no turning back. She had to see that. An hour ago the town had been a town, nothing more; and if certain merchants felt business would be better with Hank Fetterman running things, that was their business; and if Billy Lang wanted to go along with that thinking or go back to the clothing store, that was his business. Jeff Anderson hadn't needed the town. It was a place to shop and nothing more, and a man could shop as well with Hank Fetterman running things as he could with Jeff Anderson running things. But now, suddenly, that had changed, and there was tomorrow to think about, and it was exactly as he had explained it to Anton. Now, one day soon, Jeff Anderson might be explaining the same things to his own son; and a man had to show his son that he believed what he said, for if he didn't, there was nothing left. "I was wrong about Billy Lang," Jeff Anderson said. "He's not going to stand up to Hank Fetterman."

She looked into his eyes and saw the deep seriousness and knew his every thought, and in this moment they were closer than they had ever been before; and she remembered thinking so many times of men and women who had been married for fifty years or more and of how they always looked alike. She said, "I have some curtains I promised Mary Svitac. Will you take them to her when you go?"

She didn't trust herself to say more, and she didn't give him a lingering embrace as a woman might who was watching her man go off to danger; but she pretended to be busy and turned her head so that his lips just brushed her temple, and it was as casual as if he were only going to his regular day's work. "And thank her for the pickles," she said.

He stalked out of the house as if he didn't like having his Sunday disturbed by such woman nonsense, but when he was halfway to the barn his stride lengthened and she saw the stiffness of his back and the set of his shoulders. She sat down then and cried.

Anton, the boy, was pouring sour milk into a trough for the pigs when Jeff rode into the Svitac yard. The world could collapse, but pigs had to be fed, and the boy was busy with his thoughts and did not see Jeff ride up. The door of the little house that was half soddy, half dugout, opened, and Mary

Svitac called something in Bohemian. The boy looked up, startled, and Jeff smiled. "Will you ride my horse over and tie him in the shade, Anton?"

The flood of hope that filled the boy's eyes was embarrassing to a man, and Jeff dismounted quickly, keeping his head turned. He took the bundle of curtains from behind the saddle, and handed the reins to the boy; then walked on to the sod house where Mary Svitac stood, the shawl tied under her chin framing her round, expressionless face. He handed her the curtains. "Those pickles you gave us were fine, Mrs. Svitac. Elaine wanted me to bring these curtains over."

Mary Svitac let her rough fingers caress the curtain material. "I will give you all the pickles," she said. "We don't need the curtains. We don't stay here no more."

Rudy's thick voice came from the dark interior of the sod house; and now Jeff could see him there, sitting in a chair, a man dulled with work and disappointments, a man with a limited knowledge of English who had come to a new country with a dream, and found grasshoppers and drought and blizzards and neighbors who tried to drive him out. He looked up. "We don't stay," he said.

"Can I come in for a minute, Mrs. Svitac?" Jeff asked.

"I make coffee," she said.

He stooped to pass through the low door, and he took off his hat and sat down. Now that his eyes were accustomed to the darkness of the room, he saw the big lithograph there on the wall, the only decoration. Rudy Svitac stared unblinkingly at the floor, and a tear ran unashamed down the side of his nose. "We don't stay," he said.

"Sure, Rudy," Jeff Anderson said softly. "You stay."

Mary Svitac started to cry. There were no tears, for the land had taken even that away from her. There were just sobs—dry, choking sounds as she made her coffee—but they were woman sounds, made for her man; and she was willing to give up fifteen years of work if her man would be safe. "They will fight with us," she said. "They put cows in my Rudolph's corn. They tear down our fence. Soon they come to break my house. Is too much. Rudolph does not know fight. Rudolph is for plant the ground and play wiolin—"

"You stay, Rudy," Jeff Anderson said. "The law will take care of you. I promise you that."

Rudy Svitac shook his ponderous head. "Law is for Hank Fetterman," he said. "Is not for me."

"It's not so, Rudy," Jeff said. "You ask Anton. He knows."

"I ask Anton," Rudy Svitac said. "He says I am right. Law is for Hank Fetterman."

The boy came to the door and stood there, peering inside the room. His face was white, drawn with worry; but the hope was still in his eyes and a confidence was there. He didn't say anything. He didn't need to. Jeff could hear the sound of horses approaching—Jeff stood up and the feeling that was in him was an old and familiar feeling—a tightening of all his muscles. He went to the corner of the room and took Rudy Svitac's rifle from its place, and he levered in a shell, leaving the rifle at full cock. He stepped through the door then, and he put his hand on the boy's head. "You explain again to your father about the law," he said. "You know, Anton, like we talked before."

"I know," Anton Svitac said.

Jeff stepped swiftly through the door into the sunlight, and he saw Hank Fetterman and the same two riders who had been with him at the saloon coming toward the soddy. Only Hank was armed, and this could be handy later, when Hank talked to the judge. If we had expected trouble, all three of us would have been armed, Judge, Hank Fetterman could say. They rode stiffly, holding their horses in. Jeff Anderson stood the cocked rifle by the fencepost, placing it carefully. He pushed his hat back on his head and felt the sun on his back as he leaned there, one foot on a fence rail, watching the pigs eat the sour milk.

He knew when the riders were directly beside him, and he turned, his elbows leaning on the top rail of the fence behind him. His hat was pushed back, but his face was in shade, for he had moved to where he was between the sun and the riders. Hank Fetterman said, "We're seeing a lot of each other, neighbor."

"Looks that way," Jeff said.

Hank Fetterman quieted his horse with a steady hand. His eyes never left Jeff Anderson's face. "I asked you once today if you was a friend of the Bohunks," he said. "Maybe I better ask it again."

"Maybe it depends on what you've got on your mind, Hank."

"The Bohunk's been eating my beef," Fetterman said, "I'm sick of it."

"You sure that's it, Hank?" Jeff asked quietly. "Or is it just that there's something that eats on you and makes you want to tear down things other folks have taken years to build up?"

There were small white patches on either side of Hank Fetterman's mouth. "I said the Bohunk was eating my beef," Hank Fetterman said. His lips didn't move. "You doubting my word?"

"No," Jeff said. "I'm calling you a liar."

He saw the smoldering anger in Hank Fetterman, the sore, whisky-nursed anger, and then the cattleman felt the full shock as the flat insult in Jeff's voice reached through to him. He cursed and half twisted in the saddle, blinking directly into the sun. "You forgetting you ain't a lawman any more?" he demanded.

"You decide, Hank," Jeff said.

They looked at each other, two men who had killed before and knew the meaning of it, two men who respected a gun and understood a gun. They said nothing and yet they spoke a silent language, and the man who had been a lawman said, I'm telling you to back down, Fetterman; and the man who wanted to be king said, You'll have to be big enough to make me. No actual words, and yet they knew; and they faced each other with muscles tense and faces drawn, and appeared at ease. Jeff Anderson had dealt himself into the game, and he had checked the bet.

Hank Fetterman saw the rifle by the post. He knew it was cocked and loaded. He wondered if Jeff Anderson was actually as quick and as accurate as men said he was; and because he was Hank Fetterman, he had to know, because if he backed down now, it was over for him and he knew it. He jerked his horse around, trying to avoid that direct glare of the sun, and he made his decision. His hand went for his gun.

Jeff Anderson saw the move coming. It seemed to him that he had plenty of time. He had placed the rifle carefully and now he held it, hip high, gripping it with one hand, tilting it up and pulling the trigger all at the same time. He didn't hear the sound of the rifle's explosion. You never did, he remembered; but he saw the thin film of gunsmoke, and he saw Hank Fetterman's mouth drop open, saw the man clawing at his chest. He didn't feel the sickness. Not yet—

Time passed as if through a film of haze, and nothing was real. Then they were gone and a canvas was stretched over the still form of Hank Fetterman, and Rudy Svitac was whipping his team toward town to get the coroner. Now the sickness came to Jeff Anderson. He stood by the barn, trembling, and he heard the boy come up behind him. The boy said, "This was in the street in town, Mr. Anderson." The boy held out the tin star. "I told my father how the law was for everybody in America. Now he knows."

Jeff Anderson took the tin star and dropped it into his pocket.

Elaine saw him through the front window. She had been watching a long time, and she had been praying, silently; and now she said, "Thank God," and she went and sat down, and she was like that when he came into the room. She wanted to ask him about it, but her throat kept choking; and then he was kneeling there, his head in her lap, and he was crying deep inside, not making a sound. "It's all right, Jeff," she said. "It's all right."

For that was the thing he had to know—that it was all right with her. He had to know that she loved him for the man he was and not for the man he had tried to become. He couldn't change any more than Billy Lang could change. She had never told him to take off his gun—not in words—but she had wanted him to, and he had understood, and he had tried. No woman could ask for greater love than that a man to try to change himself. And no woman need be afraid when she had such love. She thought of young Anton Svitac and of her own son who was to be, and she was calm and sure.

A long time later she picked up Jeff's coat and laid it across her arm. The tin star fell to the floor. For a long time she looked at it, then she bent her knees and reached down and picked it up and put it back into the coat pocket. She went into the bedroom then and hung the coat carefully. From the bureau drawer she took a clean white pleated-front shirt and laid it out where he could see it. Marshal Jeff Anderson had worn a clean white pleated-front shirt to the office on Monday morning for as long back as she could remember. She didn't expect him to change his habits now.

Elmer Kelton is a major and widely respected name in modern western fiction, as evidenced by his unprecedented four Spur awards and three Cowboy Hall of Fame Western Heritage awards. While writing for western novels during the 1950s and 1960s, he also edited several ranching magazines, including *The Ranch Magazine* and *Livestock Weekly*. His work deals mainly with the settlement of Texas, from its early days as a frontier filled with danger and opportunity to the days of the oil boom. His more than thirty novels include such classics as *The Man Who Rode Midnight*, *The Day the Cowboys Quit*, and *The Good Old Boys*, all modern benchmarks of western fiction.

The Burial of Letty Strayhorn

Elmer Kelton

Greenleaf Strayhorn frowned as he rode beyond the dense live oak motte and got his first clear look at Prosperity. The dry west wind, which had been blowing almost unbroken for a week, picked up dust from the silent streets and lifted it over the frame buildings to lose it against a cloudless blue sky. He turned toward the brown packhorse that trailed the young sorrel he was riding. His feeling of distaste deepened the wrinkles which had resulted from long years of labor in the sun.

"Wasn't much of a town when we left here, Letty, and I can't see that it's got any better. But you wanted to come back."

Prosperity had a courthouse square but no courthouse. Even after voting some of its horses and dogs, it had lost the county-seat election to rival Paradise Forks, a larger town which could rustle up more horses and dogs. Greenleaf hoped the dramshop was still operating. He had paused in Paradise Forks only long enough to buy a meal cooked by someone other than himself, and that had been yesterday. He was pleased to see the front door open. If the sign out front had been repainted during his twelve-year absence, he could not tell it.

"*Finest in liquors, wines, and bitters,*" he read aloud. "*Cold beer and billiards*. Our kind of a place. Mine, anyway. You never was one for self-indulgence."

The sorrels' ears poked forward distrustfully as a yellow dog sauntered out to inspect the procession. Greenleaf tightened his knee grip, for the young horse was still prone to regard with great suspicion such things as dogs, chickens, and flying scraps of paper. It had pitched him off once already on this trip. Greenleaf was getting to an age when rodeoing was meant to be a spectator sport, not for personal participation. The dog quickly lost interest in rider and horses and angled off toward the live oak motte to try and worry a rabbit or two.

Greenleaf tied up the horses in front of the saloon, loosening the girth so his saddle horse could breathe easier. He checked the pack on the brown horse and found it still snug. Seeing no others tied nearby, he knew the saloon was enjoying another in a long succession of slow days.

He stepped up onto the board sidewalk, taking an extralong stride to skip over a spot where two planks had been removed. Somebody had evidently fallen through in the relatively distant past. The rest of the boards were badly weathered, splintered, and worn. It was only a matter of time until they, too, caused someone embarrassment, and probably skinned shins.

The whole place looked like the tag end of a hot, dry summer. Whoever had named this town Prosperity was a terrible prophet or had a wicked sense of humor, he thought.

A black cat lay curled in the shade near the front door. It opened one eye in response to Greenleaf's approach, then closed the eye with minimum compromise to its rest.

The bartender sat on a stool, his head upon his arms atop the bar. He stirred to the jingling of spurs and looked up sleepy-eyed.

"Beer," Greenleaf said. "A cold one if you've got it."

The man delivered it to him in a mug and gave him a squinting appraisal. "Ain't your name Greenleaf Shoehorn?"

"Strayhorn."

"A name like Greenleaf ain't easily forgot. The rest of it . . ." He shrugged. "Didn't you used to work on Old Man Hopkins's place?"

"And married his daughter Letty."

Memory made the bartender smile. "Anybody who ever met Letty would remember her. A mighty strong-willed woman. Where's she at?"

"Outside, on a horse."

The bartender frowned. "You'd leave her in the hot sun while you come in here for a cool drink?" He walked to the door. "All I see is two horses."

"She's under the tarp on the packhorse, in a lard can. Her ashes, I mean."

The bartender's face fell. "She's dead?"

"Took by a fever two weeks ago. Last thing she asked me was to bring her back here and bury her on the homeplace alongside her mama and papa. It was so far, the only way I could do it was to bring her ashes."

Soberly the bartender refilled the mug Greenleaf had drained. "Sorry about Letty. Everybody liked her. Everybody except Luther Quinton. He hated all the Hopkinses, and everybody that neighbored them."

"It always makes it easier when you hate the people you set out to rob. Less troublin' on the conscience."

"He still owns the old Hopkins place. He may not take it kindly, you buryin' Letty there. Asked him yet?"

"Wasn't figurin' on askin' him. Just figured on doin' it."

The bartender's attention was drawn to the front window. "If you *was* thinkin' about askin' him, this'd be the time. That's him comin' yonder."

Greenleaf carried his beer to the door, where he watched as the black cat raised up from its nap, stretched itself luxuriously, and meandered out into the windy street, crossing Quinton's path. Quinton stopped abruptly, turning back and taking a path that led him far around the cat. It stopped in the middle of the deserted street to lick itself.

The bartender remarked, "Superstitious, Luther is. Won't buy anything by the dozen because he's afraid they may throw in an extra one on him. They say he won't even keep a mirror in his house because he's afraid he might break it."

"He probably just doesn't like to look at himself. I never liked lookin' at him either." Quinton had long legs and a short neck. He had always reminded Greenleaf of a frog.

Quinton came to the door, looking back to be sure the cat had not moved. He demanded of the bartender, "How many more lives has that tomcat got? I've been hopin' a wagon might run over him in the street."

"She ain't a tomcat, and there ain't enough traffic. She's liable to live for twenty years."

"I'd haul her off and dump her, but I know she'd come back."

Quinton's attention shifted to Greenleaf, and his eyes narrowed with recognition. "Speakin' of comin' back . . ." He pointed a thick, hairy finger. "Ain't you the hired hand that married the Hopkins girl?"

"Letty. Yep, I'm the one."

"There's no accountin' for some people's judgment. Wonder she ain't killed and scalped you before now. Has Indian blood in her, don't she?"

"Her mama was half Choctaw."

"Probably some kind of a medicine woman. That Letty laid a curse on me the day I took over the Hopkins place. Cow market went to hell. Calf crop dropped to half. Rain quit and the springs dried up. I had nothin' but bad luck for over a year."

"Only a year? She must not've put her whole heart into it."

Dread was in Quinton's eyes. "She back to cause me more misery?"

"She died."

Relief washed over Quinton's round, furrowed face like sunshine breaking through a dark cloud. He was not one to smile easily, but he ventured dangerously near. "I'm mighty sorry to hear it." He gulped down a glass of whiskey in one long swallow. "Mighty sorry."

Greenleaf grunted. "I can see that." He turned to the bartender. "Old Brother Ratliff still doin' the preachin'?"

The bartender nodded. "You'll find him at the parsonage over by the church. My sympathies about Letty."

Greenleaf thanked him and walked out. He had not expected this to be a pleasant homecoming, and running into Luther Quinton had helped it live down to his expectations. Untying the two horses, he looked a moment at the pack on the second animal, and a catch came in his throat. He had worked his way through the darkest of his grief, but a lingering sadness still shadowed him. He wanted to fulfill his promise to Letty, then put this place behind him for once and all. His and Letty's leavetaking from here had created a residue of memories bitter to the taste.

Not all the fault had been Quinton's. Letty's father should have known he was dealing himself a busted flush when he tried farming on land where the average rainfall was only about fifteen inches a year, and half of that tended to come in one night if it came at all. Letty's stubborn nature was a natural heritage from both sides of her family. She had tried to keep on farming even though her father had accomplished four crop failures in a row. He had died of a seizure in the middle of a diatribe against the bank for letting him borrow himself so deeply into the hole and refusing to let him dig the hole any deeper.

All Quinton had done, really, was to buy the notes from the frustrated banker and foreclose on Letty. Quinton had acquired several other properties the same way. He was not a hawk that kills its prey but rather a buzzard which feeds on whatever has died a natural death.

Greenleaf had not considered Brother Ratliff an old man when he had lived here, but like the town, the minister had aged a lot in a dozen years. Greenleaf had to knock on the door a third time before it swung inward and a tall, slightly stooped gentleman peered down at him, cocking his head a little to one side to present his best ear. From Ratliff's gaunt appearance, Greenleaf judged that the Sunday offering plate had been coming back but little heavier than it went out.

"May I be of service to you, friend?"

"I'm Greenleaf Strayhorn. You may not remember, but you tied the knot for me and Letty Hopkins a long time ago."

The minister smiled broadly and made a gesture that invited him into the spare little house. "I do remember. Quite a beautiful bride, she was. Have you brought her with you?"

"In a manner of speakin', yes sir. I was wonderin' if you'd be kind enough to say some fittin' words over her so I can put her ashes in the ground?"

The minister's smile died. "The Lord calls all of us home eventually, but it would seem He has called her much too early. I hope she had a good life to compensate for its shortness."

"We did tolerable well. Got us a nice little ranch up north, though we wasn't blessed with kids. She just never could shake loose from her old family homeplace. The memory of it was always there, itchin' like a wool shirt. She wanted me to bring her back."

"It's a sad thing to preach a funeral, but part of my calling is to comfort the bereaved and commend the soul to a better land. When would you want me to perform the service?"

"Right now, if that's not too soon."

The minister put on his black coat and walked with Greenleaf to the church next door. "Would you mind pulling the bell rope for me, son? The devil has afflicted my shoulder with rheumatism."

Afterward, Greenleaf unwrapped the pack and fetched the lard can containing all that was left in the world of Letty Strayhorn. He placed it in front of the altar. A dozen or so citizens came, curious about the reason for the bell to ring in the middle of the week. Among them was the bartender, who knew. He had removed his apron and put on a coat, though the church was oppressively warm. Its doors and windows had been kept shut because the wind would have brought in too much dust.

The sermon was brief, for Brother Ratliff did not know all that much to say about Letty's past, just that she had been a hard-working, God-fearing woman who held strong opinions about right and wrong and did not easily abide compromise.

At the end of the closing prayer he said, "Now, if any of you would like to accompany the deceased to her final resting place, you are welcome to go with us to the old Hopkins farm."

A loud voice boomed from the rear of the church. "No you ain't! The place is mine, and that woman ain't fixin' to be buried in any ground that belongs to me!"

The minister was first surprised, then dismayed. "Brother Quinton, surely you would not deny that good soul the right to be buried amongst her own."

"Good soul? A witch, I'd call her. A medicine woman, somethin' from the Indian blood in her."

"She has passed on to another life. She can do you no harm now."

"I'm takin' no chances. You want her buried, bury her here in town. You ain't bringin' her out to my place."

Apologetically the minister looked back to Greenleaf. "I am sorry, Brother Strayhorn. I may argue with Brother Quinton's logic, but I cannot argue with his legal rights."

Greenleaf stood up and studied Quinton's physical stature. He decided he could probably whip the man, if it came to a contest. But he would no doubt end up in jail, and he still would not be able to carry out Letty's final wish.

"She's goin' to be disappointed," he said.

The town cemetery was a depressing place, the site picked for convenience rather than for beauty. His sleeves rolled up, Greenleaf worked with a pair of posthole diggers that belonged to the minister. Brother Ratliff, looking too frail to help in this kind of labor, sat on a marble gravestone and watched as the hole approached three feet in depth. The length of the handles would limit Greenleaf's digging. The bartender had come to the cemetery but had left after a few minutes to reopen the saloon lest he miss out on any thirsty customers. Or perhaps he had feared he might be called upon to lend a hand with the diggers.

Ratliff said, "It matters not where the body lies."

"So the old song says," Greenleaf responded, turning into the wind. Though its breath was warm, it felt cool against his sweaty face and passing through his partially soaked shirt. "But I feel like I'm breakin' a promise. I never got to do everything I wanted to for Letty while she was livin', but at least I never broke a promise to her."

"You made your promise in good faith. Now for reasons beyond your control you cannot fulfill it. She would understand that. Anyway, you brought her back to her hometown. That's close."

"I remember a couple of times my stomach was growlin' awful loud at me, and I bore down on a whitetail deer for meat but missed. Close wasn't good enough. I was still hungry."

"You've done the best you could."

"No, I ain't." Greenleaf brought the diggers up out of the hole and leaned on their handles while he pondered. "Mind lendin' me these diggers a little longer, Preacher?"

Ratliff studied him quizzically. "You'd be welcome to keep them. Should I ask you what for?"

"A man in your profession ain't supposed to lie. If I don't tell you, you won't have to lie to anybody that might ask you."

Greenleaf used the diggers to rake dirt back into the hole and tamp it down. The lard can still sat where he had placed it beside a nearby gravestone. "We had a full moon last night. It ought to be just as bright tonight."

The minister looked up at the cloudless sky. "Unless it rains. I would say our chance for rain is about as remote as the chance of Luther Quinton donating money for a new church. Would you like for me to go with you?"

"You've got to live here afterward, Preacher. I don't." Greenleaf finished filling the hole. "If I was to leave you the money, would you see to it that a proper headstone is put up for her?"

"I would consider it a privilege."

"Thanks." Greenleaf extended his hand. "You don't just know the words, Preacher. You know the *Lord.*"

.   .   .

EVEN IF THE moon had not been bright, Greenleaf could have found the old Hopkins place without difficulty. He had ridden the road a hundred times in daylight and in darkness. Nothing had changed in the dozen years since he had last traveled this way. He rode by the deserted house where the Hopkins family had lived while they struggled futilely to extract a good living from a soil that seemed always thirsty. He stopped a moment to study the frame structure. The porch roof was sagging, one of its posts buckled out of place. He suspected the rest of the house looked as desolate. The wind, which had abated but little with moonrise, moaned through broken windows.

"Probably just as well we've come at night, Letty. I doubt you'd like the looks of the place in the daytime."

Memories flooded his mind, memories of coming to work here as hired help, of first meeting Letty, of gradually falling in love with her. A tune ran through his brain, a tune she had taught him when they had first known one another and that they had often sung together. He dwelled at length upon the night he had brought her back here after their wedding in town. Life had seemed golden then . . . for a while. But reality had soon intruded. It always did, after so long. It intruded now.

"I'd best be getting' about the business, Letty, just in case Luther Quinton is smarter than I think he is."

The small family cemetery lay halfway up a gentle hillside some three hundred yards above the house. Rocks which the plow had turned up in the field had been hauled to the site to build a small protective fence. Greenleaf dismounted beside the gate and tied the saddle horse to the latchpost. He let the packhorse's rein drop. The brown would not stray away from the sorrel. He untied the rope that bound the diggers to the pack, then unwrapped the pack.

Carefully he lifted down the lard can. He had been amazed at how little it weighed. Letty had never been a large woman, but it had seemed to him that her ashes should represent more weight than this. Carrying the can under one arm and the diggers under the other, he started through the gate.

He had never been of a superstitious nature, but his heart almost stopped when he saw three dark figures rise up from behind the gravestones that marked the resting places of Letty's mother and father. He gasped for breath.

The voice was not that of a ghost. It belonged to Luther Quinton. "Ain't it strange how you can tell some people *no* and they don't put up an argument? Tell others and it seems like they can't even hear you."

The shock lingered, and Greenleaf had trouble getting his voice back. "I guess it's because *no* doesn't always make much sense."

"It don't have to. All that counts is that this place belongs to me, and I don't want you on it, you or that woman of yours either. Lucky for me I set a man to watchin' you in town. He seen you fill that hole back up without puttin' anything in it but dirt."

"Look, Luther, you hurt her enough when she was livin'. At least you could let her rest in peace now. Like the preacher said, she's in no shape to do you any harm. She just wanted to be buried next to her folks. That don't seem like much to ask."

"But it is. You heard her when she laid that curse on me after I took this place. She named a dozen awful things that was fixin' to happen to me, and most of them did. Anybody that strong ain't goin' to quit just because they're dead." Quinton shook his head violently. "I'm tellin' you, she's some kind of an Indian medicine woman. If I was to let you bury her here, I'd never be shed of her. She'd be risin' up out of that grave and hauntin' my every move."

"That's a crazy notion. She never was a medicine woman or anything like that. She wasn't but a quarter Indian in the first place. The rest was white."

"All I know is what she done to me before. I don't aim to let her put a hex on me again."

"You can't watch this place all the time. I can wait. Once she's in the ground, you wouldn't have the guts to dig her up."

"I could find twenty men who'd do it for whiskey money. I'd have them carry her over into the next county and throw her in the river, can and all."

Frustration began to gnaw at Greenleaf. Quinton had him blocked.

Quinton's voice brightened with a sense of victory. "So take her back to town, where you ought to've buried her in the first place. Since you seem to enjoy funerals, you can have another one for her."

"I hope they let me know when *your* funeral takes place, Luther. I'd ride bareback two hundred miles to be here."

Quinton spoke to the two men beside him. "I want you to ride to town with him and be sure he doesn't do anything with that can of ashes. I want him to carry it where you can watch it all the way."

One of the men tied up Greenleaf's pack and lashed the diggers down tightly against it. The other held the can while Greenleaf mounted the sorrel horse, then handed it up to him.

Quinton said, "If I ever see you on my place again, I'm liable to mistake you for a coyote and shoot you. Now git!"

To underscore his order, he drew his pistol and fired a shot under the young sorrel's feet.

That was a bad mistake. The horse bawled in fright and jumped straight up, then alternated between a wild runaway and fits of frenzied pitching in a semicircle around the little cemetery. Greenleaf lost the reins at the second jump and grabbed at the saddlehorn with his left hand. He was handicapped by the lard can, which he tried to hold tightly under his right arm. He did not want to lose Letty.

It was a forlorn hope. The lid popped from the can, and the ashes began streaming out as the horse ran a few strides, then whipped about, pitched a few jumps and ran again. The west wind caught them and carried them away. At last Greenleaf felt himself losing his seat and his hold on the horn. He bumped the rim of the cantle and kicked his feet clear of the stirrups to keep from hanging up. He had the sensation of being suspended in midair for a second or two, then came down. His feet landed hard on the bare ground but did not stay beneath him. His rump hit next, and he went rolling, the can bending under his weight.

It took him a minute to regain his breath. In the moonlight he saw one of Quinton's men chasing after the sorrel horse. The packhorse stood where it had been all along, watching the show with only mild interest.

Quinton's second man came, finally, and helped Greenleaf to his feet. "You hurt?"

"Nothin' seems to be broke except my feelin's." Greenleaf bent down and picked up the can. Most of the ashes had spilled from it. He waited until Quinton approached, then poured out what remained. The wind carried part of them into Quinton's face.

The man sputtered and raged and tried desperately to brush away the ashes.

"Well, Luther," Greenleaf said, "you really done it now. If I'd buried her here, you'd've always known where she was. The way it is, you'll never know where she's at. The wind has scattered her all over the place."

Quinton seemed about to cry, still brushing wildly at his clothing. Greenleaf thrust the bent can into his hand. Quinton made some vague shrieking sound and hurled it away as if it were full of snakes.

The first Quinton man brought Greenleaf his horse. Greenleaf's hip hurt where he had fallen, and he knew it would be giving him unshirted hell tomorrow. But tonight it was almost a good pain. He felt strangely elated as he swung up into the saddle. He reached down for the packhorse's rein.

"This isn't what Letty asked for, but I have a feelin' she wouldn't mind. She'd've liked knowin' that no matter where you go on this place, she'll be there ahead of you. And she won't let you forget it, not for a minute."

Riding away, he remembered the old tune Letty had taught him a long time ago. Oddly, he felt like whistling it, so he did.

Loren D. Estleman is generally considered the best Western writer of his generation. Such novels as *Aces & Eights*, *The Stranglers*, and *Bloody Season* rank with the very best Western novels ever written. As will be seen here, Estleman brings high style to his writing, the sentences things of beauty in and of themselves. Few writers of prose can claim that. He has brought poetry, historical truth, and great wisdom to the genre. His finest short western fiction was collected in *The Best Western Stories of Loren D. Estleman*.

Hell on the Draw

Loren D. Estleman

In the weeks to come there would be considerable debate and some brandishing of weapons over who had been the first to lay eyes on Mr. Nicholas Pitt of Providence; but the fact of the matter is the honor belonged to Ekron Fast, Persephone's only blacksmith. It was he, after all, who replaced the shoe the stranger's great black hammerhead had thrown just outside town, and as everyone who lived there knew, a traveler's first thought upon reaching water or civilization in that dry Huachuca country was his horse. Nor was Pitt's a horse for a former cow man like Ekron to forget.

"Red eyes," he declared to the gang at the Fallen Shaft that Wednesday night in July. "Eighteen—hell, *twenty* hands if he was one, that stud, with nary a speck of any color but black on him except for them eyes. Like burning pipeplugs they was. Feature that."

"Oklahoma Blood Eye." Gordy Wolf, bartender at the Shaft, refilled Ekron's glass from a measured bottle, collected his coin, and made a note of the transaction in the ledger with a gnawed stub of pencil. As a half-breed Crow he couldn't drink, and so the owner required him to keep track of what came out of stock. "I seen it in McAlester. Thisyer dun mare just up and rolled over on the cavalry sergeant that was riding her, snapped his neck like dry rot. Your Mr. Pip better watch that don't happen to him."

"Fermented mash, more 'n likely, both cases." This last came courtesy of Dick Wagner, who for the past eleven years had stopped off at the Shaft precisely at six forty-five for one beer on his way home from the emporium. He chewed sen-sen in prodigious amounts to keep his wife Lucy from detecting it on his breath.

"Pitt, not Pip," said Ekron. "Mr. Nicholas Pitt of Providence. Where's that?"

"East a ways," Wagner said. "Kansas I think."

"He didn't talk like no Jayhawker I ever heard. 'There's a good fellow,' says he, and gives me that there ten-cent piece."

"This ain't no ten-cent piece." Gordy Wolf was staring at the coin Ekron had given him for the drink. It had a wavy edge and had been stamped crooked with the likeness of nobody he recognized. He bit it.

"Might I see it?"

Gordy Wolf now focused his good eye on Professor the Doctor Webster Bennett, late of the New York University classical studies department, more lately of the Brimstone Saloon across the street. The bartender's hesitation did not mean he suspected that the coin would not be returned; he was just unaccustomed to having the good educator conscious at that hour. Professor the Doctor Bennett's white linen and carefully brushed broadcloth had long since failed to conceal from anyone in Persephone that beneath it, at any hour past noon, was a sizeable bag.

Handed the piece, Professor the Doctor Bennett stroked the edge with his thumb, then raised his chin from the bar and studied the coin on both sides, at one point holding it so close to his pinkish right eye he seemed about to screw it in like a monocle. Finally he returned it.

"Roman. Issued, I would say, something after the birth of Christ, and not very long after. The profile belongs to Tiberius."

"It cover Ekron's drink?"

"I rather think it will." He looked at Ekron. "I would hear more of your Mr. Pitt."

"He ain't *my* Mr. Pitt. Anyway I don't much look at folks, just the animals they ride in on. Seen his clothes; fine city ones they was, and a duster. Hogleg tied down on his hip like you read in the nickel novels. And there's something else."

"Gunfighter?" Wagner sat up straight. His greatest regret, aside from having chosen Lucy for his helpmeet, was that he had come West from Louisiana too late to see a real gunfight. The great pistoleers were all dead or gone East to act on the stage. All except one, of course, and he had proved frustrating.

"Or a dude," said Gordy Wolf. "Tenderfoot comes out here, wants everyone to think he's Wild Bill."

Ekron spat, missing the cuspidor by his standard margin. "Forget the damn gun, it don't count. Leastwise not till it goes off. Gordy, you're injun. Man comes in off that desert country up North. Babocomari's dry till September, Tucson's a week's ride, gila and roadrunner's the only game twixt here and Iron Springs. What you figure he's got to have in provisions and truck?"

"Rifle, box of cartridges. Grain for the horse. Bacon for himself and maybe some tinned goods. Two canteens or a skin. That's if he's white. Apache'd do with the rifle and water."

"Well, Mr. Nicholas Pitt of Providence didn't have none of that."

"What you mean, just water?"

"I mean nothing. Not water nor food nor rifle nor even a blanket roll to keep the chill off his *cojones* in the desert at night. Man rides in with just his hip gun and saddle and nary a bead of sweat on man nor mount, and him with nothing behind him but a hunnert miles of sand and alkali." He jerked down his whiskey and looked around at his listeners. "Now, what would you call a man like that, if not the Devil his own self?"

Thus, in addition to having been first to spot the stranger who would mean so much to the town's fortunes, Ekron Fast settled upon him the appelation by which he would be commonly known when not directly addressed. From that time forward, His Own Self, uttered in silent but generally agreed-upon capitals, meant none other and required no illumination.

At the very moment that this unconscious christening was taking place, Guy Dante, manager at the Belial Hotel, was in the throes of a similar demonstration, albeit with somewhat less theater, for his wife. Angel Dante had come in perturbed to have found Dick Wagner gone and the emporium closed and therefore a trip wasted to purchase red ink with which to keep the books. As was his custom, Guy had been bleating on while she unpinned her hat and removed her gloves, and so went unheeded for the crucial first minute of his speech.

". . . registered with no mark like I ever say, and him from his clothes and deportment a city gentleman who should certainly have enjoyed a considerable education," he finished.

"What mark? What gentleman? Oh, Mr. Dante, sometimes I believe you talk sideways just to increase my burden." She tugged on green velvet penwipers for another go at the books.

"Room six. He registered while you were out. I just sent Milton up with water for his bath. Weren't you listening?"

She didn't acknowledge the question. In truth she was slightly hard of hearing and preferred to have people think she was rude rather than advertise the fact that she was seven years older than her husband; a piece of enlightenment that would have surprised many of the town's citizens, who assumed that the difference was much greater. "I don't smell the stove," she said.

"He said cold water would be more than satisfactory. Here's his mark I was telling you about." He shoved the registration book at her.

She seated her spectacles in the dents alongside her nose and examined the two-pronged device scratched deeply into the creamy paper. She ran a finger over it. "It looks like some kind of brand. He must be a cattleman."

"He didn't look like one. What would a cattleman be doing in this country?"

"Perhaps he knows something. Perhaps the railroad is coming and he's here to check out the prospect for shipping beef. Oh, Mr. Dante, why did you give him six? Nine's the president."

"He asked for six."

"Land. I hope you had the presence to have Milton carry up his traps."

"He didn't have any. And he didn't talk like any cattleman either. He asked about the Brimstone. Wanted to know if it's for sale."

"An entrepreneur, in Persephone?" She cast a glance up the stairs, removing her spectacles as if the portly, diamond-stickpinned figure she associated with an entrepreneur might appear on the landing and see them. "Land. He must know something."

"If he does, this town sure isn't it. Nor Ned Harpy. He'd sell his sister before he'd let that saloon go. And for a smaller price to boot."

"Nevertheless we must make him comfortable. Prosperity may be involved."

Dante made that braying noise his wife found distressing. "I hope he tells us when it's fixed to start. Wait till you see what he gave me for the room."

Only the manager's familiar bray rose above the first floor, where Milton heard it on his way to room six. Inside he hung up the fine striped suit he had finished brushing and asked the man splashing behind the screen if he wanted his boots blacked as well. Milton made beds, served meals, and banished dirt and dust from the Belial with an industry that come naturally to the son of a stablehand.

"If you would, lad." The man's whispery voice barely rose above the lapping in the tub. It reminded Milton of a big old rattler shucking its skin. "There something on the bureau for you. Much obliged." Then he laughed, which was worse than when he spoke.

Milton picked up the boots, handsome black ones with butter-soft tops that flopped over and a curious two-pointed design on each one that looked like a cow's hoofprint. They were made of a wonderful kind of leather he had never seen or felt before, as dark as his father's skin. His skin was much lighter than his father's. He knew that some mean folks around town said he wasn't Virgil's son at all, sired as like as not by some unparticular plantation owner—disregarding that Milton was only thirteen and born well after Mr. Lincoln did his duty. Such folks could go to hell.

He got a chill then, in that close room in July in Arizona, and took his mind off it by examining the strange coin he had picked up from the dresser. Confederate pewter, most like. No wonder Mr. Pitt had laughed. Only he didn't think that was the reason. Damn little about strangers made sense—those few that found their way here after the last of the big silver interests had hauled its wagon east—but this one less than most. Where were his possibles? Why weren't his clothes caked and stinking of man and horse, instead of just dusty? And how was it, after Milton had filled the bathtub himself with buckets of water ice-cold from the pump, that steam was rolling out under the screen where the stranger was bathing?

JOSH MARLOWE RODE up from Mexico in the middle of a September rainstorm with water funneling off his hatbrim fore and aft and shining on his back oilskin. Charon's hoofs splashed mud up over his boots and made sucking sounds when they pulled clear. The gray snorted its misery.

Josh concurred. In times past he had preferred entering a town in weather that kept folks indoors. There were some short fuses then who'd throw down on him the second they recognized him but wouldn't later when they had a chance to think of it, making arrivals the most dangerous time in a gunman's experience. But that was before he'd given up the road. Persephone was home, and now that there was no danger he discovered he hated riding in the rain.

Peaceable though he was these days, he clung to his old custom of coming in the back way. He dismounted behind the livery, found the back door locked, stepped back, and kicked it until Virgil opened it from inside. He stood there like always with coal-oil light at his back and his old Colt's Dragoon gleaming in his big black fist.

"Virgil, now many times I tell you to snuff that lantern when a stranger comes?"

The stablehand's barn-door grin shone in the bad light. He stuck the big pistol under his belt. "Balls, Mr. Josh. You ain't no stranger."

Josh left the point short of argument and handed him the reins. "How's Milton?"

"Gettin' uppity. Hotel work's got him thinking he's town folks." He led the gray inside.

The barrel stove was glowing. Josh slung his saddle and pouches over an empty stall and warmed his hands. When he turned to put heat on his backside he spotted the black standing in its stall. He whistled. Reflection from the fire made its eyes look red.

"That there's Mr. Pitt's horse." Virgil began rubbing down Charon with burlap. "You stand clear of that animal, Mr. Josh. He's just plain evil."

"Who might Mr. Pitt be?"

"That's right, you been gone."

"Two months trailing grandee beef to Mexico City. This Pitt with the railroad? Credit won't acquire a mount like that."

"If he is, the railroad done bought the Brimstone. Mr. Pitt, he runs the place now."

"Horseshit. Ned Harpy told me he'd die before he sold out."

"I reckon he wasn't pulling your leg."

Josh saw the stablehand wasn't smiling. "The hell you say."

The black horse reared, screamed, plunged, and kicked its stall. The hammering mingled with a long loud peal of thunder. Even Charon shied from it.

"You see what I mean about that animal," Virgil said, when it had calmed down. "It happened real quick, Mr. Josh. Mr. Ned, he got mad when that Mr. Pitt wouldn't take no as an answer and pulled on him right there in the gameroom. Only Mr. Pitt filled his hand first and just drilled that man full of holes. He was dead when he hit the floor. Mrs. Harpy, she sold out and went back East."

"Ned was fast."

"Near as fast as you." Virgil was grave. "You stay out of the Brimstone, Mr. Josh."

He grinned. "Save that talk for your boy. I gave all that up years ago."

"I hopes so, Mr. Josh. I surely does. You can't beat that man. Nobody can."

From there Josh went to the Fallen Shaft, where he closed the door against the wind and rain and piano music clattering out of the Brimstone. Gordy Wolf was alone. He took his elbows off the bar.

"Josh Marlowe. Gouge out my eyes and pour vinegar in the holes if it ain't. What can I draw you, Josh?"

"Tanglefoot. Where is everybody?" He slapped water off his hat and hooked a heel over the rail.

Gordy Wolf shook his head, poured, and made a mark in the ledger. "You could touch off a Hotchkiss in here since they put the piano in across the street. Nobody'd mind."

"What about Professor the Doctor Webster Bennett? He'd never desert the Shaft."

"He's give up the Creature. Says it don't fit with teaching school."

"That's what the council said when they booted him for falling on his face during sums. Then they closed down the schoolhouse."

"Mr. Pitt bought it and opened it back up. Professor the Doctor ain't got but six pupils and one of them's near as old as him. Way he struts and fluffs his feathers you'd think he's still learning Eyetalian and Greek to them rich men's sons back home."

"This the same Pitt killed Ned Harpy?"

"If there's two I'd hear about it."

"From what Virgil said I didn't take him to be one for the community."

"Before the school he bought the Belial Hotel from Old Man Merry and deeded it to Guy and Angel Dante and then he bought the emporium from Dick Wagner and made him manager at the Brimstone."

"I can't feature Lucy Wagner sitting still for that."

"Lucy went back to New Orleans. She got on worse with Mr. Pitt than she did with Dick. You wouldn't know Dick now. He's got him a red vest and spats."

"What's Pitt's purpose? When the mines played out I gave Persephone five years."

"He told Ekron Fast there's future here. Then he bought him a new forge and an autymobile."

"Ain't no autymobiles twixt here and Phoenix."

"There one now. 'Thisyer's the future I been telling you about,' he says to Ekron. 'Master it.' Ekron run it straight into an arroyo. But he fixed it with his new forge."

"I reckon he's one stranger who's made himself popular," Josh said.

"He's got him an eye for what every man he meets wants more'n any-thing, plus a pocket deep enough to get it for him."

"Except Ned Harpy."

"Nobody much liked Ned anyway. If Mr. Pitt was to run for mayor to-morrow I reckon he'd get everybody's vote but two."

"How is it he ain't throwed his loop over you and Virgil?"

The half-breed put an elbow on the bar and leaned in close enough for Josh to discover that his ledger-keeping had not prevented him from sam-pling the Shaft's stock. "On account of Virgil's a Christian man," he said. "And on account of I ain't. Mr. Pitt, he gets what falls between."

"That's heathen talk."

"It ain't neither. Just because they threwed me out of the mission school after a week don't mean I didn't hear what they had to teach."

Josh drank whiskey. "I got to meet this fellow."

"How long's it been since you wore a pistol?" Gordy Wolf kept his good eye on him.

"Three years."

"You'd best not."

"Talking's all I'm after."

"When your kind meet his kind it don't stop at talking."

"What kind's mine, Christian or Ain't?"

"I seen you struggling with both."

He stopped grinning and drained his glass. "It's a damn shame the mis-sion school didn't keep you, Gordy. You'd of made a right smart preacher."

"Call me what you like. I'm just saying you'd best climb on that gray horse and ride out and forget all about Persephone. That Mr. Pitt is hell on the draw."

Thunder cracked.

TWO MONTHS WAS hardly long enough for the Brimstone to change as much as it had since Josh's last visit. It was one thing to cover the knotty walls with scarlet cloth and take down the prizefighter prints behind the bar to make room for a gilt-framed painting of a reclining naked fat lady holding an apple and laughing; quite another to rip out the old pine bar and replace it with one made from gnarled black oak with what looked like horned evil children carved into the corners. Such items, like the enormous chandelier that now swung from the center rafter, its thousand candles filling the room with oppressive heat, required more time than that to order and deliver. Let alone make, for what catalogue house stocked statuary representing serpents amorously entwined with more naked femininity like the two Amazons thus engaged on either side of the batwing doors?

Mr. Pitt's tastes were apparently not excessive for Persephone's nightlife, however. The main room was packed. Under an awning of lazily turning smoke the drinkers' voices rose above the noise from the piano, where a thickish man in a striped suit and derby was playing something fit to raise blisters on a stump. The strange, fast melody was unknown to Josh, who decided he had been below the border a mite too long.

"Look what the wind blew up from Mexico!"

Gordy Wolf hadn't lied about the spats and red vest. They were accompanied by green silk sleeve garters, a platinum watch chain with a dyed rabbit's-foot fob, and an eastern straw hat tipped forward at such a steep angle the former merchant had to slant his head back to see in front of him.

"Howdy, Dick." Josh sentenced his hand to serious pumping by one heavy with rings.

"What you think of the old place?" Dick Wagner asked. His eyes looked wild and he was grinning to his molars.

"Talks up for itself, don't it?"

"Loud and proud. Lucy'd hate it to death." He roared and clapped a hand on Josh's shoulder. "Keep! Draw one on the house for my gunslinging friend here."

"After I talk to the owner. He around?"

"That's him banging the pianny."

Josh stared at the derbied piano player. He was built like a nailkeg and very fair—a fact that surprised Josh, though he could not own why—and wore jaunty reddish chin-whiskers that put the former gunman in mind of an elf he had seen carved on the door of Irish Mike's hospitable house in St. Louis. As Josh approached him he turned glass-blue eyes on the newcomer. "I'll warrant you're Marlowe." He went on playing the bizarre tune.

"I reckon news don't grow much grass in a town this size."

"Nor does your reputation. I am Nicholas Pitt, originally of Providence. You'll excuse me for not clasping hands."

"It sounds a difficult piece."

"A little composition of my own. But it's not the reason. I only touch flesh with someone when we've reached accord."

Something in Pitt's harsh whisper made Josh grateful for this eccentricity. "I admired your horse earlier this evening."

"Beelzebub? I've had him forever. Ah, thank you, Margaret. Can I interest you in a libation, Marlowe?" He quit playing and accepted a tall glass from a plump girl in a spangled corset. She looked to Josh like one of old Harry Bosch's daughters. He shook his head. Pitt shrugged and drank. A thread of steam rose from the liquid when he lowered it. "I watched you as you came in. You don't approve of the renovations." It was a statement.

"I ain't used to seeing the place so gussy."

"The gameroom is unoccupied. I'll show it to you if you'll mosey in there with me." Laughing oddly, he rose. His coat-frock swayed, exposing briefly the shiny black handle of a Colt's Peacemaker strapped to his hip.

The side room was similarly appointed, with the addition of faro and billiard tables covered in red felt. Milton, the black stablehand's son, sat in the dealer's chair polishing a cuspidor.

"That will be all, lad." Pit tossed him a silver dollar.

Josh laid a hand on Milton's shoulder as he was headed for the door. "Your pa know you're here?"

"No sir. I get a whuppin'. But Mr. Pitt he pays better than the hotel." He lowered his voice. "'Specially since he started paying real money." He left.

"Good lad. But I have hopes for him." Pitt took another sip and set his glass on the billiard table, where it boiled over.

"Who are you?" Josh asked.

"I am a speculator."

"Persephone's past speculating."

"That's where you're wrong, Marlow. My commodity is most plentiful here."

"What's your commodity?"

"Something that is valued by only three in town at present. Milton's father Virgil, because he understands it. The half-breed Gordy Wolf, because he does not possess it. And I."

"What about me?"

"You have been a signal disappointment. When you came to this territory, that item which you are pleased to call yours was more than half mine. Since then you have begun to reclaim it."

"You came to take it back?"

Pitt laughed. It sounded like scales dragging over stone. "You exalt yourself. What is your soul against the soul of an entire town?"

"Then Virge and Gordy was right. You're him."

"Succinctly put. Gary Cooper would be proud."

"Who?"

"Perhaps I should explain myself. But where to start? Aha. Has it ever occurred to you in your wanderings that the people you meet are a tad too colorful, their behavior insufferably eccentric, their language over-folksy? That they themselves are rather—well, *broad*? Half-breed Crows tending bar, drunken college professors, henpecked merchants, gossipy blacksmiths, Negro liverymen who talk as if they just stepped off the plantation—really, where does one encounter these types outside of entertainment?"

"Keep cranking, Mr. Pitt. You ain't drawed a drop yet."

"There. That's just what I mean. Why can't you say simply that you don't follow? I don't suppose you'd understand the concept of alternate earths."

Josh said nothing.

"There is, if you will, a Master Earth, against which all the lesser alternate earths must be measured. Each earth has an equal number of time frames, and it's my privilege to move in and out of these frames among the Master and alternate earths. Now, on Master Earth, the American West within this frame is quite different from the one in which you and I find ourselves. *This* West, with its larger-than-life characters and chivalric codes of conduct, is but a mythology designed for escapist entertainment on Master Earth. That earth's West is a much drearier place. Are you still with me?"

"Sounds like clabber."

"How to put it." Pitt worried a whiskered lip between small ivory teeth. "You were a gunfighter. Were you ever struck by the absurdity of this notion that the faster man in a duel is the moral victor, when the smart way to settle a fatal difference would be to ambush your opponent or shoot him before he's ready?"

"We don't do things that way here."

"Of course not. But on Master Earth they do. Or did. I get my tenses tangled jumping between time frames. In any case being who and what I am, I thought it would be fine sport to do my speculating in this alternate West. The fact that I am mortal here lends a nice edge to those splendid fast-draw contests like the one I enjoyed with Ned Harpy. His soul was already mine when I came here, but I couldn't resist the challenge." He sighed heavily; Josh felt the heat. "I'm aggrieved to say I've found none to compare with it. I'd expected more opposition."

"You talk like you got the town sewed up."

"I bagged the entire council this very afternoon when I promised them they'd find oil if they drilled north of Cornelius Street. The rest is sweepings."

"What do you need with Milton?"

"The souls of children hold no interest for me. But his father's would be a prize. I'm certain a trade can be arranged. Virgil will make an excellent pair of boots when these wear out." He held up a glossy black toe and laughed. Wind and rain lashed the windows, howling like demons.

"You trade often?"

Pitt cocked an eyebrow under the derby. "When the bargain is sufficient. What are you proposing?"

"I hear you're fast against saloonkeepers. How are you with a genuine gunman?"

"Don't be ludicrous. You haven't been in a fight in years."

"You yellowing out?"

Pitt didn't draw; the Peacemaker was just in his hand. Lightning flashed, thunder roared, a windowpane blew in and rain and wind extinguished the lamps in the room. All at once they re-ignited. The Peacemaker was in its holster. Pitt smiled. "What will you use for a gun?"

"I'll get one."

"That won't be necessary." He opened a drawer in the faro table and took out a glistening gray leather gun belt with a slate-handled converted Navy Colt in the holster. "I think you'll find this will fit your hand."

Josh accepted the rig and drew out the pistol. The cylinder was full. "I sold this set in Tucson. How'd you come by it?"

"I keep track of such things. What are the spoils?"

"Me and the town if you win. If I win you ride out on that red-eyed horse and don't come back. Leave the town and everybody in it the way you found them."

"That won't be necessary. In the latter event I'd be as dead as you in the former. In this world, anyway. What is hell for a gunfighter, Marlowe? Eternity on a dusty street where you take on all challengers, your gun hand growing swollen and bloody, never knowing which man you face is your last? I'll see you're kept interested."

"Stop jawing and go to fighting."

Smiling, Pitt backed up several paces, spread his feet, and swept his coatfrock behind the black-handled pistol, setting himself. Josh shot him.

The storm wailed. Pitt staggered back against the billiard table and slid to the floor. Black blood stained his striped vest. The glass-blue eyes were wide. "Your gun was already out! You didn't give me a chance!"

Josh shrugged. "Did you think you were the only one who could travel between worlds?"

Glendon Swarthout wrote a number of highly successful novels, most notably *The Shootist*, that also became a highly successful movie. But he also wrote a number of novels that, while less successful commercially, secured his lasting place in the Western Writers Hall of Fame. *The Shootist* is one of the most important Western novels ever published. It completely destroys, then carefully rebuilds, the myth of the Western gunfighter, and was the perfect vehicle for John Wayne's last movie. The prose is impeccable, as it is in such other Swarthout novels as *They Came to Cordura* and *Skeletons*. An educated man, a professor in fact, he seems to have had a first-rate understanding of the gears and mechanisms of American popular fiction. With *The Shootist*, he demonstrated that he could successfully write literature, as well. Swarthout was born in 1918 and his books reflect the concerns and obsessions of his generation, culminating in the sentimental but well-written novel *Luck and Pluck*.

The Attack on the Mountain

Glendon Swarthout

This is about a general and a petticoat and three squaws and a rat roast and a sergeant and some other soldiers and a mutt dog and an old maid and a message.

The general was Nelson A. Miles. He followed George Crook in charge of the military department of Arizona, in which vast command the Apaches, still feisty in the 80s were accustomed to breaking out of the agencies, stealing horses and cattle, burning ranches, deceasing the settlers, and being beat-all scampish. Tender in the beam, Miles was disinclined to spend much time in the saddle, as Crook had done, preferring to reign over military reviews and fancy-do's in towns with the locals and let the terrain and the latest in tactics conduct his campaign for him.

To this end he scattered his cavalry in troops across that area most pested by the Indians, ready to strike at any raiding band close-range, and also set up the most intricate, cosmographical system of observation and communication ever seen in the West. The finest telescopes and heliographs were obtained from the chief signal officer in Washington. The heliostat consisted of a mirror set on a tripod and covered with a shutter; by means of a lever which alternately removed and interposed the shutter, long or short flashes of light coded out words, the distance depending on the sun's brillance and the clearness of the atmosphere. Infantrymen were trained at

Signal Corps school at Fort Myer, in Virginia, then shipped west and stuck up on peaks so as to form a network. There were twenty-seven stations, not only in Arizona but in New Mexico and even more were eventually added, reaching down into Sonora, Mexico. The entire system covered a zigzag course of over four hundred miles, a part of it being pieced out by telegraph. It was a monument to science and to General Miles' administrative genius, and it was not worth a tinker's damn.

The Apaches took to moving by night. By day they observed the observers, using their own means of communication—fire, smoke, sunlight on a glittering conch shell. They yanked down the telegraph lines, cut them, and spliced them with wet rawhide which dried to look like wire, the cuts then being almost impossible for linemen to detect, thus degutting the system.

But whatsoever General Field Order No. 7 establisheth on April 20th, 1886, at Fort Bowie must endure. The station could at least transmit messages like the following:

RELAY C O FORT HUACHUCA PREPARE POST
INSPECTION AND REVIEW GENL MILES

So much for the general.

On Bill Williams Mountain, five thousand feet up, set on a ledge, there were five men of the 24th Infantry and two mules and a mutt dog. This was the way they passed their time. Sergeant Ammon Swing was in command. He copied the messages sent and received, made sure there was always an eye to the telescope, and allowed himself only the luxury of an occasional think about Miss Martha Cox. Corporal Bobyne had charge of the heliograph. After two weeks training in the code, he worked the shutter with a flourish, youngsterlike. Private Takins cooked. He never bathed, and over the months built up such a singular oniony odor that they said of him he could walk past the pot and season the stew. The guards were Corporal Heintz and Private Mullin. Reckoning to grow potatoes, Heintz, a stubborn Dutchman from Illinois, hoed and hilled at a great rate while the studious Mullin took up botany, cataloging specimens of yucca, nopal, and hediondilla. In their brush corral the two mules tucked back their ears and pondered whom to kick next. Their names were Annie and Grover, the latter after Mr. Cleveland, who was then serving his first term in 1886. The mutt dog chased quail and was in turn hunted by sand fleas, who had better luck.

There was no call for the men to be lonely or the mules mean or the dog to mope. Only six miles away, down in the valley, was Cox's Tanks, a ranch from which water was packed up twice weekly on muleback; only twelve miles off, along the range at a pass, was the Rucker Canyon Station; and only thirty-four miles to the south was Fort Buford, whence supplies were hauled once a month. The five men had high, healthy air to breathe, the goings-on over a hundred square miles of nothing to watch, a branding sun by day and low fierce stars by night.

In addition, they could gossip via heliograph with Rucker:

YOU SEEN ANY PACHES? NOPE   HEINTZ
GROWED ANY TATER YET?   NOPE

But after May and June on Bill Williams Mountain they began to be lorn. In July they commenced talking to themselves more than to each other. One day in August the dog turned his eyes heavenward and ran at full speed toward the top of the mountain and death. Dogs had been known to commit suicide in that way hereabouts.

OUR DOG RUN AWAY
SO DID OURN

So much for the mutt.

When they rousted out one September morning there was smoke columning a few hundred yards down the ledge. Taking Mullin with him, Sergeant Swing went out to reconnoiter, snaking along through the greasewood until they reached a rock formation. What they spied was a mite insulting. They had Apaches on their hands, all right, but squaws instead of braves—three of them, and a covey of kids running about. The ladies had come during the night, built a bungalow of brush and old skins and set up housekeeping. The smoke issued from a stone-lined pit in which they were baking mescal, a species of century plant and a staple of the Apache diet. Ollas and conical baskets were scattered about. The squaws wore calico dresses, which meant they had at one time been on an agency, and one of them was missing the tip of her nose. The whites had not as yet succeeded in arguing the Apache warriors out of their age-old right to snick off a little when they suspected their womenfolk of being unfaithful. But the final indignity was dealt the sergeant when he and Mullin crawled out of the rocks. Two youngsters, who had watched their every move, skittered laughingly back to their mamas.

Apaches or not, they were the station's first real company in six months and the men were glad of them. Sergeant Swing was not. He could not decide if he should start an official message to department headquarters and if he did, how to word it so that he would not sound ridiculous.

While he hesitated young Bobyne shuttered the news to Rucker Canyon anyway:

THREE SQUAWS COME   SARGE
DUNNO WHAT TO DO

The reply was immediate:

HAVE DANCE   INVITE US

When this was decoded, since no one but Bobyne could read Morse, there was general laughter.

"Folderol," the sergeant says.

"You tink dem squaws vill 'tack us?" Heintz asks, winking at the others. "Zhould ve zhoot dem kids?"

Swing ruminated. "You fellers listen. If you expect them desert belles come up to cook and sew for us, your expecter is busted. Where there's squaws there's billy-bound to be bucks sooner or later." He said further that he was posting a running guard at once. He wanted someone on the telescope from sunup to dark. "And here's the gist of it," he concludes. "We will stay shy of them Indians. Nobody to go down there calling, and if they come up here you treat them as kindly as 'rantulas, which they are."

"Dats too ztiff," Heintz protests.

"Sarge, you mean we ain't even to be decent to the kiddies?" complains Mullin.

"Not as you love your mother," is the answer, "and calculate to see her again."

They grudged off to their posts and the sergeant went to sit by a joshua tree and study his predicament. He was more alarmed than he had let on. The news along the system had for two weeks been all bad. The most varminty among the Warm Springs chiefs had left the agency with bands and were raiding to the south—Naiche and Mangas together, Kaytennay by himself. With their example before him, it would be beneath Geronimo's dignity down in Mexico to behave much longer. General Miles had cavalry rumping out in all directions, but there had as yet been neither catch nor kill. He had heard that the first thing sought by the Apaches on breakouts was weapons. What more logical than to camp a few squaws and kids near a heliograph station, cozy up to the personnel, then smite them suddenly with braves, wipe out the sentimental fools and help yourself to rifles and cartridges? Apaches had been known to wait days, even weeks, for their chance. And how was a mere sergeant to control men who had not mingled with humankind for six months?

Had he been an oathing man, Ammon Swing would have. He had in him a sense of duty like a rod of iron. A small compact individual, he wore a buggy-whip mustache which youthened his face and made less New

England his expression. Pushing back his hat, he let his gaze lay out, first at the far mountains on the sides of which the air was white as milk, then lower, at the specks of Cox's Tanks upon the valley floor. This brought to mind Miss Martha Cox, with whom he might be in love and might not. The sister of Jacob Cox, she was a tanned leathery customer as old as the sergeant, which put her nigh on forty-four, too old and sensible for male and female farandoles. She ran the ranch with her brother, plowed with a pistol round her waist, spat and scratched herself like a man, and her reputation with a rifle, after twenty years of raids, caused even the Apaches to give the Cox spread leeway. Swing had seen her five times in six months during his turns to go down with Annie and Grover to pack water. Only once, the last trip, had anything passed between them.

"Ain't you considerable mountain-sore, Mister Swing?"

"Suppose I am," says he.

"Seems to me settling down would be suitable to you."

"Ma'am?"

"Sure," says she. "Marry up and raise a fam'ly and whittle your own stick."

"Too old, Miss Cox."

"Too old?"

"Old as you are," says he.

He knew his blunder when he saw the turkey-red under her tan. She squinted at the mules, then gave him a granite eye.

"Mister Swing, if ever you alter your mind, I know the very one would have you."

"Who, ma'am?"

"Annie," says she.

For the next few days Ammon Swing was much put on. The little Indians soon swarmed over the station, playing games, ingratiating themselves with the soldiers, eventually sitting on their knees to beg for trinkets. Shoo as hard as he might, the sergeant could not put a stop to it. Down the ledge the three squaws went on baking mescal and inevitably there commenced to be visiting back and forth. Takins was the first caught skulking off.

"Takins," says the sergeant, "I told you to stay shy of them."

"I be only humin, Sarge," grumbles the cook, which was doubtful, considering his fragrance.

"You keep off, that's an order!" says Swing, losing his temper. "Or I'll sent you back to Buford to the guardhouse!"

"You will, Sarge?" Takins grins. "Nothin' I'd like better 'n to git off this cussed mountin'!"

Thus it was that the sergeant's authority went to pot and his command to pieces. Men on guard straggled down the ledge to observe the baking and weaving of baskets and converse sociably in sign. The ladies in turn, led by Mrs. Noseless, a powerful brute of a woman, paid daily calls on the station to watch the operation of the heliostat and giggle at the unnatural ways of the whites.

Three days passed. Then a new factor changed the situation on Bill Williams Mountain from absurd to desperate. The supply party from Fort Buford did not arrive. Takins ran entirely out of salt beef and hardtack. Ammon Swing was reduced to swapping with the squaws for mescal, which tasted like molasses candy and brought on the bloat; but the commodity for which the Apaches were most greedy turned out to be castor oil, of which he had only two bottles in his medicine chest. He considered butchering Annie or Grover, but that would mean one less mule to send down to Cox's Tanks for water.

Water! He could not wait on that. But to obtain it, and food as well, would short him by two men. If an attack were ever to come it would come when the station had only three defenders. Worse yet, it was his turn to go down the mountain day after next, his and Takins's, and he wanted very much to go to Cox's again. Why he wanted to so much he would not admit even to himself.

The next morning he traded the last drop of castor oil to the squaws for mescal. In the afternoon the water casks went dry.

At day-die Ammon Swing called Heintz to him and said he was sending him down for water and food with Takins. It was his own turn, but he should stay in case of attack.

The Dutchy puffed his cheeks with pleasure. "Goot. You be zorry."

"Why?"

"I ask dis voman to vedding. I ask before, bud zhe zay no. Dis time zhe zay yez, I tink."

One end of the iron rod of duty in the sergeant stuck in his crop. "Why?" he inquires again.

"I goot farmer. Zhe needs farmer to raunch. Alzo zhe iz nod much young. Nod many chanzes more vill zhe get. You change your mind, Zarge?"

"No," says Ammon Swing.

As soon as Heintz and Takins and Annie and Grover had started down in the morning Sergeant Swing would have bet a month's pay this was the day. Something in the pearl air told him. He ordered Mullin and Bobyne to stand guard near the heliostat and have hands on their weapons at all times. They would change off on the telescope. No man was to leave the sight of the other two.

The morning inched.

They had not had food for twenty-four hours nor water for eighteen. Nor would they until Heintz and Takins returned. The squaws did not come to visit nor the kids to play.

One message winked from Rucker Canyon and was shuttered on:

RELAY GENL MILES REQUESTS
PLEASURE COL AND MRS. COTTON OFFICERS
BALL HEADQUARTERS FT BOWIE 22 AUGUST

By noon they were so thirsty they spit dust and so hungry their bellies sang songs. It had never been so lonesome on Bill Williams Mountain.

Then they had visitors. The three squaws came waddling along the ledge, offspring after them, and surrounded a pile of brush not twenty yards off. In one hand they held long forked sticks and in the other small clubs. Mrs. Noseless started a fire. The soldiers had no notion what the Indians could be up to. When all was ready, the fire burned down to hot coals, the squaws and kids began to squeal and shout and poke into the brush pile. Curious, the soldiers came near.

What they soon saw was that the Apaches had discovered a large convention of field rats. Under the brush the animals cast up a mound of earth by burrowing numerous tunnels. When a stick was thrust into one end of the tunnel, the animal, seeking an escape route, would dart to the opening of another and hesitate for an instant, half in and half out to scan for his enemy. In that split second another Indian would pin the rat down with forked stick, pull it toward him, bash it over the head with his club, and with a shout of triumph eviscerate it with a stroke of the knife and pitch it into the fire. In a trice the hair was burned off, the carcass roasted to a turn, impaled on the stick and the juicy tidbit lifted to a hungry mouth. Starved and horrified, the soldiers were drawn to the banquet despite themselves. There seemed no end to the victuals or the fun.

A little girl ran laughing to Bobyne with a rat. The young man sniffed, tasted, and with a grin of surprise put down his rifle and commenced to feast. Mullin was next served. Then a squaw bore a plump offering to the sergeant. It was done exactly to his liking, medium rare. He could no longer resist. The taste was that of rodent, sort of like the woodchuck he had shot and cooked as a sprout. He had, however, to keep his eyes closed.

What opened them was the terrible silence immediately smashed by a scream.

For an instant as the food fell from his hands he was stricken with shock and fright. The kids vanished. A dying Mullin staggered toward him, screaming. An arrow transfixed his body, driven with such force into his back that it pierced him completely, feathers on one side, head and shaft on the other.

One squaw ran full speed toward the tents to plunder, holding high her grimy calico skirt.

Like deer, three Apache bucks leaped from their hiding place in the greasewood and sped toward him, letting arrows go from bows held at waist level.

Another squaw made for the heliograph and, giving the tripod a kick, toppled the instrument onto rock, shattering the mirror.

An arrow skewered through the fleshy part of Swing's left leg. He cried out with pain and went down on one knee, reaching for his rifle.

Young Bobyne retrieved his and began to blaze away at the oncoming bucks when Mrs. Noseless seized him from behind in powerful arms and hurled him backward into the fire of hot coals as she might have barbecued a rat, kneeling on him and setting his hair afire and bashing in his skull with her club.

Shooting from one knee, Ammon Swing brought down one of the bucks at twenty yards and another point-blank. But it was too late to fire at the third, who swept a long knife upward from a hide boot.

He had only time to glimpse the contorted brown face and yellow eye-balls and hear the death yell as a bullet slammed life and wind out of the Apache and the buck fell heavily upon him. He lay wondering if he were dead, stupified by the fact that the bullet had not been his own.

Then the buck was dragged off him by Miss Martha Cox. She took the Indian's knife, knelt, and slitting the trouser leg began to cut through the arrow shaft on either side of his thigh.

"Soldiers and wimmen," she snorts.

"You shoot him?" he groans.

"Sure."

He asked about Heintz and Takins. Dead, the both of them, she told him—ambushed on the way down. When they had not shown at the ranch, she rode up to find out why.

She had the arrow cut off close to the meat now and bound his leg with shirt cloth. As he sat up she said he would bleed a little; what was danger-ous was the chance of infection, since the Apaches had as much fondness for dirty arrows as they did for dirty everything else. He was to ride her horse down as fast as he could manage. Her brother would have the tools to pull the shaft piece, and water for the wound.

Ammon Swing saw that she wore the best she owned, a long dress of gray taffeta and high-button shoes. When furbished, she was near to hand-some.

"Heintz was intending to ask you to marry."

"I figured it would be you coming down today," says she. "So I got out my fancies. Ain't had them on in ten year."

"Oh?" says he. "Well, help me."

With her arm round his waist he was hobbling toward her horse when he caught the flash from the Mogollon Station, to the south.

"Message." He stopped. "I ain't trained to read it, but it better be put down."

"It better not," says she, bossy.

But he made her fetch pencil and paper from a tent and wait while he transcribed the signals according to length, long and short. When the flashes ceased, he cast a glum look at his own shattered heliograph nearby.

"Ought to relay this," says he. "It's maybe important."

"Mister Swing," says she, "infection won't wait. You army around up here much longer and you might have to make do without a leg."

He did not even hear. He sat down on a boulder and tried to think how the Sam Hill to send the message on to Rucker Canyon. The piece of shaft twinged as though it were alive, the pain poisoning all the way to his toes. There was no other mirror. There was neither pot nor pan bright enough to reflect sun. Miss Martha Cox kept after him about infection, but the more he knew she was right the more dutiful and mule-headed he became. He would not leave with chores undone. Such a stunt would do injustice to his dead. Suddenly he gave a finger snap.

"Making apology, ma'am, but what do you have on beyunder that dress?"

"Well I never!" says she, coloring up real ripe for a woman who had just put down a rifle after a killing.

"Would you please remove same?"

"Oh!" she cries.

The sergeant gave a tug at his buggy whip. "Govermint business, ma'am."

With a female stamp of her foot she obeyed, hoisting the taffeta over her head. Above she wore a white corset cover laced with pink ribbon and below, a muslin petticoat so overstarched it was as stiff and glittering as galvanized tin, touching evidence that it had been a long time since she had made starch.

"We are in luck, ma'am," says he. "We have a clear day and the whitest unspeakabout this side of Heaven, and I calculate they will see us."

Being most gentlemanly, he escorted her near the lip of the ledge facing Rucker Canyon, took her dress and, reading from the paper, began to transmit the message by using her dress as a shutter, shading her with it, then sweeping it away for long and short periods corresponding to the code letters he had transcribed. And all the while poor Miss Martha Cox was forced to stand five thousand feet high in plain sight of half the military department of Arizona, being alternately covered and revealed, a living heliograph, flashing in the sun like an angel descended from above and blushing like a woman fallen forever into sin. When her ordeal and her glory were ended, and Rucker blinked on and off rapidly to signify receipt, she snatched her dress to herself. To his confusion, a tear splashed down one of her leathery cheeks while at the same time she drew up breathing brimstone.

"Ammon Swing," cries she, "no man has ever in all my days set eyes on me in such a state! Either I put my brother on your evil trail or you harden your mind to marrying me this minute!"

"Already have," says he.

Thoughtfully she pulled on the gray taffeta. "We better kiss on it," says she.

"Folderol," says he. But they did.

Then she helped him on her horse and together they went down Bill Williams Mountain.

So much for the petticoat, the three squaws, the rat roast, the sergeant, the other soldiers, and the old maid.

The signals reaching Rucker Canyon Station twelve miles off were less distinct than usual, but by means of the telescope and much cussing they could be deciphered and sent on:

RELAY COL AND MRS. COTTON ACCEPT
WITH PLEASURE OFFICERS BALL
BOWIE 22 AUGUST

So much for the message.

Bill Pronzini has worked in virtually every genre of popular fiction. Though he's best known as the creator of the Nameless mystery novels, he has written several first-rate Westerns, as well as a half-dozen remarkable novels of dark suspense. This is not to slight his western stories at all, with novels such as *Starvation Camp, Quincannon,* and *Firewind* establishing him as a master of the Western. In addition to his novels, Pronzini is an especially gifted short-story writer, several of his pieces winning prestigious awards, including the Shamus.

Fear

Bill Pronzini

He sat with his back to the wall, waiting.

Shadows shrouded the big room, thinned by early daylight filtering in through the plate-glass front window. Beyond the glass he could see Boxelder's empty main street, rain spattering the puddled mud that wagon wheels and horses' hooves had churned into a quagmire. Wind rattled the chain-hung sign on the outer wall: R. J. CABLE. SADDLEMAKER.

Familiar shapes surrounded him in the gloom. Workbenches littered with scraps of leather, mallets, cutters, stamping tools. A few saddles, finished and unfinished—not half as many as there used to be. Wall racks hung with bridles and hackamores, saddlebags and other accessories. Once the tools and accomplishments of his trade had given him pleasure, comfort, a measure of peace. Not anymore. Even the good odors of new leather and beeswax and harness oil had soured in his nostrils.

It was cold in the shop; he hadn't bothered to lay a fire when he had come in at dawn, after another sleepless night. But he took little notice of the chill. He had been cold for a long while now, the kind of gut-cold that no fire can ever thaw.

His hands, twisted together in his lap, were sweating.

He glanced over at the closed door to the storeroom. A seed company calendar was tacked to it—not that he needed a calendar to tell him what day this was. October 26, 1892. The day after Lee Tarbeaux was scheduled to be released from Deer Lodge Prison. The day Tarbeaux would return to Boxelder after eight long years.

The day Tarbeaux had vowed to end Reed Cable's life.

His gaze lingered on the storeroom door a few seconds longer. The shot gun was back there—his father's old double-barreled Remington that he'd brought from home yesterday—propped in a corner, waiting as he was. He thought about fetching it, setting it next to his stool. But there was no need yet. It was still early.

He scrubbed his damp palms on his Levi's, then fumbled in a vest pocket for his turnip watch. He flipped the dustcover, held the dial up close to his eyes. Ten after seven.

How long before Tarbeaux came?

Noon at the earliest; there were a lot of miles between here and Deer Lodge. If he could work, it would make the time go by more quickly . . . but he couldn't. His hands were too unsteady for leathercraft. It would be an effort to keep them steady enough to hold the shotgun when the time came.

A few more hours, he told himself. Just a few more hours. Then it'll finally be over.

He sat watching the rainswept street. Waiting.

IT WAS A quarter past twelve when Lee Tarbeaux reached the outskirts of Boxelder. The town had grown substantially since he'd been away—even more than he'd expected. There were more farms and small ranches in the area, too—parcels deeded off to homesteaders where once there had been nothing but rolling Montana grassland. Everything changes, sooner or later, he thought as he rode. Land, towns, and men, too. Some men.

He passed the cattle pens near the railroad depot, deserted now in the misty rain. He'd spent many a day there when he had worked for Old Man Kendall—and one day in particular that he'd never forget, because it had been the beginning of the end of his freedom for eight long years. Kendall was dead now; died in his sleep in '89. Tarbeaux had been sorry to hear it, weeks after it had happened, on the prison grapevine. He'd held no hard feelings toward the old cowman or his son Bob. The Kendalls were no different from the rest of the people here; they'd believed Cable's lies and that there was a streak of larceny in Tarbeaux's kid-wildness. You couldn't blame them for feeling betrayed. Only one man to blame and that was Reed Cable.

Tarbeaux rode slowly, savoring the chill October air with its foretaste of winter snow. The weather didn't bother him and it didn't seem to bother the spavined blue roan he'd bought cheap from a hostler in the town of Deer Lodge—something of a surprise, given the animal's age and condition. Just went to show that you couldn't always be sure about anybody or anything, good or bad. Except Reed Cable. Tarbeaux was sure Cable was the same man he'd been eight years ago. Bits and pieces of information that had filtered through the prison walls added weight to his certainty.

Some of the buildings flanking Montana Street were familiar: the Boxelder Hotel, the sprawling bulk of Steinmetz Brewery. Many others were not. It gave him an odd, uncomfortable feeling to know this town and yet not know it—to be home and yet to understand that it could never be home again. He wouldn't stay long. Not even the night. And once he left, he'd never come back. Boxelder, like Deer Lodge, like all his foolish kid plans, were part of a past he had to bury completely if he was to have any kind of future.

A chain-hung shingle, dancing in the wind, appeared in the gray mist ahead: R. J. CABLE. SADDLEMAKER. The plate-glass window below the sign showed a rectangle of lamplight, even though there was a "closed" sign in one corner. Tarbeaux barely glanced at the window as he passed, with no effort to see through the water-pocked glass. There was plenty of time. Patience was just one of the things his stay in the penitentiary had taught him. Besides, he was hungry. It had been hours since his meager trailside breakfast.

He tied the roan to a hitch rail in front of an eatery called the Elite Cafe. It was one of the new places; no one there knew or recognized him. He ordered hot coffee and a bowl of chili. And as he ate, he thought about the things that drive a man, that shape and change him for better or worse. Greed was one. Hate was another. He knew all about hate; he'd lived with it a long time. But it wasn't the worst of the ones that ate the guts right out of a man.

The worst was fear.

WHEN CABLE SAW the lone, slicker-clad figure ride by outside, he knew it was Lee Tarbeaux. Even without a clear look at the man's face, shielded by the tilt of a rain hat, he knew. He felt a taut relief. It wouldn't be much longer now.

He extended a hand to the shotgun propped beside his stool. He'd brought it out of the storeroom two hours ago, placed it within easy reach. The sick feeling inside him grew and spread as he rested the weapon across his knees. His damp palms made the metal surfaces feel greasy. He kept his hands on it just the same.

His thoughts drifted as he sat there, went back again, as they so often did these days, to the spring of '84. Twenty years old that spring, him and Lee Tarbeaux both. Friendly enough because they'd grown up together, both of them town kids, but not close friends. Too little in common. Too much spirit in Tarbeaux and not enough spirit in him. Lee went places and did things he was too timid to join in on.

When Tarbeaux turned eighteen he'd gone to work as a hand on Old Man Kendall's K-Bar Ranch. He'd always had a reckless streak and it had widened out over the following two years, thanks to a similar streak in Old Man Kendall's son Bob. Drinking, whoring, a few saloon fights. No serious trouble with the law, but enough trouble to make the law aware of Lee Tarbeaux.

Not a whisper of wildness in Reed Cable, meanwhile. Quiet and steady—that was what everyone said about him. Quiet and steady and honest. He took a position as night clerk at the Boxelder Hotel. Not because he wanted the job; saddlemaking and leather work were what he craved to do with his life. But there were two saddlemakers in town already, and neither was interested in hiring an apprentice. He'd have moved to another town except that his ma, who'd supported them since his father's death, had taken sick and was no longer able to work as a seamstress. All up to him then. And the only decent job he could find was the night clerk's.

Ma'd died in March of that year. One month after Tarbeaux's aunt—the last of his relatives—passed away. And on a day in late April Bob Kendall and Lee Tarbeaux and the rest of the K-Bar crew drove their roundup beeves in to the railroad loading pens. Old Man Kendall wasn't with them: he'd been laid up with gout. Bob Kendall was in charge, but he was a hammerhead as well as half wild: liquor and women and stud poker were all he cared about. Tarbeaux was with him when the cattle buyer from Billings finished his tally and paid off in cash. Seventy-four hundred dollars, all in greenbacks.

It was after bank closing hours by the time the deal was done. Bob Kendall hadn't cared to go hunting Banker Weems to take charge of the money. He wanted a running start on his night's fun, so he turned the chore over to Lee. Tarbeaux made a halfhearted attempt to find the banker, and then his own itch got the best of him. He went to the hotel, where his old friend Reed had just come on shift, where the lobby was otherwise deserted, and laid the saddlebags full of money on the counter.

"Reed," he said without explanation, "do me a favor and put these bags in the hotel safe for tonight. I or Bob Kendall'll be back to fetch 'em first thing in the morning."

It was curiosity that made him open the bags after Tarbeaux left. The sight of all that cash weakened his knees, dried his mouth. He put the saddlebags away in the safe, but he couldn't stop thinking about the money. So many things he could do with it, so many ambitions he could make a reality. A boldness and a recklessness built in him for the first time. The money grew from a lure into a consuming obsession as the hours passed. He might've been able to overcome it if his mother had still been alive, but he was all alone—with no prospects for the future and no one to answer to but himself.

He took the saddlebags from the safe an hour past midnight. Took them out back of the hotel stables and hid them in a clump of buck brush. Afterward he barely remembered doing it, as if it had all happened in a dream.

Bob Kendall came in alone at eight in the morning, hung over and in mean spirits, just as the day clerk arrived to serve as a witness. There was a storm inside Reed Cable, but outwardly he was calm. Saddlebags? He didn't know anything about saddlebags full of money. Tarbeaux hadn't been in last evening, no matter what he claimed. He hadn't seen Lee in more than two weeks.

In a fury Bob Kendall ran straight to the sheriff, and the sheriff arrested Tarbeaux. The hardest part of the whole thing was facing Lee, repeating the lies, and watching the outraged disbelief in Tarbeaux's eyes turn to blind hate. But the money was all he let himself think about. The money, the money, the money. . . .

It was his word against Tarbeaux's, his reputation against Tarbeaux's. The sheriff believed him, the Kendalls believed him, the townspeople believed him—and the judge and jury believed him. The verdict was guilty, the sentence a minimum of eight years at hard labor.

Tarbeaux had made his vow of vengeance as he was being led from the courtroom. "You won't get away with this, Reed!" he yelled. "You'll pay and pay dear. As soon as I get out I'll come back and make sure you pay!"

The threat had shaken Cable at the time. But neither it nor his conscience had bothered him for long. Tarbeaux's release from Deer Lodge was in the far future; why worry about it? He had the money, he had his plans—and when one of the town's two saddlemakers died suddenly of a stroke, he soon realized the first of his ambitions.

CABLE SHIFTED POSITION on the hard stool. That was then and this was now, he thought bitterly. The far future had become the present. Pain moved through his belly and chest; a dry cough racked him. He sleeved sweat from his eyes, peered again through the front window. A few pedestrians hurried by on the west sidewalk; none was Lee Tarbeaux.

"Come on," he said aloud. "Come on, damn you, and get it over with!"

TARBEAUX FINISHED HIS meal, took out the makings, and rolled a smoke to savor with a final cup of coffee. Food, coffee, tobacco—it all tasted good again, now that he was free. He'd rushed through the first twenty years of his life, taking everything for granted. And he'd struggled and pained his way through the last eight, taking nothing for granted. He'd promised himself that when he got out he'd make his remaining years pass as slowly as he could, that he'd take the time to look and feel and learn, and that he'd cherish every minute of every new day.

He paid his bill, crossed the street to Adams Mercantile—another new business run by a stranger—and replenished his supplies of food and tobacco. That left him with just three dollars of his prison savings. He'd have to settle someplace soon, at least long enough to take a job and build himself a stake. After that . . . no hurry, wherever he went and whatever he did. No hurry at all.

First things first, though. The time had come to face Reed Cable.

He felt nothing as he walked upstreet to where the chain-hung sign rattled and danced. It had all been worked out in his mind long ago. All that was left was the settlement.

Lamplight still burned behind the saddlery's window. Without looking through the glass, without hesitation, Tarbeaux opened the door and went in under a tinkling bell.

Cable sat on a stool at the back wall, an old double-barreled shotgun across his knees. He didn't move as Tarbeaux shut the door behind him. In the pale lamp glow Cable seemed small and shrunken. His sweat-stained skin was sallow, pinched, and his hands trembled. He'd aged twenty years in the past eight—an old man before his thirtieth birthday.

The shotgun surprised Tarbeaux a little. He hadn't figured on a willingness in Cable to put up a fight. He said as he took off his rain hat, "Expecting me, I see."

"I knew you'd come. You haven't changed much, Lee."

"Sure I have. On the inside. Just the opposite with you."

"You think so?"

"I know so. You fixing to shoot me with that scattergun?"

"If you try anything I will."

"I'm not armed."

"Expect me to believe that?"

Tarbeaux shrugged and glanced slowly around the shadowed room. "Pretty fair leather work," he said. "Seems you were cut out to be a saddlemaker, like you always claimed."

"Man's got to do something."

"That's a fact. Only thing is, he ought to do it with honest money."

"All right," Cable said.

"You admitting you stole the K-Bar money, Reed? No more lies?"

"Not much point in lying to you."

"How about the sheriff and Bob Kendall? Ready to tell them the truth, too—get it all off your chest?"

Cable shook his head. "It's too late for that."

"Why?"

"I couldn't face prison, that's why. I couldn't stand it."

"I stood it for eight years," Tarbeaux said. "It's not so bad, once you get used to it."

"No. I couldn't, not even for a year."

"Man can be in prison even when there's no bars on his windows."

Cable made no reply.

"What I mean, it's been a hard eight years for you, too. Harder, I'll warrant, than the ones I lived through. Isn't that so?"

Still no reply.

"It's so," Tarbeaux said. "You got yourself this shop and you learned to be a saddlemaker. But then it all slid downhill from there. Starting with Clara Weems. You always talked about marrying her someday, having three or four kids—your other big ambition. But she turned you down when you asked for her hand. Married that storekeeper in Billings, instead."

The words made Cable's hands twitch on the shotgun. "How'd you know that?"

"I know plenty about you, Reed. You proposed to two other women: they wouldn't have you, either. Then you lost four thousand dollars on bad mining stock. Then one of your horses kicked over a lantern and burned down your barn and half your house. Then you caught consumption and were laid up six months during the winter of '90 and '91—"

"That's enough," Cable said, but there was no heat in his voice. Only a kind of desperate weariness.

"No, it's not. Your health's been poor ever since, worsening steadily, and there's nothing much the sawbones can do about it. How much more time do they give you—four years? Five?"

"Addled, whoever told you that. I'm healthy enough. I've got a long life ahead of me."

"Four years—five, at the most. *I'm* the one with the long life ahead. And I aim to make it a good life. You remember how I could barely read and write? Well, I learned in prison and now I can do both better than most. I learned a trade, too. Blacksmithing. One of these days I'll have my own shop, same as you, with my name on a sign out front bigger than yours."

"But first you had to stop here and settle with me."

"That's right. First I have to settle with you."

"Kill me, like you swore in court you'd do. Shoot me dead."

"I never swore that."

"Same as."

"You think I still hate you that much?"

"Don't you?"

"No," Tarbeaux said. "Not anymore."

"I don't believe that. You're lying."

"You're the liar, Reed, not me."

"You want me dead. Admit it—you want me dead."

"You'll be dead in four or five years."

"You can't stand to wait that long. You want me dead here and now."

"No. All I ever wanted was to make sure you paid for what you did to me. Well, you're paying and paying dear. I came here to tell you to your face that I know you are. That's the only reason I came, the only settlement I'm after."

"You bastard, don't fool with me. Draw your gun and get it over with."

"I told you, I'm not armed."

Cable jerked the scattergun off his knees, a gesture that was meant to be provoking. But the muzzle wobbled at a point halfway between them, held there. "Make your play!"

Tarbeaux understood then. There was no fight in Cable; there never had been. There was only fear. He said, "You're trying to *make* me kill you. That's it, isn't it? You want me to put you out of your misery."

It was as if he'd slapped Cable across the face. Cable's head jerked; he lurched to his feet, swinging the Remington until its twin muzzles were like eyes centered on Tarbeaux's face.

Tarbeaux stood motionless. "You can't stand the thought of living another five sick, hurting years, but you don't have the guts to kill yourself. You figured you could goad me into doing it for you."

"No. Make your play or I'll blow your goddamn head off!"

"Not with that scattergun. It's not loaded, Reed. We both know that now."

Cable tried to stare him down. The effort lasted no more than a few seconds; his gaze slid down to the useless shotgun. Then, as if the weight of the weapon was too much for his shaking hands, he let it fall to the floor, kicked it clattering under one of the workbenches.

"Why?" he said in a thin, hollow whisper. "Why couldn't you do what you vowed you'd do? Why couldn't you finish it?"

"It is finished," Tarbeaux said.

And it was, in every way. Now he really was free—of Cable and the last of his hate, of the past. Now he could start living again.

He turned and went out into the cold, sweet rain.

CABLE SLUMPED AGAIN onto his stool. Tarbeaux's last words seemed to hang like a frozen echo in the empty room.

It is finished.

For Tarbeaux, maybe it was. Not for Reed Cable. It wouldn't be finished for him for a long, long time.

"Damn you," he said, and then shouted the words. "Damn you!" But they weren't meant for Lee Tarbeaux this time. They were meant for himself.

He kept on sitting there with his back to the wall.

Waiting.

Peggy S. Curry (1911–1987) wrote the kind of quiet Western stories that escaped the attention of all but a few practiced eyes. It seems that every generation produces a number of excellent writers who are never quite given their proper due or recognition. Her slight body of work, most of which appeared in such slick magazines as *The Saturday Evening Post* and *Collier's,* fell somewhere between traditional Western fiction and main-stream literature. Her literary influences seemed to run more to Willa Cather and Katherine Anne Porter that to any Western writers. Curry was born in Ayrshire, Scotland, and this influence can also be felt in her work. Readers are encouraged to read any of her fourteen or so other stories, especially "In the Silence," which is one of the true masterpieces of American literature.

Geranium House

Peggy Simson Curry

We heard about them long before we saw them. News traveled fast in those days even though we didn't have telephones in the valley. Old Gus, the mailman, gave us the full report. "They come in from Laramie in a two-wheeled cart," he said, "him ridin' and her walking' beside the cart and the old sway-bellied horse pullin' it. That cart was mostly filled with plants, and she was carrying one in her arms, just like most women carry a baby."

"Where they going to live?" my uncle Rolfe asked.

"They moved into that old homestead shack on the flats," Gus said. "Been there since the Indians fired the west range, that shack. Used to belong to a man named Matt but he died a spell ago, and I guess they're welcome to it." He sucked on the end of his drooping brown mustache and added, "Him now, he don't look like he'd be much—his pants hangin' slack and his shoulders humped worsen my granddad's. But her! You'd have to see her, Rolfe. What she's got ain't anything a man could put words to."

As soon as Gus finished his coffee and started back to town in his buggy, my mother mixed a batch of bread. "We'll take over a couple of loaves and a cake," she said. "A woman deserves better than that dirt-roofed cabin on the flats."

My uncle Rolfe stood looking out the kitchen window. He was big and handsome in a wild, blackheaded way. He was always splitting his shirts and popping off buttons, and he never cared what he had on or how it fitted.

Uncle Rolfe came to live with us and take over part of the ranch when my father died, and you'd never have thought he was my mother's brother, for she was small and neat and had pale brown hair.

"Anne," Uncle Rolfe said, "I wouldn't be in a hurry to rush over and welcome a couple of squatters. We don't know anything about them and they don't come from much when they have to put up in a dead man's shack on the flats. What's more, they won't stay long."

The color flew high in my mother's cheeks. "You don't understand about a woman," she said. "You don't know how much it helps to have a friend of her own kind in this big lonesome country. You've been a bachelor too long to see a woman's side of things, Rolfe Annister."

"Well," he said, "I aim to leave them alone."

But the next morning when we were ready to go, Uncle Rolfe got in the buggy. "Won't hurt me to meet them, I guess." Then he turned to me and smiled. "Billy, you want to drive this morning?"

I was thirteen that spring morning in the mountain country, and nothing ever sounded better than the clop-clop of the horses' hooves and the singing sound of the buggy wheels turning along the dirt road. The meadowlarks were whistling and Uncle Rolfe began humming under his breath, the way he did sometimes when the sky was soft and the grass coming green.

It was six miles to the homesteader's cabin and we were almost there before we saw it, for it sat low on the flat land among the sagebrush and was the same silver-gray color. The river ran past it but there weren't any trees along the water, only a few scrubby willows still purple from the fall, for they hadn't leafed out yet.

First thing we noticed was the color in the windows of the old cabin, big blossoms of red and pink and white. My mother stepped out of the buggy and stared. "Geraniums!" she exclaimed. "I never saw anything so beautiful!"

The two-wheeled cart was beside the door and so old and bleached it might have been part of the land. And we saw the horse picketed in the sagebrush. Like Gus had said, he was a pack of bones with a belly slung down like a hammock.

My mother carefully carried her box with the cake and bread to the front door and knocked. She was wearing her new gloves, the ones Uncle Rolfe had bought her in Denver when he shipped the cattle.

The door opened slowly and all I saw that first moment was the woman's eyes, big and dark and shining. She was young and her hair was so blond it looked almost white and was drawn back tight until it made her eye seem larger and blacker. She was brown-skinned and tall and she looked strong. Her dress was clean but so worn my mother would have used it for a rag.

"I'm Anne Studer," My mother said. "We're your neighbors. This is my brother, Rolfe, and my son, Billy."

The woman seemed to forget my mother and Uncle Rolfe. She bent over and put her hand on my head and smiled down into my face. "Billy," she said, and her hand stroked my head and I could feel she loved me, for the warmth came right out of her hand.

She asked us to come in and then I saw the bed on the floor near the stove and the man there in the blankets. His face was thin and gray and he sat up coughing. "Sam," she said, "we've got company—our neighbors."

He didn't try to get up but just lay there, and I thought how terrible it was he didn't have any bunk or bedstead, only the floor under him. Then he smiled at us and said, "The trip was too much for me, I guess. We've come a long way. Melora, will you put on the coffee?"

The woman went to the old stove that had pools of velvety-looking rust on the lids and she set a small black pot on it and filled the pot with water from the bucket. Her arms were soft and rounded but strong lifting the bucket.

No one said anything for a few moments and I could hear a rustling that seemed to come from all the corners of the room.

"You've got lots of mice," my uncle Rolfe said.

Melora smiled at him. "I know. And we forgot to bring traps."

Mother looked around and drew her skirts close to her, her mouth pinching into a thin line. I saw her touch the shiny lid of a tin can with her toe. The can lid was nailed over a hole in the rotting wooden floor.

Melora cut the cake, saying what a beautiful cake it was, and glancing at my mother, who still had that tight look on her face. Then she poured coffee into two battered tin cups and three jelly glasses. "Billy," she said to me, "if I'd been expecting you, I'd surely have fixed lemonade and put it in the river to cool." She stroked my head again and then walked over to one of the geraniums and I could see her fingers busy among the leaves. Her hands moved so softly and quietly in the plant that I knew she was loving it just as she had loved me when she touched me.

We didn't stay long and Melora walked to the buggy with us. She shook my mother's hand and said, "You were good to come. Please come back soon—and please bring Billy."

Driving home, my mother was silent. Uncle Rolfe finally said, "I knew we shouldn't go there. Makes a man feel low in his mind to see that. He's half dead, and how are they going to live?"

"I'm going to ride over with mousetraps," I said. "I'll set them for her."

My mother gave me a strange look. "You're not going alone," she said firmly.

"No," my uncle Rolfe said. "I'll go with him."

A few nights later we rode to the house on the flats and Uncle Rolfe set twelve mousetraps. Sam was in bed and Melora sat on an old spike keg, her hands folded in her lap. We'd just get started talking when a trap would go off and Uncle Rolfe would take it outside, empty it, and set it again.

"Sam's asleep now," Melora said. "He sleeps so much—and it's just as well. The mice bother him."

"Isn't there any other place you can go?" Uncle Rolfe asked, a roughness in his voice. "You can't live off this land. It won't grow anything but sagebrush."

"No, we haven't any other place to go," Melora replied, and her strong shoulders sagged. "We've no kin and Sam needs this climate. I've got more plants coming from Missouri—that's where we used to live. I'll sell my geraniums. We'll manage—we always have."

She walked out in the night with us when we were leaving. She put her arm around me and held me hard against her. "So young," she said, "so alive—I've been around death a long time. Sam—look at Sam. And our babies died. We had two. And now, now I'll never have another child—only the geraniums." Her voice broke and I knew she was crying. Her arms swept me closer and there was something about the way she clung to me that made me hurt inside.

"Come on, Billy," Uncle Rolfe said gruffly. I pulled away from Melora and got my horse. I could still hear her sobbing as we rode away.

We were riding quietly in the dark when my uncle Rolfe began to talk to himself, as though he'd forgotten I was there. "Beautiful," he said, "and needing a strong red-blooded man to love her. Needing a child to hold in her arms—and there she is, tied to *him*. Oh Lord, is it right?"

A week later my uncle Rolfe wrapped a piece of fresh beef in a white sack and rode off toward the flats. My mother watched him go, a frown on her forehead. Then she said to me. "Billy, you bring in the milk cows at five o'clock. I don't think your uncle Rolfe will be back by then."

The next morning I saw a pink geranium on the kitchen table and a piece of brown wrapping paper beside it. On the paper was written in strong sloping letters, "For Anne from Melora."

It wasn't long till everybody in the valley spoke of the cabin on the flats as "Geranium House." On Sundays, before the haying season started, the ranchers drove out in their buggies and they always went past the cabin on the flats. The women stopped to admire the flowers and usually bought one or two plants. They told my mother how beautiful Melora was and how kind—especially to the children.

"Yes," my mother would say and get that pinched look about her mouth.

One morning in early August when Gus brought the mail, he told us

Melora had been driving all over the valley in the cart, selling geraniums and visiting with the women. "And she's got a new horse to pull the cart," he said, "a big black one."

That afternoon my mother saddled her horse and taking me with her went riding through the horse pasture. "I'm looking for the black gelding," she said. "Seems to me I haven't noticed him around lately."

We rode until sundown but we didn't find the gelding. I said he might have jumped the fence and gotten out on the range or into one of the neighbor's pastures.

"Yes," she said, frowning. "I suppose he could have."

She asked Uncle Rolfe about the black gelding and Uncle Rolfe let on like he didn't hear her. "Well," my mother said tartly, "there's such a thing as carrying goodwill toward your neighbors too far."

"You haven't," he said angrily. "You never bothered to go back. And she must be lonely and tired of looking at a sick man every day."

"She hasn't returned my call," my mother said, her chin in the air. "I'm not obligated to go there again. Besides, there's something about her—the way she looks at Billy—"

"You've forgotten, Anne, what it is to hunger for love, for a child to be part of you—for a man's arms around you in the night."

Tears came into my mother's eyes. "No, Rolfe! I haven't forgotten. But I've got Billy—and when I saw her eyes and her hands on the geraniums—Rolfe, it isn't that I don't like her. It's—it hurts me to be around her."

Uncle Rolfe put his hand on her shoulder. "I'm sorry, Anne, I shouldn't have said a word."

"If she comes here," my mother said, "I'll make her welcome, Rolfe."

And then one warm morning I saw the two-wheeled cart driving up in front of the house, and I saw that the horse pulling it was our black gelding.

"Billy!" Melora called to me. "How are you, Billy?" And she got out of the cart and put her arms around me and I could feel the warmth coming from her body and covering me like a wool blanket in winter.

My mother came to the door and asked Melora in. "How's Sam?" she said.

Melora put her hand to her eyes as though she wanted to brush something away. She was thinner than when I'd last seen her and her eyes burned bigger and brighter in her face that now had the bones showing under the fine-tanned skin. But still she looked strong, the way a wire is tight and strong before it breaks. "Sam," she said, "Sam's all right. As good as he'll ever be. It's a weakness, a sickness born in him—as it was in our babies. Anne, I didn't know Sam was a sick man when I married him. He never told me."

Uncle Rolfe came in with his black hair looking wilder than usual. The color burned in Melora's cheeks and her eyes lighted. "Hello, Rolfe," she said, "and thank you for being so kind to Sam."

"That's all right," Uncle Rolfe said gruffly.

"I went to town to see the minister," Melora said, still looking at Uncle Rolfe. "I asked him to find me a baby I could adopt—like you suggested. He said 'no.'"

"He did!" Uncle Rolfe sounded shocked.

"He said I had nothing to take care of a baby," Melora went on. "He said I had my hands full now. I begged him to help me, but he just sat there with a face like stone and said it wasn't my lot in life to have a child."

"The fool!" Uncle Rolfe muttered.

My mother set food on the table and asked Melora to stay and eat with us.

Melora shook her head. "I'm going home and fix something for Sam. He can't eat much this hot weather but I tell him he must try. And he gets so lonesome when I'm gone."

My uncle Rolfe went out and helped her into the cart. He stood for a long time looking down the road after she left.

Two weeks later we saw the buggy of Gus, the mailman, coming up the road. It wasn't the day for bringing mail. The horses were running and a big cloud of dust rose behind the buggy. My mother and I stepped onto the porch just as Uncle Rolfe rode in from the haying field with a piece of machinery across the saddle in front of him. My uncle Rolfe dismounted and waited for Gus. The buggy rattled to a stop. The horses were panting and sweating, for it was a hot morning.

"Melora's taken Sadie Willard's baby," Gus said, "and drove off with it."

"Oh no!" My mother twisted her hands.

"Happened a little while ago," Gus said. "Sadie went to feed the chickens and when she came back she saw Melora's cart going over the hill in front of the house. She thought that was strange. She went in the house and looked everywhere and the baby was gone. She sent the sickle grinder to the hay field after Jim and just as I left Jim come in and said he'd get the neighbors and they'd go after Melora. It's a terrible thing and Jim's about crazy and Sadie sittin' cryin' like her heart would break."

Uncle Rolfe looked at my mother. "Anne, you take the lunch to the meadow at noon for our hay hands. Billy, you come with me." He jammed his big hat lower on his black head and we started for the barn.

The heat waves shimmered all around us on the prairie as we rode toward Geranium House. When we got there our horses were covered with lather, but there wasn't any sign of the cart or Melora. Everything looked still and quiet and gray except for the flowers blooming in the windows and around the outside of the cabin.

Uncle Rolfe pushed the door open and Sam was propped up on some pillows, reading an old newspaper. There were two bright spots of color in his thin cheeks. "Hello, Rolfe," he said. "Thought you'd be making hay."

"Where's Melora?" Uncle Rolfe asked.

"Melora? She left me a lunch and said she was going to drive up to the timber and get some water lilies. A lily pond she found awhile ago, I guess. I don't know where it is, though."

"I do," Uncle Rolfe said.

"Folks are lookin' for her," I said, my voice rising with excitement. "I bet they're goin' to—" Uncle Rolfe's big hand covered my mouth and he shoved me toward the door.

"What's wrong?" Sam said. "Has something happened to Melora?" And his face twisted like he was going to cry.

"No," Uncle Rolfe said gently, "nothing's wrong with Melora. You just take it easy, Sam."

It took us awhile to reach the timber, for it was so hot we couldn't crowd the horses and there was no wind moving to cool things off. The smell of pines was thick, almost clogging my nose, and I could see big thunderclouds building up behind the mountains.

I didn't know where the pond was but Uncle Rolfe rode right to it. It was a small pond and very smooth, with the blue dragonflies hanging over the yellow lilies. Uncle Rolfe got off his horse and I followed. He took a few steps and stopped, staring.

There sat Melora under an aspen tree, holding the baby against her breast and her eyes closed and her mouth smiling. She didn't look like any ordinary woman sitting there. She looked like the pictures of saints they have in Sunday school books.

Uncle Rolfe said, "Melora—"

She opened her eyes and looked at us. Then she said in a small frightened voice. "I only wanted to have him a little while to myself—to feel him in my arms. I meant no harm to him." She got up then, holding the baby carefully. "He's asleep and don't you bother him."

"They're looking for you," Uncle Rolfe said. "Melora, you shouldn't have done this. The women will never be your friends again."

Melora bowed her head and began to cry. The sun came through the trees and made her hair shine until it looked like a halo. "I only wanted to hold him," she said. "I only wanted to have him in my arms a little while."

"Hush!" Uncle Rolfe said roughly. "Where's the cart?"

"I hid it in the trees."

Then Uncle Rolfe took hold of her arm and said to me, "You bring the horses, Billy."

Melora cried all the way through the timber until we reached the cart. Then she sat stiff and quiet, holding the baby. I rode along behind, leading Uncle Rolfe's horse.

When we got to the cabin on the flats there were several buggies and saddle horses there, and men were standing by the front door, their faces dark and angry. Inside the cabin I could hear Sam shouting hoarsely, "She meant no harm, I tell you! She's good, a good woman with no mean thing in her!"

Uncle Rolfe took the baby and gave it to Sadie's husband, Jim Willard, and the baby wakened and started to cry. Jim Willard stared at Melora, his face ugly. "You get outta this country!" he shouted. "We've got no place for baby stealers in the valley. If you ain't gone by tomorrow night, I'll burn this shack to the ground!"

Melora shrank back, pressed against the wheel of the cart, her eyes filled with a terrible look of pain and her lips moving but no word coming out. The men began to mutter and shift restlessly and someone said, "Why don't we load their stuff and start 'em out of the valley now?"

Jim Willard kicked at one of the geranium plants that sat beside the cabin door. His big boot ground the blossom into the dirt. Melora gave a little cry and covered her face with her hands.

"That's enough, Jim!" Uncle Rolfe's voice was cold. He moved to stand close to Melora, his shaggy black head lifted, his fists clenched. "You men go home and leave her be. She's got no other place to go and her man's sick. I'll take care of things. I'll be responsible for her—and for him, too."

One of the men moved forward toward Melora, and Uncle Rolfe's big hand grabbed him and shoved him aside, spinning him away like a toy man. There was some arguing then but Uncle Rolfe stood silent with that fierce look in his eyes. After awhile the men got on their horses and in their buggies and went away. Melora walked slowly into the house and we could hear Sam half crying as he spoke her name, and then her voice, soft and warm, "I'm here, Sam. Now don't you fret. Sleep now, and when you waken I'll have supper ready."

"Come on, Billy," Uncle Rolfe said. His voice sounded old and tired. We rode slowly toward home.

It was black that night in the mountain country, black and sultry, the window curtains hanging motionless. When I went to bed it was too hot to sleep and I could hear thunder rumbling in the distance. Lightning began to play through the house, flashing streaks of blue and red, and I heard my uncle Rolfe moving in the bedroom next to mine. I heard his boots on the floor and then his steps going to the kitchen and a door closing. I got out of bed and ran through the dark house and when the lightning flared again, I saw my uncle Rolfe walking toward the barn. A little later, when the lightning glowed so bright it made me shiver, I saw my uncle Rolfe ride past the window, his hat pulled low on his black head. He was headed toward the flats.

I was awake a long time, for it was hard to sleep with the thunder getting close and loud and the lightning popping all around. When the storm broke I got up again and closed the door of Uncle Rolfe's room. A little later my mother came into the kitchen and lighted the lamp and heated some milk for us to drink. We sat close together in the kitchen until the storm went over and a cool wet wind began to blow through the house.

I never knew when Uncle Rolfe got home that night but the next morning he was at the breakfast table. And all the rest of the summer he didn't ride toward the flats again.

It was far into fall and I was going to country school when Gus came one Saturday morning and brought my mother two large red geranium plants with the penciled message on brown wrapping paper. "To Anne with love, from Melora."

"Pretty," Gus said. "Never did see such geraniums as are in that house now. And Melora, she's bloomin' like the flowers."

Uncle Rolfe put down the local paper he'd just started to open and turned to look at Gus.

"Yes sir," Gus went on, "she always was a woman a man had to look at more than once, but now she's downright beautiful. Sam, he's not much better. Might be he'd die tomorrow and might be he'd live a few years yet. Never can tell about things like that. And I guess if he did die, somebody'd look out for a woman like Melora."

"I expect so," my mother said, pouring coffee for Gus.

"The Lord's favored her, make no mistake about that," Gus went on, "for she's going to have that baby she's been hankerin' for. The women, they've all forgive her for what she did and been up there with baby clothes and buyin' her geraniums again." Gus sighed and sucked at the end of his drooping brown mustache. "Only the Lord's doing would give a woman a baby when she needed it so bad and didn't have but a shell of a man to love her."

My mother lifted her head and stared at my uncle Rolfe, a strange softness in her eyes and around her mouth. My uncle Rolfe looked back at my mother and it seemed to me they said a lot of things to each other without speaking a word. Then my uncle Rolfe opened the local paper and began to read the news.

Every aficionado of Western fiction has his or her opinion as to the finest story ever written about the Old West. It is safe to say, though, that not a few of them would cast their votes for Eugene Manlove Rhodes's (1869–1934) brilliant novella *"Pasó por Aquí,"* first published in 1927. He has been called "The connoisseur's Western writer," and indeed his fiction is not only superb entertainment but of high literary merit as well. If *"Pasó por Aquí"* is the standout among his longer works, *The Proud Sheriff*, *Stepsons of Light*, and *Copper Streak Trail* are not far behind; and of his shorter works, "The Trouble Man" certainly ranks as one of the best.

The Trouble Man

Eugene Manlove Rhodes

Billy Beebe did not understand. There was no disguising the unpalatable fact: Rainbow treated him kindly. It galled him. Ballinger, his junior in Rainbow, was theme for ridicule and biting jest, target for contumely and abuse; while his own best efforts were met with grave, unfailing courtesy.

Yet the boys liked him; Billy was sure of that. And so far as the actual work was concerned, he was at least as good a roper and brand reader as Ballinger, quicker in action, a much better rider.

In irrelevant and extraneous matters—brains, principle, training, acquirements—Billy was conscious of unchallenged advantage. He was from Ohio, eligible to the presidency, of family, rich, a college man; yet he had abandoned laudable moss-gathering, to become a rolling bounding, riotous stone. He could not help feeling that it was rather noble of him. And then to be indulgently sheltered as an honored guest, how beloved soever! It hurt.

Not for himself alone was Billy grieved. Men paired on Rainbow. "One stick makes a poor fire"—so their word went. Billy sat at the feet of John Wesley Pringle—wrinkled, wind-brown Gamaliel. Ballinger was the disciple of Jeff Bransford, gay, willful, questionable man. Billy did not like him. His light banter, lapsing unexpectedly from Broad Doric to irreproachable New English, carried in solution audacious, glancing disrespect of convention, established institutions, authorities, axioms, "accepted theories of irregular verbs"—too elusive for disproof, too intolerably subversive to be ignored. That Ballinger, his shadow, was accepted man of action, while

Billy was still an outsider, was, in some sense, a reflection on Pringle. Vicarious jealousy was added to the pangs of wounded self-love.

Billy was having ample time for reflection now, riding with Pringle up the Long Range to the Block roundup. Through the slow, dreamy days they threaded the mazed ridges and canyons falling eastward to the Pecos from Guadalupe, Sacramento, and White Mountain. They drove their string of thirteen horses each; rough circlers, wise cutting horses, sedate night horses and patient old Steamboat, who, in the performance of pack duty, dropped his proper designation to be injuriously known as "the Wagon."

Their way lay through the heart of the Lincoln County War country— on winding trails, by glade and pine-clad mesa; by clear streams, bell-tinkling, beginning, with youth's eager haste, their journey to the far-off sea; by Seven Rivers, Bluewater, the Feliz, Penasco, and Silver Spring.

Leisurely they rode, with shady halt at midday—leisurely, for an empire was to be worked. It would be months before they crossed the divide at Nogal, "threw in" with Bransford and Ballinger, now representing Rainbow with the Bar W, and drove home together down the west side.

While Billy pondered his problem Pringle sang or whistled tirelessly— old tunes of amazing variety, ranging from Nancy Lee and Auld Robin Gray to La Paloma Azul or the Nogal Waltz. But ever, by ranch house or brook or pass, he paused to tell of deeds there befallen in the years of old war, deeds violent and bloody, yet half redeemed by hardihood and un-flinching courage.

Pringle's voice was low and unemphatic; his eyes were ever on the long horizon. Trojan nor Tyrian he favored, but as he told the Homeric tale of Buckshot Roberts, while they splashed through the broken waters of Rui-doso and held their winding way through the cutoff of Cedar Creek, Billy began dimly to understand.

Between him and Rainbow the difference was in kind, not in degree. The shadow of old names lay heavy on the land; these resolute ghosts yet shaped the acts of men. For Rainbow the Roman *virtus* was still the one virtue. Whenever these old names had been spoken, Billy remembered, men had listened. Horseshoers had listened at their shoeing; card-players had listened while the game went on; by campfires other speakers had ceased their talk to listen without comment. Not ill-doers, these listeners, but quiet men, kindly, generous; yet the tales to which they gave this trib-ute were too often of ill deeds. As if they asked not "Was this well done?" but rather "Was this done indeed—so that no man could have done more?" Were the deed good or evil, so it were done utterly it commanded admiration—therefore imitation.

Something of all this he got into words. Pringle nodded gravely. "You've got it sized up, my son," he said. "Rainbow ain't strictly up-to-date and still holds to them elder ethics, like Norval on the Grampian Hills,

William Dhu Tell, and the rest of them neck-or-nothing boys. This Mr. Rolando, that Eusebio sings about, give our sentiment to a T-Y-ty. He was some scrappy and always blowin' his own horn, but, by jings, he delivered the goods as per invoice and could take a major league lickin' with no whimperin'. This Rolando he don't hold forth about gate money or individual percentages. 'Get results for your team,' he says. 'Don't flinch, don't foul, hit the line hard, here goes nothing!'

"That's a purty fair code. And it's all the one we got. Pioneerin' is troublesome—pioneer is all the same word as pawn, and you thrown away a pawn to gain a point. When we drive in a wild bunch, when we top off the boundin' bronco, it may look easy, but it's always a close thing. Even when we win we nearly lose; when we lose we nearly win. And that forms the stay-with-it-Bill-you're-doin'-well habit. See?

"So, we mostly size a fellow up by his abilities as a trouble man. Any kind of trouble—not necessarily the fightin' kind. If he goes the route, if he sets no limit, if he's enlisted for the war—why, you naturally depend on him.

"Now, take you and Jeff. Most ways you've got the edge on him. But you hold by rules and formulas and laws. There's things you must do or mustn't do—because somebody told you so. You go into a project with a mental reservation not to do anything indecorous or improper; also, to stop when you've taken a decent lickin'. But Jeff don't aim to stop while he can wiggle; and he makes up new rules as he goes along, to fit the situation. Naturally, when you get in a tight place you waste time rememberin' what the authorities prescribe as the neat thing. Now, Jeff consults only his own self, and he's mostly unanimous. Mebbe so you both do the same thing, mebbe not. But Jeff does it first. You're a good boy, Billy, but there's only one way to find out if you're a square peg or a round one."

"How's that?" demanded Billy, laughing, but half vexed.

"Get in the hole," said Pringle.

"Aw, stay all night! What's the matter with you fellows? I haven't seen a soul for a week. Everybody's gone to the roundup."

Wes' shook his head. "Can't do it, Jimmy. Got to go out to good grass. You're all eat out here."

"I'll side you," said Jimmy decisively. "I got a lot of stored-up talk I've got to get out of my system. I know a bully place to make camp. Box canyon to hobble your horses in, good grass, and a little tank of water in the rocks for cookin'. Bring along your little old wagon, and I'll tie on a hunk o' venison to feed your faces with. Get there by dark."

"How come you didn't go to the work your black self?" asked Wes' as Beebe tossed his rope on the wagon and let him up.

Jimmy's twinkling eyes lit up his beardless face. "They left me here to play shinny-on-your-own-side," he explained.

"Shinny?" echoed Billy.

"With the Three Rivers sheep," said Jimmy. "I'm to keep them from crossing the mountain."

"Oh, I see. You've got an agreement that the east side is for cattle and the west side for sheep."

Jimmy's face puckered. "Agreement? H'm, yes, least ways, I'm agreed I didn't ask them, but they've got the general idea. When I ketch 'em over here I drive them back. As I don't ever follow 'em beyond the summit they ought to savvy my the'ries by this time."

Pringle opened the gate. "Let's mosey along—they've got enough water. Which way, kid?"

"Left-hand trail," said Jimmy, falling in behind.

"But why don't you come to an understanding with them and fix on a dividing line?" insisted Beebe.

Jimmy lolled sidewise in his saddle, cocking an impish eye at his inquisitor. "Reckon ye don't have no sheep down Rainbow way? Thought not. Right there's the point exactly. They have a dividing line. They carry it with 'em wherever they go. For the cattle won't graze where sheep have been. Sheep pertects their own range, but we've got to look after ours or they'd drive us out. But the understanding's all right, all right. They don't speak no English, and I don't know no *paisano* talk, but I've fixed up a signal code they savvy as well's if they was all college aluminums."

"Oh, yes—sign talk," said Billy. "I've heard of that." Wes' turned his head aside.

"We-ell, not exactly. Sound talk'd be nearer. One shot means 'Git!' two means 'Hurry up!' and three—"

"But you've no right to do that," protested Billy, warmly. "They've got just as much right here as your cattle, haven't they?"

"Surest thing they have—if they can make it stick," agreed Jimmy cordially. "And we've got just as much right to keep 'em off if we can. There ain't really no right to it. It's Uncle Sam's land we both graze on, and Unkie is some busy with conversation on natural resources, and keepin' republics up in South America and down in Asia, and selectin' texts for coins and infernal revenue stamps, and upbuildin' Pittsburgh, and keepin' up the price of wool and fightin' all the time to keep the laws from bein' better 'n the Constitution, like a Bawston puncher trimmin' a growin' colt's foot down to fit last year's shoes. Shucks! *He* ain't got no time to look after us. We just got to do our own regulatin' or git out."

"How would you like it yourself?" demanded Billy.

Jimmy's eyes flashed. "If my brain was to leak out and I subsequent took to sheep herdin', I'd like to see any dern puncher drive me out," he declared belligerently.

"Then you can't complain if—"

"He don't," interrupted Pringle. "None of us complain—nary a mur-

mur. If the sheep men want to go they go, an' a little shootin' up the con-
tagious vicinity don't hurt 'em none. It's all over oncet the noise stops. Besides, I think they mostly sorter enjoy it. Sheep herdin' is mighty dull
business, and a little excitement is mighty welcome. It gives 'em something
to look forward to. But if they feel hostile they always get the first shot for
keeps. That's a mighty big percentage in their favor, and the reports on file
with the War Department shows that they generally get the best of it.
Don't you worry none, my son. This ain't no new thing. It's been goin' on
ever since Abraham's outfit and the LOT boys got to scrappin' on the Jordan range, and then some before that. After Abraham took to the hill
country, I remember, somebody jumped one of his wells and two of
Isaac's. It's been like that, in the short-grass countries ever since. Human
nature's not changed much. By Jings! There they be now!"

Through the twilight the winding trail climbed the side of a long ridge.
To their left was a deep, impassable canyon; beyond that a parallel ridge;
and from beyond that ridge came the throbbing, drumming clamor of a
sheep herd.

"The son of a gun!" said Jimmy. "He means to camp in our box canyon.
I'll show him!" He spurred by the grazing horses and clattered on in the
cad, striking fire from the stony trail.

On the shoulder of the further ridge heaved a gray fog, spreading,
rolling slowly down the hillside. The bleating, the sound of myriad tram-
pling feet, the multiplication of bewildering echoes, swelled to a steady, un-
changing, ubiquitous tumult. A dog suddenly topped the ridge; another;
then a Mexican herder bearing a long rifle. With one glance at Jimmy beyond the blackshadowed gulf he began turning the herd back, shouting to
the dogs. They ran in obedient haste to aid, sending the stragglers scurry-
ing after the main bunch.

Jimmy reined up, black and gigantic against the skyline. He drew his
gun. Once, twice, thrice, he shot. The fire streamed out against the growing dark. The bullets, striking the rocks, whined spitefully. The echoes took
up the sound and sent it crashing to and fro. The sheep rushed huddling
together, panic-stricken. Herder and dogs urged them on. The herder
threw up a hand and shouted.

"That boy's shootin' might close to that *paisano*," muttered Pringle.
"He orter quit now. Reckon he's showin' off a leetle." He raised his voice
in warning. "Hi! You Jimmy!" he called. "He's agoin'! Let him be!"

"*Vamos! Hi-i!*" shrilled Jimmy gaily. He fired again. The Mexican
clapped hand to his leg with an angry scream. With the one movement he
sank to his knees, his long rifle fell to a level, cuddled to his shoulder, spitting fire. Jimmy's hand flew up. His gun dropped; he clutched at the saddle
horn, missed it, fell heavily to the ground. The Mexican dropped out of
sight behind the ridge. It had been but a scant minute since he first

appeared. The dogs followed with the remaining sheep. The ridge was bare. The dark fell fast.

Jimmy lay on his face. Pringle turned him over and opened his shirt.

He was quite dead.

FROM MALAGRA TO Willow Spring, the next available water, is the longest jump on the Bar W range. Working the "Long Lane" fenced by Malpais and White Mountain is easy enough. But after cutting out and branding there was the long wait for the slow day herd, the tedious holding to water from insufficient troughs. It was late when the day's "cut" was thrown in with the herd, sunset when the bobtail had caught their night horses and relieved the weary day herders.

The bobtail moves the herd to the bed ground—some distance from camp, to avoid mutual annoyance and alarm—and holds it while night horses are caught and supper eaten. A thankless job, missing the nightly joking and banter over the day's work. Then the first guard comes on and the bobtail goes, famished, to supper. It breakfasts by starlight, relieves the last guard, and holds cattle while breakfast is eaten, beds rolled and horses caught, turning them over to the day herders at sunup.

Bransford and Ballinger were two of the five bobtailers, hungry, tired, dusty, and cross. With persuasive, soothing song they trotted around the restless cattle, with hasty, envious glances for the merry groups around the chuck wagon. The horse herd was coming in; four of the boys were butchering a yearling; beds were being dragged out and unrolled. Shouts of laughter arose; they were baiting the victim of some mishap by making public an exaggerated version of his discomfiture.

Turning his back on the camp, Jeff Bransford became aware of a man riding a big white horse down the old military road from Nogal way. The horse was trotting, but wearily; passing the herd he whinnied greeting, again wearily.

The cattle were slow to settle down. Jeff made several circlings before he had time for another campward glance. The horse herd was grazing off, and the boys were saddling and staking their night horses; but the stranger's horse, still saddled, was tied to a soapweed.

Jeff sniffed. "Oh, Solomon was sapient and Solomon was wise!" he crooned, keeping time with old Summersault's steady fox trot. "And Solomon was marvelously wide between the eyes!" He sniffed again, his nose wrinkled, one eyebrow arched one corner of his mouth pulled down; he twisted his mustache and looked sharply down his nose for consultation, pursing his lips. "H'm! That's funny!" he said aloud. "That horse is some tired. Why don't he turn him loose? Bransford, you old fool, sit up and take notice! 'Eternal vigilance is the price of liberty.'"

He had been a tired and a hungry man. He put his weariness by as a garment, keyed up the slackened strings, and rode on with every faculty on the alert. It is to be feared that Jeff's conscience was not altogether void of offense toward his fellows.

A yearling pushed tentatively from the herd. Jeff let her go, fell in after her, and circled her back to the bunch behind Clay Cooper. Not by chance. Clay was from beyond the divide.

"Know the new man, Clay?" Jeff asked casually, as he fell back to preserve the proper interval.

Clay turned his head. "Sure. Clem Littlefield, Bonita man."

When the first guard came at last Jeff was on the farther side and so the last to go in. A dim horseman overtook him and waved a sweeping arm in dismissal.

"We've got 'em! Light a rag, you hungry man!"

Jeff turned back slowly, so meeting all the relieving guard and noting that Squatty Robinson, of the V V, was not of them, Ollie Jackson taking his place.

He rode thoughtfully into camp. Staking his horse in the starlight he observed a significant fact. Squatty had not staked his regular night horse, but Alizan, his favorite. He made a swift investigation and found that not a man from the east side had caught his usual night horse. Clay Cooper's horse was not staked, but tied short to a mesquite, with the bridle still on.

Pete Johnson, the foreman, was just leaving the fire for bed. Beyond the fire the east-side men were gathered, speaking in subdued voices. Ballinger, with loaded plate, sat down near them. The talking ceased. It started again at once. This time their voices rose clear and distinct in customary bandiage.

"Why, this is face up," thought Jeff. "Trouble. Trouble from beyond the divide. They're going to hike shortly. They've told Pete that much, anyhow. Serious trouble—for they've kept it from the rest of them. Is it to my address? Likely. Old Wes' and Beebe are over there somewhere. If I had three guesses the first two'd be that them Rainbow chasers was in a tight."

He stumbled into the firelight, carrying his bridle, which he dropped by the wagon wheel. "This day's sure flown by like a week," he grumbled, fumbling around for cup and plate. "My stomach was just askin' was my throat cut."

As he bent over to spear a steak the tail of his eye took in the group beyond and intercepted a warning glance from Squatty to the stranger. There was an almost imperceptible thrusting motion of Squatty's chin and lips; a motion which included Jeff and the unconscious Ballinger. It was enough. Surmise, suspicion flamed to certainty. "My third guess," reflected Jeff sagely, "is just like the other two. Mr. John Wesley Pringle has been doing a running high jump or some such stunt, and has plumb neglected to come down."

He seated himself cross-legged and fell upon his supper vigorously, bandying quips and quirks with the bobtail as they ate. At last he jumped up, dropped his dishes clattering in the dishpan, and drew a long breath.

"I don't feel a bit hungry," he announced plaintively. "Gee! I'm glad I don't have to stand guard. I do hate to work between meals." He shouldered his roll of bedding. "Good-bye, old world—I'm going home!" he said, and melted into the darkness. Leo following, they unrolled their bed. But as Leo began pulling off his boots Jeff stopped him.

"Close that aperture in your face and keep it that way," he admonished guardedly. "You and me has got to do a ghost dance. Project around and help me find them Three Rivers men."

The Three Rivers men, Crosby and Os Hyde, were sound asleep. Awakened, they were disposed to peevish remonstrance.

"Keep quiet!" said Jeff. "Al, you slip on your boots and go tell Pete you and Os is goin' to Carrizo and that you'll be back in time to stand your guard. Tell him out loud. Then you come back here and you and Os crawl into our bed. I'll show him where it is while you're gone. You use our night horses. Me and Leo want to take yours."

"If there's anything else don't stand on ceremony," said Crosby. "Don't you want my toothbrush?"

"You hurry up," responded Jeff. "D'ye think I'm doin' this for fun? We're It. We got to prove an alibi."

"Oh!" said Al.

A few minutes later, the Three Rivers men disappeared under the tarp of the Rainbow bed, while the Rainbow men, on Three Rivers horses, rode silently out of camp, avoiding the firelit circle.

Once over the ridge, well out of sight and hearing from camp, Jeff turned up the draw to the right and circled back toward the Nogal road on a long trot.

"Beautiful night," observed Leo after an interval. "I just love to ride. How far is it to the asylum?"

"Leo," said Jeff, "you're a good boy—a mighty good boy. But I don't believe you'd notice it if the sun didn't go down till after dark." He explained the situation. "Now, I'm going to leave you to hold the horses just this side of the Nogal road, while I go on afoot and eavesdrop. Them fellows'll be makin' big medicine when they come along here. I'll lay down by the road and get a line on their play. Don't you let them horses nicker."

Leo waited an interminable time before he heard the eastside men coming from camp. They passed by, talking, as Jeff had prophesied. After another small eternity Jeff joined him.

"I didn't get all the details," he reported. "But it seems that the Parsons City People has got it framed up to hang a sheepman some. Wes' is dead set against it—I didn't make out why. So there's a deadlock and we've got the casting vote. Call up your reserves, old man. We're due to ride around Nogal and beat that bunch to the divide."

It was midnight by the clock in the sky when they stood on Nogal divide. The air was chill. Clouds gathered blackly around Capitan, Nogal Peak, and White Mountain. There was steady, low muttering of thunder; the far lightnings flashed pale and green and rose.

"Hustle along to Lincoln, Leo," commanded Jeff, "and tell the sheriff they state, positive, that the hangin' takes place prompt after breakfast. Tell him to bring a big posse—and a couple of battleships if he's got 'em handy. Meantime, I'll go over and try what the gentle art of persuasion can do. So long! If I don't come back the mule's yours."

He turned up the right-hand road.

"WELL?" SAID PRINGLE.

"Light up!" said Uncle Peter. "Nobody's goin' to shoot at ye from the dark. We don't do business that way. When we come we'll come in daylight, down the big middle of the road. Light up. I ain't got no gun. I come over for one last try to make you see reason. I knowed thar weren't use talking' to you when you was fightin' mad. That's why I got the boys to put it off till mawnin'. And I wanted to send to Angus and Salado and the Bar W for Jimmy's friends. He ain't got no kinnery here. They've come. They all see it the same way. Chavez killed Jimmy, and they're goin' to hang him. And, since they've come, there's too many of us for you to fight."

Wes' lit the candle. "Set down. Talk all you want, but talk low and don't wake Billy," he said as the flame flared up.

That he did not want Billy waked up, that there was not even a passing glance to verify Uncle Pete's statement as to being unarmed, was, considering Uncle Pete's errand and his own position, a complete and voluminous commentary on the men and ethics of that time and place.

Pete Burleson carefully arranged his frame on a bench, and glanced around.

On his cot Billy tossed and moaned. His fevered sleep was tortured by a phantasmagoria of broken and hurried dreams, repeating with monsterous exaggeration the crowded hours of the past day. The brain-stunning shock and horror of sudden, bloody death, the rude litter, the night-long journey with their awful burden, the doubtful aisles of pine with star galaxies wheeling beyond, the gaunt, bare hill above, the steep zigzag to the sleeping town, the flaming wrath of violent men—in his dream they came and went. Again, hasty messengers flashed across the haggard dawn; again, he shared the pursuit and capture of the sheepherder. Sudden clash of unyielding wills; black anger; wild voices for swift death, quickly backed by wild, strong hands; Pringle's cool and steady defiance; his own hot,

resolute protest; the prisoner's unflinching fatalism; the hard-won respite—
all these and more—the lights, the swaying crowd, fierce faces black and
bitter with inarticulate wrath—jumbled confusedly in shifting, unsequenced
combinations leading ever to some incredible, unguessed catastrophe.

Beside him, peacefully asleep, lay the manslayer, so lately snatched from
death, unconscious of the chain that bound him, oblivious of the menace
of the coming day.

"He takes it pretty hard," observed Uncle Pete, nodding at Billy.

"Yes. He's never seen any sorrow. But he don't weaken one mite. I tried
every way I could think of to get him out of here. Told him to sidle off
down to Lincoln after the sheriff. But he was dead on to me."

"Yes? Well, he wouldn't 'a' got far, anyway," said Uncle Pete dryly.
"We're watching every move. Still, it's a pity he didn't try. We'd 'a' got him
without hurtin' him, and he'd 'a' been out o' this."

Wes' made no answer. Uncle Pete stroked his grizzled beard reflectively.
He filled his pipe with cut plug and puffed deliberately.

"Now, look here," he said slowly. "Mr. Procopio Chavez killed Jimmy,
and Mr. Procopio Chavez is going to hang. It wa'n't no weakenin' or
doubt on my part that made me call the boys off yesterday evenin'. He's
got to hang. I just wanted to keep you fellers from gettin' killed. There
might 'a' been some sense in your fighting then, but there ain't now.
There's too many of us."

"Me and Billy see the whole thing," said Wes', unmoved. "It was too
bad Jimmy got killed, but he was certainly mighty brash. The sheepherder
was goin' peaceable, but Jimmy kept shootin', and shootin' close. When
that splinter of rock hit the Mexican man he thought he was shot, and he
turned loose. Reckon it hurt like sin. There's a black-and-blue spot on his
leg big as the palm of your hand. You'd 'a' done just the same as he did.

"I ain't much enthusiastic about sheepherders. In fact, I jerked my gun
at the time; but I was way down the trail and he was out o' sight before I
could shoot. Thinkin' it over careful, I don't see where this Mexican's got
any hangin' comin'. You know, just as well as I do, no court's goin' to hang
him on the testimony me and Billy's got to give in."

"I do," said Uncle Pete. "That's exactly why we're goin' to hang him
ourselves. If we let him go it's just encouragin' the *pastores* to kill up some
more of the boys. So we'll just stretch his neck. This is the last friendly
warnin', my son. If you stick your fingers between the anvil and the hammer you'll get 'em pinched. 'Tain't any of your business, anyway. This ain't
Rainbow. This is the White Mountain and we're strictly home rulers. And,
moresoever, that war talk you made yisterday made the boys plumb sore."

"That war talk goes as she lays," said Pringle steadily. "No hangin' till after the shootin'. That goes."

"Now, now—what's the use?" remonstrated Uncle Pete. "Ye'll just get yourself hurted and 'twon't do the greaser any good. You might mebbe so stand us off in a good, thick 'dobe house, but not in this old shanty. If you want to swell up and be stubborn about it, it just means a grave apiece for you all and likely for some few of us."

"It don't make no difference to me," said Pringle, "if it means diggin' a grave in a hole in the cellar under the bottomless pit. I'm goin' to make my word good and do what I think's right."

"So am I, by Jupiter! Mr. Also Ran Pringle, it is a privilege to have known you!" Billy, half awake, covered Uncle Pete with a gun held in a steady hand. "Let's keep him here for a hostage and shoot him if they attempt to carry out their lynching," he suggested.

"We can't, Billy. Put it down," said Pringle mildly. "He's here under flag of truce."

"I was tryin' to save your derned fool hides," said Uncle Pete benignantly.

"Well—'tain't no use. We're just talkin' round and round in a circle, Uncle Pete. Turn your wolf loose when you get ready. As I said before, I don't noways dote on sheepmen, but I seen this, and I've got to see that this poor devil gets a square deal. I got to!"

Uncle Pete sighed. "It's a pity!" he said. "A great pity! Well, we're comin' quiet and peaceful. If there's any shootin' done you all have got to fire the first shot. We'll have the last one."

"Did you ever stop to think that the Rainbow men may not like this?" inquired Pringle. "If they're anyways dissatisfied they're liable to come up here and scratch your eyes out one by one."

"Jesso. That's why you're goin' to fire the first shot," explained Uncle Pete patiently. "Only for that—and likewise because it would be a sorter mean trick to do—we could get up on the hill and smoke you out with rifles at long range, out o' reach of your six-shooters. You all might get away, but the sheepherder's chained fast and we could shoot him to kingdom come, shack and all, in five minutes. But you've had fair warnin' and you'll get an even break. If you want to begin trouble it's your own lookout. That squares us with Rainbow."

"And you expect them to believe you?" demanded Billy.

"Believe us? Sure! Why shouldn't they?" said Uncle Pete simply. "Of course they'll believe us. It'll be so." He stood up and regarded them wistfully. "There don't seem to be any use o' sayin' any more, so I'll go. I hope there ain't no hard feelin's?"

"Not a bit!" said Pringle, but Billy threw his head back and laughed angrily. "Come, I like that! By Jove, if that isn't nerve for you! To wake a man up and announce that you're coming presently to kill him, and then to expect to part the best of friends!"

"Ain't I doin' the friendly part?" demanded Uncle Pete stiffly. He was both nettled and hurt. "If I hadn't thought well of you fellers and done all I could for you, you'd 'a' been dead and done forgot about it by now. I give you all credit for doin' what you think is right, and you might do as much for me."

"Great Caesar's ghost! Do you want us to wish you good luck?" said Billy, exasperated almost to tears. "Have it your own way, by all means— you gentle-hearted old assassin! For my part, I'm going to do my level best to shoot you right between the eyes, but there won't be any hard feeling about it. I'll just be doing what I think is right—a duty I owe to the world. Say! I should think a gentleman of your sportsmanlike instincts would send over a gun for our prisoner. Twenty to one is big odds."

"Twenty to one is a purty good reason why you could surrender without no disgrace," rejoined Uncle Pete earnestly "You can't make nothin' by fightin', cause you lose your point, anyway. And then, a majority of twenty to one—ain't that a good proof that you're wrong?"

"Now, Billy, you can't get around that. That's your own argument," cried Pringle, delighted. "You've stuck to it right along that you Republicans was dead right because you always get seven votes to our six. *Nux vomica*, you know."

Uncle Pete rose with some haste. "Here's where I go. I never could talk politics without gettin' mad," he said.

"Billy, you're certainly making good. You're a square peg. All the same, I wish," said Wes' Pringle plaintively, as Uncle Pete crunched heavily through the gravel, "that I could hear my favorite tune now."

Billy stared at him. "Does your mind hurt your head?" he asked solicitously.

"No, no—I'm not joking. It would do me good if I could only hear him sing it."

"Hear who sing what?"

"Why, hear Jeff Bransford sing 'The Little Eohippus'—right now. Jeff's got the knack of doing the wrong thing at the right time. Hark! What's that?"

It was a firm footstep at the door, a serene voice low chanting:

> *There was once a little animal*
> *No bigger than a fox,*
> *And on five toes he scampered—*

"Good Lord!" said Billy. "It's the man himself."

Questionable Bransford stepped through the half-open door, closed it, and set his back to it.

"That's my cue! Who was it said eavesdroppers never heard good of themselves?"

. . .

HE WAS SMILING, his step was light, his tones were cheerful, ringing. His eyes had looked on evil and terrible things. In this desperate pass they wrinkled to pleasant, sunny warmth. He was unhurried, collected, confident. Billy found himself wondering how he had found this man loud, arbitrary, distasteful.

Welcome, question, answer; daybreak paled the ineffectual candle. The Mexican still slept.

"I crawled around the opposition camp like a snake in the grass," said Jeff. "There's two things I observed there that's mightily in our favor. The first thing is, there's no whiskey goin'. And the reason for that is the second thing—and our one best big chance. Mister Burleson won't let 'em. Fact! Pretty much the entire population of the Pecos and tributary streams had arrived. Them that I know are mostly bad actors, and the ones I don't know looked real horrid to me; but your Uncle Pete is the bell mare. 'No booze!' he says, liftin' one finger; and that settled it. I reckon that when Uncle Simon Peter says 'Thumbs up!' those digits'll be elevated accordingly. If I can get him to see the gate the rest will only need a little gentle persuasion."

"I see you persuading them now," said Billy. "This is a plain case of the irresistible force and the immovable body."

"You will," said Jeff confidently. "You don't know what a jollier I am when I get down to it. Watch me! I'll show you a regular triumph of mind over matter."

"They're coming now," announced Wes' placidly. "Two by two, like the animals out o' the ark. I'm glad of it. I never was good at waitin'. Mr. Bransford will now oblige with his monologue entitled 'Givin' a bull the stop signal with a red flag.' Ladies will kindly remove their hats."

It was a grim and silent cavalcade. Uncle Pete rode at the head. As they turned the corner Jeff walked briskly down the path, hopped lightly on the fence, seated himself on the gatepost, and waved an amiable hand.

"Stop, look, and listen!" said this cheerful apparition.

The procession stopped. A murmur, originating from the Bar W contingent, ran down the ranks. Uncle Pete reined up and demanded of him with marked disfavor: "Who in merry hell are you?"

Jeff's teeth flashed white under his brown mustache. "I'm Ali Baba," he said, and paused expectantly. But the allusion was wasted on Uncle Pete. Seeing that no introduction was forthcoming, Jeff went on: "I've been laboring with my friends inside, and I've got a proposition to make. As I told Pringle just now, I don't see any sense of us getting' killed, and killin' a lot of you won't bring us alive again. We'd put up a pretty fight—a very pretty fight. But you'd lay us out sooner or later. So what's the use?"

"I'm mighty glad to see someone with a leetle old horse sense," said

Uncle Pete. "Your friends is dead game sports all right, but they got mighty little judgment. If they'd only been a few of us I wouldn't 'a' blamed 'em a might for not givin' up. But we got too much odds of 'em."

"This conversation is taking an unexpected turn," said Jeff, making his eyes round. "I ain't named giving up that I remember of. What I want to do is to rig up a compromise."

"If there's any halfway place between a hung Mexican and a live one," said Uncle Pete, "mebbe we can. And if not, not. This ain't no time for triflin', young fellow."

"Oh, shucks! I can think of half a dozen compromises," said Jeff blandly. "We might play seven-up and not count any turned-up jacks. But I was thinking of something different. I realize that you outnumber us, so I'll meet you a good deal more than halfway. First, I want to show you something about my gun. Don't anybody shoot, 'cause I ain't going to. Hope I may die if I do!"

"You will if you do. Don't worry about that," said Uncle Pete. "And mebbe so, anyhow. You're delayin' the game."

Jeff took this for permission. "Everybody please watch and see there is no deception."

Holding the gun, muzzle up, so all could see, he deliberately extracted all the cartridges but one. The audience exchanged puzzled looks.

Jeff twirled the cylinder and returned the gun to its scabbard. "Now!" he said, sparkling with enthusiasm. "You all see that I've only got one cartridge. I'm in no position to fight. If there's any fighting I'm already dead. What happens to me has no bearing on the discussion. I'm out of it.

"I realize that there's no use trying to intimidate you fellows. Any of you would take a bit chance with odds against you, and here the odds is for you. So, as far as I'm concerned, I substitute a certainty for chance. I don't want to kill up a lot of rank strangers—or friends, either. There's nothing in it.

"Neither can I go back on old Wes' and Billy. So I take a halfway course. Just to manifest my entire disapproval, if anyone makes a move to go through that gate I'll use my one shot—and it won't be on the man goin' through the gate, either. Nor yet on you, Uncle Pete. You're the leader. So if you want to give the word, go it! I'm not goin' to shoot you. Nor I ain't goin' to shoot any of the Bar W push. They're free to start the ball rolling."

Uncle Pete, thus deprived of the initiatory power, looked helplessly around the Bar W push for confirmation. They nodded in concert. "He'll do whatever he says," said Clay Cooper.

"Thanks," said Jeff pleasantly, "for this unsolicited testimonial. Now, boys, there's no dare about this. Just cause and effect. All of you are plumb safe to make a break—but one. To show you that there's nothing personal about it, no dislike or anything like that, I'll tell you how I picked that one.

I started at some place near both ends or the middle and counted backward, or forward, sayin' to myself, 'Intra, mintra, cutra, corn, apple seed and briar thorn,' and when I got to 'thorn' that man was stuck. That's all. Them's the rules."

That part of Uncle Pete's face visible between beard and hat was purple through the brown. He glared at Jeff, opened his mouth, shut it tightly, and breathed heavily through his nose. He looked at his horse's ears, he looked at the low sun, he looked at the distant hills; his gaze wandered disconsolately back to the twinkling indomitable eyes of the man on the gatepost. Uncle Pete sighed deeply.

"That's good! I'll just about make the wagon by noon," he remarked gently. He took his quirt from his saddle horn. "Young man," he said gravely, flicking his horse's flank, "any time you're out of a job come over and see me." He waved his hand, nodded, and was gone.

Clay Cooper spurred up and took his place, his black eyes snapping. "I like a damned fool," he hissed, "but you suit me too well!"

The forty followed; some pausing for quip or jest, some in frowning silence. But each, as he passed that bright, audacious figure, touched his hat in salute to a gallant foe.

Squatty Robinson was the last. He rode close up and whispered confidentially, "I want you should do me a favor, Jeff. Just throw down on me and take my gun away. I don't want to go back to camp with any such tale as this."

"You see, Billy," explained Jeff, "you mustn't dare the denizens—never! They dare. They're uncultured; their lives ain't noways valuable to society and they know it. If you notice, I took pains not to dare anybody. Quite otherhow. I merely stated annnoyin' consequences to some other fellow, attractive as I could, but impersonal. Just like I'd tell you: 'Billy, I wouldn't set the oil can on the fire—it might boil over.'

"Now, if I'd said: 'Uncle Pete, if anybody makes a break I'll shoot your eye out, anyhow,' there'd 'a' been only one dignified course open to him. Him and me would now be dear Alphonsing each other about payin' the ferryman.

"S'pose I'd made oration to shoot the first man through the gate. Every man Jack would have come a-snuffin'—each one tryin' to be first. The way I put it up to 'em, to be first wasn't no graceful act—playin' safe at some one else's expense—and then they seen that someone else wouldn't be gettin' an equitable vibration. That's all there was to it. If there wasn't any first there couldn't conveniently be any second, so they went home. B-r-r! I'm sleepy. Let's go bye-bye. Wake that dern lazy Mexican up and make him keep watch till the sheriff comes!"

Like Jack London, Rex Beach (1877–1949) was lured by the excitement and adventure of the 1898 Yukon Gold Rush and subsequently spent a number of years prospecting in the Yukon and later in Alaska. Also like London, he wrote often and well of the "Land of the Midnight Sun" (as well as of the American West, South America, and other exotic locales). His first book, a collection of "Northern" and Western stories, *Pardners,* was published in 1905; his best novel, *The Spoiler,* appeared a year later and was a runaway bestseller. Beach's work is little known among modern readers, a regrettable fact. "The Weight of Obligation," a harrowing tale of the frozen north and of the test of a friendship, remains as fresh and vital as when it was initially published.

The Weight of Obligation

Rex Beach

This is the story of a burden, the tale of a load that irked a strong man's shoulders. To those who do not know the North it may seem strange, but to those who understand the humors of men in solitude, and the extravagant vagaries that steal in upon their minds, as fog drifts with the night, it will not appear unusual. There are spirits in the wilderness, eerie forces which play pranks; some droll or whimsical, others grim.

Johnny Cantwell and Mortimer Grant were partners, trailmates, brothers in soul if not in blood. The ebb and flow of frontier life had brought them together, its hardships had united them until they were as one. They were something of a mystery to each other, neither having surrendered all his confidence, and because of this they retained their mutual attraction. Had they known each other fully, had they thoroughly sounded each other's depths, they would have lost interest, just like husbands and wives who give themselves too freely and reserve nothing.

They had met by accident, but they remained together by desire, and so satisfactory was the union that not even the jealousy of women had come between them. There had been women, of course, just as there had been adventures of other sorts, but the love of the partners was larger and finer than anything else they had experienced. It was so true and fine and unselfish, in fact, that either would have smilingly relinquished the woman of his desires had the other wished to possess her. They were young, strong men, and the world was full of sweethearts, but where was there a partnership like theirs, they asked themselves.

The spirit of adventure bubbled merrily within them, too, and it led them into curious byways. It was this which sent them northward from the states in the dead of winter, on the heels of the Stony River strike; it was this which induced them to land at Katmai instead of Illiamna, whither their land journey should have commenced.

"There are two routes over the coast range," the captain of the *Dora* told them, "and only two. Illiamna Pass is low and easy, but the distance is longer than by way of Katmai. I can land you at either place."

"Katmai is pretty tough, isn't it?" Grant inquired.

"We've understood it's the worst pass in Alaska." Cantwell's eyes were eager.

"It's a heller! Nobody travels it except natives, and they don't like it. Now, Illiamna—"

"We'll try Katmai. Eh, Mort?"

"Sure! They don't come hard enough for us, Cap. We'll see if it's as bad as it's painted."

So, one gray January morning they were landed on a frozen beach, their outfit was flung ashore through the surf, the lifeboat pulled away, and the *Dora* disappeared after a farewell toot of her whistle. Their last glimpse of her showed the captain waving good-bye and the purser flapping a red tablecloth at them from the afterdeck.

"Cheerful place, this," Grant remarked, as he noted the desolate surroundings of dune and hillside.

The beach itself was black and raw where the surf washed it, but elsewhere all was white, save for the thickets of alder and willow which protruded nakedly. The bay was little more than a hollow scooped out of the Alaskan range; along the foothills behind there was a belt of spruce and cottonwood and birch. It was a lonely and apparently unpeopled wilderness in which they had been set down.

"Seems good to be back in the north again, doesn't it?" said Cantwell, cheerily. "I'm tired of the booze, and the streetcars, and the dames, and all that civilized stuff. I'd rather be broken in Alaska—with you—than a banker's son, back home."

Soon a globular Russian half-breed, the Katmai trader, appeared among the dunes, and with him were some native villagers. That night the partners slept in a snug log cabin, the roof of which was chained down with old ships' cables. Petellin, the fat little trader, explained that roofs in Katmai had a way of sailing off seaward when the wind blew. He listened to their plan of crossing the divide and nodded.

It could be done, of course, he agreed, but they were foolish to try it, when the Illiamna route was open. Still, now that they were here, he would find dogs for them, and a guide. The village hunters were out after meat, however, and until they returned the white men would need to wait in patience.

There followed several days of idleness, during which Cantwell and Grant amused themselves around the village, teasing the squaws, playing games with the boys, and flirting harmlessly with the girls, one of whom, in particular, was not unattractive. She was perhaps three-quarters Aleut, the other quarter being plain coquette, and, having been educated at the town of Kodiak, she knew the ways and the wiles of the white man.

Cantwell approached her, and she met his extravagant advances more than halfway. They were getting along nicely together when Grant, in a spirit of fun, entered the game and won her fickle smiles for himself. He joked his partner unmercifully, and Johnny accepted defeat gracefully, never giving the matter a second thought.

When the hunters returned, dogs were bought, a guide was hired, and, a week after landing, the friends were camped at timberline awaiting a favorable moment for their dash across the range. Above them white hillsides rose in irregular leaps to the gash in the saw-toothed barrier which formed the pass; below them a short valley led down to Katmai and the sea. The day was bright, the air clear, nevertheless after the guide had stared up at the peaks for a time he shook his head, then re-entered the tent and lay down. The mountains were "smoking;" from their tops streamed a gossamer veil which the travelers knew to be drifting snow clouds carried by the wind. It meant delay, but they were patient.

They were up and going on the following morning, however, with the Indian in the lead. There was no trail; the hills were steep; in places they were forced to unload the sled and hoist their outfit by means of ropes, and as they mounted higher the snow deepened. It lay like loose sand, only lighter; it shoved ahead of the sled in a feathery mass; the dogs wallowed in it and were unable to pull, hence the greater part of the work devolved upon the men. Once above the foothills and into the range proper, the going became more level, but the snow remained knee-deep.

The Indian broke trail stolidly; the partners strained at the sled, which hung back like a leaden thing. By afternoon the dogs had become disheartened and refused to heed the whip. There was neither fuel nor running water, and therefore the party did not pause for luncheon. The men were sweating profusely from their exertions and had long since become parched with thirst, but the dry snow was like chalk and scoured their throats.

Cantwell was the first to show the effects of his unusual exertions, for not only had he assumed a lion's share of the work, but the last few months of easy living had softened his muscles, and in consequence his vitality was quickly spent. His undergarments were drenched; he was fearfully dry inside; a terrible thirst seemed to penetrate his whole body; he was forced to rest frequently.

Grant eyed him with some concern, finally inquiring, "Feel bad, Johnny?"

Cantwell nodded. Their fatigue made both men economical of language.

"What's the matter?"

"Thirsty!" The former could barely speak.

"There won't be any water till we get across. You'll have to stand it."

They resumed their duties; the Indian *swish-swished* ahead, as if wading through a sea of swan's down; the dogs followed listlessly; the partners leaned against the stubborn load.

A faint breath finally came out of the north, causing Grant and the guide to study the sky anxiously. Cantwell was too weary to heed the increasing cold. The snow on the slopes above began to move; here and there, on exposed ridges, it rose in clouds and puffs; the clean-cut outlines of the hills became obscured as by a fog; the languid wind bit cruelly.

After a time Johnny fell back upon the sled and exclaimed, "I'm—all in, Mort. Don't seem to have the—guts." He was pale, his eyes were tortured. He scooped a mitten full of snow and raised it to his lips, then spat it out, still dry.

"Here! Brace up!" In a panic of apprehension at this collapse Grant shook him; he had never known Johnny to fail like this. "Take a drink of booze; it'll do you good." He drew a bottle of brandy from one of the dunnage bags and Cantwell seized it avidly. It was wet; it would quench his thirst, he thought. Before Mort could check him he had drunk a third of the contents.

The effect was almost instantaneous, for Cantwell's stomach was empty and his tissues seemed to absorb the liquor like a dry sponge; his fatigue fell away, he became suddenly strong and vigorous again. But before he had gone a hundred yards the reaction followed. First his mind grew thick, then his limbs became unmanageable and his muscles flabby. He was drunk. Yet it was a strange and dangerous intoxication, against which he struggled desperately. He fought it for perhaps a quarter of a mile before it mastered him; then he gave up.

Both men knew that stimulants are never taken on the trail, but they had never stopped to reason why, and even now they did not attribute Johnny's breakdown to the brandy. After a while he stumbled and fell, then, the cool snow being grateful to his face, he sprawled there motionless until Mort dragged him to the sled. He stared at his partner in perplexity and laughed foolishly. The wind was increasing, darkness was near, they had not yet reached the Bering slope.

Something in the drunken man's face frightened Grant and, extracting a ship's biscuit from the grub-box, he said, hurriedly, "Here, Johnny. Get something under your belt, quick."

Cantwell obediently munched the hard cracker, but there was no moisture on his tongue; his throat was paralyzed; the crumbs crowded themselves from the corners of his lips. He tried with limber fingers to stuff
them down, or to assist the muscular action of swallowing, but finally expelled them in a cloud. Mort drew the parka hood over his partner's head,
for the wind cut like a scythe and the dogs were turning tail to it, digging
holes in the snow for protection. The air about them was like yeast; the
light was fading.

The Indian snowshoed his way back, advising a quick camp until the
storm abated, but to this suggestion Grant refused to listen, knowing only
too well the peril of such a course. Nor did he dare take Johnny on the sled,
since the fellow was half asleep already, but instead whipped up the dogs
and urged his companion to follow as best he could.

When Cantwell fell, for a second time, he returned, dragged him forward, and tied his wrists firmly, yet loosely, to the load.

The storm was pouring over them now, like water out of a spout; it
seared and blinded them; its touch was like that of a flame. Nevertheless
they struggled on into the smother, making what headway they could. The
Indian led, pulling at the end of a rope; Grant strained at the sled and
hoarsely encouraged the dogs; Cantwell stumbled and lurched in the rear
like an unwilling prisoner. When he fell his companion lifted him, then beat
him, cursed him, tried in every way to rouse him from his lethargy.

After an interminable time they found they were descending and this
gave them heart to plunge ahead more rapidly. The dogs began to trot as
the sled overran them; they rushed blindly into gullies, fetching up at the
bottom in a tangle, and Johnny followed in a nerveless, stupefied condition. He was dragged like a sack of flour, for his legs were limp and he
lacked muscular control, but every dash, every fall, every quick descent
drove the sluggish blood through his veins and cleared his brain momentarily. Such moments were fleeting, however; much of the time his mind
was a blank, and it was only by a mechanical effort that he fought off unconsciousness.

He had vague memories of many beatings at Mort's hands, of the slippery clean-swept ice of a stream over which he limply skidded, of being carried into a tent where a candle flickered and a stove roared. Grant was
holding something hot to his lips, and then—

It was morning. He was weak and sick; he felt as if he had awakened
from a hideous dream. "I played out, didn't I?" he queried, wonderingly.

"You sure did," Grant laughed. "It was a tight squeak, old boy. I never
thought I'd get you through."

"Played out! I—can't understand it." Cantwell prided himself on his
strength and stamina, therefore the truth was unbelievable. He and Mort
had long been partners, they had given and taken much at each other's

hands, but this was something altogether different. Grant had saved his life, at risk of his own; the older man's endurance had been the greater and he had used it to good advantage. It embarrassed Johnny tremendously to realize that he had proven unequal to his share of the work, for he had never before experienced such an obligation. He apologized repeatedly during the few days he lay sick, and meanwhile Mort waited upon him like a mother.

Cantwell was relieved when at last they had abandoned camp, changed guides at the next village, and were on their way along the coast, for somehow he felt very sensitive about his collapse. He was, in fact, extremely ashamed of himself.

Once he had fully recovered he had no further trouble, but soon rounded into fit condition and showed no effects of his ordeal. Day after day he and Mort traveled through the solitudes, their isolation broken only by occasional glimpses of native villages, where they rested briefly and renewed their supply of dog feed.

But although the younger man was now as well and strong as ever, he was uncomfortably conscious that his trailmate regarded him as the weaker of the two and shielded him in many ways. Grant performed most of the unpleasant tasks, and occasionally cautioned Johnny about overdoing. This protective attitude at first amused, then offended Cantwell; it galled him until he was upon the point of voicing his resentment, but reflected that he had no right to object, for, judging by past performances, he had proven his inferiority. This uncomfortable realization forever arose to prevent open rebellion, but he asserted himself secretly by robbing Grant of his self-appointed tasks. He rose first in the mornings, he did the cooking, he lengthened his turns ahead of the dogs, he mended the harness after the day's hike had ended. Of course the older man objected, and for a time they had a good-natured rivalry as to who should work and who should rest—only it was not quite so good-natured on Cantwell's part as he made it appear.

Mort broke out in friendly irritation one day. "Don't try to do everything, Johnny. Remember I'm no cripple."

"Humph! You proved that. I guess it's up to me to do your work."

"Oh, forget that day on the pass, can't you?"

Johnny grunted a second time, and from his tone it was evident that he would never forget, unpleasant though the memory remained. Sensing his sullen resentment, the other tried to rally him, but made a bad job of it. The humor of men in the open is not delicate; their wit and their words become coarsened in direct proportion as they revert to the primitive; it is one effect of the solitudes.

Grant spoke extravagantly, mockingly, of his own superiority in a way which ordinarily would have brought a smile to Cantwell's lips, but the latter did not smile. He taunted Johnny humorously on his lack of physical prowess, his lack of good looks and manly qualities—something which had never failed to result in a friendly exchange of badinage; he even teased him about his defeat with the Katmai girl.

Cantwell did respond finally, but afterward he found himself wondering if Mort could have been in earnest. He dismissed the thought with some impatience. But men on the trail have too much time for their thoughts; there is nothing in the monotonous routine of the day's work to distract them, so the partner who had played out dwelt more and more upon his debt and upon his friend's easy assumption of pre-eminence. The weight of obligation began to chafe him, lightly at first, but with ever-increasing discomfort. He began to think that Grant honestly considered himself the better man, merely because chance had played into his hands.

It was silly, even childish, to dwell on the subject, he reflected, and yet he could not banish it from his mind. It was always before him, in one form or another. He felt the strength in his lean muscles, and sneered at the thought that Mort should be deceived. If it came to a physical test he felt sure he could break his slighter partner with his bare hands, and as for endurance—well, he was hungry for a chance to demonstrate it.

They talked little; men seldom converse in the wastes, for there is something about the silence of the wilderness which discourages speech. And no land is so grimly silent, so hushed and soundless, as the frozen north. For days they marched through desolation, without glimpse of human habitation, without sight of track or trail, without sound of a human voice to break the monotony. There was no game in the country, with the exception of an occasional bird or rabbit, nothing but the white hills, the fringe of aldertops along the watercourses, and the thickets of gnarled, unhealthy spruce in the smothered valleys.

Their destination was a mysterious stream at the headwaters of the unmapped Kuskokwim, where rumor said there was gold, and whither they feared other men were hastening from the mining country far to the north.

Now it is a penalty of the White Country that men shall think of women. The open life brings health and vigor, strength and animal vitality, and these clamor for play. The cold of the still, clear days is no more biting than the fierce memories and appetites which charge through the brain at night. Passions intensify and imprisonment, recollections come to life, longings grow vivid and wild. Thoughts change to realities, the past creeps close, and dream figures are filled with blood and fire. One remembers pleasures and excesses, women's smiles, women's kisses, the invitation of outstretched arms. Wasted opportunities mock at one.

Cantwell began to brood about the Katmai girl, for she was the last; her eyes were haunting and distance had worked its usual enchantment. He reflected that Mort had shouldered him aside and won her favor, then boasted of it. Johnny awoke one night with a dream of her, and lay quivering.

"Hell! She was only a squaw," he said, half aloud. "If I'd really tried—"

Grant lay beside him, snoring; the heat of their bodies intermingled. The waking man tried to compose himself, but his partner's stertorous breathing irritated him beyond measure; for a long time he remained motionless, staring into the gray blur of the tent-top. He had played out. He owed his life to the man who had cheated him of the Katmai girl, and that man knew it. He had become a weak, helpless thing, dependent upon another's strength, and that other now accepted his superiority as a matter of course. The obligation was insufferable, and—it was unjust. The north had played him a devilish trick, it had betrayed him, it had bound him to his benefactor with chains of gratitude which were irksome. Had they been real chains they could have galled him no more than at this moment.

As time passed the men spoke less frequently to each other. Grant joshed his mate roughly, once or twice, masking beneath an assumption of jocularity his own vague irritation at the change that had come over them. It was as if he had probed at an open wound with clumsy fingers.

Cantwell had by this time assumed most of those petty camp tasks which provoke tired trailers, those humdrum duties which are so trying to exhausted nerves, and of course they wore upon him as they wear upon every man. But, once he had taken them over, he began to resent Grant's easy relinquishment; it rankled him to realize how willingly the other allowed him to do the cooking, the dishwashing, the fire-building, the bed-making. Little monotonies of this kind form the hardest part of winter travel, they are the rocks upon which friendships founder and partnerships are wrecked. Out on the trail, nature equalizes the work to a great extent, and no man can shirk unduly, but in camp, inside the cramped confines of a tent pitched on boughs laid over the snow, it is very different. There one must busy himself while the other rests and keeps his legs out of the way if possible. One man sits on the bedding at the rear of the shelter, and shivers, while the other squats over a tantalizing fire of green wood, blistering his face and parboiling his limbs inside his sweaty clothing. Dishes must be passed, food divided, and it is poor food, poorly prepared at best. Sometimes men criticize and voice longings for better grub and better cooking. Remarks of this kind have been known to result in tragedies, bitter words and flaming curses—then, perhaps, wild actions, memories of which the later years can never erase.

It is but one prank of the wilderness, one grim manifestation of its silent forces.

Had Grant been unable to do his part Cantwell would have willingly accepted the added burden, but Mort was able, he was nimble and "handy," he was the better cook of the two; in fact, he was the better man in every way—or so he believed. Cantwell sneered at the last thought, and the memory of his debt was like bitter medicine.

His resentment—in reality nothing more than a phase of insanity begot of isolation and silence—could not help but communicate itself to his companion, and there resulted a mutual antagonism, which grew into a dislike, then festered into something more, something strange, reasonless, yet terribly vivid and amazingly potent for evil. Neither man ever mentioned it—their tongues were clenched between their teeth and they held themselves in check with harsh hands—but it was constantly in their minds, nevertheless. No man who has not suffered the manifold irritations of such an intimate association can appreciate the gnawing canker of animosity like this. It was dangerous because there was no relief from it: the two were bound together as by gyves; they shared each other's every action and every plan; they trod in each other's tracks, slept in the same bed, ate from the same plate. They were like prisoners ironed to the same staple.

Each fought the obsession in his own way, but it is hard to fight the impalpable, hence their sick fancies grew in spite of themselves. Their minds needed food to prey upon, but found none. Each began to criticize the other silently, to sneer at his weaknesses, to meditate derisively upon his peculiarities. After a time they no longer resisted the advance of these poisonous thoughts, but welcomed it.

On more than one occasion the embers of their wrath were upon the point of bursting into flame, but each realized that the first ill-considered word would serve to slip the leash from those demons that were straining to go free, and so managed to restrain himself.

The crisis came one crisp morning when a dog-team whirled around a bend in the river and a white man hailed them. He was the mail carrier, on his way out from Nome, and he brought news of the "inside."

"Where are you boys bound for?" he inquired when greetings were over and gossip of the trail had passed.

"We're going to the Stony River strike," Grant told him.

"Stony River? Up the Kuskokwim?"

"Yes!"

The mailman laughed. "Can you beat that? Ain't you heard about Stony River?"

"No!"

"Why, it's a fake—no such place."

There was a silence; the partners avoided each other's eyes.

"MacDonald, the fellow that started it, is on his way to Dawson. There's a gang after him, too, and if he's caught it'll go hard with him. He wrote the letters—to himself—and spread the news just to raise a grubstake. He cleaned up big before they got on to him. He peddled his tips for real money."

"Yes!" Grant spoke quietly. "Johnny bought one. That's what brought us from Seattle. We went out on the last boat and figured we'd come in from this side before the breakup. So—fake! By God!"

"Gee! You fellers bit good." The mail carrier shook his head. "Well! You'd better keep going now; you'll get to Nome before the season opens. Better take dog-fish from Bethel—it's four bits a pound on the Yukon. Sorry I didn't hit your camp last night; we'd 'a' had a visit. Tell the gang that you saw me." He shook hands ceremoniously, yelled at his panting dogs, and went swiftly on his way, waving a mitten on high as he vanished around the next bend.

The partners watched him go, then Grant turned to Johnny, and repeated, "Fake! By God! MacDonald stung you."

Cantwell's face went as white as the snow behind him, his eyes blazed. "Why did you tell him I bit?" he demanded, harshly.

"Hunh! *Didn't* you bite? Two thousand miles afoot; three months of hell; for nothing. That's biting some."

"*Well!*" The speaker's face was convulsed, and Grant's flamed with an answering anger. They glared at each other for a moment. "Don't blame me. You fell for it, too."

"I—" Mort checked his rushing words.

"Yes, *you!* Now, what are you going to do about it? Welch?"

"I'm going through to Nome." The sight of his partner's rage had set Mort to shaking with a furious desire to fly at his throat, but, fortunately, he retained a spark of sanity.

"Then shut up, and quit chewing the rag. You—talk too damned much."

Mort's eyes were bloodshot; they fell upon the carbine under the sled lashings, and lingered there, then wavered. He opened his lips, reconsidered, spoke softly to the team, then lifted the heavy dog whip and smote the malamutes with all his strength.

The men resumed their journey without further words, but each was cursing inwardly.

"So! I talk too much," Grant thought. The accusation stuck in his mind and he determined to speak no more.

"He blames me," Cantwell reflected, bitterly. "I'm in wrong again and he couldn't keep his mouth shut. A hell of a partner he is!"

All day they plodded on, neither trusting himself to speak. They ate their evening meal like mutes; they avoided each other's eyes. Even the guide noticed the change and looked on curiously.

There were two robes and these the partners shared nightly, but their hatred had grown so during the past few hours that the thought of lying side by side, limb to limb, was distasteful. Yet neither dared suggest a division of the bedding, for that would have brought further words and resulted in the crash which they longed for, but feared. They stripped off their furs, and lay down beside each other with the same repugnance they would have felt had there been a serpent in the couch.

This unending malevolent silence became terrible. The strain of it increased, for each man now had something definite to cherish in the words and the looks that had passed. They divided the camp work with scrupulous nicety, each man waited upon himself and asked no favors. The knowledge of his debt forever chafed Cantwell; Grant resented his companion's lack of gratitude.

Of course they spoke occasionally—it was beyond human endurance to remain entirely dumb—but they conversed in monosyllables, about trivial things, and their voices were throaty, as if the effort choked them. Meanwhile they continued to glow inwardly from a white heat.

Cantwell no longer felt the desire to merely match his strength against Grant's; the estrangement had become too wide for that; a physical victory would have been flat and tasteless; he craved some deeper satisfaction. He began to think of the ax—just how or when or why he never knew. It was a thin-bladed, polished thing of frosty steel, and the more he thought of it the stronger grew his impulse to rid himself once and for all of that presence which exasperated him. It would be very easy, he reasoned; a sudden blow, with the weight of his shoulders behind it—he fancied he could feel the bit sink into Grant's flesh, cleaving bone and cartilage in its course—a slanting downward stroke, aimed at the neck where it joined the body, and he would be forever satisfied. It would be ridiculously simple. He practiced in the gloom of evening as he felled spruce trees for firewood; he guarded the ax religiously; it became a living thing which urged him on to violence. He saw it standing by the tent fly when he closed his eyes to sleep; he dreamed of it; he sought it out with his eyes when he first awoke. He slid it loosely under the sled lashings every morning, thinking that its use could not long be delayed.

As for Grant, the carbine dwelt forever in his mind, and his fingers itched for it. He secretly slipped a cartridge into the chamber, and when an occasional ptarmigan offered itself for a target he saw the white spot on the breast of Johnny's reindeer parkas, dancing ahead of the Lyman bead.

The solitude had done its work; the north had played its grim comedy to the final curtain, making sport of men's affections and turning love to rankling hate. But into the mind of each man crept a certain craftiness. Each longed to strike, but feared to face the consequences. It was lonesome, here among the white hills and the deathly silences, yet they reflected that it would be still more lonesome if they were left to keep step with nothing more substantial than a memory. They determined, therefore, to wait until civilization was nearer, meanwhile rehearsing the moment they knew was inevitable. Over and over in their thoughts each of them enacted the scene, ending it always with the picture of a prostrate man in a patch of trampled snow which grew crimson as the other gloated.

They paused at Bethel Mission long enough to load with dried salmon, then made the ninety-mile portage over lake and tundra to the Yukon. There they got their first touch of the "inside" world. They camped in a barabara where white men had slept a few nights before, and heard their own language spoken by native tongues. The time was growing short now, and they purposely dismissed their guide, knowing that the trail was plain from there on. When they hitched up, on the next morning, Cantwell placed the ax, bit down, between the tarpaulin and the sled rail, leaving the helve projecting where his hand could reach it. Grant thrust the barrel of the rifle beneath a lashing, with the butt close by the handlebars, and it was loaded.

A mile from the village they were overtaken by an Indian and his squaw, travelling light behind hungry dogs. The natives attached themselves to the white men and hung stubbornly to their heels, taking advantage of their tracks. When night came they camped alongside, in the hope of food. They announced that they were bound for St. Michaels, and in spite of every effort to shake them off they remained close behind the partners until that point was reached.

At St. Michaels there were white men, practically the first Johnny and Mort had encountered since landing at Katmai, and for a day at least they were sane. But there were still three hundred miles to be travelled, three hundred miles of solitude and haunting thoughts. Just as they were about to start, Cantwell came upon Grant and the A. C. agent, and heard his name pronounced, also the word "Katmai." He noted that Mort fell silent at his approach, and instantly his anger blazed afresh. He decided that the latter had been telling the story of their experience on the pass and boasting of his service. So much the better, he thought, in a blind rage; that which he planned doing would appear all the more like an accident, for who would dream that a man could kill the person to whom he owed his life?

That night he waited for a chance.

They were camped in a dismal hut on a windswept shore; they were alone. But Grant was waiting also, it seemed. They lay down beside each other, ostensibly to sleep; their limbs touched; the warmth from their bodies intermingled, but they did not close their eyes.

They were up and away early, with Nome drawing rapidly nearer. They had skirted an ocean, foot by foot; Bering Sea lay behind them, now, and its northern shore swung westward to their goal. For two months they had lived in silent animosity, feeding on bitter food while their elbows rubbed.

Noon found them floundering through one of those unheralded storms which make coast travel so hazardous. The morning had turned off gray, the sky was of a leaden hue which blended perfectly with the snow underfoot, there was no horizon, it was impossible to see more than a few yards in any direction. The trail soon became obliterated and their eyes began to play tricks. For all they could distinguish, they might have been suspended in space; they seemed to be treading the measure of an endless dance in the center of a whirling cloud. Of course it was cold, for the wind off the open sea was damp, but they were not men to turn back.

They soon discovered that their difficulty lay not in facing the storm but in holding to the trail. That narrow, two-foot causeway, packed by a winter's travel and frozen into a ribbon of ice by a winter's frosts, afforded their only avenue of progress, for the moment they left it the sled plowed into the loose snow, well-nigh disappearing and bringing the dogs to a standstill. It was the duty of the driver, in such case, to wallow forward, right the load if necessary, and lift it back into place. These mishaps were forever occurring, for it was impossible to distinguish the trail beneath its soft covering. However, if the driver's task was hard it was no more trying than that of the man ahead, who was compelled to feel out and explore the ridge of hardened snow and ice with his feet, after the fashion of a man walking a plank in the dark. Frequently he lunged into the drifts with one foot, or both; his glazed mukluk soles slid about, causing him to bestride the invisible hogback, or again his legs crossed awkwardly, throwing him off his balance. At times he wandered away from the path entirely and had to search it out again. These exertions were very wearing and they were dangerous, also, for joints are easily dislocated, muscles twisted, and tendons strained.

Hour after hour the march continued, unrelieved by any change, unbroken by any speck or spot of color. The nerves of their eyes, wearied by constant nearsighted peering at the snow, began to jump so that vision became untrustworthy. Both travelers appreciated the necessity of clinging to the trail, for, once they lost it, they knew they might wander about indefinitely until they chanced to regain it or found their way to the shore, while always to seaward was the menace of open water, of airholes, or cracks which might gape beneath their feet like jaws. Immersion in this temperature, no matter how brief, meant death.

The monotony of progress through this unreal, leaden world became almost unbearable. The repeated strainings and twistings they suffered in walking the slippery ridge reduced the men to weariness; their legs grew clumsy and their feet uncertain. Had they found a camping place they would have stopped, but they dared not forsake the thin thread that linked them with safety to go and look for one, not knowing where the shore lay. In storms of this kind men have lain in their sleeping bags for days within a stone's throw of a roadhouse or village. Bodies had been found within a hundred yards of shelter after blizzards have abated.

Cantwell and Grant had no choice, therefore, except to bore into the welter of drifting flakes.

It was late in the afternoon when the latter met with an accident. Johnny, who had taken a spell at the rear, heard him cry out, saw him stagger, struggle to hold his footing, then sink into the snow. The dogs paused instantly, lay down, and began to strip the ice pellets from between their toes.

Cantwell spoke harshly, leaning upon the handlebars, "Well! What's the idea?"

It was the longest sentence of the day.

"I've—hurt myself." Mort's voice was thin and strange; he raised himself to a sitting posture, and reached beneath his parka, then lay back weakly. He writhed, his face was twisted with pain. He continued to lie there, doubled into a knot of suffering. A groan was wrenched from between his teeth.

"Hurt? How?" Johnny inquired, dully.

It seemed very ridiculous to see that strong man kicking around in the snow.

"I've ripped something loose—here." Mort's palms were pressed in upon his groin, his fingers were clutching something. "Ruptured—I guess." He tried again to rise, but sank back. His cap had fallen off and his forehead glistened with sweat.

Cantwell went forward and lifted him. It was the first time in many days that their hands had touched, and the sensation affected him strangely. He struggled to repress a devilish mirth at the thought that Grant had played out—it amounted to that and nothing less; the trail had delivered him into his enemy's hands, his hour had struck. Johnny determined to square the debt now, once for all, and wipe his own mind clean of that poison which corroded it. His muscles were strong, his brain clear, he had never felt his strength so irresistible as at this moment, while Mort, for all his boasted superiority, was nothing but a nerveless thing hanging limp against his breast. Providence had arranged it all. The younger man was impelled to give raucous voice to his glee, and yet—his helpless burden exerted an odd effect upon him.

He deposited his foe upon the sled and stared at the face he had not met for many days. He saw how white it was, how wet and cold, how weak and dazed, then as he looked he cursed inwardly, for the triumph of his moment was spoiled.

The ax was there, its polished bit showed like a piece of ice, its helve protruded handily, but there was no need of it now; his fingers were all the weapons Johnny needed; they were more than sufficient, in fact, for Mort was like a child.

Cantwell was a strong man, and, although the north had coarsened him, yet underneath the surface was a chivalrous regard for all things weak, and this the trail-madness had not affected. He had longed for this instant, but now that it had come he felt no enjoyment, since he could not harm a sick man and waged no war on cripples. Perhaps, when Mort had rested, they could settle their quarrel; this was as good a place as any. The storm hid them, they would leave no traces, there could be no interruption.

But Mort did not rest. He could not walk; movement brought excruciating pain.

Finally Cantwell heard himself saying, "Better wrap up and lie still for a while. I'll get the dogs under way." His words amazed him dully. They were not at all what he had intended to say.

The injured man demurred, but the other insisted gruffly, then brought him his mittens and cap, slapping the snow out of them before rousing the team to motion. The load was very heavy now, the dogs had no footprints to guide them, and it required all of Cantwell's efforts to prevent capsizing. Night approached swiftly, the whirling snow particles continued to flow past upon the wind, shrouding the earth in an impenetrable pall.

The journey soon became a terrible ordeal, a slow, halting progress that led nowhere and was accomplished at the cost of tremendous exertion. Time after time Johnny broke trail, then returned and urged the huskies forward to the end of his tracks. When he lost the path he sought it out, laboriously hoisted the sledge back into place, and coaxed his four-footed helpers to renewed effort. He was drenched with perspiration, his inner garments were steaming, his outer ones were frozen into a coat of armor; when he paused he chilled rapidly. His vision was untrustworthy, also, and he felt snow-blindness coming on. Grant begged him more than once to unroll the bedding and prepare to sleep out the storm; he even urged Johnny to leave him and make a dash for his own safety, but at this the younger man cursed and bade him hold his tongue.

Night found the lone driver slipping, plunging, lurching ahead of the dogs, or shoving at the handlebars and shouting at the dogs. Finally during a pause for rest he heard a sound which roused him. Out of the gloom to the right came the faint, complaining howl of a malamute; it was answered by his own dogs, and the next moment they had caught a scent which swerved them shoreward and led them scrambling through the drifts. Two hundred yards, and a steep bank loomed above, up and over which they rushed, with Cantwell yelling encouragement; then a light showed, and they were in the lee of a low-roofed hut.

A sick native, huddled over a Yukon stove, made them welcome to his mean abode, explaining that his wife and son had gone to Unalaklik for supplies.

Johnny carried his partner to the one unoccupied bunk and stripped his clothes from him. With his own hands he rubbed the warmth back into

Mortimer's limbs, then swiftly prepared hot food, and, holding him in the hollow of his aching arm, fed him, a little at a time. He was like to drop from exhaustion, but he made no complaint. With one folded robe he made the hard boards comfortable, then spread the other as a covering. For himself he sat beside the fire and fought his weariness. When he dozed off and the cold awakened him, he renewed the fire; he heated beeftea, and, rousing Mort, fed it to him with a teaspoon. All night long, at intervals, he tended the sick man, and Grant's eyes followed him with an expression that brought a fierce pain to Cantwell's throat.

"You're mighty good—after the rotten way I acted," the former whispered once.

And Johnny's big hand trembled so that he spilled the broth.

His voice was low and tender as he inquired, "Are you resting easier now?"

The other nodded.

"Maybe you're not hurt badly, after—all. God! That would be awful—" Cantwell choked, turned away, and, raising his arms against the log wall, buried his face in them.

THE MORNING BROKE clear; Grant was sleeping. As Johnny stiffly mounted the creek bank with a bucket of water he heard a jingle of sleigh-bells and saw a sled with two white men swing in toward the cabin.

"Hello!" he called, then heard his own name pronounced.

"Johnny Cantwell, by all that's holy!"

The next moment he was shaking hands vigorously with two old friends from Nome.

"Martin and me are bound for Saint Mike's," one of them explained. "Where the deuce did you come from, Johnny?"

"The 'outside,' started for Stony River, but—"

"Stony River!" The newcomers began to laugh loudly and Cantwell joined them. It was the first time he had laughed for weeks. He realized the fact with a start, then recollected also his sleeping partner, and said,

"Shh! Mort's inside, asleep!"

During the night everything had changed for Johnny Cantwell; his mental attitude, his hatred, his whole reasonless insanity. Everything was different now, even his debt was cancelled, the weight of obligation was removed, and his diseased fancies were completely cured.

"Yes! Stony River," he repeated, grinning broadly. "I bit!"

Martin burst forth gleefully, "They caught MacDonald at Holy Cross and ran him out on a limb. He'll never start another stampede. Old Man Baker gun-branded him."

"What's the matter with Mort?" inquired the second traveler.

"He's resting up. Yesterday, during the storm, he"—Johnny was upon the point of saying "played out," but changed it to—"had an accident. We thought it was serious, but a few days' rest'll bring him around all right. He saved me at Katmai, coming in. I petered out and threw up my tail, but he got me through. Come inside and tell him the news."

"Sure thing."

"Well, well!" Martin said. "So you and Mort are still partners, eh?"

"*Still* partners!" Johnny took up the pail of water. "Well, rather! We'll always be partners." His voice was young and full and hearty as he continued, "Why, Mort's the best damned fellow in the world. I'd lay down my life for him."

With the exception of Louis L'Amour, no writer of popular Westerns attracted a larger and more faithful audience in the fifties, sixties, and seventies than Luke Short (Frederick D. Glidden). From 1936, when his first novel, *The Feud at Single Shot,* was published, until his death in 1975, he wrote more than fifty novels whose aggregate sales in hardcover and paperback exceeded thirty million copies. Among his most memorable titles are *Fiddlefoot, Saddle by Starlight, High Vermillion, Silver Rock,* and *King Colt.* Many of his short stories, and many of his longer works as well, appeared in such magazines as *Collier's* and *The Saturday Evening Post.* It was in the pages of the latter that "Top Hand," considered by many to be the finest of his short tales, first saw print in 1943.

Top Hand

Luke Short

Gus Irby was out on the boardwalk in front of the Elite, giving his swamper hell for staving in an empty beer barrel, when the kid passed on his way to the feed stable. His horse was a good one and it was tired, Gus saw, and the kid had a little hump in his back from the cold of a mountain October morning. In spite of the ample layer of flesh that Gus wore carefully like an uncomfortable shroud, he shivered in his shirt sleeves and turned into the saloon, thinking without much interest *Another fiddle-footed dry-country kid that's been paid off after roundup.*

Later, while he was taking out the cash for the day and opening up some fresh cigars, Gus saw the kid go into the Pride Café for breakfast, and afterward come out, toothpick in mouth, and cruise both sides of Wagon Mound's main street in aimless curiosity.

After that, Gus wasn't surprised when he looked around at the sound of the door opening, and saw the kid coming toward the bar. He was in a clean and faded shirt and looked as if he'd been cold for a good many hours. Gus said good morning and took down his best whiskey and a glass and put them in front of the kid.

"First customer in the morning gets a drink on the house," Gus announced.

"Now I know why I rode all night," the kid said, and he grinned at Gus. He was a pleasant-faced kid with pale eyes that weren't shy or sullen or bold, and maybe because of this he didn't fit readily into any of Gus's handy character pigeonholes. Gus had seen them young and fiddle-footed before, but they were the tough kids, and for a man with no truculence in him, like Gus, talking with them was like trying to pet a tiger.

Gus leaned against the back bar and watched the kid take his whiskey and wipe his mouth on his sleeve, and Gus found himself getting curious. Half a lifetime of asking skillful questions that didn't seem like questions at all, prompted Gus to observe now, "If you're goin' on through you better pick up a coat. This high country's cold now."

"I figure this is far enough," the kid said.

"Oh, well, if somebody sent for you, that's different." Gus reached around lazily for a cigar.

The kid pulled out a silver dollar from his pocket and put it on the bar top, and then poured himself another whiskey, which Gus was sure he didn't want, but which courtesy dictated he should buy. "Nobody sent for me, either," the kid observed. "I ain't got any money."

Gus picked up the dollar and got change from the cash drawer and put it in front of the kid, afterward lighting his cigar. This was when the announcement came.

"I'm a top hand," the kid said quietly, looking levelly at Gus. "Who's lookin' for one?"

Gus was glad he was still lighting his cigar, else he might have smiled. If there had been a third man here, Gus would have winked at him surreptitiously; but since there wasn't, Gus kept his face expressionless, drew on his cigar a moment, and then observed gently, "You look pretty young for a top hand."

"The best cow pony I ever saw was four years old," the kid answered pointedly.

Gus smiled faintly and shook his head. "You picked a bad time. Round-up's over."

The kid nodded, and drank down his second whiskey quickly, waited for his breath to come normally. Then he said, "Much obliged. I'll see you again," and turned toward the door.

A mild cussedness stirred within Gus, and after a moment's hesitation he called out, "Wait a minute."

The kid hauled up and came back to the bar. He moved with an easy grace that suggested quickness and work-hardened muscle, and for a moment Gus, a careful man, was undecided. But the kid's face, so young and without caution, reassured him, and he folded his heavy arms on the bar top and pulled his nose thoughtfully. "You figure to hit all the outfits, one by one, don't you?"

The kid nodded, and Gus frowned and was silent a moment, and then he murmured, almost to himself, "I had a notion—oh, hell, I don't know."

"Go ahead," the kid said, and then his swift grin came again. "I'll try anything once."

"Look," Gus said, as if his mind were made up. "We got a newspaper here—the Wickford County Free Press. Comes out every Thursday, that's today." He looked soberly at the kid. "Whyn't you put a piece in there and say 'Top hand wants a job at forty dollars a month'? Tell 'em what you can do and tell 'em to come see you here if they want a hand. They'll all get it in a couple days. That way you'll save yourself a hundred miles of ridin'. Won't cost much either."

The kid thought awhile and then asked, without smiling, "Where's this newspaper at?"

Gus told him and the kid went out. Gus put the bottle away and doused the glass in water, and he was smiling slyly at his thoughts. Wait till the boys read that in the Free Press. They were going to have some fun with that kid, Gus reflected.

JOHNNY MCSORLEY STEPPED out into the chill thin sunshine. The last silver in his pants pocket was a solid weight against his leg, and he was aware that he'd probably spend it in the next few minutes on the newspaper piece. He wondered about that, and figured shrewdly it had an off chance of working.

Four riders dismounted at a tie rail ahead and paused a moment, talking. Johnny looked them over and picked out their leader, a tall, heavy, scowling man in his middle thirties who was wearing a mackinaw unbuttoned.

Johnny stopped and said, "You know anybody lookin' for a top hand?" and grinned pleasantly at the big man.

For a second Johnny thought he was going to smile. He didn't think he'd have liked the smile, once he saw it, but the man's face settled into the scowl again. "I never saw a top hand that couldn't vote," he said.

Johnny looked at him carefully, not smiling, and said, "Look at one now, then," and went on, and by the time he'd taken two steps he thought, *Vote, huh? A man must grow pretty slow in this high country.*

He crossed the street and paused before a window marked WICKFORD COUNTY FREE PRESS. JOB PRINTING. D. MELAVEN, ED. AND PROP. He went inside, then. A girl was seated at a cluttered desk, staring at the street, tapping a pencil against her teeth. Johnny tramped over to her, noting the infernal racket made by one of two men at a small press under the lamp behind the railed-off office space.

Johnny said "Hello," and the girl turned tiredly and said, "Hello, bub." She had on a plain blue dress with a high bodice and a narrow lace collar, and she was a very pretty girl, but tired, Johnny noticed. Her long yellow hair was worn in braids that crossed almost atop her head, and she looked,

Johnny thought, like a small kid who has pinned her hair up out of the way for her Saturday night bath. He thought all this and then remembered her greeting, and he reflected without rancor, *Damn, that's twice*, and he said, "I got a piece for the paper, sis."

"Don't call me sis," the girl said. "Anybody's name I don't know, I call him bub. No offense. I got that from pa, I guess."

That's likely, Johnny thought, and he said amiably, "Any girl's name I don't know, I call her sis. I got that from ma."

The cheerful effrontery of the remark widened the girl's eyes. She held out her hand now and said with dignity, "Give it to me. I'll see it gets in next week."

"That's too late," Johnny said. "I got to get it in this week."

"Why?"

"I ain't got money enough to hang around another week."

The girl stared carefully at him. "What is it?"

"I want to put a piece in about myself. I'm a top hand, and I'm lookin' for work. The fella over there at the saloon says why don't I put a piece in the paper about wantin' work, instead of ridin' out lookin' for it."

The girl was silent a full five seconds and then said, "You don't look that simple. Gus was having fun with you."

"I figured that," Johnny agreed. "Still, it might work. If you're caught shorthanded, you take anything."

The girl shook her head. "It's too late. The paper's made up." Her voice was meant to hold a note of finality, but Johnny regarded her curiously, with a maddening placidity.

"You D. Melaven?" he asked.

"No. That's pa."

"Where's he?"

"Back there. Busy."

Johnny saw the gate in the rail that separated the office from the shop and he headed toward it. He heard the girl's chair scrape on the floor and her urgent command, "Don't go back there. It's not allowed."

Johnny looked over his shoulder and grinned and said, "I'll try anything once," and went on through the gate, hearing the girl's swift steps behind him. He halted alongside a square-built and solid man with a thatch of stiff hair more gray than black, and said, "You D. Melaven?"

"Dan Melaven, bub. What can I do for you?"

That's three times, Johnny thought, and he regarded Melaven's square face without anger. He liked the face; it was homely and stubborn and intelligent, and the eyes were both sharp and kindly. Hearing the girl stop beside him, Johnny said, "I got a piece for the paper today."

The girl put in quickly, "I told him it was too late, pa. Now you tell him, and maybe he'll get out."

"Cassie," Melaven said in surprised protest.

"I don't care. We can't unlock the forms for every out-at-the-pants puncher that asks us. Beside, I think he's one of Alec Barr's bunch." She spoke vehemently, angrily, and Johnny listened to her with growing amazement.

"Alec who?" he asked.

"I saw you talking to him, and then you came straight over here from him," Cassie said hotly.

"I hit him for work."

"I don't believe it."

"Cassie," Melaven said grimly, "come back here a minute." He took her by the arm and led her toward the back of the shop, where they halted and engaged in a quiet, earnest conversation.

Johnny shook his head in bewilderment, and then looked around him. The biggest press, he observed, was idle. And on a stone-topped table where Melaven had been working was a metal form almost filled with lines of type and gray metal pieces of assorted sizes and shapes. Now, Johnny McSorley did not know any more than the average person about the workings of a newspaper, but his common sense told him that Cassie had lied to him when she said it was too late to accept his advertisement. Why, there was space to spare in that form for the few lines of type his message would need. Turning this over in his mind, he wondered what was behind her refusal.

Presently, the argument settled, Melaven and Cassie came back to him, and Johnny observed that Cassie, while chastened, was still mad.

"All right, what do you want printed, bub?" Melaven asked.

Johnny told him and Melaven nodded when he was finished, said, "Pay her," and went over to the type case.

Cassie went back to the desk and Johnny followed her, and when she was seated he said, "What do I owe you?"

Cassie looked speculatively at him, her face still flushed with anger. "How much money have you got?"

"A dollar some."

"It'll be two dollars," Cassie said.

Johnny pulled out his lone silver dollar and put it on the desk. "You print it just the same; I'll be back with the rest later."

Cassie said with open malice, "You'd have it now, bub, if you hadn't been drinking before ten o'clock."

Johnny didn't do anything for a moment, and then he put both hands on the desk and leaned close to her. "How old are you?" he asked quietly.

"Seventeen."

"I'm older'n you," Johnny murmured. "So the next time you call me 'bub' I'm goin' to take down your pigtails and pull 'em. I'll try anything once."

Once he was in the sunlight, crossing toward the Elite, he felt better. He smiled—partly at himself but mostly at Cassie. She was a real spitfire, kind of pretty and kind of nice, and he wished he knew what her father said to her that made her so mad, and why she'd been mad in the first place.

Gus was breaking out a new case of whiskey and stacking bottles against the back mirror as Johnny came in and went up to the bar. Neither of them spoke while Gus finished, and Johnny gazed absently at the poker game at one of the tables and now yawned sleepily.

Gus said finally, "You get it in all right?"

Johnny nodded thoughtfully and said, "She mad like that at everybody?"

"Who? Cassie?"

"First she didn't want to take the piece, but her old man made her. Then she charges me more for it than I got in my pocket. Then she combs me over like I got my head stuck in the cookie crock for drinkin' in the morning. She calls me bub, to boot."

"She calls everybody bub."

"Not me no more," Johnny said firmly, and yawned again.

Gus grinned and sauntered over to the cash box. When he came back he put ten silver dollars on the bar top and said, "Pay me back when you get your job. And I got rooms upstairs if you want to sleep."

Johnny grinned. "Sleep, hunh? I'll try anything once." He took the money, said "Much obliged," and started away from the bar and then paused. "Say, who's this Alec Barr?"

Johnny saw Gus's eyes shift swiftly to the poker game and then shuttle back to him. Gus didn't say anything.

"See you later," Johnny said.

He climbed the stairs whose entrance was at the end of the bar, wondering why Gus was so careful about Alec Barr.

A gunshot somewhere out in the street woke him. The sun was gone from the room, so it must be afternoon, he thought. He pulled on his boots, slopped some water into the washbowl and washed up, pulled hand across his cheek and decided he should shave, and went downstairs. There wasn't anybody in the saloon, not even behind the bar. On the tables and on the bar top, however, were several newspapers, all fresh. He was reminded at once that he was in debt to the Wickford County Free Press for the sum of one dollar. He pulled one of the newspapers toward him and turned to the page where all the advertisements were.

When, after some minutes, he finished, he saw that his advertisement was not there. A slow wrath grew in him as he thought of the girl and her father taking his money, and when it had come to full flower, he went out of the Elite and cut across toward the newspaper office. He saw, without really noticing it, the group of men clustered in front of the store across from the newspaper office. He swung under the tie rail and reached the opposite boardwalk just this side of the newspaper office and a man who was lounging against the building. He was a puncher and when he saw Johnny heading up the walk he said, "Don't go across there."

Johnny said grimly, "You stop me," and went on, and he heard the puncher say, "All right, getcher head blown off."

His boots crunched broken glass in front of the office and he came to a gingerly halt, looking down at his feet. His glance raised to the window, and he saw where there was a big jag of glass out of the window, neatly wiping out the WICKFORD except for the "W" on the sign and ribboning cracks to all four corners of the frame. His surprise held him motionless for a moment, and then he heard a voice calling from across the street, "Clear out of there, son."

That makes four times, Johnny thought resignedly, and he glanced across the street and saw Alec Barr, several men clotted around him, looking his way.

Johnny went on and turned into the newspaper office and pit was like walking into a dark cave. The lamp was extinguished.

And then he saw the dim forms of Cassie Melaven and her father back of the railing beside the job press, and the reason for his errand came back to him with a rush. Walking through the gate, he began firmly, "I got a dollar owed—" and ceased talking and halted abruptly. There was a six-shooter in Dan Melaven's hand hanging at his side. Johnny looked at it, and then raised his glance to Melaven's face and found the man watching him with a bitter amusement in his eyes. His glance shuttled to Cassie, and she was looking at him as if she didn't see him, and her face seemed very pale in that gloom. He half gestured toward the gun and said, "What's that for?"

"A little trouble, bub," Melaven said mildly. "Come back for your money?"

"Yeah," Johnny said slowly.

Suddenly it came to him, and he wheeled and looked out through the broken window and saw Alec Barr across the street in conversation with two men, his own hands, Johnny supposed. That explained the shot that wakened him. A little trouble.

He looked back at Melaven now in time to hear him say to Cassie, "Give him his money."

Cassie came past him to the desk and pulled open a drawer and opened the cash box. While she was doing it, Johnny strolled soberly over to the desk. She gave him the dollar and he took it, and their glances met. She's been crying, he thought, with a strange distress.

"That's what I tried to tell you," Cassie said. "We didn't want to take your money, but you wouldn't have it. That's why I was so mean."

"What's it all about?" Johnny asked soberly.

"Didn't you read the paper?"

Johnny shook his head in negation, and Cassie said dully, "It's right there on page one. There's a big chunk of government land out on Artillery Creek coming up for sale. Alec Barr wanted it, but he didn't want anybody bidding against him. He knew pa would have to publish a notice of sale. He tried to get pa to hold off publication of the date of sale until it would be too late for other bidders to make it. Pa was to get a piece of the land in return for the favor, or money. I guess we needed it all right, but pa told him no."

Johnny looked over at Melaven, who had come up to the rail now and was listening. Melaven said, "I knew Barr'd be in today with his bunch, and they'd want a look at a pull sheet before the press got busy, just to make sure the notice wasn't there. Well, Cassie and Dad Hopper worked with me all last night to turn out the real paper, with the notice of sale and a front-page editorial about Barr's proposition to me, to boot."

"We got it printed and hid it out in the shed early this morning," Cassie explained.

Melaven grinned faintly at Cassie, and there was a kind of open admiration for the job in the way he smiled. He said to Johnny now, "So what you saw in the forms this mornin' was a fake, bub. That's why Cassie didn't want your money. The paper was already printed." He smiled again, that rather proud smile. "After you'd gone, Barr came in. He wanted a pull sheet and we gave it to him, and he had a man out front watching us most of the morning. But he pulled him off later. We got the real paper out of the shed on to the Willow Valley stage, and we got it delivered all over town before Barr saw it."

Johnny was silent a moment, thinking this over. Then he nodded toward the window. "Barr do that?"

"I did," Melaven said quietly. "I reckon I can keep him out until someone in this town gets the guts to run him off."

Johnny looked down at the dollar in his hand and stared at it a moment and put it in his pocket. When he looked up at Cassie, he surprised her watching him, and she smiled a little, as if to ask forgiveness.

Johnny said, "Want any help?" to Melaven, and the man looked at him thoughtfully and then nodded. "Yes. You can take Cassie home."

"Oh, no," Cassie said. She backed away from the desk and put her back against the wall, looking from one to the other. "I don't go. As long as I'm here, he'll stay there."

"Sooner or later, he'll come in," Melaven said grimly. "I don't want you hurt."

"Let him come," Cassie said stubbornly. "I can swing a wrench better than some of his crew can shoot."

"Please go with him."

Cassie shook her head. "No, pa. There's some men left in this town. They'll turn up."

Melaven said "Hell," quietly, angrily, and went back into the shop. Johnny and the girl looked at each other for a long moment, and Johnny saw the fear in her eyes. She was fighting it, but she didn't have it licked, and he couldn't blame her. He said, "If I'd had a gun on me, I don't reckon they'd of let me in here, would they?"

"Don't try it again," Cassie said. "Don't try the back either. They're out there."

Johnny said, "Sure you won't come with me?"

"I'm sure."

"Good," Johnny said quietly. He stepped outside and turned upstreet, glancing over at Barr and the three men with him, who were watching him wordlessly. The man leaning against the building straightened up and asked, "She comin' out?"

"She's thinkin' it over," Johnny said.

The man called across the street to Barr, "She's thinkin' it over," and Johnny headed obliquely across the wide street toward the Elite. *What kind of a town is this, where they'd let this happen?* he thought angrily, and then he caught sight of Gus Irby standing under the wooden awning in front of the Elite, watching the show. Everybody else was doing the same thing. A man behind Johnny yelled, "Send her out, Melaven," and Johnny vaulted up onto the boardwalk and halted in front of Gus.

"What do you aim to do?" he asked Gus.

"Mind my own business, same as you," Gus growled, but he couldn't hold Johnny's gaze.

There was shame in his face, and when Johnny saw it his mind was made up. He shouldered past him and went into the Elite and saw it was empty. He stepped behind the bar now and, bent over so he could look under it, slowly traveled down it. Right beside the beer taps he found what he was looking for. It was a sawed-off shotgun and he lifted it up and broke it and saw that both barrels were loaded. Standing motionless, he thought about this now, and presently he moved on toward the back and went out the rear door. It opened on to an alley, and he turned left and went up it, thinking, *It was brick, and the one next to it was painted brown, at least in front.* And then he saw it up ahead, a low brick store with a big loading platform running across its rear.

He went up to it, and looked down the narrow passageway he'd re-membered was between this building and the brown one beside it. There was a small areaway here, this end cluttered with weeds and bottles and tin cans. Looking through it he could see a man's elbow and segment of leg at the boardwalk, and he stepped as noiselessly as he could over the trash and worked forward to the boardwalk.

At the end of the areaway, he hauled up and looked out and saw Alec Barr some ten feet to his right and teetering on the edge of the high board-walk, gun in hand. He was engaged in low conversation with three other men on either side of him. There was a supreme insolence in the way he exposed himself, as if he knew Melaven would not shoot at him and could not hit him if he did.

Johnny raised the shotgun hip high and stepped out and said quietly, "Barr, you goin' to throw away that gun and get on your horse or am I goin' to burn you down?"

The four men turned slowly, not moving anything except their heads. It was Barr whom Johnny watched, and he saw the man's bold baleful eyes gauge his chances and decline the risk, and Johnny smiled. The three other men were watching Barr for a clue to their moves.

Johnny said "Now," and on the heel of it he heard the faint clatter of a kicked tin can in the areaway behind him. He lunged out of the areaway just as a pistol shot erupted with a savage roar between the two buildings.

Barr half turned now with the swiftness with which he lifted his gun across his front, and Johnny, watching him, didn't even raise the shotgun in his haste; he let go from the hip. He saw Barr rammed off the high boardwalk into the tie rail, and heard it crack and splinter and break with the big man's weight, and then Barr fell in the street out of sight.

The three other men scattered into the street, running blindly for the opposite sidewalk. And at the same time, the men who had been standing in front of the buildings watching this now ran toward Barr, and Gus Irby was in the van. Johnny poked the shotgun into the areaway and without even taking sight he pulled the trigger and listened to the bellow of the explosion and the rattling raking of the buckshot as it caromed between the two buildings. Afterward, he turned down the street and let Gus and the others run past him, and he went into the Elite.

It was empty, and he put the shotgun on the bar and got himself a glass of water and stood there drinking it, thinking, *I feel some different, but not much.*

He was still drinking water when Gus came in later. Gus looked at him long and hard, as he poured himself a stout glass of whiskey and downed it. Finally, Gus said, "There ain't a right thing about it, but they won't pay you a bounty for him. They should."

Johnny didn't say anything, only rinsed out his glass.

"Melaven wants to see you" Gus said then.

"All right." Johnny walked past him and Gus let him get past him ten feet, and then said, "Kid, look."

Johnny halted and turned around and Gus, looking sheepish, said, "About that there newspaper piece. That was meant to be a rawhide, but damned if it didn't backfire on me."

Johnny just waited, and Gus went on. "You remember the man that was standing this side of Barr? He works for me, runs some cows for me. Did, I mean, because he stood there all afternoon sickin' Barr on Melaven. You want his job? Forty a month, top hand."

"Sure," Johnny said promptly.

Gus smiled expansively and said, "Let's have a drink on it."

"Tomorrow," Johnny said. "I don't aim to get a reputation for drinkin' all day long."

Gus looked puzzled, and then laughed. "Reputation? Who with? Who knows—" His talk faded off, and then he said quietly, "Oh."

Johnny waited long enough to see if Gus would smile, and when Gus didn't, he went out. Gus didn't smile after he'd gone either.

With the publication of his classic short novel, *Shane*, in 1949, Jack Schaefer (1907–1991) established himself as one of the premier Western writers of all time. The books which followed—*First Blood, The Canyon, Company of Cowards, Monte Walsh*, and such collections as *The Big Range, The Kean Land and Other Stories*, and *The Collected Stories of Jack Schaefer*—firmly cemented that reputation. Nowhere was his talent better displayed than in his short stories, and no short story of his is better than "Sergeant Houck"—a realistic and moving tale of what happens when a young woman, captured by Indians and forced to mate with and bear the child of one of the tribe, is rescued by a cavalry troop.

Sergeant Houck

— ✦ —

Jack Schaefer

Sergeant Houck stopped his horse just below the top of the ridge ahead. The upper part of his body was silhouetted against the sky line as he rose in his stirrups to peer over the crest. He urged the horse on up and the two of them, the man and the horse, were sharp and distinct against the copper sky. After a moment he turned and rode down to the small troop waiting. He reined beside Lieutenant Imler.

"It's there, sir. Alongside a creek in the next hollow. Maybe a third of a mile."

Lieutenant Imler looked at him coldly. "You took your time, Sergeant. Smack on the top, too."

"Couldn't see plain, sir. Sun was in my eyes."

"Wanted them to spot you, eh, Sergeant?"

"No, sir. Sun was bothering me. I don't think—"

"Forget it, Sergeant. I don't like this either."

Lieutenant Imler was in no hurry. He led the troop slowly up the hill. The real fuss was fifty-some miles away. Captain McKay was hogging the honors there. Here he was, tied to this sideline detail. Twenty men. Ten would have been enough. Ten and an old hand like Sergeant Houck.

With his drawn saber pointing forward, Lieutenant Imler led the charge up and over the crest and down the long slope to the Indian village. There were some scattered shots from bushes by the creek, ragged pops indicating poor powder and poorer weapons, probably fired by the last of the old men left behind when the young braves departed in war paint ten days before. The village was silent and deserted.

Lieutenant Imler surveyed the ground they'd taken. "Spectacular achievement," he muttered to himself. He beckoned Sergeant Houck to him.

"Your redskin friend was right, Sergeant. This is it."

"Knew he could be trusted, sir."

"Our orders are to destroy the village. Send a squad out to round up any stock. There might be some horses around. We're to take them in." Lieutenant Imler waved an arm at the thirty-odd skin-and-pole huts. "Set the others to pulling those down. Burn what you can and smash everything else.

"Right, sir."

Lieutenant Imler rode into the slight shade of the cottonwoods along the creek. He wiped the dust from his face and set his campaign hat at a fresh angle to ease the crease the band had made on his forehead. Here he was, hot and tired and way out at the end of nowhere with another long ride ahead, while Captain McKay was having it out at last with Grey Otter and his renegade warriors somewhere between the Turkey Foot and the Washakie. He relaxed to wait in the saddle, beginning to frame his report in his mind.

"Pardon, sir."

Lieutenant Imler looked around. Sergeant Houck was standing nearby with something in his arms, something that squirmed and seemed to have dozens of legs and arms.

"What the devil is that, Sergeant?"

"A baby, sir. Or rather, a boy. Two years old, sir."

"How the devil do you know? By his teeth?"

"His mother told me, sir."

"His mother?"

"Certainly, sir. She's right here."

Lieutenant Imler saw her then, standing beside a neighboring tree, shrinking into the shadow and staring at Sergeant Houck and the squirming child. He leaned to look closer. She wore a shapeless, sacklike covering with slits for her arms and head. She was sun- and windburned dark yet not as dark as he expected. And there was no mistaking the color of her hair. It was light brown and long and coiled in a bun on her neck.

"Sergeant! It's a white woman!"

"Right, sir. Her name's Cora Sutliff. The wagon train she was with was wiped out by a raiding party. She and another woman were taken along. The other woman died. She didn't. The village bought her. She's been in Grey Otter's lodge." Sergeant Houck smacked the squirming boy briskly and tucked him under one arm. He looked straight at Lieutenant Imler. "That was three years ago, sir."

"Three years? Then that boy—"

"That's right, sir."

· · ·

CAPTAIN MCKAY LOOKED up from his desk to see Sergeant Houck stiff at attention before him. It always gave him a feeling of satisfaction to see this great, granite man. The replacements they were sending these days, raw and unseasoned, were enough to shake his faith in the service. But as long as there remained a sprinkling of these case-hardened old-time regulars, the army would still be the army.

"At ease, Sergeant."

"Thank you, sir."

Captain McKay drummed his fingers on the desk. This was a ridiculous situation and the solid, impassive bulk of Sergeant Houck made it seem even more so.

"That woman, Sergeant. She's married. The husband's alive—wasn't with the train when it was attacked. He's been located. Has a place about twenty miles out of Laramie. The name's right and everything checks. You're to take her there and turn her over with the troop's compliments."

"Me, sir?"

"She asked for you. The big man who found her. Lieutenant Imler says that's you."

Sergeant Houck considered this expressionlessly. "And about the boy, sir?"

"He goes with her." Captain McKay drummed on the desk again. "Speaking frankly, Sergeant, I think she's making a mistake. I suggested she let us see that the boy got back to the tribe. Grey Otter's dead and after that affair two weeks ago there's not many of the men left. But they'll be on the reservation now and he'd be taken care of. She wouldn't hear of it; said if he had to go she would, too." Captain McKay felt his former indignation rising again. "I say she's playing the fool. You agree with me, of course."

"No, sir. I don't."

"And why the devil not?"

"He's her son, sir."

"But he's—Well, that's neither here nor there, Sergeant. It's not our affair. We deliver her and there's an end to it. You'll draw expense money and start within the hour."

"Right, sir." Sergeant Houck straightened up and started for the door.

"Houck."

"Yes, sir."

"Take good care of her—and that damn kid."

"Right, sir."

CAPTAIN MCKAY STOOD by the window and watched the small cavalcade go past toward the post gateway. Lucky that his wife had come with him to this godforsaken station lost in the prairie wasteland. Without her they would have been in a fix with the woman. As it was, the woman looked like a woman now. And why shouldn't she, wearing his wife's third-best crinoline dress? It was a bit large, but it gave her a proper feminine appearance. His wife had enjoyed fitting her, from the skin out, everything except shoes. Those were too small. The woman seemed to prefer her worn moccasins anyway. And she was uncomfortable in the clothes. But she was decently grateful for them, insisting she would have them returned or would pay for them somehow. She was riding past the window, sidesaddle on his wife's horse, still with that strange shrinking air about her, not so much frightened as remote, as if she could not quite connect with what was happening to her, what was going on around her.

Behind her was Private Lakin, neat and spruce in his uniform, with the boy in front of him on the horse. The boy's legs stuck out on each side of the small, improvised pillow tied to the forward arch of the saddle to give him a better seat. He looked like a weird, dark-haired doll bobbing with the movements of the horse.

And there beside the woman, shadowing her in the midmorning, was that extra incongruous touch, the great hulk of Sergeant Houck, straight in his saddle, taking this as he took everything, with no excitement and no show of any emotion, a job to be done.

They went past and Captain McKay watched them ride out through the gateway. It was not quite so incongruous after all. As he had discovered on many a tight occasion, there was something comforting in the presence of that big man. Nothing ever shook him. You might never know exactly what went on inside his close-cropped skull, but you could be certain that what needed to be done he would do.

They were scarcely out of sight of the post when the boy began squirming. Private Lakin clamped him to the pillow with a capable right hand. The squirming persisted. The boy seemed determined to escape from what he regarded as an alien captor. Silent, intent, he writhed on the pillow. Private Lakin's hand and arm grew weary. He tickled his horse forward with his heels until he was close behind the others.

"Beg pardon, sir."

Sergeant Houck shifted in his saddle and looked around. "Yes?"

"He's trying to get away, sir. It'd be easier if I tied him down. Could I use my belt, sir?"

Sergeant Houck held in his horse to drop back alongside Private Lakin. "Kids don't need tying," he said. He reached out and plucked the boy from in front of Private Lakin and laid him, face down, across the withers of his own horse and smacked him sharply. Then he set him back on the pillow. The boy sat still, very still. Sergeant Houck pushed his left hand into his left side pocket and pulled out a fistful of small, hard biscuits. He passed these to Private Lakin. "Stick one of these in his mouth when he gets restless."

Sergeant Houck urged his horse forward until he was beside the woman once more. She had turned her head to watch and she stared sidewise at him for a long moment, then looked straight forward again.

They came to the settlement in the same order: the woman and Sergeant Houck side by side in the lead, Private Lakin and the boy tagging behind at a respectful distance. Sergeant Houck dismounted and helped the woman down and handed the boy to her. He saw Private Lakin looking wistfully at the painted front of the settlement's one saloon and tapped him on one knee. "Scat," he said and watched Private Lakin turn his horse and ride off, leading the other two horses.

Then he led the woman into the squat frame building that served as general store and post office and stage stop. He settled the woman and her child on a preserved-goods box and went to the counter to arrange for their fares. When he came back to sit on another box near her, the entire permanent male population of the settlement was assembled just inside the door, all eleven of them staring at the woman.

". . . that's the one . . ."

". . . an Indian had her . . ."

". . . shows in the kid . . ."

Sergeant Houck looked at the woman. She was staring at the floor and the blood was leaving her face. He started to rise and felt her hand on his arm. She had leaned over quickly and clutched his sleeve.

"Please," she said. "Don't make trouble account of me."

"Trouble?" said Sergeant Houck. "No trouble." He stood up and confronted the fidgeting men by the door. "I've seen kids around this place. Some of them small. This one needs decent clothes and the store here doesn't stock them."

The men stared at him, startled, and then at the wide-eyed boy in his clean but patched, skimpy cloth covering. Five or six of them went out through the door and disappeared in various directions. The others scattered through the store. Sergeant Houck stood sentinel, relaxed and quiet, by his box, and those who had gone out straggled back, several embarrassed and empty-handed, the rest proud with their offerings. Sergeant Houck took the boy from the woman's lap and stood him on his box. He measured the offerings against the small boy and chose a small red-checked shirt and a small pair of overalls. He set the one pair of small scuffed shoes aside. "Kids don't need shoes," he said. "Only in winter."

WHEN THE COACH rolled in, it was empty, and they had it to themselves for the first hours. Dust drifted steadily through the windows and the silence inside was a persistent thing. The woman did not want to talk. She had lost all liking for it and would speak only when necessary. And Sergeant Houck used words with a natural economy, for the sole simple purpose of conveying or obtaining information that he regarded as pertinent to the business immediately in hand. Only once did he speak during these hours and then only to set a fact straight in his mind. He kept his eyes fixed on the scenery outside as he spoke.

"Did he treat you all right?"

The woman made no pretense of misunderstanding him. "Yes," she said.

The coach rolled on and the dust drifted. "He beat me once," she said and four full minutes passed before she finished the thought. "Maybe it was right. I wouldn't work."

They stopped for a quick meal at a lonely ranch house and ate in silence while the man there helped the driver change horses. It was two mail stops later, at the next change, that another passenger climbed in and plopped his battered suitcase and himself on the front seat opposite them. He was of medium height and plump. He wore city clothes and had quick eyes and features that seemed small in the plumpness of his face. He took out a handkerchief and wiped his face and took off his hat to wipe all the way up his forehead. He laid the hat on top of the suitcase and moved restlessly on the seat, trying to find a comfortable position.

"You three together?"

"Yes," said Sergeant Houck.

"Your wife then?"

"No," said Sergeant. He looked out the window on his side and studied the far horizon.

THE COACH ROLLED on and the man's quick eyes examined the three of them and came to rest on the woman's feet.

"Begging your pardon, lady, but why do you wear those things? Moccasins, aren't they? They more comfortable?"

She shrank back farther in the seat and the blood began to leave her face.

"No offense, lady," said the man. "I just wondered—" He stopped. Sergeant Houck was looking at him.

"Dust's bad," said Sergeant Houck. "And the flies this time of year. Best to keep your mouth closed." He looked out the window again, and the only sounds were the running beat of the hooves and the creakings of the old coach.

A front wheel struck a stone and the coach jolted up at an angle and lurched sideways and the boy gave a small whimper. The woman pulled him onto her lap.

"Say," said the man. "Where'd you ever pick up that kid? Looks like—" He stopped. Sergeant Houck was reaching up and rapping against the top of the coach. The driver's voice could be heard shouting at the horses, and the coach stopped. One of the doors opened and the driver peered in. Instinctively he picked Sergeant Houck.

"What's the trouble, soldier?"

"No trouble," said Sergeant Houck. "Our friend here wants to ride up with you." He looked at the plump man. "Less dust up there. It's healthy and gives a good view."

"Now, wait a minute," said the man. "Where'd you get the idea—"

"Healthy," said Sergeant Houck.

The driver looked at the bleak, impassive hardness of Sergeant Houck and at the twitching softness of the plump man. "Reckon it would be," he said. "Come along, I'll boost you up."

The coach rolled along the false-fronted street of a mushroom town and stopped before a frame building tagged "Hotel." One of the coach doors opened, and the plump man retrieved his hat and suitcase and scuttled into the building. The driver appeared at the coach door. "Last meal here before the night run," he said.

When they came out, the shadows were long, and fresh horses had been harnessed. As they settled themselves again, a new driver, whip in hand, climbed up to the high seat and gathered the reins into his left hand. The whip cracked and the coach lurched forward and a young man ran out of the low building across the street carrying a saddle. He ran alongside and heaved the saddle up on the roof inside the guardrail. He pulled at the door and managed to scramble in as the coach picked up speed. He dropped onto the front seat, puffing deeply. "Evening, ma'am," he said between puffs. "And you, General." He leaned forward to slap the boy gently along the jaw. "And you too, bub."

Sergeant Houck looked at the lean young man, at the faded Levi's tucked into high-heeled boots, the plaid shirt, the amiable competent young face. He grunted a greeting, unintelligible but a pleasant sound.

"A man's legs ain't made for running," said the young man. "Just to fork a horse. That last drink was near too long."

"The army'd put some starch in those legs," said Sergeant Houck.

"Maybe. Maybe that's why I ain't in the army." The young man sat quietly, relaxed to the jolting of the coach. "Is there some other topic of genteel conversation you folks'd want to worry some?"

"No," said Sergeant Houck.

"Then maybe you'll pardon me," said the young man. "I hoofed it a lot of miles today." He worked hard at his boots and at last got them off and tucked them out of the way on the floor. He hitched himself up and over on the seat until he was resting on one hip. He put an arm on the windowsill and cradled his head on it. His head dropped down and he was asleep.

Sergeant Houck felt a small bump on his left side. The boy had toppled against him. Sergeant Houck set the small body across his lap with the head nestled into the crook of his right arm. He leaned his head down and heard the soft little last sigh as drowsiness overcame the boy. He looked sidewise at the woman and dimly made out the outline of her head falling forward and jerking back up and he reached his left arm along the top of the seat until his hand touched her far shoulder. He felt her shoulder stiffen and then relax as she moved closer and leaned toward him. He slipped down lower in the seat so that her head could reach his shoulder and he felt the gentle touch of her brown hair on his neck above his shirt collar. He waited patiently and at last he could tell by her steady deep breathing that all fright had left her and all her thoughts were stilled.

The coach reached a rutted stretch and began to sway and the young man stirred and began to slide on the smooth leather of his seat. Sergeant Houck put up a foot and braced it against the seat edge and the young man's body rested against it. Sergeant Houck leaned his head back on the top of the seat. The stars came out in the clear sky and the running beat of the hoofs had the rhythm of a cavalry squad at a steady trot and gradually Sergeant Houck softened slightly into sleep.

SERGEANT HOUCK AWOKE, as always, all at once and aware. The coach had stopped. From the sounds outside, fresh horses were being buckled into the traces. The first light of dawn was creeping into the coach. He raised his head and he realized that he was stiff.

The young man was awake. He was inspecting the vast leather sole of Sergeant Houck's shoe. His eyes flicked up and met Sergeant Houck's eyes and he grinned.

"That's impressive footwear," he whispered. "You'd need starch in the legs with hooves like that." He sat up and stretched, long and reaching, like a lazy young animal. "Hell," he whispered again. "You must be stiff as a branding iron." He took hold of Sergeant Houck's leg at the knee and hoisted it slightly so that Sergeant Houck could bend it and ease the foot down to the floor without disturbing the sleeping woman leaning against him. He stretched out both hands and gently lifted the sleeping boy from Sergeant Houck's lap and sat back with the boy in his arms. The young man studied the boy's face. "Can't be yours," he whispered.

"No," whispered Sergeant Houck.

"Must have some Indian strain."

"Yes."

The young man whispered down at the sleeping boy. "You can't help that, can you, bub?"

"No," said Sergeant Houck suddenly, out loud. "He can't."

The woman jerked upright and pulled over to the window on her side, rubbing at her eyes. The boy woke up, wide awake on the instant and saw the unfamiliar face above him and began to squirm violently. The young man clamped his arms tighter. "Morning ma'am," he said. "Looks like I ain't such a good nursemaid."

Sergeant Houck reached out a hand and picked up the boy by a grip on the small overalls and deposited him in a sitting position on the seat beside the young man. The boy sat very still.

THE SUN CLIMBED into plain view and now the coach was stirring the dust of a well-worn road. It stopped where another road crossed and the young man inside pulled on his boots. He bobbed his head in the direction of a group of low buildings up the side road. "Think I'll try it there. They'll be peeling broncs about now and the foreman knows I can sit a saddle." He opened the door and jumped to the ground and turned to poke his head in. "Hope you make it right," he said. "Wherever you're heading." The door closed and he could be heard scrambling up the back of the coach to get his saddle. There was a thump as he and the saddle hit the ground and then voices began outside, rising in tone.

Sergeant Houck pushed his head through the window beside him. The young man and the driver were facing each other over the saddle. The young man was pulling the pockets of his Levi's inside out. "Lookahere, Will," he said. "You know I'll kick in soon as I have some cash. Hell, I've hooked rides with you before."

"Not now no more," said the driver. "The company's sore. They hear of this they'd have my job. I'll have to hold the saddle."

"You touch that saddle and they'll pick you up in pieces from here to breakfast."

Sergeant Houck fumbled for his inside jacket pocket. He whistled. The two men turned. He looked hard at the young man. "There's something on the seat in here. Must have slipped out of your pocket."

The young man leaned in and saw the two silver dollars on the hard seat and looked up at Sergeant Houck. "You've been in spots yourself," he said.

"Yes," said Sergeant Houck.

The young man grinned. He picked up the two coins in one hand and swung the other to slap Sergeant Houck's leg, sharp and stinging and grateful. "Age ain't hurting you any, General," he said.

The coach started up and the woman looked at Sergeant Houck. The minutes passed and still she looked at him.

"If I'd had brains enough to get married," he said, "might be I'd have a son. Might have been one like that."

The woman looked away, out her window. She reached up to pat at her hair and the firm line of her lips softened in the tiny imperceptible beginnings of a smile. The minutes passed and Sergeant Houck stirred again.

"It's the upbringing that counts," he said and settled into silent immobility, watching the miles go by.

It was near noon when they stopped in Laramie and Sergeant Houck handed the woman out and tucked the boy under one arm and led the way to the waiting room. He settled the woman and the boy in two chairs and left them. He was back soon, driving a light buckboard wagon drawn by a pair of deep-barreled chestnuts. The wagon bed was well padded with layers of empty burlap bags. He went into the waiting room and picked up the boy and beckoned to the woman to follow. He put the boy down on the burlap bags and helped the woman up on the driving seat.

"Straight out the road, they tell me," he said. "About fifteen miles. Then right along the creek. Can't miss it."

He stood by the wagon, staring along the road. The woman leaned from the seat and clutched at his shoulder. Her voice was high and frightened. "You're going with me?" Her fingers clung to his service jacket. "Please! You've got to!"

Sergeant Houck put a hand over hers on his shoulder and released her fingers. "Yes. I'm going." He put the child in her lap and stepped to the seat and took the reins. The wagon moved forward.

"You're afraid," he said.

"They haven't told him," she said, "about the boy."

Sergeant Houck's hands tightened on the reins and the horses slowed to a walk. He clucked sharply to them and slapped the reins on their backs and they quickened again into a trot. The wagon topped a slight rise and the road sloped downward for a long stretch to where the green of trees and tall bushes showed in the distance. A jackrabbit started from the scrub growth by the roadside and leaped high and leveled out, a gray brown streak. The horses shied and broke rhythm and quieted to a walk under the firm pressure of the reins. Sergeant Houck kept them at a walk, easing the heat out of their muscles, down the long slope to the trees. He let them step into the creek up to their knees and dip their muzzles in the clear running water. The front wheels of the wagon were in the creek and he reached behind him to find a tin dipper tucked among the burlap bags and leaned far out to dip up water for the woman and the boy and himself. He backed the team out of the creek and swung them into the wagon ruts leading along the bank to the right.

The creek was on their left and the sun was behind them, warm on their backs, and the shadows of the horses pushed ahead. The shadows were longer, stretching farther ahead, when they rounded a bend along the creek and the buildings came in sight, the two-room cabin and the several lean-to sheds and the rickety pole corral. A man was standing by one of the sheds and when Sergeant Houck stopped the team he came toward them and stopped about twenty feet away. He was not young, perhaps in his middle thirties, but with the young look of a man on whom the years have made no mark except that of the simple passing of time. He was tall, soft, and loose-jointed in build, and indecisive in manner and movement. His eyes wavered as he looked at the woman, and the fingers of his hands hanging limp at his sides twitched as he waited for her to speak.

She climbed down her side of the wagon and faced him. She stood straight and the sun behind her shone on her hair. "Well, Fred," she said. "I'm here."

"Cora," he said. "It's been a long time, Cora. I didn't know you'd come so soon."

"Why didn't you come get me? Why didn't you, Fred?"

"I didn't rightly know what to do, Cora. It was all so mixed up. Thinking you were dead. Then hearing about you. And what happened. I had to think about things. And I couldn't get away easy. I was going to try maybe next week."

"I hoped you'd come. Right away when you heard."

His body twisted uneasily while his feet remained flat and motionless on the ground. "Your hair's still pretty," he said. "The way it used to be."

Something like a sob caught in her throat and she started toward him. Sergeant Houck stepped down on the other side of the wagon and walked off to the creek and knelt to bend and wash the dust from his face. He stood drying his face with a handkerchief and watching the little eddies of the current around several stones in the creek. He heard the voices behind him.

"Wait, Fred. There's something you have to know."

"That kid? What's it doing here with you?"

"It's mine, Fred."

"Yours? Where'd you get it?"

"It's my child. Mine."

There was silence and then the man's voice, bewildered, hurt. "So it's really true what they said. About that Indian."

"Yes. He bought me. By their rules I belonged to him. I wouldn't be alive and here now, any other way. I didn't have any say about it."

There was silence again and then the man spoke, self-pity creeping into his tone. "I didn't count on anything like this."

Sergeant Houck walked back to the wagon. The woman seemed relieved at the interruption. "This is Sergeant Houck," she said. "He brought me all the way."

The man nodded his head and raised a hand to shove back the sandy hair that kept falling forward on his forehead. "I suppose I ought to thank you, soldier. All that trouble."

"No trouble," said Sergeant Houck.

The man pushed at the ground in front of him with one shoe, poking the toe into the dirt and studying it. "I suppose we ought to go inside. It's near suppertime. I guess you'll be taking a meal here, soldier, before you start back to town."

"Right," said Sergeant Houck. "And I'm tired. I'll stay the night, too. Start in the morning. Sleep in one of those sheds."

The man pushed at the ground more vigorously. The little pile of dirt in front of his shoe seemed to interest him a great deal. "All right, soldier. Sorry there's no quarters inside." He turned quickly and started for the cabin.

THE WOMAN TOOK the boy from the wagon and followed him. Sergeant Houck unharnessed the horses and led them to the creek for a drink and to the corral and let them through the gate. He walked quietly to the cabin doorway and stopped just outside.

"For God's sake, Cora," the man was saying, "I don't see why you had to bring that kid with you. You could have told me about it. I didn't have to see him."

"What do you mean?"

"Why, now we've got the problem of how to get rid of him. Have to find a mission or some place that'll take him. Why didn't you leave him where he came from?"

"No! He's mine!"

"Good God, Cora! Are you crazy? Think you can foist off a thing like that on me?"

Sergeant Houck stepped through the doorway. "Thought I heard something about supper," he said. He looked around the small room, then let his eyes rest on the man. "I see the makings on those shelves. Come along, Mr. Sutliff. A woman doesn't want men cluttering about when she's getting a meal. Show me your place before it gets dark."

He stood, waiting, and the man scraped at the floor with one foot and slowly stood up and went with him.

THEY WERE WELL beyond earshot of the cabin when Sergeant Houck spoke again. "How long were you married? Before it happened?"

"Six years," said the man. "No, seven. It was seven when we lost the last place and headed this way with the train."

"Seven years," said Sergeant Houck. "And no child."

"It just didn't happen. I don't know why." The man stopped and looked sharply at Sergeant Houck. "Oh. So that's the way you're looking at it."

"Yes," said Sergeant Houck. "Now you've got one. A son."

"Not mine," said the man. "You can talk. It's not *your* wife. It's bad enough thinking of taking an Indian's leavings." He wiped his lips on his sleeve and spat in disgust. "I'll be damned if I'll take his kid."

"Not his anymore. He's dead."

"Look, man. Look how it'd be. A damn little half-breed. Around all the time to make me remember what she did. A reminder of things I'd want to forget."

"Could be a reminder that she had some mighty hard going. And maybe come through the better for it."

"*She* had hard going! What about me? Thinking she was dead. Getting used to that. Maybe thinking of another woman. Then she comes back—and an Indian kid with her. What does that make me?"

"Could make you a man," said Sergeant Houck. "Think it over." He turned away and went to the corral and leaned on the rail, watching the horses roll in the sweat-itches out of the dry sod. The man went slowly down by the creek and stood on the bank, pushing at the dirt with one shoe and kicking small pebbles into the water. The sun, holding to the horizon rim, dropped suddenly out of sight and dusk came swiftly to blur the outlines of the buildings. The woman appeared in the doorway and called and they went in. There was simple food on the table and the woman stood beside it. "I've already fed him," she said and moved her head toward the door to the inner room.

Sergeant Houck ate steadily and reached to refill his plate. The man picked briefly at the food before him and stopped, and the woman ate nothing at all. The man put his hands on the table edge and pushed back and stood up. He went to a side shelf and took a bottle and two thick cups and set them by his plate. He filled the cups a third full from the bottle and shoved one along the table boards toward Sergeant Houck. He lifted the other. His voice was bitter. "Happy homecoming," he said. He waited and Sergeant Houck took the other cup and they drank. The man lifted the bottle and poured himself another drink.

The woman looked quickly at him and away. "Please, Fred."

The man paid no attention. He reached with the bottle toward the other cup.

"No," said Sergeant Houck.

The man shrugged. "You can think better on whiskey. Sharpens the mind." He set the bottle down and took his cup and drained it. Sergeant Houck fumbled in his right side pocket and found a short straight straw there and pulled it out and put one end in his mouth and chewed slowly on it. The man and the woman sat still, opposite each other at the table, and seemed to forget his quiet presence. They stared everywhere except at each other. Yet their attention was plainly concentrated on one another. The man spoke first. His voice was restrained, carrying conscious patience.

"Look, Cora. You wouldn't want to do that to me. You can't mean what you said before."

Her voice was determined. "He's mine."

"Now, Cora. You don't want to push it too far. A man can take just so much. I didn't know what to do after I heard about you. But I was all ready to forgive you. And now you—"

"Forgive me!" She knocked against her chair rising to her feet. Hurt and bewilderment made her voice ragged as she repeated the words. "Forgive me?" She turned and ran into the inner room. The handleless door banged shut behind her.

The man stared after her and shook his head and reached again for the bottle.

"Enough's enough," said Sergeant Houck.

The man shrugged in quick irritation, "For you maybe," he said and poured himself another drink. "Is there any reason you should be nosying in on this?"

"My orders," said Sergeant Houck, "were to deliver them safely. Both of them."

"You've done that," said the man. He lifted the cup and drained it and set it down carefully. "They're here."

"Yes," said Sergeant Houck. "They're here." He stood up and stepped to the outside door and looked into the night. He waited a moment until his eyes were accustomed to the darkness and could distinguish objects faintly in the starlight. He stepped out and went to the pile of straw behind one of the sheds and took an armload and carried it back by the cabin and dropped it at the foot of a tree by one corner. He sat on it, his legs stretched out, his shoulders against the tree, and broke off a straw stem and chewed slowly on it. After awhile his jaws stopped their slow slight movement and his head sank forward and his eyes closed.

SERGEANT HOUCK WOKE up abruptly. He was on his feet in a moment, and listening. He heard the faint sound of voices in the cabin, indistinct but rising as the tension rose in them. He went toward the doorway and stopped just short of the rectangle of light from the lamp.

"You're not going to have anything to do with me!" The woman's voice was harsh with stubborn anger. "Not until this has been settled right!"

"Aw, come on, Cora." The man's voice was fuzzy, slow-paced. "We'll talk about that in the morning."

"No!"

"All right!" Sudden fury made the man's voice shake. "You want it settled now! Well, it's settled! We're getting rid of that damn kid first thing tomorrow!"

"No!"

"What gave you the idea you've got any say around here after what you did? I'm the one to say what's to be done. You don't be careful, maybe I won't take you back."

"Maybe I don't want you to!"

"So damn finicky all of a sudden! After being with the Indian and maybe a lot more!"

Sergeant Houck stepped through the doorway. The man's back was to him, and he spun him around and his right hand smacked against the side of the man's face and sent him staggering against the wall.

"Forgetting your manners won't help," said Sergeant Houck. He looked around, and the woman had disappeared into the inner room. The man leaned against the wall, rubbing his cheek, and she came out, the boy in her arms, and ran toward the outer door.

"Cora!" the man shouted. "Cora!"

She stopped, a brief hesitation in flight. "I don't belong to you," she said and was gone through the doorway. The man pushed out from the wall and started after and the great bulk of Sergeant Houck blocked the way.

"You heard her," said Sergeant Houck. "She doesn't belong to anybody now. Nobody but that boy."

The man stared at him and some of the fury went out of his eyes and he stumbled to his chair at the table and reached for the bottle. Sergeant Houck watched him a moment, then turned and quietly went outside. He walked toward the corral and as he passed the second shed, she came out of the darker shadows and her voice, low and intense, whispered at him.

"I've got to go. I can't stay here."

Sergeant Houck nodded and went on to the corral. He harnessed the horses quickly and with a minimum of sound. He finished buckling the traces and stood straight and looked toward the cabin. He walked to the doorway and stepped inside. The man was leaning forward in his chair, his elbows on the table, staring at the empty bottle.

"It's finished," said Sergeant Houck. "She's leaving now."

The man shook his head and pushed at the bottle with one forefinger. "She can't do that." He looked up at Sergeant Houck and sudden rage began to show in his eyes. "She can't do that! She's my wife!"

"Not anymore," said Sergeant Houck. "Best forget she ever came back." He started toward the door and heard the sharp sound of the chair scraping on the floor behind him. The man's voice rose, shrilling up almost into a shriek.

"Stop!" The man rushed to the wall rack and grabbed the rifle there and held it low and aimed it at Sergeant Houck. "Stop!" He was breathing deeply and he fought for control of his voice. "You're not going to take her away!"

Sergeant Houck turned slowly. He stood still, a motionless granite shape in the lamplight.

"Threatening an army man," said Sergeant Houck. "And with an empty gun."

The man wavered and his eyes flicked down at the rifle. In the second of indecision Sergeant Houck plunged toward him and one huge hand grasped the gun barrel and pushed it aside and the shot thudded harmlessly into the cabin wall. He wrenched the gun from the man's grasp and his other hand took the man by the shirtfront and pushed him down into the chair.

"No more of that," said Sergeant Houck. "Best sit quiet." He looked around the room and found the box of cartridges on a shelf and he took this with the rifle and went to the door. "Look around in the morning and you'll find these." He went outside and tossed the gun up on the roof of one of the sheds and dropped the little box by the pile of straw and kicked some straw over it. He went to the wagon and stood by it and the woman came out of the darkness, carrying the boy.

THE WAGON WHEELS rolled silently. The small creakings of the wagon body and the thudding rhythm of the horses' hooves were distinct, isolated sounds in the night. The creek was on their right and they followed the road back the way they had come. The woman moved on the seat, shifting the boy's weight from one arm to the other, until Sergeant Houck took him by the overalls and lifted him and reached behind to lay him on the burlap bags. "A good boy," he said, "has the Indian way of taking things without yapping. A good way."

The thin new tracks in the dust unwound endlessly under the wheels and the waning moon climbed through the scattered bushes and trees along the creek.

"I have relatives in Missouri," said the woman. "I could go there."

Sergeant Houck fumbled in his side pocket and found a straw and put this in his mouth and chewed slowly on it. "Is that what you want?"

"No."

They came to the main-road crossing and swung left and the dust thickened under the horses' hooves. The lean dark shape of a coyote slipped from the brush on one side and bounded along the road and disappeared on the other side.

"I'm forty-seven," said Sergeant Houck. "Nearly thirty of that in the army. Makes a man rough."

The woman looked straight ahead and a small smile showed in the corners of her mouth.

"Four months," said Sergeant Houck, "and this last hitch's done. I'm thinking of homesteading on out in the Territory." He chewed on the straw and took it between a thumb and forefinger and flipped it away. "You could get a room at the settlement."

"I could," said the woman. The horses slowed to a walk, breathing deeply, and he let them hold the steady, plodding pace. Far off a coyote howled and others caught the signal and the sounds echoed back and forth in the distance and died away into the night silence.

"Four months," said Sergeant Houck. "That's not so long."

"No," said the woman. "Not too long."

A breeze stirred across the brush and she put out a hand and touched his shoulder. Her fingers moved down along his upper arm and curved over the big muscles there and the warmth of them sank through the cloth of his worn service jacket. She dropped her hand in her lap again and looked ahead along the ribbon of the road. He clucked to the horses and urged them again into a trot and the small creakings of the wagon body and the dulled rhythm of the hooves were gentle sounds in the night.

The late moon climbed and its pale light shone slantwise down on the moving wagon, on the sleeping boy and the woman looking straight ahead, and on the great solid figure of Sergeant Houck.

Americans love success stories, and few success stories match that of John Jakes. Following a long career in advertising, during which he wrote innumerable novels and short stories, he found his literary fortunes waning. Then, in the 1970s, he was commissioned to write the American Bicentennial series and very quickly became one of the world's bestselling authors. He has written virtually every kind of fiction, and excels at all of them, but the Western seems to bring out his best work and most passionate feelings. He is particularly good with characters common to the American frontier, and the protagonists in the story chosen for his book, "Manitow and Ironhand" are no exception.

Manitow and Ironhand

A TALE OF THE STONY MOUNTAINS

—◆—

John Jakes

Dedicated to the memory of Karl May.

THE FREE TRAPPER, a strapping shaggy white man of indeterminate age, waded into his secret stream about a quarter mile above the wide beaver dam. His darting glance revealed no dangers; nor did he truly expect any, this far into the wilderness.

His buckskin shirt was wet, and soiled by many hasty meals. His buckskin leggings were stagged at the knees, where he'd sewn on pieces of fine English blanket, which wouldn't shrink. Leggings and his wool-lined moccasins were last year's tipi of a Crow chief of his acquaintance.

Shadows of quaking aspens and bending willows were growing longer. It was nearing the twilight hour, the ideal time for setting out traps. He would set this one, his fifth of the afternoon, then one more before returning to his campsite, there to rest until he rose before daybreak to clear the traps. He shifted his campsite nightly; a professional precaution of those who worked alone. Also, he now had eighty plews to protect—a valuable mixed bale of beaver, marten, and otter, weighing nearly a hundred pounds. So far the spring trapping season had been bountiful.

The late afternoon air was light and warm, but the water was still icy from the melted snows. The soft-burbling stream froze his bones and set his hands to aching, the good right one and the mangled left one he concealed with a filthy mitten except when he was at his trade, as now. He went by the name "Old Ironhand," though he really wasn't old, except in spirit. The snowy white streaks in his long hair were premature. There was a bitter cynicism in his eyes, the oldest part of him.

Once his name had been Ewing. Ewing Something. It was a name he no longer used, and struggled to remember. Ever since he'd split with the Four Flags outfit, and Mr. Alexander Jaggers—ever since they'd crippled his left hand, causing him to compensate with exercises that strengthened the other one, welding five digits into a weapon—to the free trappers and those who still gave allegiance to the large outfits, he was Old Ironhand.

He waded along, carrying the seven-pound trap and chain in his left hand, the pin pole in his right. He moved carefully, the small sounds of his passage undetectable because of the water's purl. This was a fine stream; he'd been working it for a year. It yielded fat mature beaver, fifty to sixty pounds each, with choice tails he charred, skinned, then boiled as a mealtime delicacy. Hip deep in his secret stream, he felt good as he approached a natural beaver slide worn into the bank at the water's edge. The shadowed air was sweet. The trees were a-bud, the mountain peaks pristine as a new wedding dress, the sky a pale pink, like a scene from a book about fairyland. He saw a mockingbird singing alertly on a bush. It was 1833, in the Stony Mountains, far from the civilized perfidy of other white men.

He laid the pin pole on the bank. He crouched in the water and lowered the trap to the bottom, drawing out the chain with its ring at the end. By now he was bent like a bow, half his beard immersed. The water smelled icy and clean.

He pushed the pin pole through the ring on the chain. Then he grasped the pole with both hands and began to twist it into the marly bottom. He leaned and pushed and twisted with his great right hand bloodless-white around the pole. If the trapped beaver didn't gnaw his paw off and escape—if he died as he should, by drowning—the pole would site his carcass.

In order to leave as little man-scent as possible, Ironhand worked obliquely backward toward the bank, to a willowy branch he'd already selected for its pronounced droop. He unstoppered his horn of medicine, which he compounded from secret ingredients added to the musky secretions of beaver glands, and with this he coated the end of the drooping branch. The strongly scented end of the branch hung near the pin pole.

Hands on his hips, he inspected his work. Though by now his teeth were chattering—the spring warmth was leaching from the plum-colored shadows—he was satisfied. Felt better than he had in a long spell. One more trap to place, then he'd have his supper, and a pipe.

He was turning to move on to the next location when the rifle shot rang out. The bullet hit him high in the back. Toppling, he thought not of the awful hot pain but instead of his failure to hear the rifleman stealing up for the cowardly ambush. *Careless damn fool! Should've kept your eyes skinned!* He was reasonably sure of his attacker's identity, but that wasn't much damn satisfaction as the muddy bank hurled up to strike him.

And that was all there was.

SOMEONE HAD DRAGGED him to level ground.

Someone had rolled him on his back.

Someone had built a fire whose comforting heat played along the left side of his seamed face, and the back of his ruined hand. The fire was vivid, shooting off sparks as brilliant as the mountain stars. A curtain of smoke blew away on a puff of breeze.

He elbowed himself to a raised position, clenching his teeth against the pain. The Samaritan was squatting on the other side of the fire. A young Indian, with a well-sculpted nose, firm mouth, light brown skin that shimmered bronze in the firelight. His glowing dark eyes were not unfriendly, only carefully, unemotionally observant.

Bluish-black hair hung like a veil down his back, to his waist. His costume consisted of moccasins ornamented with porcupine quills and bright trade beads, fringed leggings, a hunting coat of elk leather. Around his neck hung a small medicine bag that nestled inside his coat against his bare chest. Outside the coat, ornamentation was a three-strand necklace of bear claws. A double-barrel rifle rested within his reach.

"I put medicine on you. The ball is still there. It must come out. Do you understand?"

"Delaware," Ironhand grunted, not as a question. He understood perfectly.

"Yes." The Indian nodded. "I am Manitow."

"My pardner, the one they killed at the rendezvous two year ago, he was Delaware. Named after the great old chief Tammany. Fine man." So were most of the members of the tribe who roved the Stony Mountains. The Delaware had been driven from Eastern hunting grounds eighty to ninety years ago; had migrated over the Mississippi and successfully taken up farming on the plains. A few, more restless and independent, had pushed farther on to the mountains. Enemies of the Delaware, including ignorant whites, sneered at them as Petticoat Indians. That was not only stupid but dangerous. Ironhand knew the Delaware to be keen shots, excellent horsemen, superb trackers and readers of sign. They were honest, quick to learn, resourceful in the wilderness. You could depend on them unless for some reason they hated you.

The Delaware could find the remotest beaver streams as handily as a magnet snapped bits of iron to itself. Thus they were prized pardners of the free trappers, or prized employees of the outfits such as Four Flags.

The white man licked his dry lips, then said, "I'm called Old Ironhand."

"I have heard of you. Who shot you?"

"I think it was the Frenchman, *Petit Josep. Petit Josep Clair de Lune.* Little Joe Moonlight."

"Works for Jaggers."

"I worked for Jaggers . . . "

"I know that. Don't talk anymore. The ball must come out." In a calm, almost stately way, Manitow rose from his crouch. His hair shimmered, black as the seepage of one of the oil springs that produced the tar trappers like Ironhand rubbed on their arthritic joints.

Without being told, Ironhand rolled over to his belly. It hurt hellishly. In the firelight a long rustfree knife sparkled in Manitow's hand; an authentic Green River—Ironhand glimpsed the GR, *George Rex,* stamped into the blade in England. It was a knife as good as Ironhand's own, which he'd left with his possibles bag, his bale of plews, and his carbine, in what he'd presumed was a safe clearing upstream.

Manitow laid the knife on the ground. From a pocket in his coat he took the all-purpose awl most Delaware carried. He placed this beside the knife. One or the other, or maybe both, would mine for lead in Ironhand's back. The trapper stared at the implements with bleary eyes and made a heavy swallowing sound.

Manitow knelt beside him. With a gentle touch he lifted Ironhand's bloody shirt high enough to expose the wound glistening with smelly salve. With the fingers of his left hand Manitow spread the dark brown edges of the wound. A swift, sharp inhale from Ironhand was the only sound.

"Be sure you get it out," he said. "I don't want to go down with the sun. That bastard Jaggers has to pay. Little Joe Moonlight will pay. Go ahead, dig."

"I don't have whiskey," Manitow said.

"I don't need any whiskey," Ironhand said. "Dig."

A NIGHT BIRD trilled in the darkness. Old Ironhand listened drowsily. He was coming awake; hadn't died under Manitow's ministrations, which had hurt infernally. He had, however, fainted at the moment the Indian worked the rifle ball out of the wound with bloody fingers, ending the ordeal.

Ironhand's eyes fluttered open. Against a morning sky the color of lemons, Manitow crouched by the fire as he had the night before; a small dented pot, blue enamelware, sat in the embers.

A white mist floated on the high peaks. The air nipped; Manitow had found a colorful trade blanket as a coverlet for the trapper. Ironhand heard a nickering; tried to rise up.

"Your horses are safe, with mine," Manitow said. "Your gun and plews also." Small comfort, now that Ironhand realized the outfit was still after him.

Manitow stretched out his hand, offering a strip of *charqui,* the smoked buffalo meat that was a staple of frontiersmen. The trapper caught the meat between his teeth. He lay back, gazing at the sky, and chewed.

The enamel pot lid clinked when Manitow lifted it. "Coffee is boiling. Ready soon."

Ironhand grunted and kept chewing. A hawk sailed in heaven, then plunged and vanished in the mists. The cold ground smelled of damp and made him think of death, not springtime. On his back under his shirt, where the Indian had prospected for lead, a thick pad of some kind told him Manitow had improvised a dressing.

"You have been a trapper for many years," the Indian said in a reflective way.

Old Ironhand pushed the jerky into his cheek, like a cud, while he answered. "Twenty years next summer."

"All that time. And a man stalks you and you don't see any sign?"

"I wasn't looking for none."

"You didn't hear him?"

His anger was sudden, overriding his pain. "I was in the stream. It makes noise. I was thinking about my traps. I thought the outfit was done with me. Christ, they did me enough damage—why not?"

Manitow's grunt seemed to scorn that naive conclusion. The damn Indian made Ironhand uneasy with his quiet, unruffled manner. His air of wisdom annoyed and puzzled the trapper, because of Manitow's relative youth.

"Done with you?" Manitow repeated. "Not when the fur trade is sickly and you steal profits from the company by working for yourself and selling to others."

"You sure"—a gasp of pain punctuated the sentence—"seem to know a devil of a lot about me. How come?"

Ironhand's head was rolled to the side now; his old reddened eyes stared. Almost shyly, Manitow dropped his own gaze to the smoldering fire, from which he pulled the dented pot. He poured steaming coffee into Ironhand's own drinking cup.

"Help me sit up. Then answer my damn question."

There followed a slow and elaborate ritual of raising him, Manitow gently pulling on his forearms rather than pushing at his back. Resting on his elbows worsened Ironhand's pain again, but his position enabled him to suck some of the bitter hot coffee out of the cup Manitow held to his lips. At length the Indian said, "The people in the Stony Mountains know Old Ironhand. They know the evil ways of Four Flags, too. For five winters and summers I have been north, Canada, hunting and trapping. Even so far away, we heard of the crimes of Four Flags. No more talk. Rest awhile now."

"I've got to go," the trapper protested, wriggling on his elbows and accidentally falling back, a terrific jolt that made him cry out. "Got to go," he repeated in a hoarse voice. "Catch that Little Joe . . ."

"In a day or two. No sooner."

The Indian's flat declaration angered the trapper again. Then a bolt of guilt struck him; he was being an ungrateful bastard. After licking a drop of coffee from his droopy mustache, he said, "I didn't thank you proper yet. For taking care of my wound and all. For coming along when you did. That was a piece of luck."

Manitow silently watched the ethereal mist drifting over the hidden peaks.

"Anyway—it's a debt I owe."

Manitow's eyes, black and opaque, met his again. "I am sorry I did not come in time to stop the assassin. Fortunately he was a bad shot."

"Little Joe has a big opinion of himself. I 'spect he thought he couldn't miss."

"And I was coming close, so he couldn't wait to find out. I was not far behind him, though approaching from a different direction. That's why I didn't see his sign, only heard his rifle. Until then I did not know there were two hunting you."

Confusion was followed by a stab of fear. "Two? Who else . . . ?"

Manitow stared.

"You? Why?"

"To see what kind of man you were. Are. I hold you responsible."

"For what?"

"The death of my brother. The one who was your pardner."

Ah, Christ, Christ, Ironhand cried silently, stunned harder than he was when the rifle ball struck him. *He's no friend. He saved me for the pleasure of killing me himself.*

BUT THERE WAS no apparent hostility in the Indian's speech or demeanor. He merely asked the trapper to give him a brief history of the quarrel that had led to his brother's death, and the cowardly attack by the lackey of Four Flags.

"I'd have to go back a few years," Old Ironhand said. "The summer rendezvous of '28. I had quit as a brigade leader for the outfit a year before, but on good terms with Jaggers—we had an agreement that Four Flags would take all my plews and I'd work for no other." Four Flags was a fur company as big and powerful as Astor's. English, French, Russian, and American interests had pooled money to establish it. The boss west of St. Louis was Alexander Jaggers, who headquartered at Kirk's Fort.

The annual summer rendezvous was a combination trade mart and revel; a great gathering where spring plews were sold, and trappers bought new equipment pack-trained out from St. Louis, all in the midst of much drinking and horse racing and woman swapping and other familiar entertainments of the frontier. Manitow said that before he went to Canada he had come down from the Wind Rivers several times, to the barren and unlovely Upper Valley of the Green, there to take part in the rendezvous himself. Ironhand didn't remember meeting him, or hearing his name.

Speaking slowly, taking occasional sips of the cooling coffee, the trapper explained that it was at the summer rendezvous of '28 that he saw his first black silk topper. A disreputable German merchant of traps, cutlery, and other metalware was wearing it. The hat was already hard-used, soiled by filthy stains, and pierced by a bullet front and back. Ironhand had quickly understood it was the enemy when the peddler said, "These they are wearing on the Continent now. Gents in the East are taking up the fashion. It's the modern style, beaver hats will go out, you mark me. Also my cousin in Köln writes me to say inventors are perfecting machines to manufacture fine felting cheaply from all kinds of materials, even paper. This trade will die. Is dying now."

The following two years confirmed it. In the great days, the high days of the trade, when Ironhand was still a brigade leader, the company paid as much as $9 a plew to certain free trappers to keep them working exclusively for Four Flags. By 1830 all was changed; average plews selling for $4 at St. Louis slipped to $3.75, no matter who trapped the animals. Then buyers at the summer rendezvous refused to go above $3.50. Ironhand was haunted by memories of the silk topper.

ALEXANDER JAGGERS WAS a short, prim Scot; a Glaswegian. A bachelor, his two passions were Four Flags and his religion. When he first came out to Kirk's Fort in 1822, he had transported a compact gleaming Philadelphia-made pump organ on which he played and sang Christian hymns in a stentorian voice.

In 1831 Jaggers spoke to Ironhand about the price of plews. They were still dropping. Every free trapper working for Four Flags would have to accept $3, St. Louis, or further business was impossible. Ironhand refused.

Alexander Jaggers showed no visible anger, merely turned his back, swished up his coattails, sat at the organ, and began to play and sing "Saviour, Like a Shepherd Lead Us." But to bring Ironhand in line, discipline him, show him his error, Jagger's henchman, Little Joe Moonlight, set on Ironhand's pardner at the summer rendezvous.

Little Joe, a mustachioed weasel-chinned fellow, turned up with a couple of the bravos who frequently backed his most brutal plays. They cornered Ironhand's pardner while the trapper was occupied with a comely Snake woman, the Snake women being universally conceded as the most attractive, and the most generous with their favors, of all the women of the many tribes.

Little Joe and his cronies pretended they were merely sporting with Tammany, hazing him, before the accident happened. As Ironhand learned afterward, Little Joe and his bravos seized the Indian's wrist and swung him round and round in circles, cracking his arm like a whip. Tammany tried to fight them but the odds were wrong; he was soon reeling.

One of the bravos knocked the bung from a small whiskey keg and poured the contents over the Delaware. The bravos and Little Joe roared. But they swore ever afterward that the dousing was supposed to be the end of it. How the stray ember from a nearby cook fire accidentally fell on Tammany, igniting the spirits, was a mystery. Damn shame, but a mystery. Little Joe and his bravos fled the rendezvous before Ironhand could catch up to them. Ironhand's pardner lived a day and a night, in broiled black agony, before the mercy of death.

Ironhand, who at the time went by his old name, left the encampment at once. He rode night and day for Kirk's Fort, there to confront Alexander Jaggers, who never personally went to the rendezvous. Little Joe Moonlight had beaten Ironhand to the fort and was hovering in Jagger's quarters when Ironhand, full of drink, kicked the door down and leaped on the Scot to strangle him.

"Little Joe whistled up his bravos," Ironhand said to Manitow. "They swarmed on me. Looking pious as a deacon, Mr. Jaggers said that in a spirit of Christian forgiveness, Little Joe would only break the hand I used least."

He held up the twisted crooked fingers; Manitow had removed the dirty mitten while he slept.

The misshapen claw was sufficient to suggest the scene: Little Joe's helpers knocking Ironhand to the floor, stomping him into a stupor. Little Joe slapping Ironhand's outstretched arm over a table while the bravos held fast to the groggy trapper's shoulders; the bravos had flung him to a kneeling position.

Gleefully, Little Joe raised a trade hatchet and smashed the blunt end of the blade on the outstretched hand. At the organ, his back turned to the mayhem, Mr. Jaggers pumped and sang:

> *"We've a story to tell to the nations*
> *That shall turn their hearts to the right!*
> *A story of truth and mercy!*
> *A story of peace and light!"*

Little Joe Moonlight grasped Ironhand's index finger, bent it, and broke it. Then he broke the middle finger. Next the ring finger. After a few more blows with the now-bloody hatchet, he broke the little finger. To Ironhand's everlasting disgust, when Little Joe bent the thumb backward and that snapped, he screamed. More than once. Sweaty-cheeked, Mr. Jaggers pumped faster, and sang to drown the noise:

> *"We've a song to be sung to the nations*
> *That shall lift their hearts to the Lord!*
> *A song that shall conquer evil*
> *And shatter the spear and sword!*
> *For the darkness shall turn to dawning . . ."*

He remembered his hand lying on the table like a bloody red piece of buffalo hump. He remembered starting to swoon.

> *"And the dawning to noonday bright!*
> *And Christ's great kingdom shall come on earth,*
> *The kingdom of Love and Light!"*

Then Ironhand heard Little Joe, his voice very distant, as though he were shouting in a windy cave. "You don't need to play no more, Mr. Jaggers, he's all done screaming."

Little Joe lifted his head by the hair and let it fall, *thump . . .*

Out of some perverse piety that governed him, Mr. Jaggers rushed Ironhand to a comfortable bunk in the fort barracks, and saw to it that he was given excellent treatment until he recovered his senses.

His hand, of course, was permanently maimed. This Mr. Jaggers totally ignored when he and Ironhand parted. Jaggers shook the trapper's right hand—the left was already concealed by the first of many mittens. "The account book is closed, laddie." It was not, but Ironhand was too enraged to do anything except glare. "We part as competitors, but eternal friends. Christ counsels forgiveness above all."

"Forgiveness," Ironhand muttered, waving his mitten in an obvious way. Mr. Jaggers merely beamed and pumped the other hand . . .

"That was two years back," Ironhand explained to Manitow in a weary voice. "After awhile I came to believe his crazy cant about forgiving and forgetting. I wanted to mend my life, so I didn't take after him as I could have. I sold my plews to Astor, though they say he's tired of falling prices too and will get out. . . . What a fool I was, wouldn't you say? Trying to get on with keeping alive, forgetting Jaggers?"

The spring sun had burned off the spectral mist; the snow peaks were brilliant against hazy lavender sky. Ironhand was exhausted from speaking. Manitow chewed on a strip of *charqui* and considered what he'd heard. At last he said, "Many traps are set in this wilderness. You were caught in the cruelest of all. Trust."

And do I dare trust you, you ring-tailed savage? Not so far's as I could throw you. I daren't turn my back.

Still, there were necessities.

"Will you help me up? I have to pee."

"Clasp my arm with both hands."

Ironhand braced his boot heels and was slowly, painfully raised to standing position. His eyes were close to Manitow's a moment but he could read nothing there, except what he imagined was there—an intent to murder. The trap of trust, was it? Well, not a second time . . .

As he hobbled toward a grove of white birch trees, he bit out, "This time I won't turn my cheek. I'm going after that pissant who does the dirty work for Jaggers."

"I will go with you."

Ironhand twisted around, causing a hell-hot pain in his bandaged back. "Why? So's you can pass judgment?"

His face a smooth bronze mask, Manitow said, "It may be so."

I won't turn my back, you red devil . . .

But he hobbled on, grasping Manitow's arm for support; for the present he was at the mercy of the unavoidable necessities.

THEY RODE SOUTHEAST, the direction of Kirk's Fort. The fort stood sixty miles beyond the foothills of the Stony Mountains, at the confluence of two shallow muddy streams. It was the jumping-off place for St. Louis. Ironhand presumed it was also the destination of the quarry whose sign they were following. He was in constant pain, but it was bearable. Hate was a stronger painkiller than opium.

He trailed his three pack mules behind his old roan. Manitow could have sped ahead because he had a better horse, which he rode with only a scrap of blanket and his moccasined heels. The Indian's horse was small, with spots like swollen inkblots on his white rump. The trapper enviously compared his faithful but sorry saddle animal, Brownie, with the other horse, which the Cayuse tribe had bred and sold to the Indian. Cayuse and Nez Perce horses were the best a man could find. Ironhand had evidence of it the first morning. He woke in his odorous blankets to find Manitow gone. A distant drumming stilled sudden alarm. Somewhere in the foothills Manitow was galloping his spotted horse.

Another thing bred envy, in the same dark inner place as Ironhand's suspicion of murder being planned: Manitow's skill with sign. The second noon, examining horse dung, Ironhand said, "He's near a day in front of us."

Manitow shook his head. "Less than half a day. Moving slowly. Not fearful he will be caught."

Ironhand's cheeks turned red above his beard that still held crumbs of ship's biscuit from breakfast. "Why 'n hell not? He knows he didn't put me down for good."

"That may be so, it may not. I will show you why he doesn't worry." Manitow led him to a clump of stunted shrubbery, stepped around it, pointed. Ironhand saw more droppings. "There are three now. Your assassin and two more."

"Since when in hell—?"

"Sunset, yesterday."

"You damn well should've told me."

Manitow smiled. "It would have spoiled our supper. If I had told you then, would you have stopped this chase?"

"Not likely."

The Indian bobbed his head, vindicated.

They talked intermittently as they tracked Little Joe Moonlight and his companions moving southeast ahead of them. Manitow expressed no surprise at the treatment the trapper had received from Four Flags. "Theft, ambush, murder—it is the way of the strong companies against the single weak rebel. It is the way of those while men who are evil."

Which should have soothed Ironhand's suspicion a little, since it was clear from Manitow's voice and expression which side he favored. But Ironhand wasn't soothed. He continued to insist that Manitow ride ahead of him; they had sorted that out before they started. Ironhand still believed Manitow would try to murder him at the first opportunity.

They exchanged stories of their trials in the wilderness. Manitow pushed up the sleeve of his hunting coat to reveal a snakelike scar on his left forearm. Ironhand, who had seen plenty of horrors in his time, was nevertheless a little sick at the sight of the healed tissue, because of what had made it. Manitow had survived the bites of a rabid wolf, in the land of the Apaches, far south. He didn't explain why he had been in the land of the Apaches.

Ironhand told of nearly starving to death several times during his career. "I slew my mules and drank their blood once. I ate my moccasins twice. Another time, all I could find to feed on after five days were ants from an anthill." Manitow seemed to find these exploits unremarkable; almost to be expected.

He did express admiration for Ironhand's carbine. The trapper explained that it was a custom creation from the armory of the legendary

Wyatt Henry of St. Louis. The revolving magazine, Henry's unique design, held five rounds.

Manitow asked to handle the piece. Ironhand said no. Manitow looked at him, and seemed to sneer just before he trotted his spotted horse ahead again.

As the mountains fell behind, the twisted gullies straightened; the shale ridges sank; the spring prairie rose up to greet them. They saw a migratory herd of buffalo passing southward in a dust cloud that boiled nearly to the apex of the sky. "Thousands upon thousands of shaggy brothers," Manitow said. Ironhand growled something under his breath; he already knew the herd was huge; they had been watching it the best part of an hour. The upstart savage was beginning to anger as well as worry him.

Or was it the sign they'd read—two unknown bravos and a third smug killer lolling their way toward Kirk's Fort without concern? Manitow insisted the trio was only a couple of hours ahead now.

A sunlit dust seemed to float above the silent plain surrounding them. The sky was tawny, like the earth, only a few cottonwoods with twisted shapes breaking the horizon. The vista had the serene quality of a landscape painting, but the diffuse light and dust gave it a touch of the unreal, like a picture from one of those fables of old Greek gods Ironhand dimly remembered reading from a hornbook when he was a child, in a civilized place somewhere.

At sunset they stopped to camp and eat. The trapper took some kindling from a parfleche strapped to a mule. Manitow watched him build a small pyramid of sticks, then said, "If you cook they will see the smoke."

"Hardly matters, does it? We'll find each other one way or another. That's the idea."

Late next day they approached a wide turgid stream Ironhand identified as Paint River, though the only artist's color represented in its flow was dirty brown. Natural features surrounding Kirk's Fort had been named by the fur men passing through.

While they watered and rested their animals, Ironhand advised the Indian that one more day would bring them to the headquarters of Four Flags. "I have to speed. Leave the mules. Catch them before they're safe inside the fort."

"Even with three against you?"

Ironhand answered with a nod.

Manitow sighted ahead. "I will go on a little way."

He didn't ask permission, hitting his spotted horse with his heels and splashing on across Paint River. Ironhand hunkered down on the long narrow hump of an island in the middle of the water, where they'd pulled up. What the hell was the upstart savage about?

Manitow galloped away till he was a speck, then galloped back. He threw himself off his spotted horse, looking unhappy.

"One has gone on ahead, leaving two. Their tracks turn north. I think they saw the smoke and are circling back."

Ironhand's gaze crawled to stunted trees on the northern horizon. Nothing moved there, nor anyplace. Manitow said, "We should camp. I do not think you need to chase your enemy anymore. He will find you. He knows you are hurt. But he will think you are alone."

Ironhand scowled, gripping his Henry rifle with his powerful right hand. "I am. Isn't your fight."

"I am here, so it will be. There is no reason not to cook again. Have you any sticks left in the saddlebag?"

IRONHAND SLEPT BADLY, rolling around with his carbine clutched against his middle, the way he'd slept with it nightly since he met the prowling Indian. A new moon shed pale light on the plain, which was flat for miles in every direction save north, where a pronounced tilt raised the horizon. Along that horizon the crooked trees stood out. If there were a fight on this barren hump of island, would he have to look out for Manitow and Little Joe Moonlight at the same time? A threat of death from two directions?

He wished he could sleep but it was impossible. Manitow lay to his left, hands crossed on his shirt bosom, profile sharp in the pale moonshine. The Indian breathed softly, steadily, like a small boy sleeping without care.

He must have dozed. He woke to Manitow barking his name. Ironhand floundered to his knees, saw Manitow standing beyond the mules and pointing to the stunted trees. Two riders were pounding down the inclined plain, riding with their knees and reins in their teeth. Each held a brace of revolvers. Four guns against his one.

"Protect yourself," Manitow cried, diving under the belly of a snorting, bucking mule. Seizing Ironhand, he tried to throw him to the ground. Little Joe Moonlight and his burly pardner were riding hell-bent for the hump island, but Ironhand refused to cower. He shook off the Indian and took his fighting stance with his carbine at his shoulder. His blood was up; he didn't care that he presented a perfect target.

The riders were closer. He distinctly saw Little Joe's mean white triangular face, his long Chinese-style mustaches, his leering smirk. Still short of the river bank, Little Joe and his pardner opened up with all four barrels. Ironhand stood his ground and squeezed his trigger. Manitow tackled him. Yelling, Ironhand toppled. Only the fall prevented one of the flying bullets from finding him.

He didn't realize this; all his anger was directed against the damned

Indian. He screamed oaths, trying to get up as Little Joe Moonlight galloped into the stream, closely followed by his henchman. Manitow snatched his double-barrel rifle from its saddle loop. The blued metal flashed.

The charging horses tossed up fans of moonlit water. Little Joe passed to the left of Ironhand and the Indian, the henchman to the right. They were firing continuously. One of their bullets hit Manitow's rifle, a lucky shot that blew apart the breech. Manitow leaped back, momentarily blinded. A bullet hit Ironhand's left thigh just as he stood up. With a cry he fell a second time. The back of his head struck the earth. Stars danced.

The mules bucked and bellowed. Two of them tore their picket pins out and ran into the stream, braying, Ironhand heard the attackers splash to the bank of Paint River behind him and there wheel for another charge. His back wound, cruelly bruised by his fall, hurt nearly as much as the thigh wound bleeding into the leg of his hide trousers. He had to get up . . . *had* to. Tried it and, with a howl of despair and fury, fell back again. He heard the attacking horses coming on, in the river.

Standing over the wounded trapper, Manitow said, "Give me the rifle."

He'll use it to kill me . . .

"The rifle!"

Don't dare, I can't trust . . .

"White man, if you don't, we'll die."

There was a halo of hoof-driven dust around Manitow's head. He looked like some ghost of one of his primitive ancestors. His outstretched brown hand opened, demanding. "White man—*obey me!*"

The hooves were thunderous. Risking all, the supreme act of trust, Ironhand flung the carbine upward and Manitow snatched it and put it to his shoulder. Bullets were flying again but Manitow stood firm and fired and kept firing. As the horse of Little Joe's henchman passed within Ironhand's field of vision, the trapper saw the nameless bravo lift in his saddle as if being jerked to heaven. The bravo's horse ran out from under him and he crashed and rolled into the brown water, staining it with blood from his open belly.

Ironhand was shouting without realizing it. "Stop firing, there are only five—"

Too late; some part of his brain had already counted five shots. Manitow had exhausted the magazine in one volley.

And Little Joe Moonlight, his long thin mustaches whipping against his cheeks, was unhurt.

He wheeled his horse in the water, making him dance to the island, then stand still while Little Joe raised his revolver with his shooting hand, clasped it with his other hand and pointed it at Manitow's head at close range.

It all happened quickly. Ironhand acted from instinct, coming upright,

dizzy and tortured by pain but willing it not to matter. He leaped at Little
Joe Moonlight and his prancing horse. Little Joe was angrily heeling the
animal while trying to steady himself for the shot. Manitow crouched and
pulled his knife to throw it but Little Joe would fire first. There was no
cover to keep the Indian from death.

The horse sidestepped again; Little Joe screamed a filthy oath. He realized too late that his mount had sidestepped *toward* Ironhand. . . .

Ironhand's face contorted into a bestial parody of a grin. His filthy mitten closed on Little Joe's right arm. Little Joe understood his peril and
shrieked girlishly. Ironhand brought his huge right hand upward from his
hip at great speed while pulling his enemy out of the saddle. The angle was
right; the edge of the trapper's hand struck Little Joe's windpipe with
speed and force.

Paralyzed, Little Joe dropped his revolver. Two streams of blood
spurted from his nostrils. Ironhand threw Little Joe on the sere ground
and knelt on his chest with one knee. He snatched his knife from the thong
at his waist. Poised to cut Little Joe's throat, Ironhand started at a touch
on his shoulder.

"Wait. Look at him. His spirit is gone. It flew before he touched the
earth."

Ironhand changed position so that he could press an ear to his enemy's
chest. He hunched that way for a long space, then raised his head, starting
to shake from shock. Manitow was right again. The heart of Little Joe
Moonlight had stopped.

Ironhand lurched up. His wounded leg would barely support him. His
back was screaming with pain. He poked his knife at the thong loop on his
belt and missed. He missed a second time. Manitow took the knife from
him and put it in place, giving the thong an extra twist to secure the hilt.

Ironhand raked a trembling hand through his dirty beard. "I—didn't
want to give you the rifle."

"Why?"

"I knew you'd kill me after you saved yourself."

"Why?"

"Your brother—"

"The white man's mind," Manitow said with enormous disgust. "Don't
you think I had a hundred opportunities to kill you before this?"

"But you said I was responsible—"

"That was before I met you. I wanted to learn what sort you are. I
learned. You learned nothing, you were full of poison bile of fear. You're
like all the rest of the whites, even though not as bad as some. It's lucky
you broke down and gave me the rifle or the story would end differently."

He stepped forward suddenly—it seemed menacing until Ironhand realized the true import. Then he felt a fool. Manitow supported his back

and forearm gently. "Now you had better lie down before you fall down, white man." He no longer sounded scornful.

STIFF AND SORE in heavy bandages, Ironhand rode alone up the dirt track to the gate of Kirk's Fort. Draped in a U over the neck of his horse Brownie was the smelly corpse of Little Joe Moonlight.

Kirk's Fort was old and famous on the plains. It was a large rectangular stockade with a blockhouse at every corner. Cabins and warehouse buildings formed two of its walls. Ironhand passed through the palisade by the main gate, which opened on a long dirt corridor of sheds and shops. A second inner gate led to the quadrangle, where Indians were never admitted; all trading was done in the corridor, though even here there were precautions. Bars on the shop windows; iron shutters on the windows of the storehouse that held trade goods.

A toothless fort Indian sat against the wall, looking sadly displaced in a white man's knitted cap and a white soldier's discarded blouse. He popped his eyes at Ironhand, whom he recognized. The trapper rode on through the second gate and straight across the trampled soil of the quadrangle to the Four Flags headquarters building. Company employees appeared around corners or from doorways of the accounting office, the strongbox room, the powder house, staring at Ironhand in a bewildered way. Someone called a greeting he didn't acknowledge. No one stopped him as he kicked the office door open and lumbered through, Little Joe's stiffening body folded over his shoulder, his Henry carbine tucked under his arm.

Alexander Jaggers was occupied with familiar things: his quill, his account books. Seeing the looming figure, he exclaimed, "Ewing! Laddie— what's this? Ye dinna hae the courtesy to knock or announce yersel—"

He was stopped by Ironhand slipping the Henry onto the seat of a chair, then laying the body of Little Joe Moonlight on top of the wide wooden desk. It disarranged the account books and overturned the ink pot, which dripped its contents on the old floor.

"He met with an accident. It happens often in the mountains," Ironhand said with a meaningful look at the master of Four Flags.

Jaggers reddened, puffing out his cheeks. He darted a hand to a drawer of the desk but Ironhand was quicker. He leaped on the desk, over Little Joe's corpse, and pushed Jaggers, toppling him and his chair at the same time. Jaggers flailed, kicking his legs in the air and yelling decidedly unChristian oaths.

Ironhand jumped down and retrieved his Henry rifle from the chair. He took aim and emptied the revolving magazine, five rounds, into Mr. Jagger's pump organ in the corner. After the roar of the volley, the organ exhaled once, loudly, like a man with pierced lungs gasping his last.

The trapper stepped to the pump organ and attacked its wood cabinet with his right hand. The hand beat and smashed like a hammer; a mace; a sledge. Thin veneers cracked and snapped. Jaggers was screaming and vainly trying to rise, but his fall had sprung some leg muscle, and each attempt was more futile than the last; he continued to wail on his back, heels in the air.

Ironhand locked his two hands together, the good with the ruined, and brought this huge hammerhead of flesh and bone down on the frame of the organ, breaking it in two as if it were a man's spine.

Jaggers screamed misery and rage.

Ironhand picked up his Henry and walked out without a backward look.

THE DAYLIGHT WAS waning too soon. Sunset was many hours away. But the sky and the prairie were dark, and the air was damp. Away in the north, thunder was bumping.

The dew and damp produced a ground mist that congealed and spread rapidly. As Ironhand rode to the cottonwood grove two miles west of the fort, he craned around in his saddle—at no small cost in pain—and saw the corner blockhouses floating above murky gray mist-clouds, like ogres' castles in the sky in a fairytale.

When he reached the grove, Manitow woke up, scratched his back, stood, asked, "Where for you now?"

"Back to the mountains. Back to the beaver. It's the only trade I know. They aren't all wearing silk toppers in New York town yet, I wager."

Manitow paused before saying, "I know secret streams, Old Ironhand. Three or four, locked so far in the Stony Mountains you would never find them alone."

"Hmm. Well. Let's see. I'd like a pardner again. A free trapper needs a pardner. But I never paid your brother any sort of fee, like many do. We split what the plews brought in."

"That would be agreeable."

"If you think you can trust me not to cost you your life?" Ironhand asked, a sudden flash of sourness.

Manitow took it calmly, seriously. "The old Scot will trouble you no more, I think. But can you trust me?"

Ironhand's wreck of a face seemed to relax. "We crossed that river awhile back."

Slowly, with graceful ceremonious moves, Manitow the Delaware drew from his waist his splendid long Green River knife. He held it out, handle first.

With equal ceremony, Ironhand took his equally fine knife from its thong. He held it out the same way. Among the men of the mountains, white and red, there was no more significant gesture of trust.

"Pardner."

"Pardner."

They exchanged knives. Manitow kissed the fingers of his right hand and raised them over his head in a mystical gesture. Ironhand laughed, deep and rumbling. They mounted up and rode away together into the storm.

Afterword

The western writer Karl May probably did more to promote the splendor and excitement of the West to non-Americans than anyone except Buffalo Bill Cody, king of the scouts, the arena show, and the dime novel. Yet not many fans of the genre, perhaps excluding specialist scholars, know of him.

Surely it is because Karl May was born in Saxony in 1842, wrote only in German, and visited America just once—four years before his death in 1912. By that time he had written seventy-four volumes, forty of them set in "the American Wild West."

May was decidedly an odd bird for this sort of missionary work. He knew about the West only through reading—some of which was done in prison. May was jailed four times in his early life, for assorted thefts and swindles. During his longest sentence, four years, he ran a prison library.

May's youth was hard. He was afflicted with spells of near-blindness. He came from what we would call a dysfunctional family. Of thirteen brothers and sisters, nine died.

When old enough, he entered a preparatory school for teachers. He was expelled for stealing. It didn't seem to teach him a lesson; other crimes— other incarcerations—followed.

But reading somehow turned him around, much as it turns around quite a few convict-writers. In 1875 Karl May published the first of his westerns.

His white hero had different names in different stories: Old Surehand; Old Firehand; Old Shatterhand. He was a *Westmänner* (Westman)—not a native frontiersman but a strong, suave, cultured European who quickly adapted to the rigors and perils of the West by means of intelligence and physical strength. Old Shatterhand possessed a "mighty fist" useful for dispatch of villains. But he also carried firepower, in the form of a fantastic repeating rifle customcrafted by the "legendary" gunsmith, Mr. Henry of St. Louis. This *Henrystutzen* (Henry carbine) with its revolving chamber holding twenty-five rounds is not to be confused with the more familiar Henrys; there is no connection beyond the name.

Partnered with May's Surehand/Shatterhand character was a young Indian, first introduced to readers around 1892. Winnetou is a consistently

brave and brainy Apache chief educated by a Christian tutor, hence recep-
tive to the "civilized" ways of Europe, and the white man with whom he
adventures.

The two heroes wandered all over the map of the West, meeting again
and again by remarkable coincidence, and removing an untold number of
malefactors. In one historical quarterly, a scholar did a body count of four
representative May novels totaling 2,300 pages. The number of persons
going to their rewards was 2,012. They were dispatched by shooting,
scalping, knifing, drowning, poisoning—and sixty-one were put down by
the "mighty fist" previously cited.

May had a fair grasp of Western geography, except in one respect. In addition to familiar settings of mountains and deserts, he repeatedly used "an
impenetrable cactus forest"—exact location unspecified.

May's works have been translated into many languages but seldom, if at
all, into English. Yet they've sold upwards of fifty million copies, and continue to sell. You find long shelves of May in almost every bookshop in
Germany, just as you find long shelves of L'Amour throughout the United
States.

At least thirty films have been made from May's novels. An entire publishing house devoted to them was founded in 1913. At summer encamp-
ments similar to those of American Civil War reenactors, mild-mannered
fans gather in costume to act out the exploits of their two heroes. Now
doctoral dissertations are being written about Karl May.

So it seemed fitting, and an enjoyable challenge, to pay respects to him
with a story about a couple of Westerners who battle a decidedly rotten
crew from a fur trust. The story takes place in what May sometimes called
the Stony Mountains.

I have used variations of the names of his two leading characters, and
kept the marvelous repeating Henry (reduced to an arbitrary five shots).
Those are the only resemblances. Ironhand is not a "blond Teutonic super-
man who speaks a dozen languages fluently and lards his conversations
with little sermons about God and Christianity." Manitow is neither a chief
nor an Apache. My intent was to create *un hommage* to an important figure in the literature of the West, not to write a pastiche of May's work,
which I can't translate very well anyway with my rudimentary German. I
wanted a story bathed in a diffuse pastel-colored mist, like a legend. A
story not overly realistic. In short, the kind of Western story someone
might have written from afar.

One other note: The hymn Mr. Jaggers sings is reverse anachronism; it
was composed years after the period of the story. But in context, the lyrics
proved irresistible.

Evan Hunter is one of popular fiction's modern masters. As Ed McBain, he created the 87th Precinct, one of the most popular mystery series of all time; and as Hunter he has written many novels that have captured wide public acclaim, including *The Blackboard Jungle* and *Last Summer*. His Westerns contain many elements of his mysteries, including ruthless criminals and hard-bitten lawmen. "The Killing at Triple Tree" is one of his best.

The Killing at Triple Tree

Evan Hunter

I saw the rider appear over the brow of the hill, coming at a fast gallop. He loomed black against the scrub oak lining the trail, dropped into a small gulley, and splashed across the narrow creek. I lost sight of him behind an outcropping of gray boulders, and when he appeared again it was right between the ears of the sorrel I was riding, like a target resting on the notched sight of a rifle.

The sorrel lifted her head, blocking the rider from view for a moment. She twitched her ears and snorted, and I laid my hand on her neck and said, "Easy, girl. Easy now."

The rider kept coming, dust pluming up around him. He was mounted on a roan, and the lather on the horse's flanks told me he'd been riding hard for a long time. He came closer, and then yelled, "Johnny! Hey, Johnny!"

I spurred the sorrel and galloped down the road to meet him. He'd reined in, and he stood in his stirrups now, the sweat beading his brow and running down his nose in a thin trickle.

"Johnny! Christ, I thought I'd never find you."

The rider was Rafe Dooley, one of my deputies, a young kid of no more than nineteen. He'd been tickled to death to get the badge, and he wore it proudly, keeping it polished bright on his vest.

"What's the matter, Rafe?"

He swallowed hard and passed the back of his hand over his forehead. He shook the sweat from his hand, then ran his tongue over the dryness of his lips. It took him a long time to start speaking.

"What the hell is it, Rafe?"

"Johnny, it's . . . it's . . ." He stopped again, a pained expression on his face.

"Trouble? Is it trouble?"

He nodded wordlessly.

"What kind of trouble? For God's sake, Rafe, start . . ."

"It's May, Johnny. She . . ."

"May?" My hands tightened on the reins. "What's wrong? What happened?"

"She's . . . she's dead, Johnny."

For a second, it didn't register. I was staring at the drop of sweat working its way down Rafe's nose, and I kept staring at it, almost as if I hadn't heard what he'd said. It began to seep in then, not with sudden shock, but a sort of slow comprehension, building inside me, the way thunderheads build over the mountains.

"What?" I asked. "What did you say, Rafe?"

"She's dead," he said, and he almost began crying. His face screwed up, and he began shaking his head from side to side. "I didn't want to tell you. I wanted them to send someone else. Johnny, I didn't want to be the one. She's dead, Johnny. She's dead."

I nodded, and then I shook my head, and then I nodded again. "What . . . what happened? How . . ."

"You'll see her, Johnny," he said. "Please, don't make me talk about it. Please, Johnny. Please."

"Where?"

"In town. Johnny, I didn't want to tell . . ."

"Come on, Rafe."

DOC TALMADGE HAD pulled a sheet over her.

I stared at the white fabric outlining her body, and I almost knew it was her before I'd seen her face. Doc stood near the table and reached for the sheet.

"It's May, Johnny," he said. "You sure you want to see her?"

"I'm sure."

"Johnny . . ."

"Pull back the sheet, Doc."

Doc Talmadge shrugged, let out his breath, and pulled his brows together in a frown. He took the end of the sheet in careful fingers, gently pulled it back over her face.

Her hair lay beneath her head like a nest of black feathers, cushioning the softness of her face. Her eyes were closed, and her skin was like snow, white and cold. Her lips were pressed together into a narrow line, and a trickle of blood was drying at one corner of her mouth.

"I . . . I didn't wash her off," Doc said. "I wanted you to . . ."

Her shoulders were bare, and I saw the purple bruises just above the hollow of her throat. I took the sheet from Doc's hands and pulled it all the way down. She was wearing a skirt, but it had been torn to tatters. She was barefoot, and there were scratches on the long curve of her legs. She wore no blouse. The bruises above her waist were ugly against the swell of her breasts.

I pulled the sheet over her and turned away.

"Where'd they find her?" I asked.

"The woods. Just outside of town. She had a basket with her, Johnny, and some flowers in it. I guess she was just . . ." —he took another deep breath—"picking flowers."

"Who did it?" He turned to me.

"I don't know, Johnny."

"A posse out?"

"We were waiting for you. We figured . . ."

"Waiting? Why? Why in Christ's name were you waiting?"

Doc seemed to pull his neck into his collar. "She . . . she's your wife, Johnny. We thought . . ."

"Thought, hell! The sonovabitch who did this is roaming around loose, and you all sat around on your fat duffs! What the hell kind of thinking is that?"

"Johnny . . ."

"Johnny, Johnny, Johnny! Shut up! Shut up and get out in the street and get some riders for me. Get some riders for me, Doc. Get some riders . . ." I bunched my fists into balls, and I turned my face away from Doc because it had hit me all of a sudden and I didn't want him to see his town marshal behaving like a baby. "Get me some riders," I said, and then I choked and didn't say anything else.

"Sure, Johnny. Sure."

THEY SHOWED ME the spot where May had been attacked.

A few scattered flowers were strewn over the ground. Some of the flowers were stamped into the dirt, where the attacker's boots had trod on them. May's blouse was on the ground, too, the buttons gone from it, and some of the material torn when the blouse had been ripped.

We followed her tracks to where the attacker must have first spotted her. There was a patch of daisies on a green hillock near the edge of the woods. The trail ran past the hillock, and any rider on the trail would have had no difficulty in spotting a girl picking flowers there. Beyond the hillock, we found the rider's sign. The sign was easy to read, with the horse's right hind leg carrying a cracked shoe. We saw the spot some fifty feet from the hillock, where the rider had reined in and sat his saddle for a while, it seemed. The dead ashes of a cigarette lay in the dust of the trail, and it was easy to get the picture. The rider had come around the bend, seen May on the hillock, and pulled in his horse. He had watched her while he smoked a cigarette, and then started for the hillock. The tracks led around the daisy patch, with clods of earth and grass pulled out of the hill where the horse had started to climb. May must have broken away at about that time and started into the woods, with the rider after her. We found both her shoes a little ways from the hillock, and the rider's tracks following across the floor of the forest. He'd jumped from his horse, it looked like, and grabbed her then, taking what he wanted, and then strangling her to death.

We followed the tracks to the edge of the forest, the sign of the cracked hind shoe standing out like an elephant's print. When they reached the trail again, they blended with a hundred hoofprints to form a dusty, tangled puzzle.

I looked at the muddled trail.

"It don't look good, Johnny," Rafe said.

"No."

"What are we going to do?"

"Split up. You come with me, Rafe. We'll head away from town. The rest of you head back to town and on through toward Rock Falls. Stop anyone you meet on the trail. If you find a rider on a horse with a cracked shoe, bring him in."

"Bring him in, Johnny?" one of the possemen asked.

"You heard me."

"Sure. I just thought . . ."

"Bring him in. Let's go, Rafe."

We turned our mounts and started riding away from the woods, and away from the scene of May's attack. There was an emptiness inside me, and a loneliness, as if someone had deliberately drained all feeling from me, as if someone had taken away my life and left only my body. We rode in silence because there was nothing to say. Rafe looked at me from time to time, uneasy in my company, the way a man would be in a funeral parlor when the corpse was someone he knew.

We'd been riding for an hour when Rafe said, "Up ahead, Johnny."

We reined in, and I looked at the cloud of dust in the distance.

"A rider."

"Going like hell afire," Rafe said.

"I'll take him, Rafe," I said softly. "Get back to town."

"Huh?"

"Get back to town. I'll bring him in."

"But, Johnny, I thought you wanted my . . ."

"I don't want anything, Rafe. Just get the hell back to town and leave me alone. I'll take care of this."

"Sure. I'll see you, Johnny."

Rafe turned his mount, and I waited until he was out of sight before I started after the rider. I gave the sorrel the spurs, and I rode hard because the rider was out to break all records for speed. The distance between us closed, and when I was close enough, I fired a shot over my head. I saw the rider's head turn, but he didn't stop, so I poured on a little more, closing the gap until I was some thirty feet behind him.

"Hey!" I yelled. "Hey, you!"

The rider pulled up this time, and I brought my horse up close to his, wheeling around to get a good look at him.

"What's your hurry, mister?" I asked.

He was tall and rangy, and he sat his saddle with the practiced ease of years of experience. He wore a gray hat pulled low over his eyes, and a shock of unruly brown hair spilled from under his hat onto his forehead. A blue bandana was knotted around his throat, and his shirt and trousers were covered with dust and lather.

"What's it to you?" he asked. His voice was soft, mildly inquisitive, not in the least offensive.

"I'm the marshal of Triple Tree."

"So?"

"You been through town lately?"

"Don't even know where your town is," he said.

"No?"

"Nope. Why? Somebody rob a bank or something?"

"Something," I said. "Want to get off your mount?" He was riding a sorrel that could have been a twin to my own horse.

"Nope, can't say that I do. Suppose you tell me what's on your mind, marshal?"

"Suppose I don't."

The rider shrugged. He wasn't a bad-looking fellow, and a half-smile lurked at the corners of his mouth and in the depths of his blue eyes. "Marshal," he said, "this here's a free country. You don't want to tell me what you're all het up about, that's fine with me. Me, I'll just mosey along and forget I ever . . ."

"Just a second, mister."

"Yes, marshal?" He moved his hands to his saddle horn, crossed them there. He wore a single Colt .44 strapped to his waist, the holster tied to his thigh with a leather thong.

"Where are you bound?"

"Nowheres in particular. Down the road a piece, I suppose. Might be able to pick up some work there. If not, I'll ride on a little more."

"What kind of work?"

"Punching. Cattle drive. Shoveling horse manure or cow dung. I ain't particular."

"How come you didn't ride through Triple Tree?"

"I crossed over the mountains yonder," he said. "Spotted the trail and headed for it. Any law against that?"

"What's your name?"

The rider smiled. "Jesse James. My brother Frank's right behind that tree there."

"Don't get funny," I told him. "I'm in no mood for jokes."

"You *are* in a pretty sour mood, ain't you, marshal?" He wagged his head sorrowfully. "Something you et, maybe?"

"What's your name, mister?"

"Jack," he said simply, drawling the word.

"Jack what?"

"Hawkins. Jack Hawkins."

"Get off your horse, Hawkins."

"Why?"

I was through playing games. I cleared leather and rested the barrel of my gun on my saddle horn. "Because I say so. Come on, swing down."

Hawkins eyed the .44 with respect. "My, my," he said. He swung his long legs over the saddle, and looked at the gun again. "My!"

"You better drop your gun belt, Hawkins."

Hawkins's eyes widened a bit. "I'll bet a bank *was* robbed," he said. "Hell, marshal, I ain't a bank robber." He loosened his belt and dropped the holstered .44 to the road.

"Back away a bit."

"How far, marshal?"

"Listen . . ."

"I just asked . . ."

I fired two shots in quick succession, both plowing up dirt a few inches from his toe boots.

"Hey!"

"Do as I say, goddamnit!"

"Sure, sure." A frown replaced the smile on his face, and he stood watching me tight-lipped.

I walked around the side of his horse and lifted the right hind hoof. I stared at it for a few seconds, and then dropped it to the dust again.

"Where's her shoe?" I asked.

"On her hoof," Hawkins replied. "Where the hell do you suppose it would be?"

"She's carrying no shoe on that hoof, Hawkins."

He seemed honestly surprised. "No? Must have lost it. I'll be damned if everything doesn't happen to me."

"Was the shoe cracked? Is that why she lost it?"

"Hell, no. Not that I know of."

I looked at him, trying to read meaning in the depths of his eyes. I couldn't tell. I couldn't be sure. A horse could lose a shoe anytime. That didn't mean it was carrying a cracked shoe, before the shoe got lost.

"You better mount up," I said.

"Why?"

"We're taking a little ride back to Triple Tree."

"You intent on pinning that bank job on me, ain't you? Marshal, I ain't been in a bank in five years."

"How long is it since you've been in the woods?"

"What?"

"Mount up!"

Hawkins cursed under his breath and reached for his gun belt in the dust.

"I'll take care of that," I said. I hooked it with my toe and pulled it toward me, lifting it and looping it over my saddle horn.

Hawkins stared at me for a few seconds, then shook his head and swung into his saddle. "Here goes another day shot up the behind," he said. "All right, marshal, let's get this goddamned farce over with."

THE TOWN WAS deserted.

The afternoon sun beat down on the dusty street with fierce intensity. The street was lonely, and we rode past the blacksmith shop in silence, past the saloon, past the post office, past my office, up the street with the sound of our horses' hooves the only thing to break the silence.

"Busy little town you got here," Hawkins said.

"Shut up, Hawkins."

He shrugged. "Whatever you say, marshal."

The silence was strange and forbidding. It was like walking in on some-one who'd been talking about you. It magnified the heat, made the dust swirling up around us seem more intolerable.

When the voice came, it shattered the silence into a thousand brittle shards.

"Marshal! Hey, marshal!"

I wheeled the sorrel and spotted old Jake Trilby pushing open the batwings on the saloon. He waved and I walked the horse over to him, waiting while he put his crutch under his arm and stepped out onto the boardwalk.

"Where is everyone, Jake?"

"They got him, marshal," he said. "The feller killed your wife."

"What?"

"Yep, they got him. Caught him just outside of Rock Falls. Ridin' a horse with a cracked right hind shoe. Had blood on his clothes, too. He's the one, all right, marshal. He's the one killed May, all right."

"Where? Where is he?"

"They didn't wait for you this time, marshal. They knowed you wanted action."

"Where are they?"

"Out hangin' him. If he ain't hanged already by this time." Old Jake chuckled. "They're givin' it to him, marshal. They're showin' him."

"Where, Jake?"

"The oak down by the fork. You know where. Heck, marshal, he's dancin' on air by now."

I turned the sorrel and raked my spurs over her belly. She gave a leap forward and as we rode past Hawkins, I tossed him his gun belt. A surprised look covered his face, and then I didn't see him anymore because he was behind me, and I was heading for the man who killed her.

I SAW THE tree first, reaching for the sky with heavy branches. A rope had been thrown over one of those branches, and it hung limply now, its ends lost in the milling crowd beneath the tree. The crowd was silent, a tight knot of men and women forming the nucleus, a loose unraveling of kids on the edges. I couldn't see the man the crowd surrounded until I got a little closer. I pushed the sorrel right into the crowd and it broke apart like a rotten apple, and then I saw the man sitting on the bay under the tree, his hands tied behind him, the rope knotted around his neck.

"Here's Johnny," someone shouted, and then the cry seemed to sweep over the crowd like a small brush fire. "Here's Johnny."

"Hey, Johnny!"

"We got him, Johnny!"

"Just in time, Johnny!"

I swung off the horse and walked over to where Doc Talmadge was pulling rope taut.

"Hello, Johnny," he said, greeting me affably. "We got the bastard, and this time we didn't wait for you. Another few minutes and you'd have missed it all."

"Put that rope down, Doc," I said.

Doc's eyes widened and then blinked. "Huh? What, Johnny?"

"What the hell do you think you're doing?"

"I was just fixin' to tie the rope around the trunk here. After that, we going to take that horse from underneath this sonova . . ."

"What's the matter, Johnny?" someone called.

"Come on, Johnny," another voice prodded. "Let's get on with this."

The sky overhead was a bright blue, and the sun gleamed in it like a fiery eye. It was a beautiful day, with a few clouds trailing wisps of cotton close to the horizon. I glanced up at the sky and then back to the man sitting the bay.

He was narrow faced, with slitted brown eyes and jaws that hadn't been razor-scraped in days. His mouth was expressionless. Only his eyes spoke, and they told of silent hatred. His clothes were dirty, and his shirt was spattered with blood.

I walked away from Doc, leaving him to knot the rope around the tree trunk. The crowd fell silent as I approached the man on the bay.

"What's your name?" I asked.

"Dodd," he said.

"This your horse?"

"Yep."

I walked around behind the horse and checked the right hind hoof. The shoe was cracked down the center. I dropped the hoof and walked back to face Dodd.

I stared at him for a few minutes, our eyes locked. Then I turned to the crowd and said, "Go on home. Go on. There'll be no hanging here today."

Rafe stepped out of the crowd and put his hands on his hips. "You nuts, Johnny? This is the guy who killed May. He killed your wife!"

"We don't know that," I said.

"We don't know it? Jesus, you just saw the broken shoe. What the hell more do you want?"

"He's got blood all over his shirt, Johnny," Doc put in. "Hell, he's our man."

"Even if he is, he doesn't hang," I said tightly.

An excited murmur went up from the crowd and then Jason Bragg shouldered his way through and stood in front of me, one hand looped in his gun belt. He was a big man, with corn yellow hair and pale blue eyes. He was a farmer with a wife and three grown daughters. When he spoke now, it was in slow and measured tones.

"Johnny, you are not doing right."

"No, Jason?"

Jason shook his massive head, and pointed up to Dodd. "This man is a killer. We know he's a killer. You're the marshal here. It's your job to . . ."

"It's my job to do justice."

"Yes, it's your job to do justice. It's your job to see that this man is hanged!" He looked at me as if he thought I was some incredible kind of insect. "Johnny, he killed *your own wife!*"

"That doesn't mean we take the law into our own hands."

"Johnny . . ."

"It doesn't mean that this town will get blood on its hands, either. If you hang this man, you'll all be guilty of murder. You'll be just as much a killer as he is. Every last one of you! You'll be murdering in a group, but you'll still be murdering. You've got no right to do that."

"The hell we ain't!" someone shouted.

"Come on, Johnny, quit the goddamned stalling!"

"What is this, a tea party?"

"We got our man, now string him up!"

"That's the man killed your wife, Johnny."

Jason Bragg cleared his throat. "Johnny, I got a wife and three girls. You remember my daughters when they were buttons. They're young ladies now. We let this one get away with what he's done, and this town won't be safe for anyone anymore. My daughters . . ."

"He won't get away with anything," I said. "But you're not going to hang him."

"He killed your wife!" someone else shouted.

"He's ridin' the horse that made the tracks."

"Shut up!" I yelled. "Shut up, all of you!"

There was an immediate silence, and then, cutting through the silence like a sharp-edged knife, a voice asked, "You backin' out, marshal?"

The heads in the crowd turned, and I looked past them to see Hawkins sitting his saddle on the fringe of the crowd.

"Keep out of this, stranger," I called. "Just ride on to wherever the hell you were going."

"Killed your wife, did he?" Hawkins said. He looked over to Dodd, and then slowly began rolling a cigarette. "No wonder you were all het up back there on the trail."

"Listen, Hawkins . . ."

"You seemed all ready to raise six kinds of hell a little while ago. What's the matter, a hangin' turn your stomach?"

The crowd began to murmur again, and Hawkins grinned.

"Hawkins," I started, but he raised his voice above mine and shouted, "Are you sure this is the man?"

"Yes!" the crowd yelled. "Yes!"

"Ain't no two ways about it. He's the one! Even got scratches on his neck where May grabbed at him."

I glanced quickly at Dodd, saw his face pale, and saw the deep fresh scratches on the side of his neck at the same time.

"Then string him up!" Hawkins shouted. "String him higher 'n the sun! String him up so your wives and your daughters can walk in safety. String him up even if you've got a yellow-livered marshal who . . ."

"String him up!" the cry rose.

The crowd surged forward and Doc Talmadge brought his hand back to slap at the bay's rump. I took a step backward and pulled my .44 at the same time. Without turning my back to the crowd, I swung the gun down, chopping the barrel onto Doc's wrist. He pulled back his hand and let out a yelp.

"First man moves a step," I said, "gets a hole in his gut!"

Jason Bragg took a deep breath. "Johnny, don't try to stop us. You should be ashamed of yourself. You should . . ."

"I like you, Jason," I said. "Don't let it be you." I cocked the gun, and the click was loud in the silence.

"Johnny," Rafe said, "you don't know what you're doing. You're upset, you're . . ."

"Stay where you are, Rafe. Don't move an inch."

"You going to let him stop you?" Hawkins called.

No one answered him.

"You going to let him stop justice?" he shouted.

I waited for an answer, and when there was none, I said, "Go home. Go back to your homes. Go back to your shops. Go on, now. Go on."

The crowd began to mumble, and then a few kids broke away and began running back to town. Slowly, the women followed, and then Jason Bragg turned his back to me and stumped away silently. Rafe looked at me sneeringly and followed the rest. Doc Talmadge was the last to go, holding his wrist against his chest.

Hawkins sat on his sorrel and watched the crowd walking back to town. When he turned, there was a smile on his face.

"Thought we were going to have a little excitement," he said.

"You'd better get out of town, Hawkins. You'd better get out damned fast."

"I was just leavin', marshal." He raised his hand in a salute, wheeled his horse, and said, "So long, chum."

I watched while the horse rode up the dusty trail, parting the walkers before it. Then the horse was gone, and I kept watching until the crowd turned the bend in the road and was gone, too.

I walked over to Dodd.

He sat on the bay with his hands tied behind him, his face noncommittal.

"Did you kill her?" I asked

He didn't answer.

"Come on," I said. "You'll go before a court anyway, and there's no one here but me to hear a confession. Did you?"

He hesitated for a moment, and then he nodded briefly.

"Why?" I asked.

He shrugged his thin shoulders.

I looked into his eyes, but there was no answer there, either.

"I appreciate what you done, marshal," he said suddenly, his lips pulling back to expose narrow teeth. "Considering everything . . . well, I just appreciate it."

"Sure," I said. "I'm paid to see that justice is done."

"Well, I appreciate it."

I stepped behind him and untied his hands, and then I loosened the noose around his neck.

"That feels good," he said, massaging his neck.

"I'll bet it does." I reached into my pocket for the makings. "Here," I said, "roll yourself a cigarette."

"Thanks. Say, thanks."

His manner grew more relaxed. He sat in the saddle and sprinkled tobacco into the paper. He knew better than to try a break, because I was still holding my .44 in my hand. He worked on the cigarette, and he asked, "Do you think . . . do you think it'll go bad for me?"

I watched him wet the paper and put the cigarette into his mouth.

"Not too bad," I said.

He nodded, and the cigarette bobbed, and he reached into his pocket for a match.

I brought the .44 up quickly and fired five fast shots, watching his face explode in soggy red chunks.

He dropped out of the saddle.

The cigarette falling to the dust beside him.

Then I mounted up and rode back to town.

Marcia Muller is the author of more than twenty novels and several dozen short stories, a number of which have Western themes. She shows her considerable talent in this field in "Sweet Cactus Wine," one of the few Western stories about pioneer women and how they coped with the myriad problems of the frontier. Her other Western stories, including "The Time of the Wolves," often feature strong, independent women making their own way in the West. In this wry-humored, ironic, and immensely satisfying story, we meet the widow Katy (or Kathryn, as she prefers to be called), a woman not to be trifled with. When a rejected suitor starts shooting up her cacti, why, she just naturally sets out to do something about it. Something very fitting, indeed . . .

Sweet Cactus Wine

Marcia Muller

The rain stopped as suddenly as it had begun, the way it always does in the Arizona desert. The torrent had burst from a near-cloudless sky, and now it was clear once more, the land nourished. I stood in the doorway of my house, watching the sun touch the stone wall, the old buckboard and the twisted arms of the giant saguaro cacti.

The suddenness of these downpours fascinated me, even though I'd lived in the desert for close to forty years, since the day I'd come here as Joe's bride in 1866. They'd been good years, not exactly bountiful, but we'd lived here in quiet comfort. Joe had the instinct that helped him bring the crops—melons, corn, beans—from the parched soil, an instinct he shared with the Papago Indians who were our neighbors. I didn't possess the knack, so now that he was gone I didn't farm. I did share one gift with the Papagos, however—the ability to make sweet cactus wine from the fruit of the saguaro. That wine was my livelihood now—as well as, I must admit, a source of Saturday-night pleasure—and the giant cacti scattered around the ranch were my fortune.

I went inside to the big rough-hewn table where I'd been shelling peas when the downpour started. The bowl sat there half full, and I eyed the peas with distaste. Funny what age will do to you. For years I'd had an overly hearty appetite. Joe used to say, "Don't worry, Katy. I like big women." Lucky for him he did, because I'd carried around enough lard for two such admirers, and I didn't believe in divorce anyway. Joe'd be surprised if he could see me now, though. I was tall, yes, still tall. But thin. I guess you'd call it gaunt. Food didn't interest me any more.

I sat down and finished shelling the peas anyway. It was market day in Arroyo, and Hank Gardner, my neighbor five miles down the road, had taken to stopping in for supper on his way home from town. Hank was widowed too. Maybe it was his way of courting. I didn't know and didn't care. One man had been enough trouble for me and, anyway, I intended to live out my days on these parched but familiar acres.

Sure enough, right about suppertime Hank rode up on his old bay. He was a lean man, browned and weathered by the sun like folks get in these parts, and he rode stiffly. I watched him dismount, then went and got the whiskey bottle and poured him a tumblerful. If I knew Hank, he'd had a few drinks in town and would be wanting another. And a glassful sure wouldn't be enough for old Hogsbreath Hank, as he was sometimes called.

He came in and sat at the table like he always did. I stirred the iron pot on the stove and sat down too. Hank was a man of few words, like my Joe had been. I'd heard tales that his drinking and temper had pushed his wife into an early grave. Sara Gardner had died of pneumonia, though, and no man's temper ever gave that to you.

Tonight Hank seemed different, jumpy. He drummed his fingers on the table and drank his whiskey.

To put him at his ease, I said, "How're things in town?"

"What?"

"Town. How was it?"

"Same as ever."

"You sure?"

"Yeah, I'm sure. Why do you ask?" But he looked kind of furtive.

"No reason," I said. "Nothing changes out here. I don't know why I asked." Then I went to dish up the stew. I set it and some corn bread on the table, poured more whiskey for Hank and a little cactus wine for me. Hank ate steadily and silently. I sort of picked at my food.

After supper I washed up the dishes and joined Hank on the front porch. He still seemed jumpy, but this time I didn't try to find out why. I just sat there beside him, watching the sun spread its redness over the mountains in the distance. When Hank spoke, I'd almost forgotten he was there.

"Kathryn"—he never called me Katy; only Joe used that name—"Kathryn, I've been thinking. It's time the two of us got married."

So that was why he had the jitters. I turned to stare. "What put an idea like that into your head?"

He frowned. "It's natural."

"Natural?"

"Kathryn, we're both alone. It's foolish you living here and me living over there when our ranches sit next to each other. Since Joe went, you haven't farmed the place. We could live at my house, let this one go, and I'd farm the land for you."

Did he want me or the ranch? I know passion is supposed to die when you're in your sixties, and as far as Hank was concerned mine had, but for form's sake he could at least pretend to some.

"Hank," I said firmly, "I've got no intention of marrying again—or of farming this place."

"I said I'd farm it for you."

"If I wanted it farmed, I could hire someone to do it. I wouldn't need to acquire another husband."

"We'd be company for one another."

"We're company now."

"What're you going to do—sit here the rest of your days scratching out a living with your cactus wine?"

"That's exactly what I plan to do."

"Kathryn . . ."

"No."

"But . . ."

"No. That's all."

Hank's jaw tightened and his eyes narrowed. I was afraid for a minute that I was going to be treated to a display of his legendary temper, but soon he looked placid as ever. He stood, patting my shoulder.

"You think about it," he said. "I'll be back tomorrow and I want a yes answer."

I'd think about it, all right. As a matter of fact, as he rode off on the bay I was thinking it was the strangest marriage proposal I'd ever heard of. And there was no way old Hogsbreath was getting any yesses from me.

HE RODE UP again the next evening. I was out gathering cactus fruit. In the springtime, when the desert nights are still cool, the tips of the saguaro branches are covered with waxy white flowers. They're prettiest in the hours around dawn, and by the time the sun hits its peak, they close. When they die, the purple fruit begins to grow, and now, by midsummer, it was splitting open to show its bright red pulp. That pulp was what I turned into wine.

I stood by my pride and joy—a fifty-foot giant that was probably two hundred years old—and watched Hank come toward me. From his easy gait, I knew he was sure I'd changed my mind about his proposal. Probably figured he was irresistible, the old goat. He had a surprise coming.

"Well, Kathryn," he said, stopping and folding his arms across his chest, "I'm here for my answer."

"It's the same as it was last night. No. I don't intend to marry again."

"You're a foolish woman, Kathryn."

"That may be. But at least I'm foolish in my own way."

"What does that mean?"

"If I'm making a mistake, it'll be one I decide on, not one you decide for me."

The planes of his face hardened, and the wrinkles around his eyes deepened. "We'll see about that." He turned and strode toward the bay.

I was surprised he had backed down so easy, but relieved. At least he was going.

Hank didn't get on the horse, however. He fumbled at his saddle scabbard and drew his shotgun. I set down the basket of cactus fruit. Surely he didn't intend to shoot me!

He turned, shotgun in one hand.

"Don't be a fool, Hank Gardner."

He marched toward me. I got ready to run, but he kept going, past me. I whirled, watching. Hank went up to a nearby saguaro, a twenty-five footer. He looked at it, turned, and walked exactly ten paces. Then he turned again, brought up the shotgun, sighted on the cactus, and began to fire. He fired at its base over and over.

I put my hand to my mouth, shutting off a scream.

Hank fired again, and the cactus toppled.

It didn't fall like a man would if he were shot. It just leaned backwards. Then it gave a sort of sigh and leaned farther and farther. As it leaned it picked up momentum, and when it hit the ground there was an awful thud.

Hank gave the cactus a satisfied nod and marched back toward his horse.

I found my voice, "Hey, you! Just what do you think you're doing?"

Hank got on the bay. "Cactuses are like people, Kathryn. They can't do anything for you once they're dead. Think about it."

"You bet I'll think about it! That cactus was valuable to me. You're going to pay!"

"What happens when there're no cactuses left?"

"What? What?"

"How're you going to scratch out a living on this miserable ranch if someone shoots all your cactuses?"

"You wouldn't dare!"

He smirked at me. "You know, there's one way cactuses *aren't* like people. Nobody ever hung a man for shooting one."

Then he rode off.

I stood there speechless. Did the bastard plan to shoot up my cacti until I agreed to marry him?

I went over to the saguaro. It lay on its back, oozing water. I nudged it

gently with my foot. There were a few round holes in it—entrances to the
caves where the Gila woodpeckers lived. From the silence, I guessed the
birds hadn't been inside when the cactus toppled. They'd be mighty surprised when they came back and found their home on the ground.

The woodpeckers were the least of my problems, however. They'd just
take up residence in one of the other giants. Trouble was, what if Hank carried out his veiled threat? Then the woodpeckers would run out of nesting
places—and I'd run out of fruit to make my wine from.

I went back to the granddaddy of my cacti and picked up the basket. On
the porch I set it down and myself in my rocking chair to think. What was
I going to do?

I could go to the sheriff in Arroyo, but the idea didn't please me. For
one thing, like Hank had said, there was no law against shooting a cactus.
And for another, it was embarrassing to be in this kind of predicament at
my age. I could see all the locals lined up at the bar of the saloon, laughing
at me. No, I didn't want to go to Sheriff Daly if I could help it.

So what else? I could shoot Hank, I supposed, but that was even less appealing. Not that he didn't deserve shooting, but they could hang you for
murdering a man, unlike a cactus. And then, while I had a couple of Joe's
old rifles, I'd never been comfortable with them, never really mastered the
art of sighting and pulling the trigger. With my luck, I'd miss Hank and kill
off yet another cactus.

I sat on the porch for a long time, puzzling and listening to the night
sounds of the desert. Finally I gave up and went to bed, hoping the old
fool would come to his senses in the morning.

He didn't, though. Shotgun blasts on the far side of the ranch brought
me flying out of the house the next night. By the time I got over there,
there was nothing around except a couple of dead cacti. The next night it
happened again, and still the next night. The bastard was being cagey, too.
I had no way of proving it actually was Hank doing the shooting. Finally I
gave up and decided I had no choice but to see Sheriff Daly.

I put on my good dress, fixed my hair, and hitched up my horse to the
old buckboard. The trip into Arroyo was hot and dusty, and my stomach
lurched at every bump in the road. It's no fun knowing you're about to become a laughing-stock. Even if the sheriff sympathized with me, you can
bet he and the boys would have a good chuckle afterward.

I drove up Main Street and left the rig at the livery stable. The horse
needed shoeing anyway. Then I went down the wooden sidewalk to the
sheriff's office. Naturally, it was closed. The sign said he'd be back at two,
and it was only noon now. I got out my list of errands and set off for the
feed store, glancing over at the saloon on my way.

Hank was coming out of the saloon. I ducked into the shadow of the covered walkway in front of the bank and watched him, hate rising inside me. He stopped on the sidewalk and waited, and a moment later a stranger joined him. The stranger wore a frock coat and a broad-brimmed black hat. He didn't dress like anyone from these parts. Hank and the man walked toward the old adobe hotel and shook hands in front of it. Then Hank ambled over to where the bay was tied, and the stranger went inside.

I stood there, frowning. Normally I wouldn't have been curious about Hank Gardner's private business, but when a man's shooting up your cacti you develop an interest in anything he does. I waited until he had ridden off down the street, then crossed and went into the hotel.

Sonny, the clerk, was a friend from way back. His mother and I had run church bazaars together for years, back when I still had the energy for that sort of thing. I went up to him and we exchanged pleasantries.

Then I said, "Sonny, I've got a question for you, and I'd just as soon you didn't mention me asking it to anybody."

He nodded.

"A man came in here a few minutes ago. Frock coat, black hat."

"Sure. Mr. Johnson."

"Who is he?"

"You don't know?"

"I don't get into town much these days."

"I guess not. Everybody's' talking about him. Mr. Johnson's a land developer. Here from Phoenix."

Land developer. I began to smell a rat. A rat named Hank Gardner.

"What's he doing, buying up the town?"

"Not the town. The countryside. He's making offers on all the ranches." Sonny eyed me thoughtfully. "Maybe you better talk to him. You've got a fair-sized spread there. You could make good money. In fact, I'm surprised he hasn't been out to see you."

"So am I, Sonny. So am I. You see him, you tell him I'd like to talk to him."

"He's in his room now. I could . . ."

"No," I held up my hand. "I've got a lot of errands to do. I'll talk to him later."

But I didn't do any errands. Instead I went home to sit in my rocker and think.

THAT NIGHT I didn't light my kerosene lamp. I kept the house dark and waited at the front door. When the evening shadows had fallen, I heard a rustling sound. A tall figure slipped around the stone wall into the dooryard.

I watched as he approached one of the giant saguaros in the dooryard.

He went right up to it, like he had the first one he'd shot, turned and walked exactly ten paces, then blasted away. The cactus toppled, and Hank ran from the yard.

I waited. Let him think I wasn't home. After about fifteen minutes, I got undressed and went to bed in the dark, but I didn't rest much. My mind was too busy planning what I had to do.

The next morning I hitched up the buckboard and drove over to Hank's ranch. He was around back, mending a harness. He started when he saw me. Probably figured I'd come to shoot him. I got down from the buckboard and walked up to him, a sad, defeated look on my face.

"You're too clever for me, Hank. I should have known it."

"You ready to stop your foolishness and marry me?"

"Hank," I lied, "there's something more to my refusal than just stubbornness."

He frowned. "Oh?"

"Yes. You see, I promised Joe on his deathbed that I'd never marry again. That promise means something to me."

"I don't believe in . . ."

"Hush. I've been thinking, though, about what you said about farming my ranch. I've got an idea. Why *don't* you farm it for me? I'll move in over here, keep house and feed you. We're old enough everyone would know there weren't any shenanigans going on."

Hank looked thoughtful, pleased even. I'd guessed right; it wasn't my fair body he was after.

"That might work. But what if one of us died? Then what?"

"I don't see what you mean."

"Well, if you died, I'd be left with nothing to show for all that farming. And if I died, my son might come back from Tucson and throw you off the place. Where would you be then?"

"I see." I looked undecided, fingering a pleat in my skirt. "That *is* a problem." I paused. "Say, I think there's a way around it."

"Yeah?"

"Yes. We'll make wills. I'll leave you my ranch in mine. You do the same in yours. That way we'd both have something to show for our efforts."

He nodded, looking foxy. "That's a good idea, Kathryn. Very good."

I could tell he was pleased I'd thought of it myself.

"And, Hank, I think we should do it right away. Let's go into town this afternoon and have the wills drawn up."

"Fine with me." He looked even more pleased. "Just let me finish with this harness."

THE WILL SIGNING, of course, was a real solemn occasion. I even sniffed a little into my handkerchief before I put my signature to the document. The lawyer, Will Jones, was a little surprised by our bequests, but not much. He knew I was alone in the world, and Hank's son John was known to be more of a ne'er-do-well than his father. Probably Will Jones was glad to see the ranch wouldn't be going to John.

I had Hank leave me off at my place on his way home. I wanted, I said, to cook him one last supper in my old house before moving to his in the morning. I went about my preparations, humming to myself. Would Hank be able to resist rushing back into town to talk to Johnson, the land developer? Or would he wait a decent interval, say a day?

Hank rode up around sundown. I met him on the porch, twisting my handkerchief in my hands.

"Kathryn, what's wrong?"

"Hank, I can't do it."

"Can't do what?"

"I can't leave the place. I can't leave Joe's memory. This whole thing's been a terrible mistake."

He scowled. "Don't be foolish. What's for supper?"

"There isn't any."

"What?"

"How could I fix supper with a terrible mistake like this on my mind?"

"Well, you just get in there and fix it. And stop talking this way."

I shook my head. "No, Hank, I mean it. I can't move to your place. I can't let you farm mine. It wouldn't be right. I want you to go now, and tomorrow I'm going into town to rip up my will."

"You what?" His eyes narrowed.

"You heard me, Hank."

He whirled and went toward his horse. "You'll never learn, will you?"

"What are you going to do?"

"What do you think? Once your damned cactuses are gone, you'll see the light. Once you can't make any more of that wine, you'll be only too glad to pack your bags and come with me."

"Hank, don't you dare!"

"I do dare. There won't be a one of them standing."

"Please, Hank! At least leave my granddaddy cactus." I waved at the fifty-foot giant in the outer dooryard. "It's my favorite. It's like a child to me."

Hank grinned evilly. He took the shotgun from the saddle and walked right up to the cactus.

"Say good-bye to your child."

"Hank! Stop!"

He shouldered the shotgun.

"Say good-bye to it, you foolish woman."

"Hank, don't you pull that trigger!"

He pulled it.

Hank blasted at the giant saguaro—one, two, three times. And, like the others, it began to lean.

Unlike the others, though, it didn't lean backwards. It gave a great sigh and leaned and leaned and leaned forwards. And then it toppled. As it toppled, it picked up momentum. And when it fell on Hank Gardner, it made an awful thud.

I stood quietly on the porch. Hank didn't move. Finally I went over to him. Dead. Dead as all the cacti he'd murdered.

I contemplated his broken body a bit before I hitched up the buckboard and went to tell Sheriff Daly about the terrible accident. Sure was funny, I'd say, how that cactus toppled forward instead of backward. Almost as if the base had been partly cut through and braced so it would do exactly that.

Of course, the shotgun blasts would have destroyed any traces of the cutting.

Brian Garfield grew up surrounded by pulp authors such as Nelson Nye, Elliot Arnold, and Luke Short—not just their fiction, but the writers themselves. He began writing at the age of twelve, and sold his first novel when he was eighteen years old. Although he has written many Westerns, he's probably best known for such major historical novels as *Wild Times*. The trouble with this assessment is that it overlooks some equally fine work he did with the traditional western in the early seventies, *Sliphammer, Valley of the Shadow,* and *Gun Down* being particularly effective.

Peace Officer

Brian Garfield

It was hot. A gauze of tan dust hung low over the street.

Matt Paradise rode his horse into Aztec, coming off the coach road at four in the afternoon, and when he passed a drygoods store at the western end of the street a lady under a parasol smiled at him. Matt Paradise tipped his hat, rode on by, and mutters *sotto voce,* "A friendly face, a sleepy town. Don't I wish."

He was a big-boned young man. He took off his hat to scrape a flannel sleeve across his forehead, and exposed to view a wild, thick crop of bright red hair. He had a bold face, vividly scarred down the right cheek. His eyes were gold-flecked, hard as jacketed bullets. There was the touch of isolation about him. He carried a badge, pinned to the front of his shirt.

An intense layer of heat lay along the earth. He found the county sheriff's office, midway down a block between the hardware store and the barbershop; he dismounted there and climbed onto the dusty boardwalk with legs stiffened from a long day's hot ride.

He rested his shoulder against the frame of the open door and waited for his eyes to accustom themselves to the gloom inside. A voice reached forward from the dimness: "Something I can do for you?"

"Sun's pretty strong this time of year," Matt Paradise said. "I can't make you out yet. Sheriff Morgan?"

"I am."

Matt Paradise took three paces into the office. As his pupils began to dilate he took in the office—not very much different from a dozen other sheriffs' offices in Arizona Territory—and its occupant.

Sheriff John Morgan was stripped down to a faded pink undershirt. The empty right sleeve was pinned up at the shoulder.

Morgan was middle-aged. His shoulders were heavy, and his belly was beginning to swell out over his belt line. His face was craggy and weathered, topped by a sidewise slash of hair that was going thin and of salt-and-pepper color.

And so this—*this*—was the legendary Morgan, the peace officer who had cleaned up Coyotero County single-handed. This tired man, getting older, with his chin softening up. Morgan's eyes were pouched. His left hand drummed nervously on the desk. Matt Paradise masked his shock behind squinted eyes. The years had reduced John Morgan to a kind of bookmark, which only marked the place where a great lawman had been. The disappointment of it made Paradise guard his voice:

"Name's Paradise. Arizona Rangers."

Morgan touched his stiff mustache. He seemed to notice Paradise's badge for the first time. He tried to make his voice sound friendly: "Glad to see you."

Paradise wanted to turn around and ride out of town and not look back.

Morgan said, "Business or just traveling through?"

Just traveling through, Paradise wanted to say. But he fastened his will around him. "Business, I'm afraid."

"Afraid, Ranger?"

Matt Paradise inhaled deeply. *Better get it over with. Why beat around the bush? You poor, tired old man.* He said, almost harshly, "Your house isn't in order, Sheriff. I've been sent down here to help you clean it out."

He saw color rise in Morgan's cheeks, and he wanted to look away, but he held the sheriff's sad glance.

"You're just a kid," Sheriff Morgan said. "I don't want any amateur help, Ranger."

"Afraid you've got it, Sheriff, whether you want it or not."

He saw an abrupt touch of sullenness in Morgan's glance, and he thought, *I pity you, Morgan, but I've got to lay it on the line so there's no mistake.* He said, "You're getting fat—where you sit and where you think."

Instantly, Morgan's eyes showed cruel hatred. Paradise walked forward to the desk and spoke flatly. "Doc Wargo has been in this town for two weeks and you haven't done anything about it."

"That's right," Morgan said evenly. "Wargo's broken no laws in this county. I can't touch him." His eyes gleamed brutally.

"The Territory wants him for murder, Sheriff, and you know it. You've received two wires from our headquarters, to arrest Wargo and deliver him to Prescott for trial."

Morgan sighed out a long breath. "Ranger, you're young and impatient and there are certain things you've got to learn. This country isn't easy on anybody, young fellow, and if you want to survive very long, you learn that certain stones are better left unturned. There's a difference between making a stand and rocking the boat. Now, with this business, I'm alone in this office, no deputies, and I had my right arm shot off a year ago in a fight. What kind of chance do you think I'd stand if I went after Wargo and his gang?"

"Gang?" Matt Paradise murmured. "He's got one man with him, the way I hear it."

"Ernie Crouch isn't one man, Ranger. He's a crowd."

"So you're not lifting a finger."

"I am not," Morgan told him. "You can do whatever you like, Ranger, but I hate to see you come so far just to get killed. Those two haven't made any trouble in my county. And until they do, I leave them alone. That's my policy." He shook his head. "Go on home, son. You can't fight Wargo and Crouch."

"How do you know, Sheriff?" Paradise said softly. "You've never tried."

He expected Morgan to explode, but Morgan just sat and looked at him as if he were slightly crazy. Then Morgan said, "The only times lawmen have tried to close Doc Wargo down, he's closed them down. Do you understand what I'm telling you, boy? You ever handled anything like this before?"

"Maybe."

"And you think you can handle Wargo and Crouch, do you?"

"If I didn't," said Matt Paradise, "I wouldn't be here."

Morgan scrutinized the hang of Paradise's twin revolvers. "How good do you think you are with those things?"

"Good enough. Nobody's killed me yet."

"Suit yourself, then."

It made Paradise lean forward and plant both palms on the desk. He brought his face near the level of Morgan's. "Don't you care, Sheriff? Don't you care at all? All the legends about John Morgan—are they all lies?"

Morgan's left hand reached the desk and gripped its edge. "Legends are for the far past, boy. That was a lot of miles ago. Let me tell you what a smart man does. When the likes of Doc Wargo takes over your town, you just hunker down and take it like a jackrabbit in a hailstorm. Because sooner or later the hailstorm moves on. Wargo will move on too, and if he's not prodded, he won't hurt anybody in the meantime."

"And you're willing to take the chance on that, are you?"

Morgan sat back and studied him. "Tell me something. What do you do with all your time, Ranger? Just ride around hunting up trouble for yourself?"

"Trouble and I are old friends," Paradise said. "We understand each other."

"Sure."

"I'm arresting Doc Wargo," Paradise told him. "Do I get your help or not?"

"I'll think about it," the sheriff said, and turned away in his chair to reach for a newspaper.

"You've got five seconds." Paradise said flatly.

The sheriff looked up angrily, but before he could reply, a figure barred the door, blocking out the light. Paradise turned and his eyes fixed themselves on the girl.

She had long eyes. Smooth dark hair gracefully surrounded her face. Looking at the rich warm tone of her flesh, Paradise knew she was the most stunning human creature he had ever seen.

He stared at her until she blushed. Suddenly she gave him a blinding smile. Her smile was as good as a kiss.

Morgan said in a cranky tone, "You want something, Terry?"

She had a smoky voice. Her eyes did not stray from Paradise when she answered the sheriff. "Nothing important, Dad. I didn't know you were busy. I'll see you later."

Her body turned away before her head did. She gave Paradise a last, level glance, and was gone.

"My daughter," Morgan said unnecessarily. He grunted getting out of his chair. "I'll go down to the Occidental with you. That's where Wargo's putting up."

"You'll back my play?"

"I don't know," the sheriff said. He put on a severe, flat-crowned hat. "Come on."

When they reached the street, the girl Terry was a block away, just turning a corner. She wore riding trousers and a cotton blouse that hugged her at waist and breasts. She went out of sight and around the corner. Morgan said, "That your horse?"

"Yes."

"Nice-looking animal. What'll I do with it if you get dead?"

"Give it to your daughter," Paradise said, and walked away.

Morgan caught up and they went down the street together. The merciless orange sun burned wherever it struck. Heat clung to the street like melted tar.

The Occidental was the biggest building in town. The sign on the tall front was painted in a crescent shape: *Gaming Tables—SALOON—Dancing.* It looked as though there were hotel bedrooms on the second floor.

It was four-thirty. The sun burst through the west-facing windows upon an almost deserted, long, low-ceilinged room. An aproned bartender polished glasses at the backbar. Three men sat playing cards at a table. That was all.

Paradise recognized Wargo right away, from the reward flyer portraits. Wargo was a neat, slight, lizard of a man; his hair was Indian black. He wore sleeve garters and celluloid collar and cuffs; no coat, no hat. Cigar smoke trailed from Wargo's mouth and nostrils. He watched the two new-comers come forward.

At Wargo's right sat a slope-chinned card player, evidently a house gam-bler. At Wargo's left sat an enormous shape, the biggest man Paradise had ever seen. That would be Ernie Crouch. *Ernie Crouch isn't one man, Ranger. He's a crowd*. All Crouch's fat looked hard; hard as granite. He had a placid bovine face, but his deep-slit eyes were shrewd and he was festooned like a gun collector after an auction: knives and guns bristled all over—at his boot tops; at his waist; in sheathes sewn to his butternut trousers. Paradise could have walked around inside one leg of Crouch's trousers.

Crouch was sitting on two chairs, side by side, one under each buttock.

He looked like a puppeteer, with Doc Wargo his marionette. But actu-ally, Paradise knew, it was the other way around.

Doc Wargo spoke, in a voice surprisingly deep for his small body. "Hello, Sheriff. Where've you been keeping yourself?" His face was amused. When Morgan made no answer, Wargo murmured, "I hear you're getting old."

Morgan's eyes flickered when they touched Wargo's. Paradise took a pace forward, and seeing the look on Paradise's face, Wargo started to rise.

"Keep your seat," Paradise said coolly.

Wargo's eyes, triangular like a snake's, became wicked. A mustache drooped past the edges of his mouth. "What's this—what's this?"

Sheriff Morgan had stepped back, and suddenly Paradise felt the cold muzzle of a revolver against his back ribs. Morgan said gently, "I changed my mind. I'm sworn to keep the peace. It wouldn't be peaceful if you let these two men kill you, would it?"

Paradise's jaw muscles rippled. "You're all through, Sheriff, as of right now."

"Maybe."

Wargo was smiling gently. "What's this all about?"

Paradise ignored the gun in his back. He spoke to Wargo: "What hap-pened to Carlos Ramirez?"

"I killed him."

"Why?"

"I forget," Wargo murmured. He halved his smile. "You'd better beg your pardon and get out of here."

Ernie Crouch spoke without stirring on his chairs. "He's one of them Rangers, Doc."

"I can see that for myself," Wargo snapped. "Ramirez was a Ranger, wasn't he?"

"He was," Paradise said bleakly.

"Go on," Wargo told him. "Clear out of here before you do something that'll make me have to kill you."

Paradise glanced over his shoulder at Morgan. The sheriff had backed away, but his gun was leveled on Paradise. Paradise said, "This badge of mine won't die, Wargo, any more than Ramirez's died. It will get up and come after you, on another man's shirt."

While he was talking, he took a pace back, and whipped his elbow around behind him. It jarred against the gun in Morgan's fist, turning the gun away. Paradise whipped his left hand around and down, yanked the gun out of Morgan's grip, and pushed the surprised sheriff back. Morgan windmilled his single arm and almost lost his footing.

Paradise wheeled, starting to talk: "You're under arrest—"

But Crouch, as soundless as he was enormous, was on top of him. Crouch batted the gun away as if it were paper; he swatted Paradise contemptuously across the cheek and Paradise caromed back against the edge of the bar. The scar on his face went ghostly white. A half-full tumbler of whiskey stood on the bar. He made a grab for it. Crouch was shifting forward; Paradise could hear Wargo's husky chuckling in the background. Crouch began to swing.

Paradise flung the whiskey in Crouch's fleshy face.

Crouch yelled and clawed at his stung eyes. Paradise stepped in and brought the heel of his left hand up under Crouch's pointed nose. The blow smashed in: he heard the crush of cartilage, felt the spurt of blood on his palm. Agony exploded in his wrist—it was like pounding a concrete wall—but Crouch backpedaled in pain.

Paradise still had the empty tumbler in his right hand. He smashed it, edge first, down on top of Crouch's head—smashed it down once and again. Crouch sagged against the bar and began to slip to the floor.

Paradise didn't wait. He turned, dropping the glass, reaching for his gun.

But Doc Wargo had him covered with a nickel-plated revolver. Wargo was still in his chair; he looked slightly amused. "Nice job," he remarked.

Paradise's hands became still. He glanced at Morgan. Morgan was looking at the floor. Wargo's glance flicked casually to the crumpled mountain of the dazed Ernie Crouch, and then his face hardened. He said in an acid voice, "I'm in a charitable mood, which is why I'm not gut-shooting you here and now. But remember this, Ranger. The next time you call me, I'm going to see you."

"You'll see me all of a sudden," Paradise replied grimly.

"I'll see you," Wargo answered, "in Boot Hill with dirt in your face. You've got till dawn tomorrow to ride out of here. After that you're fair game for me and Ernie."

Paradise massaged the soreness in his left hand. "I'll see you at sunup, then. If you're smart, you'll be on the run."

"From one man?"

"From the badge, Wargo."

"Get out of here," Wargo said softly.

His gun lifted.

Morgan came across the floor and touched Paradise on the arm. "Come on. You can't fight the drop."

They went outside and Paradise stood on the walk looking back at the saloon, half-expecting Wargo to explode out the door with a gun blazing. Morgan said, "He won't come after you. Not till morning. He's a skunk, maybe, but he keeps his word. You've got twelve hours. Get on your horse and use it."

Sweat rolled freely along the sheriff's flushed face. He spoke earnestly: "You don't have to finish the job, Paradise. Nobody cares."

"I care."

"You can't win it, man!"

Paradise said, "You can't always go by that. Doesn't that badge mean anything at all to you?"

Morgan looked away. Fear had robbed him of his dignity. Fear: it quivered in his eyes. Paradise said, "You don't want to hear this, and I don't particularly want to say it, but you'd better sort yourself out fast, Sheriff. Because if you don't back my play in the morning, you'll be out of a job and behind bars."

Morgan did not meet his eye. "I'm dead, Paradise. I just haven't got the guts to lie down." The one-armed sheriff turned, then, and walked away slowly.

His wife said, "Do you like my dress?"

"It looks good with your hair."

"John, you haven't even looked at it."

Sweat dripped from Morgan's scarlet face. He was staring vacantly out the window of the bedroom. Heat pressed down on the desert from the burning sky; the sun was about to go down.

She said, "Being frightened is a natural human reaction, like breathing."

"Will you please shut up?" he demanded. He turned in his chair; his voice dropped. "I'm sorry, Kit. You don't deserve that. You don't deserve any part of me."

"Come sit by me. Please, John."

He crossed to the loveseat and put his arm around her shoulders. She dropped her head against him. She said, "You're not cast in bronze. You can do anything you want."

"Sure."

"The Ranger," she said. "Does he have any chance at all?"

"I'm a sheriff, not an oracle. He handled himself pretty well against Ernie Crouch. Maybe he can do it. He doesn't look like the type to come out last in a gunfight. But then, neither does Doc Wargo."

He got up, restless. He passed the mirror and stopped in front of it. "I barely recognize that man," he said, looking at his image in the glass; he turned to face her: "Take a look at me, Kit. Take a good look."

His mouth twisted. "I lost a lot more than an arm in that fight last year." His face was sweat-drenched and greenish. "My guts spilled out with the arm." His voice climbed, pitched to a driving high recklessness: "Let the fool get himself killed. Let him die, to prove some stupid pride. Let him—"

"John! Pull yourself together. You've got to get hold of yourself!"

"Why?" he asked miserably. "Why?" He looked at her, and curbed his tongue.

AT EIGHT O'CLOCK, in the residue of the day's torpid heat, Matt Paradise presented himself at the door of the sheriff's house. He was wearing a clean shirt and string tie, and a black, dusty coat that had become shiny with long use.

The sheriff's daughter answered the door. For a moment their eyes locked. Paradise regarded her gravely, saying nothing. She said, "My father is in the back. I'll get him."

"I didn't come to see your father, Terry."

She wore a dove-gray dress. Her dark hair was swept back, pinned with a bow. She said, "You came courting," and he could see that she was laughing quietly.

He smiled and put out his hand. She considered it for a little while before she put her slender hand into his big fingers. He said to her, "You are the promise I made to myself when I was a kid."

"That must have been a very long time ago." She was still laughing at him. He pulled her forward. She closed the door behind her, and they walked down the road, hand in hand. Her head was at his shoulder. They did not speak until they reached the turning in the road, where the wagon tracks swung into the head of the town's main street. Here a cluster of tall heavy cottonwood trees surrounded the bubbling of a spring, and there was grass on a precious half acre of earth. With a finger Matt Paradise brushed back a stray lock of her hair. He watched for her quick, slanting smile.

She said, "You want to kiss me, don't you?"

"Yes."

"Why don't you stop looking at me and do it?"

Her arms were folded. She leaned against him, moved her face up; he kissed her. Her arms did not stir. He put his hands softly on the gloss of her hair, holding her without pressure. It was a gentle kiss; yet it rocked him.

She smiled and laid her head on his chest. She made him feel drunk. She whispered, "Does everyone feel like this, or are we very special?"

"Don't ask any questions."

"Then I won't."

He said, "I'm crazy in love with you."

"I know." She was smiling. "A woman knows when she's loved." Abruptly, she walked away from him. She said, "I can't breathe when I'm with you."

HE WAS GOING to leave her at the door, but her mother came from the parlor into the doorway. "Won't you come in?"

"No, thank you," Paradise said.

"Do you mind terribly if I insist?" The woman stepped aside to make room. She was handsome; she had not begun to thicken up.

John Morgan was striding back and forth in the parlor. He became still when they entered. "Well, then," he said.

Terry said, "I'm going to marry him."

Morgan said, "Then you'd better do it fast, because he's likely to be dead in the morning."

"I can live a lifetime in one night," she said, looking at Paradise.

Morgan uttered a monosyllabic curse. Trembling in anger, he raised one arm. His hand was formed into a fist. His wife stepped in front of him. "She's a woman, John."

"I know that. She's grown."

"Yes. And she needs what every woman needs."

His wife turned to Paradise. He had not spoken. Now he said, "You have a wonderful daughter."

"Yes, I think so."

"That doesn't just happen," Paradise said.

"Thank you," said Mrs. Morgan.

"For Pete's sake," Morgan exploded. "Terry! Do you have any notion what it's like to marry a Ranger? He spends his life from town to town, from fight to fight—"

"I know," she said calmly.

"How long have you thought about this? How long did take you to make this decision? Two hours? Ten minutes?" He was roaring.

She said, "I've had all the time I need. And all the advice." She stood her ground and met her father's glance. She cried joyously, "Do you know what it feels like to love?"

"I knew your mother for years before I married her."

"That's not what I asked you."

"How do you know he's any better than the fly-by-night cowhands around here? One night's fling and then gone? How do you—"

She said, "Maybe he *is* just toying with my affections. All right. Maybe I'm just in a mood to have my affections toyed with!"

Morgan's sight was blurring. "I don't believe any of this," he muttered. "It's all a bad dream. It can't be happening. It's a nightmare." He swung his arm up in a gesture of frustrated anger, toward Paradise. He said bitterly, "Just the kind of moth-eaten son-in-law I've always wanted. What kind of a coffin do you want, Paradise?"

Mrs. Morgan pulled her husband's arm down. She said to him. "You've lost your nerve, John, and that's no crime. But you can't stand to see another man face up to the things you're afraid of."

She turned to her daughter and begged, "I made him into what he is, Terry. It's my fault. I washed him up because I wouldn't stop harping at him, trying to get him to hang up his guns. I kept trying to talk him into turning his back and running away."

She bowed, beaten. "I succeeded all too well. Don't make the same mistake, Terry. Follow your man to the ends of the earth, but never tell him to turn back."

THE SUN WOULD be up in a little while. Matt Paradise stood within the darkened, empty sheriff's office. Waiting laid a frost on his nerves. For the tenth time he took out his guns and checked their loads.

Someone came down the street, tramping on heavy feet. Paradise moved close to the door.

Morgan came in, weaving slightly. He carried a whiskey bottle by the neck. His eyes were stained with a bleak darkness. He put the bottle down and hitched his gun around. "You need help."

Paradise looked him in the eye. "And where am I going to get it?" He turned away. "You're drunk."

"Not really. I haven't done the bottle much damage yet."

"I didn't think you'd have the guts to come."

"I didn't either," Morgan admitted. "But I didn't have the guts not to."

After a moment he added, "You don't start a life over again, I guess. You just try to do the best you can with what's left of it. But maybe that's enough. *Whatsoever thy hand findeth to do, do it with thy might.*" He moved back into the office, an amorphous shape in the poor light. "If you survive this, you really mean to marry her?"

"I do."

"She's a wildcat."

"I know."

"Just thought I'd better warn you," Morgan muttered absently. "It's getting to be time."

"Yeah." Paradise pulled the door open and stepped out onto the walk. His eyes were ominous. Morgan came out beside him, and they stood there watching the dawn pink up. Morgan said, "Going to be another hot one today. Hot as blazes."

"There they are," Paradise said. "Spread out a little."

Morgan shifted three paces to his left. On the porch of the Occidental, half a block away to the southwest, the little shape of Wargo and the big shape of Crouch came out off the boardwalk onto the street, cuffing up dust.

Wargo's bass voice rolled across the hundred feet separating them. "You're all through, Ranger. Last chance—get on your horse and ride."

"I guess the cards are dealt," Paradise said. "Play your hand, Doc, or throw it in."

Crouch looked like a granite block set to motion. He waddled, lumbering out to a point in the exact center of the street. The pink dawn caught him on one cheek and threw that side of his face into blood-colored relief. He was carrying so much armament that it was possible he might get confused as to which gun to reach for.

Wargo's nickel-plated revolver hung at his right hip, and his right hand was inches from it. He said, "You in this, Sheriff?"

"I'm in it."

"Too bad," Wargo murmured. "All right, then—"

He didn't finish the sentence; his gun came curling up.

Paradise whipped his Colt forward; as it settled in his grasp he heard the sharp crack of Wargo's revolver: The little gunman was fast, amazingly fast. The fist-sized blow of the bullet smashed Paradise half around in his tracks. He didn't know exactly where he was hit, didn't have time to care; he was still on his feet and as he turned his gun back toward target, he heard a mushroom roar of sound from his left.

The old sheriff was fast, too: That was his gun roaring. Morgan's bullet punched a hole in the front of Ernie Crouch's shirt. Dust puffed up. Crouch hardly stirred. He had guns in both hands, rising, but Paradise had no time for that; all in the space of this tiny split second, Wargo was cocking his gun for another shot, taking his deliberate time about it.

Paradise fired.

In slack-jawed disbelief, Doc Wargo shuddered back. His body went loose, and he fell down and began to curl up like a piece of bacon in a hot frying pan.

Morgan's gun was booming methodically, and every shot found a place in his ample target; but none of it seemed to trouble Ernie Crouch. Both guns lifted irrevocably in his ham fists and both guns went off, once each, before Crouch finally tilted like an axed redwood tree and crashed to the earth with a blow that seemed to shake the town.

The stink of powder smoke was acrid in Paradise's nostrils. He had only fired one shot; the wind drifted Morgan's smoke past his face. He looked down at himself and saw the long ugly bleeding slice, curving around his ribs, and he thought, *If the damn fool had used something bigger than that .38, he'd have killed me with that bullet.* The slug had been deflected by his rib.

Wargo was dead and Crouch was down, evidently dying, coughing blood into the street. Five bullets in his chest, Crouch still found the energy to yank back his trigger and pour lead into the street. Then, finally, the guns were stilled.

Paradise turned to look for Morgan.

The sheriff was walking backward with slow little steps. He swayed back against the wall and came away, leaving behind a red smear; he eyed Paradise petulantly and sat down, clumsy.

Paradise ran to him. Morgan looked up and said, "I guess that's all."

"You'll be all right, Sheriff."

"Not with two slugs in my lungs. So long Paradise. Like I said," he grinned weakly, "the kind of son-in-law I always wanted." He passed out, and Paradise knew he would never awaken.

The crowd was gathering, gingerly coming closer, gathering boldness. When he looked up the street he saw the two slim women there, and he knew they had seen the whole thing. They walked forward now, breaking into a skirt-flying run.

Paradise put his gun away in the holster and waited for them. They knelt over Morgan, and Paradise said, "I tolled him into this. It was my fault. If it didn't sound hollow, I'd say I'm sorry."

"Don't be sorry," Mrs. Morgan told him. "Don't ever be sorry. He's all right now. Nothing can hurt him any more."

Terry's tears were glistening in the dawn light. Paradise lifted her by the shoulders and walked away with his arm around her. There was nothing that needed saying. She pulled his arm down off her shoulders and grasped him by the hand, and turned against him; he held her close and said, "Cry it out."

She said, "He died well?"

"Yes."

She reached up and pulled his shaggy red head down. Her cheeks were wet. He held her silently while the sun came up.

Ed Gorman is a Midwesterner, born in Iowa in 1941; growing up in Minneapolis, Minnesota; Marion, Iowa; and finally settling down in Cedar Rapids, Iowa. While primarily a suspense novelist, he was written half a dozen Western novels and published a collection of Western stories. His novel *Wolf Moon* was a Spur nominee for Best Paperback Original. About his Western novels, *Publisher's Weekly* said, "Gorman writes Westerns for grown-ups," which the author says he took as a high compliment, and was indeed his goal in writing his books.

Wolf Moon

Ed Gorman

The wolves lived on a perch high in the mountains so that the leader of the pack could see anything that threatened his mate or their pups. Behind the perch was a cave that served as a den. It was a shared responsibility to bring their pups food. It was not easy. The land was filled with two-legs and their guns. That was why they lived so high up, near where the jagged peaks touched the clouds.

Of course, the wolf knew that man was a devious foe. He did not always show himself when he meant to destroy the wolves.

The leader remembered last spring, when four of the pups had wandered off to hunt and had found for themselves a piece of buffalo meat that a rancher had poisoned with strychnine. The pups had died long and terrible deaths cuddled up against the belly of their mother, while she cried for hours into the dark and indifferent night.

Only one pup had lived, and about this last son the leader and his wife were protective to the point of mania. When the pup slept, the leader sat just outside the den, so that nobody could get inside without killing him first. When the pup accompanied the mother on a small hunt, she never once let him stray, despite the wolf ritual of letting the pups wander off and find their own food.

By the time he was six months, and by the time the white and bitter snows came, the pup stood thirty inches high at the shoulder and measured six feet from the tip of his nose to the tip of his tail. An Indian boy with a white man's lasso managed to get the rope over the pup's neck one day but, incredibly, the pup's powerful jaws cleaved the rope with a single bite. The Indian boy ran off, convinced he had encountered a dire and supernatural being.

By the summer, leader and mate began giving their huge and eager pup a little more freedom.

Because of this, the pup was drinking from a winding mountain stream the day he heard the shots from up on the ledge where the den was.

In fear and rage the pup made his way quickly up the shifting rocks of the mountain.

He saw his mother lying dead, her head exploded from several bullets, her limp body hanging over the edge of a promontory.

At this same moment, his father was being held up by his rear paws and a shaggy and filthy man was gutting him with a bowie knife.

The shaggy man saw the pup. "Schroeder, look at that pup!"

For the first time, the pup set eyes on the sleek and handsome human named Schroeder. He was everything the other man was not—well-attired in fancy hunting clothes, well-spoken, composed and radiating a self-confidence that was almost oppressive.

Schroeder turned now and beheld the pup. His face showed true awe as he studied the imposing animal. He said, simply, "I don't care how long it takes you, Greenleaf. I want that pup. Do you understand me?"

And so the hunt began.

It took the wolfer known as Greenleaf four days, but finally with the help of two Indian trackers, he captured the pup and turned him over to Schroeder. His reward was $1,000 cash and a night in a Denver whorehouse with a former slave girl named (by her madam) Esmerelda.

Schroeder never saw Greenleaf again and didn't care. He had the pup. And he had his very special plans for the pup.

Part I

The first thing I did after leaving the saloon was find an alley and throw up. We'd been two hard days riding and I still hadn't gotten over the killing yet. I had never robbed a bank before, and I had certainly never seen a man die before, either, especially one of my own brothers. The man named Schroeder had killed him without hesitation or mercy.

So tonight I'd had too much to drink, trying to forget how I'd been changed from eighteen-year-old farm boy to bank robber in the course of forty-eight hours. And trying to forget how Glen had looked dying there by the side of the road when we were dividing the money with Schroeder.

After I finished in the alley, I went back to the dusty street. The water wagon had worked most of the afternoon, but by now, near midnight, the dust rose like ghosts from the grave. The eighty-degree temperature didn't make things any more pleasant, either.

The sleeping room Don and I rented was over the livery stable. The owner had built two small rooms up there and put in cots and a can to piss in and fancied himself in the hotel business. He wanted Yankee cash up front and he wanted a promise not to smoke in bed. All the hay in the stalls below would go up like tinder, he said. We wouldn't have put up with his rules, Don and I, but there were no other rooms to be had.

The livery was dark. You could hear the horses talking to themselves in their sleep. The windless air was sweet and suffocating with the aroma of their shit.

I took the outside stairs leading up to the sleeping rooms. Halfway up I heard the moan. I stopped, just standing there, feeling my stomach and bowels do terrible things. Despite the fact that I looked like a big, jovial, sunbaked farm boy, I was given to nerves and the stomach of an old man.

I eased my .45 from my holster.

I'd recognized the moan as belonging to my older brother, Don. You don't grow up with somebody and not know all the sounds he makes.

The night sky was black and starry. The animals below were still jibbering and snorting as they slept. The saloon music was distant now, and lonely in the hot night air.

I started climbing the stairs on tiptoes.

When I got to the landing, I found the door leading to the hall was ajar. I eased it open, gripping my gun tighter.

The shadows were so deep I had the momentary sense of going blind.

He moaned again, Don did, behind the door down the hall and to the right.

I tiptoed over, put my hand on the knob, and gave it an inward push.

You could smell the dying on him. The blood and the seeping poisons.

In the pale light of the moon-facing window he lay on his cot as if the undertaker had already done him up. He lay unmoving with his hands folded primly on his belly and his raw, naked feet arranged precisely side by side, sticking straight up in a way that was almost funny.

Then I got foolish, because he was my brother and all, and because my other brother had passed on less than forty-eight hours ago.

I went straight into the room without considering that somebody might be behind the door.

Don moaned just as I reached his cot. I could see the wounds now, deep knife slashes across his neck and chest and arms. At least, I thought they were knife slashes.

The growl came up from the gravelike darkness behind the door. Hearing it, Don made a whimpering dying-animal noise that scared me because I knew he had only minutes to go.

I turned toward the growl and there they stood—a handsome, trim man in a dark suit much too hot for this kind of summer night, and a timber wolf so big and well-muscled he had to go at least one hundred eighty pounds. But size wasn't the only thing that made the lobo remarkable. His coat glowed silver—there was no other way to think of it except glowing—and his eyes glowed yellow, the color of a midnight moon.

The animal I'd never seen before. The man was plenty familiar. He was Schroeder, the man who'd hired us to rob the bank he was part owner of. Afterward we were supposed to split the money four ways—three for us brothers, one for Schroeder. But he'd double-crossed us, killing Glen in the process. But we'd been suspicious of Schroeder and had stashed the money under the foundation of a little white country church. It had taken Schroeder a day and a half to figure out that we'd double-crossed him right back.

Now he was here to get the rest of the money.

He used a few Indian words I didn't understand. And then the lobo, growling again, sprang.

He went right for my gun hand, teeth tearing into my wrist, knocking my gun to the floor before I could possibly fire a shot.

The lobo then did to me what he'd done to my brother, whose wounds I now knew had been caused by teeth, not a knife.

He came for me then. He was so well-trained he didn't even make much noise. He just worked his slashing teeth and ripping claws over my face and chest and belly.

I wasn't awake long, of course, not with all the pain, not with all the blood.

There was just the lobo, that glowing lunging body, and those haunted glowing eyes . . .

For a time all I could hear was my own screaming. Then I couldn't hear much of anything at all.

Part 2

Three months later, a judge named Emmanuel Byers sentenced me to twelve years in territorial prison for my part in the bank robbery.

You hear a lot of stories about prison, and most of them, unfortunately, are true. I was put in a steel five-by-seven cell on the south wing. There were two canvas hammocks for sleeping and one chair for sitting. If you took instruction in reading and writing, as I did, you were allowed to keep a book in your cell. I learned to read and write so well that a lady reporter came out one time and wrote a piece about me. She was especially impressed with the fact that I could recite whole chunks of Shakespeare from memory.

Most of the time I did what most prisoners did. I worked at the quarry. The owner paid the warden eighty cents a day per man. The warden, it was said, paid forty cents to the territorial government and kept the rest for himself. This was in the summer. In the winter I worked on the river, cutting and storing ice for the Union Pacific Railroad. The warden had a cousin who was some kind of railroad vice-president, and the cousin was said to pay plenty for us men, with the warden and himself dividing the spoils.

The first man I bunked with was an Indian who had stabbed to death a man he insisted was a Negro. His lawyer eventually got an old Negro woman to swear that the dead man had been colored, which saved the Indian's life. The judge, learning that the victim was only one more shabby black man, called off the Indian's scheduled execution and let him go free after six months.

During all this time, I wrote letters to Gillian, a young woman I'd known my last two years on the farm. Her father had run the general store. She'd been my partner at harvest moon dances and on the sledding hills near Christmas. I loved her, though I'd never been able to quite say that out loud, and she loved me, a sentiment she expressed frequently. The first three or four times I'd written her, she hadn't responded. I imagined she was still upset over the fact that the man she loved was a bank robber, though as I pointed out in those letters, it was Don and Glen who'd been the robbers, I'd just sort of gone along this one time to see what it was like. Also to their credit, as I noted in those same letters, nobody had ever been killed or even shot during any of their robberies. Eventually she started writing back, though she admitted that she had to be careful her father didn't find out. He was a typical townsman in his belief that criminals of any stripe should be hanged and utterly forgotten.

About seven months into my sentence, I got a letter from Gillian with a new address. She said her father had found out about her writing me and had demanded that she stop. She'd refused. And so she was now living in the mountains in a gold-mining town where, after a few weeks, she'd met a dandy named Reeves, a man who reminded her an awful lot of Schroeder, at least as I'd described him. One day this Reeves got his photograph in the local paper. He'd just become co-owner of the town's largest bank. The other owner was a retiring Yankee major named Styles. This Reeves fellow would run everything from now on. The photograph showed that Gillian had good instincts. It was Schroeder himself, back in the banking business under a new name and in a new town. I wondered how long it would take him to arrange a robbery of his new bank.

ONE DAY AT the quarry a fierce murderer named Maples, a man nobody troubled, not even the guards, started making fun of a fifteen-year-old boy who was serving time for killing his father. The boy was pretty and slender as a girl. It was whispered that Maples was sweet on the boy but that the boy wouldn't oblige him in any way. This day at the quarry Maples suddenly went crazy. For no reason that anybody could see, he grabbed the boy and hurled him into the water. Then Maples, still crazed and angrier than anybody had seen him, ran down into the water himself and grabbed the boy, who was just now getting up, and held the boy down under the water till he drowned. Several times the boy surfaced, screaming and puking, but Maples just kept holding his head under until the deed was done. I started down into the water, but an old con who'd always looked out for me grabbed my arm and whispered, "Maples'll just kill you next, kid, if 'n you go down there." And I knew he was right. And so I just stood there like all the other men in that hot dusty quarry and watched one man kill another.

My fourth year there tuberculosis walked up and down the cell blocks. More than two hundred men died in four months.

In all my time inside I had only one fight, when a new man, trying to impress everybody, made fun of my face, how it was all scarred up from the wolf that time. I don't know why it bothered me so much, but it did and I damned near killed him with my fists. For that I got what the guards called a "shower bath," which meant stripping me naked and directing a stream of high-pressure water from a hose to my face, chest, and crotch. When you fell down, they kept spraying away, till your balls were numb and your nose and mouth ran with blood. I was so sick with diarrhea afterward, I lost twenty pounds in the next week and a half.

In a way, even though I'd been angry when the warden told me I couldn't grow a beard, I was grateful for how scarred my face was. Sure, people looked away when they first saw me—I was a monster now, not a human being—but my appearance always reminded me of why, lying there in the doc's office right after the white wolf attacked me—why, despite the physical pain from the bites and slashes, and the mental pain of having seen both my brothers die—why I wanted to go on living.

I wanted to repay Schroeder for how he'd betrayed us. That was my one reason for existing.

Parole was not a major event. Early in the morning of a certain day, a guard took me forward to the warden's office, where I received ten dollars, a suggestion that I read every day the Bible the warden had just handed me, and a plea to stay away from bad people like myself. When you wait so many years for something you expect to feel exuberant. I didn't feel much of anything at all. I just wanted to see Gillian and hear more about Schroeder.

A buggy took me to the train depot, where I sat for an hour on a hard little bench and let the locals gawk at me. It probably wasn't real hard to see that I'd just gotten out of prison.

BY THE TIME *it was a year and a half old, the wolf was no longer a pup. Nor was it exactly a wolf. Its weight of 160 pounds marked its maturity, but the tasks it performed belonged not to the wolf family—which was essentially peaceful except for hunting—but to a predatory state that could only be man-made.*

Schroeder, using methods a wolfer named Briney had shown him, built an enormous cage for the animal and let him out only when there was a task to be performed—or only when the wolf was being trained.

Schroeder believed that violence begat violence, and so he was remarkably cruel with the wolf. When the animal failed to perform properly, Schroeder beat the animal until it crawled and whimpered. Thus broken, it once again became malleable.

Schroeder trained the animal for eight months before testing it.

One chill March day, Schroeder took a husky about the same size as the wolf and put it in the cage, locked the door, and spoke aloud the Indian command for "kill," which was supposed to turn the wolf into a frenzied beast.

The wolf did not turn on the husky.

Schroeder spent an hour alternately calling out the command and threatening the animal.

When it was finally clear that the wolf would not attack the husky, Schroeder opened the cage, withdrew the dog, and then began beating the wolf until the animal seemed ready to turn on its master.

But Schroeder had been ready for that. He clubbed the animal across the skull with a ball bat. The animal collapsed into unconsciousness.

This training continued until the year that Schroeder met the Chase brothers and arranged for them to rob the bank of which he was part owner.

By then the wolf was obedient, as he proved when he murdered the one Chase brother and cruelly attacked the other.

The wolf no longer remembered the smell of smoky autumn winds and the taste of cool clear creek water and the beauty of sunflowers in the lazy yellow sunlight. He no longer even remembered his mother and father.

There was just the cage. There was just his master. There was just the whip. There was just the prey he was sometimes ordered to kill and rend.

He was still called a wolf, of course, by everyone who saw him.

But he was no longer a true wolf at all. He was something more. And something less.

ON A FINE sunny dawn, the roosters stirring, the wolf awoke to find that he had company in the large cage.

A raccoon had burrowed under the wire and was just now moving without any fear or inhibition toward the wolf.

Instinctively the wolf knew something was wrong with the raccoon. For one thing, such an animal was not very often brave, not around a wolf anyway.

And for another, there was the matter of the raccoon's mouth, and the curious foamy substance that bearded it. Something was very wrong with this raccoon.

It struck before the wolf had time to get to its feet.

It ripped into the wolf's forepaw and brought its jaws tight against the bone.

The wolf cried out in rage and pain, utterly surprised by the speed and savagery with which the raccoon had moved.

In moments the raccoon was dead, trapped in the teeth and jaws of the wolf as it slammed the chunky body of the raccoon again and again against the bars of the cage.

And then the wolf, still enraged, eviscerated it, much as the wolf had been taught to eviscerate humans.

Then it was done.

The wolf went back to his favorite end of the cage and lay down. His forepaw still hurt and he still cried some, but oddly, he was tired, exhausted, and knew he needed sleep.

When he woke, he stared down at the forepaw. A terrible burning had infected it.

He still wondered about the raccoon and where it had gotten all that nerve to come into his cage and attack him.

Soon enough the wolf went back to sleep, the inexplicable drowsiness claiming him once again.

Part 3

In the summer of '98 the folks in Rock Ridge were just starting to sink the poles and string the wire for telephones. I knew this because all three of the town's newspapers told me about it right on the front page, in the kind of civic-pride tone most mining-town papers use to prove that they really are, after all, a bunch of law-abiding Christian people.

On a sunny June morning filled with bird song and silver dew, I sat in a crowded restaurant located between a lumberyard and a saddlery. The place smelled of hot grease, tobacco smoke, and the sweaty clothes of the laborers.

Near midnight I'd pitched from my dry and dusty mount and taken a room down the street at the Excelsior Hotel. I didn't know exactly what to expect from Gillian yet.

According to the *Gazeteer*, Rock Ridge was a town of four thousand souls, five banks, twelve churches (I found it curious that the *Gazeteer* folks would list banks before houses of the Lord), two schools, ten manufacturing plants, and a police department of "eighteen able and trustworthy men, among the finest in all the West." (On a following page was a small story about how a prisoner had died of a "mysterious fall" in his jail cell, and how his widowed mother was planning to sue the town, which of course told me a hell of a lot more about the police force than all of the newspaper's glowing adjectives.)

I was just about to ask for another cup of coffee when the front door opened up and a man in a dark blue serge uniform with shiny gold buttons on the coat came in, the coat resembling a Union Army jacket that had been stripped of all insignia. He wore a Navy Colt strapped around his considerable belly and carried in his right hand a long club that had an impressive number of knicks and knocks on it, not to mention a few dark stains that were likely blood that soap hadn't been able to cleanse. The contrast of his natty white gloves only made the club look all the more brutal. He had a square and massive blond head and intelligent blue eyes that were curiously sorrowful. He was probably my age, on the lee side of thirty.

He made a circuit, the policeman, like a mayor up for re-election, ultimately offering a nod, a handshake, a smile, or a soft greeting word to virtually everybody in the place. And they grinned instantly and maybe a little too heartily, like kids trying hard not to displease a mean parent. They were afraid of him, and some of them even despised him, and the more they grinned and the more they laughed at his little jokes, the more I sensed their fear.

When he was done, he walked over to a plump serving woman who had long been holding a lone cup of coffee for him. He thanked her, looked around, and then settled his eyes on me.

He came over, pulled out a chair, sat down, and put forth a hand that looked big and strong enough to choke a full-grown bear.

"You'd be Mr. Chase?"

I nodded.

"Got your name at the hotel desk. Always like to know who's staying over in our little town."

I said nothing, just watched him. Hick law, I figured, trying to intimidate me into pushing on. He wouldn't know anything about my time in prison, but he wouldn't want me around town, either, not unless I had some reason for being here.

"Name's Ev Hollister. I'm the chief of police."

"Nice to meet you."

"This is a friendly place."

"Seems to be."

"And we're always happy to welcome strangers here."

"I appreciate that."

"Long as we know their business." When he finished with this line, he shot me one of his empty white smiles.

"Maybe looking for a place to settle."

"You have any special trade?"

Yeah, I wanted to say, bank robbing. Which bank would you suggest I hit first? "Nothing special. Little of this, little of that."

"Little of this, little of that, huh?"

"Uh-huh." I gave him one of my own empty white smiles. "All strictly legal of course."

"Glad you said that."

"Oh?"

He took some of his coffee and wiped his mouth with the back of his hand. He was proud of those hands the way a man is proud of a certain gun. They were outsize, powerful hands. "Cholera came through here three months ago."

"Bad stuff."

"Struck the Flannery family especially hard."

"They kin of yours?"

"No, but they gave this town two of the best officers I ever had. Brothers. About your age and build. Damned good men." He looked at me straight and hard. "You ever thought of being a police officer?"

I could imagine the men back in territorial prison listening in on this conversation. They'd be howling.

"Guess not, Chief."

"Well, if you stay around her, you should consider it. The work is steady and the pay ain't bad, forty-eight dollars a month. And folks have a lot of respect for a police officer."

My mind drifted back to the mother of the youngster who'd died in a "mysterious fall" in his jail cell. I wondered how much respect she had for police officers.

"Well, I sure do appreciate the interest, Chief. How about I think it over for a couple days?"

"Lot of men would jump at the chance to be on my police force." There was just a hint of anger in his tone. He wasn't use to getting turned down.

I put forth my hand.

He stood up and made a big pretense of not seeing my hand sticking out there.

"You think it over," he said, and left.

The smile was back on him as soon as he reached the front of the place, where he flirted with a couple of ladies at a table and told a bawdy joke to an old man with a hearing horn. I knew it was bawdy by the way the old guy laughed, that burst of harsh pleasure.

Through the window, I watched Chief Hollister make his way down the street. The water wagon was out already, soaking down the dust as much as possible. A telephone pole was being planted on a corner half a block away. Ragged summertime kids stood watching, fascinated. Later they'd spin tales of how different a place Rock Ridge would be with telephones.

Up in the hills you could see the mines, watch the smoke rise and hear the hard rattling noise of the hoists and pumps and mills. In prison an ex-miner had told me what it was like to be twenty three hundred feet down when the temperature hit one hundred twenty and they had to lower ice down the shaft because that low your tools got so hot you sometimes couldn't hold them. And sometimes you got so dehydrated and sick down there that you started puking up blood—all so two or three already rich men in New York could get even richer.

And who would keep all those miners in line if they ever once started any kind of real protest?

None other than the dead-eyed man I'd just met, Rock Ridge's esteemed police chief, Ev Hollister. Over in Leadville they'd recently given a police chief and two of his officers $500 each for killing three miners who were trying to lead a strike. Law was the same in all mining towns.

I paid my money, went down to the livery and got my horse, and rode out to see Gillian.

Part 4

It was a hardscrabble ranch house with a few hardscrabble outbuildings on the edge of some jack pines in the foothills of the blue, aloof mountains. It was not quite half a mile out of town.

In the front yard a very pretty little girl of eight or so spoke with great intimacy to a dun pony no taller than she was. The little girl wore a blue gingham dress that set off her shining blond pigtails just fine. When she looked me full in the face, I saw the puzzlement in her eyes, the same puzzlement as in mine. She favored her mother, and that tumbled me into sorrow. I guess I hadn't any right to expect that Gillian would go without a man all these years. As for the little girl staring at me—I was long conditioned to people studying my scars, repelled and snake-charmed at the same time, but then I remembered my new blond beard that covered the scars. They couldn't be seen now except in the strongest sunlight. Yet the little girl still stared at me.

"I don't think I've ever seen eyes that blue," I said.

She smiled.

"Are you enjoying the summer?"

She nodded. "I'm Annie. I bet I know who you are. You're Chase. My mom talks about you all the time."

It was a day of orange butterflies and white fluffy dandelions and quick silken birds the color of blooded sunsets. And now fancy little conversations.

"I was going to write you a letter once," Annie said.

"You were?"

"Uh-huh, but Mom said I better not because of your major."

She smiled, sweet and shy and pure little girl there in the bright prairie morning.

"She said you were in the cavalry and that you had a real mean major named Thomkins who didn't want you to get letters."

I handled it best I could. "He was pretty mean all right."

"My mom's inside."

"You think it'd be all right if I went and saw her?"

"She's baking bread. She'll give you some if you ask."

I grinned. "Then I'll make sure to ask."

She put her tiny hand up in mine and led me up the earthen path to the slab front door of the ranch house. As we walked, I saw to the west a hillock where a well had been dug, probably an artesian that had failed because the water would not rise. Easier to walk to the distant creek and lug it back in buckets. Or make one of those homemade windmills you could now buy kits for.

I could smell bread baking. It reminded me of my own ma and our own kitchen, back before all the troubles came to us Chase boys, and for a moment I was Annie's age again, all big eyes and empty rumbling belly.

Annie pushed open the door and took me into the cool shadows of the house. The layout seemed to be a big front room with a hallway leading to a big kitchen in back. Between were two bedrooms set one on each side of the hallway. There wasn't much furniture, a tumbledown couch and chairs, a painting of an aggrieved Jesus, and a splendid vase lamp with an ornately painted globe. The flooring was hardwood shined slick and bright and covered occasionally with shaggy blue throw rugs.

In the kitchen, I found Gillian just taking a loaf of bread from the oven and setting it on the windowsill to cool. To clear room, she had to *shush* a cardinal away, and looked guilty doing it.

When she saw me there, led in by her little daughter, her face went blank and she paused, as if considering what to feel. I'd once promised Gillian I'd marry her, and never had; and when I was sent off to prison, she in turn promised she'd wait. But the birth of Annie had put the lie to that. I guess neither one of us knew what to feel, standing here and facing each other across a canyon of eight hard and lonely years.

She was still pretty—not beautiful, not cute, pretty—with a long fragile neck and fine shining golden hair, Annie's hair, and a frank blue gaze that was never quite without a hint of grief. She'd had one of those childhoods that not even a long life could outlive. She wore gingham, which she always had, and a white frilly apron, and even from here I could see how years of work had made her quick, slender hands raw. She was neither old nor young now, but that graceful in-between when a girl becomes full woman. She looked good as hell to me, and I felt tongue-lost as a boy, having no idea what to say.

"This is my mom," Annie said.

I laughed. "I'm glad you told me that, honey."

"He wants some bread."

"Oh, he does, does he?" Gillian said.

"And jam," Annie said definitively.

"Doesn't he know how to speak for himself?" Gillian said.

"He's so hungry, he can't talk."

I wondered, what had happened to that shy little girl who'd greeted me on the walk?

Gillian gaped at me a moment longer and said, "That sure is some beard you got there, Chase."

A FEW MINUTES later Gillian shooed Annie outside and set about fixing me up with that warm fresh bread and strawberry jam her daughter wanted me to have.

As she sliced the bread and poured us both coffee, she asked me how my first night here had gone, and I told her, with a laugh, all about how the chief of police had tried to recruit me.

"Maybe you should do it," she said.

"Huh?"

She sat down my bread and coffee, slid the jam pot over to my side of the table, and then sat down across from me. "Maybe you should do it."

"Be a policeman?"

"There are worse ways to make a living."

"Seems you're forgetting where I've been the last few years."

"Hollister doesn't know where you've been. And he wouldn't have any reason to check unless you did something wrong."

We didn't speak for a time. She sat there and watched me eat. I tried not to smack my lips. I'd shared a cell with a man who snorted when he ate. I knew how aggravating noisy eaters could be.

When only my coffee was left, I looked up at her. "I'd appreciate it if you'd tell me about Schroeder."

"I was hoping you'd forget about Schroeder. Anyway, he calls himself Reeves now."

"What does he do?"

"Runs a bank. Has a partner who's very old, and lives in a big mansion by himself."

"The bank been robbed since 'Reeves' bought in?"

"No, but I imagine it's just a matter of time." She watched me the way Annie had when I'd first come into the yard. "Why don't you forget about him, Chase? That part of your life is gone now."

"He killed my brothers."

"They'd want you to go on with your life, Chase." She'd known both my brothers. While to the town they'd been bank robbers, to her they were never more than rambunctious boys who'd eventually settle down. "I knew them, Chase, and what they wanted for you. They didn't want you to be the way they were."

And then she was crying.

We were sitting in the kitchen with the scent of bread sweet on the air and a jay on the window ledge and the breeze soft and warm on the underside of the curtains.

And I didn't know what to do.

I just went over to her and knelt down beside her and took her tiny hand and held it gently as I could. I kept saying over and over, "Oh, Gillian, come on now; oh, Gillian, please," and things like that, but neither words nor touches helped, she just sat there and cried without sound, her frail body shaking with her grief.

And then Annie was in the doorway saying. "Did Chase hurt you, Mommy?"

Gillian got herself together quickly, brought apron to nose and eyes to daub tears, and cleared her throat sternly to speak. "No, hon, he didn't hurt me."

"I wouldn't like him if he hurt you, Mommy."

"It's fine, honey, really. You go on back outside now."

Annie looked at me for a time, confused and ready to hate me if Gillian said to, and then turned and slowly left the doorway.

We sat in silence again until she said, "I don't want you to come out here anymore."

"Oh, God, Gillian. You don't know how long I've waited to—"

"I was hoping prison would change you. Force you to grow up and forget about Reeves." She sounded as if she were about to start crying again. "But is hasn't. I was just fooling myself all those years while I waited."

I wanted to point out that she'd been doing more than "waiting," what with having a daughter during that time. But the words died in my throat, and I felt guilty for making Gillian carry on this way.

She put her head down on the table and started crying again, her slender shoulders shaking miserably. I leaned over and kissed her on the back of the head and slipped out through the gathering blue shadows of the afternoon.

As I walked over to my horse, Annie looked up from combing her pony and said, "Is my mommy still sad?"

I swung up in the saddle and said, "Right now she is. But if you go in and see her, she won't be."

She nodded solemnly, put down the brush she was using, and set off walking to the ranch house.

Part 5

"You got a name, son?"

"Chase."

"You got a first name?"

"Sorry. Guess people usually call me plain 'Chase.' First name's Robert."

"Well, son, I wish I could help you, but I can't. See that Indian out there on the loading dock?"

"Yessir."

"That sonofabitch does the work of three white men and he don't complain half as much as they do."

"Good worker, huh?"

"Good? Hell, great. That's why I don't need nobody right now. But I tell ya. If you're around town in three, four weeks, you try me again, 'cause you never can tell."

"That's right. You never can tell."

"Good luck, son, you shouldn't have no problem, big strong young man like you."

"Yessir. And thank you, sir."

That's how it went all afternoon. I went up and down the alleys, knocking on the back doors of every business I could find, and it was always the same story. Just hired me somebody last week; or business been a little slow lately; or why don't ya try down the street, son?

Near dusk, when I was walking into the lumberyard, I saw Chief Hollister and he gave me a smirk as if he knew that I wasn't getting anywhere and that I'd been damned foolish to turn down his offer.

As I had been.

Part 6

That night, I sat in a chair next to Annie's bed reading aloud a book called *Standard Fairy Tales*. Nearby a kerosene lantern flickered light through the cottage.

"How tall was Jack's beanstalk?"

"Didn't you already ask me that?"

She giggled. "Uh-huh."

"It was eighty feet tall."

"Last time you said it was sixty feet tall."

"I lied."

She giggled again. "You don't lie. My mom says you're a good man."

I looked up from my book to Gillian in the rocker in the corner. She was knitting. The rocker squeaked pleasantly back and forth, back and forth, as a slow summer rain pattered on the full-grown leaves of the elm trees on either side of the house.

"You said I was a good man?" I asked Gillian.

She smiled her easy smile. "I believe I said something like that, yes."

"Well, I just want you to know that I'm mighty grateful. It's nice to have somebody thinking nice thoughts about me."

"Did you really like my roast beef tonight?"

"I like it very much."

"You didn't think it was tough?"

"I thought it was tender."

"You really mean that?"

"I really mean that."

Truth was, the meat had been tough as hell. Cooking had never been one of Gillian's strengths. Great baker—breads and rolls and pies—but terrible, terrible cook.

"I like to close my eyes and hear you read, Chase. I like it as much as Annie does."

"I'll read some more."

"I remember when you wrote and told me—when you were away, I mean—how that man taught you to read."

"When you were in the Army?" Annie said.

"Yes," I looked over at Gillian again. "When I was in the Army."

"Tell me about the Army. You promised."

"When we have a little more time, I'll tell you."

"Don't we have time now?"

"Nope."

"How come?"

"Because we've got to find out what the giant's going to do to Jack."

"Go on, Chase," Gillian said. "Annie and I'll close our eyes and you read."

So they closed their eyes and I read.

LATER ON THAT night, after Annie fell asleep, Gillian and I went down to the willow by the creek that ran in the back of her yard, and made love standing up, the way we used to sometimes in the old days.

When her dress was down and my pants were up, we walked along the creek listening to the frogs and the crickets and the owls. The rain had stopped and everything smelled minty and fresh in the midnight moon.

"You never did answer that one letter of mine, Chase."

"Which letter was that?"

"The one where I asked you if you'd ever say you loved me."

"I guess I figured you knew."

We walked a little more in silence. Stars filled the sky and everything smelled cool and fresh after the rain.

"Annie sure likes you."

"I sure like her."

"Says she hopes she sees you some more."

"Hope I see her some more."

We came to the small leg of river that ran below a railroad bridge. The water was silver in the moonlight.

I skipped rocks across the surface and she laughed and said it was good to see me acting so young; she'd been afraid that prison would make of me what prison had earlier made of an uncle of hers, a scared old man in a thirty-year-old's body.

About halfway back to the cabin I said, "Who's Annie's father, Gillian?"

"I was wondering when you'd ask me that."

"She's mine, isn't she?"

"Yes," Gillian said, "yes, she is."

Part 7

Just in case you think that a policeman's life is filled with the kind of derring-do you read about in yellow-backs or eastern newspapers, consider the fact that I spent my first two days walking all over town handing out circulars that came from Chief Hollister. They read:

> Cleanup notice is hereby given to property owners that all rubbish and disease breeding matter must be removed from their premises at once, or the work will be done by my officers at the owners' expense. The town board, sitting as a board of health, has ordered all pigsty and other nuisances to be abated. This order will be rigidly enforced.
>
> (Signed) Chief of Police, Ev Hollister

As you might expect, humans being humans, very little in the town was cleaned up by the owners, so most of us men, fine and shiny in our blue serge uniform coats with the bright brass buttons and the snug white gloves—most of us had to do the cleaning up. The men called it the "pig shit detail," and you got on it by drawing the smallest straw. I got on it twice in three weeks, which meant that Gillian had to do some extra hard cleaning of my uniform. But I don't mean to sound as if I was unhappy. I wasn't. My second weekend as an officer, Gillian and I got married, and my third weekend we sat Annie down and told her that I was her father and that we'd all be living together now forever. Annie cried and Gillian cried and I tried not to, but as I hugged them to me, I couldn't help myself. I cried at least a little bit, too. The hell of it was, I wasn't even sure why we were all crying. It was something the two females understood, not me.

In my first three weeks as an officer, I did not get into a gunfight, ward off an Indian attack, save a stagecoach from plunging into a ravine, rush an infant from a burning building, or even help an old lady across a busy street.

What I did do was spend from five in the afternoon till midnight, six nights a week, walking around the town and making sure that everything was locked up tight. Because what you had in a town like this, a mining town where bitter men drank a lot, were robberies. So my job was to walk a six-block area every night and rattle the doors on most of the businesses. I had been given the right to shoot on sight any burglar who offered me any resistance at all. I had also been given the key to most businesses so that in case I had to get inside, suspecting that a burglar might have hidden in there during business hours, I didn't have to bother Hollister or any of the merchants who were all home, presumably sleeping. At first, having the keys made me nervous—I'd never been one for much responsibility—but then as Gillian said over Sunday dinner, "You should be proud the merchants have that kind of trust in you, Chase."

Somewhere during those first few weeks, I gave up any notion of getting back at Reeves. I had convinced myself that Gillian was right, my brothers would have wanted me to pick up my life after prison and do something decent with it. Every once in a while I'd glimpse Reeves swaggering down the street but I'd just turn my head and look the other way. I had a wife and daughter now and they were all that mattered.

Summer became Indian summer and Indian summer became autumn. By now most people in town knew me and seemed to like me. I enjoyed the feeling.

"That uniform looks good on you."

"Thank you."

"I'm glad I spotted you in the restaurant that day." It was just afternoon, and you could smell the whiskey on him but you couldn't exactly say he was drunk yet.

I nodded. "Me too, Chief."

I'd been going to the back for a drink of water, passing Hollister's office on the way. He'd called me in and started talking, sitting behind his desk with his feet up and his hands folded on his stomach.

He smiled. "Merchants're always asking me how I think you're doing."

"The keys?"

He nodded. "Yup. They want to make sure you're the kind of man they can trust. They like you and they want to keep it that way."

"So do I."

"We had a fellow here—three, four years ago, I guess—good fellow, too, least he was when he started, but by the end he was breaking into the stores himself and then reporting all these burglaries."

"He might have been good but he doesn't sound too smart."

Hollister started to say something but then peeked out his window and saw a fancy black surrey pull up outside the two-story redbrick police station. The surrey belonged to his wife. She was always out and about in it. She had the kind of red-haired society-lady good looks that went just fine with a surrey like this one, and so naturally people resented her and whispered tales of her supposed infidelity. The police officers especially liked to tell such tales. It gave them a way to get back at Hollister, who always made it clear that he was at least one cut above us. He had been brought here by the merchants, and it was with the merchants he was friends. I'd even seen him eat lunch up to Casey's Restaurant with Reeves.

A minute later his eyes strayed from me and fixed on something over my shoulder. He smiled in a way that made him look ten years younger.

"Come on in and meet officer Chase," Hollister said in a smooth social voice.

I turned and saw her. She was a beauty all right, cat-green eyes to complement the silken red hair, nose and mouth and neck classical as a piece of sculpture. As she came into the room, she brought a scent of sweet cachet with her. In her crisp white blouse and full, dark green skirt, her hair caught up with a comb at the back of her head, she looked like a very beautiful schoolmarm.

"H-How are you d-doing?" she said to her husband.

That was the dirtiest part of the joke about Mrs. Hollister. Here you had all this beauty and grace and poise—she'd been schooled back East—and yet it was all marred by her very bad stutter, something she was clearly ashamed of. A lot of beautiful women like to flirt. They are saucy of eye and brazen of gait. But not Claire Hollister. She always walked with her eyes downcast, moving quickly, as if she wished she were invisible.

"Just a minute, hon," Hollister said, taking her hand and stroking it gently. "I'll finish with Chase here and you can tell me about your day."

Hollister was a hard man and a dangerous man and a proud man, yet right now, speaking so softly to his wife, I heard real tenderness in him and I was almost shocked by it. He had a locked room upstairs where he took prisoners at night after he'd been drinking awhile. There was no tenderness in him then. None at all.

"I just wanted to say you're doing a good job, Chase, and that I'm glad you got married. A man needs some responsibility. Otherwise he's not much better than a hobo."

It was like an awards ceremony, all the nice words, only there wasn't any plaque.

"Thanks," I said.

I turned toward the door. Claire Hollister nervously got out of my way. She was a skittish woman, which made no sense with that beautiful, sad face of hers.

"N-Nice to m-meet y-you," she said, and dropped her eyes, ashamed of herself.

"Nice to meet you," I said, and left.

Part 8

With all the walking I did, I was pretty tired when I got home every night around one o'clock, the honky-tonk piano music still in my ears, the beery scent of the taverns I patrolled still on me. I'd eat the light meal Gillian had set out for me and then I'd go into Annie's room and kneel down by her bed and just look at her little face made silver by the moonlight, the stray damp wisp of blond hair making her look even younger than she was, and then I'd close my eyes and say the best prayer I knew how, a prayer that Annie and Gillian would always be safe in the invisible arms of the Lord, and a prayer that Hollister would never find out about my prison record and that I'd go on to be a good policeman who eventually got promoted. And then I'd lean over and kiss Annie on the forehead, her kid skin warm to my lips, and then I'd go into our bedroom and strip down to my underwear and climb in next to Gillian and hold her gently and think of how long she'd waited for me and how true she'd been and how her faith had given me this new life of mine, and all I could pray for then was that I would never give in to my worst self and go after Reeves.

THE FIRST TIME I ever saw Lundgren and Mars they were stepping off the train just about suppertime of an early November evening. Kids and dogs ran down the dark streets toward mothers calling them in for the night.

I don't suppose anybody else would have made anything special of them. They were just two middle-aged men in dark business suits, each carrying a carpetbag, each wearing a bowler, one tall and thin, the other short and heavyset. They stood on the depot platform looking around at the town. They tried very hard to give the impression that they were important men.

I was making my early rounds. After some months as a policeman, I'd already developed flat feet, bunions, and a suspicious eye for everybody and everything, and that included these two strangers.

I decided to follow them. They went down the boardwalk past the noise of player pianos and the smells of cigars and the laughter of whores, up past the livery where the Mex was rubbing down a horse that had just been brought in, and down past the gunsmith's.

I stayed half a block behind them, rattling doorknobs as I went, making sure the town was locked up tight. In the hills there was talk of a miner's strike. Socialism was just starting to get a grip on the miners. Hollister had told us to watch out for trouble.

This particular night, the two strangers ended their walk at the front door of the Whitney Hotel, the town's best hotel, and a place that always boasts of two presidents having slept in its hallowed beds.

When I'd given them sufficient time to find rooms for themselves, I walked up to the massive registration desk, turned the guest register around and stared at the names I'd been looking for.

"I don't remember inviting you to look at our registration book," said Hartley, the night man. Because he wears a cravat and attends all the musicales at the opera house, he seems to find himself superior to people like me.

But by now I didn't care what he'd said. I had their names and that was all I wanted.

"Next time I'd appreciate it if you'd ask me first," he said, petulant as ever.

"I'll be sure to do that," I said, being just sarcastic enough so he'd get the message but not so sarcastic that he could say anything.

Half an hour later I sat on the stoop of the police station, taking my dinner break.

In chill evening, the first stars showing, I heard the jingle of a bicycle bell and here came Gillian with Annie up on the handlebars, bringing me my dinner as they did every once in awhile as sort of a special treat.

"It's getting nippy," Gillian said, handing me down a roast beef sandwich and an apple. "You can smell winter in the wind sometimes now."

Annie came over and sat down next to me. She couldn't get used to the idea yet that I was really her father.

"Did you shoot anybody tonight, Daddy?"

"Nope. But I wrestled a bear."

She giggled. "You did not."

"And when I got done with the bear, I wrestled an alligator."

More giggling. "Huh-uh."

"What're we going to do with this kid, anyway?" I said to Gillian. "She doesn't believe anything her old pappy tells her."

"Mrs. Dirks sent a note home with Annie today. She said Annie's one of her best students."

I gave Annie a hug and she gave me a wet kiss. The temperature was dropping fast. Her little nose and cheeks were cold as creek stones.

"I'll have some stew hot when you get home."

"I'd appreciate that."

"I told Annie that maybe Sunday the three of us could to see the motor car over in Carleton County."

"That'd be fun."

"Goodie!" Annie said.

A minute later Annie was back up on the handlebars and Gillian was turning the bike in the direction of our cottage.

"Sleep tight," I said to Annie.

"I love you, Daddy."

"I love you, too, sweet potato."

And then they were gone, phantoms in the gray, starry gloom, the two most important people in my life.

AROUND TEN I was finishing up with my second long patrol and just thinking of walking over to the bridge to roll myself a cigarette—I liked watching the river flow, and I couldn't even tell you why—when I looked down the street and saw two familiar shapes standing in the street in front of the Whitney Hotel. One tall, one short. Lundgren and Mars.

They stood for a time finishing off stogies, and then they flipped the butts into the street and walked on over to the livery. The Mex fixed them up with horses and saddles.

Five minutes later, seeming in no particular hurry, and seeming easy and confident on their mounts, the two of them rode out of town. I thought of going after them—they made me damned curious—but I knew it would take too long to get a horse saddled and follow them.

I stood there in the middle of the dark street, the bawdy sounds of saloons behind me in the distance, the sounds of their horses loud but fading into the night.

Where would they be going at this time of night?

Part 9

In the morning, after chores, I went into town earlier than usual. I couldn't stop thinking about Lundgren and Mars and what they might be doing in town.

The roan was fresh when I got him at the livery. A Mexican rubbing down a palomino gave me directions to the Reeves place.

An hour later, just as I rounded a copse of pines, I saw a massive Victorian house, a tower soaring up the center and seeming to touch the sky; a half-dozen spires; and three full floors. The front porch was vast and shadowy; the eaves elaborately carved. The grounds, enclosed within a black iron fence, looked relentlessly groomed. To the west was a large stable, to the east a vivid red barn.

It would take a whole lot of bank robbing to buy a place like this.

Just as I nudge the roan forward, I heard a rifle being cocked behind me.

"Howdy," a man's voice said.

He knew I'd heard his Winchester.

I tugged my roan to a halt.

"I said howdy, mister. Ain't you gonna howdy me back?"

"I'll howdy you all over the place if you'll put the rifle down."

"Just want to know your business out here."

"Far as I could tell, this is a public road."

"Yeah, but you ain't been on the road for ten minutes now. You been on Mr. Reeves's property."

A horsefly, having partaken of the splash the roan had just emptied on the road, buzzed near my face, loud in the sunny silence.

"You gonna say anything, mister?"

"I'm gonna say that I'm an old friend of Mr. Reeves's."

"No offense, mister, in case you are and all, but a lot of people say that to get inside here. They're usually looking for handouts."

"With me it's the truth, though."

"You got any way of proving that?"

"You just go tell Mr. Reeves that the man who helped him with his bank in Dunkirk is here."

"Didn't know Mr. Reeves ever lived in Dunkirk."

"You do now."

Now it was the guard's turn for quiet.

The cry of jays and the screech of hawks played against the lazy baying of the cows.

His shod horse took a few steps forward and he came around so he could take his first good look at me.

"You don't look like no businessman, son. Don't take that personal."

"Didn't say I was a businessman. All I said was that I'd given Mr. Reeves a little help."

He was fat and fifty but quick for his size, and his dark eyes gave you the feeling that he was capable of just about anything. He held a Winchester in gloved hands and spat tobacco in sickening streams, chawing not a habit I'd ever taken to as either participant or spectator. His sweaty white Stetson looked too big for him, as if his head was shrinking in the heat.

"Name's Hanratty. What's yours?"

I told him. He looked as if he thought if was a fake.

"You ride ahead of me," he said.

"Past the gate?"

He nodded.

We went inside, along a cinder path, to the right of which an old black man was now raking leaves.

We ground-tied the horses in front of the long, shadowy porch. He took me up and inside the house. Two feet inside, a tiny, white-haired man in a white shirt, paisley vest, and dark trousers appeared. He had a tanned simian face with bright, brown, intelligent eyes. He reminded me of a smart monkey. He carried a dust cloth in his right hand and a small bottle of sweet-smelling furniture polish in the other.

"Fenton, this man would like to see Mr. Reeves."

Fenton looked at me as if Hanratty had just told him some kind of joke.

"I see," he said.

"He looks unlikely as hell, I got to admit that." Hanratty laughed.

"Very unlikely," Fenton said. "And the nature of your business, sir?"

"Mr. Reeves and I once did a little business with a bank in Dunkirk."

"Dunkirk, sir?"

"Yes, he'll know what I mean."

"I see."

"So I wish you'd tell him I'm out here."

Fenton glanced at Hanratty again, then disappeared down the hall.

"I got to get back to my post," Hanratty said. "Good luck." He grinned and leaned to my ear. "Reeves ain't any nicer than he was when you knew him before, believe me."

I grinned back. "Nice to know some things never change."

I stood alone in the shadowy vestibule. Directly ahead of me a large, carpeted staircase rose steeply to a landing that glowed in sunlight. On the wall of the landing was a huge painting of Reeves in an Edwardian suit, trying hard to look like the illegitimate son of J. P. Morgan or some other robber baron. To my right was a wall with three doors on it, each leading to hushed rooms. The floor was parquet; almost everything else was dark wood, mostly mahogany. The effect was of being in a very fancy library.

Far down the hall, to the left of the staircase, a door opened. Footsteps—and Fenton—approached.

"Mr. Reeves will see you now."

He stayed several feet away. He didn't know what I had but he sure didn't want to catch it.

I went down the hall, the rowels of my spurs musical in the silence. I knocked on the door Fenton had just left, but nobody responded.

The door was open an inch or so. I pushed it open a bit more and peeked through. The room was a den with expensive leather furniture, a mahogany desk big enough to have a hoe-down on, and enough leather-bound books to humble a scholar. There was a genuine Persian rug on the floor, and an imposing world globe sitting in its cradle on the wide ledge of a mullioned window.

I still didn't see anybody.

I took two steps inside, my feet finding the Persian rug. By the fourth step, hearing a human breath behind me, I'd figured it out, but by then it was too late. He did the same thing he'd done to me that night in my brother's room.

He came out from behind the door and brought something heavy down across the back of my skull.

My hat went flying and so did I.

"YOU SONOFABITCH. WHAT the hell're you doing here?"

I was still on the floor, just now starting to pull myself up. I daubed the back of my head with careful fingers, finding a mean little lump and some blood.

Reeves sat behind his desk, a snifter of brandy near his hand. He was older and heavier, the hair gray-shot, and these days he looked like a successful politician in his dark suit and white shirt and black string tie.

"You're lucky I didn't kill you."

"I don't feel so lucky," I said, touching the back of my head again.

I got to my feet in sections and stood wobbling in front of his desk. Not until then did I realize he'd slipped my .45 from its holster. I wondered how long I'd been out.

"As far as I'm concerned, our business is finished," he said. "You understand me?"

I reached down and picked up my dusty black hat and got it set just right on my head. I was taking everything slow and easy so as to not give him any warning.

I grabbed his snifter and splashed brandy in his face and then I dove across his desk and hit him twice before he finally pitched over backward in his fancy leather chair.

I could hear Fenton running down the hall—then banging on the closed door.

"Sir? Sir? Are you all right?"

He knew better than to let Fenton in. Otherwise I'd tell Fenton a few things he just might not know about his boss man.

"I'm fine. I just knocked the globe over is all."

"You're sure, sir?"

"Of course I'm sure. Now you get back to your dusting. We're having company tonight, remember?"

"Yes, sir." Fenton didn't believe him, but what could he say?

We got to our feet and took our respective places—him in back of the desk, ever in command, and me, dusty and busted, in front—ever the supplicant.

"You killed my brothers," I said.

He smiled. "Does that mean you're going to kill me?" But before I could answer, he said, "I've got something for you."

He opened a drawer, pulled out my .45, and slid it across the polished surface of his desk.

"Pick it up."

I just stared at it.

"Go ahead. Pick it up."

I picked it up.

"Now ease the hammer back and point the gun right at me."

He was a smug sonofabitch, sitting there in a couple hundred dollars' worth of clothes and a lifetime's worth of arrogance.

I had the gun but he was giving orders.

"You're right, Chase—if that's what you're calling yourself these days—I did kill your brothers, and you know why? Because they let me. Because they were just like you, a couple of goddamned farm boys who just couldn't wait to rob banks because it was going to be so easy and so much fun." He shook his head. "Prison's filled with farm boys, as you no doubt found out." He leaned forward. He was het up now, a blaze-eyed minister delivering the truth to the unwashed. "It's a rough goddamned business, Chase, and I ought to know. I've survived in it twenty years now and it's made me a rich man and I haven't spent one hour behind bars."

"What happened to your partner after we stuck up his bank?"

The smile again. "Well, for once my partner figured something out for himself—figured out that I helped set up the robbery to make things go easy. He was about to turn me in, so I killed him."

"You killed him?"

He shook his head, as if he were trying to explain a complicated formula to a chimp.

"I killed him, Chase. And that's the goddamned point which you never will understand. It's the nature of this business—of any business—to do what you need to when you need to." He sat back and made little church steeples of his well-tended fingers. "I'm able to do what I need to. How about you? Can you point that .45 of yours at me and pull the trigger?"

"You sonofabitch."

"Never forget I gave you this chance."

I cursed him again.

"Show me you're not a dumb goddamned farm boy like your brothers."

I wanted to kill him, I really did, but I also knew that I wouldn't. Not under these circumstances.

"Go ahead, Chase. Otherwise you're wasting my time and your own."

The gun felt good and right in my hand, and I could imagine the jerk of his body when the bullet struck his heart, and the red bloom of blood on the front of his lacy white shirt, and I could see my poor brother Don dying from the cuts and slashes the wolf had put on him, and I wanted so bad to pull that trigger, to empty the gun in his face.

"You sonofabitch."

"You said that before, Chase. Several times." He stared a me. "I want you to learn something from this."

I didn't say anything.

"I want you to learn that you should go somewhere and buy yourself a little farm and find yourself a nice plump little farm girl and marry her and have yourself a bunch of kids and forget all about your dead brothers and forget all about me." He nodded to the .45 in my hand. "Because you had your chance. And you chose not to take it. And so what's the point of wasting your life hating me or trying to pay me back?"

Before he'd reached to a right-hand drawer. Now he reached to a left-hand one.

He drew out a pack of greenbacks bank-wrapped with a paper strip around the middle.

He threw the pack on the desk.

"There's five thousand dollars there. That's about what your cut of the job would have been as I recall. Probably a bit more, in fact. Take it, Chase; take it and get on that horse of yours and get the hell out of this county—get the hell out of this state, in fact—and go start the kind of life I told you to. All right?"

I stared at the greenbacks. I just kept thinking of my brother Glen's eyes when I'd cradled him in my arms as he was dying off the side of the stagecoach road, after Reeves had double-crossed us and taken the money and killed Glen because Glen had said something smart to him.

I could still hear the sounds Glen had made, those terrible sounds in his throat, dying sounds, of course, the way I'd once heard a calf strangle on its own umbilical cord one snowy night in the barn.

I stood up and pushed the money back to him and settled my gun in my holster.

"Oh, shit," he said. "You're still going to come after me, aren't you?"

"Two men came into town last night, name of Lundgren and Mars. And I'll bet I know why."

"Lundgren and Mars. Don't know anything about them."

But I could see the truth in his eyes. He knew damned well why they were here.

He tried to look relaxed, but mentioning the two men had infuriated him.

"You set foot on my property again, Chase, and I'll personally blow your fucking head off. Is that understood?"

I just stared at him awhile, shook my head, and went back to the hallway.

When I got to the porch, Fenton was polishing some gold candelabras in the sunlight.

He said nothing, just watched me walk down the steps and start over to my horse.

It was then I heard the growl from somewhere on the other side of the house. I stopped, knowing right away the origin of the growl. The wolf that had killed my brother, the wolf of glowing coat and midnight-yellow eyes.

Fenton stopped his work and stared at me. "He's a killer, that one. The master would be just as well off shut of him, if you want my opinion. He's too dangerous."

I didn't say anything. I walked around the side of the house, and there, in a large cage made of galvanized wire, paced the wolf. In the sunlight his coat shone ivory; but his eyes, when his head swung up suddenly, were still the same old yellow. An Indian was dumping raw meat through a small door in the cage. On the hot wind you could smell the wolf's shit and the high hard stink of the grass he'd pissed in.

I walked closer and he started growling again, that low rumble I'd first heard when my brother Don was dying in his bed that long ago night.

The Indian, still on his haunches, looked over his shoulder. "He don't like you, man." He had graying hair worn long and a faded denim shirt and work pants. His feet were brown and bare.

"So I gather."

"He's a bad one, this wolf."

"Yeah," I said. "I know."

The Indian pointed to a hole in the ground where a small animal had burrowed up into the cage. "Raccoon. Should've seen what the wolf did to that little bastard." The Indian grinned with teeth brown as his skin.

I knelt down next to the Indian, gripping the wire with two fingers for support.

The wolf, who had been growling and going into a crouch, lunged at me suddenly, hurling himself against the cage and ripping his teeth across the two fingers I had inside the cage.

The pain was instant and blinding.

I fell back on my haunches, grabbing my bloody fingers and gritting my teeth and trying not to look like a nancy in front of the Indian who stood above me grinning again with his bad teeth and saying, "I told you, man, that wolf just plain don't like you."

I got to my feet, still hurting, but I pretended that the pain was waning. "Maybe I'll come back here some night and kill that sonofabitch."

The wolf was still glaring at me, still in a crouch, and still growling.

"He'd like to fight you, man. He really would."

I glared back at the wolf and left.

Hanratty was still at his post behind the jack pines, Winchester laid across his saddle. He waved, friendly as always in his way, but he didn't fool me at all. If he had to, he'd kill me fast and sure and never pay me another thought.

THAT AFTERNOON, HOLLISTER held one of his weekly meetings for the entire eighteen-man police force.

We stood in the back of his office, at full attention the way he'd ordered, while he gnawed on our asses the way a military man would.

He had plenty of complaints. One officer, and he said the man would know who he was, was found sleeping down by the mill. The officer would be docked ten dollars from his next check—this was damned near a fourth of the man's pay.

Then he held up his whistle and showed it around as if we'd never seen anything like it before. "Some of you seem to think it's embarrassing to use this—but I want you to use it anyway. Anytime there's a crime, anytime you're pursuing somebody, I want that whistle blown so that the citizens and your fellow officers know that you're carrying out your duties. When your fellow officers hear the whistle, they're supposed to lend you a hand. And when the citizens hear it, they're supposed to get out of your way." He held the whistle up for us to see again, put it to his lips, and filled the slow golden afternoon air with an ear-shattering blow. Then he said, "If I catch anybody forgetting to use his whistle, I'll fine him five dollars." There was the usual grumbling.

The final matter was drunks. "Our friends Hayes and Croizer have been getting overeager again. Last Monday night they arrested two miners who were walking home drunk. How many times do we have to go over this, boys? We're not here to make the lives of working men any harder. Those poor bastards catch plenty of hell during the day—they don't need us to add to it. The rule is—unless a drunkard is causing some kind of trouble, he's to be left alone. If he's having trouble walking, then walk him home if you've got the time, or find a citizen to go get the drunkard's wife or son to take him home. But I sure as hell don't want any more people arrested just because they've got a snootful. Understood?"

We nodded.

"Good," Hollister said. "Now get to work."

We were just turning to leave when Hollister said, "Chase, I need to speak with you."

I turned around and faced him. He sat himself down and took a pipe from a drawer and put the pipe in his mouth and his feet on the desk.

"I kind of got my ass chewed on because of you, Chase."

I couldn't figure out what he was talking about but I got a sick feeling in my stomach. Hollister was known to fire men almost on a whim—especially if he'd been drinking, and he had that look now—and I could feel that old prison fear in my chest. But instead of getting locked in . . . this time I was going to get locked out—of a good job and wages.

"Because of me?" I said.

"That fop of a night clerk at the Whitney Hotel."

"Oh."

"You sound as if you know what I'm talking about."

I shrugged. "Hell, all I did was look at the guest register."

He smiled. "Without asking that sweet little man's permission."

I laughed. "So he complained?"

"Oh, did he complain. He had a letter waiting for me on my desk this morning. He was filled with civic outrage."

He sucked on his unlit pipe. "Western towns like ours hate police departments. Just about everything we do, the people consider infringing on their rights in some way."

He wasn't exaggerating. Two towns over, a group of outraged citizens, angered that the police chief had imposed a curfew following three drunken murders, took two young policemen hostage and threatened to kill them unless the police chief packed up and left town. The outraged mob had been led by the mayor and a minister. Eastern papers liked to talk about how the "Wild West" had been tamed now that a new century was about to turn. But that didn't mean that police forces—too often crooked and violent—had found acceptance, because in most places they sure hadn't . . . not yet, anyway.

"Why were you looking in the register anyway?"

For the first time I noticed that he was watching me carefully. He seemed suspicious of me.

"I saw two men get off a train. They didn't look right to me. I just wanted to see what names they registered under."

"Didn't look right to you?"

"Slickers, was how I had them pegged. Remember that confidence game that man named Rawlins was running on old folks a month ago? That's how they looked to me."

I didn't tell him about them taking late-night horses from the livery and riding out of town.

"You ask them their business?" Hollister said.

"No."

"That would've been better than bothering that sonofabitch at the Whitney. He's very popular with the 'landed gentry,' as they like to be called, and the 'landed gentry' likes to see us as a group of barbarians. This only gives them something to bitch about."

"I won't bother him anymore."

"I'd appreciate that, Chase. You're doing a good job. I don't want to see you get in any political trouble with one of the mighty."

"I appreciate the advice."

He looked at my bandaged fingers. I'd put some iodine on them. They still smarted from the wolf bite.

"What's wrong with your fingers?"

I didn't want to tell him about Reeves. "I cut them when I was sawing some logs."

He laughed. "You're about as handy as I am."

When he laughed, he pushed a little breath up on the air. Pure bourbon.

I said good-bye and left his office. Before I even reached the doorway, I heard him sliding a drawer open.

I glanced back over my shoulder just as he was turning his chair to the wall so he could lift up his silver flask and tip it to his lips.

Part 10

Before work the next morning I took Annie up into the hills. She wanted to collect leaves.

I found some hazel thickets and showed her how to dig into the mice nests surrounding them. You could find near a quart of nuts that the mice had already shelled and put away for bitter winter. But we didn't take any of course, because the food belonged to them.

Annie made a collection of the prettiest leaves she could find, taking care to pluck some extras for her mother, and then we stood on an old Indian bridge and watched clear creek water splash rocks and slap against a ragged dam some beavers had recently built. Annie counted eight frogs and six fish from up on the bridge.

We took the east trail back, watching sleek fast horses the color of saddle leather run up grassy slopes in the late morning sun.

When we got near the house, she stopped at the abandoned well. Four large ragged rocks formed a circle around the well, inside of which Gillian had placed a piece of metal to cover the hole.

Now, expertly, Annie bent down, lifted the piece of metal up, took one of her leaves, and closed her eyes and said, "I have to be quiet now and keep my eyes closed."

"How come?"

"Because I'm making a wish."

"Oh."

"Mommy always says that's what you have to do for God to hear you."

"Be quiet and close your eyes?"

"Uh-huh. And drop something down the well that you really like."

And with that she let the pretty autumn leaf go from her hand. It floated gently down into the darkness.

Gillian had told me about the well, how it was pretty shallow, and how the folks who had the house before her got sick drinking from it.

"You glad you're my pop?" Annie said, opening her eyes. She'd heard a boy at school call his daddy his "pop" and had decided she liked it.

"I sure am."

"Well, I sure am, too." She smiled and put her hand in mine. "I always knew you were my pop."

"You did?"

"In my dreams I always had a pop. I couldn't exactly see him real good but he was always there. And then the day I saw you in front of our house—well, I knew you were my pop."

"Aw, honey," I said, feeling sad for all the years she hadn't had a pop. "Honey, you don't have to worry about not having a pop anymore. I'll always be here."

"Always?" she said, squinting up at me in the sunshine.

"Always," I said, then reached down and swung her up in my arms and carried her home just that way, her blonde hair flying and her laughter clear and pure. The only thing that spoiled it was the sore throat and aching muscles I had. I was apparently getting sick.

AROUND TEN THAT night, I just happened to be standing half a block from the Whitney Hotel. And Lundgren and Mars just happened to be standing on the porch of that same hotel. They couldn't see me because I was in the shadows of an overhang.

Lundgren smoked a cigar. Mars just looked around. He seemed nervous. I wondered why.

Fifteen minutes after coming out onto the porch, Lundgren flipped his cigar away exactly as he'd done the night before, and then, also as he'd done the night before, led his shorter friend down the street to the livery where the Mex gave them two horses already rubbed down and rested and saddled.

Lundgren and Mars rode out of town, taking the same moonlit road as last night.

I finished my rounds of the block then cut west over by the furrier, where the smell of pelts was sour on the cold night. Moving this fast didn't make me feel any better. The damned head cold I'd been getting was still with me.

The alley behind the Whitney was busy with the usual drunks. Henry, a half-breed, had pissed his pants and was sleeping, mouth open and slack, propped up against a garbage can. A hobo with but one finger on his left hand was having some kind of nightmare, his whole body shaking and cries of "Mother! Mother!" caught in his throat. And there was Jesse—Jesse as in female, Jesse as in mother of three, Jesse as in town drunk. Most nights her kids (the father having been killed four years earlier in the mines) kept tight rein on her, but every once in awhile she escaped and wandered the town like a graveyard ghost, and usually fell over unconscious in an alley.

I debated waking them and making them leave. But that would only mean that one or two of them would possibly remember me.

I made sure as I could that they were all sleeping, and then I climbed onto the fire escape that ran at an angle down the back of the Whitney.

I moved fast. I could always say that I was following a suspicious character up here. But I wouldn't want to use that excuse unless I had to.

Lundgren and Mars were staying on the fourth floor. I pulled the screen door open and went in. The hallway was empty. I started toward 406. In one of the rooms I passed, an old man was coughing so hard I thought he'd puke. The corridor smelled of whiskey and tobacco and sweat and kerosene from the lamps.

I was two doors from 406 when 409 opened up and a man came out. He was so drunk he looked like a comic in an opera-house skit. He wore a messy black suit and a bowler that looked ready to slide off his bald head. He was weaving so hard, he nearly fell over backward.

I pressed flat to the wall and stayed that way while the drunk managed to get his door closed and locked.

He didn't once glance to his left. If he had, he would have seen me for sure.

He tottered off, still a clown in an opera-house turn.

Shaking, neither my stomach nor my bowels in good condition, I went to 406 and got it open quickly. You learn a lot of useful things in prison.

The room was dark. Some kind of jasmine-scented hair grease was on the air. I felt my way across the room, touching the end of the bed, a bureau, and a closet door. By now I was able to see.

I started in the bureau, working quickly. I found nothing special, the usual socks and underwear and shirts without their collars or buttons.

I then moved to the closet. Nothing there, either.

I was just starting to pick up one of the two carpetbags sitting on a straight-backed chair when I heard footsteps in the corridor.

I paused, pulling my revolver.

In the street below there was a brief commotion as a few drunks made their way from one saloon to another. In the distance a surrey jingled and jangled its way out of town.

The footsteps in the hallway had stopped.

Where had the man gone? Was it Lundgren or Mars coming back?

My breathing was loud and nervous in the darkness. My uniform coat felt as if it weighed a hundred pounds. My whole chest was cold and greasy with sweat.

And then I heard him, whistling, or trying to—the drunk down the way, the one who'd barely been able to get his door locked. Easy enough to figure out what had happened. He had made his way down the stairs only to find that the people in the saloon wouldn't serve him. Too drunk. So he'd come back up here.

It took him several minutes to insert key into lock, to turn doorknob, to step across threshold, to walk across floor, to fall across bed, springs squeaking beneath his weight. Within thirty seconds he was snoring.

I went back to work.

I took the first carpetbag to the bed and dumped everything out. The contents included an unloaded .45, a few more shirts without celluloid collars, and a small framed picture of a large, handsome woman I guessed was his wife. I took it over to the window and hiked back the curtain. A lone strip of silver moonlight angled across the back of the picture: SHARON LUNDGREN, 1860–1889, BELOVED WIFE OF DUNCAN LUNDGREN. So he was a widower, Lundgren was. It made him human for me, and for some reason, I didn't want him to be human.

The second carpetbag didn't yield much more—not at first anyway. Mars was a collector of pills and salves and ointments. The bag had enough of these things to stock a small pharmacy. He seemed to be a worrier, Mars did.

I had almost given up on the bag when my fingers felt, way in the back, an edge of paper. I felt farther. An envelope. I pulled it out, winnowing it upward through tins of muscle ointment and small bottles of pills that rattled like an infant's toy.

I went back to the window and the moonlight.

I turned the envelope face up. In the left upper hand I saw the name and address of the letter writer. My old friend Schroeder, known hereabouts as Reeves.

The letter was brief, inviting Lundgren and Mars here to "increase their fortunes by assisting me in a most worthy endeavor."

I didn't have to wonder about what that "worthy endeavor" might be. Not when Reeves owned half a bank in town here.

I put the envelope back in the carpetbag and the carpetbag back on the chair.

I went to the door, eased it open, stuck my head out. The hallway was empty. In the hall I relocked the door, checked again to make sure that nobody was watching me, and then walked quickly to the screen door and the fire escape.

I knew now that I wasn't done with Reeves. Not at all, no matter how much I'd promised Gillian otherwise.

Part 11

"He's going to do it again."

"He?"

"Schroeder. Reeves. Whatever name he goes by."

"Do what?"

"Hire two people to rob his bank and then double-cross them. Take the money and kill them."

"You sure?"

"Positive. Those two men I saw in town?"

"They're the ones?"

"They're the ones. I got into their hotel room tonight. They had a letter from Reeves."

She didn't say anything for a long time. We were in bed. The window was soft silver with moonlight. Annie muttered in her sleep. The air smelled of dinner stew and tobacco from my pipe. Somewhere an owl sang lonely into the deep sweet night.

"You promised to stay clear of it, Chase."

"I was just telling you who they are."

"You'll get in trouble. I know it."

"I didn't mean to make you mad."

She was silent. "I thought we had a nice life," she said after a time.

"We do."

"Then why do you want to spoil it?"

"I won't spoil it, Gillian. I promise."

"You promise," she said. "Men are always promising, and it doesn't mean anything."

I tried to kiss her but she wouldn't let me. She rolled over on her side, facing the wall.

"You know I love you, Gillian."

She was silent.

"Gillian?"

Silent.

I rolled over. Thought. Felt naked and alone. My sore throat was getting worse, too, and every once in awhile, I'd shiver from chills.

I couldn't stop thinking about Gillian. How she knew what was going to happen now, with Reeves and all. How betrayed she must feel.

I tried to make it better for her.

"I'm not your father Gillian," I said. "I'm not going to hurt you and I'm not going to run out on you the way he did. Do you understand that?"

But she didn't speak then, either.

After an hour or so I slept.

Part 12

Next night, I made my rounds early. I had some business to do.

Lundgren and Mars put in their usual appearance at the usual time, strolling down the street to the livery, picking up their horses, and riding out of town just as the moon rose directly over the river.

I rode a quarter mile behind them out the winding stage road.

They went just where I thought they would, straight to Reeves's fancy Victorian. But just before reaching the grounds, they angled eastward toward the foothills.

Half an hour's ride brought them to a cabin along a leg of the river. I ground-tied my horse a long ways back and slipped into the small woods to the west of the cabin. Everything smelled piney and was sticky to the touch.

When I got close enough to see through a window, I watched Lundgren and Mars talking with Reeves. He poured them bourbon. There was some quick rough laughter, as if a joke might have been told, and then quiet talk for twenty minutes I couldn't hear at all.

At one point I thought I heard a woman's voice, but I wasn't sure.

When they came out, Lundgren and Mars and Reeves, they were laughing again.

They stood making a few more jokes and dragging on their stogies and making their plans for the robbery.

"You don't forget about that side door," Reeves said.

"No, sir, I won't," Lundgren said.

Mars went over to his horse and hopped up. His small size made it look like a big effort.

"Talk to you boys soon," Reeves said, cheery as a state legislator on Flag Day.

Lundgren and Mars rode away, into dew-covered fields shimmering silver with moonlight.

Reeves stood there for a time watching them go, the chink of saddle and bridle, the heavy thud of horse hooves fading in the distance.

A woman joined him suddenly, as if from nowhere, slipping out the door and into his arms. Silhouetted in the lantern light from inside, they stood there kissing for a very long time, until it was obvious that they now wanted to do a lot more than kiss. It took me awhile to realize who she was.

A few minutes later Reeves slid his arm around her waist and escorted her back inside. They turned out the lights and walked back out and closed the door and got up in Reeves' black buggy.

Just before he whipped the horse, I heard her say, "K-Kinda ch-chilly out h-here t-tonight."

And then they were gone into the night.

THERE WAS A potbellied stove on the ground floor of the police station, and when I got back there, two men stood next to it, holding tin cups of steaming black coffee in wide peasant hands. Winter was on the air tonight.

Kozlovsky nodded upstairs. "Don't know where the hell you been, Chase, but the chief's been lookin' for you for the last hour and a half."

Benesh shook his head. "He's been drinkin' since late afternoon so I'd watch yourself, Chase. Plus he's got a prisoner up there in his little room. Some farmhand who got all liquored up because of some saloon whore. He made the mistake of making a dirty remark to the chief."

In their blue uniforms, the flickering light from the stove laying a coat of bronze across their faces, they might have been posing for a photograph in the *Police Gazette*.

"I'd better go see him," I said coughing. I was feeling worse.

The two men glanced at each other as I left.

The "room" they'd referred to was on the second floor, way in the back beyond the cells, which were dark now, men resting or sleeping on their cots, like zoo animals down for the night. Every time I came up here, I thought of prison, and every time I thought of prison, I thought of all those old men I'd known who'd spent most of their adult lives in there. Then I always got scared. I didn't want to die in some human cage smelling of feces and slow pitiful death.

Halfway to the room, I heard the kid moaning behind the door ten yards away. I also heard the sharp popping noise of an open hand making contact with a face. The closer I got the louder the moaning got.

I knocked.

"Yeah?"

"Chief, it's me. Chase."

A silence. Then footsteps. The door yanked open, the chief, sweating, wearing only his uniform trousers and shirt, his jacket on a coat hook, stood there with his hands on his hips, scowling at me. For all that the police officers and some of the citizens talked about Hollister's "torture room," it was a pretty unspectacular place, just bare walls and a straight-back chair in the middle of an empty room. Right now, no more than half-conscious, thick hairy wrists handcuffed behind him in the chair, sat a beefy farm kid. His nose was broken and two of his front teeth were gone. His face gleamed with sweat and dark blood, and his eyes showed terror and confusion.

"I've been looking for you," Hollister said.

"That's what I heard. I had to go home. My daughter Annie's been sick."

"Nobody could find you for over an hour, Chase. Don't give me any horseshit about your poor little daughter. Now you go downstairs and wait for me in my office."

He was drunk but you probably wouldn't have noticed it if you didn't know him. The voice was half a pitch higher and there was something wild and frightening in the blue eyes.

"You want me to put him in a cell?" I said, indicating the farm kid.

"I'll put him in a cell when I'm ready to put him in a cell."

"I wouldn't want to see you get in any trouble, Chief."

"I'll worry about that, Chase. You just go downstairs to my office and wait for me."

Just as the door closed, I glimpsed the kid in the straight-backed chair. His brown eyes looked right at me, pleading, pleading. I thought of the kid that day in the quarry, coming up and crying out for mercy . . .

A moment later I heard a fist collide with a face. The kid screamed, and soon enough came another punch.

He was on the other side of a locked door now. There was nothing I could do.

I went back through the cells.

A man was lying awake on the cot, his eyes very white in the gloom. As I walked past his cell he said, "He gonna kill somebody someday, beatin' folks like that."

I just kept walking. Apparently the man was a drifter and hadn't heard that a prisoner had already died here in what the newspaper called a "mysterious fall."

Twenty minutes later Hollister walked into his office, sat down behind his desk, took a small round gold tin of salve from a drawer and proceeded to rub the salve onto the knuckles of his right hand. They looked pretty bad, swollen and bloody. He had his uniform jacket on now, and he once again appeared in control of himself.

"The sonofabitch tried to hit me," he said.

"That's a pretty neat trick when you're handcuffed."

He glared at me. "Are you accusing me of lying?"

I stared at my hands in my lap.

"Somebody in this town doesn't like you, Chase."

"Oh?" I raised my eyes and met his. He was sober now. Apparently, beating up people had a good effect on him.

He opened the center drawer of his desk, extracted a white business envelope, and tossed it across his wide desk to me.

"This was waiting for me when I got to work this morning," he said. "What is it?"

"You know how to read?"

I nodded.

"Then read it for yourself."

I opened the envelope, took out a folded sheet of white paper, and read what had been written on it in blue ink. The penmanship was disguised to look as if it was a child's.

The message was just one sentence long.

"It's a lie," I said.

"Is it?

"Yes."

He took out his pipe, stuck it in his teeth, and leaned back in his chair.

"It wouldn't be the first time, you know."

"The first time for what?" I said.

"The first time an ex-convict ended up as a police officer."

"I'm not an ex-convict."

"Whoever sent me that letter thinks you are."

"Somebody's just making trouble."

"How long were you in?"

"I wasn't in."

"Up to the territorial prison, were you? I hear it's not so bad there, at least not as bad as it used to be."

"I wouldn't know."

"The warden is a good friend of mine. I'm going to wire him and ask him a few things."

"Ask him anything you want."

He stared at me a long, silent moment. The clock on the west wall tocked. Out in front, around the potbellied stove, a man laughed.

"Your name really Chase?"

"Yes."

"Why were you in prison?"

"I wasn't in prison."

"Be a man, Chase. Tell me the truth."

"I robbed a bank."

"There. You said it. Now we can cut out the horseshit." He stared at me some more, tilted back in his chair. "You shoot anybody when you robbed this bank?"

"No."

"You ever shoot anybody?"

"No."

"So you're not a violent man?"

I shrugged. "Not so far, anyway."

He smiled around his pipe. "That's an honest way to put it. 'Not so far, anyway.'" He sat up in the chair. "I'm going to make some inquiries about you."

"Your friend the warden?"

"You can be a sarcastic sonofabitch, you know that?" He shook his head. "What I was going to say, Chase, is that except for your disappearance tonight, you've been a damned good officer. Everybody likes you and trusts you, especially the merchants, and that's very important to me. So believe it or not, I'm not going to fire you just because you raised some hell when you were younger. You've got a family now, and that changes a man. Changes him a lot." Hard to believe this was the same man who, half an hour ago, had been beating a handcuffed prisoner. "I'm going to write the warden, like I said, and if your story checks out—if you really didn't shoot anybody and if you were a good prisoner—then I'm going to forget all about that letter."

He put his hand out, palm up, and I laid the letter on it.

He checked the clock. "Hell, I'd better be going home. My wife was visiting her cousin tonight and she'll probably be getting home about now."

"You want me to keep working tonight?"

"Of course I do, Chase. If you've been honest with me tonight, you don't have anything to worry about."

"I appreciated this, Chief."

"Get back to work, Chase, and forget about anything except doing a good job."

I stood up, nodded good-bye, and left.

I had a cup of coffee out next to the stove and then I went back to work.

Ev Hollister was one complicated sonofabitch, and those are the men you always have to be extra careful of.

Part 13

The young man with the white shirt and the celluloid collar and the fancy red arm garters peered at me from behind the bars of his teller's cage and said, "Three other police officers have their accounts here, too, Mr. Chase." He had a face like a mischievous altar boy. He wore rimless glasses to make himself look older.

I smiled. "Then I must be doing the right thing."

I hadn't ever wanted to step inside any bank that Reeves owned. But I wanted to see the place that Lundgren and Mars were going to rob, because by now I knew what I was going to do.

The layout was simple. For all its finery, the flocked wallpaper, the oak paneling, the elegant paintings, the massive black safe built into the wall, which resembled a huge and furious god—for all of that, the bank was really just one big room divided up by partitions into four different areas. The safe would be relatively easy to get to because, except for a wide mahogany desk, nothing stood in the way. Women in bustles and picture hats, and men in dark suits and high-top shoes, walked around, conducting whispery business. The air smelled of gardenia perfume and cigar smoke.

I looked over at the side door that Lundgren and Reeves had talked about the other night. It used to open onto the alley, I was told, before the bank had been remodeled. Now it was never opened for any reason, though I had the key to it on my ring.

"She's a beauty, isn't she?"

"Beg pardon?"

"The safe," the teller said. "Barely six months old. Straight from Boston. I doubt even nitro could open it." He smiled. "Saw you looking at her. Must make the police feel a lot safer."

"A lot."

"But that's Mr. Reeves for you."

"Oh?"

"Sure. Always buying the best and the newest and the most reliable."

Yes, I thought, and probably spending his partner's money to do it.

I started hacking then, so much so that it got embarrassing. This morning my throat had been so sore, I could barely swallow, and the chills now came on with a sudden violence.

"Well, here's my first deposit," I said when I'd finished hacking.

I handed the teller ten dollars. He found a smart little blue bankbook and took an imposing rubber stamp and opened the book and stamped something bold and black on the first page. He turned the page over and wrote $10.00 in the credit column. Then he wrote the date in the proper place and gave me the book.

"It's nice to have you as a customer, Mr. Chase."

"Thank you. I'm sure I'll like doing business here."

"I shouldn't say this, being so partial and all, but I think we're the best bank in the whole territory."

"I'm sure you are."

With that I turned and started back to the front of the bank. Then the front door opened and there stood Reeves, sleek and slick as always, staring right at me.

He was obviously angry to find me here, but he couldn't say anything with all the customers wandering around.

He came in, closing the door on the bright but chill afternoon.

He walked right up to me and said, "I'm glad to see you're still wearing that uniform."

"The chief is a more understanding man than you give him credit for."

"Maybe I'll just have to write him another little note about you." He frowned. "Why the hell don't you just get out of this town, Chase? I'd even be willing to give you some money if you just took that wife and daughter of yours and left."

"How much?"

"Maybe ten thousand."

"Maybe?"

"Ten thousand for sure."

I grinned at him. "No, thanks, I kind of like it here. Especially when I get a chance to ruin your day like this every once in awhile." I started out the door and then said, quietly, "Be sure to give Lundgren and Mars my best wishes."

He looked around to see if anybody was watching. They weren't. "You don't know what you're getting into, farm boy."

"See you around," I said, and left.

I stood on the boardwalk for awhile, enjoying the pale, slanting sunlight, enjoying the town, really, the clatter of wagons and horse-drawn trolleys, the spectacle of pretty town women going about their shopping, the way folks greeted me as they passed. They like me, the town folks, and I enjoyed that feeling.

I was a happy man just then, and I walked down the street with my lips puckered into a whistle. I tried not to notice how bad my throat was hurting.

Part 14

That night, feeling even sicker, I dragged myself home and went right to bed . . .

In the darkness.

"Chase?"

"Huh?"

"I wanted to wake you up. You were having the nightmare again. About the kid, I think."

"Oh."

"I'm sorry you had to see that, Chase."

"Yeah."

"It must have been terrible to see."

I was sweating, but it was cold sweat and I wanted to vomit. There was just darkness. And Gillian next to me in her flannel nightgown.

"I said a prayer tonight, Chase."

"How come?"

"That you wouldn't go through with it." Silence. "I know it's on your mind."

"It could work out for us. A lot of money. Going somewhere and buying a farm."

We were silent for a long time.

"Annie saw me praying—I mean, I was down on my knees with my hands folded, just like I was in church—and she asked me what I was praying for, and I told her that I was praying for Pop, that Pop would always do the right thing."

The miners got paid on Fridays. On Friday morning the bank always got extra cash for payroll. Today was Friday. Lundgren and Mars would hit the bank today sometime.

"You hear me, Chase? About my praying?"

"You know I love you and Annie?"

"It'll come to no good, Chase. Men like Reeves just go on and on. I hate to say this, but sometimes evil is more powerful than good. I don't understand why God would let that be, but He does."

Just the darkness, and Gillian next to me . . .

I wanted to be content and peaceful. I really did. But I just kept thinking of how easy it would be to take that money from Lundgren and Mars.

I started coughing hard, the way I'd been doing lately. She held me tight, as if she could make my illness go away. Sometimes she was so sweet I didn't know what to do with myself. Because I wasn't sweet at all.

"Chase, I want you to go see the doc tomorrow. I mean it. No more excuses."

I didn't say anything.

I lay back.

The sweat was cold on me. I was shivering.

"Chase. There's something that needs saying."

I didn't say anything.

"You listening, Chase?"

"Uh-huh."

"Chase, if you go through with this, I'll take Annie and leave. I swear."

I wanted to cry—just plain goddamn bawl—and I wasn't even sure why.

"I love you, Gillian."

But then I went and ruined it all by coughing so hard I had to throw my legs over the side of the bed and just sit there hacking. Maybe Gillian was right. Maybe I needed to see the doc.

When I finally laid back down again, Gillian had rolled over to face the wall.

"Honey? Gillian?"

But she wasn't speaking anymore.

Both of us knew what was going to happen, and there wasn't much to be said now.

"You're going to do it, Chase," she said after a time. And I drew her to me and held her. And I could smell her warm tears as I kissed her cheek. "I know you are, Chase. I know you are."

Part 15

I got up early, before the ice on the creek had melted off, put on street clothes and went into town. My bones ached but I tried not to notice. The sounds of roosters and waking dogs filled the chill air. The sky was a perfect blue and the fallen leaves were bright as copper pennies at the bottom of a clear stream. The fever had waned. I felt pretty good.

I went directly to the restaurant, ordered breakfast, and took up my place by the window. I wanted to keep a careful eye on the street. I knew what was going to happen this morning.

Reeves arrived first, riding a big chestnut. In his black suit and white Stetson he was trying, as usual, to impress everybody, including himself.

He dismounted at the livery, left his horse off and then came back up the street to the bank. Ordinarily, like most of the merchants, he stopped in here for coffee before the business day started.

But today he took a key from his vest pocket and walked around to the alley on the west side of the bank, and then vanished inside.

I had more coffee and rolled a cigarette and listened reluctantly as a waitress told me about a terrible incident next county over where a two-year-old had crawled into a pig pen where two boars promptly ripped him apart and then ate him. She had a sure way of getting your day off to a happy start.

The stagecoach came in twenty minutes later, a dusty, creaking Concord with a bearded Jehu and two guards up top bearing Winchesters. If you hadn't already guessed that they were transporting money, the two men with the rifles certainly gave you a big hint.

The Concord stopped right in front of the bank.

The front door opened and Reeves came out. He looked dramatic with a fancy silver pistol in his right hand and his eyes scanning the tops of buildings on the other side of the street.

The two guards jumped down. One hefted a long canvas bag and went inside. The Jehu had taken one of the Winchesters and was watching the street carefully. Reeves stood right where he was, looking vigilant for all the townspeople to see.

It took three minutes and it was very slick. They'd all obviously done this many times. At this point, anybody who tried to take the money sack would likely be outgunned.

Then the bank door closed, Reeves inside, and the two guards jumped back up top and the Jehu took the reins and snapped them against the backs of the animals, and the stagecoach pulled out.

The waitress with the dead baby story came back and gave me more coffee. She was young and chubby but with a certain insolent eroticism in the eyes, and a smile that made her seem more complicated than she probably was.

"You ever see so much money?" she said and nodded across the street. "They make that delivery every week, and every time I see it, I think of what I could do with just one of them bags of money."

"Buy yourself a house?"

"A house, hell. I'd take off for Chicago and New York and I'd have me the best time a farm girl ever had herself."

There was a certain anger in her tone that told me at least a little bit about how she'd been raised, and how she was treated in a town like this. If she had the money, she was going to tell a whole lot of people to kiss her ample ass. I understood her, but that didn't mean I liked her much. A hard woman is meaner any day than a hard man. Maybe I didn't like her because she was too much like me.

She drifted away to cheer up some other people. I kept on watching the street.

Around ten, Lundgren and Mars appeared on the steps of the Whitney Hotel. They wore their business suits and business hats and strode their important business strides as they made their way down the street amidst the clatter of wagons and the clop of horse hooves and the handful of lady shoppers on this beautiful autumn day.

They went straight to the livery.

A few minutes later they were back on this street, this time astride two big bays.

They rode straight out of town without speaking to each other or looking around.

I got up, paid my bill, went over to the livery stable, got myself a roan, and then walked it down the alleys to a place directly across from the bank.

Just after eleven, they came back into town riding two different horses. This time they were got up as dusty cowhands, not businessmen. They didn't look like their previous selves at all, which was just how they wanted it. Mars had what appeared to be a sawed-off shotgun in his scabbard.

I stood under the overhang as they rode down the street. Lundgren stayed up on his mount. Mars dropped off, grabbing the sawed-off shotgun. I wondered about the shotgun. I couldn't believe Reeves wanted anybody killed. A robbery would get you a jury trial and a prison stretch. A killing would get you hanged some frosty midnight while a lynch mob stood beneath you, grinning.

They pulled blue bandanas up over their faces.

Mars started moving quickly now, up on the boardwalk. But instead of going in the front door the way I figured he would, he ducked into the alley and went through the side door. He had a key and he used it quick and smart. He opened the door and went inside.

It sure didn't make any sense, him having a key.

Lundgren leaned over and put his hand on the Winchester in his scabbard. He was ready for trouble when Mars came boiling out of the door.

I rode my horse to the edge of town, ten feet away from the small roundhouse where an engine was being worked on. You could smell the hot oil on the cool fall air.

Five minutes went by before I heard the shotgun blast which was followed by a long, nervous silence and then horses running hard down the dusty main street out of town.

Six-shooter fire followed the horses. I imagined it was Reeves, emptying his chambers, making it look good for the townspeople.

Lundgren and Mars appeared a few minutes later, riding hard. At the fork they headed west, which was where I expected them to head. I gave them a five-minute lead and went after them, keeping to grass so I wouldn't raise any dust.

They'd had it all planned and planned well.

They rode straight to the river, where business clothes and fresh horses were waiting for them. In a couple of minutes they wouldn't look anything at all like the robbers. And they'd be riding very different horses.

They took care of the robbery horses first, leading them to the edge of the muddy rushing river where Mars took a Colt and shot both the animals in the head. The horses jerked only once, then collapsed to the ground without a sound. Lundgren and Mars pushed them into the river, where they made small splashes and then vanished. All I could think of was the hayseed kid the old con had drowned that day in the quarry. I cursed Mars. The sonofabitch could have just shooed the animals up into the foothills.

I also kept thinking of the shotgun blast back at the bank. Anybody who could kill an innocent animal the way they had would have no trouble killing a human.

They took the long sack of money, wrapped it in a red blanket, and cinched it across the back of Mars's mount.

They stripped down to their long johns and then put on their business suits and climbed up on their business horses and took off riding again, though this time they went slow and leisurely, like easterners eager to gasp at the scenery. At the river they threw all their robbery clothes into the rushing, muddy water.

Fifteen minutes later they came to the crest of a hill and looked down on the cabin where they'd been meeting Reeves, and where Reeves had been meeting Ev Hollister's wife.

They rode straight down the dead brown autumn grass, coming into a patch of hard sunlight just as they reached the valley.

A few minutes later, Lundgren tied up the horses and Mars lugged the money sack into the big, fancy cabin.

I sat there for awhile, rolling myself a cigarette and giving them a little time.

After awhile I grabbed the rifle from my scabbard and started working my way down the hill.

Part 16

I went down the hill at an angle to the cabin and then along a line of scrub pines to the right of the place. There were no side windows, so that helped make my appearance a complete surprise.

I crawled low under the front window then stood up when I was directly in front of the door.

I raised my boot and placed it right above the doorknob, where it would do the most good. If my kick didn't open the door the first time, I was likely going to get a chest full of lead before I had a second chance.

The door slammed backward.

I put two bullets straight into a Rochester lamp hanging over a large mahogany table that looked just right for both a good meal and a poker game.

The Rochester lamp exploded into several large noisy chunks.

I went inside.

Lundgren and Mars were standing by the bunk beds, the money fanned out on the lower bunk.

They were just now going for their guns, but it was too late.

I crushed Lundgren's gun hand with a bullet. His cry filled the room.

"Throw the gun down," I said to Mars.

Lundgren had already dropped his when the bullet went smashing into flesh and bone.

"Who the hell are you?" Mars said.

"Who the hell do I look like?" I said. "I'm a police officer from town."

"I'm impressed."

"You want me to shoot your hand up the way I did his?"

"Asshole," he said.

But he dropped his gun.

"Fill the sack."

"What?"

"Fill the sack."

"That's our money," Mars said. He was one of those belligerent little men whose inferiority about their size makes them dangerous.

"Do it," Lundgren said.

He had sat himself down on a chair and was holding his hand out away from him and staring at it. He was big and blond and Swedish. Tears of pain made his pale blue eyes shine. He was sweating a lot already and gritting tobacco-stained teeth.

"You heard what your partner said," I said to Mars.

"Maybe I don't care what my partner said."

I pointed the rifle directly at his chest. "I don't give a damn about killing you. After what you did to those horses, I'd even enjoy it."

"Do it," Lundgren said again. "Give him the goddamned money."

He was almost pathetic, Lundgren was, so big and swaggering before, and only whimpering and whining now. You just never know anything about a man till he faces adversity.

"He isn't going to turn this money in," Mars said, staring at me.

"What?" Lundgren said.

"You heard me. He isn't going to turn this money in. This is for himself."

"Bullshit. He's a police officer."

"So what he's a police officer? Half the goddamned cops we know in Denver are crooked. Why shouldn't they have crooked cops in a burg like this?"

"Fill the sack," I said.

Mars glared at me now, a tough little man in a brown business suit and a comic black bowler. He looked out of place amidst the expensive appointments of a stone fireplace, a small library filled with leather-bound classics, and leather furniture good enough to go in the territorial governor's office. He didn't belong in such a world.

"Fill it," I said.

"I'm going to find you, you piece of shit, and when I find you, I'm going to cut your balls off and feed them to you, the way the Arabs do, you understand me?"

In two steps I stood right in front of him. As I brought the rifle down, I thought of how he'd killed the horses, and so I put some extra power into it.

I got him just once, but I got him square in the mouth, and so the butt of my rifle took several teeth and cut his lip so deep a piece of it just hung there like a flap.

He didn't give me the satisfaction of letting me hear his pain. Unlike Lundgren, he was tough. He had tears in his eyes and he kept making tight fists of his hands, but beyond his initial cry, he wasn't going to give me any-thing.

"Now fill it," I said.

This time he filled it, all the while sucking on the blood bubbling in his mouth.

When he finished, I said, "Tie it shut."

"You tie it shut."

I hit him again, this time with the butt of the rifle right against his ear.

The blow drove him to his knees and he fell over clutching his head. This time he couldn't stop himself from moaning.

"Get up and tie the sack and hand it to me, you piece of shit."

"You hurt him enough," Lundgren said.

"Not as bad as he hurt those horses."

Mars got to his feet slowly, in a daze, swearing and whimpering and showing me, for the first time, fear.

He tied the bag shut with cord and then raised it and dropped it at my feet.

I couldn't get the horses out of my mind. I hit him again, a good clean hit against his temple.

He went down quick and final, out for a long time. His head made a hollow sound when it crashed against the floor.

"You sonofabitch," Lundgren said. "He'll hunt you down, you wait and see."

He was still holding his hand. Blood had dripped on his nice black boots and all over the floor.

I hefted the bag, holding the rifle in my right hand.

"You'll want to know my name so you can tell Reeves," I said.

"How the hell do you know about Reeves?"

I didn't answer his question. "My name's Chase. He'll know who I am."

"You sonofabitch. You're fucking with the wrong people, you better be-lieve that."

I backed up to the door.

"Remember the name," I said. "Chase."

"You don't worry. I won't forget it. And neither will Mars."

I went out the door and into the warming sunshine of late morning. I could smell the smoky hills and hear a jay nearby.

I walked around the cabin to where they'd ground-tied their horses. I shooed one away and then climbed up on the other.

I went up the hill fast. When I got to my own horse, I jumped down, put the money sack across his back, and then shooed the other horse away. He went straight across the hill and disappeared behind some scrub pines.

I got up on the roan and rode away.

Part 17

An hour later, I dismounted, eased the money sack down from the horse and then carried it, along with a good length of rope, over to the abandoned well near our house.

I knelt down, lifted up the metal cover, and peered down inside. Sometimes you could go down a couple of hundred feet and still hit shale. But Gillian had said this one had been easy, the water right there, just waiting. I took out my spike and the hammer I'd grabbed from my saddlebag and drove the spike deep into the shale on the side of the well. Then I took a piece of rope and tied one end to the top of the money bag and the other end to the spike. And then I fed the money bag, an inch of rope at a time, down into the well, stopping just short of the waterline. Nobody would think to look here. I pulled the cover over the well again and stood up.

Overhead, an arcing falcon soared against the autumn sky, swooping down when its prey was clearly in sight. I stood and watched until it carried a long black wriggling silhouette of a snake up into the air.

I stood there and thought about it all, what I'd done and what lay ahead, and what Gillian would say and how broken-hearted she'd be unless I could convince her that I'd done the right thing; and then I got on my horse and rode into town.

Part 18

Three hours after the robbery, people still stood in the street, staring at the bank and talking about everything that had happened.

On my way to the station, an old man carrying a hearing horn stopped me and said, "You catch those bastards, hang 'em right on the spot far as I'm concerned."

I nodded.

"That kid just died," he said, "a few minutes ago."

I rode another half block and saw Dr. Granville, a pleasant, chubby middle-aged man always dressed in a black three-piece suit to match his black bag. He was a real doctor, educated at a medical school back East, not just a prairie quack the way so many of them are.

He was crossing the dusty street, and when he saw me, he said, "Terrible business. I remember delivering that kid, the one that got killed. Hell, he wasn't twenty years old yet."

I went down the street. I was stopped by half a dozen citizens who wanted to express their anger over what had happened to the clerk.

I took my horse to the station and tied him up in back and went inside.

I was just passing Ev Hollister's office when I heard a familiar voice.

"I'm doing what I have to, Hollister, nothing more and nothing less."

He spoke, as usual, with a small degree of anger and a great degree of pomposity.

He sounded riled and he sounded rattled, and I wanted to get a look at him this way, so I leaned in the door frame and watched him as he bent over the chief's desk.

"Something I can do for you?" Hollister said when he saw me.

"I just rode in from town and heard that the bank was robbed."

As I said this, Reeves turned around and faced me. His look of displeasure was deep and pure.

"Yeah, and one of the tellers was killed. Had a gun in his cash drawer. Just a kid, too. Briney."

Briney was the youngster who'd opened my account. The one with the rimless glasses and the altar boy smile.

"Specifically against my orders," Reeves said. "I specifically forbid my tellers to keep guns in their drawers. I didn't want anything like this to happen."

Reeves wasn't angry only at me. He was also angry at Lundgren and Mars. A robbery would get a town riled. But the murder of a young man would put them in the same mind as that old man I'd just seen on the street. They'd want a hanging.

Reeves scowled at me. "What I want to know is how the robber got the key to the side door of the bank."

That had troubled me, too.

Hollister shifted forward in the chair behind his desk and started cleaning his pipe bowl with a pocketknife.

"Reeves here thinks the robbers got the key from somebody who had access to the bank."

"One of the employees?" I said.

Hollister shook his head. "Huh-uh. Bank employees aren't given keys."

"Could one of the employees have stolen it?" I said.

"Reeves says no." Hollister spoke as if Reeves weren't here. "Says the only person with a key is himself."

"And one other man," Reeves said, his eyes fixed on my face. "You."

I looked at Hollister. His face was drawn and serious. "You know where the keys are, Chase?"

"In the drawer in the back room. Where I always leave them when I finish my shift at night."

"You never take them home?"

"Never. You said not to."

Hollister nodded somberly toward the back. "Why don't you go get that ring of keys and bring it up here?"

I looked at Reeves. He was still scowling. "All right," I said.

My bones were still aching and I was starting to cough some, but those problems were nothing compared to what I was beginning to suspect.

In the back room, where Hollister posts the bulletins and directives for the men, I got into the desk where all the junior officers sit when they have to write out reports.

Left side, second drawer down, I found the keys. Usually there were seventeen in all. Today there were sixteen. I counted them again, just to make sure that my nerves hadn't misled me. Sixteen. The bank key was missing.

I sat there for a long time and thought about it. It was pure Reeves and it was pure beautiful, the way he was about to tie me in with Lundgren and Mars.

I went back up front. I set the keys on Hollister's desk.

He looked down at them and said, "Well, Chase?"

"There's one missing."

"You know which one that is?"

"Yes, sir."

"The bank key?"

"Yes, sir," I said.

"I knew it," Reeves said. "I goddamn knew it."

"I didn't take that key, Chief."

Hollister nodded. "I believe you, Chase, but I'm afraid Reeves here doesn't."

I met Reeves's gaze now. There was a faint smile on his eyes and mouth. He was starting to enjoy himself. If only one person had the key to the bank other than himself, then who else could the guilty party be?

I stood there feeling like the farm boy I was. I'd never been gifted with a devious mind. Reeves had not only robbed his own bank, he had also managed to set me up in the process—set me up and implicate me in the robbery.

"A little later," Hollister said quietly, "you and I should talk, Chase."

I nodded.

"Why don't you go ahead and start your shift now?" Hollister said.

"Yes, Chase, you do that," Reeves said. "But you can skip the bank. Thanks to you, there isn't any money left in there."

IT WAS A long afternoon. The sun was a bloody red ball for a time and then vanished behind the piney hills, leaving a frosty dusk. Dinner bells clanged in the shadows and you could hear the *pock-pock-pock* of small feet running down the dirt streets for home. The only warmth in the night were the voices of mothers calling in their young ones. If there was concern and a vague alarm in the voices—after all, you could never be quite sure that your child really was safe—there was also love, so much so that I wanted to be seven or eight again and heading in to the dinner table myself, for muttered "Praise the Lords" and some giggly talk with my giggly little sister and some of my mother's muffins and hot buttery sweet corn.

There were a lot of fights early that night. The miners, learning that they would have no money tomorrow, demanded credit and got it and drank up a lot of the money they would eventually get. In all, I broke up four fights. One man got a bloody eye with the neck of a bottle shoved in his face, and another man got two broken ribs when he was lifted up and thrown into the bar. The miners had to take their anger out on somebody, and who was more deserving than a friend? Like most drunkards, they saw no irony in this.

Just at seven Gillian and Annie brought my dinner, cooked beef and wheat bread. It was too cold for them to stay, so they started back right away—but not before Gillian said, "Annie, would you wait outside a minute?"

She studied both of us. Obviously, just as I did, Annie sensed something wrong. She looked hurt and scared, and I wanted to say something to her, but when Gillian was in this kind of mood, I knew better.

Annie went out the back door of the station, leaving Gillian and me next to the potbellied stove in the empty room.

"There was a robbery this morning, Chase," she said.

"So I heard."

"Reeves's bank."

"Right."

"He did it again, didn't he?"

"Did what?"

"Did what? God, Chase, don't play dumb. You know how mad that makes me."

"There was a robbery, yes, and it was Reeves's bank, yes, but other than that, I don't know what you're talking about."

She studied me just as Annie had. "Chase."

"Yeah?"

"I made up my mind about something."

"Oh?"

"If you take that bank robbery money, I'm going through with what I said. About leaving you. I'm going to pack Annie and I up and go and that's a promise. I don't want our daughter raised that way."

"He killed my two brothers."

"Don't give me that kind of whiskey talk, Chase. Your brothers are dead and I'm sorry about that, but no matter what you do, you can't bring them back. But you can give Annie a good life, and I'm going to see that you do or I'm taking her away."

"I love you, Gillian."

"This isn't the right time for that kind of talk, Chase, and you know it."

She walked to the door and turned around and looked at me. "If you break her heart, Chase, or let her down, I'm never going to forgive you."

She went right straight out without saying another word, or giving me a chance to speak my own piece.

THE FIGHTS WENT on all night. A Mex took a knife to a miner who kept calling him a Mex, and two miners who should have known better got into a drunken game of Russian roulette. They both managed to miss their own heads, but they shot the hell out of the big display mirror behind the bar.

Just at eleven, when I was finishing my second sweep of the businesses, making sure all the doors were locked, making sure that no drunken miners had sailed rocks through any of the windows. I was walking past an alley and that was when they got me.

They didn't make any noise and they surprised me completely.

Mars hit me on the side of the head with the butt of a .45, and Lundgren dragged me into the shadows of the alley.

"Where's our money?" Lundgren said.

I didn't answer. Wouldn't. Because no matter what he did to me, it wasn't going to be his money ever again.

Mars took the first three minutes. He worked my stomach and my ribs and my chest.

At one point I started throwing up, but that didn't slow him down any. He had a rhythm going, and why let a little vomit spoil everything?

By the time Mars finished, I was on my knees and trying to pitch forward.

Lundgren had better ideas.

He grabbed me by the hair and jerked me to my feet and then started using his right knee expertly on my groin.

He must have used it six, seven times before I couldn't scream anymore, before I felt the darkness overwhelm me there in the dust that was moist with my own blood and sweat and piss . . .

Just the darkness . . .

Part 19

Six years ago, two Maryknoll nuns on their way to California stopped through here. They stayed just long enough, I'm told, to set up an eight-bed hospital. It's nothing fancy, you understand, but there's a small surgery room in addition to the beds, and everything is white and very clean and smells of antiseptic.

Doc Granville got me into his examination room but then had to go out to get a man some pills. Apparently, people felt comfortable stopping by at any hour. While I was in the room alone, I looked through his medical encyclopedia. There was something I needed to look up.

When I was finished, I went back to the table and laid down and Doc Granville came in and got to work.

He daubed some iodine on the cut across my forehead. I winced. "Hell, son, that don't hurt at all."

"If you say so."

"Miners do this to you? I know they're raising hell because their paychecks are going to be late."

"I didn't get a real good look at them. But I think it was Mexes."

"You must be at least a little bit tough."

"Why's that?"

"That beating you took. And you're up and around."

I thought of mentioning what I'd just read. I decided not to. Things were complicated enough. "I'm not up and around yet."

He laughed. "I don't hand out that many compliments, son. Just accept it with some grace and keep your mouth shut."

I smiled at him. For all his grumpiness, he was a funny bastard, and a pretty decent man at that.

The pain was considerable. He had me on the table with my head propped up. He'd fixed the cuts on my face and then carefully examined my ribs. They were sore. Not broken, he said, but probably bruised. I tried not to think about it.

He was about to say something else when knuckles rapped on the white door behind him.

"I told you I'd be out in five minutes, nurse. Now you just hold on to your britches."

"It's not the nurse."

And it wasn't.

"Your boss," Granville said in a soft voice.

I nodded.

"They're going to hurt like a bitch when you get up, those ribs of yours."

"I imagine."

"Nothing I can do for it except tape it up the way I did."

"I appreciate it."

He went to the door and opened it.

Hollister, in his blue serge, walked into the room with the kind of military precision and stiffness he always used when he was trying to hide the fact he'd been drinking.

He nodded to Granville and came straight over to me. He scowled when he saw my face.

"What the hell happened?"

So I told him the Mex story, the same one I'd told Granville. It was better the second time around, the way a tall tale usually is, but as I watched him, I could see he didn't believe a word of it.

"Mexes, huh?"

"Uh-huh."

"Two of them."

"Uh-huh."

"I'm told you didn't sound your whistle," he said.

"I didn't have time."

"Or use your weapon."

"I didn't have time for that, either."

"They just grabbed you . . ."

"Grabbed me as I was walking past an open alley."

"And dragged you . . ."

"Dragged me into the alley and—"

"Why did they drag you into the alley?"

"Because I saw them in the alley, fighting—one of them even had a knife—and I told them to stop, and they turned on me."

"Just like that?"

"Just like that."

"Before you could do anything?"

"Before I could do anything."

Granville was watching me, too. He was pretending to be sterilizing some of his silver instruments, but he was really watching Hollister try to break my story.

Hollister suddenly became aware of the doc. "You do me a favor, Doc?"

"Sure, Ev."

"Wait outside."

"If you want."

"I'd appreciate it."

"Sure."

Doc looked like a kid disappointed because he had to stay home while all his friends went off and did something fun.

Doc went out and closed the door.

Hollister didn't talk at first. He went over and picked up a straight-backed chair and set it down next to the table I was lying on. Then he took out his pipe and filled it and took out a stick match and struck it on the bottom of his boot. The room smelled briefly of phosphorous from the match head and then of sweet pipe tobacco.

He still didn't say anything for a long time, but when he did speak, it sure was something I paid attention to.

"Only one way those two boys that stuck up the bank could've gotten that key."

I didn't say anything.

He said, "How much did they promise you, Chase?"

I still didn't say anything. I just lay there with my ribs hurting every other time I inhaled. I had never felt more alone.

"Reeves estimates that they got away with fifty thousand. If they didn't give you at least a third of it, you're not a very good businessman."

"I didn't have anything to do with the robbery, Chief. I honestly didn't."

"I took a chance on you, being an exconvict and all."

"I know that and I appreciate it."

"And now here I am kicking myself in the ass for doing it."

"I'm sorry, Chief."

"Every single merchant in this town knows what happened, how you threw in with those robbers."

"I didn't, Chief. I really didn't"

I closed my eyes. There was nothing else to say.

"They didn't hesitate to kill that clerk at the bank this morning, and they sure won't hesitate to kill you." He puffed on his pipe. "That beating they gave you was just a down payment, Chase."

He was trying to scare me. I thought of scaring him right back by telling him about that wife of his and Reeves.

He stood up and walked over to the table and faced me.

He jabbed a hard finger into my taped-up ribs.

I let out a cry.

"They worked you over pretty good. Maybe you should take a few days off."

"Is that an order?"

He sighed. "I can't prove you actually gave them that key, so I'm not going to fire you, even though every merchant in town wants me to."

"That's white of you."

He shook his head. "Chase, I thought you were smarter than all this."

"I didn't throw in with them, no matter what you say."

"Then where did they get the key?"

I stayed quiet. I didn't want to drag Reeves into this. That would only complicate things.

"You got any answer for that, Chase?"

"I don't know where they got the key."

"But not from you?"

"Not from me."

He took the last noisy drags of his pipe. "You've got a nice wife and a nice little girl. You don't want to spoil things for them."

"I sure don't."

"Then I'm going to ask you once more, and I want you to tell me the truth."

"You don't even have to ask. I didn't give them the key."

He walked over to the door. His boots walked heavy on the boards of the floor.

"You going to tell me why they came after you?"

"I told you. It was two Mexes."

"Right. Two Mexes."

"And they were drunk."

"Real drunk, I suppose."

"Right," I said. "Real drunk."

He looked sickened by me. "You're wasting your goddamned life, Chase. You've gotten yourself involved in something that's going to bring down your whole family. And you're going to wind up in prison again. Or worse."

He didn't even look at me anymore. He just walked through the doorway, slamming the door hard behind him.

I lay there, quiet, still hurting from where he'd jammed his finger into my rib.

Part 20

Gillian put a match to the kerosene lamp and then held the light close to my face and looked over what they'd done to me.

I watched her closely in the flickering lamplight, older looking tonight than usual, her eyes moving swiftly up and down my face, showing no emotion at all when she got to the black and blue places. She didn't touch me. I knew she was angry.

I'd been home ten minutes, sitting at the kitchen table, rolling a cigarette in the dark, trying to wake neither Gillian nor Annie, but then I'd dropped my cigarette, and when I went to get it, my rib hurt so bad I made a noise, and that had awakened Gillian.

Now she finished with her examination and set the lamp down in the middle of the table and went around and sat across the table from me.

She just kept biting her lip and frowning.

"Two Mexes," I said, keeping my voice low with Annie asleep in the other room.

"Don't say anything, Chase."

"I'm just trying to explain—"

"You're not trying to explain anything. You're lying, that's what you're doing."

"But Gillian, listen—"

"You got yourself involved in that robbery somehow, and it all went wrong just the way I knew it would, and now Reeves is after you."

She started crying. No warning at all.

I sat there in the lamp-flick dark with the woman I'd loved so long, knowing how much I'd let her down. To get Reeves the way I wanted to get Reeves meant destroying her in the process.

"I'm so sorry, Gillian."

"No, you're not."

"Well, I wish I was sorry, at any rate. I just wish I didn't hate him so much."

"And I just wish Annie didn't love you so much."

She went to bed. I sat there a long time. After awhile I blew out the lamp and just sat in the moonlight. I had some whiskey and I rolled two cigarettes and I sort of talked to my dead brothers the way you sort of talk to dead folks, and I thought of Annie in her white dress in the sunshine and I thought of sad Gillian, who'd been done nothing but wrong by men all her life.

It was near dawn when I went to bed and slid in beside her.

Part 21

The next day, I fell back into my routine as husband and father and policeman.

Before work I went up the hill and knelt down by the deserted well. The day was gray and overcast. The wind, as I pulled the well cover back, was cold and biting. I could smell snow on the air.

Last night I'd dreamt that I'd run up the hill to the well only to find it empty. Behind me stood Lundgren and Mars. When I found that they'd taken the money, they'd started laughing, and then Lundgren had leaned over and pushed me down the well.

The rope still dangled from the spike. I reached down and gripped it and pulled the canvas money sack up the long dark hole.

I put the sack on the ground and greedily tore it open and reached inside.

I pulled up a handful of greenbacks and just stared at them momentarily. I gripped the money tight, as if I had my hands around Reeves's neck.

"You're destroying this family, Chase. That's what you're doing."

In the wind, I hadn't heard Gillian come up the hill. She stood no more than two feet behind me. She wore a shawl over her faded gingham dress. She looked old again, and scared and weary, and I tried hard not to hate myself for what I was doing.

"This money is going to save us, Gillian," I said, packing it all back up again, leaning to the well and feeding the rope down the long dark tunnel. I didn't let go until I'd tested the rope. Snug and firm. The spike held. The money was back in a safe place. I pulled the cover over the well and dusted my hands off and stood up.

I took her by the arms and tried to kiss her. She wouldn't let me. She just stood stiff. Her skin was covered with goose bumps from the icy wind.

She wouldn't look at me. I spoke to her profile, to her sweet little nose and her freckles and her tiny chin.

"All we need to do is wait a few months, and then we can leave town with all this money. Tell Hollister that one of your relatives died and left you a farm in Missouri or somewhere. Even if he suspects, he can't prove it. I'll wrap the money in bundles and put it in a trunk and send the trunk on ahead to wherever we decide to go."

When she finally turned and looked at me, she seemed sadder than I'd ever seen her.

"And won't that be a nice life for Annie, Chase? Watching her father scared all the time because somebody might find the money he stole?"

"I won't be scared, Gillian, because nobody will know except you and me. And it's not stolen money, anyway, not really—it's just what Reeves rightfully owes me."

"Listen to yourself, Chase," she said. "You've convinced yourself that what you're doing is right. But all you're doing is destroying this family. You wait and see. You wait and see."

She started crying, and then she was running down the hill, pulling her shawl tighter around her.

I started after her but decided there was no point. Not right now, anyway.

All I could do was stand there in the bitter wind, feeling like a kid who'd just been scolded. I wanted to speak up on my own behalf, but I knew better, knew that no matter what I said or how long I talked, straight and true Gillian would remain straight and true.

After awhile I walked back down the hill to the house. Gillian was fixing stew at the stove. She didn't once turn around and look at me as I got into my police uniform, or say good-bye as I stood in the doorway and said, "I love you, Gillian. You and Annie are my life. And this is all going to work out. We're going to have the money and have a good life away from here. I promise you that, Gillian. I promise you that."

But there was just her back, her tired-beaten shoulders, and her arm stirring the ladle through the stew.

Part 22

When I got to town, the funeral procession was just winding its way up the hill to the graveyard. A lone man in a Union uniform walked behind the shiny black horse-drawn hearse, beating out a dirge on a drum.

I went to the police station, checked over the sheet listing the arrests thus far that day, checked to see if the new and more comfortable shoes I'd ordered had come in yet, and then started out the front door. There was still time for a cup of coffee at the restaurant before my rounds began.

As I walked to the front of the station, I felt various eyes on me.

A cop named Docey said, "Some of us were talkin' last night, Chase."

"Oh?"

"There were six of us talkin', and five of us voted that you should quit." He was leaning against the front door, a pudgy red-bearded man with red freckles on his white bald head. "We got enough problems without people thinkin' we're crooked."

"I didn't slip that key to the robbers, in case that's what you're talking about."

He grabbed me then. He pushed away from the door and took his big Irish hands and grabbed the front of my uniform coat. I heard the two other cops grunt in approval.

I couldn't afford any more physical pain. I used my knee and I went right up straight and he went down fast and sure.

He rolled around on the floor clutching his groin and swearing. The other two started toward me but then realized that if Docey couldn't handle me—Docey being a mean mick ex-railroad man—they couldn't either.

I opened the front door, about to step out on the boardwalk into the bitter blustering day, and I saw her shiny black surrey pull up.

In her dark cape and royal-blue organdy dress, red hair caught beneath a small hat, Claire Hollister was not only beautiful, she was also exotic, like a frightened forest creature you see only once or twice a year for mere moments.

As she stepped down from the surrey, she nodded good day to me.

"Afternoon, ma'am."

"Afternoon." She smiled. "D-Did y-you h-happen t-to see that h-husband of m-mine in there?" As always, her eyes reflected her humiliation.

"I think he's still at the funeral, ma'am."

"Oh. W-Would y-you l-leave a n-note telling h-him I was h-here?"

"Sure."

She turned back to her surrey. As she seated herself and lifted the reins, I saw how sad her face was even in profile. I couldn't imagine why a woman like this—a woman I sensed was decent and honorable—would give herself to a man like Reeves. Sometimes I suspected I didn't know anything about women at all.

After she was gone, I went back inside. I had to pass Docey and the other two cops, but they just scowled at me and let me go.

I wrote the chief a note and took it into his office. I started to set the note on his desk but then I noticed an envelope addressed to him. It bore the same handwriting as the note that had told him I was a jailbird.

I stood very still, staring at the envelope, making sure I was alone in the office, listening hard for any footsteps in the hallway.

I had to be quick. And I certainly couldn't risk reading it in here.

I snapped the envelope up, stuffed it inside my serge uniform coat, and walked straight out of the office and straight down the hallway and straight to the door, where Docey was still standing up and grimacing.

"You'll get yours, Chase, just you wait and goddamn see," he said.

Snow was still on the wind. The people on the street didn't dawdle now, they scurried like all other animals, trying to prepare themselves for the bitter winter soon to come. I imagined the general store, with its bacon and hams and coffee and cheeses and pickled fish and candy and tobacco and blankets and toys, was going to be doing a very good business the next few days as people set things in for the fury of winter.

I went over to the restaurant and ordered a cup of coffee. By the time the waitress came back with my steaming cup, I had already read the letter twice, and I sure didn't like what Reeves had written.

Part 23

Dear Chief Hollister,

As an upright citizen of this town, I've warned you before about your man Chase. While everybody suspects he gave the robber the key that let him in the bank, nobody can prove it. Till now . . .

Ask Hartley, the night clerk at the Whitney, about the robbers and Chase meeting behind the hotel two nights before the robbery.

If he tells the truth, you'll see that Chase was in on this meeting all along.

So Reeves had got to Hartley, the night clerk at the hotel where Lundgren and Mars had been staying. Wouldn't take much to bribe a man like Hartley. Just as it wouldn't take much to convince Hollister of Hartley's story, that I had met with Lundgren and Mars to plan the robbery.

Even if I burned this particular letter, Reeves would send Hollister another one. And keep sending him letters until Hollister decided to put me behind bars . . . a perfect target for the lynch mob Reeves would quickly stir up.

I wanted to run. I thought about Mexico and warm blue waters and sandy yellow beaches and Gillian and Annie and I living in a fine stucco house . . .

But if I ran now, it would be like signing a confession, admitting that I'd been part of the robbery.

I sipped coffee. I smoke a cigarette. I thought things through.

I had only one hope. I had to strike a bargain with Reeves.

"Yes?"

"Wondered if I could talk to you a minute, Chief."

"About what?"

"I might be a little late getting to today."

Hollister waved me into his office.

"By the way, your wife was here. I just wanted to make sure you got my note."

"I got it. Now what's this about being late?"

"Couple hours is all."

"For what?"

"Some personal things."

"Personal things, huh?"

"Not anything to do with the robbery, if that's what you're thinking."

He picked up his pipe. He'd been cleaning it with his pocketknife. Now he went back to it.

"You're not telling me the truth yet, Chase."

"I am. You just don't happen to believe the truth."

"You've got those jailhouse eyes, Chase. You think you look like every other man in this town, but you don't. Prison does something to people, and it sure as hell did something to you."

"I didn't help anybody rob that bank."

He put the pipe in his mouth and drew on it. There was a sucking sound in the empty bowl. "You could always turn them over."

"The robbers?"

"Lundgren and Mars are their names, in case you need help remembering."

"I don't know where they are."

"Uh-huh."

"I don't."

"Take the two hours." He sounded disgusted. "I don't know why you'd want to waste a fine wife and daughter the way you are."

"I'll be back by four-thirty."

"Don't hurry on my account. I'm getting damned tired of seeing your face, in fact."

Part 24

Even on a cold drab day like this one, Reeves' Victorian house was impressive and sightly. I sat on my horse staring at it, trying not to notice that

I was working up another fever and that my stomach was getting sick again.

Hanratty, the guard, appeared just when I expected him to, and leveled his carbine at me just when I was sure he would. He came out from behind the scrub pines, seated on a big bay.

"Nice uniform you got there, Chase. Maybe I could get Reeves to get me one like it."

"Maybe if you did an extra-good job, he just might do that."

Hanratty was bundled up inside a sheep-lined jacket, with his hat pulled down near his ears. He spat a stream of juice right near my horse's foreleg. "He'd be real happy to hear you went for your gun and I was forced to kill you. That's one way I could get me a uniform like that." He grinned. "Every time he works that wolf of his these days, he's always callin' out your name. And that goddamned wolf goes crazy, believe me. Crazy as all hell." He frowned. "Except the past couple days. Animal ain't hisself."

"All right if I go see Reeves?"

"It's your ass, son. He might put a couple holes in you."

I smiled. "I'm a policeman."

"Where you're concerned, I don't reckon that would make a whole lot of difference to him."

I rode up to the mansion and ground-tied my horse. Before going up the steps, I walked over the side of the house and looked at the wolf in his cage.

The wolf, crouched on the ground, watching me carefully, wailed out something that resembled a song, a wolf song, I guessed. I'd never heard anything like it. It was angry for sure, but even more, it was sad.

I walked a few feet closer to the large, oblong cage that stank of feces and raw decaying meat and I saw that Hanratty hadn't been exaggerating about the wolf's anger, either.

He got up on all fours, let out another terrible piercing sound, and then flung himself at the cage. His eyes burned with the same yellow glow I'd seen that night he'd killed my brother.

His bared teeth dripped with drool, and his entire body trembled as he slammed again and again and again into the wire, trying to tear through the wall to get to me. The reverberating wire made a tinny kind of music.

I had my gun in hand and ready, just in case.

"Maybe I'll put you in there with him," said a voice behind me, the words accompanied by the nudge of cold metal against the back of my neck. "What the hell're you doing here, anyway, Chase?"

"Talk a deal."

"Deal?" Reeves laughed. "What the hell's that supposed to mean?"

"Let's go inside and I'll tell you."

He wore a riding costume, a fancy eastern riding costume, one of those things with jodhpurs and knee-length riding boots. He was real pretty.

"You're really serious, aren't you?" he said.

"Yes."

He laughed again. "Then you're a crazy bastard, Chase. A crazy, crazy bastard. Men like me don't make deals with men like you."

"If you ever want to see any of that bank money again, Reeves, you'd better invite me inside."

The wolf was exhausted. He'd spent himself and lay now panting, his entire body heaving with hot breath, and making those funny sounds again.

"Something's wrong with your wolf," I said.

"You and that goddamned Hanratty. The wolf's just got some kind of bug is all. Wolves get bugs just the same as humans. If he was really sick, he wouldn't be able to throw himself against the cage that way.

"Be sure to wipe that mud off your boots before you go inside," Reeves said. "I don't want some hayseed tracking up my good hardwood floors."

"I take it you're inviting me inside," I said, but when I turned around, Reeves was already up near the front porch, as if he didn't even want to be seen with me, not even on his own land.

I turned back to the keening wolf and listened to his terrible sounds echo off the surrounding hills, like a distress call of some kind that nobody was answering.

"YOU HAVE TWO minutes, and then I want you the hell off my property."

We were in his office, the same one where he'd coldcocked me that day.

"I have your money," I said. He was behind his desk. He hadn't invited me to sit down.

"I'm well aware of the fact that you have my money."

"But I'm willing to make a deal."

"You heard what I said about deals, Chase."

"You get half and I get half."

"I get half of my own money and you get the other half? That sounds like a hell of a deal, all right."

"Otherwise you get nothing."

"We'll see who gets nothing, Chase. This isn't over yet."

I sat down. He didn't look especially happy about it. "You want to hear about it?"

I could tell he did but he didn't want to say he did—he didn't want to give any sign that I was in control here—so I went on anyway.

"You get ahold of Ev Hollister and tell him you made a mistake about me. Tell him that you forgot that one day you hung your coat up over at the Whitney while you were having lunch, and when you got back, you found your wallet missing. The bank key was in there. But while you went to the manager to complain, somebody slipped your wallet back into your coat."

"In other words, somebody had a duplicate key made?"

"Exactly."

"And why would he believe this?"

"Because it's you talking. Because you're a prominent citizen and he'd have no reason to suspect you're lying."

"And for this I get half my money back?"

"Right."

"And what do you get, Chase?"

"I get half the money and I get a chance to ease me and my family out of this town without this cloud hanging over me. I'll buy a farm in Missouri and disappear for the rest of my life with Gillian and Annie."

"Every jailbird's dream."

"I'm tired of your sarcasm, Reeves."

He smirked. "A jailbird sits in his cell and dreams up all these sweet little stories about how good life will be after he pulls just one more job." He leaned forward in his seat. "I should put a bullet in your face right here and right now." His anger was overtaking him now. He started spitting when he spoke. "You've got my money, you stupid hayseed asshole, and I'm going to take it back and you're going to regret ever having anything to do with me."

He waved his hand, spitting and glaring, blood spreading across his cheeks. "Now get the hell out of here."

"I figured out a peaceful way to end all this," I said. "I thought you'd want to listen."

He said nothing. Just glared.

I stood and picked up my hat and walked out of his den and down the hall, my boot heels loud in the silence, and out the front door.

I put my hat on and watched the wolf a moment. He was still crying, still that high mournful call, and still crouching, as if exhausted—until he saw me . . . and then he was up on all fours and leaping into the air and hurtling himself against the cage.

"He sure don't like you," an old Indian cleaning woman said, as she beat a rug against the porch railing.

"I guess he doesn't," I said.

On the way out, Hanratty waved to me and called, "Good to see you're still alive." I waved and rode on.

I just kept thinking of what Reeves had said, how every jailbird sits in his cell and thinks of how pretty things will be after he pulls that final job. Not till the very moment he'd said that had I ever thought of myself as a jailbird—just as a kid who'd gotten himself in some trouble, was all—but in his hard, bitter words I'd recognized myself. And now I felt every bit the hayseed he'd said I was. Trying to make a deal with him had been very foolish.

After a few more days, I'd gather up Gillian and Annie and the money, and in the middle of the night we'd light out and never be seen by any of these folks again . . .

Part 25

The rain started just after dinner time. Except for the light in the saloon windows, the stores and streets were dark as I made my rounds trying doors, checking alleys, peering into storage shacks.

I was starting down Main, past three of the rowdier saloons, when I saw the two drunken miners weaving down the street toward me. They were laughing and stumbling their way home to warm houses and irritated wives and disappointed children.

Then they saw who I was and stopped and one of them said, "There's that sonofabitch."

"Who?"

"Goddamn cop who was in on that goddamn bank robbery."

"No shit?"

"Where they killed the poor goddamned clerk with a goddamned double-barrel shotgun."

"Poor sumbitch."

By now I was abreast of them, making my way through the cold and the night and the lashing rain. They were too drunk to notice the downpour, or care about it, anyway.

There wasn't much I could do about them not liking me, the two drunks. I'd feel sorry for myself a few minutes and then the whole thing would be over.

Then the first drunk hit me.

I hadn't been expecting it and I didn't have time to do anything about it.

His punch came out of the gloom and struck me right on the jaw.

He'd hit me hard enough to daze me. There was pain and there was an even deeper darkness, and then I felt a second punch slam into my stomach.

It should have brought me down, that punch. It drove deep into my belly right below the ribs and it was expert enough and vicious enough to wind me for the moment.

But then rage and frustration took over. Suddenly this drunk became the whole town, everybody who smirked about me, everybody who whispered.

I threw down my nightstick, not wanting to make this an official act in any way, and without even being able to see yet, connected with a strong right to the drunk's face.

"Hey!" yelled the second drunk, as if defending myself was against some unwritten code.

But I didn't even slow down. I just kept punching. I even got a knee straight up between the first drunk's legs, and when he started to buckle, I grabbed him by the hair and started hitting him at will with my right fist.

By now I could see. The guy was bloody, though the rain did a good job of washing him up. He hadn't been intimidated by my uniform, but his friend was. He stood three feet away and called me names.

At first I wasn't aware of the crowd surrounding us, not until there were twenty people or so. They'd drifted down from the taverns, animals who could smell blood on the wind, animals whose taste for violence was never sated, miners, merchants, cowboys, drifters—it was a taste and thrill that cut across all lines of class and intelligence and color. Most men, and a sad number of women, loved watching other men hurt each other.

And I was hurting him, hurting him bad, and I couldn't stop. If anything, I was piling more and more punches into his body. The crowd was with me now, frenzied, caught up in my rhythms as I slammed punches first to the head then to the chest then to the belly, the same pattern again and again. He was bleeding so badly, his blood was flying across my own face.

"That's enough, Chase!"

At first the voice seemed far away and not quite recognizable. Familiar, yet . . .

And so I kept on swinging and slugging and—

And then, too late, I recognized the voice and I saw him, peripherally, step up next to me and raise his own nightstick and bring it down and—

And then there was just the eternal cosmic night, cold and dark, not life yet not quite death, either. Just pain and—blankness.

The crowd noise grew distant—and then faded entirely . . .

I DIDN'T GET my eyes open right away. Couldn't. The pain across the back of my head was too considerable.

I became aware that my arms were stretched out behind me and my wrists were bound together. I became aware that my ankles were also bound. I became aware of some other presence near me. I had to open my eyes. Had to.

I almost smiled. He was treating me as a respected guest and he didn't even know it. None of his men ever got to see the inside of the room where Ev Hollister worked over his prisoners. But now Ev Hollister was letting me see it for myself.

"You were out a long time," he said.

He sat in a straight-backed chair directly across from the one I was sitting in.

"Afraid I tapped you a little harder than I meant to," he said.

There were dark brown splatters all over the wall the dried blood of the prisoners he'd worked over in his time. There were also dents and nicks and small holes in the wall. When he got done punching the prisoners, he sometimes like to throw them around the room. Everybody likes a little variety in his life.

I brought my eyes back to Hollister.

"You look pissed, Chase. Real pissed."

"Why'd you bring me into this room? I'm not a prisoner."

He smiled. It was a drunken smile, pleasing but crooked and not quite coordinated properly. "You're not a prisoner yet, you mean, Chase. This whole town's just like that miner who swung on you. They hate you, Chase, and they hold you responsible for the clerk's death and they're putting a lot of pressure on me to arrest you whether I've got evidence or not. These are simple folks, Chase, they're not like you and me with our fine respect for the written law." He tried to smile about empty, high-minded words, but what came out was a smirk.

I decided I might as well tell him. Maybe it was what he'd been wanting all along, anyway. "I'm planning to clear out in the next few days. Gillian and Annie and me. Gone for good."

"Well," he said, "now that's a damned sensible idea."

"So all your troubles will be over."

"The next few days?"

"So how about untying me?"

"You and your wife and daughter?"

"Right."

"As far away as you can get with no plans to ever come back?"

"That's the plan."

He stood up. The crooked smile was back. So was the drunken glaze of the eyes. He walked four steps between my chair and his, and then he backhanded me so hard I went over backward, cracking my head on the floor.

I tried to struggle back up but it was no use. Lying on my back and tied up made me vulnerable to anything he wanted to do. But the fall had loosened the rope on my wrists.

He kicked me hard in the ribs.

The pain hadn't even had time to register properly before he walked around the chair and kicked me hard in the other rib, the one that I'd bruised awhile back.

I closed my eyes and coasted on the blackness and the physical grief spreading across my rib cage and up into my chest and arms. Every few minutes, I'd become aware of my sore throat again. . . .

"Where are those two peckers?" he said.

I didn't want to give him another excuse to kick me. I answered right away. "I don't know."

"Like hell you don't Chase. You stick up a bank with two men and you don't know where they are?"

"I don't. I'm telling you the truth."

"Then you've got the money, don't you?"

"No."

"Bullshit."

"Honest, Chief, I—"

He kicked me again. This was enough to shrivel my scrotum into the size of a walnut and to send tears streaming down my cheeks. The toe of his boot had found the exact spot where the doc had bandaged my rib.

"Where's the money?"

"Don't . . . know."

"You sonofabitch."

And I could sense it, the frenzy, the way I was sure all his other prisoners had been able to sense it. When he was sober, he was a decent, humane man who ran an honest police department and had a genuine regard for the people he served.

But when he drank . . .

This time he walked around in front of me and looked straight down.

"You know where I'm going to kick you this time?"

"Please don't. Please." I didn't care how I sounded. I just didn't want anymore pain.

"Then you tell me, Chase. You tell me where those men are and where that money is or I swear you won't get out of this room alive."

"I don't know. I really don't."

My groin wasn't all that easy a target, what with my ankles bound and all, but his boot toe was unerring and he found the spot with very little trouble.

I screamed. I tried praying, but all that came out was curses, and I tried biting my lip, but I bit down so hard I filled my mouth with blood.

And he kicked me again.

Almost instinctively, I kept working my hands free from the ropes behind me. But even if my hands were free, he had a gun and a nightstick and—

"You tell me, Chase, you tell me where those men are and that money is."

My body was cold with sweat. My face was swollen from the punches of the miner. My ribs and groin hurt so much I was starting to drift into unconsciousness. . . .

"I'm giving you five seconds, Chase."

He was raising his boot. He was picking his spot.

"Five seconds, Chase."

"Please, Chief," I said again, and it wasn't even me speaking now, it was the scared little boy I'd been all the time I was growing up. "Please don't, Chief."

"Three seconds."

His foot came up even higher.

"Two seconds, Chase."

Oh and he was enjoying it, seeing me writhe on the floor, hearing me whimper.

"You sonofabitch," he said.

And was just starting to lift his leg when—

Somebody banged on the door.

"Chief, Chief, you'd better get out here."

He was angry, Ev Hollister was. It was as if somebody had interrupted him having sex at the crucial moment.

"What the hell is it, Fenady?"

"Those two men we been looking for? Lundgren and Mars?"

Hollister's face changed. Anger gone, replaced with curiosity.

"What about them?"

"Somebody found them in a field the other side of Chase's cabin. And brought them in."

"They're dead?"

"Yeah. Back-shot."

Hollister smiled down at me. "Didn't know where they were, eh, Chase?"

This time he didn't give any warning. He just took two steps to the right, where he could get a better angle, and then brought his toe down swiftly and surely into my rib cage.

Fenady probably winced when he heard me scream. Even the cops who hate prisoners hate to hear human beings worked over the way Hollister works them over.

Hollister looked down at me. "I'm going out there and check those men over. When I come back, I want you to tell me what you did with the money after you killed those two men."

"But I—"

I'd started to say that I hadn't back-shot anybody, that Reeves had done it and made it look as if I had, the way he made it look as if my key had been used in the robbery.

But what was the point of talking now? Hollister wouldn't believe me no matter how many times I told him the truth.

He went over to the door, unlocked it and went out.

Part 26

The ropes slid off my wrists with no trouble. But bending down to un-cinch my ankles, I felt nauseous and dizzy. Because of the beating, the sick-ness was getting worse.

Through the door I could hear the commotion far down the hall, in the front office.

As I started unwrapping the rope again, I thought of how long I'd suf-fered at Reeves's hands. Most of my adult life he'd ruled me in one way or another. I'd been a kid when I helped pull the robbery he set me up for. And now he'd convinced Hollister that I'd back-shot the two men who had allegedly been my partners.

I reached the door, eased it open, peered down the hall and started on tiptoes down the stairs and toward the back door. I reached the ground floor and continued to tiptoe down the hall and—

I got two steps away from the doorknob when somebody shouted, "Hey!"

I turned and saw Krause, a big red-faced German cop, lunging for me with his nightstick.

He swung and I ducked. His stick hit the door above my head so hard that it snapped in two.

I knew I had no chance other than to grab the knob, throw the door open, and dive into the night outside.

Krause swore and lumbered toward me, but his jaw intersected with the edge of the door just as it was opening. He was knocked to his knees. I turned around, kicked him in the throat, and then pushed him over back-ward. As I hit the alley, he was swearing at me in German.

All I could do was run. I had no idea where I was going.

I came to the head of an alley and stopped, leaning out from the shad-ows to get a look at the street. Mrs. Hollister had pulled her fancy black surrey over by the general store and was watching all the men running in the street. Apparently all the shouting over the death of Lundgren and Mars had brought her out of the house. They lived near the downtown area.

I ducked back into the alley, pausing to catch my breath, then I started running again.

I went two blocks and then collapsed against a building, my breath com-ing in hot raw gasps.

There was moonlight and the deep shadows of the alley and the sweet smell of newly sawed lumber from a nearby store that had recently gone up.

And behind me I could hear the shouts. "He escaped! Chase escaped!"

They would come looking for me now, the human equivalents of blood-hounds, and there wouldn't be just policemen, but eager private citizens, too, eager for some sport.

I pushed away from the wall and started staggering down the alley.

When I reached the last building, I pressed myself against it and peeked around the corner.

They already had torches lit, and they were coming toward me three abreast. They hadn't seen me yet but it would be only moments before they did.

I heard noise at the far end of the alley and turned to find three men with torches approaching. They would see me any time now.

I looked frantically around the alley. All I could find was a large barrel in which the general store threw food that had spoiled. Even on a cold night like this one, the contents of the barrel reeked. In the summer it had been noisy with flies twenty-four hours a day.

I had no choice. I jerked open the lid and crawled inside, hoping that the shadows would hide me sufficiently from the oncoming men.

I sank deep into a fetid, swampy mixture of rotted produce. For a long time I had to hold my breath. I was afraid I'd vomit and the men would certainly hear me.

Their voices and their footsteps came closer.

The two groups met in the alley, near where I crouched in the barrel.

"I never did like that bastard," one man said. "Just something about him."

"Strange is what he is," another said. "You ever get a good look in sunlight at how scarred up his face is underneath that beard? Very strange how a man would come to get scars like that. Kind've gives me the willies."

"Enough talk," a third man said, sounding important. "You three take the Fourth Street alleys and we'll take Third Street. No way he could've gotten out of town yet."

"Oh, he's here somewhere all right," said another man.

As one of them turned around, he nudged the barrel. I froze. I had the sense that they could all hear my heartbeat like an Indian drum deep in the forest late at night.

"He could be hidin' right here," the man said. "In this alley. Maybe we should check it out before we go over to Third Street."

"Hell, Hawkins, look around. Where the hell would he hide?"

"Right over there in that privy, for one thing."

Another man laughed. "Yep, he's sittin' in there takin' a crap and readin' a Sears catalog."

More laughter.

"Well, it sure wouldn't hurt to check it out," Hawkins said, sounding petulant.

"Be my guest."

Hawkins walked away. Ten, maybe fifteen paces. The privy was right behind the back door of the restaurant halfway down the alley.

"Stick you head down that hole in there and see if he's hidin' down there!" one of the men said, laughing.

There was no response from Hawkins, none I could hear anyway.

Bugs and mites were crawling on me, species that apparently didn't relent in November weather. I wanted to scratch myself but there was no room, and anyway doing so would probably make too much noise.

And then the lid was lifted.

This time my heart didn't start pounding. It stopped.

I sank as far down into the garbage as I could go and watched as a plump white hand dangled over the rim of the barrel.

One of the men was dropping his cigar in here.

"What a goddamn smell," he said. "All that produce."

"I had a little girl in South Dakota who smelled just like it." The other man laughed.

The lid was still off. The man's hand was still dangling, his cigar butt looking like a red-eyed snake.

And then he tossed it.

The lighted end of the butt struck me right in the forehead.

The pain was instant and considerable. I gritted my teeth. I made fists. I wanted to curse. But no way I could indulge myself.

The lid closed.

Hawkins returned. "Nobody there."

"Gee, what a surprise."

"Well, he coulda been there," Hawkins said.

"Yeah, and so coulda Jesus H. Christ himself."

"C'mon," said the third man. "Let's get moving. I'd like to find that sonofabitch myself. Show him that without that fancy blue uniform to protect him, he ain't jack shit."

I waited five minutes, during which time I had a pretty crazy thought. What if they actually knew I was in the barrel and had just snuck away a few feet and waited while I climbed out?

I would climb out of the barrel and they would open fire and I'd be dead. A nice, legal execution, something to talk about in saloons and taverns for the next twenty years.

I slid the lid open.

I reached up and grabbed the rim of the deep barrel.

Above me I saw the cold starry sky.

I pushed myself up, tatters of garbage clinging to me, and started to climb out of the barrel.

So far, so good, but I knew that my biggest problem was ahead of me.

How was I going to escape a town filled with torch-bearing posse members?

I scrambled from the barrel and immediately hid myself in the shadows again.

What was I going to do now?

And then I saw the buggy, the shiny black buggy, and without any thought at all I started running toward it.

Part 27

The Hollister woman wasn't expecting me.

I ran from the mouth of the alley straight at her surrey, my toe landing on the vehicle's metal step while I dove down beside her feet.

She started to scream, but all I had to say was one thing. "If you don't help me, Mrs. Hollister, I'll tell your husband about you and Reeves."

She'd been all set to cry out, her mouth forming an O, but at mention of Reeves the scream died in her throat.

"I want to go out Orely Road, and fast," I said.

She seemed confused, as if she hadn't quite recovered from the shock of seeing me jump into her surrey. But then intelligence returned to her eyes and she gathered the reins tighter, made a wide turn with horse and surrey, and started us on our way out of town. The animal was running at a good steady clip.

I kept watching her face to see if she was trying to signal the men who were running past, sounding excited as hayseeds at a county fair.

The ride, with me all curled up at her feet, was bumpy. Every time we hit a rut, she kicked me in my rib with the pointed toe of her high-button shoe. I could smell horseshit and axle grease. I wanted Gillian and Annie in my arms.

The flickering street lamps fell away after a time, as did the sound of running feet slapping the hard dirt road. Even the high, charged shouts of the eager posse.

After awhile I raised myself up enough to look out at the rutted road. Moonlight showed a narrow stage road with ice shining in the potholes, and all around an autumnal mountainous land touched with glowing frost. Bears would be sleeping deep in winter caves by now, and kids would be asking for extra blankets.

I swung up from the floor and sat down next to her.

"H-How did you know about R-Reeves?" she said, and when she stuttered, I felt ashamed of myself. I had no right to judge this woman the way I had.

"Forget I said anything. I'm not fit to pass judgment on you, Mrs. Hollister."

We didn't say anything for a time. The only sound was the crack of hooves against icy road.

I sat and watched the frozen night go by, the jet silhouettes of mountains against the darker jet of the sky, the hoarfrost quarter moon, the silver-blue underbellies of clouds . . .

"Y-You d-don't know what my h-husband's l-like when he d-drinks."

She sounded miserable and I had to stop her. "I shouldn't have said that, Mrs. Hollister. Really. I don't have any right to judge you."

She started shaking her head from side to side, reliving an old grief. "I'm a s-sinful w-woman, M-Mr. Chase. I'm a h-harlot."

We fell into silence again.

Then, "I t-told him t-today that I d-don't p-plan on s-seeing him a-anymore."

I reached over and touched her shoulder. "You should have respect for yourself, Mrs. Hollister. You could do a lot better than Reeves, believe me."

And Gillian could do a lot better than me.

She didn't say anything the rest of the way.

When the road turned westward, I took the reins from her and brought the horse to a halt.

"I hope things go right for you, Mrs. Hollister. You seem like a decent woman."

She smiled and leaned over. I thought she was going to kiss me. Instead she just touched my cheek with long fingers. Tenderly.

I jumped down and started walking to the edge of the hill, from which I could look down into the valley and see our house.

What I saw was the old farm wagon that Gillian kept in back. It was loaded down with clothes and furnishings. Gillian and Annie sat up on the seat. They'd hitched up the horse and were just now pulling out of the yard.

The sickness was getting worse all the time, but I ran anyway, ran faster than I ever had in my life.

"Gillian!" I cried into the night. "Gillian!"

Part 28

By the time I got near the wagon, it had climbed the hill and was just starting down the road.

As I came close, out of breath, my legs threatening to crumple at any moment, I heard the clang of pots and pans as the wagon bounced along the road.

I fell.

I was twenty feet at most from the wagon, and I went straight down, my toe having stumbled over a pothole.

I stayed on my hands and knees for two or three minutes, like a dog trying to regain his strength. The vast night was starry and cold; the clang of pots and pans faded in the distance; and all I could smell was the hot sweat of my sickness.

After a time I got to my feet. But I promptly sank back down. Too weak.

I stayed down till I lost sight of the wagon in the moonlight far ahead. It had rounded a curve and was now behind a screen of jack pines. By this time the clank of kitchen implements was almost endearing, like a memory of Annie's smile.

All of a sudden I was having trouble swallowing, taking saliva down in gulps. Part of the sickness, I knew.

I started off walking and slowly began running. I had to catch the wagon. Had to.

BY THE TIME I caught up with them, the fever was so bad I was partially blind, a darkness falling across my vision every minute or so.

This time Annie heard me. She stood up in the wagon and turned around and saw me.

The last thing I heard, just before I pitched forward in the sandy road, was Annie's scream.

Darkness.

Squeak of wagon; clop of horse on hard-packed road; faint scent of perfume in the bed of the wagon.

Gillian.

"You're going to see that doctor in the morning, and I'm going to personally take you."

"I can't see anything."

"You just rest."

"My eyes—"

"Rest."

"Where are we?"

"Annie's taking us back home. She convinced me to give you another chance."

"Gillian—"

"And you're going to turn that money over and you're going to face whatever punishment you've got coming, and then we're going to be a real family for the first time in our lives."

She leaned down. All I could smell in the darkness was her soft sweet scent. She kissed me on the forehead, a mother's kiss.

"Sleep, now. We'll be home soon."

And so the old farm wagon tossed and squeaked down the road, the horse plodding but true, Annie talking to him most of the time, imitating the way adults talked to their wagon horses.

After a time the darkness was gone and I could see the stars again, and I wondered what it would be like to live on one of them, so far away from human grief. But they probably had their own griefs, the people on those stars, ones just as bad as ours.

Part 29

She got me out of my sweat-soaked clothes, and put on water for hot tea. She put me in bed and had Annie come in and stand over me while she gathered up more blankets. By now the chills were pretty bad.

"Mommy said that in a little while things will be all right again and you won't be in trouble anymore."

The bedroom was lit by moonlight, and Annie, one half of her face silver, the other half shadow, looked like a painting.

"That's right, honey."

"She said some men would probably come after you. Chief Hollister, she said. Doesn't he like you anymore?"

Gillian was back with more blankets. Annie helped her spread them over me.

Annie started talking again. I held her small hand in mine and tried to say something in return but I didn't have the strength. My throat was raw, my head hurt, every bone in my body ached, and I was having a hard time making sense of words.

I slept.

AT FIRST I thought it was part of a dream, the way the horses thundered toward me from the distant hill. I often had dreams where I was being pursued by fierce men on fiercer horses.

But then I heard Gillian saying, "They're coming down the hill, Chase. The posse."

Instinct took over. In moments I was out of bed, grabbing dry clothes and a jacket and throwing them on, picking up my .45 and a fancy bone-handled knife I'd bought on a lark before going to prison.

Gillian watched me. "I thought maybe you'd turn yourself in, instead of running away."

As I buttoned the fleece-lined jacket, I said "I don't want them to take me into town tonight, Gillian. Not with everybody worked up the way they are. I've seen two lynchings in my life and they were both real scary."

"Where are you going?"

"I'm going to get the money and then wait till the posse leaves."

"But they'll find you."

The horses were closer, closer.

She came into my arms and we held each other. And then I took off, moving quickly to the back door. In moments I was out in the cold night again.

I peeked around the corner of the cabin and saw them—

Six horses coming down the dark November wind—

Six riders on the hill, three bearing torches with flames that crackled and flapped like pennants in the wind, and three with carbines already drawn from leather scabbards.

Ready to make the descent, encircle the cabin, and drag me out to meet their justice.

Part 30

The wind was raw as I dropped to my knees up there where the desert well lay. A dark cloud passed across the moon, and for a brief time all color was blanched from the land, and the rocks and plains and mountains did not seem to be of earth at all, but some strange land from my prison nightmares.

I jerked the lid from the well and plunged my hand down into the chilly darkness below. All I could feel was the cold, empty blackness of the grave.

They would be coming up here looking for me, the posse would. There was only one place I could hide.

I wound the top of the rope tight around one of the large rocks at the mouth of the well. I tugged it several times, making sure that it was strong enough to hold me. The rock must have weighed two hundred pounds. It would be fine. But the rope was frayed . . .

I didn't have any choice.

I grabbed the rope end, climbed up over the rocks around the opening of the well and started my descent, feeding myself rope as I went.

Dirt and small rocks from the sides of the well fell to the water below, making a hollow splashing sound when they hit.

If I fell, nobody would ever find me. I'd hit my head or drown or I'd be trapped down there and freeze to death.

I kept on moving down, inch by inch. I kept thinking of sad Gillian there at the last moment . . . wanting only the one thing I couldn't give her . . . wanting to be safe from my hatred of Reeves.

There was a sour smell just as I got so low that darkness took me entirely. Gases . . .

Far up above me I saw a portion of the well opening and a piece of cold midnight sky.

I was tightening my grip on the rope when another wave of blindness overwhelmed me. All I could do was hold on and hope it would pass.

And it was there, blind, suspended halfway down a well, that I whispered the word to myself, the word I'd been avoiding the past few days . . .

Then the voices, harsh male voices on the witch's wind down from the mountains.

Coming up the hill—

Looking for me.

"Here's a well!" somebody shouted.

They would find the cover off and put a torch down into the darkness and find me.

"The hell with the well! Look over there in that stand of jack pines."

This was Ev Hollister's voice. He was leading his own posse.

I went lower and lower in case they came back and looked down the well. They wouldn't have much trouble finding me, if they wanted to look. It was a very shallow well.

The heels of my boots touched water.

I stopped my descent, just hung there listening to the voices of the posse fade in and out on the wind.

Obviously they'd given up; the voices were moving back down the hill, in the direction of the house.

I just kept thinking of that word I'd been so afraid to say the past couple of days . . .

I felt the top of the money sack.

I grasped it and began to pull it up and—

The rope started to give at the very top.

Even as I hung there, I could feel it begin to fray and weaken.

In a moment I would be dropped into the water and entombed forever . . . terrible fever pictures came to me. I would be prisoner down here forever, till I was only white bones for greasy black snakes to wind in and out of, and for the rats to perch on as, crimson-eyed, they surveyed the well . . . I felt as if I was suffocating.

Distant starlight in the midnight sky was my only guide now.

I stabbed my heels against the shale walls of the well. Propped up this way, I could at least keep from being pitched into the water.

With one hand dredging up the money sack, by boot heels digging into the wall . . .

I started to climb.

All I could hope was that Hollister and his men would be gone by the time I reached the top.

I just kept looking straight up at the bright indifferent stars above. In prison I'd read about how many worlds our stars shine on, so many that our little world hardly matters at all.

Even with everybody on our planet screaming, nobody in the universe could hear us anyway. . . .

I knew I was getting sicker all the while, my mind fixing on things like astronomy, my bones and joints aching so bad I could hardly keep a grip on the rope or the sack.

And every few feet the rope would fray a little more and I would feel the tug and jerk as it threatened to tear apart completely . . .

But I kept on climbing.

I have no idea how long it took me.

By the time I reached the top, I was gasping for breath.

I threw the bag over the top of the well first. It landed on the frosty earth with a satisfying thump.

And then I wrapped both hands in the rope and climbed the rest of the way up, cutting my hands on hemp and jagged rock alike, till hot blood flowed from my palms.

But I didn't care . . .

I lay for long minutes on the hard cold earth. The chill air felt cool and cleansing on my fevered skin.

I got to my feet, grabbed the money sack, and started walking back up the hill.

Beyond the hill were Gillian and Annie . . .

When I reached the other side, I swung wide eastward, so I could come up behind a copse of jack pines. From here I could see the front of the cabin clearly . . . yet I was so well-hidden that nobody could see me.

Five riders with torches and horses. The wind-whipped flames made the faces of the men look like burnished masks.

There was a sixth horse, its saddle empty, standing ground-tied. Where was its rider?

Gillian stood in the doorway—Annie clinging to her like a very small child—talking to the men.

Suddenly a man came from the cabin. He was toting a Winchester. He'd obviously been searching the place, seeing if I was hiding there.

It was Hollister. He got back up on his horse.

There was more talk between the men and Gillian, the words lost in the midnight wind.

And then they left. Abruptly. Just turned their horses and headed westward, the light from their torches diminishing as they reached the edge of the great forest, where they likely thought I'd gone.

Gillian and Annie stood outside the cabin for long moments watching the men disappear into the great pines.

And then, just as I was about to call out for Gillian, I felt the darkness overwhelm me again, felt all my strength go, and my body begin to sink to the ground.

Once again I slept . . .

Part 31

The prison dreams came again . . . watching the teenager drown as the old con held him under . . . listening to the screams of the men as whips lashed their backs . . . seeing a wolf silhouetted against the full golden moon as he stood on the hill overlooking the prison . . .

Even in my sleep my teeth chattered from the cold of my skin and baked in the heat of my insides.

I wanted Gillian . . . I wanted Annie . . .

And then the scream.

At first I counted it as part of my nightmares. Only when its intensity and pitch were sustained did I realize that it was Annie screaming.

I crawled to my feet, covered with pine, so dry I could barely part my lips. I felt at my side for my .45. Still there.

Annie kept on screaming.

I staggered across the clearing.

The cabin was dark but the front door was flung wide, and there in the doorway I saw him crouching—

The wolf.

His yellow eyes gleamed and across his face were dark damp streaks of—blood.

I tried to understand what had gone on here . . .

Reeves had come here to get the money and had brought his wolf along with him.

He growled but moved cautiously away so I could go inside.

I went into the cabin.

And saw Annie at the entrance to our bedroom door.

Her flannel gown had been shredded by wolf claws, and she lay bloody and unconscious, half propped up against the door frame, her golden hair darkened by splashes of her own blood.

I stumbled toward her, paying no attention to the snarl and growl of the wolf behind me. I reached the door and looked in on the bed and there—

Gillian had not been so lucky. She had been eviscerated.

The wolf had ripped most of her clothes off and had then torn open her throat and stomach.

I struggled toward her, fell next to her on the bed, felt for a pulse I knew my fingers would never feel.

Gillian—

She looked like a fawn that had been attacked by a ravenous predator, and when I put my fingers to her lips . . . she was already getting cold. I must have been out longer than I realized.

I took out by .45 and went over to Annie.

Beneath her bloody flesh I felt a pulse in both neck and wrist, and I snatched her up like an infant and carried her in the crook of my left arm.

I kept my right hand free to use the gun.

The gray lobo still crouched in the front doorway. A growl rumbling up its chest and throat. Waiting for me.

I raised my .45, sighted, began to squeeze the trigger, and—

He sprang.

He was so heavy yet so fast that he knocked my gun away before I could shoot accurately.

Two, three shots went wild in the darkness, the flame red-yellow in the shadows.

And then the wolf was on top of me, Annie having rolled out of my grasp as I was knocked to the floor.

He was all muscle beneath the blood-soaked gray fur, all madness in yellow eyes and blood-dripping mouth.

All I knew was to protect my throat. Once his teeth or claws reached it . . .

I rolled left and right, right and left, trying to keep him off balance until I could roll away from him completely.

By now I was beyond pain, he had ripped and bitten me so often, first across the forehead and then across the chest, and then across the belly, heat and saliva and urgent, pounding body slamming into me again and again.

And finally I started to feel myself give up. No more strength; maybe not even any more determination. Too much pain and weakness. Overwhelming . . .

And then I heard, as if I were unconscious and dreaming again, a terrified but very angry voice saying, "Leave my daddy alone! Leave my daddy alone!" She was awake now, and had found my .45, which she held up with surprising confidence.

And then there were two huge booming shots in the gloom, and the sudden cry of a wolf seriously wounded, and then the cry of a young child as she collapsed again to the floor.

The wolf, shocked, bleeding badly already from the bullets in his chest and stomach—the wolf began to crawl out the front door, crying so sadly even I felt a moment of sorrow for it.

I slowly got to my feet and crawled over to Annie.

I took her to me and held her, and at first I couldn't tell if the crying was hers or mine.

"I'm sorry I brought all this on, Annie," I said. "Your mother was right. I shouldn't have tried to get Reeves."

But she was unconscious in my arms, and my words were wasted.

And then I heard the wet snort of a horse near the front doorway.

I lay Annie down carefully, grabbed my .45, and ran to the doorway.

In the moonlit grass before the door, Reeves knelt next to the wounded wolf, stroking the animal as it crouched, growling, at the sight of me.

To Reeves's left his horse stood waiting for him. And then—

Reeves brought his right hand up—

I barely had time to duck inside before the bullet tore away an inch of wood from the door frame.

Two more shots, quickly. And then silence.

Before I could crawl back to the door frame, I heard Reeves swing up on his horse—saddle leather creaking—and start to ride away.

By the time I reached the door frame and steadied my hand enough to squeeze off some shots, Reeves was fast becoming a silhouette on the hill— fast-retreating horse and rider with the gray lobo running alongside.

I fired twice but only to sate my rage. From the distance, I had no hope of hitting him.

I FORCED MYSELF to ladle up some water for Annie. The mere smell of it still nauseated me.

I got her on the floor in the kitchen, dragged out a blanket, and propped her head up on a pillow I'd taken from the back of the rocking chair.

Every few moments I felt her wrist for a pulse. I had to keep reassuring myself that she was still alive.

I raised her head and gave her water. Her eyes fluttered open but remained so only briefly.

I was just starting to examine her wounds when I heard, on the distant hill, the sound of a rider coming fast.

Reeves. Come back for the fight that was inevitable.

I kissed Annie on the forehead and then grabbed my gun and moved to the doorway, keeping to the shadows so he couldn't see me.

As I leaned against the wall, waiting for him, I heard Annie moan. She needed a doctor, and quickly. After I finished Reeves . . .

The rider stopped short a few hundred feet from the cabin. Eased off his saddle. Ground-tied his beast. Grabbed his carbine from the scabbard. Crouched and started moving toward the cabin. All this in black silhouette against the silver moonlight.

Pain and my sickness were taking their toll on my eyesight again.

Not until the rider was very close to the door, just now getting his carbine ready, did I realize it was not Reeves at all, but Hollister, who must have doubled back and let the rest of the posse continue on. Good lawman that he was, he'd known that I couldn't leave without seeing Gillian and Annie one more time.

Now I knew how I'd get Annie taken care of.

I pressed back against the wall and let Hollister come through the door. Soft jingle of spur, faint creak of holster leather, hard quick rasp of tobacco lungs, scent of cold wind on his dark uniform.

He got four steps in and saw Annie where I'd rested her on the floor and then said, "My God!"

And set his carbine down on the kitchen table.

And rushed to little Annie. And knelt beside her. And lifted her head gently and tenderly upward so that he could see her face better. He no longer cared about his own safety—he knew I could be hiding anywhere in the cabin, but he didn't care. His overwhelming concern was Annie.

It's a funny thing about a man, how he can be crooked the way Hollister was with his prisoners when he was drunk, but be absolutely straight otherwise. Despite the animal he sometimes became in that little locked room of his in the police station, he held in his heart love and pity and duty, and I was watching all three at work now.

He rested Annie's head again and then started to stand up.

I stepped from the shadows, put my .45 on him.

"I want you to take her to the doc. Reeves brought his wolf out here. The wolf has rabies." I paused, wondering if I could actually say it out loud. "And so do I."

"Rabies!" he said. "You sure about that?"

"Yeah, I'm sure. That's why I've been so sick the last few days. One day I went out to Reeves's and the wolf bit me. There's a shot the doc can give her. You need to get her there now and fast."

"But what about you? Won't you need the shot?"

"It's too late for me. All I'm worried about is Annie here."

We stood in the shifting darkness of the big front room, wind like ghosts whistling through the front door, fire guttering in the far grate.

"That posse'll find some way to kill you, Chase, if they ever catch up with you."

"I know."

"Why don't you come in with me?"

"I want to finish my business with Reeves."

"You keep mentioning Reeves. What the hell's he got to do with this?"

So I gave him a quick history.

"I'll be damned," he said.

"I just want you to get Annie to the doc."

"All right." Then he looked around. "Where's your wife?"

"Bedroom. You don't want to see her."

"The wolf?"

"Yeah."

"I'm sorry, Chase."

"Help me with Annie."

We bundled her in blankets and carried her out in the moonlight to Hollister's horse. He got up first and got himself ready, and then I handed her up. He cradled her across his saddle.

"She's a sweet little girl, Chase."

"She sure is."

"I'll get her to the doc right away."

"Wait here."

I went to the pines where I'd been hiding and got the money and brought it back and then tied the cord to Hollister's saddle horn.

"There's the bank money," I said.

"You're pretty hard to figure out, Chase."

"Look who's talking."

He smiled. "I guess you're right."

I reached up and touched Annie's leg and stood there for a long moment with tears in my throat and a silent prayer on my lips.

And then Hollister was riding off, a dark shape against the moon-silver top of the hill, and then just receding hoofbeats in the night.

Part 32

I took Gillian's horse.

In an hour I slid off the animal and started working my way to the poplars on the west side of Reeves's mansion. There would be an armed guard in those poplars.

The fever was getting worse. Every few minutes my vision would black out again and I'd feel a spasm of ice travel down my back and into my buttocks and legs. Then the dehydration would fix my tongue to the roof of my mouth.

The frost gave the land a fuzzy look, as if a silver moss had suddenly grown over everything. The stuff was cold on the palms of my hands, and when the fever got especially bad, I'd stop and put a cooling hand to my cheek.

From the size of him, I knew the man on duty had to be Hanratty. Reeves probably knew I was coming, so he put his best man on the job. Hanratty had likely been sleeping down in the bunkhouse when Reeves had roused him. Hanratty was day guard, not night guard.

He didn't hear me till I was close, too close, and just as he turned, I brought the butt of the carbine down against the side of his head.

He managed to swear and to glare at me, but then he sank in sections to the ground. I had nothing against Hanratty, but I wanted to make sure he didn't wake up and follow me into the house. I kicked him in the side of the head. He'd be out a long time but eventually he'd wake up. He was luckier than Gillian had been.

The first thing I wanted a look at was the wolf's cage.

I crept around the edge of the sweet-smelling jack pines for a good look. The cage was empty, its door flung wide.

The wolf was inside with Reeves.

I slipped through the shadows to the Victorian estate house. In the moonlight the cupolas and captain's walk had an exotic aspect, troubling the plain line of prairie and the jagged barren stretch of mountains beyond, too fancy by half for such a landscape.

I was two steps from the front porch when I saw the man step from the shadows around the doorway.

The tip of his .45 glinted in the moonlight.

I put two bullets into him with my pistol before he could fire even once.

The noise was raucous in the vast prairie silence. The smell of gun smoke filled my nostrils.

Inside, in addition to the wolf, Reeves would have one, maybe two more men. And because of the gunfire, they now knew I was here.

I went around back, dropping to my knees halfway when blackness rushed up and knocked me down. The chills kept getting worse. I threw up, scared halfway through that I was going to choke on my own vomit. Panic . . .

When I was on my feet again, I reached the wide porch that ran the entire length of the rear.

The guard posted there wasn't very good. He was smoking a cigarette and the fire end made an easy target.

I put two shots into his face.

He made a grunting sound and fell facedown onto the porch.

I crouched, moving over to the porch door, got it open and then half crawled up the three steps.

Ahead of me lay the darkened kitchen door. Beyond that waited Reeves . . .

On my way across the porch, I nudged a chair. The scraping noise could be heard clearly in the silence. The men inside would be able to chart every step of my progress.

I eased the kitchen door open. The scent of beef and spices filled the air.

Three more steps up and I stood in the kitchen. It was long and wide, with a fancy new ice box that stood out even in the gloom.

I got four steps across the linoleum floor when the gunny appeared in the archway leading to the dining room and shot me dead-on in the shoulder.

Pain joined my sickness and spun me around entirely. But as I was spinning, I knew enough to put a shot of my own into him. I got him in the stomach.

I beat him with my fists until I knew he was dead. I'd actually done him a favor. Dying gut-shot was an experience nobody should have to go through.

Only as I started walking again did I realize how badly I was bleeding from my shoulder. I almost had to smile. There was so little left of me. The sickness had taken most of me; the gunshot claimed what remained.

I had just enough life left to finish what I needed to finish. . . .

When I got to the bottom of the staircase, my footsteps hollow on the parquet floor, I heard the wolf.

He was crying, and his cry was very much like my own. But that wasn't surprising. We were both dying of the same disease.

I started up the sweeping staircase, grasping my weapon tight in my hand. With the shoulder in such sudden pain, I had to hold my gun very tight.

I reached the landing and stopped, staring up into the gloom above me. No lights shone; not even moonlight lent highlights to the darkness. Reeves had drawn all the heavy curtains.

I started up the remaining six steps . . .

One, two, three steps, each one an agony for a man in my condition, my legs feeling as if they were weighted down by massive invisible boulders . . .

The gunshot flared against the shadows, there was even a certain beauty to it.

I threw myself on the stairs. The bullet ripped into the wainscoting behind me.

Four, five, six rifle shots cracked and roared and echoed down the sweeping stairway.

All I could do was lie there and listen to them, and listen to the wolf crying all the time.

I tried to remember how much I hated the beast for what he'd done to my brother and to my wife and daughter. And yet no matter how much I hated him, I hated Reeves even more, for what he'd trained the wolf to become.

I started crawling on my belly up the stairs. I didn't have much strength left. I needed to spend it while there was still time.

When I reached the top step, still lying flat, I raised my head an inch and stared deep into the gloom.

Reeves was crouched beneath a large gilt-framed painting of himself. A very aristocratic pose, that one.

Next to him crouched the wolf, eyes yellow in the darkness, the cry still in its throat, forlorn as the cry of a wolf lost in a blizzard some prairie midnight.

Reeves saw me peeking up over the stairs and squeezed off several more shots. Apparently he had two or three rifles with him. He wouldn't need to reload for a while.

A silence, then, as I lay on the stairs, my body trembling from the chill, my throat constricted for want of water.

And then a whisper, a word of Indian I did not understand, the same word used that night when the wolf attacked me in my brother's room.

And then I heard the wolf, his paws scratching the floor as he began to pad over to the top of the stairs; a deep, chesty sound coming from him.

I raised my eyes and looked up directly into his as he lowered his blood-spattered head and prepared to lunge at me. He was still bleeding from the bullets Annie had put in him.

I slowly raised myself to my feet, sighting the .45 on his chest.

And he dove at me, all slashing teeth and furious noise.

He knocked me backward down the steps. My gun had fallen from my hands. I could defend my throat only by keeping my arms folded over my face.

Meanwhile we tumbled over and over down the stairs.

When we reached the landing, he renewed his attack, ripping flesh from my forearms so he could weaken me further and reach my throat. His teeth cut so deep that soon he was gnawing on raw bone. . . .

I was in the kind of delirium—fever, pain, fear, rage—a kind of dream state in which I functioned automatically.

Perhaps this was hell . . . a battle with the beast lasting for all eternity.

And then I remembered the knife I'd taken from our cottage. The bone-handled bowie . . .

Reaching it would mean that I would have to take one of my arms from my face . . . but there was little choice.

I started rolling across the landing, trying to confuse the wolf, trying to keep him from my throat. He kept crying and biting and hurling himself at me—

And as I rolled, I found the bone handle of the knife and yanked the blade free, and as I rolled over once again and saw the beast ready to spring—

I held the blade of the bowie knife up so that when he lunged—

He came in with his head down, teeth bared, spittle and blood flying from his mouth—came in so that he impaled himself on the blade.

It went straight and deep into his chest, and for a moment in his fury he did not allow himself to feel the wound—

He just kept trying to get at my throat, to rend and rip it open so that I would look like poor Gillian there on the bed.

But then the pain of the knife I kept pushing deeper and deeper into his chest finally registered—

And he stood on top of me, hot splashing blood beginning to flow from his wound, and he began to cry so loud and so sad in the gloom that I had no choice but to pity him. He cried his wolf song of cold icy waters and long lonely hunts; of seeing brothers and sisters die in bitter winter; of finding a moonlit pond in a midnight forest and sleeping peacefully there; of finding a mate strong enough to follow him into the mountains and bear the offspring who would make them both so proud—sadness and grief and joy and pride, all that and much more in wolf song as the beast stood upon me and I in my pain and sickness and weakness and curious final strength watched as Reeves descended the stairs, wanting to finish me off since his trained wolf could no longer do the job himself.

But when he was halfway down the stairs, Reeves in his fancy ruffled shirt and expensive dark suit, his rifle aimed directly at my heart—when he was about to kill me, the wolf turned abruptly and sprang on him and proceeded to tear and rend in a frenzy so loud and vicious I wanted to cover my eyes.

All I could hear was Reeves screaming and screaming and screaming there in the moonlight of the stair landing. . . .

And when the wolf was finished, he came back and lay next to me, and took up his crying once more.

IN SOME WAY we are brothers, this wolf and I, lying here dying as the cold dark winds of November whip through this now-useless mansion. . . .

His cry is even louder now, and I wish I could comfort him, but there is no comfort for either of . . .

. . . not for a few minutes yes . . .

. . . not until the darkness.

IT IS A sunny afternoon and Gillian and Annie are coming toward me on the bicycle, and Annie on the handlebars, golden hair glowing.

And then it is dark and I am looking down at my dead brother in the bed that night and I am wanting to cry.

And then there is a barn dance and Gillian looks so beautiful in the autumn night and—

And then my mother is there, plain prairie woman, plain prairie wisdom evident in her kind gaze, and she puts out her hand so I will not be afraid in these last moments.

Dreams, phantasms, memory . . . all memory dying with me now . . .

Gillian—

Annie—

And finally the darkness
the wolf and I
and the   darkness

Dwight V. Swain was another pulp writer who eventually made the transition to paperback Westerns. He was also a teacher and a fine student of writing, turning his observations into three first-rate books.

Gamblin' Man

Dwight V. Swain

Stiff-lipped and grim, Mr. Devereaux fingered the double eagle and wondered bleakly if all hulking, loudmouthed men were scoundrels; or was it merely that Fate chose only uncommon blackguards to send his way? Even worse, why did he not discover their connivings before they'd stripped him down to twenty dollars? He had one double eagle left. His last.

Across the table the man called Alonzo Park scooped up the cards, squared the deck, and riffled it in an expert shuffle. In the process he also managed an incredibly deft bit of palming that ended with six cards missing, just as in previous games.

Almost without thinking, Mr. Devereaux left off fingering the gold piece and instead caressed his sleeve-rigged double derringer.

This table around which they played was jammed in a corner at one end of the El Dorado's bar. It was out of the way, yet close to the source of supply of the red-eye of which Park, who owned the place, seemed so fond. It was a good twenty feet to the door, twenty feet past cold-eyed, gun-slung loungers who wandered about the saloon.

Park's voice cut in, a reverberant, bull-throated bellow. The man's meaty features glistened red as his own raw forty-rod whiskey.

"Lafe! Drinks all around!"

In silent, studied apathy, Mr. Devereaux allowed the cross-eyed barkeep to refill his glass and continued his appraisal.

A sheepherder sat to his left, no gun showing. Beyond him, a rat-visaged nondescript from the livery stable, toting a rusted .45. Then Park, ostensibly unarmed; probably he favored a hideout gun. And finally, to Mr. Devereaux's right, completing the circuit, a brawny, freckle-faced young fellow, Charlie Adams, who swayed drunkenly in his chair and held solemn, incongruous converse with a long-skirted, china-headed doll over a foot tall which he kept propped on the table before him.

Mr. Devereaux's hand turned out a mediocre pair, augmented by another—equally mediocre—on the draw.

Again he weighed that last remaining gold piece and studied Park. Finally he shoved the double eagle forward.

The sheepherder and the nondescript threw in their cards. Charlie Adams hesitated, ogling Mr. Devereaux owlishly from behind the doll, then followed suit. For a moment Park, too, hung back. But only for a moment.

"Raise you, Devereaux! I'll call your bluff!"

Mr. Devereaux could feel his own blood quicken, the hackles rise along his neck. Imperceptibly, he hunched his left shoulder forward, just enough for the black frock coat to clear his armpit-holstered Colt. The sleeve-rigged derringer held an old friend's reassurance.

"And raise you back, Park," he said softly. He reached into the pot, removed his double eagle as if to replace it with something larger.

A harsh, raw note crept into Alonzo Park's bull voice. He thrust his chin belligerently forward. "Put in your money, Devereaux. Put up or shut up."

Mr. Devereaux allowed himself the luxury of a thin, wry smile. He breathed deep—and savored the fact that this very breath might be his last. He pushed the thought back down and brought out the Colt in one swift, sure gesture.

He let his voice ring, then.

"Misdeal, Park. I'm betting my gun against your stack that there are less than fifty-two cards on this table—and that we'll find the others in a hold-out on your side!"

Silence. Echoing eternities of silence, spreading out across the room. The sheepherder and the nondescript sat stiff and shriveled. Adams stared stupidly, jaw hanging, the big doll clasped to his chest.

Gun poised, feet flat against the floor, Mr. Devereaux waited. He watched the muscles in Park's bull neck knot, the hairy hands contract. "God help you, you dirty son!" Park rasped thickly. "I'll have your hide for this!"

"No doubt," Mr. Devereaux agreed. He gestured with his Colt to the livery groom. "Look under the table edge for a holdout."

The man flicked one nervous glance at the gun, then bent to obey. He came up with two aces and three assorted spades.

Mr. Devereaux let his thin smile broaden. "I win." He rose, starting to reach for Alonzo Park's stack. And he realized, even in that moment, the magnitude of his error.

That cross-eyed bartender whipped up a sawed-off shotgun with a bore that loomed big as twin water buckets. It seemed to Mr. Devereaux in that moment he could hear the faint, sweet song of angel voices.

A gun's roar cut them short.

Sheer reflex sent Mr. Devereaux floorward, wrapped in vast disbelief at finding himself alive. He glimpsed the scattergun, flying off across the room. He stared at the cross-eyed bartender, while that worthy swore and clutched at a bleeding hand.

Big Adams, drunk no longer, came to his feet. He still gripped the doll, but now the china head was gone. The muzzle of a .45 protruded from its shredded, smoldering neck. Left-handed, he reached a nickeled star from his pocket and pinned it on. His freckled, good-natured face had gone suddenly cold, his voice hard and level.

"You're under arrest, Park. The town council held a private confab last night. They decided Crooked Lance needed a marshal an' gave me the job. The first chore on the list was to clean up El Dorado."

THE DAY DRAGGED drowsily, even for Crooked Lance town. September's shimmering, brazen sun hung at two o'clock, the straggled clumps of cholla and Spanish bayonet a-ripple in its heat. The choked, close scent of sun on stone, and dust and dirt and baking 'dobe, rose faint yet all-persuasive. Even the thrumming flies droned lethargy, and the tail of breeze from distant, cloud-capped mountains alone kept the sparse shade tolerable.

Peace came to Mr. Devereaux. He loved such sleepy days as this, days for dreams and smiles and reveries. Relaxed and tranquil, he contemplated the padlocked El Dorado from his chair on the hotel porch. He wondered, in turn, how Alonzo Park liked his cell in the feedstore that served Crooked Lance as a makeshift jail.

The man was a fool, Mr. Devereaux decided soberly. Else why would he stay here, insisting on trial, instead of thankfully accepting Adams's offer to let him ride out of town unfettered, on his own agreement never to return? What possible defense could he offer? Did he actually believe he could salvage his fortunes?

The thought brought Mr. Devereaux's own financial state to mind. Adams was holding last night's poker pots as evidence till after the trial this afternoon. It left Mr. Devereaux with only the one twenty-dollar gold piece. He contemplated the coin wryly. He flipped it. His last double eagle, still.

The scuff of feet and the acrid breath of rising dust cut short his reveries. He looked around to see Crooked Lance's new marshal and a chubby, fresh-scrubbed cherub in pigtails and starched gingham round the corner hand in hand, the cherub wobbling ludicrously as she vainly tried to make her short legs match the lawman's long strides.

Adams nodded greetings, dropped into a chair beside Mr. Devereaux on the porch. He grinned boyishly.

"This here's my gal Alice, Devereaux. You better be nice to her, too. That was her doll I was totin' last night."

The cherub giggled and hid her face in her father's lap.

"You said you'd get me another dolly, Daddy. You promised." A tremor of excitement ran through her and she raised her head, eyes shining. "I know just the kind I want, Daddy. Missus Lauck's got one in her window. Blue eyes that close, and real gold hair."

Adams grinned again. He dandled her, gleeful and squealing, on one knee.

"Don't push me too fast, honey. Wait'll I draw at least one pay." Then, to Mr. Devereaux: "Guess we better mosey on over to the schoolhouse for court. Trial's set for two-thirty. Soon's it's over I can give you back your money."

Mr. Devereaux nodded, rose. Flat-crowned Stetson in hand, he stared off across the desert miles. An indefinable weariness washed over him, as if some queer, invisible shadow had crept across the turquoise sky. He caught himself wondering how it would feel to bounce a pigtailed daughter on one's knee . . .

It being Crooked Lance's first trial, the town council had voted in the mayor as judge. He sat behind the teacher's desk in the little adobe schoolhouse now, a thin, stooped, balding man, gavel in hand, gnawing his lips. He served as a barber, ordinarily, and these new responsibilities rode heavily upon him.

Mr. Devereaux chuckled benignly and let his gaze travel on. The little room was a babble of voices, the bare wood benches already filled. Whole families were out: fathers, mothers, children. Others, too—and over these he did not chuckle. Silent, too-casual men with guns lounging along the back wall. Last night they'd been lounging the same way at the El Dorado.

Adams brought in the prisoner.

Park had recovered his poise. Jaw outthrust, red face bright with what might pass for righteous indignation, he strode aggressively to his place. When, for the fraction of a second, his gaze met Mr. Devereaux's, his eyes were venomous, mocking, strangely mirthful.

Mr. Devereaux frowned despite himself. Almost without thinking, he touched his derringer's butt.

His Honor rapped for order, peered hesitantly down at the prisoner. "You want someone to help you, Park? You got a right, you know."

Park glowered. "I don't need help for what I've got to say."

Adams took the stand, told how he'd sat in on the game at Park's own table, feigning drunkenness. He'd picked that particular game, he explained, because he wanted to find out whether the El Dorado's owner, personally, was doing the cheating the council had ordered him to investigate. Further, he'd figured that table as most likely for action. Mr. Devereaux being a man who "looked like he knew his way around a deck of cards without no Injun guide, an' hard to buffalo too!"

Park's only comment was a contempt-laden snort.

As before, Mr. Devereaux frowned. Instinctively, he shrugged the black frock coat smooth about his shoulders. The Colt's weight stood out sharp in his consciousness. Then the judge was calling him forward to take the stand.

In an instant Alonzo Park was on his feet. "Your Honor!" he bellowed.

His Honor started, cringed. Finally he made a feeble pass at pounding with his gavel. "Now, Park—"

"Don't 'Now Park' me!" the prisoner roared, his face the hue of a too-ripe plum. "Now's the time I speak my piece." He glowered and his eyes swept the room. Yet somehow, to Mr. Devereaux, there seemed to be a certain theatrical note about it all, as if the man were carefully building up a part.

Park went on. "You've called me a crooked tinhorn on the say of that jackass Charlie Adams, and I've kept quiet. But I'm damned if I'll let you ring in this gun-wolf, too!"

The judge chewed his lips, looked uneasily from Park to Adams to Mr. Devereaux and back again. "What you got agin' him, Lon?" he queried uneasily.

Mr. Devereaux saw the triumph in Park's eyes, then—the murderous glee the front of indignation veiled. He stared in dismay as the man whipped out a flimsy, too-familiar pamphlet.

"This is the 'wanted' list of the Adjutant General of Texas!" Park bellowed. "You've brought me up for crooked gambling, but your chief witness is a card shark and a killer, on the dodge from a murderous charge!"

Mr. Devereaux could feel the tension leap within the room. His own breath came too fast. As from afar he heard the El Dorado's owner shout on, work himself into a frenzy.

"Your haywire marshal gave me a chance to run out if I wanted to, but I stayed. I guess that shows whether I'm guilty or not! This tinhorn planted that holdout under the table. He figured to chase me out of town so he could take over the El Dorado—"

Somewhere at the back of the room a man yelled, "Park's right! Turn him loose! That Devereaux's the one should be in jail!"

The schoolroom exploded to a screaming madhouse. A tribute, Mr. Devereaux thought dourly as he maneuvered himself against the nearest wall, to Alonzo Park and his carefully stationed loungers.

The judge brought down his gavel with a bang. It was the first time since the beginning of the trial that he had showed such force and vigor.

"Case dismissed!"

"What about Devereaux?" somebody yelled.

As if in answer, Charlie Adams shoved forward, gun out. His good-natured face had gone worried and grim.

"I got no choice, Devereaux. You're under arrest!"

A CLOUD HAD swept down during that stormy schoolhouse session, Mr. Devereaux discovered. Already it impinged on the sun's bright sphere, a scudding wall of night stretched off to the distant mountains. The wind had quickened, too; freshened. Now it came whipping through Crooked Lance in gusts and buffets, sucking up little geysers of sand that swirled and rustled like dry leaves.

"Let's go, Devereaux," Adams said. His voice was flat.

Carefully, Mr. Devereaux adjusted his flat-crowned Stetson, shrugged smooth the black frock coat. It was a useless gesture, really, now that the heavy Colt was gone. Its absence gave him a queer, off-balance feeling. The sleeve-rigged derringer alone remained to comfort. That, and the gold piece. One double eagle. He laughed without mirth and flipped it in a glittering arc. Together, Devereaux and Adams moved out into the street.

The storm came faster now, blotting out light, racing hungrily on across the desert. The wind increased with it, drove tiny stones into Mr. Devereaux's face. Dust choked him. Sand gritted between his teeth.

Voiceless, he strode on. The thing was inevitable, he supposed, a peril that went with notoriety. Periodically he was bound to be recognized. The only marvel was that any lobo vindictive as Park had been content to leave an enemy to the law.

They passed the shuttered, padlocked El Dorado. The Silver Lady, too. Grant's Drygoods. Lettie Lauck's millinery.

Lettie Lauck. Mr. Devereaux pondered the name, remembered Alice and her doll. Alice, the fresh-scrubbed cherub in her pigtails and starched gingham. He wondered, a bit wistful, if he would ever see her again.

"Turn here," Adams said.

The feedstore that served as jail had an inner storage room—zinc-lined against rats—for a cell. The marshal prodded Mr. Devereaux toward it.

Mr. Devereaux sighed. It was coming now. It had to come. He touched the derringer's butt.

Marshal Adams swung open the storeroom's heavy door. "In there."

Mr. Devereaux studied him, caressed the derringer. "You believe it, then, Charlie?" He made his voice very gentle.

"Believe what?

"The things Alonzo Park said."

Adams laughed. It had a harsh, unhappy sound. "What does it matter? Your name was in that book. You're on the owlhoot."

"A packed jury might call things murder that you wouldn't, Charlie."

He could see the sweat come to Adam's broad forehead. Then the jaw tightened.

"Sorry, Devereaux. That's twixt you an' the Adjutant Gen'ral of Texas. Folks here just hired me to hold up the law, not judge it."

Again Mr. Devereaux sighed. Nodded. The loose-holstered years went into his draw. "I'm sorry, too, Marshal. I can't take that chance." Cat-footed, he backed towards the open door.

Behind him a gun roared.

Mr. Devereaux leaped sidewise—swiveling; firing. He glimpsed only a blur of motion as the gunman jumped away. That, and Adams pitching to the floor.

THE MINUTES THAT followed never came quite clear to Mr. Devereaux. He acted by instinct, rather than logic, reloading the derringer as he ran. No need to ask himelf what would happen if Crooked Lance's shouting citizenry should find him here by the fallen marshal, gun in hand.

But the townsmen were out already, a dozen or more of them, headed across the street towards him at a dead run even as he broke cover. Mr. Devereaux turned hastily, to the tune of oaths and bullets. He ducked between two buildings, to come out seconds later in an alley.

The jail-and-feedstore combination was of frame construction set on low, stone corner posts close to the ground. Mr. Devereaux dropped, rolled into the shallow space beneath the building.

There followed an eternity of dust and rocks and cobwebs, lasting well over an hour. When his pursuers finally gave up and silence once more reigned, he wriggled forth and stumbled stiffly to his feet.

The storm had brought with it an early dusk. Wind whipped the black frock coat tight about his legs as he tried to dust away the worst of the debris from beneath the building. Aching, irritable—and infinitely cautious—he gave it up, headed for the livery barn on down the alley.

The nondescript groom sprawled asleep in the haymow. Ever wary, Mr. Devereaux prodded him awake.

Grumbling, bleary-eyed, the man rose, peered at Mr. Devereaux through the stable's gloom. His lantern jaw dropped. "You!"

Mr. Devereaux favored him with one curt nod, brought up the derringer. "At your service. And now, if you'll saddle my black stallion . . ."

The nondescript swayed, still staring. His words came out a half-coherent mumble. "I thought you was over there at Park's."

"Park's?"

"Sure. The El Dorado. One o' Park's boys got scared about you bein' holed up there. He come round huntin' Adams."

Mr. Devereaux compressed his lips to a thin, straight line.

"Adams is dead."

"Dead?" The groom eyed him queerly. "Who says he's dead? He come in here lookin' for you not half a hour ago. Doc Brand patched up that hole in his shoulder."

"He . . . wasn't killed?"

"Uh-uh. Not even crippled bad."

One o' Park's boys come huntin' . . .

Mr. Devereaux stood very still. Discovered, with a strange abstraction, that he was hanging on the beats of his own heart. All of a sudden his mouth grew dry.

The nondescript was speaking again now, eyeing the derringer as he rubbed his lantern jaw. "You carry that thing in a sleeve-rig, don't you? Adams was tellin' 'bout it while Doc Brand fixed him up."

"Indeed?" Mr. Devereaux stiffened. "In that case, perhaps you'll favor me with the loan of your Colt." He stepped close, reached the rusting gun from its holster.

"Yeah, sure." The nondescript shifted uneasily, licked his lips. "I'll get your horse up, too."

As in a dream, Mr. Devereaux followed, patted the nickering stallion's sleek jet neck. "This is a time for travel, boy," he heard himself say. "We'll give this groom our double eagle for his gun and be on our way."

"One o' Park's boys come huntin' . . ."

One of Park's men had come hunting, to tell an honest marshal where a wanted man was hiding. Only it wasn't true. He, the hunted, hadn't been there.

In his mind's eye he pictured Alonzo Park with his bull neck and meaty, flushed face. Yes, Park would use a fugitive's name to bait a trap for an honest marshal.

"Did Park's man find Adams?" he asked, and in spite of all his efforts he could not make it sound quite casual.

"Uh-uh. He'd already left."

For a long, wordless moment Mr. Devereaux stood there. Slowly drew in a deep, full breath. His lips felt stiff, unreal.

The groom shuffled his feet. "If you'll just lemme get there . . ."

Ever so faintly, Mr. Devereaux smiled. Again he patted the stallion's neck. He replaced the gold piece in his pocket.

"That won't be necessary now. I've had a change of plans." And then, after a second: "If the marshal asks for me again, you can tell him I'm at the El Dorado."

ALONZO PARK SPRAWLED in the self-same chair he'd occupied the night before, back to the bar, red-eye whiskey at his elbow.

"You scared me, Devereaux. I was beginning to be afraid you wouldn't come."

Mr. Devereaux raised his brows, allowed his curiosity to show. "You expected me, then?"

"Expected you? Of course I expected you." Park laughed. "You've got a rep for being a sentimental fool, Devereaux. They tell stories about it all the way to Montana. Last night Adams backed your play, so I knew you'd come when you heard he'd bought himself some trouble."

"And so?"

"So now we wait till Adams shows up to pinch you. Both of you'll turn up dead. Then I'll tell it that you forced me to hide you out at gunpoint. You killed Adams, and I killed you. The town will give me a vote of thanks." Again he leered. "Nice, eh?"

Wordless, Mr. Devereaux shrugged. It had seemed such a good idea this check on Park. Interception by the cross-eyed, shotgun-toting barkeep was another story. They'd nailed him cold, overlooked nothing save the derringer in their search. They'd have found it, too, except that he'd transferred it to a new hideout within his flat-crowned Stetson after the stable groom's comment on the sleeve-rig.

So, now he stood here before Alonzo Park in the echoing, dim-lit El Dorado. The scattergunner still covered him from behind the bar—grim incongruous against the background of mirrors and pyramided bottles. Two other Park gunmen crouched by the street-front windows at the far end of the room, eyes glued to cracks in the shutters.

One of the men by the windows sang out, low, tense. "It's Adams! Here he comes!"

Park grinned wolfishly. "Well, Devereaux?"

A chill rippled through Mr. Devereaux in spite of his control. He had to fight to keep his tremor from his face. "I bow to superior talent, sir!" He took off the Stetson, mopped his brow. His sweating fingers closed round the derringer's butt. His knuckles showed white.

"He'll be here in ten seconds, Lon!" the gunman said.

Mr. Devereaux turned a trifle, stared straight into the bartender's crossed eyes. The shotgun's barrels loomed like a cannon. Desperately, he tried to give his voice the right inflection.

"These maneuverings raise a thirst. Make mine Mill's Bluegrass please."

For the fraction of a second the bartender's gaze wavered toward the bottles stacked behind him.

Mr. Devereaux brought the derringer up past the Stetson's brim, fired once. A black spot the size of a dime appeared just above the man's left cheekbone.

Chill, rock-steady now, Mr. Devereaux swiveled.

Park snarled, clawed a pistol from beneath his coat.

Mr. Devereaux fired the other barrel. He watched two of Park's bared teeth disappear, the man himself totter over backwards.

Behind him, the street end of the room reverberated gunfire. He swung. Park's gunmen were already down, Charlie Adams coming forward stiff-legged, a smoking .45 in his hand. The marshal bent, twisted the pistol away from the dead Park.

"A .31. That's what Doc Brand said shot me," Adams said.

Other men were crowding through the door now, bug-eyed, excited men with loud voices. Mr. Devereaux ignored them, held his own tone steady. He even managed to inject a faint, ironic note. "You were looking for me, Marshal?"

The other's freckled face froze. "I still am. You're wanted back in Texas."

"And duty's duty?" Mr. Devereaux sighed. All of a sudden he felt very old, very weary. "So be it, Marshal. A man must play it as he sees it." Then: "Dry work, Marshal. If you don't mind, I'll have a drink."

Very carefully, he rounded the end of the bar, stared down at the fallen, cross-eyed barkeep.

"Dead." He bent, as if to move the man away. Then, instead, he snatched up the scattergun and straightened fast. "Buckshot means burying, gentlemen. Do I have any takers?"

No one moved. Then Adams let out his breath, scowled.

"Damn you, Devereaux!"

Somehow, to Mr. Devereaux, it sounded like a benediction.

Wordless, he backed through the El Dorado's open doorway, whipped loose the reins of a big, snake-eyed bay at the rail, and led the beast out of view beside the building. He fired the scattergun into the air as he booted the bay across the rump, hard.

The horse let out a snort second cousin to a Comanche war whoop and took off with a thunder of hooves. Mr. Devereaux ducked back into the shadow and stood stock-still.

The rush of feet in the El Dorado came like an echo to the big bay's thunder. Shouting, cursing, the marshal and his men boiled out the door, forked saddles and raced off in wild pursuit.

Mr. Devereaux waited till they were out of sight. He'd pick up the black stallion at the livery barn according to plan and head off south. There'd be plenty of time. Yes, plenty of time . . .

Again Lettie Lauck's shop caught his eye. It was lighted. We could see a tall young woman moving about inside.

The doll was still there, a big one, even bigger than the one Charlie Adams had carried. The eyes were wide and blue, the hair shimmering gold, the gown of silk. It was a beautiful doll.

The price tag was there, too: twenty dollars.

Almost without thinking, Mr. Devereaux reached into his pocket, fingered the double eagle. His last double eagle, still.

With a start, it came to him that the sky had cleared. The stars were out and the wind no longer blew. For an instant he almost thought he could hear Charlie Adams's shouts as he spurred his riders on. He smiled . . .

Still smiling, he stepped inside the shop. He doffed the flat-crowned Stetson politely as the tall young woman came forward.

"The doll in the window, please," said Mr. Devereaux.

Rodeo performer, rancher, miner, Max Evans, who was born in 1925, was able to experience life as it was frequently lived in the Old West . . . and to write about it. Evans is one of the genre's superstars, a one hundred percent original talent. Nobody is foolish enough to try to imitate him. He is his own man in every respect. Evans works in the most difficult yet most rewarding of all literary forms, the tragicomedy. One of Western fiction's true stylists, he's as good at making you cry as he is at making you laugh. He is also, in his own sly way, a fine reporter, setting down with no false romance the West as it really was, and really is. His novels, which include *The Rounders*, *The Hi-Lo Country*, and *The Mountain* bark, roll over, wag their tails, and leave you begging for more.

Candles in the Bottom of the Pool

Max Evans

Joshua Stone III moved along the cool adobe corridor listening to the massive walls. They were over three feet thick, the mud and straw solidified hard as granite. He appeared the same.

The sounds came to him faintly at first, then stronger. He leaned against the smooth dirt plaster and heard the clanking of armor, the twanging of bows, the screams of falling men and horses. His chest rose as his lungs pumped the excited blood. His powerful hands were grabbing their own flesh at his sides. It was real. Then the struggles of the olive conquerors and the brown vanquished faded away like a weak wind.

He opened his eyes, relaxing slightly, and stepped back, staring intently at the wall. Where was she? Would she still come to him smiling, waiting, wanting? Maybe. There was silence now. Even the singing of the desert birds outside could not penetrate the mighty walls.

Then he heard the other song. The words were unintelligible, ancient, from forever back, back, back, but he felt and understood their meaning. She appeared from the unfathomable reaches of the wall, undulating like a black wisp ripped from a tornado cloud. She was whole now. Her black lace dress clung to her body, emphasizing the delicious smoothness of her face and hands. The comb of Spanish silver glistened like a halo in her hair. His blue eyes stared at her dark ones across the centuries. They knew. She smiled with much warmth, and more. One hand beckoned for him to come. He smiled back, whispering, "Soon. Very soon."

"YES, YES, YES," she said, and the words vibrated about, over, through, under, and around everything. He stood, still staring, but there was only the dry mud now.

He turned, as yet entranced, then shook it off and entered through the heavily timbered archway into the main room. The light shafted in from the patio window, illuminating the big room not unlike a cathedral. In a way it was. *Santos* and *bultos* were all over. The darkly stained furniture was from another time, hand hewn and permanent like the house itself.

He absorbed the room for a moment, his eyes caressing the old Indian pots spotted about, the rich color of the paintings from Spain, the cochineal rugs dyed from kermes bugs. Yes, the house was old; older than America. He truly loved its feeling of history, glory, and power.

Then his gaze stopped on the only discord in the room. It was a wildly colored, exaggerated painting of himself. He didn't like the idea of his portrait hanging there. He didn't need that. He allowed it only because his niece, Aleta, had done it. He was fond of her.

Juanita, the aged servant, entered with a tray. It held guacamole salad, tostados, and the inevitable Bloody Marys. He asked her in perfect Spanish where his wife, Carole, was.

She answered in English, "On the patio, señor. I have your drinks." She moved out ahead of him, bony, stiff, bent, but with an almost girlish quickness about her. She'd been with them for decades. They'd expected her demise for years, then given up.

Carole lounged in the desert sun, dozing the liquor away. He couldn't remember when she started drinking so heavily. He had to admit that she had a tough constitution—almost as much as his own. It was usually around midnight before alcohol dulled her to retire. She removed the oversized sunglasses and sat up as Juanita placed the tray on a small table by her. The wrinkles showed around the eyes, but her figure was still as good as ever. She rubbed at the lotion on her golden legs and then reached for her drink. At her movement, he had a fleeting desire to take her to bed. Was that what had brought them together? Was that what had held them until it was too late? Maybe. She pushed the burnt blonde hair back and placed the edge of the glass against her glistening lips. He thought the red drink was going down her throat like weak blood to give her strength for the day. He gazed out across the green mass of trees, grass, and bushes in the formal garden beyond the patio. He heard the little brook that coursed through it, giving life to the oasis just as the Bloody Marys did his wife.

It was late morning, and already the clouds puffed up beyond the parched mountains, promising much, seldom giving. It was as if the desert of cacti, lizards, scorpions, and coyotes between the mountains and the *hacienda* was too forbidding to pass over. It took many clouds to give the necessary courage to one another. It rarely happened.

He picked up his drink, hypnotized by the rising heat waves of the harsh land.

"I've decided," he said.

"You've decided what?"

"It's time we held the gathering."

She took another sip, set it down, and reached for a cigarette. "You've been talking about that for three years, Joshua."

"I know, but I've made up my mind."

"When?"

"Now."

"Now? Oh God, it'll take days to prepare." She took another swallow of the red drink. "I'm just not up to it. Besides, Lana and Joseph are in Bermuda. Sheila and Ralph are in Honolulu."

"They'll come."

"You can't just order people away from their vacations." She took another swallow, pulled the bra of her bikini up, walked over and sat down on the edge of the pool, and dangled her feet in it. Resentment showed in her back. He still felt a little love for her, which surprised him. There was no question that his money and power had been part of her attraction to him. But at first, it had been good. They'd gone just about everywhere in the world together. The fun, the laughs, the adventure had been there even though some part of his business empire was always intruding. What had happened? Hell, why didn't he admit it? Why didn't she? It had worn out. It was that simple. Just plain worn out from the heaviness of the burdens of empire like an old draft horse or a tired underground coal miner.

She splashed the water over her body, knowing from his silence there was no use. "Well, we might as well get on with it. When do you call?"

He finished the drink, stood up, and moved towards the house, saying, "As I said, now."

JOSHUA ENTERED THE study. His secretary for the past ten years looked up, sensing something in his determined movement.

"All right, Charlotte."

She picked up the pad without questioning. He paced across the Navajo rugs, giving her a long list of names. Occasionally he'd run his hands down a row of books, playing them like an accordion. He really didn't like organization, but when he decided, he could be almost magical at it. There was no hesitation, no lost thought or confusion. He was putting together the "gathering" just as he'd expanded the small fortune his father had left him. It kept growing, moving.

When he finished dictating the names, he said, "We'll have food indigenous to the Southwest. Tons of it. I want for entertainment the Russian dancer from Los Angeles, Alfredo and his guitar from Juárez, the belly dancer what's-her-name from San Francisco, the mariachis from Mexico City, and the brass group from Denver."

His whole huge body was vibrating now. A force exuded from Joshua—the same force that had swayed decisions on many oil field deals, land developments, cattle domains, and, on occasion, even the stock market—but never had Charlotte seen him as he was now. There was something more, something she could not explain. Then he was done. He pushed at his slightly graying mass of hair and walked around the hand-carved desk to her. He pulled her head over to him and held it a moment against his side. They had once been lovers, but when she came to work for him that was over. There was still a tenderness between them. She was one of those women who just missed being beautiful all the way around, but she had a sensual appeal and a soft strength that was so much more. She had his respect, too, and that was very hard for him to give.

He broke the mood with, "Call Aleta and Rob first."

She took the book of numbers and swiftly dialed, asking, "Are you sure they're in El Paso?"

"Yes. Aleta's painting. She's getting ready for her show in Dallas." He took the phone. "Rob, is Aleta there?"

In El Paso, Rob gave an affirmative answer and put his hand over the phone, "Your Uncle *God* is on the horn."

Aleta wiped the paint from her hands and reached for the receiver. "Don't be so sarcastic, darling; he might leave you out of his will."

The vibrations were instantaneous down the wire between the man and the girl. She would be delighted to come.

When the conversation was over and Aleta informed her husband, he said, "The old bastard! He's a dictator. I'd just love to kill him!"

He finished with Lana and Joseph Helstrom in the Bahamas with, "No kids. Do you understand? This is not for children."

The husband turned to his wife, saying, "We're ordered to attend a gathering at Aqua Dulce."

"A gathering?"

"A party. You know how he is about labeling things."

"Oh Christ, two days on vacation and he orders us to a party."

"I could happily murder the son of a bitch and laugh for years," Joseph said, throwing a beach towel across the room against a bamboo curtain.

Finally, Joshua was finished. Charlotte got up and mixed them a scotch on the rocks from the concealed bar behind the desk. They raised their glasses, and both said at the same time, "To the gathering." They laughed together as they worked together.

Suddenly Charlotte set her glass down and, not having heard the phone conversations, stated almost omnipotently, "Half of them would delight in doing away with you."

Joshua nodded, smiling lightly. "You're wrong, love, a good two-thirds would gladly blow me apart, and all but a few of the others would wish them well."

"Touché."

"They do have a tendency to forget how they arrived at their present positions. However, that's not what concerns me. All are free to leave whenever they wish, but most don't have the guts. They like cinches but never acknowledge that on this earth no such thing exists. Even the sun is slowly burning itself to death."

"Another drink?"

"Of course. This is a moment for great celebration."

She poured the drinks efficiently, enjoying this time with him. Sensing something very special happening. Thrilled to share with him again.

They touched glasses across the desk, and he said, almost jubilantly, "To the Gods, goddamn them!"

CAROLE INSTRUCTED JUANITA in the cleaning and preparing of the house. She put old Martin the head caretaker and yard man, and his two younger sons, to trimming the garden. This last was unnecessary because old Martin loved the leisure and independence of his job. He kept everything in shape anyway. It did, however, serve its purpose. Carole felt like she was doing *something*. In fact, an excitement she hadn't felt for some time came upon her. She remembered the first really important entertaining she'd done for Joshua after their marriage. He was on a crucial Middle East oil deal.

It was in their New York townhouse in the days they were commuting around the world to various homes and apartments. She had really pulled a coup. Carole had worked closely with the sheik's male secretary and found what to her were some surprising facts. At first she'd intended to have food catered native to the guests' own country and utilize local belly dancers of the same origin. But after much consultation she served hamburgers and had three glowing, local-born blondes as dancing girls. The sheiks raved over the Yankee food they'd heard so much about and were obviously taken with the yellow-topped fair-skinned dancing girls. They were also highly captivated by Carole herself. The whole thing had been a rousing success. Joshua got his oil concessions, and she had felt an enormous sense of accomplishment.

Today, as she moved about the vast *hacienda*, she felt some of that old energy returning. There was something different though. Her excitement was mounting, but it was more like one must feel stalking a man-eating tiger and knowing that at the next parting of the bushes they would look into each other's eyes.

Joshua checked out the wine cellar. He loved the silence and the dank smell. He touched some of the ancient casks as he had the history books in the study. He was drawn to old things now, remembering, recalling, conjuring up the history of his land . . . the great Southwest. He lingered long after he knew the supply of fine wines was more than sufficient. He moved the lantern back and forth, watching the shadows hide from the moving light. Carole had long wanted him to have electricity installed down here, but he'd refused. Some things need to remain as they are, he felt. Many of the old ways were better. Many worse. He'd wondered uncounted times why men who could build computers and fly to distant planets were too blind, or stupid, to select the best of the old and the best of the new and weld them together. He knew that at least the moderate happiness of mankind was that simple. An idiot could see it if he opened up and looked. It would not happen during Joshua's brief encounter with this planet. He knew it and was disgusted by it.

He set the lantern on a shelf and stood gazing at the wall ending the cellar. It was awhile before the visions would begin coming to him. He didn't mind. Time was both nothing and everything. Then he heard the hooves of many horses walking methodically forward. It was like the beat of countless drumsticks against the earth. A rhythm, a pattern, a definite purpose in the sound. Closer. Louder. The song came as a sigh at first, then a whisper; finally it was clear and hauntingly lovely. He felt thousands of years old, perhaps millions, perhaps ageless. Colors in circular and elongated patterns danced about in the wall. Slowly they took form as if just being born. Swiftly now, they melded into shape, and he saw Cortés majestically leading his men and horses in clothing of iron. From the left came Montezuma and his followers in dazzling costumes so wildly colored they appeared to be walking rainbows. They knelt and prostrated themselves to the gods with four legs. Beauty had bent to force.

Joshua was witnessing the beginning of the Americas. The vision dissolved like a panoramic movie, and the song seeped away.

Then Oñate appeared, splashing his column across the Rio Grande at the pueblo of Juárez, and headed north up the river. The cellar suddenly reverberated with the swish of a sword into red flesh, and there was a huge, moving collage of churning, charging horses, and arrows whistling into the cracks of armor, and many things fell to the earth and became still. Oñate sat astride his horse surveying the compound of a conquered pueblo.

The song came again suddenly, shatteringly, crescendoing as Joshua's Spanish princess stood on a hill looking down. She came towards him, appearing to walk just above the earth. As she neared, smiling, with both arms out, he moved to the wall. As they came closer, he reached the wall with his arms outspread, trying to physically feel into it, but she was gone. He stayed thusly for a while, his head turned sideways, pushing his whole body against the dirt. For a moment he sagged and took a breath into his body that released him. He turned, picked up the lantern, and zombied his way up to the other world. The one here.

ALL WAS READY. The tables were filled with every delicacy of the land from which Joshua, his father, and grandfathers twice back had sprouted. The *hacienda* shined from repeated dusting and polishing. A *cantina* holding many bottles from many other lands was set up in the main room, and an even greater display was waiting for eager hands, dry throats, and tight emotions in the patio.

Carole moved about, checking over and over that which was already done. Joshua had one chore left.

"Martin, drain the pool."

Martin looked at his master, puzzled. "But sir, the guests will . . ."

"Just drain the pool."

"Well . . . yes sir."

When Carole saw this, she hurried to Martin and asked in agitated confusion what in hell's madness possessed him to do such a thing.

"It was on orders of Mr. Joshua, madam."

"Then he's mad! We cleaned the pool only yesterday!"

She found Joshua in the study and burst in just as Charlotte finished rechecking her own list and was saying, "Everything has been done, Joshua. The doctors are even releasing Grebbs from the hospital so he can make it."

"Of course, I knew you'd taken care of . . ."

"Joshua!"

He turned slowly to her.

"Have you lost all your sanity? Why did you have Martin drain the pool?"

"It's simple, my dear. Pools can become hypnotic and distracting. We have far greater forms of entertainment coming up."

She stood there unable to speak momentarily. She pushed at her hair and rubbed her perspiring palms on her hips, walking in a small circle around the room, finally giving utterance, "I know you're crazy, but do you want everyone else to know it?"

"It will give them much pleasure to finally find this flaw in my nature they have so desperately been seeking."

She turned and cascaded from the room, hurling back, "Oh, my God!"

Forty-eight hours later they came from all around the world. They arrived in jets, Rolls-Royces, Cadillacs, Mercedes, and pickup trucks. They moved to the *hacienda* magnetized.

The greetings were both formal and friendly, fearful and cheerful. Carole was at her gracious best, only half-drunk, expertly suppressing their initial dread with her trained talk. But there was a difference in the hands and arms and bodies that floated in the air towards Joshua. These appurtenances involved a massive movement of trepidation, heat, and fatherhood.

Joshua took Aleta in his grand and strong arms and lifted her from the floor in teasing love and respect. Her husband, Rob, died a little bit right there. His impulse of murder to the being of this man was intensified and verified. Rob wanted *in* desperately. He craved to become part of the Stone domain; craved to be part of the prestige and power. Marrying the favorite niece had seemed the proper first step. It hadn't worked. Joshua had never asked him, and Aleta absolutely forbade Rob to even hint at it. His lean, handsome face had a pinched appearance about it from the hatred. He had dwelled on it so long now that it was an obsession—an obsession to destroy that which he felt had ignored and destroyed him. It was unjustified. Joshua simply didn't want to see Rob subservient to him—not the husband of his artist niece. Aleta had never asked Joshua for anything but his best wishes. He felt that Rob must be as independent as she or else they wouldn't be married. He was wrong. Being a junior partner in a local stock brokerage firm didn't do it for Rob. And their being simply ordered here to Aleta's obvious joy had tilted his rage until he could hardly contain it.

Others—who were *in*—felt just as passionately about Joshua, but they all had their separate and different reasons.

Lana and Joseph Helstrom certainly had a different wish for Joshua. Joseph just hadn't moved as high in the organization as swiftly as he felt he should, and Lana had a hidden yen for Joshua. In fact, she often daydreamed of replacing Carole.

And there was the senior vice president, Grebbs, who wanted and believed that Joshua should step up to the position of chairman of the board and allow him his long overdue presidency. He had lately been entering hospitals for checkups, which repeatedly disclosed nothing wrong—but then x-rays do not show hatred or they would have been white with explosions all over his body.

None of these things bothered Joshua now. The gathering grew in momentum of sound, emotion, and color. The drinks were consumed along with the food, and the talk was of many things. People split up into ever-changing groups. Those who had been to the *hacienda* before remarked about this alteration or that. Those who were new to its centuries made many, many comments about all the priceless objects of art and craft. Whether they hated or loved the master of the house, they were somehow awed and honored to be in this museum of the spirit of man and Joshua himself.

Alfredo, the guitarist from Juárez, played. His dark head bent over his instrument, and the long delicate fingers stroked from the wood and steel the tenderness of love, the savagery of death. It seemed that these songs, too, came from the walls. Maybe somehow they did.

The music surged into the total system of Joshua. He felt stronger, truer than ever before. He was ready now to make his first move—the beginning of his final commitment. He looked about the room, observing with penetration his followers. His eyes settled on Charlotte. And then, as if knowing, unable to resist, she came to him. She handed him a new scotch and water, holding her own drink with practiced care. He turned, and she followed at his side. They wandered to the outer confines of the house—to his childhood room. She did not question. He turned on a small lamp that still left many shadows.

"My darling," he said softly, touching the walls with one hand, "this is where it all started."

She looked at him, puzzled, but with patience.

"I think I was five when I first heard the walls. It was gunfire and screams, and I knew it had once happened here. You see, this, in the days of the vast Spanish land grants, was a roadhouse, a *cantina,* an oasis where the dons and their ladies gathered to fight and fornicate. They are in the walls, you know, and I hear them. I even see them. I had just turned thirteen when I first *saw* into the walls."

Joshua's eyes gleamed like a coyote's in lantern light. His breath was growing, and there was an electricity charging through all his being. Charlotte was hypnotized at his voice and what was under it. His hand moved down the walls as he told her of some of the things he'd seen and heard. Then he turned to her and raised his glass for a toast.

"To you, dear loyal, wonderful Charlotte, my love and my thanks."

"It has all been a fine trip with you, Joshua. I could not have asked more from life than to have been a part of you and what you've done. Thank you, thank you."

He took the drink from her hand and set it on the dresser. Taking her gently by the arm, he pulled her to the wall. "Now lean against it and listen and you, too, will hear." She did so, straining with all her worth. "Listen! Listen," he whispered, and his powerful hands went around her neck. She struggled very little, and in a few moments she went limp. He held her a brief second longer, bending to kiss her on the back of the neck he'd just broken. Then with much care he picked her up, carried her to the closet, and placed her out of sight behind some luggage. He quietly closed the door, standing there a while looking at it. He moved, picked up his drink, and returned to his people.

IN THE PATIO, Misha, the Russian dancer from Kavkaz on Sunset Boulevard, was leaping wildly about, crouching, kicking. A circle formed around him, and the bulk of Joshua Stone III dominated it all. He was enjoying himself to the fullest, clapping his hands and yelling encouragement. The dance had turned everyone on a few more kilocycles. They started drinking more, talking more and louder, even gaining a little courage.

The gray, fiftyish Grebbs tugged at Joshua, trying to get his true attention. He kept bringing up matters of far-flung business interests. He might remind one in attitude of a presidential campaign manager, just after a victory, wondering if he'd be needed now. He rubbed at his crew cut hair nervously, trying to figure an approach to Joshua. His gray eyes darted about slightly. His bone-edged nose presented certain signs of strength and character, but weakness around the mouth gave him away. He was clever and did everything that cleverness could give to keep all underlings out of touch with Joshua. He had hoped for a while that this gathering had been called to announce Joshua's chairmanship, and the fulfillment of his own desperate dream.

Joshua motioned to Lotus Flower, the belly dancer, and she moved gracefully out into the patio ahead of the music. Then the music caught up with her. The Oriental lady undulated and performed the moves that have always pleased men.

As Grebbs tugged at Joshua again, he said, without taking his eyes from the dancer, "Grebbs, go talk business to your dictaphone." Just that. Now Grebbs knew. He moved away, hurting.

Lana stood with Carole. They were both watching Joshua with far different emotions.

Lana spoke first, about their mutual interest. "Has Joshua put on some weight?"

"No, it's the same old stomach."

"He's always amazed everyone with his athletic abilities."

"Really?" This last had a flint edge to it.

"Well, for a man who appears so awkward, it is rather surprising to find how swiftly and strongly he can move when he decides to. Carole, you do remember the time he leaped into Spring Lake and swam all the way across it, and then just turned around and swam all the way back. You must remember that, darling. We all had such a good time."

"Oh, I remember many things, *darling*."

Rob was saying to Joseph Helstrom, "There's something wrong here. I feel it. Here it's only September, and he's already drained the pool."

Joseph touched his heavy-rimmed glasses and let the hand slowly slide down his round face. "Yeah, he demanded we all come here on instant notice, and he's not really with us."

"The selfish bastard." Rob exhaled this like ridding himself of morning spittum.

The dancer swirled ever closer to Joshua, her head back, long black hair swishing across her shoulders. He smiled, absorbed in the movement of flesh as little beams of hatred were cast across the patio from Grebbs, Rob, Joseph—and others. Joshua didn't care—didn't even feel it. As the dance finished, Rob walked out into the garden and removed a small automatic pistol from the back of his belt under his jacket. He checked the breech and replaced the gun.

Joshua worked his way through the crowd, spoken to and speaking back in a distracted manner. His people looked puzzled after his broad back. He made his way slowly down the stairs towards the wine cellar, one hand caressing the wall. He stopped and waited. The song came from eternities away, soft, soothing, amidst the whispers of men planning daring moves.

The whole wall now spun with colors slowly forming into warriors. Then, there before Joshua's eyes was Esteban, the black man, standing amidst the Pueblo Indians. Joshua had always felt that Esteban was one of the most exciting and mysterious—even neglected—figures in the history of America. It has never been settled for sure how or why he arrived in the Southwest. However, his influence would always be there. He had started the legend of the Seven Golden Cities of Cíbola, which Coronado and many others searched for in vain. He was a major factor in the Pueblo Revolt of 1680, afterwards becoming the chief of several of these communities. He became a famous medicine man and was looked on as a god. But, like all earthly gods, he fell. A seven-year drought came upon the land of the Tewas, and when he could not dissipate it, he was blamed for it. They killed him, and the superstitious Zuñis skinned him like a deer to see if he was black all the way through.

Now, at last, Joshua was looking upon this man of dark skin and searing soul, as he spoke in the Indian tongue to his worshippers. He talked to them of survival without the rule of iron. They mumbled low in agreement. Maybe Joshua would learn some of the dark secrets before this apparition dissolved back to dried mud.

Joshua watched as up and down the river the Indians threw rock and wood at steel in savage dedication. Men died screaming in agony, sobbing their way painfully to the silence of death. The river flowed peacefully before him now, covering the entire wall and beyond. Then the feet splashed into his view, and he saw the remnants of the defeated Spanish straggle across the river back into Mexico.

Joshua's Spanish lady in black lace sat on a smooth, round rock staring across a valley dripping with the gold of autumn. She was in a land he'd never seen. She turned her head toward him and gave a smile that said so much he couldn't stand it. He reached towards the wall, and she nodded her head up and down and faded away with the music. Silence. More silence. Then, "Joshua."

He turned. It was Lana. She moved to him, putting her hands on his chest. "Joshua, what is it? You're acting so strangely."

"Did you see? Did you hear?" he asked, looking over her head.

"I . . . I . . . don't know what you mean, darling. See what?"

"Nothing. Nothing." He sighed.

"Can I help? Is there *anything* I can do?"

He pulled her against him and kissed her with purpose. She was at first surprised and then gave back to him. He picked her up and shoved her violently against the wooden frame between two wine barrels.

"No, no, not here."

"There is no other time," he said. "No other place." As he reached under her, one elbow struck a spigot on a barrel. He loved her standing there while a thin stream of red wine poured out on the cellar floor, forming an immediate pool not unlike blood.

She uttered only one word, "Joshua," and the wine sound continued.

BOTH HE AND Lana were back among the people now. Carole came to him.

"Where've you been? Where is Charlotte? The phone is ringing constantly. Where is she?"

"She's on vacation."

"Today? I can't believe you, Joshua. You always bragged about how she was there when you needed her."

"We don't need her now."

"You really are mad. Mad! Today of all days we need her to answer the phone."

"Take the damned phone off the hook. No one ever calls good news on a phone, anyway. If they have anything good to say, they come and see you personally." He walked away and left her standing there looking after him in much confusion.

All afternoon he had been wanting to visit his old friend Chalo Gonzales from the Apache Reservation. They met when they were kids. Chalo's father had worked the nearby orchards and alfalfa field for Joshua's father. He and Chalo hunted, fished, adventured together off and on for years. He'd gone with him to the reservation many times and learned much of nature and Indian ways. Chalo had given him as much as anyone—things of real value. He found him dressed in a regular business suit and tie, but he wore a band around his coarse, dark hair.

"Ah, amigo, let's walk in the garden away from this . . ." and he made a gesture with his arm to the scattered crowd. "How does it go with you and your people?"

"Slow, Joshua, but better. As always, there's conflict with the old and the young. The old want to stay with their own ways. The young want to rush into the outside world."

"It's the nature of youth to be impatient. It can't be helped."

"Oh, sure, that is the truth. But our young want to take the best of the old and good ways with them. They want both sides now. Now."

"That's good, Chalo. They're right."

"But nothing happens that fast. It has been too many centuries one way. You can't change it in a few years."

"It's a big problem I admit, but you will survive and finally win. You always have, you know."

"You've always given me encouragement. I feel better already."

They talked of hunts, and later adventures when they both came home for the summer from school. Chalo had been one of few to make it from his land to Bacone, the Indian college.

Joshua felt Chalo was his equal. He was comfortable with him. They stood together and talked in a far recess of the secluded garden where they could see the mountains they'd so often explored. Joshua felt a surge of love for his old friend. He knew what he must do. He'd spotted the root a few minutes back. He didn't dare risk it with his hands. Chalo was almost as strong as he was in both will and muscle.

He picked up the root and began drawing designs with it in a spot of loose ground, as men will do who are from the earth. Then, as his friend glanced away, Joshua swung it with much force, striking him just back of the ear. He heard the bone crunch and was greatly relieved to know he wouldn't have to do more. Without any wasted time, he dragged and pushed him into a thick clump of brush. He checked to see if the body was totally hidden, tossed the root in after it, walked to the wall, and looked out across the desert to the mountains again. He was very still; then he turned, smiling ineluctably, and proceeded to the party.

DUSK CAME SWIFTLY and hung awhile, giving the party a sudden subdued quality. It was the time of day that Joshua liked best. He finally escaped the clutchers and went to his study, locking the door and grinning at the phone Carole had taken off the hook and deliberately dangled across the lamp.

He drew the shades back and sat there absorbed in the hiding sun, and watched the glowing oranges and reds turn to violet and then a soft blue above the desert to the west. He knew that life started stirring there with the death of the sun. The coyotes and bobcats were already moving, sniffing the ground and the air of other living creatures. Many mice, rabbits, and birds would die this night so they could live. The great owl would soon be swooping above them in direct competition. The next day the sun would be reborn, and the vultures would dine on any remains, keeping the desert clean and in balance.

Someone knocked on the door. It was Carole.

"Joshua, are you in there?" Then louder, "Joshua, I know you're there because the door is locked from the inside. What are you doing with the door locked anyway?" Silence. "At least you could come and mix with your guests. You did *invite* them, you know." She pounded on the door now. "My God, at least speak to me. I am your wife, you know." Silence. She turned in frustration and stamped off down the hall, mumbling about his madness.

Joshua turned his lounge chair away from the window and stared at the wall across the room. There were things he had to see before he made the final move. Pieces of the past that he must reconstruct properly in his mind before he took the last step.

It did come. As always he heard it first, then saw it form, whirling like pieces of an abstract world—a new world, an old world, being broken and born, falling together again. The Spanish returned. They came now with fresh men, armor, horses, and cannon. They marched and rode up the Rio Grande setting up the artillery, blasting the adobe walls to dust. Then they charged with sabers drawn and whittled the shell-shocked Indians into slavery. They mined the gold from the virgin mountains with the Indians as their tools. And then it all vanished inwardly.

There was quiet and darkness now until he heard his name. "Joshua, Joshua, Joshua." It came floating from afar as if elongated, closer, closer. She was there. He leaned forward in the chair, his body tense, anxious. She stood by a river of emerald green. It was so clear that he could see the separate grains of white sand on its bottom. The trees, trunks thicker than the *hacienda*, rose into the sky. They went up, up past his ability to see. The leaves were as thick as watermelons, and fifty people could stand in the shade of a single leaf. The air danced with the light of four suns shafting great golden beams down through the trees.

She moved towards him through one of the beams and for a moment vanished with its brilliance. Now she was whole again, standing there before him. He ached to touch her. He hurt. An endless string of silver fish swam up the river now. The four suns penetrated the pure water and made them appear to be parts of a metallic lava flow from a far-off volcano. But they were fish, moving relentlessly, with no hesitation whatsoever, knowing their destination and fate without doubt.

Again the word came from her as she turned and walked down the river, vanishing behind a tree. "Joshua."

For a fleeting moment he heard the song. He closed his eyes. When he opened them, there was just the darkness of the room. He didn't know how long he sat there before returning to the party.

He moved directly to the bar in the patio and ordered a double scotch and water. His people were scattered out now, having dined, and were back onto the drinking and talking. The volume was beginning to rise again. It was second wind time. As the bartender served the drink, he felt something touch his hand. It was Maria Windsor.

She smiled like champagne pouring, her red lips pulling back over almost startling white teeth. She smiled with her blue eyes, too.

"It has been such a long time," she said.

"Maria, goddamn, it's good to see you." And he hugged her, picking her off the floor without intending to. She was very small and at first appeared to be delicate. But this was a strong little lady. She was a barmaid in his favorite place in El Paso when he first met her. He'd always deeply admired the polite and friendly smoothness with which she did her job. One never had to wait for a drink, the ashtray was emptied at the proper moment, and she knew when to leave or when to stand and chat. Joshua had introduced her to John Windsor, one of his junior vice presidents, and now they were married.

"I love the portrait Aleta did of you."

"Well, I feel embarrassed hanging it there, but what could I do after she worked so hard on it? How are you and John getting along?" he asked.

"How do you mean? Personally or otherwise?"

"Oh, all around I suppose."

"Good," she said. "Like all wives, I think he works too hard sometimes, but I suppose that's natural. Here he comes now."

John shook hands and greeted his boss without showing any apparent fear and revealing a genuine liking for him. He once told Maria that he'd love Joshua to his death, just for introducing her to him. He was about five eleven, straight and well-muscled, and had thick brown hair that he wore longer than anyone in the whole international organization. He, too, had a nice, white smile.

Joshua ordered a round for the three of them. He raised his glass: "My friends, you'll be receiving a memo in the next few days that I think you will enjoy. Here's to it." Several days before the party, Joshua had made out a paper giving John Windsor control of the company. It had not been delivered yet.

He left them glowing in anticipation and went to find his favorite kin, Aleta. As he moved, the eyes of hatred moved with him . . . drunker now, braver. He walked into the garden, bowing, speaking here and there, but not stopping. The moon, hung in place by galactic gravity, beamed back the sun in a blue softness. The insects and night birds hummed a song in the caressing desert breeze. The leaves on the trees moved just enough to make love. There was a combination of warmth and coolness that only the desert can give.

Aleta had seen her uncle and somehow knew he was looking for her. She came to him from where she'd been sitting on a tree that was alive but bent to the ground. She'd been studying the light patterns throughout the garden for a painting she had in mind.

"Uncle Joshua, it's time we had a visit."

He took both her hands and stood back looking at her.

"Yes, it's time, my dear. You are even more beautiful than the best of your paintings."

"Well, Uncle, that's not saying much," she said, being pleasingly flattered just the same.

He led her to an archway and opened the iron gate. They walked up a tiny, rutted wagon road into the desert. The sounds of the gathering became subdued. The yucca bushes and Joshua trees—that he'd been named after—speared the sky like frozen battalions of soldiers on guard duty forever.

"Remember when we used to ride up this trail?" she asked.

"Yes, it seems like yesterday."

"It seems like a hundred years ago to me."

He laughed. "Time has a way of telescoping in and out according to your own time. That's the way it should be. You were a tough little shit," he added with fondness. "You were the only one who could ride with me all day."

"That was simple bullheadedness. I knew I was going to be an artist someday, and you have to have a skull made of granite to be an artist."

He was amused by her even now. "But you also had a bottom made of rawhide."

They talked of some of her childhood adventures they'd shared. Then the coyotes howled off in a little draw. The strollers stood like the cacti, listening, absorbing the oldest cry left.

When the howls stopped, he spoke. "I love to hear them. I always have. I even get lonely to hear them. They're the only true survivors."

"That somehow frightens me," she said with a little shudder.

"It shouldn't. You should be encouraged. As long as they howl, people have a chance here on earth. No longer, no less. It is the final cry for freedom. It's hope."

They walked on silently for a spell. "You really are a romantic, Uncle. When I hear people say how cold you are, I laugh to myself."

"You know, Aleta darling, you're the only person who never asked me for anything."

"I didn't have to. You've always given me love and confidence. What more could you give?"

"I don't know. I wish I did."

"No, Uncle, there's no greater gift than that."

"Aleta, the world is strange. Mankind has forgotten what was always true—that a clean breath is worth more than the most elegant bank building. A new flower opening is more beautiful than a marble palace. All things rot. Michelangelo's sculpture is even now slowly breaking apart. All empires vanish. The largest buildings in the world will turn back to sand. The great paintings are cracking, the negatives of the best films ever made are right now losing their color and becoming brittle. The tallest mountains are coming down a rock at a time. Only thoughts live. You are only what you think."

"That's good," she said, "then I'm a painting, even if I am already beginning to crack."

He liked her words and added some of his own: "You know, honey, the worms favor the rich."

"Why?"

He rubbed his great belly. "Because they're usually fatter and more easily digestible."

"Do you speak of yourself?"

"Of course," he smiled. The coyotes howled again, and he said, "I love you, my dear Aleta."

"And I love you."

He stroked her hair and moved his hand downward. It had to be swift, clean. With all his strength, even more than he'd ever had before. He grabbed her long, graceful neck and twisted her head. He heard the bones rip apart. She gasped only once, and then a long sigh of her last breath exuded from her. He gathered her carefully in his arms and walked out through the brush to the little draw where the coyotes had so recently hunted. Then he stretched her out on the ground with her hands at her sides and gently brushed her hair back. She slept in the moonlight.

He walked swiftly back to the *hacienda*. As he left the garden for the patio, Rob stepped in front of him.

"Joshua, have you seen Aleta?"

"Of course, my boy, of course."

"Well, where is she?"

"Look, I don't follow your wife around. She's certainly more capable than most of taking care of herself." Joshua moved on. Rob followed him a few steps, looking at his back with glazed eyes.

Grebbs grabbed at him in one last desperate hope that Joshua was saving the announcement to the last.

"Joshua, I have to talk with you. Please."

Joshua stopped and looked at the man. He was drunk, and that was something Grebbs rarely allowed himself to be in public. He looked as if pieces of flesh were about to start dropping down into his clothing. His mouth was open, slack and watery.

Joshua said, with a certainty in his voice that settled Grebb's question, "Grebbs, you're a bad drinker. I have no respect for bad drinkers." And he moved on.

Grebbs stared at the same back the same way Rob had. He muttered, actually having trouble keeping from openly crying, "The bastard. The dirty bastard. I'll kill you! You son of a bitch!"

The thing some of these people had been uttering about Joshua now possessed them. A madness hovered about, waiting for the right moment, and then swiftly moved into them. Now all the people of music started playing at once. The Russian was dancing even more wildly, if not so expertly. The belly dancer swished about from man to man, teasing. The mariachis walked about in dominance for a while, then the brass group would break through. It was a cacophony of sound that entered the heads of all there . . . throbbing like blood poison.

Carole started sobbing uncontrollably. Lana began cursing her husband, Joseph, in vile terms—bitterly, with total malice. Joseph just reached out and slapped her down across the chaise lounge, and a little blood oozed from the corner of her mouth. He could only think of a weapon, any weapon to use on the man who he felt was totally responsible for the matrix of doom echoing all around. We always must have something to hate for our own failures and smallness. But this did not occur to Joseph, or Lana, or Carole, or the others. Only Alfredo, the guitarist, sat alone on the same old bent tree that Aleta had cherished, touching his guitar with love.

Maria took John aside and told him they were leaving, that something terrible was happening. She was not—and could not be—a part of it. He hesitated but listened. They did finally drive away, confused, but feeling they were right.

Grebbs dazedly shuffled to the kitchen looking for a knife, but old Juanita and her two sisters were there. He then remembered an East Indian dagger that lay on the mantel in the library as a paperweight. In his few trips to the *hacienda* he'd often studied it, thinking what a pleasure it would be to drive it into the jerking heart of Joshua Stone III.

He picked it up and pulled the arched blade from the jeweled sheath. He touched the sharp unused point with shaking fingers. At that precise instant, Rob felt in the back of his belt and touched the automatic. He removed it and put it in his jacket pocket. Joseph Helstrom looked about the patio for an instrument to satisfy his own destructive instincts.

Joshua entered the door to the cellar, shut it, and shoved the heavy iron bolt into place. He called on all his resources now in another direction. An implosion to the very core of time struck Joshua. Now, right now, he must visualize all the rest of the history of his land that occurred before his first childish awareness. Then, and only then, could he make his last destined move. It began to form. The long lines of Conestoga wagons tape-wormed across the prairies and struggled through the mountain passes, bringing goods and people from all over the world to settle this awesome land. They came in spite of flood, droughts, blizzards, Indian attacks, and disease. They were drawn here by the golden talk of dreamers, and promising facts.

The ruts of the Santa Fe Trail were cut so deep they would last a century. The mountain men took the last of the beaver from the sweet, churning waters of the mountains above Taos and came down to trade, to dance the wild fandangos, to drink and pursue the dark-eyed lovelies of that village of many flags.

A troop of cavalry charged over the horizon into a camp of Indians, and the battle splashed across the adobe valleys in crimson. Thousands of cattle and sheep were driven there and finally settled into their own territories. Cowboys strained to stay aboard bucking horses, and these same men roped and jerked steers, thumping them hard against the earth. They gambled and fought and raised hell in the villages of deserts and mountains, creating written and filmed legends that covered the world more thoroughly than Shakespeare.

The prospectors walked over the mountains searching for—and some finding—large deposits of gold, silver, and copper. And, as always, men of money took away the rewards of their labors and built themselves great palaces.

And Joshua saw the Italians, Chinese, and many other nationalities driving the spikes into the rail ties. The trains came like the covered wagons before them—faster, more powerful—hauling more people and goods than ever before. The double-bitted axes and two-man saws cut the majestic pines of the high places, taking away the shelter of the deer, lion, and bear.

Now Joshua closed his eyes, for he knew all the rest. When he opened them, he heard the song begin again. It was both older and newer each time he heard it. There was a massive adobe church, and his lady walked right through the walls and into the one he sat staring at. Now, as she spoke his name, he knew his final move was near. For the first time, he turned away from her and headed for the door. She smiled, somehow exactly like the song.

As he opened the door and pulled it shut, he felt a presence come at him. He was so keyed up, so full of his feelings, that he just stepped aside and let it hurtle past. It was Grebbs. He'd driven the dagger so deep into the door that he couldn't pull it out to strike again. Grebbs had missed all the way. Joshua gathered him up around the neck with one hand, jerked the dagger from the door with the other, and smashed him against the wall. He shoved the point of the dagger just barely under the skin of Grebb's guts. Grebb's eyes bulged, and he almost died of fright right there, but the hand of his master cut any words off. It was quite a long moment for the corporate vice president.

"What I should do, Grebbs, is cut your filthy entrails out and shove them down your dead throat. But that's far too easy for you."

Joshua dropped him to the floor and drove the knife to the hilt in the door. He then strode up the stairs three at a time, hearing only a low broken sob below him.

As he entered the world of people again, Carole grabbed at him, visibly drunk and more. She said, "God! God! What are you doing?" He moved on from her as she shrieked, "You don't love me!" He ignored this, too, and when she raked her painted claws into the back of his neck, he ignored that as well. She stood looking at her fingers and the bits of bloody flesh clinging to her nails.

Rob blocked his way, again demanding attention. "I'm asking you for the last time! Do you hear me? Where is Aleta?"

He pushed the young man aside, saying as he went, "I'll tell you in a few minutes." This surprised and stopped Rob right where he stood.

Then Joshua raised his arms and shouted, "Music, you fools! Play and dance!" The drunken musicians all started up again, jerky, horrendously out of synchronization.

Joshua went to the kitchen and very tenderly lifted an exhausted and sleeping Juanita from her chair. He explained to her two sisters that he would take Juanita to her room on the other side of the *hacienda*. They were glad and went on cleaning up. He led her slowly out a side door. On the other side of many walls could be heard the so-called music sailing up, dissipating itself in the peaceful desert air.

As he walked the bent old woman along, he spoke to her softly, "It's time for you to rest, Juanita. You've been faithful all these decades. Your sisters can do the labors. You will have time of your own now. A long, long time that will belong just to you. You've served many people who did not even deserve your presence."

There was an old well near the working shed where her little house stood. They stopped here.

"Juanita, you are like this—this dried-up well. It gave so much for so long, it now has no water left."

He pulled the plank top off. Juanita was weary and still partially in the world of sleep. Joshua steadied the bony old shoulders with both his hands. He looked at her in the moonlight and said, "Juanita, you are a beautiful woman."

She twitched the tiniest of smiles across her worn face and tilted her head just a little in an almost girlish move.

Then he said, "Juanita, I love you." He slipped a handkerchief from his pocket, crammed it into her mouth, jerked her upside down, and hurled her head-first into the well. There was just a crumpled thud. No more.

In the patio, the music was beginning to die. A dullness had come over the area. A deadly dullness. But heads started turning, one, two, three at a time towards the *hacienda* door. Their center of attention, Joshua, strode amongst them. There were only whispers now. Joshua saw a movement and stopped. The heavy earthen vase smashed to bits in front of him. He looked up, and there on a low wall stood Helstrom like a clown without makeup. He too, had missed.

Joshua grabbed him by both legs and jerked him down against the bricks of the patio floor. He hit, and his head bounced. Joshua gripped him by the neck and the side of one leg and tossed him over and beyond the wall.

He turned slowly around, his eyes covering all the crowd. No one moved. Not at all. He walked back through them to the house and in a few moments returned. He carried a huge silver candelabra, from the first Spanish days, with twenty lighted candles. He walked with it held high. None moved, except to get out of his way. Alfredo sat on the edge of the empty pool. His feet dangled down into its empty space. He tilted his head the way only he could do and softly, so very softly, strummed an old Spanish love song—a song older than the *hacienda*. Joshua walked to the steps of the pool and with absolute certainty of purpose stepped carefully down into it. It seemed a long time, but it was not. He placed the candelabra in the deepest part of the pool, stepped back, and looked into the flames. Then he raised his head and stared upwards at all the faces that now circled the pool to stare down at him. He turned in a complete circle so that he looked into the soft reflections in each of their eyes. He was all things in that small turn. None of them knew what *they* were seeing. He walked back up the steps, and there stood Rob.

Joshua said, "Come now, Rob, and I'll tell you what you really want to know."

Alfredo went on singing in Spanish as if he were making quiet love. The circle still looked downwards at the glowing candles.

Near the largest expanse of wall on the whole of the *hacienda*, Joshua said quietly to Rob, "I killed her. I took her into the desert and killed sweet Aleta."

Rob was momentarily paralyzed. Then a terrible cry and sound of murder burst from him as he ripped the edge of his pocket, pulling out the gun. He fired right into the chest of Joshua, knocking him against the wall. He pulled at the trigger until there was nothing left. Joshua stayed upright for a moment, full of holes, and then fell forward, rolling over, face up. The crowd from the pool moved towards Rob, hesitantly, fearfully. They made a half-circle around the body.

Rob spoke, not looking away from Joshua's dead, smiling face as if afraid he'd rise up again, "He killed Aleta."

Grebbs, saying things unintelligible like a slavering idiot, pushed his way through the mass, stopping with his face above Joshua's. Then he vented a little stuttering laugh. It broke forth louder and louder, and haltingly the others were caught up with him. They laughed and cried at the same time, not knowing really which they were doing. None thought to look at the wall above the body. It didn't matter, though, for all those who might have seen were already there. On a thin-edged hill stood Charlotte the dedicated, Aleta the beloved, Chalo the companion, and old Juanita the faithful. They were in a row, smiling with contentment. Just below them, the lady in black lace walked forward to meet Joshua.

As he moved into the wall, there came from his throat another form of laughter that far, far transcended the hysterical cackling in the patio. He glanced back just once, and the song overcame the mirth. He took her into his arms and held her. They had waited so very long. It was over. They walked, holding hands, up the hill to join those he loved, and they all disappeared into a new world.

The wall turned back to dirt.

None could stay at the *hacienda* that night. Just before the sun announced the dawn, the last candle in the bottom of the pool flickered out. The light was gone.

It has been said that no one wrote the traditional Western story better than Ernest Haycox (1899–1950). Such novels as *The Earth Breakers, Alders, Alder Gulch, Long Storm, The Wild Bunch,* and *Bugles in the Afternoon,* and such collections as *Murder on the Frontier, Pioneer Loves, By Rope and Lead,* and *Rough Justice,* offer eloquent testimony in support of that claim. The story we've chosen, "Stage to Lordsburg," was made into John Ford's landmark movie *Stagecoach,* starring John Wayne. In Haycox's hands, the simplest, and sometimes most conventional, theme became something moving, powerful, memorable. The ability to capture the true essence of life in the old West is what set Ernest Haycox apart from other Western writers of his time, and what continues to make his work popular with modern readers. His stories and novels invariably have an unsurpassed sense of realism and truth about them.

Stage to Lordsburg

Ernest Haycox

This was one of those years in the Territory when Apache smoke signals spiraled up from the stony mountain summits and many a ranch cabin lay as a square of blackened ashes on the ground and the departure of a stage from Tonto was the beginning of an adventure that had no certain happy ending. . . .

The stage and its six horses waited in front of Weilner's store on the north side of Tonto's square. Happy Stuart was on the box, the ribbons between his fingers and one foot teetering on the brake. John Strang rode shotgun guard and an escort of ten cavalrymen waited behind the coach, half asleep in their saddles.

At four-thirty in the morning this high air was quite cold, though the sun had begun to flush the sky eastward. A small crowd stood in the square, presenting their final messages to the passengers now entering the coach. There was a girl going down to marry an infantry officer, a whiskey drummer from St. Louis, an Englishman all length and bony corners and bearing with him an enormous sporting rifle, a gambler, a solid-shouldered cattleman on his way to New Mexico and a blond young man upon whom both Happy Stuart and the shotgun guard placed a narrow-eyed interest.

This seemed all until the blond man drew back from the coach door; and then a girl known commonly throughout the Territory as Henriette came quietly from the crowd. She was small and quiet, with a touch of paleness in her cheeks and her quite dark eyes lifted at the blond man's un-expected courtesy, showing surprise. There was this moment of delay and then the girl caught up her dress and stepped into the coach.

Men in the crowd were smiling but the blond one turned, his motion like the swift cut of a knife, and his attention covered that group until the smiling quit. He was tall, hollow-flanked, and definitely stamped by the guns slung low on his hips. But it wasn't the guns alone; something in his face, so watchful and so smooth, also showed his trade. Afterwards he got into the coach and slammed the door.

Happy Stuart kicked off the brakes and yelled, "Hi!" Tonto's people were calling out their last farewells and the six horses broke into a trot and the stage lunged on its fore and aft springs and rolled from town with dust dripping off its wheels like water, the cavalrymen trotting briskly behind. So they tipped down the long grade, bound on a journey no stage had at-tempted during the last forty-five days. Out below in the desert's distance stood the relay stations they hoped to reach and pass. Between lay a coun-try swept empty by the quick raids of Geronimo's men.

The Englishman, the gambler and the blond man sat jammed together in the forward seat, riding backward to the course of the stage. The drum-mer and the cattleman occupied the uncomfortable middle bench; the two women shared the rear seat. The cattleman faced Henriette, his knees al-most touching her. He had one arm hooked over the door's window sill to steady himself. A huge gold nugget slid gently back and forth along the watch chain slung across his wide chest and a chunk of black hair lay below his hat. His eyes considered Henriette, reading something in the girl that caused him to show her a deliberate smile. Henriette dropped her glance to the gloved tips of her fingers, cheeks unstirred.

They were all strangers packed closely together, with nothing in com-mon save a destination. Yet the cattleman's smile and the boldness of his glance were something as audible as speech, noted by everyone except the Englishman, who sat bolt upright with his stony indifference. The army girl, tall and calmly pretty, threw a quick side glance at Henriette and af-terwards looked away with a touch of color. The gambler saw this inter-change of glances and showed the cattleman an irritated attention. The whiskey drummer's eyes narrowed a little and some inward cynicism made a faint change on his lips. He removed his hat to show a bald head already beginning to sweat; his cigar smoke turned the coach cloudy and ashes kept dropping on his vest.

The blond man had observed Henriette's glance drop from the cattle-man; he tipped his hat well over his face and watched her—not boldly but as though he were puzzled. Once her glance lifted and touched him. But he had been on guard against that and was quick to look away.

The army girl coughed gently behind her hand, whereupon the gambler tapped the whiskey drummer on the shoulder. "Get rid of that." The drummer appeared startled. He grumbled, "Beg pardon," and tossed the smoke through the window.

All this while the coach went rushing down the ceaseless turns of the mountain road, rocking on its fore and aft springs, its heavy wheels slamming through the road ruts and whining on the curves. Occasionally the strident yell of Happy Stuart washed back. "Hi, Nellie! By God—!" The whiskey drummer braced himself against the door and closed his eyes.

Three hours from Tonto the road, making a last round sweep, let them down upon the flat desert. Here the stage stopped and the men got out to stretch. The gambler spoke to the army girl, gently: "Perhaps you would find my seat more comfortable." The army girl said "Thank you," and changed over. The cavalry sergeant rode up to the stage, speaking to Happy Stuart.

"We'll be goin' back now—and good luck to ye."

The men piled in, the gambler taking the place beside Henriette. The blond man drew his long legs together to give the army girl more room, and watched Henriette's face with a soft, quiet care. A hard sun beat fully on the coach and dust began to whip up like fire smoke. Without escort they rolled across a flat earth broken only by cacti standing against a dazzling light. In the far distance, behind a blue heat haze, lay the faint suggestion of mountains.

The cattleman reached up and tugged at the ends of his mustache and smiled at Henriette. The army girl spoke to the blond man. "How far is it to the noon station?"

The blond man said courteously: "Twenty miles." The gambler watched the army girl with the strictness of his face relaxing, as though the run of her voice reminded him of things long forgotten.

The miles fell behind and the smell of alkali dust got thicker. Henriette rested against the corner of the coach, her eyes dropped to the tip of her gloves. She made an enigmatic, disinterested shape there; she seemed past stirring, beyond laughter. She was young, yet she had a knowledge that put the cattleman and the gambler and the drummer and the army girl in their exact places; and she knew why the gambler had offered the army girl his seat. The army girl was in one world and she was in another, as everyone in the coach understood. It had no effect on her for this was a distinction she had learned long ago. Only the blond man broke through her indifference. His name was Malpais Bill and she could see the wildness in the corners of his eyes and in the long crease of his lips; it was a stamp that would never come off. Yet something flowed out of him toward her that was different than the predatory curiosity of other men; something unobtrusively gallant, unexpectedly gentle.

Upon the box Happy Stuart pointed to the hazy outline two miles away.

"Injuns ain't burned that anyhow." The sun was directly overhead, turning the light of the world a cruel brass-yellow. The crooked crack of a dry wash opened across the two deep ruts that made this road. Johnny Strang shifted the gun in his lap. "What's Malpais Bill ridin' with us for?"

"I guess I wouldn't ask him," returned Happy Stuart and studied the wash with a troubled eye. The road fell into it roughly and he got a tighter grip on his reins and yelled: "Hang on! Hi, Nellie! Goddamn you, hi!" The six horses plunged down the rough side of the wash and for a moment the coach stood alone, high and lonely on the break, and then went reeling over the rim. It struck the gravel with a roar, the front wheels bouncing and the back wheels skewing around. The horses faltered but Happy Stuart cursed at his leaders and got them into a run again. The horses lunged up the far side of the wash two and two, their muscles bunching and the soft dirt flying in yellow clouds. The front wheels struck solidly and something cracked like a pistol shot; the stage rose out of the wash, teetered crosswise, and then fell ponderously on its side, splintering the coach panels.

Johnny Strang jumped clear. Happy Stuart hung to the handrail with one hand and hauled on the reins with the other; and stood up while the passengers crawled through the upper door. All the men, except the whiskey drummer, put their shoulders to the coach and heaved it upright again. The whiskey drummer stood strangely in the bright sunlight shaking his head dumbly while the others climbed back in. Happy Stuart said, "All right, brother, git aboard."

The drummer climbed in slowly and the stage ran on. There was a low, gray 'dobe relay station squatted on the desert dead ahead with a scatter of corrals about it and a flag hanging limp on a crooked pole. Men came out of the dobe's dark interior and stood in the shade of the porch gallery. Happy Stuart rolled up and stopped. He said to a lanky man: "Hi, Mack. Where's the goddamned Injuns?"

The passengers were filing into the dobe's dining room. The lanky one drawled: "You'll see 'em before tomorrow night." Hostlers came up to change horses.

The little dining room was cool after the coach, cool and still. A fat Mexican woman ran in and out with the food platters. Happy Stuart said: "Ten minutes," and brushed the alkali dust from his mouth and fell to eating.

The long-jawed Mack said: "Catlin's ranch burned last night. Was a troop of cavalry around here yesterday. Came and went. You'll git to the Gap tonight all right but I do' know about the mountains beyond. A little trouble?"

"A little," said Happy, briefly, and rose. This was the end of rest. The passengers followed, with the whiskey drummer straggling at the rear, reaching deeply for wind. The coach rolled away again, Mack's voice pursuing them. "Hit it a lick, Happy, if you see any dust rollin' out of the east."

Heat had condensed in the coach and the little wind fanned up by the run of the horses was stifling to the lungs; the desert floor projected its white glitter endlessly away until lost in the smoky haze. The cattleman's knees bumped Henriette gently and he kept watching her, a celluloid toothpick drooped between his lips. Happy Stuart's voice ran back, profane and urgent, keeping the speed of the coach constant through the ruts. The whiskey drummer's eyes were round and strained and his mouth was open and all the color had gone out of his face. The gambler observed this without expression and without care; and once the cattleman, feeling the sag of the whiskey drummer's shoulder, shoved him away. The Englishman sat bolt upright, staring emotionlessly at the passing desert. The army girl spoke to Malpais Bill: "What is the next stop?"

"Gap Creek."

"Will we meet soldiers there?"

He said: "I expect we'll have an escort over the hills into Lordsburg."

And at four o'clock of this furnace-hot afternoon the whiskey drummer made a feeble gesture with one hand and fell forward into the gambler's lap.

The cattleman shrugged his shoulders and put a head through the window, calling up to Happy Stuart: "Wait a minute." When the stage stopped everybody climbed out and the blond man helped the gambler lay the whiskey drummer in the sweltering patch of shade created by the coach. Neither Happy Stuart nor the shotgun guard bothered to get down. The whisky drummer's lips moved a little but nobody said anything and nobody knew what to do—until Henriette stepped forward.

She dropped to the ground, lifting the whiskey drummer's shoulders, and head against her breasts. He opened his eyes and there was something in them that they could all see, like relief and ease, like gratefulness. She murmured: "You are all right," and her smile was soft and pleasant, turning her lips maternal. There was this wisdom in her, this knowledge of the fears that men concealed behind their manners, the deep hungers that rode them so savagely, and the loneliness that drove them to women of her kind. She repeated, "You are all right," and watched this whiskey drummer's eyes lose the wildness of what he knew.

The army girl's face showed shock. The gambler and the cattleman looked down at the whiskey drummer quite impersonally. The blond man watched Henriette through lids half closed, but the flare of a powerful interest broke the severe lines of his cheeks. He held a cigarette between his fingers; he had forgotten it.

Happy Stuart said: "We can't stay here."

The gambler bent down to catch the whiskey drummer under the arms. Henriette rose and said, "Bring him to me," and got into the coach. The blond man and the gambler lifted the drummer through the door so that he was lying along the back seat, cushioned on Henriette's lap. They all got in and the coach rolled on. The drummer groaned a little, whispering: "Thanks—thanks," and the blond man, searching Henriette's face for every shred of expression, drew a gusty breath.

They went on like this, the big wheels pounding the ruts of the road while a lowering sun blazed through the coach windows. The mountain bulwarks began to march nearer, more definite in the blue fog. The cattleman's eyes were small and brilliant and touched Henriette personally, but the gambler bent toward Henriette to say: "If you are tired—"

"No," she said. "No. He's dead."

The army girl stifled a small cry. The gambler bent nearer the whiskey drummer, and then they were all looking at Henriette; even the Englishman stared at her for a moment, faint curiosity in his eyes. She was remotely smiling, her lips broad and soft. She held the drummer's head with both her hands and continued to hold him like that until, at the swift fall of dusk, they rolled across the last of the desert floor and drew up before Gap Station.

The cattleman kicked open the door and stepped out, grunting as his stiff legs touched the ground. The gambler pulled the drummer up so that Henriette could leave. They all came out, their bones tired from the shaking. Happy Stuart climbed from the box, his face a gray mask of alkali and his eyes bloodshot. He said: "Who's dead?" and looked into the coach. People sauntered from the station yard, walking with the indolence of twilight. Happy Stuart said, "Well, he won't worry about tomorrow," and turned away.

A short man with a tremendous stomach shuffled through the dusk. He said: "Wasn't sure you'd try to git through yet, Happy."

"Where's the soldiers for tomorrow?"

"Other side of the mountains. Everybody's chased out. What ain't forted up here was sent into Lordsburg. You men will bunk in the barn. I'll make out for the ladies somehow." He looked at the army girl and he appraised Henriette instantly. His eyes slid on to Malpais Bill standing in the background and recognition stirred him then and made his voice careful. "Hello, Bill. What brings you this way?"

Malpais Bill's cigarette glowed in the gathering dusk and Henriette caught the brief image of his face, serene and watchful. Malpais Bill's tone was easy, it was soft. "Just the trip."

They were moving on toward the frame house whose corner seemed to extend indefinitely into a series of attached sheds. Lights glimmered in the windows and men moved around the place, idly talking. The unhitched horses went away at a trot. The tall girl walked into the station's big room, to face a soldier in a disheveled uniform.

He said: "Miss Robertson? Lieutenant Hauser was to have met you here. He is at Lordsburg. He was wounded in a brush with the Apaches last night."

The tall army girl stood very still. She said: "Badly?"

"Well," said the soldier, "yes."

The fat man came in, drawing deeply for wind. "Too bad—too bad. Ladies, I'll show you the rooms, such as I got."

Henriette's dove-colored dress blended with the background shadows. She was watching the tall army girl's face whiten. But there was a strength in the army girl, a fortitude that made her think of the soldier. For she said quietly, "You must have had a bad trip."

"Nothing—nothing at all," said the soldier and left the room. The gambler was here, his thin face turning to the army girl with a strained expression, as though he were remembering painful things. Malpais Bill had halted in the doorway, studying the softness and the humility of Henriette's cheeks. Afterwards both women followed the fat host of Gap Station along a narrow hall to their quarters.

Malpais Bill wheeled out and stood indolently against the wall of this desert station, his glance quick and watchful in the way it touched all the men loitering along the yard, his ears weighing all the night-softened voices. Heat died from the earth and a definite chill rolled down the mountain hulking so high behind the house. The soldier was in his saddle, murmuring drowsily to Happy Stuart.

"Well, Lordsburg is a long ways off and the damn mountains are squirmin' with Apaches. You won't have any cavalry escort tomorrow. The troops are all in the field."

Malpais Bill listened to the hoofbeats of the soldier's horse fade out, remembering the loneliness of a man in those dark mountain passes, and went back to the saloon at the end of the station. This was a low-ceilinged shed with a dirt floor and whitewashed walls that once had been part of a stable. Three men stood under a lantern in the middle of this little place, the light of the lantern palely shining in the rounds of their eyes as they watched him. At the far end of the bar the cattleman and the gambler drank in taciturn silence. Malpais Bill took his whiskey when the bottle came, and noted the barkeep's obscure glance. Gap's host put in his head and wheezed, "Second table," and the other men in there began to move out. The barkeep's words rubbed together, one tone above a whisper. "Better not ride into Lordsburg. Plummer and Shanley are there."

Malpais Bill's lips were stretched to the long edge of laughter and there was a shine like wildness in his eyes. He said, "Thanks, friend," and went into the dining room.

When he came back to the yard night lay wild and deep across the desert and the moonlight was a frozen silver that touched but could not dissolve the world's incredible blackness. The girl Henriette walked along the Tonto road, swaying gently in the vague shadows. He went that way, the click of his heels on the hard earth bringing her around.

Her face was clear and strange and incurious in the night, as though she waited for something to come, and knew what it would be. But he said: "You're too far from the house. Apaches like to crawl down next to a settlement and wait for strays."

She was indifferent, unafraid. Her voice was cool and he could hear the faint loneliness in it, the fatalism that made her words so even. "There's a wind coming up, so soft and good."

He took off his hat, long legs braced, and his eyes were both attentive and puzzled. His blond hair glowed in the fugitive light.

She said in a deep breath: "Why do you do that?"

His lips were restless and the sing and rush of strong feeling was like a current of quick wind around him. "You have folks in Lordsburg?"

She spoke in a direct, patient way as though explaining something he should have known without asking. "I run a house in Lordsburg."

"No," he said, "it wasn't what I asked."

"My folks are dead—I think. There was a massacre in the Superstition Mountains when I was young."

He stood with his head bowed, his mind reaching back to fill in that gap of her life. There was a hardness and a rawness to this land and little sympathy for the weak. She had survived and had paid for her survival, and looked at him now in a silent way that offered no explanations or apologies for whatever had been; she was still a pretty girl with the dead patience of all the past years in her eyes, in the expressiveness of her lips.

He said: "Over in the Tonto Basin is a pretty land. I've got a piece of a ranch there—with a house half built."

"If that's your country why are you here?"

His lips laughed and the rashness in him glowed hot again and he seemed to grow taller in the moonlight. "A debt to collect."

"That's why you're going to Lordsburg? You will never get through collecting those kind of debts. Everybody in the Territory knows you. Once you were just a rancher. Then you tried to wipe out a grudge and then there was a bigger one to wipe out—and the debt kept growing and more men are waiting to kill you. Someday a man will. You'd better run away from the debts."

His bright smile kept constant, and presently she lifted her shoulders with resignation. "No," she murmured, "You won't run." He could see the sweetness of her lips and the way her eyes were sad for him; he could see in them the patience he had never learned.

He said, "We'd better go back," and turned her with his arm. They went across the yard in silence, hearing the undertone of men's drawling talk roll out of the shadows, seeing the glow of men's pipes in the dark corners. Malpais Bill stopped and watched her go through the station door; she turned to look at him once more, her eyes all dark and her lips softly sober, and then passed down the narrow corridor to her own quarters. Beyond her window, in the yard, a man was murmuring to another man: "Plummer and Shanley are in Lordsburg. Malpais Bill knows it." Through the thin partition of the adjoining room she heard the army girl crying with a suppressed, uncontrollable regularity. Henriette stared at the dark wall, her shoulders and head bowed; and afterwards returned to the hall and knocked on the army girl's door and went in.

SIX FRESH HORSES fiddled in front of the coach and the fat host of Gap Station came across the yard swinging a lantern against the dead, bitter black. All the passengers filed sleep-dulled and miserable from the house. Johnny Strang slammed the express box in the boot and Happy Stuart gruffly said: "All right, folks."

The passengers climbed in. The cattleman came up and Malpais Bill drawled: "Take the corner spot, mister," and got in, closing the door.

The Gap host grumbled: "If they don't jump you on the long grade you'll be all right. You're safe when you get to Al Schrieber's ranch." Happy's bronze voice shocked the black stillness and the coach lurched forward, its leather springs squealing.

They rode for an hour in this complete darkness, chilled and uncomfortable and half asleep, feeling the coach drag on a heavy-climbing grade. Gray dawn cracked through, followed by a sunless light rushing all across the flat desert now far below. The road looped from one barren shoulder to another and at sunup they had reached the first bench and were slamming full speed along a boulder-strewn flat. The cattleman sat in the forward corner, the left corner of his mouth swollen and crushed, and when Henriette saw that her glance slid to Malpais Bill's knuckles. The army girl had her eyes closed, her shoulders pressing against the Englishman, who remained bolt upright with the sporting gun between his knees. Beside Henriette the gambler seemed to sleep, and on the middle bench Malpais Bill watched the land go by with a thin vigilance.

At ten they were rising again, the juniper and scrub pine showing on the slopes and the desert below them filling with the powdered haze of another hot day. By noon they reached the summit of the range and swung to follow its narrow rock-ribbed meadows. The gambler, long motionless, shifted his feet and caught the army girl's eyes.

"Schrieber's is directly ahead. We are past the worst of it."

The blond man looked around at the gambler, making no comment; and it was then that Henriette caught the smell of smoke in the windless air. Happy Stuart was cursing once more and the brake blocks began to cry. Looking through the angled vista of the window panel Henriette saw a clay and rock chimney standing up like a gaunt skeleton against the day's light. The house that had been there was a black patch on the ground, smoke still rising from pieces that had not been completely burnt.

The stage stopped and all the men were instantly out. An iron stove squatted on the earth, with one section of pipe stuck upright to it. Fire licked lazily along the collapsed fragments of what had been a trunk. Beyond the location of the house, at the foot of a corral, lay two nude figures grotesquely bald, with deliberate knife slashes marking their bodies. Happy Stuart went over there and had his look; and came back.

"Schrieber's. Well—"

Malpais Bill said: "This morning about daylight." He looked at the gambler, at the cattleman, at the Englishman who showed no emotion. "Get back in the coach." He climbed to the coach's top, flattening himself full length there. Happy Stuart and Strang took their places again. The horses broke into a run.

The gambler said to the army girl: "You're pretty safe between those two fellows," and hauled a .44 from a back pocket and laid it over his lap. He considered Henriette more carefully than before, his taciturnity breaking. He said: "How old are you?"

Her shoulders rose and fell, which was the only answer. But the gambler said gently, "Young enough to be my daughter. It is a rotten world. When I call to you, lie down on the floor."

The Englishman had pulled the rifle from between his knees and laid it across the sill of the window on his side. The cattleman swept back the skirt of his coat to clear the holster of his gun.

The little flinty summit meadows grew narrower, with shoulders of gray rock closing in upon the road. The coach wheels slammed against the stony ruts and bounced high and fell again with a jar the springs could not soften. Happy Stuart's howl ran steadily above this rattle and rush. Fine dust turned all things gray.

Henriette sat with her eyes pinned to the gloved tips of her fingers, remembering the tall shape of Malpais Bill cut against the moonlight of Gap Station. He had smiled at her as a man might smile at any desirable woman, with the sweep and swing of laughter in his voice; and his eyes had been gentle. The gambler spoke very quietly and she didn't hear him until his fingers gripped her arm. He said again, not raising his voice: "Get down."

Henriette dropped to her knees, hearing gunfire blast through the rush and run of the coach. Happy Stuart ceased to yell and the army girl's eyes were round and dark. The walls of the canyon had tapered off. Looking upward through the window on the gambler's side, Henriette saw the weaving figure of an Apache warrior reel nakedly on a calico pony and rush by with a rifle raised and pointed in his bony elbows. The gambler took a cool aim; the stockman fired and aimed again. The Englishman's sporting rifle blasted heavy echoes through the coach, hurting her ears, and the smell of powder got rank and bitter. The blond man's boots scraped the coach top and round small holes began to dimple the paneling as the Apache bullets struck. An Indian came boldly abreast the coach and made a target that couldn't be missed. The cattleman dropped him with one shot. The wheels screamed as they slowed around the sharp ruts and the whole heavy superstructure of the coach bounced high into the air. Then they were rushing downgrade.

The gambler said quietly, "You had better take this," handing Henriette his gun. He leaned against the door with his small hands gripping the sill. Pallor loosened his cheeks. He said to the army girl: "Be sure and keep between those gentlemen," and looked at her with a way that was desperate and forlorn and dropped his head to the window's sill.

Henriette saw the bluff rise up and close in like a yellow wall. They were rolling down the mountain without brake. Gunfire fell off and the crying of the Indians faded back. Coming up from her knees then she saw the desert's flat surface far below, with the angular pattern of Lordsburg vaguely on the far borders of the heat fog. There was no more firing and Happy Stuart's voice lifted again and the brakes were screaming on the wheels, and going off, and screaming again. The Englishman stared out of the window sullenly; the army girl seemed in a deep desperate dream; the cattleman's face was shining with a strange sweat. Henriette reached over to pull the gambler up, but he had an unnatural weight to him and slid into the far corner. She saw that he was dead.

At five o'clock that long afternoon the stage threaded Lordsburg's narrow streets of 'dobe and frame houses, came upon the center square, and stopped before a crowd of people gathered in the smoky heat. The passengers crawled out stiffly. A Mexican boy ran up to see the dead gambler and began to yell his news in shrill Mexican. Malpais Bill climbed off the top, but Happy Stuart sat back on his seat and stared taciturnly at the crowd. Henriette noticed then that the shotgun messenger was gone.

A gray man in a sleazy white suit called up to Happy. "Well, you got through."

Happy Stuart said: "Yeah. We got through."

An officer stepped through the crowd, smiling at the army girl. He took her arm and said, "Miss Robertson, I believe. Lieutenant Hauser is quite all right. I will get your luggage—"

The army girl was crying then, definitely. They were all standing around, bone-weary and shaken. Malpais Bill remained by the wheel of the coach, his cheeks hard against the sunlight and his eyes riveted on a pair of men standing under the board awning of an adjoining store. Henriette observed the manner of their waiting and knew why they were here. The blond man's eyes, she noticed, were very blue and a flame burned brilliantly in them. The army girl turned to Henriette, tears in her eyes. She murmured: "If there is anything I can ever do for you—"

But Henriette stepped back, shaking her head. This was Lordsburg and everybody knew her place except the army girl. Henriette said formally, "Good-bye," noting how still and expectant the two men under the awning remained. She swung toward the blond man and said, "Would you carry my valise?"

Malpais Bill looked at her, laughter remote in his eyes, and reached into the luggage pile and got her battered valise. He was still smiling as he went beside her, through the crowd and past the two waiting men. But when they turned into an anonymous and dusty little side street of the town, where the houses all sat shoulder to shoulder without grace or dignity, he had turned sober. He said: "I am obliged to you. But I'll have to go back there."

They were in front of a house no different from its neighbors; they had stopped at its door. She could see his eyes travel this street and comprehend its meaning and the kind of traffic it bore. But he was saying in that gentle melody-making tone: "I have watched you for two days." He stopped, searching his mind to find the thing he wanted to say. It came out swiftly. "God made you a woman. The Tonto is a pretty country."

Her answer was quite barren of feeling. "No. I am known all through the Territory. But I can remember that you asked me."

He said: "No other reason?" She didn't answer but something in her eyes pulled his face together. He took off his hat and it seemed to her he was looking through his hot day to that far-off country and seeing it fresh and desirable. He murmured: "A man can escape nothing. I have got to do this. But I will be back."

He went along the narrow street, made a quick turn at the end of it, and disappeared. Heat rolled like a heavy wave over Lordsburg's housetops and the smell of dust was very sharp. She lifted her valise, and dropped it and stood like that, mute and grave before the door of her dismal house. She was remembering how tall he had been against the moonlight at Gap Station.

There were four swift shots beating furiously along the sultry quiet, and a shout, and afterwards a longer and longer silence. She put one hand against the door to steady herself, and knew that those shots marked the end of a man, and the end of a hope. He would never come back; he would never stand over her in the moonlight with the long gentle smile on his lips and with the swing of life in his casual tone. She was thinking of all that humbly and with the patience life had beaten into her. . . .

She was thinking of all that when she heard the strike of boots on the street's packed earth; and turned to see him, high and square in the muddy sunlight, coming toward her with his smile.

Although he died at a tragically young age, Les Savage, Jr. (1922–1958) was a prolific writer of Western and historical fiction, publishing twenty-four novels and well over a hundred short stories, novelettes, and novellas in his sixteen-year career. Even more remarkable than his output is the consistently high level of quality he attained, whether in the novel length or in the shorter forms. Savage's fiction is highly atmospheric, assiduously accurate as to period, and vividly evoked, as evidenced by such novels as *Treasure of the Brasada*, *The Hide Rustlers*, and *Return to Warbow*. He was meticulous about plot, inventive, innovative, and loved to experiment. His painstaking research is apparent in all that he wrote, as is his intimate grasp of the terrain wherever a story would be set, his vital familiarity with the characteristics of flora in the changing seasons, and the way of horses, mules, and men.

King of the Buckskin Breed

Les Savage, Jr.

"I'll Wait In The Hills. . . ."

In the spring of 1840, Fort Union had stood at the confluence of the Yellowstone and the Missouri for eleven years. And in that same spring, Victor Garrit came down out of the mountains for the first time in three years. He came down on a Mandan pony, still shedding its winter coat, with his long Jake Hawkins rifle held across the pommel of the buffalo saddle. Those years of running the forest alone had changed his youthful handsomeness, had hollowed his face beneath its prominent cheekbones, had settled his black eyes deep in their sockets. It gave his face the sharp edge of a honed blade, and made a thin slice of his mouth which might have left him without humor but for the quirk which came and went at one tip. He stopped twenty feet out from the huge double-leaved gate in the palisaded wall, calling to the guard.

The small door in one of the leaves opened and John Farrier stepped through. Chief factor of Fort Union since 1832, his square and beefy figure in its three-point blanket coat and black boots was known from New Orleans to the Canadian Territories. He greeted Garrit with a broad grin.

"We saw you coming in, Vic."

"Your Indian runner found me in Jackson Hole last month," Garrit said. "He said you were in trouble, and would give me amnesty if I came."

"You've got my protection, as long as you're here," Farrier told him. He scratched thoughtfully at his curly red beard. "You know Yellowstone Fur is in a hole, Vic. The Blackfoot trouble has kept my company trappers from working their lines for two years. If we don't get any fur this year we go under. The free trappers have been operating over beyond the Blackfoot country. They'll have their rendezvous in Pierre's Hole this year. If we can get a train of trade goods through and get their furs, we'll be in business again."

Garrit's eyes had never been still, roving from point to point along the palisaded wall in the suspicious restlessness of some wild thing. "And you want me to take the pack train through?"

"You're the only man can do it, Vic. I can't get any of these mangy lard-eaters around the post to take the chance, not even for double wages and a bonus. The trader's here, but he had to get all of his crew from St. Looey." The factor put a freckled hand on Garrit's knee. "Yellowstone might forget a lot of what happened in the past, if you saved the day for them, Vic."

Garrit's black eyes never seemed to lose their gleam, in their shadowed sockets, and it only added to the wildness of his gaunt face. "You'd go under if the company went under, wouldn't you, John?" he asked.

Defeat pinched at Farrier's eyes, making him look old. "You know I plan on retiring soon. I couldn't do it without Yellowstone's pension."

The quirk at the tip of Garrit's lips became a fleeting grin. "You've been my only friend up here, John. I don't think I'd be alive today without you. Where's the trader?"

A broad smile spread Farrier's beard, he slapped Garrit affectionately on the knee, turned to lead him back inside. There were a dozen company trappers and *engagés* gathered on the inside of the door, gaping at Garrit as he rode through. He followed Farrier past the great fur press in the middle of the compound to the hitch rack before the neat factor's house. He dismounted, still carrying his Jake Hawkins, and followed Farrier through the door. Then he halted, shock filling his face with a bloodless, putty hue.

Enid Nelson sat in a chair by the crude desk, rising slowly to her feet with sight of Garrit. And beside her, John Bruce took a sharp step forward, staring at Garrit with red anger filling his heavy-jawed face.

"Damn you, Farrier," he half-shouted. "You didn't tell me it would be Garrit. What are you trying to do?"

Farrier dropped his hand on Garrit's tense shoulder. "I gave him my word he'd have my protection, Bruce."

"Protection, hell!" Bruce stormed. "As an officer of Yellowstone Fur, I order you to put this man under arrest immediately."

"John—" Enid wheeled toward him, her voice sharp. "You can't ask Farrier to go back on his word!"

Bruce glared at Garrit, breathing heavily, held by Enid's angry eyes for a moment. Three years of soft living had put a little weight around his belly, but he still bore a heavy-shouldered handsomeness, in the buffalo coat and cowhide breeches of a trader. Garrit was not looking at him, however. Since he had first entered, his eyes had been on Enid. She was a tall girl, auburn-haired, with a strong beauty to her wide-set eyes, her full lips. The Palatine cloak with its pointed hood, the tight bodice holding the swell of her mature figure, the skirt of India muslin—all brought the past to Garrit with poignant impact.

Bruce finally made a disgusted sound. "I'd rather go alone than be guided by a wanted man."

"You'd never make it ten miles alone," Farrier said. "The trader for Hudson's Bay tried it last year. The Blackfeet caught him. He lost his whole pack train. He was lucky to get his men back alive."

"Those weren't Blackfeet," Garrit said thinly.

Bruce stared at him blankly a moment, then a derisive smile curled on his lips. "Don't tell me you're still harping on that Anne Corday fable."

Garrit's head lifted sharply. He turned to pace restlessly across the room, glancing at the walls, like some animal suspicious of a cage. "It's no fable," he said. His voice had lost its accustomed softness. "Anne Corday was with those Indians that got the Hudson's Bay trade goods last year. The same woman that got my pack train down on the Platte."

Farrier stopped John Bruce's angry retort with an upheld hand. "There may be something to it, Bruce. The few trappers of ours that have gotten through haven't been able to keep any pelts on their lines. Their traps have been cleaned out more systematically than any Indians would ever do it."

Enid turned to Bruce, catching his arm. "John, if Garrit's the only one who can get you through, let him do it."

"And let him take another five thousand dollars' worth of trade goods whenever he feels like it?" Bruce said. "I'm not that foolish, Enid. And you have no right to give him amnesty, Farrier. When the company hears about this, there's liable to be a new factor at Fort Union."

He turned and stamped out the other door, leaving an empty silence in the room. But Farrier winked at Garrit.

"They sent Bruce up here to learn the ropes so he could take over when I retire. But he can hardly be factor if there ain't any Yellowstone Fur, can he? And there won't be any Yellowstone Fur if he don't get through to the rendezvous. And he won't get through unless you take him. When he cools off, he'll see how simple it is."

With a sly grin he followed Bruce out. Slowly, reluctantly, Garrit looked back at Enid. His weather-darkened face appeared even more gaunt. When he finally spoke, his voice had lowered to a husky murmur.

"It's funny. I've dreamed of seeing you again, for three years. And when it comes—I don't know what to say."

A smile came hesitantly to her soft lips. She moved toward him, reached out a hand shyly, impulsively, to touch his mouth.

"That quirk's still there, isn't it?"

The touch of her hand was like satin, bringing the past back so painfully that it made him pull away, turn from her, start to pace again.

"It's the only thing that hasn't changed, in you," she said. "I don't think I'd have recognized you, at a distance. You must have lost twenty pounds. You're dark as an Indian. And so restless, Vic. Like some animal."

"The woods do that to a man, I guess," he said. "You got to be half animal to stay alive in the Blackfoot country." His deepset eyes filled with that restive gleam as he glanced around the walls. "I never saw such a small room."

She shook her head from side to side, staring at him with hurt, troubled eyes. "Was it worth it?"

He turned sharply to her. "Would you spend five years in jail for something you didn't do?"

"Don't you want to come back, Vic?"

"Come back." He looked at her an instant, the pain naked in his eyes. Then he turned away stiffly, voice low and tight. "More than anything else in the world, Enid. It's the only thing that keeps me going."

"Things have changed, Vic."

The gaunt hollows beneath his prominent cheekbones deepened, as he realized what she meant. "You . . . and Bruce?"

"I tried to wait, Vic." She turned her face away, as if unable to meet his eyes. "You have no idea how hard it was." Then she wheeled back, catching at his arm, the words tumbling out. "You've got to understand. I did wait, you've got to believe me, but it was so long, not hearing from you, then someone brought word you were dead—"

"It's all right, Enid. I understand. I had no right to ask that you wait." He paused, then brought the rest out with great effort. "I suppose you and John plan to be married after he makes good on this trip?"

"Oh, Vic—" It was torn from her, and she wheeled around, face in her hands, shoulders shaking with sobs. He stared at her, helplessly. He wanted to go to her, to take her in his arms, more than anything else he'd wanted in these three years. He started to, then his hands dropped, and he stopped again, as he realized he had no right. She was tortured enough, in her dilemma. Even though she knew he was alive now, it did not change things. He had no more to offer her than he'd had three years ago, when he fled.

Finally, in a barely audible voice, he said, "For your sake, and for

Farrier's, I hope Bruce decides to let me take him through. Tell them I'll wait in the hills to the west. These walls are getting too tight."

Hell—Cat's Brew

John Bruce's pack train left Fort Union on the twelfth of April, following the Yellowstone River south. There were ten men and thirty mules, loaded with the tobacco, Du Pont powder, Missouri lead, knives, traps, flints, vermilion, bridles, spurs, needles and thread for which the free trappers and Indians at Pierre's Hole would trade their furs.

The cavalcade toiled through the rolling grasslands south of the Missouri, forded countless creeks swollen and chocolate with spring. They passed the mouth of the Powder River where the sand lay black and fine as Du Pont on the sloping banks, and fighting their way through clay flats turned viscid as glue by the rains, finally gained the mountains.

There had not been too much talk between John Bruce and Garrit during the days in the lowlands. But now, as they pulled to the first ridge ahead of the toiling mules, and halted their horses among the pines, Bruce let out a relieved sigh.

"Thank the Lord we're though that clay. I thought I'd go crazy. I never saw such country."

Garrit sat staring off westward at the undulant sea of hoary ridges and valleys, rolling away as far as he could see. "It's a good country. You've just got to get used to it," he said. His broad chest swelled as he drew a deep breath of air, syrupy with the perfumes of pine and wild roses. "Take a whiff of that. Like wine."

Bruce frowned closely at him. "Don't tell me you actually like it— running like an animal all these years in this wilderness."

Garrit tilted his narrow, dark head to one side. "It's funny," he said. "A man doesn't think about liking it, or not liking it. He just lives it. Maybe he should stop to appreciate it more often."

"I used to see those mountain men come into St. Looey," Bruce said. "I never could understand what made them come back here, year after year, till some blizzard got them, or some Indian."

Garrit glanced at him, the humor leaving his face. "No," he said. "You wouldn't understand."

Surprise widened Bruce's sullen eyes. Then his lips clamped shut, and the antipathy dropped between them again. "You want to be careful, Garrit," he said. "I still think I should turn you in."

A sardonic light gleamed in Garrit's eyes. "But not till I've brought you through safe with the furs that'll make you chief factor of Fort Union."

Bruce's face grew ruddy, and he started to jerk his reins up and pull his horse over against the mountain man's. But a rider came laboring up the slope behind them, stopping Bruce's movement. It was Frenchie, a burly man in a cinnamon bear coat and elk hide leggings, a red scarf tied about his shaggy black hair, immense brass earrings dangling against his cheeks. He drew to a halt beside them, blowing like a horse.

"Now for the climbing, *hein?*" he grinned. "Looks like we go through that pass ahead."

"Not by a long shot," Garrit said. "How long you been in this country?"

"Jus' come north to work at Fort Union this spring," the Frenchman said. "Man don't have to know the country to see that pass is the easiest way through."

"Exactly why we don't take it," Garrit said. "The Blackfeet have caught three pack trains in there the last two years. They don't think there's any other way through Buffalo Ridge. But I know a trail over that hogback to the south."

"These mules are already worn down from that clay," Bruce said angrily. "I'm not taking them ten miles out of our way to climb over a peak when there's a perfect pass through—"

"Farrier sent me along to keep your hair on your head," Garrit said thinly. There was no quirk left at the tip of his lips. "Any time you want to go on alone, just say so."

Bruce grew rigid in the saddle, his eyes drew almost shut. For a moment, there was no sound but the stertorous breathing of the animals, standing in a long line behind them. Finally Bruce settled into the saddle.

"All right," he said, sullenly. "What do we do?"

"It's getting late. I'll scout ahead. I want to be sure what we're going into. If I'm not back by the time you reach that river in the valley below us, make camp there."

Garrit heeled his horse down off the crest and into timber. As the men disappeared behind, the only sound that broke the immense stillness was the sardonic crackle of pine cones underfoot. He could not help his usual grin at the sound. There was something sly and chuckling about it, like the forest having its own private little joke on him. It always brought him close to the mountains, the solitude, and it made him realize what a contrast his present sense of freedom was to the restive confinement he had felt in the fort.

But thought of Fort Union brought the picture of Enid back to him, and his exhilaration faded. Through all these years he had carried with him constantly the painful desire to return to her, to the life they had known. Seeing her at Fort Union had been a knife twisted in the wound. He still felt a great, hollow sickness when he thought of her being promised to Bruce. Could she be mistaken in her feelings? He had seen something in her eyes, something she had been afraid to put in words. If he cleared his name, so he could go back to her, would she realize—

He shook his head, trying to blot out the thoughts. He realized he had climbed halfway up to the next ridge without looking for sign. A man was a fool to dream in this country. His head began to move from side to side in the old, wolfish way, eyes picking up every little infraction of the normal rule of things.

It was near dusk when he found the sign. He was five or six miles beyond the pack train, emerging from a fringe of quaking aspen along a stream in the bottom of a canyon, and he caught sight of the early berry bush ahead. A few of the red-black berries were scattered on the ground, and half a dozen of the limbs had been sliced cleanly near the root. As he approached, a magpie began scolding far up the slope. It was another of the forest sounds that invariably turned the quirk at the tip of his lips to a grin. There was something irrepressibly clownish about the raucous chatter.

Just keep talking, you joker, he thought. *Long as you jabber I'm safe.*

He got down to study the moccasin tracks about the early berry bushes. They were only a few hours old, for the grass they had pressed down had not yet risen straight again. As he stood up, the magpie's scolding broke off abruptly. It made his narrow head snap around. The weather seams deepened around his eyes, squinting them almost shut, as he searched the shadowy timber. Then he hitched his horse and headed for the trees. An animal look was in his face now and he ran with a wolfish economy of motion. He reached a dense mat of buckbrush and dropped into it and became completely motionless. He could still see his horse. It had begun to browse peacefully. The timber was utterly still.

After a long space, he began to load his gun. He measured a double load of Du Pont into his charge cup and dumped it down the barrel of his Jake Hawkins. He slid aside the brass plate in the stock, revealing the cavity filled with bear grease. He wiped a linen patch across this, and stuck it to his half-ounce ball of Galena. He rammed the lead home, and then settled down to wait.

FOR TEN MINUTES he was utterly motionless. His eyes had grown hooded, the quirk had left his lips. The fanwise sinews of his fingers gleamed through the darker flesh of his hands, as they lay so softly, almost caressingly, against the long gun.

Then the man appeared, coming carefully down through the timber. He saw the horse and stopped. The brass pan of his Springfield glittered dully in the twilight. Garrit knew the conflict that was going on within him. But finally, as Garrit knew it would be, the temptation was too great, and the horse decoyed him out.

He approached the animal, frowning at it. At last he began to unhitch it.

"Don't do that, Frenchie," Garrit said.

The burly Frenchman wheeled toward the sound of his voice. Surprise dug deep lines into his greasy jowls.

"By gar," he whispered. "You are an Indian."

Garrit's voice was silken with speculation. "I thought you were the Indian."

"Ho-ho!" The man's laugh boomed through the trees. "That is the joke. He thought I was Indian. And I find his horse and think the Indian take his scalp."

"Shut up," Garrit said sharply. "Don't you know better 'n to make that much noise out here? I found sign down by the creek. Some Blackfeet had cut early berry branches for arrows."

Frenchie sobered. "We better go then, *hein?* My horse she's up on the ridge. Bruce he got worry about you and sent me to look." Garrit unhitched his horse and began the climb beside the man. Frenchie sent him an oblique glance. "You really belong to the woods, don't you?"

"How do you mean?"

"I was five feet from you and never see you. Like you was part tree or something."

"A man learns that or doesn't stay alive."

"Is more than that. Some men belong, some don't. Them that do will never be happy any place else."

It touched something in Garrit that he could not define. "Maybe so," he shrugged.

"For w'y you guide Bruce through like this? You hate him."

"It's for Farrier," Garrit said. "He's been my only friend up here. He'll go down with the company if they don't get any pelts this year."

"And for Anne Corday?"

Garrit glanced at him sharply. "What do you know about her?"

Frenchie shook his head. "Nothing. Except this is the first trade goods to go through mountains this year. Is like honey to bear. Five thousand dollar worth of honey. You have been hunting three year for Anne Corday without the success. Wouldn't it be nice if you were along when she show up to get these pack train?"

Garrit was looking straight ahead, his dark face somber and withdrawn. He would not admit it to Frenchie, but the man had struck the truth. Part of his motive in taking the train through had been his debt to Farrier. But another part was his realization of what a strong lure this train would be to the men with Anne Corday. If he could catch them in the act, with John Bruce as witness . . .

"It's funny you should talk that way," Garrit said. "Most men won't admit Anne Corday exists."

"I only know the stories I hear. You were youngest man ever trusted with Yellowstone Fur's trade goods for the rendezvous. Engaged to Enid Nelson in St. Looey. Big future ahead with the company." He sent Garrit that oblique look. "How did it really happen? I hear different story every time."

Garrit's eyes lost their focus, looking back through the years. "We had brought the trade goods by boat to the mouth of the Platte. Gervais Corday was camped there. He said he'd been a free trapper till Yellowstone Fur squeezed him out. He'd fought them and some Yellowstone man had shot him. They had to take his arm off. It made him bitter as hell toward the company."

"I would be bitter too," Frenchie said softly.

Garrit hardly heard him. "Anne Corday was his daughter. He'd married a Blackfoot squaw and kept Anne up there with the Indians. We were the first white men to see her. I guess no white man has ever really seen her since. It was raining. The Corday's invited us into their shelter. There was whiskey. You don't pay attention to how much you're drinking, with a girl like that around. She danced with me, I remember that. She got us so drunk we didn't know what was going on. And her pa and his men got away with our goods."

"But why were you accused of taking the furs?"

"Cheyennes caught us before we got back to St. Looey. My crew was wiped out. I was the only one left alive. I had to get back the rest of the way on foot. It took me months. Nobody would believe my story. Too many traders had worked that dodge on Yellowstone, and had taken the trade goods themselves. If there had been witnesses, or someone had known of the Cordays, or had seen them, it would have been different. But I was completely without proof."

"And nobody has seen Anne Corday since," Frenchie mused. "She mus' have been very beautiful woman."

Garrit nodded slowly. "I can still see her—"

He broke off, as he became aware of the expression on Frenchie's face. The man tried to hide it. But Garrit had seen the sly curl of the lips. Hot anger wheeled Garrit into Frenchie, bunching his hand in the filthy pelt of the cinnamon bear coat and yanking the man off-balance.

"Damn you. You don't believe a word I'm saying. You were just leading me on—"

For a moment they stood with their faces not an inch apart. Garrit's lips were drawn thin, his high cheekbones gleamed against the taut flesh. Finally the Frenchman let his weight settle back against Garrit's fist, chuckling deep in his chest.

"Do not be mad with Frenchie for making the joke, *M'sieu*."

Garrit shoved him away with a disgusted sound, trying to read what lay in those sly, pouched eyes. "Don't make another mistake like that," he said thinly. "It's no joke with me."

IT WAS FULL night when they got back to camp. The mules were out in timber on the picket line, grazing on the buffalo grass and cottonwood bark, indifferently guarded by a pair of buffalo-coated men. The pack saddles were lined up on one side of a roaring fire. Garrit came in at a trot, calling to the trader.

"Bruce, don't you know better 'n to build a fire like that in Indian country? Get those mules and saddle up. We can't stay here now—"

He broke off as the men about the fire parted. There was a horse near the blaze, with two willow poles hooked in a V over its back. From this *travois* the men had just lifted the woman, putting her on a buffalo pallet by the fire. Before they closed in around her again, Garrit caught a glimpse of the Indian sitting on the ground beside the pallet, head in his arms. Bruce pushed his way free, a flat keg of Monongahela in one hand.

"We can't move now, Garrit. The woman is sick. Our interpreter's been talking with them. Game has been scarce this spring. She's so weak she can hardly talk. The man had tied himself to the horse to stay on."

"That's an old dodge," Garrit said. "They've probably got a hundred red devils waiting, now, out in the trees, to jump you."

"Wouldn't you have run into them on your way back?"

Garrit shook his head darkly. "You just got to learn the hard way, don't you? If she's hungry, that whiskey won't help."

"I was just giving the men a drink. I thought a shot might revive her."

"You were what?"

"Giving the men some," Bruce said irritably. "Now don't tell me I can't do that. Farrier said he gave his men a drink every other night."

"I suppose you had some too?"

"I did. How else can a man keep his sanity out in this godforsaken country?"

Garrit shook his head disgustedly, glancing at the laughing, joking, red-faced men. "From the looks of them they've had more than their share. If you want to get anywhere tomorrow, cork that keg up right now."

He turned to walk over to the group and push his way through, to stare down at the woman. She was in an elk hide dress with openwork sleeves, whitened by bleaching, a stripe of vermilion paint was in the part of her black hair, and more was blotched on her cheeks. She lay with her head thrown back, eyes closed, breathing shallowly.

He felt the blood begin to pound in his temples. He felt shock spread its thin sickness through his belly. Suddenly, he found himself on his knees beside her, his hand grasping her arm, jerking at her.

"Open your eyes; you're no more starving than I am. Get up—"

The Indian man raised his head from his arms, calling weakly to Garrit, "*Kola, kola—*"

"Friend, hell," Garrit said savagely. "*Ma yan levi kuwa na—*"

Bruce shoved his way through, grabbing at him. "Garrit, what are you doing?"

"I'm telling him to come over here," Garrit said hotly. "He isn't weak, and this isn't any Indian. It's Anne Corday."

"Let her go," Bruce said roughly. "You're crazy. You can't treat a sick woman that way."

"She isn't sick, damn you, she's Anne Corday—"

Bruce pulled him back so hard he sat down. He jumped to his feet like a cat, whirling on Bruce, so enraged he started to hit him. Then he became aware of the men, sitting down around the campfire. Only one was still standing, and he was rubbing at his eyes, a stupid look on his face. The others were dropping their heads onto their arms, or lying back in their buffalo robes. A couple were beginning to snore stertorously. Even Bruce's eyes had a heavy-lidded look to them.

"What's the matter?" Garrit said.

"Nothing." Bruce shook his head. "Just sleepy."

"How much of that whiskey did you drink?"

Bruce yawned heavily. "Maybe a little more 'n I should. But it wouldn't do this. Just been a long day."

"Long day, hell." Garrit spotted the keg of whiskey, walked savagely over to it. He picked it up, uncorked it, sniffed. "She did this," he said, wheeling on Bruce. "That's laudanum, she's put laudanum in the whiskey—"

Then he stopped. Bruce had sat down against one of the saddles, arms supported on his knees, and his heavy head had fallen onto those arms. Garrit's eyes flashed back around the men. Frenchie was not among them. He realized he had been too intent on the whiskey. It was too late. Even as he started to wheel, with the heavy grunt in his ears, the blow struck his head.

The Fight

He regained consciousness to the sense of throbbing pain at the base of his skull. Someone was shaking him gently.

More pain dug new seams about his eyes, as he opened them.

"I thought you'd never come around," John Bruce was telling him. "It's lucky that Frenchman didn't split your head open."

He helped Garrit sit up. It was dawn, with the timber drenched in a pearl-gray mist all about them. The men were gathered around him, grimacing, rubbing their eyes, staring stupidly at each other. One of them was feeding a spitting fire, another was at the edge of camp, retching.

"We came out of it a couple of hours ago," Bruce said. "Been trying ever since to revive you."

Garrit shook his head again, winced at the pain. "How could they have got that laudanum in the whiskey?"

"When I gave her a drink, she tried to hold the keg," Bruce said. "She dropped it, spilled some. The Indian picked it up. There was a little confusion for a minute, there, when they could have put it in. I never would have believed laudanum would do that."

"If you drink enough," Garrit muttered. "Farrier used it at Fort Union once. The Indians got so drunk they were going to start a massacre. He spiked their whiskey with laudanum and it knocked them out." He sent a dismal glance to where the pack saddles had stood, beyond the fire. "Did they get everything?"

"Even the animals," Bruce said. "We're stranded."

"Did you send that Frenchman after me?"

"No. He just disappeared."

"I guess he was trying to keep me from coming back," Garrit mused. Then he looked up at Bruce, wide-eyed. "Now will you believe me?"

The man shook his dark head. "I've thought Anne Corday was a myth for so long, it's hard to accept it, even now. I might as well join you in the mountains. This will finish me with Yellowstone Fur."

"It will finish Yellowstone Fur, if we don't get that pack train back."

Bruce's black brows rose in surprise. "What chance have we got? They have a night's start on us, and they're riding. We'll be lucky to get back to Fort Union on foot, as it is."

"A crowd like this will never make it back through that Blackfoot country on foot," Garrit told him. "Your best bet is to hole up while I go after our horses. If you can hold these men here till I get back you still might get a chance to stay with Yellowstone Fur."

Bruce protested, but Garrit finally convinced him it was their only chance. He drew a map in the earth. There was a creek in the next valley that ran ten miles northward into a canyon so narrow and tortuous it could not be reached by horses. Bruce was to do his hunting now, try to get enough meat to last the men several weeks, and then walk in the water of the creek to its head. This would leave ten miles of his backtrail covered, and in such an inaccessible place, he would be comparatively safe from Indians, if he did not move around.

Bruce finally agreed, and Garrit made up a pack of smoked buffalo meat and dried corn, rolled it in one three-point blanket, and took up the trail.

They had not bothered to hide their tracks. They led northwest from the Yellowstone, toward the heart of the Blackfoot country. It convinced him more than ever that he had not been mistaken. Only someone with connections in the tribe would have dared head so boldly into their land. And Anne Corday's mother had been a Blackfoot.

He left the mountains for a while, and hit the high plains, rolling endlessly away from him, so devoid of timber in most places that he could not travel much during the day for fear of being seen. On the third day he reached the Little Belts. After the endless plains, it was like coming home. He plunged gratefully into the shadowed timber on the first of the rolling slopes.

Now it was the real running. It brought out all the animal attributes bred in him these last years. There was an intense wolfishness to his unremitting dog-trot, long body slack, head down and turning incessantly from side to side, eyes gleaming balefully in their shadowed sockets, not missing a sign. He ran on their trail till he could run no more and then crawled into a thicket and lay in stupefied sleep and then woke and ran again.

He began to see tepee rings, circles of rocks in parks or open meadows that marked the campsite of an Indian band. It made him even more watchful. On the fourth day he sighted the first Indians. He was climbing a slope, with a magpie scolding in the firs. Despite his aching weariness, he could not help his faint grin at the sound. *Just keep talking, you joker.*

His moccasins crushed resiliently into the mat of pine needles, and for another hundred yards he climbed steadily. Then the magpie broke off sharply. He stopped, staring up the slope, and wheeled and darted for a dense clump of chokecherry.

He was on his belly, hidden in the brush, when the Indians appeared. They passed within fifty yards of him and never knew he was there, a part of Blackfeet on the move, with their pack horses, their wives, their children. The scent of their tobacco floated to him, and it was not willow-bark *kinnikinnik*, but the rank plug cut the traders used. There were new axes on their saddles, and new iron bridles on their horses. They had been trading their furs with Anne Corday.

The band of spare horses made his mouth water. But he could not try for one in broad daylight, and since they were heading in the wrong direction, he did not want to lose half a day by following them south to their night camp. So he ran on.

On the fifth day he ran out of food and was afraid to shoot game for fear he would be heard. But he knew the Indian tricks. He found *tinipsila* roots and ate them raw and later on came across some bulrushes by a stream and ate the white part like celery. And farther up the stream were wild strawberries and a few service berries that only an Indian could swallow with a straight face. It gave him enough nourishment to keep running.

THAT NIGHT HE found three more tepee rings in a shallow valley. The grass had not begun to grow up around the circled rocks, so he knew they had been planted recently. The horse droppings leading north were fresh enough to have been left that morning. It was the way he wanted it.

He followed the trail by moonlight, his lank figure fluttering through the shadow-black timber like a lost animal. He found the new camp near dawn. Three tepees formed pale cones in the center of a clearing, with the horses grazing on picket ropes.

Under ordinary circumstances, he would have moved more slowly, but the squaws would be rising soon, and he wanted to get away before that. So he had to approach the horses directly, not giving them time to get used to him. He picked out a pinto with lots of wind in its heavy throttle. Before he could reach it, however, one of the animals spooked and whinnied.

This brought the dogs from where they had been sleeping near the embers of last night's fire, and their baying raised the camp. They circled him in a pack, snapping at his legs and yapping crazily. Kicking them off, he pulled the pinto's picket pin and ran down the rope to the plunging horse. The first Indian to jump through the door flap had a clumsy London fusil.

He saw that he couldn't get it loaded in time, and started to run for Garrit. The mountain man threw all his weight onto the picket rope, pulling the pinto down so he could throw the loose end around its fluttering snout in a war-bridle. He did not have time to unknot the other end from about its neck. He pulled his green River Knife and slashed it.

The Indian reached him then, leaping through the pack of dogs to swing viciously with his clubbed fusil. Garrit ducked and the butt of the gun thumped against the pinto's flank. Holding the plunging horse with one hand he threw his Green River, blade first, with the other. There was but a foot between them, and he saw it sink to the hilt in the man's shoulder.

The Indian staggered back, face contorted with pain. Garrit scooped up the rifle he had been forced to drop and threw himself aboard the horse, kicking its flanks. He raced out of camp with the dogs yapping at his heels and the other Indians stopping halfway between the tepees and the herd to load their fusils and fire after him. The short-range London guns would not reach him, however, and he plunged unhurt into timber.

He knew they would follow and ran the horse for the first creek. He went south in the water, for they knew all the tricks too. After two miles of riding the shallows he went out on shore and left sign they would be sure to follow and made them a false trail leading on south till he found a talus bench that led into another creek. The pony was unshod and would not even leave shoe scars on the rocky bench. In the water he turned north again. When he could travel north no longer in the water he left it once more. He was far enough above the Indian camp to start hunting for the Cordays' sign now. It took him several hours to pick it up.

They were pushing twenty-five horses, and he could travel at three times their speed if he drove hard. And he drove hard. All day, with only time out to water the horse and shoot a buck whose haunch he roasted over a fire and ate as he rode. He gave the horse an hour's rest at sundown and then went on.

By dawn the horse was beaten down but Garrit knew he was near his quarry for all the signs were not many hours old. His belly sucked at him with its hunger and his face, covered with a week's growth of scraggly beard, had the haggard, driven look of some animal. It took all his grim purpose and the bitterness of three years' exile to push him those last miles. Then, in the late afternoon, he topped a ridge and saw the line of pack horses standing in the park below him.

He left the horse and dropped down through the trees on foot. Closing in on the camp, he became a shadow, flitting from tree to tree. Finally he bellied down and crawled like a snake through buckwheat and chokecherry bushes till he could see the whole camp.

They had evidently just finished trading with more Indians, for there was a pile of unbaled pelts heaped to one side of a campfire, and a pack saddle next to them, with some trade goods still lying on the ground. The Blackfoot who had come to Bruce's camp with the woman was busily loading another pack saddle onto one of the horses lined up near the trees. The other three were at the fire. Frenchie was on his hunkers, still wearing his immense cinnamon bear coat, sorting out the pelts they had just gotten. Gervais Corday stood above him, tall, bitter-eyed, one-armed. And Anne Corday was feeding new wood to the fire.

The weather seams deepened about Garrit's eyes, as he stared at her, giving his face an expression close to pain. This was the woman he had hunted for three years. Hers was the face he had seen in a thousand dreams. And now it was before him. Her blue-black hair no longer had the vermilion in its part. It was blown wild by the wind, and made a tousled frame for the piquant oval of her face, with its black eyes, its ripe lips. She had discarded the Indian dress for a shirt made from a red Hudson's Bay blanket, and a skirt of white doeskin with fringes that softly caressed her coppery calves. Even in his bitter triumph, he could not deny her striking, young beauty.

"Ho-ho," Frenchie chortled. "There are over twenty prime beaver here. Another year or so like this and we'll be rich."

Gervais frowned down at him. "You said this would finish Yellowstone Fur."

"Is true." The Frenchman grinned. "They don't turn this pack train into furs, they go under. But why stop? There is still American Fur, Rocky Mountain Fur. Even Hudson's Bay."

"Did they take my arm?" Gervais's voice was acid. He began to pace back and forth, slapping at his elk hide leggins with his good hand. "Did they ruin me? What do I care about Rocky Mountain or Hudson's Bay? They didn't smash my life. It is Yellowstone Fur who will pay." His voice began to shake. "They can't take a man's life and toss it away like a puff of smoke. Ruin everything he worked for so long. Cast him and his daughter upon the wilderness—"

The girl caught his arm, her voice low and placating. "Father please, don't get excited again—"

"Excited!" He turned on her with blazing eyes. "How can you talk that way? You were ruined too. All my plans for you. Instead of a great lady you're nothing but a wild animal running the forest with me."

"One fur company is just as bad as the next," Frenchie said. "You saw how American Fur pushed Lestrade off his rightful lines. If you'd fought them, I'm sure they'd have taken your arm just as quickly."

"Frenchie," the girl said sharply. "Don't start him off again. You're just twisting things around. Maybe he had reason to fight Yellowstone, but—"

"I don't know—" Gervais pulled away from his daughter, pacing again. "Perhaps Frenchie is right."

"Of course I'm right," the big Frenchman said. "What good would it do to stop now? If you take what we've made and try to start again, some other big fur company will only pinch you off again. We've got to ruin them all, Gervais. Only then will it be safe for honest men out here again. They take your arm this time; they're liable to kill you next time—"

"They won't get the chance, Frenchie," Garrit said, rising from the chokecherry bushes.

The three in the clearing and the Indian by the horses all turned in surprise. Garrit walked toward them, his Jake Hawkins held across one hip. Gervais finally let out a pent breath, speaking in a voice thin with shock.

"I thought you said you took all the horses."

"I did," Frenchie said. "The man's inhuman." Then he let out his bellowing laugh. "*Sacré bleu,* I should have kill you. The only man in the world who could have catch us on foot, and I let him live."

At that moment a quick movement from the Indian spun Garrit toward him. The man had tried to jump behind one of the horses and scoop up a loaded rifle and fire, all at the same time. His gun boomed simultaneously with Garrit's but he had tried to do too much at once. His bullet dug into the ground a foot from Garrit, while Garrit's bullet struck him in the chest, knocking him backward like a heavy blow.

But it gave Frenchie his chance. He reached Garrit before the mountain man could wheel back, with Gervais Corday rushing right in behind. Garrit was off-balance when the Frenchman grabbed his rifle. It was his first true sense of the man's bearlike strength. He felt as though his hands had been torn off with the rifle when Frenchie wrenched it free.

The big Frenchman swung it wide, clubbed, and brought it back in a vicious circle. It would have broken Garrit's head open. All he could do was drop to his knees. The heavy gun whistled over his head and smashed Gervais right in the face as he came rushing in on Frenchie's flank.

The one-armed man made a choked sound and dropped like a poled ox. Garrit came up off his knees into Frenchie, locking the rifle between them. It knocked the Frenchman back off his feet and he rolled to the ground with Garrit on top, fighting like a cat.

The quarters were too close for the rifle and the Frenchman let it go to pull his knife. Garrit tried to grasp the wrist but the Frenchman spraddled out for leverage and rolled atop Garrit.

The mountain man saw the flash of a blade and jerked his whole body aside. The knife drove into the ground. Frenchie yanked it out, but Garrit got hold of the knife-wrist with both hands and twisted it inward as he lunged upward with his whole body.

It drove the knife hilt-deep into the Frenchman. He let out a great shout of pain and flopped off Garrit. As the mountain man rolled over and came to his feet he saw Anne Corday on her knees beside her father, fumbling the pistol from his belt. Garrit ran at her, reaching her just as she raised the weapon. He kicked it out of her hand.

She threw herself up at him, clawing like an enraged cat. He caught both hands, spun aside, used her own momentum to throw her. She hit on her back so hard it stunned her, and she made no attempt to roll over or rise.

Garrit wheeled back in time to see Frenchie staggering into the trees, one hand gripped over his bloody side. Garrit got the loaded pistol and ran after the man. But by the time he reached timber, Frenchie was out of sight. Garrit heard Anne Corday groan and roll over. He didn't know how much time it would take him to find Frenchie. He couldn't risk it, he couldn't take that chance of losing the pack train again, with the girl and her father still in the clearing.

Reluctantly, he turned back to Anne Corday. The anger was gone from her face. Grief and shock rendered it blank. She was staring at her father, as if just realizing how crazily his head was twisted. Garrit knew, then, what she must have known. The blow of the rifle butt had broken Gervais Corday's neck.

"She'll Always Be Calling. . . ."

It was two days before the girl would talk to Garrit. He buried her father and the Indian up there in the Little Belts and took the pack train and started back to Bruce.

The second night he made camp on the white beach of a creek in a narrow gorge that rose a hundred feet above them and would hide the light of their fire. The girl sat on a heap of buffalo robes, watching him draw a spark with his flint and steel. When he had the blaze started, her voice came softly out of the night.

"You love this country, don't you?"

He was silent awhile, staring into the flames. "I guess you're right. The country gets into a man without him even knowing it." He paused, then slowly turned to look at her. "You don't hate me?"

"I've been mixed up these last two days." She spoke in a low, strained voice. "For a while I thought you were to blame for my father's death. But the Frenchman killed my father." She shook her head slowly. "Something like this was bound to happen sooner or later. Father was changing so. I thought he was bitter enough, at first. But he was getting worse. He was becoming a fanatic. Actually, you have as much reason to hate me. We ruined you, didn't we?"

He turned and walked to where she sat, towering above her, his face narrow and dark with thought as he gazed down at her. "I should hate you. I've tried to. But what I saw in that clearing changed a lot of things. Don't you realize how Frenchie was using your father?"

She stared at the sand, her lips still pinched and white with grief. "I realize now. The Frenchman didn't show his true colors till that afternoon. We thought he was a friend, another man who had been ruined by Yellowstone Fur. But he was nothing more than a thief, using my father's bitterness against Yellowstone to further his own ends."

"And your bitterness?"

Her face turned up to him defiantly. "Were we wrong? Wouldn't you despise the people who ruined your father?"

He dropped beside her, caught her hands. "It wasn't Yellowstone Fur itself, Anne. Has your father so filled you with his bitterness that you can't see that? There are decent men in Yellowstone. There's a man named Farrier down at Fort Union who could have turned me in, but he gave me a break."

"They sent a man out to kill my father—"

"Did your father really convince you of that? I saw a copy of the Yellowstone man's orders. He was sent to try and negotiate a new deal with your father for his territory. It was your father who started the fight. The Yellowstone man was only defending himself."

She jumped to her feet, eyes flashing. "Now you're trying to twist it up. I forgave you my father's death. Isn't that enough?" She wheeled away from him, walking to the end of the sandspit. She locked her hands, staring out into the night for a long time. Finally she said, thinly, "You think you'll take me in. You think you'll show me to all those men who don't believe Anne Corday exists, and it will clear your name."

"It's what I've been working toward for three years," he said, in a low voice.

"You'll never even get me back to Bruce," she said.

"Where would you go, if you escaped?" he said, gently.

"My mother is still with the tribe, up near Flathead Lake," Anne said. "I would be safe with any band of Blackfeet I met. But I don't need that. Don't you know who is following us?"

He felt his head lift in surprise, as he realized what she meant. "How could he, with a wound like that?"

"I know him," she said. "When he sets out to do something, nothing can stop him. You could stab him a dozen times and he could still walk a hundred miles. Frenchie is following us, Garrit, and he will catch us. You will never take me in."

GARRIT DID NOT sleep much that night. He tied Anne Corday's hands and spent most of the time scouting the gorge. It rained the next day, a spring thunderstorm that made the creeks overflow their banks and wiped out the trail of the pack train. Garrit pushed hard, knowing there was little chance of meeting Indians in the storm. But thought of the Frenchman hung more heavily upon him than any danger of Indians. If Anne Corday was right, the man would be a constant threat, hanging over them till they reached Bruce. It made Garrit jumpy, imbuing him with more than his normal restlessness.

They made a miserable camp in a cave, both of them soaking wet, and he hung a three-point for Anne to undress behind and then she wrapped the blanket around her and huddled over the fire.

"Do you remember how it was raining the first night we met, down on the Platte?" she said.

"And you took us into your shelters and let us dry our clothes and drink your whiskey and we got drunk as Indians on ration day."

"I had been drunk before. It was more than that. It's bothered me ever since."

"It has bothered me, too," she said, softly.

He stared down at her, trying to fathom the strange look in her eyes, to untangle the mixed emotions in himself. Her lips, so red, so ripe, seemed to rise toward him, until they were touching his, with her body in his arms.

After a long while, he backed away, staring down at her. There was a twisted look to her face, a shining confusion in her eyes. Then, for an instant, the expression in her face changed. Her eyes seemed to focus on something behind him. When they swung back to his face, she reached up to pull his lips down to hers once more.

Only senses developed through three years of living like an animal would have detected it. Some sound, unidentifiable in that instant, reached him. He tried to tear himself loose and twist around. He shifted far enough aside to that the knife went into his arm instead of his back.

The girl scrambled away from him, lunging for the rifle he had kept loaded at all times, these last days. Sick with pain, he tried to wheel on around and rise. He had a dim view of the Frenchman above him, the pelt of his coat matted with dried blood, a murderous light in his eyes.

Then his fist smashed Garrit across the face, knocking him back against the wall of the cave, and his other hand pulled the knife free of Garrit's upper arm. Garrit rolled over, dazed by the blow. His eyes were open, but he could barely see the Frenchman, lunging up above him, raising the knife for the kill. He tried to rise, but his stunned nerves would not answer his will. Anne Corday stood on the other side of the cave, the loaded Jake Hawkins in her hands. There was a wide-eyed vindication on her face.

The Frenchman straddled Garrit with a triumphant bellow, and the uplifted knife flashed in the firelight as it started to come down.

Then the shot boomed out, rocking the cave with its thunder. As if from a heavy blow, the Frenchman was slammed off Garrit and carried clear up against the wall of the cave. He hung there a moment, and then toppled back, to sprawl limply on the ground. Garrit shared blankly at him, until he finally realized what had happened. A Jake Hawkins packed that much punch, close up.

Slowly he turned his head, to see the girl, still holding the gun, smoke curling from its muzzle. Her face was blank, as if she was surprised what she had done. Then that same confusion widened her eyes. With a small cry, she dropped the rifle, wheeled, and ran out of the cave. He got to his feet and tried to follow, but almost fell again at the mouth and had to stop there. He heard a whinny, then the drumming of hooves. He stared out into the dripping timber, knowing he was too weak to follow her. The knowledge turned his face bleak and empty.

JOHN BRUCE'S PACK train returned to Fort Union on the first day of September. The trade goods were gone from the packs, now. They were bulging with dark brown beaver pelts and buffalo robes. The saddle-galled horses filed soddenly in through the great double-leaved gates, met by cheers and greetings of the *engagés* and hunters and trappers of the post.

Farrier took Bruce and Garrit to his office. Enid was there, in a wine dress, a pale expectancy in her face. Bruce grasped her arms, a boyish eagerness lighting his heavy features momentarily. Garrit thought the presence of himself and Farrier must have restrained them from an expression of their true feelings, for after looking into her eyes a long moment, Bruce turned to Farrier, telling him of Anne Corday. When he was finished, Farrier turned in amazement to Garrit.

"And what happened to the girl?"

Garrit stared around at the walls, feeling that constriction again. He rubbed at his arm, still sore from the knife wound Frenchie had given him. "She got away," he said, curtly. "I couldn't help it."

"Your name will be cleared anyway," Farrier said. "Bruce's whole crew is witness to what happened. You've saved Yellowstone Fur, Garrit, and they'll certainly reinstate you with honors." He scratched his beard, studying Bruce and Enid with a knowing grin. "Maybe we better go out and talk it over, while these two reunite."

Bruce had been watching Enid, whose eyes had never left Garrit. "Perhaps it is I who had better go out with you, Farrier," he said.

Enid turned sharply to him. "Bruce, I—"

"Never mind, Enid." His voice had a dead sound. "I guess I should have known how you felt, ever since you saw Garrit here last April."

He turned, shoulders dragging, and went out with a perplexed Farrier. Garrit felt sorry for the man. He knew he should have felt elation for himself, however, as he turned back to Enid, but it did not come.

"I have always wondered, Vic, why you let her make such a fool of you, that first time, on the Platte," Enid said.

He stopped, frowning deeply. "I've wondered that myself."

"Perhaps, Vic, it was because she is really the woman, and I never was," she said.

He turned to her, tried to say something. She shook her head.

"You'll never be happy with the old life. I can see that now. If you want to go to her, Vic, you're free."

He stared at her a long time, realizing she had touched the truth. And he knew now why Anne Corday's face had been with him in so many dreams. It hadn't been there as a symbol of his revenge, or vindication.

"Thank you, Enid," he said, softly.

He left the fort with but one packhorse and enough supplies to take him as far as Flathead Lake. He rode across the flats and into the timber where a magpie's scolding drew a fleeting grin to his lips. He stopped, to take one look backward, and then he turned his face toward the mountains, and rode.

Not only a writer of Western fiction, Frank Bonham (1914–1988) also produced mysteries, television scripts, and articles for magazines and journals. Starting out small, Bonham turned out several hundred Western and mystery short stories and novelettes for pulp magazines and other magazines such as *McCall's*, *Argosy*, and *The Saturday Evening Post*. During his career he published more than forty books, approximately half of them adult Westerns, including *Lost Stage Valley*, *Cast a Long Shadow*, and the novel many consider to be his masterpiece, *The Eye of the Hunter*.

Burn Him Out

———

Frank Bonham

Will Starrett squatted before the campfire in the creek bottom, drinking his coffee and watching the other men over the rim of his tin cup. In the strong light from the fire, the sweat and the dirt and the weariness made harsh masks of their faces. They were tired men. But pushing up through their fatigue was a growing restlessness. Now and then, a man's face was lost in heavy shadow as he turned away to talk with a neighbor. A head nodded vigorously, and the buzz of talk grew louder. To Starrett, listening, it was like the hum a tin of water makes as it comes to a boil. The men were growing impatient now, and drawing confidence from each other. Snatches of talk rose clearly. Without the courtesy of direct address, they were telling Tim Urban what to do.

Starrett swirled his cup to raise the sugar from the bottom and studied Urban coldly. The man leaned against the wheel of a wagon, looking cornered. He held a cup of coffee in his hand and his puffy face was mottled with sweat and dirt. On his hands and forearms was the walnut stain of grasshopper excrement. He was a man for whom Starrett felt only mild contempt. Urban was afraid to make his own decisions, and yet unable to accept outside advice. The land on which he stood, and on which they had worked all day, was Urban's. The decision about the land was his, too. But because he hesitated, so obviously, other voices were growing strong with eagerness to make up his mind for him. Tom Cowper was the most full-throated of the twenty-five who had fought the grasshoppers since dawn.

"If the damned poison had only come!" he said. "We could have been spreading it tonight and maybe had them stopped by noon. Since it ain't come, Tim—" He scowled and shook his head. "We're going to have to concoct some other poison just as strong."

"What would that be?" Starrett struck a match and shaped the orange light with his hands.

Cowper, a huge man with a purplish complexion, badger-gray hair, and tufted sideburns, pondered without meeting Starrett's eyes, and answered without opening his mind.

"Well, we've got time to think of something, or they'll eat this country right down to bedrock. We're only three miles from your own land right now. The hoppers didn't pasture on Urban's grass because they liked the taste of it. They just happened to land here. Once they get a start, or a wind comes up, they'll sweep right down the valley. We've got to stop them here."

Will Starrett looked at him and saw a big angry-eyed man worrying about his land as he might have worried about any investment. To him, land was a thing to be handled like a share of railroad stock. You bought it when prices were low, you sold it when prices were high. Beyond this, there was nothing to say about it.

When Starrett did not answer him, Cowper asked, "What is there to do that we haven't already done? If we can't handle them here on Tim's place, how can we handle them on our own?"

They all knew the answer to that, Starrett thought. Yet they waited for someone else to say it. It was Tim Urban's place to speak, but he lacked the guts to do it. Starrett dropped the match and tilted his chin as he drew on the cigarette. The fire's crackling covered the far-off infinite rattling of the grasshoppers, the night covered the sight of them. But they were still there in every man's mind, a hated, crawling plague sifting the earth like gold-seekers.

They were there with their retching green smell and their racket, as of a herd of cattle in a dry cornfield. Across two miles of good bunchgrass land they had squirmed, eating all but a few weeds, stripping leaves and bark from the trees. They had dropped from the sky upon Urban's home place the night before, at the end of a hot July day. They had eaten every scrap of harness in the yard, gnawed fork-handles and corral bars, chewed the paint off his house and left holes where onions and turnips had been in his garden.

By night, four square miles of his land had been destroyed, his only stream was coffee-colored with hopper excrement. And the glistening brown insects called Mormon crickets were moving on toward the valley's heart as voraciously as though wagon loads of them had not been hauled to a coulee all day and cremated in brush fires. And no man knew when a new hatch of them might come across the hills.

Starrett frowned. He was a dark-faced cattleman with a look of seasoned toughness, a lean and sober man, who in his way was himself a creature of the land. "Well, there's one thing," he said.

"What's that?" Cowper asked.

"We could pray."

Cowper's features angered, but it was his foreman, Bill Hamp, who gave the retort. "Pray for seagulls, like the Mormons?"

"The Mormons claim they had pretty good luck."

With an angry flourish, Hamp flung the dregs of his coffee on the ground. He was a drawling, self-confident Missourian, with truculent pale eyes and a brown mustache. The story was that he had marshaled some cowtown a few years ago, or had been a gunman in one of them.

He had been Cowper's ramrod on his other ranches in New Mexico and Colorado, an itinerant foreman who suited Cowper. He did all Cowper asked of him—kept the cows alive until the ranch could be resold at a profit. To Hamp, a ranch was something you worked on, from month to month, for wages. Land, for him, had neither beauty nor dimension.

But he could find appreciation for something tangibly beautiful like Tom Cowper's daughter, Lynn. And because Starrett himself had shown interest in Lynn, Bill Hamp hated him—hated him because Starrett was in a position to meet her on her own level.

Hamp kept his eyes on Starrett. "If Urban ain't got the guts to say it," he declared, "I have. Set fires! Burn the hoppers out!" He made a sweeping gesture with his arm.

Around the fire, men began to nod. Urban's rabbity features quivered. "Bill, with the grass dry as it is I'd be burned out!"

Hamp shrugged. "If the fire don't get it, the hoppers will," he said.

Cowper sat there, slowly nodding his head. "Tim, I don't see any other way. We'll backfire and keep it from getting out of hand."

"I wouldn't count on that," Starrett said.

"It's take the risk or accept catastrophe," Cowper declared. "And as far as its getting out of hand goes, there's the county road where we could stop it in a pinch."

"Best to run off a strip with gangplows as soon as we set the fires," Hamp said. He looked at Starrett with a hint of humor. Downwind from Tim Urban's place at the head of the valley was Starrett's. Beyond that the other ranches sprawled over the prairie. Hamp was saying that there was no reason for anyone to buck this, because only Urban could lose by the fire.

Starrett said nothing, and the opinions began to come.

Finally Cowper said, "I think we ought to take a vote. How many of you are in favor of setting fires? Let's see hands on it."

There were twenty men in the creek bottom. Cowper counted fourteen in favor. "The rest of you against?"

All but Starrett raised their hands. Hamp regarded him. "Not voting?"

"No. Maybe you'd like to vote on a proposition of mine."

"What's that?"

"That we set fire to Cowper's ranch house first."

Cowper's face contorted. "Starrett, we've got grief enough without listening to poor jokes!"

"Burning other men's grass is no joke. This is Urban's place, not yours or mine. I'm damned if any man would burn me out by taking a vote."

Bill Hamp sauntered to the wagon and placed his foot against a wheel-hub. "Set by and let ourselves be eaten out—is that your idea?"

"Ourselves?" Starrett smiled.

Hamp flushed. "I may not own land, but I make my living from it."

"There's a difference, Hamp. You need to sweat ten years for a down payment before you know what owning an outfit really means. Then you'd know that if a man would rather be eaten out than burned out, it's his own business."

Hamp regarded him stonily and said, "Are you going to stand there and say we can't fire the place to save the rest?"

Starrett saw the men's eyes in the firelight, some apprehensive, some eager, remembering the stories about Bill Hamp and his cedar-handled .45. "No," he said. "I didn't say that."

Hamp, after a moment, let a smile loosen his mouth. But Starrett was saying, "I've got nothing against firing, but everything against deciding it for somebody else. Nobody is going to make up Urban's mind for him, unless he agrees to it."

Urban asked quickly, "What would you do, Will?"

It was not the answer Starrett wanted. "I don't know," he said. "What are you going to do?"

Urban knew an ally when he saw one. He straightened, spat in the fire, and with his thumbs hooked in the riveted corners of his jeans pockets, stared at Cowper. "I'm going to wait till morning," he said. "If the poison don't come—and if it don't rain or the wind change—I may decide to fire. Or I may not."

Information passed from Cowper to Bill Hamp, traveling on a tilted eyebrow. Hamp straightened like a man stretching slowly and luxuriously. In doing so, his coat was pulled back and the firelight glinted on his cartridge belt. "Shall we take that vote again, now that Mr. Starrett's finished stumping?" he asked.

Starrett smiled. "Come right down to it, I'm even principled against such a vote."

Hamp's dark face was stiff. The ill-tempered eyes held the red catch-lights of the fire. But he could not phrase his anger for a moment, and Starrett laughed. "Go ahead," he said. "I've always wondered how much of that talk was wind."

Cowper came in hastily. "All right, Bill! We've done all we can. It's Urban's land. As far as I'm concerned, he can fight the grasshoppers himself." He looked at Starrett. "We'll know where to lay the blame if things go wrong."

He had brought seven men with him. They got up, weary, unshaven cowpunchers wearing jeans tied at the bottoms to keep the grasshoppers from crawling up their legs. Cowper found his horse and came back, mounted.

"You'll be too busy to come visit us for a while." His meaning was clear—he was speaking of his daughter. "As for the rest of it—I consider that a very dangerous principle you've laid down. I hope it never comes to a test when the hoppers have the land next to *mine*."

They slept a few hours. During the night a light rain fell briefly. Starrett lay with his head on his saddle, thinking of the men he had so nearly fought with.

Cowper would sacrifice other men's holdings to protect his own. That was his way. Urban would protest feebly over being ruined with such haste, but he would probably never fight. Hamp was more flexible. His actions were governed for the time by Cowper's. But if it came to a showdown, if the hoppers finished Urban and moved a few miles east onto Starrett's land, this dislike that had grown into a hate might have its airing.

Starrett wished Cowper had been here longer. Then the man might have understood what he was trying to say. That land was not shares of stock, not just dirt with grass growing on it. It was a bank, a feedlot, a reservoir. The money, the feed, the water were there as long as you used them wisely. But spend them prodigally, and they vanished. Your cattle gaunted down, your graze died. You were broke. But after you went back to punching cows or breaking horses, the grass came back, good as ever, for a wiser cowman to manage.

It was a sort of religion, this faith in the land. How could you explain it to a man who gypsied around taking up the slack in failing ranches by eliminating extra hands, dispensing with a useless horse-herd, and finally selling the thing at a profit?

Ranching was a business with Cowper and Hamp, not a way of life.

Just at dawn the wind died. The day cleared. An hour later, as they were riding, armed with shovels, into the blanket of squirming hoppers to shovel tons of them into the wagons and dozers, a strong wind rose. It was coming from the north, a warm, vigorous breeze that seemed to animate the grasshoppers. Little clouds of them rose and flew a few hundred yards and fell again. And slowly the earth began to shed them, the sky absorbed their rattling weight and they moved in a low cloud toward the hills. Soon the land was almost clean. Where they had passed in their crawling advance, the earth was naked, with only a few clumps of brush and skeletal trees left.

Urban leaned on the swell of his saddle by both elbows. He swallowed a few times. Then he said softly, like a man confessing a sin, "I prayed last night, Will. I prayed all night."

"Then figure this as the first installment on an answer. But this is grasshopper weather. They're coming out of the earth by the million. Men are going to be ruined if they come back out of the brush, and if the wind changes, they will. Don't turn down that poison if it comes."

That day Starrett rode into Antelope. From the stationmaster he learned that Tim Urban's poison had not come. A wire had come instead, saying that the poison had proved too dangerous to handle and suggesting that Urban try Epsom salts. Starrett bought all the Epsom salts he could find— a hundred pounds. Then he bought a ton of rock salt and ordered it dumped along the county road at the southwest border of his land.

He had just ridden out of the hot, shallow canyon of the town and turned down toward the river when he saw a flash of color on the bridge, among the elms. He came down the dusty slope to see a girl in green standing at the rail. She stood turning her parasol as she watched him drop the bridle-reins and come toward her.

"Imagine!" Lynn smiled. "Two grown men fighting over grasshoppers!"

Will held her hand, warm and small in the fragile net of her glove. "Well, not exactly. We were really fighting over foremen. Hamp puts some of the dangedest ideas in Tom's head."

"The way I heard it some ideas were needed last night."

"Not that kind. Hamp was going to ram ruination down Urban's throat."

"You have more tact than I thought," she told him. "It's nice of you to keep saying, 'Hamp.' But isn't that the same as saying 'Tom Cowper?'"

He watched the creek dimple in the rain of sunlight through the leaves. "I've been hoping it wouldn't be much longer. I could name a dozen men who'd make less fuss and get more done than Hamp. If Urban had made the same suggestion to your father, Hamp would have whipped him."

She frowned. "But if Urban had had the courage, he'd have suggested firing himself, wouldn't he? Was there any other way to protect the rest of us?"

"I don't think he was as much concerned about the rest of us as about himself. You've never seen wildfire, have you? I've watched it travel forty miles an hour. July grass is pure tinder. If we'd set fires last night, Tim would have been out of business this morning. And of course the hardest thing to replace would have been his last fifteen years."

"I know," she said. But he knew she didn't. She'd have an instinctive sympathy for Urban, he realized. She was that kind of woman. But she hadn't struggled with the land. She couldn't know what the loss of Urban's place would have meant to him.

"They won't come back, will they?" she asked.

He watched a rider slope unhurriedly down the hill toward them. "If they do, and hit me first, I hope to be ready for them. Or maybe they'll pass me up and land on Tom. . . . Or both of us. Why try to figure it?"

She collapsed the parasol and put her hands out to him. "Will—try to understand us, won't you? Dad doesn't want to be a rebel, but if he makes more fuss than you like it's only because he's feeling his way. He's never had a ranch resist him the way this one has. Of course, he bought it just at the start of a drought, and it hasn't really broken yet."

"I'll make you a bargain." Will smiled. "I'll try to understand the Cowpers if they'll do the same for me."

She looked up at him earnestly. "I do understand you—in most things. But then something happens like last night and I wonder if I understand you any better than I do some Comanche brave."

"Some Comanches," he said, "like their squaws blonde. That's the only resemblance I know of."

The horseman on the road came past a peninsula of cottonwoods and they saw it was Bill Hamp. Hamp's wide mouth pulled into a stiff line when he saw Starrett. He hauled his horse around, shifting his glance to Lynn. "Your father's looking all over town for you, Miss Lynn."

She smiled. "Isn't he always? Thanks, Bill." She opened the parasol and laid it back over her shoulder. "Think about it, Will. He can be handled, but not with a spade bit."

She started up the hill. Hamp lingered to roll a cigarette. He said, "One place he can't be handled is where she's concerned."

"He hasn't kicked up much fuss so far," said Starrett.

Hamp glanced at him, making an effort, Starrett thought, to hold the reasonless fury out of his eyes. "If you want peace with him as a neighbor, don't try to make a father-in-law out of him."

Starrett said, "Is this him talking, or you, Bill?"

"It's me that's giving the advice, yes," Hamp snapped. "I'd hate to ram it down your throat, but if you keep him riled up with your moonshining around . . ."

Starrett hitched his jeans up slowly, his eyes on the ramrod.

Lynn had stopped on the road to call to Hamp, and Hamp stared wordlessly at Will and turned to ride after her.

As he returned to the ranch, Starrett thought, *If there's any danger in him, it's because of her.*

STARRETT SPREAD THE salt in a wide belt along the foothills. Every morning he studied the sky, but the low, dark cloud did not reappear. Once he and Cowper met in town and rather sheepishly had a drink. But Bill Hamp drank a little farther down the bar and did not look at Starrett.

Starrett rode home that evening feeling better. Well, you did not live at the standpoint of crisis, and it was not often that something as dramatic as a grasshopper invasion occurred to set neighbors at each other's throats. He felt almost calm, and had so thoroughly deceived himself that when he reached the cutoff and saw the dark smoke of locusts sifting down upon the foothills in the green afterlight he stared a full ten seconds without believing his eyes.

He turned his horse and rode at a lope to his home place. He shouted at the first puncher he saw, "Ride to Urban's for the dozers!" and sent the other three to the nearest ranches for help. Then he threw some food in a sack and, harnessing a team, drove toward the hills.

There was little they could do that night, other than prepare for the next day. The hoppers had landed in a broad and irregular mass like a pear-shaped birthmark on the earth, lapping into the foothills, touching the road, spreading across a curving mile-and-a-half front over the corner of Will Starrett's land.

By morning, eighteen men had gathered, a futile breastplate to break the hoppers' spearhead. Over the undulating grassland spread the plague of Mormon crickets. They had already crossed the little area of salt Starrett had spread. If they had eaten it, it had not hurt them. They flowed on, crawling, briefly flying, swarming over trees to devour the leaves in a matter of moments, to break the branches by sheer weight and strip the bark away.

The men tied cords about the bottoms of their jeans, buttoned their shirt collars, and went out to shovel and curse. Fires were started in coulees. The dozers lumbered to them with their brown-bleeding loads of locusts. Wagon loads groaned up to the bank and punchers shoveled the squirming masses into the gully. Tom Cowper was there with Hamp and a few others.

He said tersely, "We'll lick them Will." He was gray as weathered board.

But they all knew this was a prelude to something else. That was as far as their knowledge went. They knew an army could not stop the grasshoppers. Only a comprehensive thing like fire could do that. . . .

They fought all day and until darkness slowed the hoppers' advance. Night brought them all to their knees. They slept, stifled by the smoke of grasshoppers sizzling in the coulees. In the morning Starrett kicked the campfire coals and threw on wood. Then he looked around.

They were still there. Only a high wind that was bringing a scud of rain clouds gave him hope. Rain might stop the hoppers until they could be raked and burned. But this rain might hold off for a week, or a wind might tear the clouds to rags.

There was rage in him. He wanted to fight them physically, to hurt these filthy invaders raping his land.

When he turned to harness his team, he saw Bill Hamp bending over the coffee pot, dumping in grounds. Hamp set the pot in the flames and looked up with a taunt in his eyes. Starrett had to discipline his anger to keep it from swerving foolishly against the ramrod.

The wind settled against the earth and the hoppers began to move more rapidly. The fighters lost a half-mile in two hours. They were becoming panicky now, fearing the locusts would fly again and cover the whole valley.

At noon they gathered briefly. Starrett heard Hamp talking to a puncher. He heard the word "gangplows" before the man turned and mounted his horse. He went over to Hamp. "What do we want with gangplows?"

"We might as well be prepared." Hamp spoke flatly.

"For what?" Cowper frowned.

"In case you decide to fire, Mr. Starrett," said Hamp, "and it gets out of hand."

"Shall we put it to a vote?" Starrett asked. An irrational fury was mounting through him, shaking his voice.

"Whenever you say." Hamp drew on his cigarette, enjoying both the smoke and the situation.

Starrett suddenly stepped into him, slugging him in the face. Hamp went down and turned over, reaching for his gun. Starrett knelt quickly with a knee in the middle of his back and wrenched the gun away. He moved back, and as the foreman came up he sank a hard blow into his belly. Hamp went down and lay writhing.

"IF YOU'VE GOT anything to say, say it plain!" Starrett shouted. "Don't be campaigning against me the way you did Tim Urban! Don't be talking them into quitting before we've started."

He was ashamed then, and stared angrily about him at the faces of the other men. Tim Urban did not meet his eyes. "We've pretty well started, Will," he said. "You've had our patience for thirty-six hours, and it's yours as long as you need it."

Cowper looked puzzled. He stood regarding Hamp with dismay.

After a moment Starrett turned away. "Let's go," he said.

Cowper said, "How long are we going to keep it up? Do you think we're getting anywhere?"

Starrett climbed to the wagon seat. "I'll make up my mind without help, Tom. When I do I'll let you know."

The sky was lighter than it had been in the morning, the floating continents of cloud leveled to an even gray. It was the last hope Starrett had had, and it was gone. But for the rest of the afternoon he worked and saw to it that everyone else worked. There was something miraculous in blind, headlong labor. It had built railroads and republics, had saved them from ruin, and perhaps it might work a miracle once more.

But by night the hoppers had advanced through their lines. The men headed forward to get out of the stinking mass. Driving his wagon, Starrett was the last to go. He drove his squirming load of hoppers to the coulee and dumped it. Then he mounted to the seat of the wagon once more and sat there with the lines slack in his hands, looking across the hills. He was finished. The plague had advanced to the point from which a sudden strong wind could drive the hoppers onto Cowper's land before even fire could stop them.

He turned the wagon and drove to the new campfire blazing in the dusk. As he drove up, he heard an angry voice in staccato harangue. Hamp stood with a blazing juniper branch in his hand, confronting the other men. He had his back to Starrett and did not hear him at first.

"It's your land, but my living is tied to it just as much as yours. This has got to stop somewhere, and right here is as good a piece as any! He can't buck all of you."

Starrett swung down. "We're licked," he said. "I'm obliged to all of you for the help. Go home and get ready for your own fights."

Hamp tilted the torch down so that the flames came up greedily toward his hand. "I'm saying it plain this time," he said slowly. "We start firing here—not tomorrow, but now!"

"Put that torch down," Starrett said.

"Drop it, Bill!" Tom Cowper commanded.

Hamp thrust the branch closer. "Catch hold, Mr. Starrett. Maybe you'd like to toss the first torch."

Starrett said, "I'm saying that none of you is going to set fire to my land. None of you! And you've got just ten seconds to throw that into the fire!"

Bill Hamp watched him, smiled, and walked past the wagons into the uncleared field, into the golden bunchgrass. His arm went back and he flung the torch. In the same movement he pivoted and was ready for the man who had come out behind him. The flames came up behind Hamp like an explosion. They made a sound like a sigh. They outlined the foreman's hunched body and poured a liquid spark along the barrel of his gun.

Will Starrett felt a sharp fear as Hamp's gun roared. He heard a loud smack beside him and felt the wheel stir. Then his arm took the recoil of his own gun and he was blinded for an instant by the gun-flash. His vision cleared and he saw Hamp on his hands and knees. The man slumped after a moment and lay on his back.

Starrett walked back to the fire. The men stood exactly where they had a moment before, bearded, dirty, expressionless. Taking a length of limbwood, he thrust it into the flames and roasted it until it burned strongly. Then he strode back, stopped by Hamp's body, and flung the burning brand out into the deep grass, beyond the area of flame where Hamp's branch had fallen.

He came back. "Load my wagon with the rest of this wood," he said, "and get out. I'll take care of the rest of it. Cowper, another of our customs out here is that employers bury their own dead."

Halfway home, he looked back and saw the flames burst across another ridge. He saw little winking lights in the air that looked like fireflies. The hoppers were ending their feast in a pagan fire-revel. There would not be enough of them in the morning to damage Lynn Cowper's kitchen garden.

He unsaddled. Physically and spiritually exhausted, he leaned his head against a corral bar and closed his eyes. It had been the only thing left to do, for a man who loved the land as he did. But it was the last sacrifice he could make, and no gun-proud bunchgrasser like Hamp could make it look like a punishment and a humiliation.

Standing there, he felt moisture strike his hand and angrily straightened. Tears! Was he that far gone?

Starting toward the house, he felt the drops on his face. Another drop struck, and another. Then the flood let loose and there was no telling where one drop ended and the other began, as the July storm fell from the sky.

Starrett ran back to the corral. A crazy mixture of emotions was in his head—fear that the rain had come too soon; joy that it came at all. He rode out to catch the others and enlist their aid in raking the hoppers into heaps and cremating them with rock-oil before they were able to move again.

He had not gone over a mile when the rain changed to hail. He pulled up under a tree to wait it out. He sat, a hurting in his throat. The hopper hadn't crawled out of the earth that could stand that kind of pelting. In its way, it was as miraculous as seagulls.

Another rider appeared from the darkness and pulled a winded, skittish horse into the shelter of the elm. It was Tom Cowper.

"Will!" he said. "This—this does it, doesn't it?"

"It does," Starrett replied.

Cowper said, "Have you got a dry smoke on you?"

Starrett handed him tobacco and papers. He smoked broodingly.

"Starrett," he said, "I'll be damned if I'll ever understand a man like you. You shot Hamp to keep him from setting fire to your grass—no, he's not dead—and then you turned right around and did it yourself. Now, what was the difference?"

Starrett smiled. "I could explain it, but it would take about twenty years, and by that time you wouldn't need it. But it's something about burying your own dead, I suppose."

Cowper thought about it. "Maybe you have something," he said. "Well, if I were a preacher I'd be shouting at the top of my voice now."

"I'm shouting," Starrett admitted, "but I'll bet you can't hear me."

After awhile, Cowper said, "Why don't you come along with me, when the hail stops? Lynn and her mother will be up. There'll be something to eat, and we can have a talk. That wouldn't be violating one of your customs, would it?"

"It would be downright neighborly," Starrett said.

Bill Gulick was born in Missouri in 1916. He notes, in a biographical sketch, "I write books that are set in the West—not Westerns." In such fully realized novels as *Bend of the Snake* and *Liveliest Town in the West,* one sees the distinction Gulick makes. His books are character studies as well as plot-driven stories, and his take on frontier America is almost always as exciting as his story lines. Gulick has continued to write, and write well, into the present day. He is one of those writers whose love of the craft is apparent in each and every sentence.

The Shaming of Broken Horn

Bill Gulick

Toward sundown of the second day after the train reached Fort Hall, Harlan Faber, elected wagon captain, called a meeting of the emigrant families, as was the custom when a question affecting them all had to be voted on. Well aware by now that this western land was a man's land in which a woman must keep silent, Mary Bailey told her pa she guessed she'd stay by their wagons and catch up on the mending. But her pa said, "You got a right to be there. I want you to help me make up my mind which way to vote."

"Your mind's already made up, isn't it, Pa?"

"I know what I'd like to do, sure. But I want you at that meeting. Since your ma left us, you've taken her place, seems like."

So Mary went along, carrying some mending with her to keep her hands busy, standing at the edge of the crowd with her lanky, gray-haired, slow-spoken pa, Jed, and her younger brother, Mike, who was slim, dark-eyed and, at fourteen, beginning to consider himself an adult. Mary, a pretty, black-haired, grave young lady of eighteen, had put away childish notions years ago.

Facing the crowd stood Harlan Faber. With him were Peter Kent, factor of Fort Hall; Broken Horn, the fierce-eyed Bannock chief whose imperious edict had brought on this present crisis; Tim Ramsey, guide for the wagon train; and a pair of American trappers who had drifted into the trading post the day before. Faber raised his hand for silence.

"You folks all know what this meeting's about. The trail forks here. What we got to decide is whether we want to go on to Oregon, like we'd planned, or change our plans and go to Californy."

As the wagon captain outlined the situation facing the emigrants, Mary studied the two American trappers curiously, for there were strange tales of these wild, rootless men. Both wore ragged, grease-stained buckskins and had an alert, almost savage look about them. To the stooped, older man, Charley Huff, she gave no more than a brief glance; but the younger man, Dave Allen, standing tall and straight, was so handsome and had such nice gray eyes that she stared at him shamelessly.

"If we go to Oregon," Faber was saying, "we'll have to pass through Bannock country. The Bannocks are on the warpath against Americans, Broken Horn says, an' will fight us every step of the way. But if we turn south an' head fer Californy, stayin' clear of Bannock country, Broken Horn says his bucks won't pester us. That's how matters stand. Speak up, men, an' tell me how you feel."

One by one the men spoke their sentiments, while their womenfolk listened in silence. Jed whispered, "Well, Mary?"

"It's up to you, Pa. It's whatever you want to do."

"It's the seedlings I'm thinkin' about. To bring a whole wagonload of 'em this far, then give up—"

"Jed Bailey!" Faber called out. "You got anything to say?"

New England born and bred, Jed shifted his weight from one foot to the other, cocked his head at the sky as if looking for sign of rain, then said slowly, "Does it freeze in Californy, come winter?"

Tim Ramsey said no it didn't, normally. Peter Kent and the two trappers agreed. Faber let his eyes run over the crowd. "Any more questions 'fore we take a vote?"

"Get on with it!" a man shouted. "Call the roll!"

"All right." Faber took a sheet of paper out of his pocket. "Joshua Partridge."

"Here!"

"I know you're here, you blamed fool! How do you vote?"

"Californy!"

"Frank Lutcher."

"Californy!"

"Matthew Honleiker."

"Californy!"

And so it went, down through the list until forty-nine names had been called. Now, with only one name left, the wagon captain paused, looked at Jed, then said, "Jedidiah Bailey."

Jed studied the blue sky and the far reach of parched land to the west. At last he said, "A man can't grow decent apples in country where it don't freeze."

"That ain't an answer, Jed. How do you vote?"

"Oregon."

Mary heard a murmuring run through the crowd. "Stubborn old fool . . . Jed Bailey and his damned apple trees . . . Let him git scalped. . . ."

Faber tallied the list. "Results of the vote. Fer Californy, forty-nine. Fer Oregon, one. Majority rules, as agreed. We'll pull out first thing in the mornin' fer Californy." He looked angrily at Jed. "Forty-nine of us, anyhow. I wash my hands of you, Jed Bailey. Meetin's adjourned."

The Bailey family walked back to their wagons in silence, Mary feeling proud of her pa, but not knowing how to put it into words. Mike went out to check on the grazing mules. Jed took a pair of wooden buckets and headed for the creek to get water for the seedlings. Mary readied supper. It being early July, dark came late and though the sun had sunk by the time she called her menfolk to supper—a good meat stew filled with fresh vegetables grown in the Fort Hall garden, baked beans sweetened with molasses, hot biscuits and dried-apple pie—there was still plenty of twilight left when they finished eating. Because she loved her pa and knew how worried he was, Mary treated him extra good.

"More pie, Pa?"

"Thank you kindly, Mary, but I reckon not." He gave her a gentle smile. "You're a fine cook, girl, just like your ma was. The man that marries you will get a real prize."

"Fiddlesticks!" Mary said, but the praise pleased her just the same.

Lighting his pipe, Jed brooded into the fire while Mike got out cleaning stick, rag, and oil and set to work cleaning his rifle. Busy with the dishes, Mary did not hear the visitors approach until Peter Kent said, "Good evening, Mr. Bailey. May I have a word with you?"

"Sure. What's on your mind?"

Turning around, Mary got the fright of her life, for standing an arm's reach away was that murderous-looking Indian, Broken Horn. Likely she would have screamed if she hadn't looked past him and seen Charley Huff and Dave Allen. Dave Allen was smiling at her with those nice gray eyes, and somehow she knew nothing bad could happen when he was around. But watching Broken Horn sniff animallike at the stew simmering in the iron pot and the pie keeping warm in the open Dutch oven, she did feel a mite uneasy.

"You're set on going to Oregon, I take it," Kent said. "Do you plan to wait here until an Oregon-bound train willing to fight its way through Bannock country comes along?"

"Can't hardly do that. Ours was the last train due to leave Independence this season." A questioning look came into Jed's eyes. "You got a proposition, Mr. Kent?"

"Yes. Charley and Dave here also want to go to Oregon. I'll vouch for their reliability, if you want to hire them as guides. I've talked to Chief

Broken Horn, and he's agreed—for a reasonable consideration—to let you pass through his country."

"How much?"

"One hundred dollars."

"And these gents, how much do they want?"

"Two hundred dollars—apiece."

Jed fiddled with his pipe. "That's a sight of money."

"It's a sight of a job takin' two wagons an' three greenhorns through bad Injun country," Charley grunted.

"There's one thing I must make clear," Dave said, looking first at Mary, then at Jed. "If you do hire us, you've got to do exactly as we tell you at all times."

That was a mighty bossy way for a mere guide to talk, Mary thought angrily. Finishing the dishes, she carried them to the wagon and put them away. As she turned back to the fire, her mouth flew open in horror. Chief Broken Horn, fascinated by the smell emanating from the stewpot, had lifted its lid and was plunging a dirty butcher knife into its depths. This time she did scream.

"Stop that, you heathen!"

The Indian gave no sign that he heard her. Seizing the first weapon handy—a broom leaning against the wagon wheel—she made for him. As she raised the broom to strike, Dave Allen leaped toward her and caught her wrists.

"Easy, ma'am!"

Paying no attention to the commotion, Chief Broken Horn sniffed at the piece of meat he had impaled on his knife, diagnosed it as edible and disposed of it at a single bite. Finding the sample good, he dipped his bare hand into the pot, gobbled down its contents, then, still masticating noisily, stooped and picked up the apple pie. Indignantly Mary struggled against the steel-like grip on her wrists.

"Let me go!"

The nice gray eyes weren't smiling now. "Don't you want to go to Oregon?"

"Of course I do!"

"You won't get there by beating Indian chiefs on the head with a broom. If you hit Broken Horn, he'd be so insulted he'd kill us all first chance he got!"

It was too late to save the pie anyway, so Mary let go of the broom. "All right, Mr. Allen. I won't harm your precious Indian. Now let me go."

The grin came back to his face, and he released her. "That's better." He turned to Jed. "Think you can control your daughter?"

Jed looked questioningly at Mary. Shamefaced, she dropped her gaze to the ground. She was still trembling with anger, not only at Chief Broken

Horn but also at these two trappers who, to her way of thinking, were heartlessly taking advantage of her pa. Why, five hundred dollars was half of the family's lifetime savings! But this was a man's world, and it was not her place to object.

"I'll make no trouble, Pa. I promise."

"That's sensible talk," Dave said. He nodded to Jed. "It's set, then. We'll pull out first thing in the morning."

West of Fort Hall the trail followed Snake River across flat, monotonous sagebrush desert, with mountains faint in the heat-hazed distance to the northwest and the green, swift-flowing river often lost deep in lava-walled canyons. Jed drove one wagon, Mary the other, except when the road got too bad, at which times Dave would tie his saddle horse to the tail gate, climb to the driver's seat, and take the reins. He drove as he did everything else, with a casual skill which the mules recognized and responded to, though the stubborn brutes gave Mary all kinds of trouble.

"Good mules," he said, grinning at her as the wagon topped a particularly bad grade. "How come Jed was smart enough to use mules instead of oxen?"

"Pa is a smart man."

"What's he going to do with those seedlings?"

"Raise apples. Back home he had the finest apple orchard in the state."

"Why did you leave?"

"Ma died a year ago, and it took the heart out of Pa. He got restless, hearing about the free land in Oregon and how scarce fresh fruit was out there. He kept talking about it, and I thought a change might do him good."

The wagon was on a perfectly level stretch of trail now, and there was no reason why Dave shouldn't turn the reins over to her, but he lingered. "Kind of hard on a woman, ain't it, leaving her friends and all?"

"Pa and Mike are all that matter to me."

"Most girls your age think more of catching a husband than they do of their pa and brother."

The way he put it exasperated her. "You make getting married sound like trapping."

He threw back his head and laughed heartily. "I meant no offense. But judging from what I've seen of women, most of 'em do have men on their minds when they get to be your age."

"I'll bet they pestered you no end when you lived in civilized country."

"Well, they did, if you want the truth."

"Is that why you ran away and turned trapper?"

"Nope. I just wanted to see what was on the other side of the hill."

"Did you find out?"

"Sure. Another hill—with another side to it." He stopped the wagon, handed her the reins and climbed down. Mounting his horse, he said with a grin, "Don't say anything to those mules, gal. Maybe they'll think I'm still driving and won't give you no trouble."

Angrily she watched him gallop away. Then she gave the off-wheeler a lick with the whip that made him jump as if he'd been scalded.

FOR A WEEK they traveled west without molestation, save for the torment of heat, dust, and monotony. Dave said the fact that they saw no Indians didn't mean the Indians hadn't seen them. Chief Broken Horn had ridden ahead, he said, to warn his people that the party of whites was coming; and scouts watching from ridge tops likely were noting the progress of the wagons.

"We won't be safe," Dave said, "till we're into the Blue Mountains. And we'll have company before we get out of Bannock country, you can bet on that. When we do, Charley and I will tell you how to behave. Make sure you listen."

The two trappers had brought along several extra horses to pack their gear, and when Charley suggested that one of the animals' loads be stowed in a wagon, freeing the horse for Mike to ride and accompany him on hunts for fresh meat, the old trapper made himself a friend for life.

From dawn till dusk, Mike tagged after Charley, listening with youthful awe to Charley's rambling tales of beaver trapping, Indian fighting and wilderness adventures. Mary was aware of the relationship that existed between boy and man, but she saw no harm in it.

One evening they camped in a grassy swale bare of trees, with the river five hundred feet below. It was quite a chore lugging up water for the seedlings; and by the time it was finished, Jed was done in. He lay down on the ground with a weary sigh.

"Jehoshaphat, I'm tired! Hungry too. What's for supper, Mary?"

Mary was exhausted; the fuel was scant, and what there was of it refused to burn. "Nothing," she said shortly, "unless somebody fetches me some decent firewood."

"Mike," Jed said, "cut your sister some wood. Hustle, now!"

Charley and Mike were squatting nearby, the old trapper rambling on while they boy listened intently. Mary gave her brother a sharp look. "Mike!"

"Hmm?"

"Did you hear your pa?"

"What'd he say?"

"He told you to fetch me some firewood."

"Aw, fetch it yourself. That's squaw work."

Mary stared at her brother. Jed sat up with a scowl. "What did you say, son?"

Mike flushed, gave Charley a sidelong glance and muttered, "Cutting firewood is squaw work. Ain't it, Charley?"

"Why, yeah, boy," Charley answered, scratching his ribs. "Amongst Injuns, that's how it is. The buck kills the game an' brings it home, an' his squaw skins an' cooks it."

Dave, who had just strolled up, looked at Mike and said, "Don't believe everything Charley tells you, son."

"But Charley knows all about squaws!" Mike said indignantly. "He's had dozens of 'em! . . . Haven't you, Charley?"

"Wal, not dozens—"

Mary put her hands on her hips. "I never heard the like! Stuffing a boy full of awful stories!"

"Mike, fetch Mary some wood," Dave said firmly. "Jump, now! . . . Charley, you help him."

Charley looked hurt. "Me? Me fetch wood?"

"If you want to eat, you'd better."

After supper, Mary strolled off into the twilight and sat down on a boulder overlooking the whispering river. Though she'd promised her pa she'd make no trouble, the chore of feeding four hungry, ungrateful men three times a day was getting on her nerves; and she knew if she had to listen to any more of their idle chatter, she'd likely bust loose and say something she'd regret. Hearing a quiet step behind her, she looked around. Dave had followed her.

"Nice night."

"Yes."

"You'd ought not to wander away from camp alone. Some Injun might see you and pack you home with him."

"Just let one try."

Sitting down beside her, he lighted his pipe. "Charley don't mean no harm. He just likes to tell big windies."

"Has he had many squaws?"

"Two or three."

"Did he—marry them?"

"Bought 'em."

She stared at him, not sure whether he was teasing her or telling the blunt truth. Deciding he was telling the truth, she exclaimed, "Do you mean to say Indian women are bought and sold like—like horses?"

"Sure. A man picks out a squaw he wants, dickers with her pa and settles on a price. Some come higher than others, naturally. You take a young, healthy woman that's a good cook, she'll cost a man a sight more than a run-of-the-mill squaw would."

"What if she doesn't like the man that buys her? What if she refuses to live with him?"

"Why, he beats her. That generally makes her behave."

"I think that's horrible!"

His eyes were twinkling, and now the suspicion came to her that he hadn't been telling the truth. She was dying to ask him if he'd ever owned any squaws, but blessed if she'd give him a chance to tease her further. Grinning, he held out his hand and helped her up. "Come on, you'd better get back to camp. You're too good a cook to lose."

THE BANNOCKS APPEARED while they were nooning next day. Seeing the squaws and children in the band, Dave said their intentions likely were peaceable, for Indians didn't take their families along when they had war in mind. But watching the savages set up their teepees a quarter of a mile down the valley, Mary felt uneasy.

Chief Broken Horn, accompanied by half a dozen of the leaders of the tribe, rode into camp presently. Broken Horn made a long speech, emphasized by many dramatic gestures. The gist of it was, Dave said, that Broken Horn considered himself quite a great man. Had he not made forty-nine wagons turn aside from the Oregon Trail because the American emigrants feared him? Was it not only through his generosity and by his consent that this small party was being permitted to cross his lands after paying the toll he demanded?

"Can't say as I like that kind of talk," Jed muttered.

"Let him brag," Dave said. "It don't hurt us a bit."

When the chief finished his speech, Dave frowned, then came over to Mary and said, "We're going to have company for supper."

"Chief Broken Horn?"

"Yeah. He and six of his headmen. You're to fix them a big feed, he says, with lots of stew and pie like you cooked for him back at Fort Hall."

"I didn't cook anything for him! He stole that food, and you know it."

"Well, he tells it different. Anyhow he seems to like your cooking and wants more of it."

"Do you mean to tell me I've got to feed seven of those heathen?"

"Afraid so. He says when he eats well, his dreams are good. He says if his dreams are good tonight, he'll let us go on in peace. But if his dreams are bad—"

"Now, look here!" Jed cut in angrily. "The old thief made a bargain and he's got to stick to it, good dreams or bad!"

"We've got to humor him," Dave said, shaking his head. He looked at Mary. "Can you do it? Can you rustle up enough stew and pie to make them happy?"

Mary was tired and she was scared, but most of all, right now, she was mad. Seemed like all she'd done since she'd left home was cater to men, cooking for them, washing for them, mending for them. She hadn't minded doing those chores for her own family because that was her job. But if this was a man's land, why didn't the men out here act like men? Why had Harlan Faber and the other men back at Fort Hall let an arrogant old Indian turn them aside from their original destination? Why didn't Charley and Dave make Chief Broken Horn live up to his promise with no nonsense about dreams?

"All right," she said wearily. "I'll feed them. But you'll all have to help me."

Charley and Mike had killed an antelope and two deer the evening before, so meat was no problem. There was still half a barrel of dried apples left in the wagon, plenty of beans, sugar and flour, fifty pounds of potatoes she'd bought at Fort Hall, and a few carefully hoarded onions, carrots and dried peas. While Charley chopped wood and Dave carried water, she had Mike stretch a large square of canvas on the ground beside one of the wagons—on this her guests would sit. Brushing aside her pa's objections that it was casting pearls before swine, she made him dig out the family's best china, silverware, glasses, pitcher and a white linen tablecloth, which she laid and set on the canvas ground cloth. Except for the fact that her banquet table had no legs, it looked as attractive as any she'd ever set back home."

How much food could a hungry Indian eat? She made a liberal estimate of what a normal man with a healthy appetite could do away with at one sitting and tripled it, just to be on the safe side. She took special care that there should be more apple pie than her guests could possibly consume.

After putting a quantity of dried apples to soak for several hours, she prepared two dozen pie shells. When the apples had soaked sufficiently, she filled the shells, covered them with thin strips of dough, coated them with brown sugar and baked them until they were almost done. One of her most precious culinary treasures was a square tin of grated cheese flakes, which time and the dry western air had long since drawn all moisture from, but which, when sprinkled generously over the top of an apple pie and heated for a few minutes, melted and blended with the sugar to give the pie a delightful flavor. The tin was kept in a wooden chest in the wagon, along with her spices, extracts, and family medical supplies. She asked Mike to get it for her.

Climbing into the wagon, he rummaged around, then called, "Is it the red tin?"

"No, the blue one. Hurry, Mike!"

He clambered out of the wagon and handed her the tin. Taking a tablespoon, she hurriedly ladled a liberal layer of powdery flakes over the top of each pie, set them back in the Dutch ovens to bake and turned her attention to other tasks. Some minutes later she was exasperated to find Mike, whom she had told to return the tin to the chest, curiously staring down at what remained of its contents.

"Mike, will you please quite dawdling and put that away?"

"How come you sprinkled this stuff on the pies?"

"Because it's cheese, you idiot!"

"Don't smell like cheese." He dipped finger and thumb into the tin, took a tiny pinch, sampled it. "Don't taste like cheese either."

She stared at the tin in horror. It wasn't blue. It was green. And pasted on its side was a faded label. She read it and suddenly felt faint. "Oh, my goodness!"

She ran to one of the Dutch ovens, opened it and snatched out a pie. Heedless of scorched fingers, she tried a tiny sample of the browned, delicious-looking crust. Mike did the same. He made a face.

"You going to feed these pies to the Indians?"

She closed her eyes and tried to think. The stuff wouldn't kill them, of that she was sure. It was too late to bake more pies, certainly, for even now the guests were arriving. Dressed in their finest, followed at a respectful distance by a horde of curious squaws, children, and uninvited braves, Chief Broken Horn and his subchiefs had dismounted from their horses and were walking into camp. Worn-out and nerve-ragged after her long afternoon of work, Mary felt like dropping to the ground and giving way to tears. Instead she got mad. She got so mad that she didn't care a hang what happened, just so long as those pies didn't go to waste. Opening her eyes, she gave her brother a grim look.

"I certainly am. Get me the sugar, Mike. Indians will eat anything if it's sweet enough."

Judging from the amount of food consumed and the rapidity with which it vanished, the feast was a huge success. The Indians were vastly fascinated by the plates, dishes, and silverware, though they used their bare hands more than they did the knives, forks, and spoons. The cold tea, liberally sugared, was a great hit, too, disappearing as fast as Mike could fill the glasses. And the pie brought forth approving grunts from all.

Mary had given her own menfolk strict orders not to partake of the pie, telling them that she feared there might not be enough to go round; but as the Indians one by one lapsed into glassy-eyed satiety, with half a dozen still uneaten pies before them, Dave gazed longingly at the beautiful creation on the tablecloth between himself and Chief Broken Horn. He smiled up at Mary.

"Sure does look like fine pie. Can't I have a piece?"

"No," Mary said sharply.

"Not even a little one?" he persisted, picking up the pie. "Why, if you knew how long it's been since I tasted—"

"I said 'no,'" Mary cut in, rudely snatching the pie out of his hand. Pretending that she'd done it for the sake of her guests, she turned to Chief Broken Horn and smiled. "More pie, Mr. Broken Horn?"

The Indian made a sign indicating he was full up to his chin. As he looked her over from head to toe, a greedy, acquisitive light came into his black eyes. He turned and grunted something to Dave. Dave laughed and winked at Mary.

"He says you're a better cook than his own squaw is."

"That's very kind of him."

"He wants to know if your pa will sell you. He says he'd pay a fancy price."

Mary was too tired to have much of a sense of humor right then. From the way Jed's face froze, he wasn't in a joking mood either. "I won't stand for that kind of talk in front of Mary."

"He didn't mean it as an insult," Dave said. "He meant it as a—"

Chief Broken Horn showed exactly how he had meant it by reaching up, seizing Mary's left wrist and pulling her toward him. Livid-faced, Jed leaped to his feet. Dave swore and reached for the pistol in his belt. Charley drew his knife. Mike ran and grabbed up his rifle. But Mary was too angry to wait for help from her menfolk. Quick as a wink, she drew back her right arm and plastered Chief Broken Horn full in the face with the apple pie.

For a moment there wasn't a sound. The Indians were all staring at their chief, who lay flat on his back—pawing pie out of his eyes, kicking his heels in the air in a most unchieftainlike manner.

Getting his feet under him, Chief Broken Horn gave Mary a stunned, horrified glance, then wheeled and ran for his horse as if all the hounds of hell were after him. The other Indians wasted no time in following.

Mary took a long, deep breath. Turning to look at Jed, she said in a voice filled with shame, "I'm sorry, Pa."

"Don't be," Dave said, and his nice gray eyes were hard as flint. "If you hadn't done what you did, I'd have killed him where he sat."

A body does queer things in time of stress. Suddenly becoming aware of the way her menfolk were staring at her, their weapons in their hands, their eyes filled with amazement, relief and admiration, she began to laugh. She laughed till tears ran out of her eyes, but for the life of her she couldn't stop. Dave put an arm around her shoulders and said gently, "Easy, Mary—easy."

She sighed and quietly fainted.

As dark came on and the fires burned low, they sat huddled together, their backs against a wagon for safety's sake, listening to the drums in the Indian village. Mary was frightened now, but looking around, seeing the grim looks on the faces of her menfolk as they balanced their rifles across their knees, she was sure of one thing—her men would act like men if the need arose, and she was proud of them all.

"What do you think they'll do?" Jed said.

"Hard to tell," Dave answered. "Broken Horn has lost considerable face, being made a fool of by a woman in public. If there's going to be an attack, it will likely come at dawn. He'll spend the night stirring up the young bucks. The war drums are going already."

Charley, who had been listening intently to the sounds coming from the village, interrupted, "Quiet, boy!"

"What's the matter?"

"Them drums. They don't sound like war drums to me. Sound more like medicine drums."

"What's the difference?" Mary asked.

Patiently Dave explained that when Bannocks prepared for battle, the drums were pounded in one fashion; but when there was sickness in the tribe and the medicine man was called in to recite his chants and attempt to heal the ill person, the drums were beaten in another manner. "But Charley's wrong," he added. "Chief Broken Horn isn't going to let his medicine man fool around curing sick people tonight."

"Maybe he's sick. Eating all that food—"

"He's got the stomach of a wolf. No, they're war drums, no question about that," Dave insisted.

In the faint glow of the dying fires Mary saw a bulky figure appear on the far side of camp. Dave called out a challenge in the Bannock tongue and was quickly answered by an Indian woman. He told her to approach the wagon, and she did so—her hesitant pace showing how frightened she was. She was fat, wrinkled and middle-aged. Dave asked her who she was and what she wanted. As she spoke, he translated.

"She says she's Broken Horn's squaw."

"Is he going to attack?" Jed said.

"She says no."

"So he's going to stick to his bargain after all?"

"But the young bucks might, she says, if they can work up nerve enough. They're arguing it out now."

"Can't he keep them in line?"

Mary saw Dave frown as the squaw spoke. "She says he ain't interested in anything right now except the mess of bad spirits that have crawled into his belly. She says he's sick as a dog—and so are all the other chiefs that ate with us." Dave turned and gave Mary a sharp look. "She thinks you poisoned 'em."

"I didn't!"

"How come they all took sick, then?"

Mary flushed. "Maybe it was the beans and all that cold tea they drank."

"It was the apple pie, wasn't it? You wouldn't let us eat any of it, but you made sure they stuffed themselves with it. What did you put in that pie, Mary?"

Defiantly Mary looked at Dave. "Epsom salts."

"What?"

"It won't hurt them. In fact, they made such pigs of themselves, it might even do them some good. Why, I wouldn't be surprised but what they all dream real nice dreams—when they finally get to sleep. That's what you wanted, wasn't it?"

Dave looked shaken. In fact, all her menfolk were staring at her, awe and respect in their eyes. Suddenly the squaw started gabbling furiously, pointing an accusing finger at Mary. Dave listened for a time, then he silenced her with a gesture.

"She says either you poisoned her man or cast an evil spell on him because he grabbed hold of you. Whichever it was you did, she's begging you to make him well. What shall I tell her?"

Mary smiled. "Tell her I cast a spell."

"Now, look here!"

"Tell her, please. Tell her that all white women have the power to cast spells over men when they get angry with them."

Reluctantly Dave spoke to the Indian woman. Her black eyes grew wide with fright as she stared at Mary, then she grunted a question. Dave said, "She wants to know how long the spell will last."

"Tell her two days. Tell her if her husband and the other sick chiefs lie quietly for two days and nights, thinking nothing but peaceful thoughts, they will get well. But if they let their people attack us, they will die."

An admiring grin spread over Dave's face. "Now why didn't I think of that?"

As he spoke to the squaw, Mary saw the frightened look fade from the woman's face. The squaw nodded vigorously, turned to go, hesitated; then shyly walked up to Mary, touched Mary's breast, then her own, grunted something and ran off into the darkness. Mary looked at Dave.

"What did that mean?"

Dave didn't answer for a moment. Then, an uneasy light coming into his nice gray eyes, as if he were looking into the future, he answered, "She says you know how to handle men and she's glad you hit her husband with that pie. She's been wanting to sock the old fool for years."

Donald Hamilton is best known as the creator of the Matt Helm books, which many believe is the best espionage series ever written by an American. But early in his career, Hamilton wrote a number of excellent traditional Westerns as well, including such titles as *Smoky Valley, The Big Country, Mad River,* and *The Two-Shoot Gun.* He also edited one of the seminal anthologies of the Western genre, the Western Writers of America's *Iron Men and Silver Spurs.*

The Guns of William Longley

Donald Hamilton

We'd been up north delivering a herd for Old Man Butcher the summer I'm telling about. I was nineteen at the time. I was young and big, and I was plenty tough, or thought I was, which amounts to the same thing up to a point. Maybe I was making up for all the years of being that nice Anderson boy, back in Willow Fork, Texas. When your dad wears a badge, you're kind of obliged to behave yourself around home so as not to shame him. But Pop was dead now, and this wasn't Texas.

Anyway, I was tough enough that we had to leave Dodge City in something of a hurry after I got into an argument with a fellow who, it turned out, wasn't nearly as handy with a gun as he claimed to be. I'd never killed a man before. It made me feel kind of funny for a couple of days, but like I say, I was young and tough then, and I'd seen men I really cared for trampled in stampedes and drowned in rivers on the way north. I wasn't going to grieve long over one belligerent stranger.

It was on the long trail home that I first saw the guns one evening by the fire. We had a blanket spread on the ground, and we were playing cards for what was left of our pay—what we hadn't already spent on girls and liquor and general hell-raising. My luck was in, and one by one the others dropped out, all but Waco Smith, who got stubborn and went over to his bedroll and hauled out the guns.

"I got them in Dodge," he said. "Pretty, ain't they? Fellow I bought them from claimed they belonged to Bill Longley."

"Is that a fact?" I said, like I wasn't much impressed. "Who's Longley?"

I knew who Bill Longley was, all right, but a man's got a right to dicker a bit, and besides, I couldn't help deviling Waco now and then. I liked him all right, but he was one of those cocky little fellows who ask for it. You know the kind. They always know everything.

I sat there while he told me about Bill Longley, the giant from Texas with thirty-two killings to his credit, the man who was hanged twice. A bunch of vigilantes strung him up once for horse-stealing he hadn't done, but the rope broke after they'd ridden off and he dropped to the ground, kind of short of breath but alive and kicking.

Then he was tried and hanged for a murder he had done, some years later in Giddings, Texas. He was so big that the rope gave way again and he landed on his feet under the trap, making six-inch deep footprints in the hard ground—they're still there in Giddings to be seen, Waco said, Bill Longley's footprints—but it broke his neck this time and they buried him nearby. At least a funeral service was held, but some say there's just an empty coffin in the grave.

I said, "This Longley gent can't have been so much, to let folks keep stringing him up that way."

That set Waco off again, while I toyed with the guns. They were pretty, all right, in a big carved belt with two carved holsters, but I wasn't much interested in leatherwork. It was the weapons themselves that took my fancy. They'd been used but someone had looked after them well. They were handsome pieces, smooth-working, and they had a good feel to them. You know how it is when a firearm feels just right. A fellow with hands the size of mine doesn't often find guns to fit him like that.

"How much do you figure they're worth?" I asked, when Waco stopped for breath.

"Well, now," he said, getting a sharp look on his face, and I came home to Willow Fork with the Longley guns strapped around me. If that's what they were.

I got a room and cleaned up at the hotel. I didn't much feel like riding clear out to the ranch and seeing what it looked like with Ma and Pa gone two years and nobody looking after things. Well, I'd put the place on its feet again one of these days, as soon as I'd had a little fun and saved a little money. I'd buckle right down to it, I told myself, as soon as Junellen set the date, which I'd been after her to do since before my folks died. She couldn't keep saying forever we were too young.

I got into my good clothes and went to see her. I won't say she'd been on my mind all the way up the trail and back again, because it wouldn't be true. A lot of the time I'd been too busy or tired for dreaming, and in Dodge City I'd done my best *not* to think of her, if you know what I mean. It did seem like a young fellow engaged to a beautiful girl like Junellen Barr could have behaved himself better up there, but it had been a long dusty drive and you know how it is.

But now I was home and it seemed like I'd been missing Junellen every minute since I left, and I couldn't wait to see her. I walked along the street in the hot sunshine feeling light and happy. Maybe my leaving my guns at the hotel had something to do with the light feeling, but the happiness was all for Junellen, and I ran up the steps to the house and knocked on the door. She'd have heard we were back and she'd be waiting to greet me, I was sure.

I knocked again and the door opened and I stepped forward eagerly. "Junellen—" I said, and stopped foolishly.

"Come in, Jim," said her father, a little turkey of a man who owned the drygoods store in town. He went on smoothly: "I understand you had quite an eventful journey. We were waiting to hear all about it."

He was being sarcastic, but that was his way, and I couldn't be bothered with trying to figure what he was driving at. I'd already stepped into the room, and there was Junellen with her mother standing close as if to protect her, which seemed kind of funny. There was a man in the room, too, Mr. Carmichael from the bank, who'd fought with Pa in the war. He was tall and handsome as always, a little heavy nowadays but still dressed like a fashion plate. I couldn't figure what he was doing there.

It wasn't going at all the way I'd hoped, my reunion with Junellen, and I stopped, looking at her.

"So you're back, Jim," she said. "I heard you had a real exciting time. Dodge City must be quite a place."

There was a funny hard note in her voice. She held herself very straight, standing there by her mother, in a blue-flowered dress that matched her eyes. She was a real little lady, Junellen. She made kind of a point of it, in fact, and Martha Butcher, Old Man Butcher's kid, used to say about Junellen Barr that butter wouldn't melt in her mouth, but that always seemed like a silly saying to me, and who was Martha Butcher anyway, just because her daddy owned a lot of cows?

Martha'd also remarked about girls who had to drive two front names in harness as if one wasn't good enough, and I'd told her it surely wasn't if it was a name like Martha, and she'd kicked me on the shin. But that was a long time ago when we were all kids.

Junellen's mother broke the silence, in her nervous way: "Dear, hadn't you better tell Jim the news?" She turned to Mr. Carmichael. "Howard, perhaps you should—"

Mr. Carmichael came forward and took Junellen's hand. "Miss Barr has done me the honor to promise to be my wife," he said.

I said, "But she can't. She's engaged to me."

Junellen's mother said quickly, "It was just a childish thing, not to be taken seriously."

I said, "Well, I took it seriously!"

Junellen looked up at me. "Did you, Jim? In Dodge City, did you?" I didn't say anything. She said breathlessly, "It doesn't matter. I suppose I could forgive . . . But you have killed a man. I could never love a man who has taken a human life."

Anyway, she said something like that. I had a funny feeling in my stomach and a roaring sound in my ears. They talk about your heart breaking, but that's where it hit me, the stomach and the ears. So I can't tell you exactly what she said, but it was something like that.

I heard myself say, "Mr. Carmichael spent the war peppering Yanks with a peashooter, I take it."

"That's different—"

Mr. Carmichael spoke quickly. "What Miss Barr means is that there's a difference between a battle and a drunken brawl, Jim. I am glad your father did not live to see his son wearing two big guns and shooting men down in the street. He was a fine man and a good sheriff for this county. It was only for his memory's sake that I agreed to let Miss Barr break the news to you in person. From what we hear of your exploits up north, you have certainly forfeited all right to consideration from her."

There was something in what he said, but I couldn't see that it was his place to say it. "You agreed?" I said. "That was mighty kind of you, sir, I'm sure." I looked away from him. "Junellen—"

Mr. Carmichael interrupted. "I do not wish my fiancée to be distressed by a continuation of this painful scene. I must ask you to leave, Jim."

I ignored him. "Junellen," I said, "is this what you really—"

Mr. Carmichael took me by the arm. I turned my head to look at him again. I looked at the hand with which he was holding me. I waited. He didn't let go. I hit him and he went back across the room and kind of fell into a chair. The chair broke under him. Junellen's father ran over to help him up. Mr. Carmichael's mouth was bloody. He wiped it with a handkerchief.

I said, "You shouldn't have put your hand on me, sir."

"Note the pride," Mr. Carmichael said, dabbing at his cut lip. "Note the vicious, twisted pride. They all have it, all these young toughs. You are too big for me to box, Jim, and it is an undignified thing anyway. I have worn a sidearm in my time. I will go to the bank and get it, while you arm yourself."

"I will meet you in front of the hotel, sir," I said, "if that is agreeable to you."

"It is agreeable," he said, and went out.

I followed him without looking back. I think Junellen was crying, and I know her parents were saying one thing and another in high, indignant voices, but the funny roaring was in my ears and I didn't pay too much attention. The sun was very bright outside. As I started for the hotel, somebody ran up to me.

"Here you are, Jim." It was Waco, holding out the Longley guns in their carved holsters. "I heard what happened. Don't take any chances with the old fool."

I looked down at him and asked, "How did Junellen and her folks learn about what happened in Dodge?"

He said, "It's a small town, Jim, and all the boys have been drinking and talking, glad to get home."

"Sure," I said, buckling on the guns. "Sure."

It didn't matter. It would have got around sooner or later, and I wouldn't have lied about it if asked. We walked slowly toward the hotel.

"Dutch LeBaron is hiding out back in the hills with a dozen men," Waco said. "I heard it from a man in a bar."

"Who's Dutch LeBaron?" I asked. I didn't care, but it was something to talk about as we walked.

"Dutch?" Waco said. "Why, Dutch is wanted in five states and a couple of territories. Hell, the price on his head is so high now even Fenn is after him."

"Fenn?" I said. He sure knew a lot of names. "Who's Fenn?"

"You've heard of Old Joe Fenn, the bounty hunter. Well, if he comes after Dutch, he's asking for it. Dutch can take care of himself."

"Is that a fact?" I said, and then I saw Mr. Carmichael coming, but he was a ways off yet and I said, "You sound like this Dutch fellow was a friend of yours—"

But Waco wasn't there anymore. I had the street to myself, except for Mr. Carmichael, who had a gun strapped on outside his fine coat. It was an army gun in a black army holster with a flap, worn cavalry style on the right side, butt forward. They wear them like that to make room for the saber on the left, but it makes a clumsy rig.

I walked forward to meet Mr. Carmichael, and I knew I would have to let him shoot once. He was a popular man and a rich man and he would have to draw first and shoot first or I would be in serious trouble. I figured it all out very coldly, as if I had been killing men all my life. We stopped, and Mr. Carmichael undid the flap of the army holster and pulled out the big cavalry pistol awkwardly and fired and missed, as I had known, somehow, that he would.

Then I drew the right-hand gun, and as I did so I realized that I didn't particularly want to kill Mr. Carmichael. I mean, he was a brave man coming here with his old cap-and-ball pistol, knowing all the time that I could outdraw and outshoot him with my eyes closed. But I didn't want to be killed, either, and he had the piece cocked and was about to fire again. I tried to aim for a place that wouldn't kill him, or cripple him too badly, and the gun wouldn't do it.

I mean, it was a frightening thing. It was like I was fighting the Longley gun for Mr. Carmichael's life. The old army revolver fired once more and something rapped my left arm lightly. The Longley gun went off at last, and Mr. Carmichael spun around and fell on his face in the street. There was a cry, and Junellen came running and went to her knees beside him.

"You murderer!" she screamed at me. "You hateful murderer!"

It showed how she felt about him, that she would kneel in the dust like that in her blue-flowered dress. Junellen was always very careful of her pretty clothes. I punched out the empty and replaced it. Dr. Sims came up and examined Mr. Carmichael and said he was shot in the leg, which I already knew, being the one who had shot him there. Dr. Sims said he was going to be all right, God willing.

Having heard this, I went over to another part of town and tried to get drunk. I didn't have much luck at it, so I went into the place next to the hotel for a cup of coffee. There wasn't anybody in the place but a skinny girl with an apron on.

I said, "I'd like a cup of coffee, ma'am," and sat down.

She said, coming over, "Jim Anderson, you're drunk. At least you smell like it."

I looked up and saw that it was Martha Butcher. She set a cup down in front of me. I asked, "What are you doing here waiting tables?"

She said, "I had a fight with Dad about . . . well, never mind what it was about. Anyway, I told him I was old enough to run my own life and if he didn't stop trying to boss me around like I was one of the hands, I'd pack up and leave. And he laughed and asked what I'd do for money, away from home, and I said I'd earn it, so here I am."

It was just like Martha Butcher, and I saw no reason to make a fuss over it like she probably wanted me to.

"Seems like you are," I agreed. "Do I get sugar, too, or does that cost extra?"

She laughed and set a bowl in front of me. "Did you have a good time in Dodge?" she asked.

"Fine," I said. "Good liquor. Fast games. Pretty girls. Real pretty girls."

"Fiddlesticks," she said. "I know what you think is pretty. Blond and simpering. You big fool. If you'd killed him over her they'd have put you in jail, at the very least. And just what are you planning to use for an arm when that one gets rotten and falls off? Sit still."

She got some water and cloth and fixed up my arm where Mr. Carmichael's bullet had nicked it.

"Have you been out to your place yet?" she asked.

I shook my head. "Figure there can't be much out there by now. I'll get after it one of these days."

"One of these days!" she said. "You mean when you get tired of strutting around with those big guns and acting dangerous—" She stopped abruptly.

I looked around, and got to my feet. Waco was there in the doorway, and with him was a big man, not as tall as I was, but wider. He was a real whiskery gent, with a mat of black beard you could have used for stuffing a mattress. He wore two gunbelts, crossed, kind of sagging low at the hips.

Waco said, "You're a fool to sit with your back to the door, Jim. That's the mistake Hickok made, remember? If instead of us it had been somebody like Jack McCall—"

"Who's Jack McCall?" I asked innocently.

"Why, he's the fellow shot Wild Bill in the back . . ." Waco's face reddened. "All right, all right. Always kidding me. Dutch, this big joker is my partner, Jim Anderson. Jim, Dutch LeBaron. He's got a proposition for us."

I tried to think back to where Waco and I had decided to become partners, and couldn't remember the occasion. Well, maybe it happens like that, but it seemed like I should have had some say in it.

"Your partner tells me you're pretty handy with those guns," LeBaron said, after Martha'd moved across the room. "I can use a man like that."

"For what?" I asked.

"For making some quick money over in New Mexico Territory," he said.

I didn't ask any fool questions, like whether the money was to be made legally or illegally. "I'll think about it," I said.

Waco caught my arm. "What's to think about? We'll be rich, Jim!"

I said, "I'll think about it, Waco."

LeBaron said, "What's the matter, sonny, are you scared?"

I turned to look at him. He was grinning at me, but his eyes weren't grinning, and his hands weren't too far from those low-slung guns.

I said, "Try me and see."

I waited a little. Nothing happened. I walked out of there and got my pony and rode to the ranch, reaching the place about dawn. I opened the door and stood there, surprised. It looked just about the way it had when the folks were alive, and I half expected to hear Ma yelling at me to beat the dust off outside and not bring it into the house. Somebody had cleaned the place up for me, and I thought I knew who. Well, it certainly was neighborly of her, I told myself. It was nice to have somebody show a sign they were glad to have me home, even if it was only Martha Butcher.

I spent a couple of days out there, resting up and riding around. I didn't find much stock. It was going to take money to make a going ranch of it again, and I didn't figure my credit at Mr. Carmichael's bank was anything to count on. I couldn't help giving some thought to Waco and LeBaron and the proposition they'd put before me. It was funny, I'd think about it most when I had the guns on. I was out back practicing with them one day when the stranger rode up.

He was a little, dry, elderly man on a sad-looking white horse he must have hired at the livery stable for not very much, and he wore his gun in front of his left hip with the butt to the right for a cross draw. He didn't make any noise coming up. I'd fired a couple of times before I realized he was there.

"Not bad," he said when he saw me looking at him. "Do you know a man named LeBaron, son?"

"I've met him," I said.

"Is he here?"

"Why should he be here?"

"A bartender in town told me he'd heard you and your sidekick, Smith, had joined up with LeBaron, so I thought you might have given him the use of your place. It would be more comfortable for him than hiding out in the hills."

"He isn't here," I said. The stranger glanced toward the house. I started to get mad, but shrugged instead. "Look around if you want to."

"In that case," he said, "I don't figure I want to." He glanced toward the target I'd been shooting at, and back to me. "Killed a man in Dodge, didn't you, son? And then stood real calm and let a fellow here in town fire three shots at you, after which you laughed and pinked him neatly in the leg."

"I don't recall laughing," I said. "And it was two shots, not three."

"It makes a good story, however," he said. "And it is spreading. You have a reputation already, did you know that, Anderson? I didn't come here just to look for LeBaron. I figured I'd like to have a look at you, too. I always like to look up fellows I might have business with later."

"Business?" I said, and then I saw that he'd taken a tarnished old badge out of his pocket and was pinning it on his shirt. "Have you a warrant, sir?" I asked.

"Not for you," he said. "Not yet."

He swung the old white horse around and rode off. When he was out of sight, I got my pony out of the corral. It was time I had a talk with Waco. Maybe I was going to join LeBaron and maybe I wasn't, but I didn't much like his spreading it around before it was true.

I didn't have to look for him in town. He came riding to meet me with three companions, all hard ones if I ever saw any.

"Did you see Fenn?" he shouted as he came up. "Did he come this way?"

"A little old fellow with some kind of a badge?" I said. "Was that Fenn? He headed back to town, about ten minutes ahead of me. He didn't look like much."

"Neither does the devil when he's on business," Waco said. "Come on, we'd better warn Dutch before he rides into town."

I rode along with them, and we tried to catch LeBaron on the trail, but he'd already passed with a couple of men. We saw their dust ahead and chased it, but they made it before us, and Fenn was waiting in front of the cantina that was LeBaron's hangout when he was in town.

We saw it all as we came pounding after LeBaron, who dismounted and started into the place, but Fenn came forward, looking small and inoffensive. He was saying something and holding out his hand. LeBaron stopped and shook hands with him, and the little man held on to LeBaron's hand, took a step to the side, and pulled his gun out of that cross-draw holster left-handed, with a kind of twisting motion.

Before LeBaron could do anything with his free hand, the little old man had brought the pistol barrel down across his head. It was as neat and cold-blooded a thing as you'd care to see. In an instant, LeBaron was unconscious on the ground, and Old Joe Fenn was covering the two men who'd been riding with him.

Waco Smith, riding beside me, made a sort of moaning sound as if he'd been clubbed himself. "Get him!" he shouted, drawing his gun. "Get the dirty sneaking bounty hunter!"

I saw the little man throw a look over his shoulder, but there wasn't much he could do about us with those other two to handle. I guess he hadn't figured us for reinforcements riding in. Waco fired and missed. He never could shoot much, particularly from horseback. I reached out with one of the guns and hit him over the head before he could shoot again. He spilled from the saddle.

I didn't have it all figured out. Certainly it wasn't a very nice thing Mr. Fenn had done, first taking a man's hand in friendship and then knocking him unconscious. Still, I didn't figure LeBaron had ever been one for giving anybody a break; and there was something about the old fellow standing there with his tarnished old badge that reminded me of Pa, who'd died wearing a similar piece of tin on his chest. Anyway, there comes a time in a man's life when he's got to make a choice, and that's the way I made mine.

Waco and I had been riding ahead of the others. I turned my pony fast and covered them with the guns as they came charging up—as well as you can cover anybody from a plunging horse. One of them had his pistol aimed to shoot. The left-handed Longley gun went off, and he fell to the ground. I was kind of surprised. I'd never been much at shooting left-handed. The other two riders veered off and headed out of town.

By the time I got my pony quieted down from having that gun go off in his ear, everything was pretty much under control. Waco had disappeared, so I figured he couldn't be hurt much; and the new sheriff was there, old drunken Billy Bates, who'd been elected after Pa's death by the gambling element in town, who hadn't liked the strict way Pa ran things.

"I suppose it's legal," Old Billy was saying grudgingly. "But I don't take it kindly, Marshal, your coming here to serve a warrant without letting me know."

"My apologies, Sheriff," Fenn said smoothly. "An oversight, I assure you. Now, I'd like a wagon. He's worth seven hundred and fifty dollars over in New Mexico Territory."

"No decent person would want that kind of money," Old Billy said sourly, swaying on his feet.

"There's only one kind of money," Fenn said. "Just as there's only one kind of law, even though there's different kinds of men enforcing it." He looked at me a I came up. "Much obliged, son."

"Por nada," I said. "You get in certain habits when you've had a badge in the family. My daddy was sheriff here once."

"So? I didn't know that." Fenn looked at me sharply. "Don't look like you're making any plans to follow in his footsteps. That's hardly a lawman's rig you're wearing."

I said, "Maybe, but I never yet beat a man over the head while I was shaking his hand, Marshal."

"Son," he said, "my job is to enforce the law and maybe make a small profit on the side, not to play games with fair and unfair." He looked at me for a moment longer. "Well, maybe we'll meet again. It depends."

"On what?" I asked.

"On the price," he said. "The price on your head."

"But I haven't got—"

"Not now," he said. "But you will, wearing those guns. I know the signs. I've seen them before, too many times. Don't count on having me under obligation to you, when your time comes. I never let personal feelings interfere with business . . . Easy, now," he said to a couple of fellows who were lifting LeBaron, bound hand and foot, into the wagon that somebody had driven up. "Easy. Don't damage the merchandise. I take pride in delivering them in good shape for standing trial, whenever possible."

I decided I needed a drink, and then I changed my mind in favor of a cup of coffee. As I walked down the street, leaving my pony at the rail back there, the wagon rolled past and went out of town ahead of me. I was still watching it, for no special reason, when Waco stepped from the alley behind me.

"Jim!" he said. "Turn around, Jim!"

I turned slowly. He was a little unsteady on his feet, standing there, maybe from my hitting him, maybe from drinking. I thought it was drinking. I hadn't hit him very hard. He'd had time for a couple of quick ones, and liquor always got to him fast.

"You sold us out, you damn traitor!" he cried. "You took sides with the law!"

"I never was against it," I said. "Not really."

"After everything I've done for you!" he said thickly. "I was going to make you a great man, Jim, greater than Longley or Hardin or Hickok or any of them. With my brains and your size and speed, nothing could have stopped us! But you turned on me! Do you think you can do it alone? Is that what you're figuring, to leave me behind now that I've built you up to be somebody?"

"Waco," I said, "I never had any ambitions to be—"

"You and your medicine guns!" he sneered. "Let me tell you something. Those old guns are just something I picked up in a pawnshop. I spun a good yarn about them to give you confidence. You were on the edge, you needed a push in the right direction, and I knew once you started wearing a flashy rig like that, with one killing under your belt already, somebody'd be bound to try you again, and we'd be on our way to fame. But as for their being Bill Longley's guns, don't make me laugh!"

I said, "Waco—"

"They's just metal and wood like any other guns!" he said. "And I'm going to prove it to you right now! I don't need you, Jim! I'm as good a man as you, even if you laugh at me and make jokes at my expense. . . . *Are you ready, Jim?*"

He was crouching, and I looked at him, Waco Smith, with whom I'd ridden up the trail and back. I saw that he was no good and I saw that he was dead. It didn't matter whose guns I was wearing, and all he'd really said was that he didn't know whose guns they were. But it didn't matter, they were my guns now, and he was just a little runt who never could shoot for shucks, anyway. He was dead, and so were the others, the ones who'd come after him, because they'd come, I knew that.

I saw them come to try me, one after the other, and I saw them go down before the big black guns, all except the last, the one I couldn't quite make out. Maybe it was Fenn and maybe it wasn't . . .

I said, "To hell with you, Waco. I've got nothing against you, and I'm not going to fight you. Tonight or any other time."

I turned and walked away. I heard the sound of his gun behind me an instant before the bullet hit me. Then I wasn't hearing anything for a while. When I came to, I was in bed, and Martha Butcher was there.

"Jim!" she breathed. "Oh, Jim . . . !"

She looked real worried, and kind of pretty, I thought, but of course I was half out of my head. She looked even prettier the day I asked her to marry me, some months later, but maybe I was a little out of my head that day, too. Old Man Butcher didn't like it a bit. It seems his fight with Martha had been about her cleaning up my place, and his ordering her to quit and stay away from that young troublemaker, as he'd called me after getting word of all the hell we'd raised up north after delivering his cattle.

He didn't like it, but he offered me a job, I suppose for Martha's sake. I thanked him and told him I was much obliged but I'd just accepted an appointment as Deputy U.S. Marshal. Seems like somebody had recommended me for the job, maybe Old Joe Fenn, maybe not. I got my old gun out of my bedroll and wore it tucked inside my belt when I thought I might need it. It was a funny thing how seldom I had any use for it, even wearing a badge. With that job, I was the first in the neighborhood to hear about Waco Smith. The news came from New Mexico Territory. Waco and a bunch had pulled a job over there, and a posse had trapped them in a box canyon and shot them to pieces.

I never wore the other guns again. After we moved into the old place, I hung them on the wall. It was right after I'd run against Billy Bates for sheriff and won that I came home to find them gone. Martha looked surprised when I asked about them.

"Why," she said, "I gave them to your friend, Mr. Williams. He said you'd sold them to him. Here's the money."

I counted the money, and it was a fair enough price for a pair of second-hand guns and holsters, but I hadn't met any Mr. Williams.

I started to say so, but Martha was still talking. She said, "He certainly had an odd first name, didn't he? Who'd christen anybody Long Williams? Not that he wasn't big enough. I guess he'd be as tall as you, wouldn't he, if he didn't have that trouble with his neck?"

"His neck?" I said.

"Why, yes," she said. "Didn't you notice when you talked to him, the way he kept his head cocked to the side? Like this."

She showed me how Long Williams had kept his head cocked to the side. She looked real pretty doing it, and I couldn't figure how I'd ever thought her plain, but maybe she'd changed. Or maybe I had. I kissed her and gave her back the gun money to buy something for herself, and went outside to think. Long Williams, William Longley. A man with a wry neck and man who was hanged twice. It was kind of strange, to be sure, but after a time I decided it was just a coincidence. Some drifter riding by just saw the guns through the window and took a fancy to them.

I mean, if it had really been Bill Longley, if he was alive and had his guns back, we'd surely have heard of him by now down at the sheriff's office, and we never have.

Max Brand was one of many pseudonyms used by Frederick Faust (1892–1944), one of the most amazing giants of the pulp fiction field. Faust produced about one hundred twenty-five novels and more than three hundred thirty stories in many fields (among other things, he was the creator of "Dr. Kildare"), but it was as a Western writer that he achieved his greatest fame. His stories were well-plotted, reasonably true to historical fact, and always fast-moving and involving for the reader. He was so prolific that he often had three or four stories in the same magazine issue, each under a different name. He died in action as a war correspondent for *Harper's* during World War II.

Wine on the Desert

Max Brand

There was no hurry, except for the thirst, like clotted salt, in the back of his throat, and Durante rode on slowly, rather enjoying the last moments of dryness before he reached the cold water in Tony's house. There was really no hurry at all. He had almost twenty-four hours' head start, for they would not find his dead man until this morning. After that, there would be perhaps several hours of delay before the sheriff gathered a sufficient posse and started on his trail. Or perhaps the sheriff would be fool enough to come alone.

Durante had been able to see the wheel and fan of Tony's windmill for more than an hour, but he could not make out the ten acres of the vineyard until he had topped the last rise, for the vines had been planted in a hollow. The lowness of the ground, Tony used to say, accounted for the water that gathered in the well during the wet season. The rains sank through the desert sand, through the gravels beneath, and gathered in a bowl of clay hardpan far below.

In the middle of the rainless season the well ran dry but, long before that, Tony had every drop of the water pumped up into a score of tanks made of cheap corrugated iron. Slender pipe lines carried the water from the tanks to the vines and from time to time let them sip enough life to keep them until the winter darkened overhead suddenly, one November day, and the rain came down, and all the earth made a great hushing sound as it drank. Durante had heard that whisper of drinking when he was here before; but he never had seen the place in the middle of the long drought.

The windmill looked like a sacred emblem to Durante, and the twenty stodgy, tar-painted tanks blessed his eyes; but a heavy sweat broke out at once from his body. For the air of the hollow, unstirred by wind, was hot and still as a bowl of soup. A reddish soup. The vines were powdered with thin red dust, also. They were wretched, dying things to look at, for the grapes had been gathered, the new wine had been made, and now the leaves hung in ragged tatters.

Durante rode up to the squat adobe house and right through the entrance into the patio. A flowering vine clothed three sides of the little court. Durante did not know the name of the plant, but it had large white blossoms with golden hearts that poured sweetness on the air. Durante hated the sweetness. It made him more thirsty.

He threw the reins off his mule and strode into the house. The water cooler stood in the hall outside the kitchen. There were two jars made of a porous stone, very ancient things, and the liquid which distilled through the pores kept the contents cool. The jar on the left held water; that on the right contained wine. There was a big tin dipper hanging on a peg beside each jar. Durante tossed off the cover of the vase on the left and plunged it in until the delicious coolness closed well above his wrist.

"Hey, Tony," he called. Out of his dusty throat the cry was, "Throw some water into that mule of mine, would you, Tony?"

A voice pealed from the distance.

Durante, pouring down the second dipper of water, smelled the alkali dust which had shaken off his own clothes. It seemed to him that heat was radiating like light from his clothes, from his body, and the cool dimness of the house was soaking it up. He heard the wooden leg of Tony bumping on the ground, and Durante grinned; then Tony came in with that hitch and sideswing with which he accommodated the stiffness of his artificial leg. His brown face shone with sweat as though a special ray of light were focused on it.

"Ah, Dick!" he said. "Good old Dick! . . . How long since you came last! . . . Wouldn't Julia be glad! Wouldn't she be glad!"

"Ain't she here?" asked Durante, jerking his head suddenly away from the dripping dipper.

"She's away at Nogalez," said Tony. "It gets so hot. I said, 'You go up to Nogalez, Julia, where the wind don't forget to blow.' She cried, but I made her go."

"Did she cry?" asked Durante.

"Julia . . . that's a good girl," said Tony.

"Yeah. You bet she's good," said Durante. He put the dipper quickly to his lips but did not swallow for a moment; he was grinning too widely. Afterward he said, "You wouldn't throw some water into that mule of mine, would you, Tony?"

Tony went out with his wooden leg clumping loud on the wooden floor, softly in the patio dust. Durante found the hammock in the corner of the patio. He lay down in it and watched the color of sunset flush the mists of desert dust that rose to the zenith. The water was soaking through his body; hunger began, and then the rattling of pans in the kitchen and the cheerful cry of Tony's voice, "What you want, Dick? I got some pork. You don't want pork. I'll make you some good Mexican beans. Hot. Ah ha, I know that old Dick. I have plenty of good wine for you, Dick. Tortillas. Even Julia can't make tortillas like me. . . . And what about a nice young rabbit?"

"All blowed full of buckshot?" growled Durante.

"No, no. I kill them with the rifle."

"You kill rabbits with a rifle?" repeated Durante, with a quick interest.

"It's the only gun I have," said Tony. "If I catch them in the sights, they are dead. . . . A wooden leg cannot walk very far. . . . I must kill them quick. You see? They come close to the house about sunrise and flop their ears. I shoot through the head."

"Yeah? Yeah?" muttered Durante. "Through the head?" He relaxed, scowling. He passed his hand over his face, over his head.

Then Tony began to bring the food out into the patio and lay it on a small wooden table; a lantern hanging against the wall of the house included the table in a dim half circle of light. They sat there and ate. Tony had scrubbed himself for the meal. His hair was soaked in water and sleeked back over his round skull. A man in the desert might be willing to pay five dollars for as much water as went to the soaking of that hair.

Everything was good. Tony knew how to cook, and he knew how to keep the glasses filled with his wine.

"This is old wine. This is my father's wine. Eleven years old," said Tony. "You look at the light through it. You see that brown in the red? That's the soft that time puts in good wine, my father always said."

"What killed your father?" asked Durante.

Tony lifted his hand as though he were listening or as though he were pointing out a thought.

"The desert killed him. I found his mule. It was dead, too. There was a leak in the canteen. My father was only five miles away when the buzzards showed him to me."

"Five miles? Just an hour . . . Good Lord!" said Durante. He stared with big eyes. "Just dropped down and died?" he asked.

"No," said Tony. "When you die of thirst, you always die just one way. . . . First you tear off your shirt, then your undershirt. That's to be cooler. . . . And the sun comes and cooks your bare skin . . . And then you think . . . there is water everywhere, if you dig down far enough. You begin to dig. The dust comes up your nose. You start screaming. You break your nails in the sand. You wear the flesh off the tips of your fingers, to the bone." He took a quick swallow of wine.

"Without you seen a man die of thirst, how d'you know they start to screaming?" asked Durante.

"They got a screaming look when you find them," said Tony. "Take some more wine. The desert never can get to you here. My father showed me the way to keep the desert away from the hollow. We live pretty good here? No?"

"Yeah," said Durante, loosening his shirt collar. "Yeah, pretty good."

AFTERWARD HE SLEPT well in the hammock until the report of a rifle waked him and he saw the color of dawn in the sky. It was such a great, round bowl that for a moment he felt as though he were above, looking down at it.

He got up and saw Tony coming in holding a rabbit by the ears, the rifle in his other hand.

"You see?" said Tony. "Breakfast came and called on us!" He laughed.

Durante examined the rabbit with care. It was nice and fat and it had been shot through the head. Through the middle of the head. Such a shudder went down the back of Durante that he washed gingerly before breakfast; he felt that his blood was cooled for the entire day.

It was a good breakfast, too, with flapjacks and stewed rabbit with green peppers, and a quart of strong coffee. Before they had finished, the sun struck through the east window and started them sweating.

"Gimme a look at that rifle of yours, Tony, will you?" Durante asked.

"You take a look at my rifle, but don't you steal the luck that's in it," laughed Tony. He brought the fifteen-shot Winchester.

"Loaded right to the brim?" asked Durante.

"I always load it full the minute I get back home," said Tony.

"Tony, come outside with me," commanded Durante.

They went out from the house. The sun turned the sweat of Durante to hot water and then dried his skin so that his clothes felt transparent.

"Tony, I gotta be damn mean," said Durante. "Stand right there where I can see you. Don't try to get close. . . . Now listen. . . . The sheriff's gunna be along this trail some time today, looking for me. He'll load up himself and all his gang with water out of your tanks. Then he'll follow my sign across the desert. Get me? He'll follow if he finds water on the place. But he's not gunna find water."

"What you done, poor Dick?" said Tony. "Now look. . . . I could hide you in the old wine cellar where nobody . . ."

"The sheriff's not gunna find any water," said Durante. "It's gunna be like this."

He put the rifle to his shoulder, aimed, fired. The shot struck the base of the nearest tank, ranging down through the bottom. A semicircle of darkness began to stain the soil near the edge of the iron wall.

Tony fell on his knees. "No, no, Dick! Good Dick!" he said. "Look! All the vineyard. It will die. It will turn into old, dead wood, Dick. . . ."

"Shut your face," said Durante. "Now I've started, I kinda like the job."

Tony fell on his face and put his hands over his ears. Durante drilled a bullet hole through the tanks, one after another. Afterward, he leaned on the rifle.

"Take my canteen and go in and fill it with water out of the cooling jar," he said. "Snap into it, Tony!"

Tony got up. He raised the canteen, and looked around him, not at the tanks from which the water was pouring so that the noise of the earth drinking was audible, but at the rows of his vineyard. Then he went into the house.

Durante mounted his mule. He shifted the rifle to his left hand and drew out the heavy Colt from its holster. Tony came dragging back to him, his head down. Durante watched Tony with a careful revolver but he gave up the canteen without lifting his eyes.

"The trouble with you, Tony," said Durante, "is you're yellow. I'd of fought a tribe of wildcats with my bare hands, before I'd let 'em do what I'm doin' to you. But you sit back and take it."

Tony did not seem to hear. He stretched out his hands to the vines.

"Ah, my God," said Tony. "Will you let them all die?"

Durante shrugged his shoulders. He shook the canteen to make sure that it was full. It was so brimming that there was hardly room for the liquid to make a sloshing sound. Then he turned the mule and kicked it into a dogtrot.

Half a mile from the house of Tony, he threw the empty rifle to the ground. There was no sense packing that useless weight, and Tony with his peg leg would hardly come this far.

Durante looked back, a mile or so later, and saw the little image of Tony picking up the rifle from the dust, then staring earnestly after his guest. Durante remembered the neat little hole clipped through the head of the rabbit. Wherever he went, his trail never could return again to the vineyard in the desert. But then, commencing to picture to himself the arrival of the sweating sheriff and his posse at the house of Tony, Durante laughed heartily.

The sheriff's posse could get plenty of wine, of course, but without water a man could not hope to make the desert voyage, even with a mule or a horse to help him on the way. Durante patted the full, rounding side of his canteen. He might even now begin with the first sip but it was a luxury to postpone pleasure until desire became greater.

He raised his eyes along the trail. Close by, it was merely dotted with occasional bones, but distance joined the dots into an unbroken chalk line which wavered with a strange leisure across the Apache Desert, pointing toward the cool blue promise of the mountains. The next morning he would be among them.

A coyote whisked out of a gully and ran like a gray puff of dust on the wind. His tongue hung out like a little red rag from the side of his mouth; and suddenly Durante was dry to the marrow. He uncorked and lifted his canteen. It had a slightly sour smell; perhaps the sacking which covered it had grown a trifle old. And then he poured a great mouthful of lukewarm liquid. He had swallowed it before his senses could give him warning.

It was wine!

He looked first of all toward the mountains. They were as calmly blue, as distant as when he had started that morning. Twenty-four hours not on water, but on wine!

"I deserve it," said Durante. "I trusted him to fill the canteen. . . . I deserve it. Curse him!" With a mighty resolution, he quieted the panic in his soul. He would not touch the stuff until noon. Then he would take one discreet sip. He would win through.

Hours went by. He looked at his watch and found it was only ten o'clock. And he had thought that it was on the verge of noon! He uncorked the wine and drank freely and, corking the canteen, felt almost as though he needed a drink of water more than before. He sloshed the contents of the canteen. Already it was horribly light.

Once, he turned the mule and considered the return trip; but he could remember the head of the rabbit too clearly, drilled right through the center. The vineyard, the rows of old twisted, gnarled little trunks with the bark peeling off . . . every vine was to Tony like a human life. And Durante had condemned them all to death!

He faced the blue of the mountains again. His heart raced in his breast with terror. Perhaps it was fear and not the suction of that dry and deadly air that made his tongue cleave to the roof of his mouth.

The day grew old. Nausea began to work in his stomach, nausea alternating with sharp pains. When he looked down, he saw that there was blood on his boots. He had been spurring the mule until the red ran down from its flanks. It went with a curious stagger, like a rocking horse with a broken rocker; and Durante grew aware that he had been keeping the mule at a gallop for a long time. He pulled it to a halt. It stood with wide-braced legs. Its head was down. When he leaned from the saddle, he saw that its mouth was open.

"It's gunna die," said Durante. "It's gunna die. . . . What a fool I been. . . ."

The mule did not die until after sunset. Durante left everything except for his revolver. He packed the weight of that for an hour and discarded it in turn. His knees were growing weak. When he looked up at the stars they shone white and clear for a moment only, and then whirled into little racing circles and scrawls of red.

He lay down. He kept his eyes closed and waited for the shaking to go out of his body, but it would not stop. And every breath of darkness was like an inhalation of black dust.

He got up and went on, staggering. Sometimes he found himself running.

Before you die of thirst, you go mad. He kept remembering that. His tongue had swollen big. Before it choked him, if he lanced it with his knife the blood would help him; he would be able to swallow. Then he remembered that the taste of blood is salty.

Once, in his boyhood, he had ridden through a pass with his father and they had looked down on the sapphire of a mountain lake, a hundred thousand million tons of water as cold as snow. . . .

When he looked up, now, there were not stars; and this frightened him terribly. He never had seen a desert night so dark. His eyes were failing, he was being blinded. When the morning came, he would not be able to see the mountains, and he would walk around and around in a circle until he dropped and died.

No stars, no wind; the air as still as the waters of a stale pool, and he in the dregs at the bottom. . . .

He seized his shirt at the throat and tore it away so that it hung in two rags from his hips.

He could see the earth only well enough to stumble on the rocks. But there were no stars in the heavens. He was blind; he had no more hope than a rat in a well. Ah, but Italian devils know how to put poison in wine that will steal all the senses or any one of them; and Tony had chosen to blind Durante.

He heard a sound like water. It was the swishing of the soft deep sand through which he was treading; sand so soft that a man could dig it away with his bare hands. . . .

AFTERWARD, AFTER MANY hours, out of the blind face of that sky the rain began to fall. It made first a whispering and then a delicate murmur like voices conversing, but after that, just at the dawn, it roared like the hoofs of ten thousand charging horses. Even through that thundering confusion the big birds with naked heads and red, raw necks found their way down to one place in the Apache Desert.

Zane Grey (1872–1939) was a bored dentist who turned to writing stories of the American West at the age of thirty-two. He proceeded to become a legend in his own time and a world-famous Western writer. He was fascinated by every era and aspect of the West, and meticulously researched the backgrounds for his novels, whether they were about the railroads, Native Americans, or the cattlemen-sheepherders feuds. Although he sold more than ten million copies of his books before the paperback era, he became even more popular after his death, and his works continue to sell in large numbers today. Among his sixty books are such classics as *Riders of the Purple Sage*, *Last of the Plainsmen*, and *West of the Pecos*.

Tappan's Burro

Zane Grey

I

Tappan gazed down upon the newly born little burro with something of pity and consternation. It was not a vigorous offspring of the redoubtable Jennie, champion of all the numberless burros he had driven in his desert-prospecting years. He could not leave it there to die. Surely it was not strong enough to follow its mother. And to kill it was beyond him.

"Poor little devil!" soliloquized Tappan. "Reckon neither Jennie nor I wanted it to be born. . . . I'll have to hole up in this camp a few days. You can never tell what a burro will do. It might fool us an' grow strong all of a sudden."

Whereupon Tappan left Jennie and her tiny, gray lop-eared baby to themselves, and leisurely set about making permanent camp. The water at this oasis was not much to his liking, but it was drinkable, and he felt he must put up with it. For the rest of the oasis was desirable enough as a camping site. Desert wanderers like Tappan favored the lonely water holes. This one was up under the bold brow of the Chocolate Mountains, where rocky wall met the desert sand, and a green patch of *paloverdes* and mesquites proved the presence of water. It had a magnificent view down a many-leagued slope of desert growths, across the dark belt of green and the shining strip of red that marked the Rio Colorado, and on to the up-flung Arizona land, range lifting to range until the saw-toothed peaks notched the blue sky.

Locked in the iron fastness of these desert mountains was gold. Tappan, if he had any calling, was a prospector. But the lure of gold did not bind him to this wandering life any more than the freedom of it. He had never made a rich strike. About the best he could ever do was to dig enough gold to grubstake himself for another prospecting trip into some remote corner of the American Desert. Tappan knew the arid Southwest from San Diego to the Pecos River and from Picacho on the Colorado to the Tonto Basin. Few prospectors had the strength and endurance of Tappan. He was a giant in build, and at thirty-five had never yet reached the limit of his physical force.

With hammer and pick and magnifying glass Tappan scaled the bare ridges. He was not an expert in testing minerals. He knew he might easily pass by a rich vein of ore. But he did his best, sure at least that no prospector could get more than he out of the pursuit of gold. Tappan was more of a naturalist than a prospector, and more of a dreamer than either. Many were the idle moments that he sat staring down the vast reaches of the valleys, or watching some creature of the wasteland, or marveling at the vivid hues of desert flowers.

Tappan waited two weeks at this oasis for Jennie's baby burro to grow strong enough to walk. And the very day that Tappan decided to break camp he found signs of gold at the head of a wash above the oasis. Quite by chance, as he was looking for his burros, he struck his pick into a place no different from a thousand others there, and hit into a pocket of gold. He cleaned out the pocket before sunset, the richer for several thousand dollars.

"You brought me luck," said Tappan, to the little gray burro staggering around its mother. "Your name is Jenet. You're Tappan's burro, an' I reckon he'll stick to you."

JENET BELIED THE promise of her birth. Like a weed in fertile ground she grew. Winter and summer Tappan patrolled the sand beats from one trading post to another, and his burros traveled with him. Jenet had an especially good training. Her mother had happened to be a remarkably good burro before Tappan had bought her. And Tappan had patience; he found leisure to do things, and he had something of pride in Jenet. Whenever he happened to drop into Ehrenberg or Yuma, or any freighting station, some prospector always tried to buy Jenet. She grew as large as a medium-sized mule, and a three-hundred-pound pack was no load to discommode her.

Tappan, in common with most lonely wanderers of the desert, talked to his burro. As the years passed this habit grew, until Tappan would talk to Jenet just to hear the sound of his voice. Perhaps that was all which kept him human.

"Jenet, you're worthy of a happier life," Tappan would say, as he unpacked her after a long day's march over the barren land. "You're a ship of the desert. Here we are, with grub an' water, a hundred miles from any camp. An' what but you could have fetched me here? No horse! No mule! No man! Nothin' but a camel, an' so I call you ship of the desert. But for you an' your kind, Jenet, there'd be no prospectors, and few gold mines. Reckon the desert would be still an unknown waste. . . . You're a great beast of burden, Jenet, an' there's no one to sing your praise."

And of a golden sunrise, when Jenet was packed and ready to face the cool, sweet fragrance of the desert, Tappan was wont to say, "Go along with you, Jenet. The mornin's fine. Look at the mountains yonder callin' us. It's only a step down there. All purple an' violet! It's the life for us, my burro, an' Tappan's as rich as if all these sands were pearls."

But sometimes, at sunset, when the way had been long and hot and rough, Tappan would bend his shaggy head over Jenet, and talk in different mood.

"Another day gone, Jenet, another journey ended—an' Tappan is only older, wearier, sicker. There's no reward for your faithfulness. I'm only a desert rat, livin' from hole to hole. No home! No face to see. . . . Some sunset, Jenet, we'll reach the end of the trail. An' Tappan's bones will bleach in the sands. An' no one will know or care!"

WHEN JENET WAS two years old she would have taken the blue ribbon in competition with all the burros of the Southwest. She was unusually large and strong, perfectly proportioned, sound in every particular, and practically tireless. But these were not the only characteristics that made prospectors envious of Tappan. Jenet had the common virtues of all good burros magnified to an unbelievable degree. Moreover, she had sense and instinct that to Tappan bordered on the supernatural.

During these years Tappan's trail crisscrossed the mineral region of the Southwest. But, as always, the rich strike held aloof. It was like the pot of gold buried at the foot of the rainbow. Jenet knew the trails and the water holes better than Tappan. She could follow a trail obliterated by drifting sand or cut out by running water. She could scent at long distance a new spring on the desert or a strange water hole. She never wandered far from camp so that Tappan had to walk far in search of her. Wild burros, the bane of most prospectors, held no charm for Jenet. And she had never yet shown any especial liking for a tame burro. This was the strangest feature of Jenet's complex character. Burros were noted for their habit of pairing off, and forming friendships for one or more comrades. These relations were permanent. But Jenet still remained fancy free.

Tappan scarcely realized how he relied upon this big, gray, serene beast of burden. Of course, when chance threw him among men of his calling he would brag about her. But he had never really appreciated Jenet. In his way

Tappan was a brooding, plodding fellow, not conscious of sentiment. When he bragged about Jenet it was her good qualities upon which he dilated. But what he really liked best about her were the little things of every day.

During the earlier years of her training Jenet had been a thief. She would pretend to be asleep for hours just to get a chance to steal something out of camp. Tappan had broken this habit in its incipiency. But he never quite trusted her. Jenet was a burro.

Jenet ate anything offered her. She could fare for herself or go without. Whatever Tappan had left from his own meals was certain to be rich dessert for Jenet. Every meal time she would stand near the camp fire, with one great long ear drooping, and the other standing erect. Her expression was one of meekness, of unending patience. She would lick a can until it shone resplendent. On long, hard, barren trails Jenet's deportment did not vary from that where the water holes and grassy patches were many. She did not need to have grass or grain. Brittle-bush and sage were good fare for her. She could eat greasewood, a desert plant that protected itself with a sap as sticky as varnish and far more dangerous to animals. She could eat cacti. Tappan had seen her break off leaves of the prickly pear cactus, and stamp upon them with her forefeet, mashing off the thorns, so that she could consume the succulent pulp. She liked mesquite beans, and leaves of willow, and all the trailing vines of the desert. And she could subsist in an arid wasteland where a man would have died in short order.

No ascent or descent was too hard or dangerous for Jenet, provided it was possible of accomplishment. She would refuse a trail that was impassable. She seemed to have an uncanny instinct both for what she could do, and what was beyond a burro. Tappan had never known her to fail on something to which she stuck persistently. Swift streams of water, always bugbears to burros, did not stop Jenet. She hated quicksand, but could be trusted to navigate it, if that were possible. When she stepped gingerly, with little inch steps, out upon thin crust of ice or salty crust of desert sink hole, Tappan would know that it was safe, or she would turn back. Thunder and lightning, intense heat or bitter cold, the sirocco sand storm of the desert, the white dust of the alkali wastes—these were all the same to Jenet.

ONE AUGUST, THE hottest and driest of his desert experience, Tappan found himself working a most promising claim in the lower reaches of the Panamint Mountains on the northern slope above Death Valley. It was a hard country at the most favorable season; in August it was terrible.

The Panamints were infested by various small gangs of desperadoes—outlaw claim jumpers where opportunity afforded—and out-and-out robbers, even murderers where they could not get the gold any other way.

Tappan had been warned not to go into this region alone. But he never heeded any warnings. And the idea that he would ever strike a claim or dig enough gold to make himself an attractive target for outlaws seemed preposterous and not worth considering. Tappan had become a wanderer now from the unbreakable habit of it. Much to his amazement he struck a rich ledge of free gold in a canyon of the Panamints; and he worked from daylight until dark. He forgot about the claim jumpers, until one day he saw Jenet's long ears go up in the manner habitual with her when she saw strange men. Tappan watched the rest of that day, but did not catch a glimpse of any living thing. It was a desolate place, shut in, red-walled, hazy with heat, and brooding with an eternal silence.

Not long after that Tappan discovered boot tracks of several men adjacent to his camp and in an out-of-the-way spot, which persuaded him that he was being watched. Claim jumpers who were not going to jump his claim in this torrid heat, but meant to let him dig the gold and then kill him. Tappan was not the kind of man to be afraid. He grew wrathful and stubborn. He had six small canvas bags of gold and did not mean to lose them. Still, he was worried.

"Now, what's best to do?" he pondered. "I mustn't give it away that I'm wise. Reckon I'd better act natural. But I can't stay here longer. My claim's about worked out. An' these jumpers are smart enough to know it. . . . I've got to make a break at night. What to do?"

Tappan did not want to cache the gold, for in that case, of course, he would have to return for it. Still, he reluctantly admitted to himself that this was the best way to save it. Probably these robbers were watching him day and night. It would be most unwise to attempt escaping by traveling up over the Panamints.

"Reckon my only chance is goin' down into Death Valley," soliloquized Tappan, grimly.

The alternative thus presented was not to his liking. Crossing Death Valley at this season was always perilous, and never attempted in the heat of day. And at this particular time of intense torridity, when the day heat was unendurable and the midnight furnace gales were blowing, it was an enterprise from which even Tappan shrank. Added to this were the facts that he was too far west of the narrow part of the valley, and even if he did get across he would find himself in the most forbidding and desolate region of the Funeral Mountains.

Thus thinking and planning, Tappan went about his mining and camp tasks, trying his best to act natural. But he did not succeed. It was impossible, while expecting a shot at any moment, to act as if there was nothing on his mind. His camp lay at the bottom of a rocky slope. A tiny spring of water made verdure of grass and mesquite, welcome green in all that stark iron nakedness. His camp site was out in the open, on the bench near the spring. The gold claim that Tappan was working was not visible from any vantage point either below or above. It lay back at the head of a break in the rocky wall. It had two virtues—one that the sun never got to it, and the other that it was well hidden. Once there, Tappan knew he could not be seen. This, however, did not diminish his growing uneasiness. The solemn stillness was a menace. The heat of the day appeared to be augmenting to a degree beyond his experience. Every few moments Tappan would slip back through a narrow defile in the rocks and peep from his covert down at the camp. On the last of these occasions he saw Jenet out in the open. She stood motionless. Her long ears were erect. In an instant Tappan became strung with thrilling excitement. His keen eyes searched every approach to his camp. And at last in the gully below to the right he discovered two men crawling along from rock to rock. Jenet had seen them enter that gully and was now watching for them to appear.

Tappan's excitement gave place to a grimmer emotion. These stealthy visitors were going to hide in ambush, and kill him as he returned to camp.

"Jenet, reckon what I owe you is a whole lot," muttered Tappan. "They'd have got me sure. . . . But now—"

Tappan left his tools, and crawled out of his covert into the jumble of huge rocks toward the left of the slope. He had a six-shooter. His rifle he had left in camp. Tappan had seen only two men, but he knew there were more than that, if not actually near at hand at the moment, then surely not far away. And his chance was to worm his way like an Indian down to camp. With the rifle in his possession he would make short work of the present difficulty.

"Lucky Jenet's right in camp!" said Tappan, to himself. "It beats hell how she does things!"

Tappan was already deciding to pack and hurry away. On the moment Death Valley did not daunt him. This matter of crawling and gliding along was work unsuited to his great stature. He was too big to hide behind a little shrub or a rock. And he was not used to stepping lightly. His hobnailed boots could not be placed noiselessly upon the stones. Moreover, he could not progress without displacing little bits of weathered rock. He was sure that keen ears not too far distant could have heard him. But he kept on, making good progress around that slope to the far side of the canyon. Fortunately, he headed the gully up which his ambushers were stealing. On the other hand, this far side of the canyon afforded but little cover. The sun had gone down back of the huge red mass of the mountain. It had left the rocks so hot Tappan could not touch them with his bare hands.

He was about to stride out from his last covert and make a run for it down the rest of the slope, when, surveying the whole amphitheater below him, he espied the two men coming up out of the gully, headed toward his camp. They looked in his direction. Surely they had heard or seen him. But Tappan perceived at a glance that he was the closer to the camp. Without another moment of hesitation, he plunged from his hiding place, down the weathered slope. His giant strides set the loose rocks sliding and rattling. The men saw him. The foremost yelled to the one behind him. Then they both broke into a run. Tappan reached the level of the bench, and saw he could beat either of them into the camp. Unless he were disabled! He felt the wind of a heavy bullet before he heard it strike the rocks beyond. Then followed the boom of a Colt. One of his enemies had halted to shoot. This spurred Tappan to tremendous exertion. He flew over the rough ground, scarcely hearing the rapid shots. He could no longer see the man who was firing. But the first one was in plain sight, running hard, not yet seeing he was out of the race.

When he became aware of that he halted, and dropping on one knee, leveled his gun at the running Tappan. The distance was scarcely sixty yards. His first shot did not allow for Tappan's speed. His second kicked up the gravel in Tappan's face. Then followed three more shots in rapid succession. The man divined that Tappan had a rifle in camp. Then he steadied himself, waiting for the moment when Tappan had to slow down and halt. As Tappan reached his camp and dove for his rifle, the robber took time for his last aim, evidently hoping to get a stationary target. But Tappan did not get up from behind his camp duffel. It had been a habit of his to pile his boxes of supplies and roll of bedding together, and cover them with a canvas. He poked his rifle over the top of this and shot the robber.

Then, leaping up, he ran forward to get sight of the second one. This man began to run along the edge of the gully. Tappan fired rapidly at him. The third shot knocked the fellow down. But he got up, and yelling, as if for succor, he ran off. Tappan got another shot before he disappeared.

"Ahuh!" grunted Tappan, grimly. His keen gaze came back to survey the fallen robber, and then went out over the bench, across the wide mouth of the canyon. Tappan thought he had better utilize time to pack instead of pursuing the fleeing man.

Reloading the rifle, he hurried out to find Jenet. She was coming in to camp.

"Shore you're a treasure, old girl!" ejaculated Tappan.

Never in his life had he packed Jenet, or any other burro, so quickly. His last act was to drink all he could hold, fill his two canteens, and make Janet drink. Then, rifle in hand, he drove the burro out of camp, round the corner of the red wall, to the wide gateway that opened down into Death Valley.

Tappan looked back more than he looked ahead. And he had traveled down a mile or more before he began to breathe more easily. He had escaped the claim jumpers. Even if they did show up in pursuit now, they could never catch him. Tappan believed he could travel faster and farther than any men of that ilk. But they did not appear. Perhaps the crippled one had not been able to reach his comrades in time. More likely, however, the gang had no taste for a chase in that torrid heat.

Tappan slowed his stride. He was almost as wet with sweat as if he had fallen into the spring. The great beads rolled down his face. And there seemed to be little streams of fire trickling down his breast. But despite this, and his labored panting for breath, not until he halted in the shade of a rocky wall did he realize the heat.

It was terrific. Instantly then he knew he was safe from pursuit. But he knew also that he faced a greater peril than that of robbers. He could fight evil men, but he could not fight this heat.

So he rested there, regaining his breath. Already thirst was acute. Jenet stood near by, watching him. Tappan, with his habit of humanizing the burro, imagined that Jenet looked serious. A moment's thought was enough for Tappan to appreciate the gravity of his situation. He was about to go down into the upper end of Death Valley—a part of that country unfamiliar to him. He must cross it, and also the Funeral Mountains, at a season when a prospector who knew the trails and water holes would have to be forced to undertake it. Tappan had no choice.

His rifle was too hot to hold, so he stuck it in Jenet's pack; and, burdened only by a canteen of water, he set out, driving the burro ahead. Once he looked back up the wide-mouthed canyon. It appeared to smoke with red heat veils. The silence was oppressive.

Presently he turned the last corner that obstructed sight of Death Valley. Tappan had never been appalled by any aspect of the desert, but it was certain that here he halted. Back in his mountain-walled camp the sun had passed behind the high domes, but here it still held most of the valley in its blazing grip. Death Valley looked a ghastly, glaring level of white, over which a strange dull leaden haze drooped like a blanket. Ghosts of mountain peaks appeared to show dim and vague. There was no movement of anything. No wind! The valley was dead. Desolation reigned supreme. Tappan could not see far toward either end of the valley. A few miles of white glare merged at last into leaden pall. A strong odor, not unlike sulphur, seemed to add weight to the air.

Tappan strode on, mindful that Jenet had decided opinions of her own. She did not want to go straight ahead or to right or left, but back. That was the one direction impossible for Tappan. And he had to resort to a rare measure—that of beating her. But at last Jenet accepted the inevitable and headed down into the stark and naked plain. Soon Tappan reached the margin of the zone of shade cast by the mountain and was now exposed to the sun. The difference seemed tremendous. He had been hot, oppressed, weighted. It was now as if he was burned through his clothes, and walked on red-hot sands.

When Tappan ceased to sweat and his skin became dry, he drank half a canteen of water, and slowed his stride. Inured to desert hardship as he was, he could not long stand this. Jenet did not exhibit any lessening of vigor. In truth what she showed now was an increasing nervousness. It was almost as if she scented an enemy. Tappan never before had such faith in her. Jenet was equal to this task.

With that blazing sun on his back, Tappan felt he was being pursued by a furnace. He was compelled to drink the remaining half of his first canteen of water. Sunset would save him. Two more hours of such insupportable heat would lay him prostrate.

The ghastly glare of the valley took on a reddish tinge. The heat was blinding Tappan. The time came when he walked beside Jenet with a hand on her pack, for his eyes could no longer endure the furnace glare. Even with them closed he knew when the sun sank behind the Panamints. That fire no longer followed him. And the red left his eyelids.

With the sinking of the sun the world of Death Valley changed. It smoked with heat veils. But the intolerable constant burn was gone. The change was so immense that it seemed to have brought coolness.

In the twilight—strange, ghostly, somber, silent as death—Tappan followed Jenet off the sand, down upon the silt and borax level, to the crusty salt. Before dark Jenet halted at a sluggish belt of fluid—acid, it appeared to Tappan. It was not deep. And the bottom felt stable. But Jenet refused to cross. Tappan trusted her judgment more than his own. Jenet headed to the left and followed the course of the strange stream.

Night intervened. A night without stars or sky or sound, hot, breathless, charged with some intangible current! Tappan dreaded the midnight furnace winds of Death Valley. He had never encountered them. He had heard prospectors say that any man caught in Death Valley when these gales blew would never get out to tell the tale. And Jenet seemed stern. Most assuredly she knew now which way she wanted to travel. It was not easy for Tappan to keep up with her, and ten paces beyond him she was out of sight.

At last Jenet headed the acid wash, and turned across the valley into a field of broken salt crust, like the roughened ice of a river that had broken and jammed, then frozen again. Impossible was it to make even a reasonable headway. It was a zone, however, that eventually gave way to Jenet's instinct for direction. Tappan had long ceased to try to keep his bearings. North, south, east, and west were all the same to him. The night was a blank—the darkness a wall—the silence a terrible menace flung at any leaving creature. Death Valley had endured them millions of years before living creatures had existed. It was no place for a man.

Tappan was now three hundred and more feet below sea level, in the aftermath of a day that had registered one hundred and forty-five degrees of heat. He knew, when he began to lose thought and balance—when only the primitive instincts directed his bodily machine. And he struggled with all his will power to keep hold of his sense of sight and feeling. He hoped to cross the lower level before the midnight gales began to blow.

Tappan's hope was vain. According to record, once in a long season of intense heat, there came a night when the furnace winds broke their schedule, and began early. The misfortune of Tappan was that he had struck this night.

Suddenly it seemed that the air, sodden with heat, began to move. It had weight. It moved soundlessly and ponderously. But it gathered momentum. Tappan realized what was happening. The blanket of heat generated by the day was yielding to outside pressure. Something had created a movement of the hotter air that must find its way upward, to give place for the cooler air that must find its way down.

Tappan heard the first, low, distant moan of wind and it struck terror to his heart. It did not have an earthly sound. Was that a knell for him? Nothing was surer than the fact that the desert must sooner or later claim him as a victim. Grim and strong, he rebelled against the conviction.

That moan was a forerunner of others, growing louder and longer until the weird sound became continuous. Then the movement of wind was accelerated and began to carry a fine dust. Dark as the night was, it did not hide the pale sheets of dust that moved along the level plain. Tappan's feet felt the slow rise in the floor of the valley. His nose recognized the zone of borax and alkali and niter and sulphur. He had reached the pit of the valley at the time of the furnace winds.

The moan augmented to a roar, coming like a mighty storm through a forest. It was hellish—like the woeful tide of Acheron. It enveloped Tappan. And the gale bore down in tremendous volume, like a furnace blast. Tappan seemed to feel his body penetrated by a million needles of fire. He seemed to dry up. The blackness of night had a spectral, whitish cast; the gloom was a whirling medium; the valley floor was lost in a sheeted, fiercely seeping stream of silt. Deadly fumes swept by, not lingering long enough to suffocate Tappan. He would gasp and choke—then the poison gas was gone on the gale. But hardest to endure was the heavy body of moving heat. Tappan grew blind, so that he had to hold to Jenet, and stumble along. Every gasping breath was a tortured effort. He could not bear a scarf over his face. His lungs heaved like great leather bellows. His heart pumped like an engine short of fuel. This was the supreme test for his never proven endurance. And he was all but vanquished.

Tappan's senses of sight and smell and hearing failed him. There was left only the sense of touch—a feeling of rope and burro and ground—and an awful insulating pressure upon all his body. His feet marked a change from salty plain to sandy ascent and then to rocky slope. The pressure of wind gradually lessened; the difference in air made life possible; the feeling of being dragged endlessly by Jenet had ceased. Tappan went his limit and fell into oblivion.

When he came to, he was suffering bodily tortures. Sight was dim. But he saw walls of rocks, green growths of mesquite, tamarack, and grass. Jenet was lying down, with her pack flopped to one side. Tappan's dead ears recovered to a strange murmuring, babbling sound. Then he realized his deliverance. Jenet had led him across Death Valley, up into the mountain range, straight to a spring of running water.

Tappan crawled to the edge of the water and drank guardedly, a little at a time. He had to quell a terrific craving to drink his fill. Then he crawled to Jenet, and loosening the ropes of her pack, freed her from its burden. Jenet got up, apparently none the worse for her ordeal. She gazed mildly at Tappan, as if to say, "Well, I got you out of that hole."

Tappan returned her gaze. Were they only man and beast, alone in the desert? She seemed magnified to Tappan, no longer a plodding, stupid burro.

"Jenet, you—saved—my life," Tappan tried to enunciate. "I'll never—forget."

Tappan was struck then to a realization of Jenet's service. He was unutterably grateful. Yet the time came when he did forget.

II

Tappan had a weakness common to all prospectors: Any tale of a lost gold mine would excite his interest; and well-known legends of lost mines always obsessed him.

Peg-leg Smith's lost gold mine had lured Tappan to no less than half a dozen trips into the terrible shifting-sand country of southern California. There was no water near the region said to hide this mine of fabulous wealth. Many prospectors had left their bones to bleach white in the sun, finally to be buried by the ever blowing sands. Upon the occasion of Tappan's last escape from this desolate and forbidding desert, he had promised Jenet never to undertake it again. It seemed Tappan promised the faithful burro a good many things. It had been a habit.

When Tappan had a particularly hard experience or perilous adventure, he always took a dislike to the immediate country where it had befallen him. Jenet had dragged him across Death Valley, through incredible heat and the midnight furnace winds of that strange place; and he had promised her he would never forget how she had saved his life. Nor would he ever go back to Death Valley! He made his way over the Funeral Mountains, worked down through Nevada, and crossed the Rio Colorado above Needles, and entered Arizona. He traveled leisurely, but he kept going, and headed southeast toward Globe. There he cashed one of his six bags of gold, and indulged in the luxury of a complete new outfit. Even Jenet appreciated this fact, for the old outfit would scarcely hold together.

Tappan had the other five bags of gold in his pack; and after hours of hesitation he decided he would not cash them and entrust the money to a bank. He would take care of them. For him the value of this gold amounted to a small fortune. Many plans suggested themselves to Tappan. But in the end he grew weary of them. What did he want with a ranch, or cattle, or an outfitting store, or any of the businesses he now had the means to buy? Towns soon palled on Tappan. People did not long please him. Selfish interest and greed seemed paramount everywhere. Besides, if he acquired a place to take up his time, what would become of Jenet? That question decided him. He packed the burro and once more took to the trails.

A dim, lofty, purple range called alluringly to Tappan. The Superstition Mountains! Somewhere in that purple mass hid the famous treasure called the Lost Dutchman gold mine. Tappan had heard the story often. A Dutch prospector struck gold in the Superstitions. He kept the location secret. When he ran short of money, he would disappear for a few weeks, and then return with bags of gold. Wherever his strike, it assuredly was a rich one. No one ever could trail him or get a word out of him. Time passed. A few years made him old. During this time he conceived a liking for a young man, and eventually confided to him that some day he would tell him the secret of his gold mine. He had drawn a map of the landmarks adjacent to his mine. But he was careful not to put on paper directions how to get there. It chanced that he suddenly fell ill and saw his end was near. Then he summoned the young man who had been so fortunate as to win his regard. Now this individual was a ne'er-do-well, and upon this occasion he was half drunk. The dying Dutchman produced his map, and gave it with verbal directions to the young man. Then he died. When the recipient of this fortune recovered from the effects of liquor, he could not remember all the Dutchman had told him. He tortured himself to remember names and places. But the mine was up in the Superstition Mountains. He never remembered. He never found the lost mine, though he spent his life and died trying. Thus the story passed into the legend of the Lost Dutchman.

Tappan now had his try at finding it. But for him the shifting sands of the southern California desert or even the barren and desolate Death Valley were preferable to this Superstition Range. It was a harder country than the Pinacate of Sonora. Tappan hated cactus, and the Superstitions were full of it. Everywhere stood up the huge *saguaro*, the giant cacti of the Arizona plateaus, tall like branchless trees, fluted and columnar, beautiful and fascinating to gaze upon, but obnoxious to prospector and burro.

One day from a north slope Tappan saw afar a wonderful country of black timber, above which zigzagged for many miles a yellow, winding rampart of rock. This he took to be the rim of the Mogollon Mesa, one of Arizona's freaks of nature. Something called Tappan. He was forever victim to yearnings for the unattainable. He was tired of heat, glare, dust, bare rock, and thorny cactus. The Lost Dutchman gold mine was a myth. Besides, he did not need any more gold.

Next morning Tappan packed Jenet and worked down off the north slopes of the Superstition Range. That night about sunset he made camp on the bank of a clear brook, with grass and wood in abundance—such a camp site as a prospector dreamed of but seldom found.

Before dark Jenet's long ears told of the advent of strangers. A man and a woman rode down the trail into Tappan's camp. They had poor horses, and led a pack animal that appeared too old and weak to bear up under even the meager pack he carried.

"Howdy," said the man.

Tappan rose from his task to his lofty height and returned the greeting. The man was middle-aged, swarthy, and rugged, a mountaineer, with something about him that Tappan instinctively distrusted. The woman was under thirty, comely in a full-blown way, with rich brown skin and glossy dark hair. She had wide-open black eyes that bent a curious possession-taking gaze upon Tappan.

"Care if we camp with you?" she inquired, and she smiled.

That smile changed Tappan's habit and conviction of a lifetime.

"No indeed. Reckon I'd like a little company," he said.

Very probably Jenet did not understand Tappan's words, but she dropped one ear, and walked out of camp to the green bank.

"Thanks, stranger," replied the woman. "That grub shore smells good." She hesitated a moment, evidently waiting to catch her companion's eye, then she continued. "My name's Madge Beam. He's my brother Jake. . . . Who might you happen to be?"

"I'm Tappan, lone prospector, as you see," replied Tappan.

"Tappan! What's your front handle?" she queried, curiously.

"Fact is, I don't remember," replied Tappan, as he brushed a huge hand through his shaggy hair.

"Ahuh? Any name's good enough."

When she dismounted, Tappan saw that she had a tall, lithe figure, garbed in rider's overalls and boots. She unsaddled her horse with the dexterity of long practice. The saddlebags she carried over to the spot the man Jake had selected to throw the pack.

Tappan heard them talking in low tones. It struck him as strange that he did not have his usual reaction to an invasion of his privacy and solitude. Tappan had thrilled under those black eyes. And now a sensation of the unusual rose in him. Bending over his campfire tasks he pondered this and that, but mostly the sense of the nearness of a woman. Like most desert men, Tappan knew little of the other sex. A few that he might have been drawn to went out of his wandering life as quickly as they had entered it. This Madge Beam took possession of his thoughts. An evidence of Tappan's preoccupation was the fact that he burned his first batch of biscuits. And Tappan felt proud of his culinary ability. He was on his knees, mixing more flour and water, when the woman spoke from right behind him.

"Tough luck you burned the first pan," she said. "But it's a good turn for your burro. That shore is a burro. Biggest I ever saw."

She picked up the burned biscuits and tossed them over to Jenet. Then she came back to Tappan's side, rather embarrassingly close.

"Tappan, I know how I'll eat, so I ought to ask you to let me help," she said, with a laugh.

"No, I don't need any," replied Tappan. "You sit down on my roll of beddin' there. Must be tired, aren't you?"

"Not so very," she returned. "That is, I'm not tired of ridin'." She spoke the second part of this reply in lower tone.

Tappan looked up from his task. The woman had washed her face, brushed her hair, and had put on a skirt—a singularly attractive change. Tappan thought her younger. She was the handsomest woman he had ever seen. The look of her made him clumsy. What eyes she had! They looked through him. Tappan returned to his task, wondering if he was right in his surmise that she wanted to be friendly.

"Jake an' I drove a bunch of cattle to Maricopa," she volunteered. "We sold 'em, an' Jake gambled away most of the money. I couldn't get what I wanted."

"Too bad! So you're ranchers. Once thought I'd like that. Fact is, down here at Globe a few weeks ago I came near buyin' some rancher out an' trying the game."

"You did?" Her query had a low, quick eagerness that somehow thrilled Tappan. But he did not look up.

"I'm a wanderer. I'd never do on a ranch."

"But if you had a woman?" Her laugh was subtle and gay.

"A woman! For me? Oh, Lord, no!" ejaculated Tappan, in confusion.

"Why not? Are you a woman-hater?"

"I can't say that," replied Tappan, soberly. "It's just—I guess—no woman would have me."

"Faint heart never won fair lady."

Tappan had no reply for that. He surely was making a mess of the second pan of biscuit dough. Manifestly the woman saw this, for with a laugh she plumped down on her knees in front of Tappan, and rolled her sleeves up over shapely brown arms.

"Poor man! Shore you need a woman. Let me show you," she said, and put her hands right down upon Tappan's. The touch gave him a strange thrill. He had to pull his hands away, and as he wiped them with his scarf he looked at her. He seemed compelled to look. She was close to him now, smiling in good nature, a little scornful of man's encroachment upon the housewifely duties of a woman. A subtle something emanated from her— a more than kindness or gayety. Tappan grasped that it was just the woman of her. And it was going to his head.

"Very well, let's see you show me," he replied, as he rose to his feet.

Just then the brother Jake strolled over, and he had a rather amused and derisive eye for his sister.

"Wal, Tappan, she's not overfond of work, but I reckon she can cook," he said.

Tappan felt greatly relieved at the approach of this brother. And he fell into conversation with him, telling something of his prospecting since leaving Globe, and listening to the man's cattle talk. By and by the woman called, "Come an' get it!" Then they sat down to eat, and, as usual with hungry wayfarers, they did not talk much until appetite was satisfied. Afterward, before the campfire, they began to talk again, Jake being the most discursive. Tappan conceived the idea that the rancher was rather curious about him, and perhaps wanted to sell his ranch. The woman seemed more thoughtful, with her wide black eyes on the fire.

"Tappan, what way you travelin'?" finally inquired Beam.

"Can't say. I just worked down out of the Superstitions. Haven't any place in mind. Where does this road go?"

"To the Tonto Basin. Ever heard of it?"

"Yes, the name isn't new. What's in this Basin?"

The man grunted. "Tonto once was home for the Apache. It's now got a few sheep an' cattlemen, lots of rustlers. An' say, if you like to hunt bear an' deer, come along with us."

"Thanks. I don't know as I can," returned Tappan, irresolutely. He was not used to such possibilities as this suggested.

Then the woman spoke up. "It's a pretty country. Wild an' different. We live up under the rim rock. There's mineral in the canyons."

Was it that about mineral which decided Tappan or the look in her eyes?

TAPPAN'S WORLD OF thought and feeling underwent as great a change as this Tonto Basin differed from the stark desert so long his home. The trail to the log cabin of the Beams climbed many a ridge and slope and foothill, all covered with manzanita, mescal, cedar, and juniper, at last to reach the canyons of the Rim, where lofty pines and spruces lorded it over the under forest of maples and oaks. Though the yellow Rim towered high over the site of the cabin, the altitude was still great, close to seven thousand feet above sea level.

Tappan had fallen in love with this wild wooded and canyoned country.

So had Jenet. It was rather funny the way she hung around Tappan, mornings and evenings. She ate luxuriant grass and oak leaves until her sides bulged.

There did not appear to be any flat places in this landscape. Every bench was either uphill or downhill. The Beams had no garden or farm or ranch that Tappan could discover. They raised a few acres of sorghum and corn. Their log cabin was of the most primitive kind, and outfitted poorly. Madge Beam explained that this cabin was their winter abode, and that up on the Rim they had a good house and ranch. Tappan did not inquire closely into anything. If he had interrogated himself, he would have found out that the reason he did not inquire was because he feared something might remove him from the vicinity of Madge Beam. He had thought it strange the Beams avoided wayfarers they had met on the trail, and had gone round a little hamlet Tappan had espied from a hill. Madge Beam, with woman's intuition, had read his mind, and had said, "Jake doesn't get along so well with some of the villagers. An' I've no hankerin' for gun play." That explanation was sufficient for Tappan. He had lived long enough in his wandering years to appreciate that people could have reasons for being solitary.

This trip up into the Rim Rock country bade fair to become Tappan's one and only adventure of the heart. It was not alone the murmuring, clear brook of cold mountain water that enchanted him, nor the stately pines, nor the beautiful silver spruces, nor the wonder of the deep, yellow-walled canyons, so choked with verdure, and haunted by wild creatures. He dared not face his soul, and ask why this dark-eyed woman sought him more and more. Tappan lived in the moment.

He was aware that the few mountaineer neighbors who rode that way rather avoided contact with him. Tappan was not so dense that he did not perceive that the Beams preferred to keep him from outsiders. This perhaps was owing to their desire to sell Tappan the ranch and cattle. Jake offered to let it go at what he called a low figure. Tappan thought it just as well to go out into the forest and hide his bags of gold. He did not trust Jake Beam, and liked less the looks of the men who visited this wilderness ranch. Madge Beam might be related to a rustler, and the associate of rustlers, but that did not necessarily make her a bad woman. Tappan sensed that her attitude was changing, and she seemed to require his respect. At first, all she wanted was his admiration. Tappan's long unused deference for women returned to him, and when he saw that it was having some strange softening effect upon Madge Beam, he redoubled his attentions. They rode and climbed and hunted together. Tappan had pitched his camp not far from the cabin, on a shaded bank of the singing brook. Madge did not leave him much to himself. She was always coming up to his camp, on one pretext or another. Often she would bring two horses, and make Tappan ride with her. Some of these occasions, Tappan saw, occurred while visitors came to the cabin. In three weeks Madge Beam changed from the bold and careless woman who had ridden down into his camp that sunset, to a serious and appealing woman, growing more careful of her person and adornment, and manifestly bearing a burden on her mind.

October came. In the morning white frost glistened on the split-wood shingles of the cabin. The sun soon melted it, and grew warm. The afternoons were still and smoky, melancholy with the enchantment of Indian summer. Tappan hunted wild turkey and deer with Madge, and revived his boyish love of such pursuits. Madge appeared to be a woman of the woods, and had no mean skill with the rifle.

One day they were high on the Rim, with the great timbered basin at their feet. They had come up to hunt deer, but got no farther than the wonderful promontory where before they had lingered.

"Somethin' will happen to me today," Madge Beam said, enigmatically.

Tappan had never been much of a talker. But he could listen. The woman unburdened herself this day. She wanted freedom, happiness, a home away from this lonely country, and all the heritage of woman. She confessed it broodingly, passionately. And Tappan recognized truth when he heard it. He was ready to do all in his power for this woman and believed she knew it. But words and acts of sentiment came hard to him.

"Are you goin' to buy Jake's ranch?" she asked.

"I don't know. Is there any hurry?" returned Tappan.

"I reckon not. But I think I'll settle that," she said, decisively.

"How so?"

"Well, Jake hasn't got any ranch," she answered. And added hastily, "No clear title, I mean. He's only homesteaded one hundred an' sixty acres, an' hasn't proved up on it yet. But don't you say I told you."

"Was Jake aimin' to be crooked?"

"I reckon. . . . An' I was willin' at first. But not now."

Tappan did not speak at once. He saw the woman was in one of her brooding moods. Besides, he wanted to weigh her words. How significant they were! Today more than ever she had let down. Humility and simplicity seemed to abide with her. And her brooding boded a storm. Tappan's heart swelled in his broad breast. Was life going to dawn rosy and bright for the lonely prospector? He had money to make a home for this woman. What lay in the balance of the hour? Tappan waited, slowly realizing the charged atmosphere.

Madge's somber eyes gazed out over the great void. But, full of thought and passion as they were, they did not see the beauty of that scene. But Tappan saw it. And in some strange sense the color and wildness and sublimity seemed the expression of a new state of his heart. Under him sheered down the ragged and cracked cliffs of the Rim, yellow and gold and gray, full of caves and crevices, ledges for eagles and niches for lions, a thousand feet down to the upward edge of the long green slopes and canyons, and so on down and down into the abyss of forested ravine and ridge, rolling league on league away to the encompassing barrier of purple mountain ranges.

The thickets in the canyons called Tappan's eye back to linger there. How different from the scenes that used to be perpetually in his sight! What riot of color! The tips of the green pines, the crests of the silver spruces, waved about masses of vivid gold of aspen trees, and wonderful cerise and flaming red of maples, and crags of yellow rock, covered with the bronze of frostbitten sumach. Here was autumn and with it the colors of Tappan's favorite season. From below breathed up the low roar of plunging brook; an eagle screeched his wild call; an elk bugled his piercing blast. From the Rim wisps of pine needles blew away on the breeze and fell into the void. A wild country, colorful, beautiful, bountiful. Tappan imagined he could quell his wandering spirit here, with this dark-eyed woman by his side. Never before had Nature so called him. Here was not the cruelty or flinty hardness of the desert. The air was keen and sweet, cold in the shade, warm in the sun. A fragrance of balsam and spruce, spiced with pine, made his breathing a thing of difficulty and delight. How for so many years had he endured vast open spaces without such eye-soothing trees as these? Tappan's back rested against a huge pine that tipped the Rim, and had stood there, stronger than the storms, for many a hundred years. The rock of the promontory was covered with soft brown mats of pine needles. A juniper tree, with its bright green foliage and lilac-colored berries, grew near the pine, and helped to form a secluded little nook, fragrant and somehow haunting. The woman's dark head was close to Tappan, as she sat with her elbows on her knees, gazing down into the basin. Tappan saw the strained tensity of her posture, the heaving of her full bosom. He wondered, while his own emotions, so long darkened, roused to the suspense of that hour.

Suddenly she flung herself into Tappan's arms. The act amazed him. It seemed to have both the passion of a woman and the shame of a girl. Before she hid her face on Tappan's breast he saw how the rich brown had paled, and then flamed.

"Tappan! . . . Take me away. . . . Take me away from here—from that life down there," she cried, in smothered voice.

"Madge, you mean take you away—and marry you?" he replied.

"Oh, yes—yes—marry me, if you love me. . . . I don't see how you can—but you do, don't you?—Say you do."

"I reckon that's what ails me, Madge," he replied, simply.

"*Say* so, then," she burst out.

"All right, I do," said Tappan, with heavy breath. "Madge, words don't come easy for me. . . . But I think you're wonderful, an' I want you. I haven't dared hope for that, till now. I'm only a wanderer. But it'd be heaven to have you—my wife—an' make a home for you."

"Oh—Oh!" she returned, wildly, and lifted herself to cling round his neck, and to kiss him. "You give me joy. . . . Oh, Tappan, I love you. I never loved any man before. I know now. . . . An' I'm not wonderful—or good. But I love you."

The fire of her lips and the clasp of her arms worked havoc in Tappan. No woman had ever loved him, let alone embraced him. To awake suddenly to such rapture as this made him strong and rough in his response. Then all at once she seemed to collapse in his arms and to begin to weep. He feared he had offended or hurt her, and was clumsy in his contrition. Presently she replied, "Pretty soon—I'll make you—beat me. It's your love—your honesty—that's shamed me. . . . Tappan, I was party to a trick to—sell you a worthless ranch. . . . I agreed to—try to make you love me—to fool you—cheat you. . . . But I've fallen in love with you.—An' my God, I care more for your love—your respect—than for my life. I can't go on with it. I've double-crossed Jake, an' all of them. . . . Now, am I worth lovin'? Am I worth havin'?"

"More than ever, dear," he said.

"You will take me away?"

"Anywhere—any time, the sooner the better."

She kissed him passionately, and then, disengaging herself from his arms, she knelt and gazed earnestly at him. "I've not told all. I will some day. But I swear now on my soul—I'll be what you think me."

"Madge, you needn't say all that. If you love me—it's enough. More than I ever dreamed of."

"You're a man. Oh, why didn't I meet you when I was eighteen instead of now—twenty-eight, an' all that between. . . . But enough. A new life begins here for me. We must plan."

"You make the plans an' I'll act on them."

For a moment she was tense and silent, head bowed, hands shut tight. Then she spoke, "Tonight we'll slip away. You make a light pack, that'll go on your saddle. I'll do the same. We'll hide the horses out near where the trail crosses the brook. An' we'll run off—ride out of the country."

Tappan in turn tried to think, but the whirl of his mind made any reason difficult. This dark-eyed, full-bosomed woman loved him, had surrendered herself, asked only his protection. The thing seemed marvelous. Yet she knelt there, those dark eyes on him, infinitely more appealing than ever, haunting with some mystery of sadness and fear he could not divine.

Suddenly Tappan remembered Jenet.

"I must take Jenet," he said.

That startled her. "Jenet—Who's she?"

"My burro."

"Your burro. You can't travel fast with that pack beast. We'll be trailed, an' we'll have to go fast. . . . You can't take the burro."

Then Tappan was startled. "What! Can't take Jenet?—Why, I—I couldn't get along without her."

"Nonsense. What's a burro? We must ride fast—do you hear?"

"Madge, I'm afraid I—I must take Jenet with me," he said, soberly.

"It's impossible. I can't go if you take her. I tell you I've got to get away. If you want *me* you'll have to leave your precious Jenet behind."

Tappan bowed his head to the inevitable. After all, Jenet was only a beast of burden. She would run wild on the ridges and soon forget him and have no need of him. Something strained in Tappan's breast. He did not see clearly here. This woman was worth more than all else to him.

"I'm stupid, dear," he said. "You see I never before ran off with a beautiful woman. . . . Of course my burro must be left behind."

ELOPEMENT, IF SUCH it could be called, was easy for them. Tappan did not understand why Madge wanted to be so secret about it. Was she not free? But then, he reflected, he did not know the circumstances she feared. Besides, he did not care. Possession of the woman was enough.

Tappan made his small pack, the weight of which was considerable owing to his bags of gold. This he tied on his saddle. It bothered him to leave most of his new outfit scattered around his camp. What would Jenet think of that? He looked for her, but for once she did not come in at meal time. Tappan thought this was singular. He could not remember when Jenet had been far from his camp at sunset. Somehow Tappan was glad.

After he had his supper, he left his utensils and supplies as they happened to be, and strode away under the trees to the trysting-place where he was to meet Madge. To his surprise she came before dark, and, unused as he was to the complexity and emotional nature of a woman, he saw that she was strangely agitated. Her face was pale. Almost a fury burned in her black eyes. When she came up to Tappan, and embraced him, almost fiercely, he felt that he was about to learn more of the nature of womankind. She thrilled him to his depths.

"Lead out the horses an' don't make any noise," she whispered.

Tappan complied, and soon he was mounted, riding behind her on the trail. It surprised him that she headed down country, and traveled fast. Moreover, she kept to a trail that continually grew rougher. They came to a road, which she crossed, and kept on through darkness and brush so thick that Tappan could not see the least sign of a trail. And at length anyone could have seen that Madge had lost her bearings. She appeared to know the direction she wanted, but traveling upon it was impossible, owing to the increasingly cut-up and brushy ground. They had to turn back, and seemed to be hours finding the road. Once Tappan fancied he heard the thuds of hooves other than those made by their own horses. Here Madge acted strangely, and where she had been obsessed by desire to hurry she now seemed to have grown weary. She turned her horse south on the road. Tappan was thus enabled to ride beside her. But they talked very little. He was satisfied with the fact of being with her on the way out of the country. Some time in the night they reached an old log shack by the road-side. Here Tappan suggested they halt, and get some sleep before dawn. The morrow would mean a long hard day.

"Yes, tomorrow will be hard," replied Madge, as she faced Tappan in the gloom. He could see her big dark eyes on him. Her tone was not one of a hopeful woman. Tappan pondered over this. But he could not understand, because he had no idea how a woman ought to act under such circum-stances. Madge Beam was a creature of moods. Only the day before, on the ride down from the Rim, she had told him with a laugh that she was likely to love him madly one moment and scratch his eyes out the next. How could he know what to make of her? Still, an uneasy feeling began to stir in Tappan.

They dismounted, and unsaddled the horses. Tappan took his pack and put it aside. Something frightened the horses. They bolted down the road.

"Head them off," cried the woman, hoarsely.

Even on the instant her voice sounded strained to Tappan, as if she were choked. But, realizing the absolute necessity of catching the horses, he set off down the road on a run. And he soon succeeded in heading off the ani-mal he had ridden. The other one, however, was contrary and cunning. When Tappan would endeavor to get ahead, it would trot briskly on. Yet it did not go so fast but what Tappan felt sure he would soon catch it. Thus walking and running, he put some distance between him and the cabin be-fore he realized that he could not head off the wary beast. Much perturbed in mind, Tappan hurried back.

Upon reaching the cabin Tappan called to Madge. No answer! He could not see her in the gloom nor the horse he had driven back. Only silence brooded there. Tappan called again. Still no answer! Perhaps Madge had succumbed to weariness and was asleep. A search of the cabin and vicinity failed to yield any sign of her. But it disclosed the fact that Tappan's pack was gone.

Suddenly he sat down, quite overcome. He had been duped. What a fierce pang tore his heart! But it was for loss of the woman—not the gold. He was stunned, and then sick with bitter misery. Only then did Tappan re-alize the meaning of love and what it had done to him. The night wore on, and he sat there in the dark and cold and stillness until the gray dawn told him of the coming of day.

The light showed his saddle where he had left it. Nearby lay one of Madge's gloves. Tappan's keen eye sighted a bit of paper sticking out of the glove. He picked it up. It was a leaf out of a little book he had seen her carry, and upon it was written in lead pencil:

> I am Jake's wife, not his sister. I double-crossed him an' ran off with you an' would have gone to hell for you. But Jake an' his gang suspected me. They were close on our trail. I couldn't shake them. So here I chased off the horses an' sent you after them. It was the only way I could save your life.

Tappan tracked the thieves to Globe. There he learned they had gone to Phoenix—three men and one woman. Tappan had money on his person. He bought horse and saddle, and setting out for Phoenix, he let his passion to kill grow with the miles and hours. At Phoenix he learned Beam had cashed the gold—twelve thousand dollars. So much of a fortune! Tappan's fury grew. The gang separated here. Beam and his wife took stage for Tucson. Tappan had no trouble in trailing their movements.

Gambling dives and inns and freighting posts and stage drivers told the story of the Beams and their ill-gotten gold. They went on to California, down into Tappan's country, to Yuma, and El Cajon, and San Diego. Here Tappan lost track of the woman. He could not find that she had left San Diego, nor any trace of her there. But Jake Beam had killed a Mexican in a brawl and had fled across the line.

Tappan gave up for the time being the chase of Beam, and bent his efforts to find the woman. He had no resentment toward Madge. He only loved her. All that winter he searched San Diego. He made of himself a peddlar as a ruse to visit houses. But he never found a trace of her. In the spring he wandered back to Yuma, raking over the old clues, and so on back to Tucson and Phoenix.

This year of dream and love and passion and despair and hate made Tappan old. His great strength and endurance were not yet impaired, but something of his spirit had died out of him.

One day he remembered Jenet. "My burro!" he soliloquized. "I had forgotten her. . . . Jenet!"

Then it seemed a thousand impulses merged in one drove him to face the long road toward the Rim Rock country. To remember Jenet was to grow doubtful. Of course she would be gone. Stolen or dead or wandered off! But then who could tell what Jenet might do? Tappan was both called and driven. He was a poor wanderer again. His outfit was a pack he carried on his shoulder. But while he could walk he would keep on until he found that last camp where he had deserted Jenet.

October was coloring the canyon slopes when he reached the shadow of the great wall of yellow rock. The cabin where the Beams had lived—or had claimed they lived—was a fallen ruin, crushed by snow. Tappan saw other signs of a severe winter and heavy snowfall. No horse or cattle tracks showed in the trails.

To his amazement his camp was much as he had left it. The stone fireplace, the iron pots, appeared to be in the same places. The boxes that had held his supplies were lying here and there. And his canvas tarpaulin, little the worse for wear of the elements, lay on the ground under the pine where he had slept. If any man had visited this camp in a year he had left no sign of it.

Suddenly Tappan espied a hoof track in the dust. A small track—almost oval in shape—fresh! Tappan thrilled through all his being.

"Jenet's track, so help me God!" he murmured.

He found more of them, made that morning. And, keen now as never before on her trail, he set out to find her. The tracks led up the canyon. Tappan came out into a little grassy clearing, and there stood Jenet, as he had seen her thousands of times. She had both long ears up high. She seemed to stare out of that meek, gray face. And then one of the long ears flopped over and drooped. Such perhaps was the expression of her recognition.

Tappan strode up to her.

"Jenet—old girl—you hung round camp—waitin' for me, didn't you?" he said, huskily, and his big hands fondled her long ears.

Yes, she had waited. She, too, had grown old. She was gray. The winter of that year had been hard. What had she lived on when the snow lay so deep? There were lion scratches on her back, and scars on her legs. She had fought for her life.

"Jenet, a man can never always tell about a burro," said Tappan. "I trained you to hang round camp an' wait till I came back. . . . 'Tappan's burro,' the desert rats used to say! An' they'd laugh when I bragged how you'd stick to me where most men would quit. But brag as I did, I never knew you, Jenet. An' I left you—an' forgot. Jenet, it takes a human bein'— a man—a woman—to be faithless. An' it takes a dog or a horse or a burro to be great. . . . Beasts? I wonder now. . . . Well, old pard, we're goin' down the trail together, an' from this day on Tappan begins to pay his debt."

III

Tappan never again had the old *wanderlust* for the stark and naked desert. Something had transformed him. The green and fragrant forests, and brown-aisled, pine-matted woodlands, the craggy promontories and the great colored canyons, the cold granite water springs of the Tonto seemed vastly preferable to the heat and dust and glare and the emptiness of the wastelands. But there was more. The ghost of his strange and only love kept pace with his wandering steps, a spirit that hovered with him as his shadow. Madge Beam, whatever she had been, had showed to him the power of love to refine and ennoble. Somehow he felt closer to her here in the cliff country where his passion had been born. Somehow she seemed nearer to him here than in all those places he had tracked her.

So from a prospector searching for gold Tappan became a hunter, seeking only the means to keep soul and body together. And all he cared for was his faithful burro Jenet, and the loneliness and silence of the forest land.

He was to learn that the Tonto was a hard country in many ways, and bitterly so in winter. Down in the brakes of the basin it was mild in winter, the snow did not lie long, and ice seldom formed. But up on the Rim, where Tappan always lingered as long as possible, the storm king of the north held full sway. Fifteen feet of snow and zero weather were the rule in dead of winter.

An old native once warned Tappan, "See hyar, friend, I reckon you'd better not get caught up in the Rim Rock country in one of our big storms. Fer if you do you'll never get out."

It was a way of Tappan's to follow his inclinations, regardless of advice. He had weathered the terrible midnight storm of hot wind in Death Valley. What were snow and cold to him? Late autumn on the Rim was the most perfect and beautiful of seasons. He had seen the forest land brown and darkly green one day, and the next burdened with white snow. What a transfiguration! Then when the sun loosened the white mantling on the pines, and they had shed their burdens in drifting dust of white, and rainbowed mists of melting snow, and avalanches sliding off the branches, there would be left only the wonderful white floor of the woodland. The great rugged brown tree trunks appeared mightier and statelier in the contrast; and the green of foliage, the russet of oak leaves, the gold of the aspens, turned the forest into a world enchanting to the desert-seared eyes of this wanderer.

With Tappan the years sped by. His mind grew old faster than his body. Every season saw him lonelier. He had a feeling, a vague illusive foreshadowing that his bones, instead of bleaching on the desert sands, would mingle with the pine mats and the soft fragrant moss of the forest. The idea was pleasant to Tappan.

ONE AFTERNOON HE was camped in Pine Canyon, a timber-sloped gorge far back from the Rim. November was well on. The fall had been singularly open and fair, with not a single storm. A few natives happening across Tappan had remarked casually that such autumns sometimes were not to be trusted.

This late afternoon was one of Indian summer beauty and warmth. The blue haze in the canyon was not all the blue smoke from Tappan's camp fire. In a narrow park of grass not far from camp Jenet grazed peacefully with elk and deer. Wild turkeys lingered there, loath to seek their winter quarters down in the basin. Gray squirrels and red squirrels barked and frisked, and dropped the pine and spruce cones, with thud and thump, on all the slopes.

Before dark a stranger strode into Tappan's camp, a big man of middle age, whose magnificent physique impressed even Tappan. He was a rugged, bearded giant, wide-eyed and of pleasant face. He had no outfit, no horse, not even a gun.

"Lucky for me I smelled your smoke," he said. "Two days for me without grub."

"Howdy, stranger," was Tappan's greeting. "Are you lost?"

"Yes an' no. I could find my way out down over the Rim, but it's not healthy down there for me. So I'm hittin' north."

"Where's your horse an' pack?"

"I reckon they're with the gang that took more of a fancy to them than me."

"Ahuh! You're welcome here, stranger," replied Tappan. "I'm Tappan."

"Ha! Heard of you. I'm Jess Blade, of anywhere. An' I'll say, Tappan, I was an honest man till I hit the Tonto."

His laugh was frank, for all its note of grimness. Tappan liked the man, and sensed one who would be a good friend and bad foe.

"Come an' eat. My supplies are peterin' out, but there's plenty of meat."

Blade ate, indeed, as a man starved, and did not seem to care if Tappan's supplies were low. He did not talk. After the meal he craved a pipe and tobacco. Then he smoked in silence, in a slow realizing content. The morrow had no fears for him. The flickering ruddy light from the camp fire shone on his strong face. Tappan saw in him the drifter, the drinker, the brawler, a man with good in him, but over whom evil passion or temper dominated. Presently he smoked the pipe out, and with reluctant hand knocked out the ashes and returned it to Tappan.

"I reckon I've some news thet'd interest you," he said.

"You have?" queried Tappan.

"Yes, if you're the Tappan who tried to run off with Jake Beam's wife."

"Well, I'm that Tappan. But I'd like to say I didn't know she was married."

"Shore, I knew thet. So does everybody in the Tonto. You were just meat for the Beam gang. They had played the trick before. But accordin' to what I hear thet trick was the last for Madge Beam. She never came back to this country. An' Jake Beam, when he was drunk, owned up thet she'd left him in California. Some hint at worse. Fer Jake Beam came back a harder man. Even his gang said thet."

"Is he in the Tonto now?" queried Tappan, with a thrill of fire along his veins.

"Yep, thar fer keeps," replied Blade, grimly. "Somebody shot him."

"Ahuh!" exclaimed Tappan with a deep breath of relief. There came a sudden cooling of the heat of his blood.

After that there was a long silence. Tappan dreamed of the woman who had loved him. Blade brooded over the campfire. The wind moaned fitfully in the lofty pines on the slope. A wolf mourned as if in hunger. The stars appeared to obscure their radiance in haze.

"Reckon thet wind sounds like storm," observed Blade, presently.

"I've heard it for weeks now," replied Tappan.

"Are you a woodsman?"

"No, I'm a desert man."

"Wal, you take my hunch an' hit the trail fer low country."

This was well meant, and probably sound advice, but it alienated Tappan. He had really liked this hearty-voiced stranger. Tappan thought moodily of his slowly ingrowing mind, of the narrowness of his soul. He was past interest in his fellow men. He lived with a dream. The only living creature he loved was a lop-eared, lazy burro, growing old in contentment. Nevertheless that night Tappan shared one of his two blankets.

In the morning the gray dawn broke, and the sun rose without its brightness of gold. There was a haze over the blue sky. Then, swift-moving clouds scudded up out of the southwest. The wind was chill, the forest shaggy and dark, the birds and squirrels were silent.

"Wal, you'll break camp today," asserted Blade.

"Nope. I'll stick it out yet awhile," returned Tappan.

"But, man, you might get snowed in, an' up hyar thet's serious."

"Ahuh! Well, it won't bother me. An' there's nothin' holdin' you."

"Tappan, it's four days' walk down out of this woods. If a big snow set in, how'd I make it?"

"Then you'd better go out over the Rim," suggested Tappan.

"No. I'll take my chance the other way. But are you meanin' you'd rather not have me with you? Fer you can't stay hyar."

Tappan was in a quandary.

Some instinct bade him tell the man to go. Not empty-handed, but to go. But this was selfish, and entirely unlike Tappan as he remembered himself of old. Finally he spoke, "You're welcome to half my outfit—go or stay."

"Thet's mighty square of you, Tappan," responded the other, feelingly. "Have you a burro you'll give me?"

"No, I've only one."

"Ha! Then I'll have to stick with you till you leave."

No more was said. They had breakfast in a strange silence. The wind brooded its secret in the tree tops. Tappan's burro strolled into camp, and caught the stranger's eye.

"Wal, thet's shore a fine burro," he observed. "Never saw the like."

Tappan performed his camp tasks. And then there was nothing to do but sit around the fire. Blade evidently waited for the increasing menace of storm to rouse Tappan to decision. But the graying over of sky and the increase of wind did not affect Tappan. What did he wait for? The truth of his thoughts was that he did not like the way Jenet remained in camp. She was waiting to be packed. She knew they ought to go. Tappan yielded to a perverse devil of stubbornness. The wind brought a cold mist, then a flurry of wet snow. Tappan gathered firewood, a large quantity. Blade saw this and gave voice to earnest fears. But Tappan paid no heed. By nightfall sleet and snow began to fall steadily. The men fashioned a rude shack of spruce boughs, ate their supper, and went to bed early.

It worried Tappan that Jenet stayed right in camp. He lay awake a long time. The wind rose, and moaned through the forest. The sleet failed, and a soft, steady downfall of snow gradually set in. Tappan fell asleep. When he awoke it was to see a forest of white. The trees were mantled with blankets of wet snow, the ground covered two feet on a level. But the clouds appeared to be gone, the sky was blue, the storm over. The sun came up warm and bright.

"It'll all go in a day," said Tappan.

"If this was early October I'd agree with you," replied Blade. "But it's only akin' fer another storm. Can't you hear thet wind?"

Tappan only heard the whispers of his dreams. By now the snow was melting off the pines, and rainbows shone everywhere. Little patches of snow began to drop off the south branches of the pines and spruces, and then larger patches, until by midafternoon white streams and avalanches were falling everywhere. All of the snow, except in shaded places on the north sides of trees, went that day, and half of that on the ground. Next day it thinned out more, until Jenet was finding the grass and moss again. That afternoon the telltale thin clouds raced up out of the southwest and the wind moaned its menace.

"Tappan, let's pack an' hit it out of hyar," appealed Blade, anxiously. "I know this country. Mebbe I'm wrong, of course, but it feels like storm. Winter's comin' shore."

"Let her come," replied Tappan imperturbably.

"Say, do you want to get snowed in?" demanded Blade, out of patience.

"I might like a little spell of it, seein' it'd be new to me," replied Tappan.

"But man, if you ever get snowed in hyar you can't get out."

"That burro of mine could get me out."

"You're crazy. Thet burro couldn't go a hundred feet. What's more, you'd have to kill her an' eat her."

Tappan bent a strange gaze upon his companion, but made no reply. Blade began to pace up and down the small bare patch of ground before the campfire. Manifestly, he was in a serious predicament. That day he seemed subtly to change, as did Tappan. Both answered to their peculiar instincts, Blade to that of self-preservation, and Tappan, to something like indifference. Tappan held fate in defiance. What more could happen to him?

Blade broke out again, in eloquent persuasion, giving proof of their peril, and from that he passed to amaze and then to strident anger. He cursed Tappan for a nature-loving idiot.

"An' I'll tell you what," he ended. "When mornin' comes I'll take some of your grub an' hit it out of hyar, storm or no storm."

But long before dawn broke that resolution of Blade's had become impracticable. Both men were awakened by a roar of storm through the forest, no longer a moan, but a marching roar, with now a crash and then a shriek of gale! By the light of the smoldering campfire Tappan saw a whirling pall of snow already on the ground, and the forest lost in a blur of white.

"I was wrong," called Tappan to his companion. "What's best to do now?"

"You damned fool!" yelled Blade. "We've got to keep from freezin' an' starvin' till the storm ends an' a crust comes on the snow."

For three days and three nights the blizzard continued, unabated in its fury. It took the men hours to keep a space cleared for their camp site, which Jenet shared with them. On the fourth day the storm ceased, the clouds broke away, the sun came out. And the temperature dropped to zero. Snow on the level just topped Tappan's lofty stature, and in drifts it was ten and fifteen feet deep. Winter had set in without compromise. The forest became a solemn, still, white world. But now Tappan had no time to dream. Dry firewood was hard to find under the snow. It was possible to cut down one of the dead trees on the slope, but impossible to pack sufficient wood to the camp. They had to burn green wood. Then the fashioning of snowshoes took much time. Tappan had no knowledge of such footgear. He could only help Blade. The men were encouraged by the piercing cold forming a crust on the snow. But just as they were about to pack and venture forth, the weather moderated, the crust refused to hold their weight, and another foot of snow fell.

"Why in hell didn't you kill an elk?" demanded Blade, sullenly. He had become darkly sinister. He knew the peril and he loved life. "Now we'll have to kill an' eat your precious Jenet. An' mebbe she won't furnish meat enough to last till this snow weather stops an' a good freeze'll make travelin' possible."

"Blade, you shut up about killin' an' eatin' my burro Jenet," returned Tappan, in a voice that silenced the other.

Thus instinctively these men became enemies. Blade thought only of himself. Tappan had forced upon him a menace to the life of his burro. For himself Tappan had not one thought.

Tappan's supplies ran low. All the bacon and coffee were gone. There was only a small haunch of venison, a bag of beans, a sack of flour, and a small quantity of salt left.

"If a crust freezes on the snow an' we can pack that flour, we'll get out alive," said Blade. "But we can't take the burro."

Another day of bright sunshine softened the snow on the southern exposures, and a night of piercing cold froze a crust that would bear a quick step of man.

"It's our only chance—an' damn slim at thet," declared Blade.

Tappan allowed Blade to choose the time and method, and supplies for the start to get out of the forest. They cooked all the beans and divided them in two sacks. Then they baked about five pounds of biscuits for each of them. Blade showed his cunning when he chose the small bag of salt for himself and let Tappan take the tobacco. This quantity of food and a blanket for each Blade declared to be all they could pack. They argued over the guns, and in the end Blade compromised on the rifle, agreeing to let Tappan carry that on a possible chance of killing a deer or elk. When this matter had been decided, Blade significantly began putting on his rude snowshoes, that had been constructed from pieces of Tappan's boxes and straps and burlap sacks.

"Reckon they won't last long," muttered Blade.

Meanwhile Tappan fed Jenet some biscuits and then began to strap a tarpaulin on her back.

"What you doin'?" queried Blade, suddenly.

"Gettin' Jenet ready," replied Tappan.

"Ready! For what?"

"Why, to go with us."

"Hell!" shouted Blade, and he threw up his hands in helpless rage.

Tappan felt a depth stirred within him. He lost his late taciturnity and silent aloofness fell away from him. Blade seemed on the moment no longer an enemy. He loomed as an aid to the saving of Jenet. Tappan burst into speech.

"I can't go without her. It'd never enter my head. Jenet's mother was a good faithful burro. I saw Jenet born way down there on the Rio Colorado. She wasn't strong. An' I had to wait for her to be able to walk. An' she grew up. Her mother died, an' Jenet an' me packed it alone. She wasn't no ordinary burro. She learned all I taught her. She was different. But I treated her same as any burro. An' she grew with the years. Desert men said there never was such a burro as Jenet. Called her Tappan's burro, an' tried to borrow an' buy an' steal her. . . . How many times in ten years Jenet has done me a good turn I can't remember. But she saved my life. She dragged me out of Death Valley. . . . An' then I forgot my debt. I ran off with a woman an' left Jenet to wait as she had been trained to wait. . . . Well, I got back in time. . . . An' now I'll not leave her here. It may be strange to you, Blade, me carin' this way. Jenet's only a burro. But I won't leave her."

"Man, you talk like thet lazy lop-eared burro was a woman," declared Blade, in disgusted astonishment.

"I don't know women, but I reckon Jenet's more faithful than most of them."

"Wal, of all the stark, starin' fools I ever run into you're the worst."

"Fool or not, I know what I'll do," retorted Tappan. The softer mood left him swiftly.

"Haven't you sense enough to see thet we can't travel with your burro?" queried Blade, patiently controlling his temper. "She has little hoofs, sharp as knives. She'll cut through the crust. She'll break through in places. An' we'll have to stop to haul her out—mebbe break through ourselves. Thet would make us longer gettin' out."

"Long or short we'll take her."

Then Blade confronted Tappan as if suddenly unmasking his true meaning. His patient explanation meant nothing. Under no circumstances would he ever have consented to an attempt to take Jenet out of that snowbound wilderness. His eyes gleamed.

"We've a hard pull to get out alive. An' hard-workin' men in winter must have meat to eat."

Tappan slowly straightened up to look at the speaker.

"What do you mean?"

For answer Blade jerked his hand backward and downward, and when it swung into sight again it held Tappan's worn and shining rifle. Then Blade, with deliberate force, that showed the nature of the man, worked the lever and threw a shell into the magazine. All the while his eyes were fastened on Tappan. His face seemed that of another man, evil, relentless, inevitable in his spirit to preserve his own life at any cost.

"I mean to kill your burro," he said, in a voice that suited his look and manner.

"No!" cried Tappan, shocked into an instant of appeal.

"Yes, I am, an' I'll bet, by God, before we get out of hyar you'll be glad to eat some of her meat!"

That roused the slow-gathering might of Tappan's wrath.

"I'd starve to death before I'd—I'd kill that burro, let alone eat her."

"Starve an' be damned!" shouted Blade, yielding to rage.

Jenet stood right behind Tappan, in her posture of contented repose, with one long ear hanging down over her gray meek face.

"You'll have to kill me first," answered Tappan, sharply.

"I'm good fer anythin'—if you push me," returned Blade, stridently.

As he stepped aside, evidently so he could have unobstructed aim at Jenet, Tappan leaped forward and knocked up the rifle as it was discharged. The bullet sped harmlessly over Jenet. Tappan heard it thud into a tree. Blade uttered a curse. And as he lowered the rifle in sudden deadly intent, Tappan grasped the barrel with his left hand. Then, clenching his right, he struck Blade a sodden blow in the face. Only Blade's hold on the rifle prevented him from falling. Blood streamed from his nose and mouth. He bellowed in hoarse fury, "I'll kill you—fer thet!"

Tappan opened his clenched teeth. "No, Blade—you're not man enough."

Then began a terrific struggle for possession of the rifle. Tappan beat at Blade's face with his sledgehammer fist. But the strength of the other made it imperative that he use both hands to keep his hold on the rifle. Wrestling and pulling and jerking, the men tore round the snowy camp, scattering the campfire, knocking down the brush shelter. Blade had surrendered to a wild frenzy. He hissed his maledictions. His was the brute lust to kill an enemy that thwarted him. But Tappan was grim and terrible in his restraint. His battle was to save Jenet. Nevertheless, there mounted in him the hot physical sensations of the savage. The contact of flesh, the smell and sight of Blade's blood, the violent action, the beastly mien of his foe changed the fight to one for its own sake. To conquer this foe, to rend him and beat him down, blow on blow!

Tappan felt instinctively that he was the stronger. Suddenly he exerted all his muscular force into one tremendous wrench. The rifle broke, leaving the steel barrel in his hands, the wooden stock in Blade's. And it was the quicker-witted Blade who used his weapon first to advantage. One swift blow knocked Tappan down. As he was about to follow it up with another, Tappan kicked his opponent's feet from under him. Blade sprawled in the snow, but was up again as quickly as Tappan. They made at each other, Tappan waiting to strike, and Blade raining blows on Tappan. These were heavy blows aimed at his head, but which he contrived to receive on his arms and the rifle barrel he brandished. For a few moments Tappan stood up under a beating that would have felled a lesser man. His own blood blinded him. Then he swung his heavy weapon. The blow broke Blade's left arm. Like a wild beast, he screamed in pain; and then, without guard, rushed in, too furious for further caution. Tappan met the terrible onslaught as before, and watching his chance, again swung the rifle barrel.

This time, so supreme was the force, it battered down Blade's arm and crushed his skull. He died on his feet—ghastly and horrible change!—and swaying backward, he fell into the upbanked wall of snow, and went out of sight, except for his boots, one of which still held the crude snowshoe.

Tappan stared, slowly realizing.

"Ahuh, stranger Blade!" he ejaculated, gazing at the hole in the snow bank where his foe had disappeared. "You were goin' to—kill an' eat—Tappan's burro!"

Then he sighted the bloody rifle barrel, and cast it from him. He became conscious of injuries which needed attention. But he could do little more than wash off the blood and bind up his head. Both arms and hands were badly bruised, and beginning to swell. But fortunately no bones had been broken.

Tappan finished strapping the tarpaulin upon the burro; and, taking up both his and Blade's supply of food, he called out, "Come on, Jenet."

Which way to go! Indeed, there was no more choice for him than there had been for Blade. Toward the Rim the snowdrift would be deeper and impassable. Tappan realized that the only possible chance for him was down hill. So he led Jenet out of camp without looking back once. What was it that had happened? He did not seem to be the same Tappan that had dreamily tramped into this woodland.

A deep furrow in the snow had been made by the men packing firewood into camp. At the end of this furrow the wall of snow stood higher than Tappan's head. To get out on top without breaking the crust presented a problem. He lifted Jenet up, and was relieved to see that the snow held her. But he found a different task in his own case. Returning to camp, he gathered up several of the long branches of spruce that had been part of the shelter, and carrying them out he laid them against the slant of snow he had to surmount, and by their aid he got on top. The crust held him.

Elated and with revived hope, he took up Jenet's halter and started off. Walking with his rude snowshoes was awkward. He had to go slowly, and slide them along the crust. But he progressed. Jenet's little steps kept her even with him. Now and then one of her sharp hoofs cut through, but not to hinder her particularly. Right at the start Tappan observed a singular something about Jenet. Never until now had she been dependent upon him. She knew it. Her intelligence apparently told her that if she got out of this snowbound wilderness it would be owing to the strength and reason of her master.

Tappan kept to the north side of the canyon, where the snow crust was strongest. What he must do was to work up to the top of the canyon slope, and then keeping to the ridge travel north along it, and so down out of the forest.

Travel was slow. He soon found he had to pick his way. Jenet appeared to be absolutely unable to sense either danger or safety. Her experience had been of the rock confines and the drifting sands of the desert. She walked where Tappan led her. And it seemed to Tappan that her trust in him, her reliance upon him, were pathetic.

"Well, old girl," said Tappan to her, "it's a horse of another color now—hey?"

At length he came to a wide part of the canyon, where a bench of land led to a long gradual slope, thickly studded with small pines. This appeared to be fortunate, and turned out to be so, for when Jenet broke through the crust Tappan had trees and branches to hold to while he hauled her out. The labor of climbing that slope was such that Tappan began to appreciate Blade's absolute refusal to attempt getting Jenet out. Dusk was shadowing the white aisles of the forest when Tappan ascended to a level. He had not traveled far from camp, and the fact struck a chill upon his heart.

To go on in the dark was foolhardy. So Tappan selected a thick spruce, under which there was a considerable depression in the snow, and here made preparation to spend the night. Unstrapping the tarpaulin, he spread it on the snow. All the lower branches of this giant of the forest were dead and dry. Tappan broke off many and soon had a fire. Jenet nibbled at the moss on the trunk of the spruce tree. Tappan's meal consisted of beans, biscuits, and a ball of snow, that he held over the fire to soften. He saw to it that Jenet fared as well as he. Night soon fell, strange and weirdly white in the forest, and piercingly cold. Tappan needed the fire. Gradually it melted the snow and made a hole, down to the ground. Tappan rolled up in the tarpaulin and soon fell asleep.

In three days Tappan traveled about fifteen miles, gradually descending, until the snow crust began to fail to hold Jenet. Then whatever had been his difficulties before, they were now magnified a hundredfold. As soon as the sun was up, somewhat softening the snow, Jenet began to break through. And often when Tappan began hauling her out he broke through himself. This exertion was killing even to a man of Tappan's physical prowess. The endurance to resist heat and flying dust and dragging sand seemed another kind from that needed to toil on in his snow. The endless snowbound forest began to be hideous to Tappan. Cold, lonely, dreary, white, mournful—the kind of ghastly and ghostly winter land that had been the terror of Tappan's boyish dreams! He loved the sun—the open. This forest had deceived him. It was a wall of ice. As he toiled on, the state of his mind gradually and subtly changed in all except the fixed and absolute will to save Jenet. In some places he carried her.

The fourth night found him dangerously near the end of his stock of food. He had been generous with Jenet. But now, considering that he had to do more work than she, he diminished her share. On the fifth day Jenet broke through the snow crust so often that Tappan realized how utterly impossible it was for her to get out of the woods by her own efforts. Therefore Tappan hit upon the plan of making her lie on the tarpaulin, so that he could drag her. The tarpaulin doubled once did not make a bad sled. All the rest of that day Tappan hauled her. And so all the rest of the next day he toiled on, hands behind him, clutching the canvas, head and shoulders bent, plodding and methodical, like a man who could not be defeated. That night he was too weary to build a fire, and too worried to eat the last of his food.

Next day Tappan was not unalive to the changing character of the forest. He had worked down out of the zone of the spruce trees; the pines had thinned out and decreased in size; oak trees began to show prominently. All these signs meant that he was getting down out of the mountain heights. But the fact, hopeful as it was, had drawbacks. The snow was still four feet deep on a level and the crust held Tappan only about half the time. Moreover, the lay of the land operated against Tappan's progress. The long, slowly descending ridge had failed. There were no more canyons, but ravines and swales were numerous. Tappan dragged on, stern, indomitable, bent to his toil.

When the crust let him down, he hung his snowshoes over Jenet's back, and wallowed through, making a lane for her to follow. Two days of such heartbreaking toil, without food or fire, broke Tappan's magnificent endurance. But not his spirit! He hauled Jenet over the snow, and through the snow, down the hills and up the slopes, through the thickets, knowing that over the next ridge, perhaps, was deliverance. Deer and elk tracks began to be numerous. Cedar and juniper trees now predominated. An occasional pine showed here and there. He was getting out of the forest land. Only such mighty and justifiable hope as that could have kept him on his feet.

He fell often, and it grew harder to rise and go on. The hour came when the crust failed altogether to hold Tappan and he had to abandon hauling Jenet. It was necessary to make a road for her. How weary, cold, horrible, the white reaches! Yard by yard Tappan made his way. He no longer sweat. He had no feeling in his feet or legs. Hunger ceased to gnaw at his vitals. His thirst he quenched with snow—soft snow now, that did not have to be crunched like ice. The pangs in his breast were terrible—cramps, constrictions, the piercing pains in his lungs, the dull ache of his overtaxed heart.

Tappan came to an opening in the cedar forest from which he could see afar. A long slope fronted him. It led down and down to open country. His desert eyes, keen as those of an eagle, made out flat country, sparsely covered with snow, and black dots that were cattle. The last slope! The last pull! Three feet of snow, except in drifts; down and down he plunged, making way for Jenet! All that day he toiled and fell and rolled down this league-long slope, wearing toward sunset to the end of his task, and likewise to the end of his will.

NOW HE SEEMED up and now down. There was no sense of cold or weariness. Only direction! Tappan still saw! The last of his horror at the monotony of white faded from his mind. Jenet was there, beginning to be able to travel for herself. The solemn close of endless day found Tappan arriving at the edge of the timbered country, where wind-bared patches of ground showed long, bleached grass. Jenet took to grazing.

As for Tappan, he fell with the tarpaulin, under a thick cedar, and with strengthless hands plucked and plucked at the canvas to spread it, so that he could cover himself. He looked again for Jenet. She was there, somehow a fading image, strangely blurred. But she was grazing. Tappan lay down, and stretched out, and slowly drew the tarpaulin over him.

A piercing cold night wind swept down from the snowy heights. It wailed in the edge of the cedars and moaned out toward the open country. Yet the night seemed silent. The stars shone white in a deep blue sky—passionless, cold, watchful eyes, looking down without pity or hope or censure. They were the eyes of Nature. Winter had locked the heights in its snowy grip. All night that winter wind blew down, colder and colder. Then dawn broke, steely, gray, with a fire in the east.

Jenet came back where she had left her master. Camp! As she had returned thousands of dawns in the long years of her service. She had grazed all night. Her sides that had been flat were now full. Jenet had weathered another vicissitude of her life. She stood for a while, in a doze, with one long ear down over her meek face. Jenet was waiting for Tappan.

But he did not stir from under the long roll of canvas. Jenet waited. The winter sun rose, in cold yellow flare. The snow glistened as with a crusting of diamonds. Somewhere in the distance sounded a long-drawn, discordant bray. Jenet's ears shot up. She listened. She recognized the call of one of her kind. Instinct always prompted Jenet. Sometimes she did bray. Lifting her gray head she sent forth a clarion, *"Hee-haw hee-haw-haw—hee-haw how-e-e-e!"*

That stentorian call started the echoes. They pealed down the slope and rolled out over the open country, clear as a bugle blast, yet hideous in their discordance. But this morning Tappan did not awaken.